SOME BRIEF FOLLY

He stared down at her, eyes almost glazed with astonishment. Euphemia allowed her lashes to droop and her head to fall back a little. It was too much. She felt him tremble, and with a groan he crushed her to him indeed. His lips claimed her own in a hard, long kiss. A blaze of joy and desire swept her, and she returned his embrace until she was breathless and dizzied. Murmuring endearments, Hawkhurst kissed her closed eyelids, her cheek, her throat, and she lay in his arms, enraptured, conscious only of the wish that this moment might last forever. . . .

THE NOBLEST FRAILTY

Yolande knew that she should leave. Hastily. She did not know that her lips were slightly parted, her eyes dreamy, but she saw the emptiness in Craig's eyes change to an expression of tender worship that took her breath away. . . .

Her head was a whirl of confusion, impressions chasing one another at such a rate she could scarce comprehend them. . . .

D0121691

Also by Patricia Veryan:

A SHADOW'S BLISS*
ASK ME NO QUESTIONS*
HAD WE NEVER LOVED*
TIME'S FOOL*
LOGIC OF THE HEART*
THE DEDICATED VILLAIN*
CHERISHED ENEMY*
LOVE ALTERS NOT*
GIVE ALL TO LOVE*
THE TYRANT*
JOURNEY TO ENCHANTMENT
PRACTICE TO DECEIVE
SANGUINET'S CROWN*
THE WAGERED WIDOW*

Published by Fawcett Books

SOME BRIEF FOLLY

THE NOBLEST FRAILTY

Patricia Veryan

FAWCETT CREST • NEW YORK

A Fawcett Crest Book
Published by Ballantine Books
Copyright © 1981, 1983 by Patricia Veryan

Library of Congress Catalog Card Number: 95-90044

ISBN 0-449-22413-9

This edition published by arrangement with St. Martin's Press, Inc.

Manufactured in the United States of America

First Edition: June 1995

10 9 8 7 6 5 4 3 2 1

Contents

Some Brief Folly   1

The Noblest Frailty   295

Some
Brief
Folly

FOR CAROL

"Mingle some brief folly with your wisdom. To forget it in due place is sweet."

❧ *Chapter* I ❧

Obedient to her aunt's suggestion, Miss Euphemia Buchanan patted an errant curl into place, yet paid little more heed as her worthy companion prattled comfortably on about the delights of the evening ahead. The large carriage slowed as it edged into the long line of vehicles wending their way along Hill Street. Flambeaux blazed through the cold night air, hooves clattered, and wheels rumbled, but Miss Buchanan neither saw the one nor heard the others. Her fine, delicately arched, and only slightly darkened eyebrows were drawn into a faintly worried frown, her gloved fingers rearranged the rich folds of her fur pelisse nervously, and her thoughts—instead of being fixed with anticipation on the Hilby ball—wandered to the Peninsula. And how nonsensical, to worry so! She was a soldier's daughter, more—a soldier's daughter who had campaigned with her Papa and should therefore know better than to be blue as a megrim and indulging fears that were doubtless as deplorable as they were unwarranted. Simon was a splendid officer; he was probably sitting down merrily to dinner with his friends at this very moment, with not a thought in his head for either the dangers of the war or the sister who fretted for him in far-away London.

Miss Buchanan tossed her glowing head and, impatient with her dismals, entered belatedly into her aunt's rather one-sided conversation.

In its appointed time, the carriage arrived at the red carpet beside which an excited crowd waited. The steps were let down, Miss Buchanan and her aunt were handed reverently to the flagway and, having given the onlookers cause for another burst of envious admiration, passed inside.

The Hilby mansion, if not the largest house on Hill Street,

was certainly the most luxurious. Old Zebediah Hilby had amassed a fortune during the perilous days of Cromwell and had been shrewd enough to hang onto it. His descendants had combined his flair for finance with an appreciation of the good things of life. Not all their excesses had been able to put a dint in the fortune, however. As it was handed down from generation to generation, it grew rather than dwindled, and with increased wealth came an increased ability to enjoy it. For decades, therefore, the Hilby parties had been happily attended by all those of the top ten thousand fortunate enough to be invited, and this particular occasion proved no exception. The marble and jade ballroom was so crowded that by eleven o'clock the ball had already been proclaimed "a squeeze" by a smugly triumphant major domo. The musicians strove mightily but could barely be heard above the chatter. Silken gowns were crushed, shirt points wilted, and the plumes of turbans became entangled. Having observed one such imbroglio with wicked amusement, the Duke of Vaille bowed his head and murmured an enquiry into the shell-like ear of his charming partner.

"*Doing*, your grace?" echoed Miss Buchanan, opening her deep-blue eyes at him. "Why, we are waltzing, of course."

"Are you perfectly sure, my dear?" the Duke asked plaintively, his lean cheek tickled by the silk of her coppery tresses. "I'd be willing to wager my feet have not touched the floor anytime these five minutes. Of course, at my time of life, it is fortunate that I need exert no effort in order to remain upright. Still . . ."

A silvery gurgle of laughter greeted this mournful utterance. Vaille was a man upon whom the years rested lightly. He was as slender and upright at six and forty as he had been when, as a boy of nineteen, he had run off with London's leading Toast. His light brown hair might be touched with silver, but he was judged most handsome, and not a lady present would have been anything but proud to be selected his partner. "You are a naughty rascal, sir," scolded Miss Buchanan, with the familiarity of long friendship. "But since we have no need to concentrate upon our steps, at least we may enjoy a comfortable cose. Did I hear you say that you had visited poor Harry Redmond? How does he go on?"

Vaille's eyes clouded. "His father and brother despair of his recovery, I do believe, but will say only that he is doing splendidly." His mouth tightened and, saddened by the remembrance of that fine young man's valiant efforts to conceal his suffering, he added, "I only pray that they may prove right. It has been a long hard pull since they brought him home from Ciudad Rodrigo."

"Yet Harry has so much inner strength, do you not agree, sir?" Troubled despite her optimistic words, Euphemia murmured a tentative, "I suppose . . . he did not chance to mention Simon?"

The Duke said quietly, "He was able to say very little."

"And that was a very foolish question. Forgive me it, I beg you."

Pressing her gloved hand, he teased, "Dismals? An old campaigner like you, my dear?" Her answering smile was wan, and, having developed a healthy respect for women's intuition, especially when tied to so close a relationship as that enjoyed by Euphemia and her older brother, a wary look came into his eyes. "So you are worrying, little girl . . ." The immediate reawakening of her mischievous twinkle made him chuckle. "Young lady, then," he amended, acknowledging the reminder that she stood a willowy five feet and six inches in her stockings. "You heard from Simon after the Grand Rhune, did you not? I understood he came through that encounter without a scratch."

"Yes, he did. But . . ." Compelled to raise her voice, she admitted, "I *do* feel uneasy, your grace. As if . . . something . . ." And unwilling to put that chilling premonition into words, she sighed, "Perhaps it is because the fighting seems very furious now, and so many of our friends have fallen."

"Speaking of which," said Vaille, hoping to cheer her, "Sally Jersey tells me she went to see young Bolster last week, and he is much—" He checked abruptly, his narrowed gaze fixed upon the doors leading to the side hall.

Others had also turned, and the dancing was, in fact, coming to a complete halt. The music died away, then a stirring military march thundered out. Shouts of excitement rose, and every head turned, necks craning, to see the cause. Euphemia whirled around. A late-comer was entering the room, to be at once surrounded by eager friends and admirers. Very tall and well built, Colonel The Honourable Tristram Leith was magnificent in his full-dress hussar uniform, silver lace gleaming against the scarlet jacket, breeches impeccable, and a fur-trimmed pelisse slung carelessly across one broad shoulder.

"Leith is come home!" "Were you hit, Leith?" "What news from Spain?" "Oh, Lord! Have we lost then?" These shouts, mingling with more optimistic outcries, rang in Euphemia's ears. Whitening, she shrank against Vaille, and he slipped an arm about her waist. She looked up at him in mute appeal. He smiled encouragement, and his rank enabled him to make his way through the crush and guide her to the side.

Leith was quite engulfed now, and although she stood on tiptoe peering desperately over the excited throng, she could no longer discern him. Vaille's strong hands gripped her waist, and she was lifted to share the pedestal occupied by a large marble statue of Diana. At once she saw Leith's handsome head, his dark eyes full of laughter as he strove to answer the questions fired at him from every side. Snatches of that hectic interchange came to her, many followed by outbursts of cheers. "Yes, indeed! Wellington is most pleased . . . Chased them all up and down the hills south of the Nivelle . . . Grand fight! Broke through his lines . . . Soult's men ran like jackrabbits . . . Yes, it was most certainly a fine victory! We're across the Pyrenees, by God!"

In the ensuring pandemonium, Leith glanced up and saw her. His expression changed subtly. Terror lanced through her as she searched that suddenly grave face. Not Simon . . . ? Dear God! Not Simon! Vaille was shouting something, but she was conscious only of the fact that Leith was attempting to disengage himself. Such was the excitement of the crowd surrounding him, however, that he could not at once break free, and waiting, trembling, Euphemia began to feel sick lest her haunting sense of something amiss had been too well justified.

Miss Charlotte Hilby, the lovely and much-admired hostess of this elegant ball, was deeply fond of Euphemia Buchanan. She plunged into the crowd and, struggling to reach her friend, encountered her dashing young brother. "Galen!" she gasped, her famous green eyes filled with anxiety. "I must get to poor Mia!"

"Did you hear? Leith says Old Hookey's done it again! By Jove! The man's a wizard, is what!" He joined enthusiastically in a new outbreak of cheers, then went on, "We broke through Soult's lines and—" Following his sister's gaze, he ejaculated, "What the deuce? Euphemia shouldn't be cavorting about up there! Ain't seemly! Victory, Pyrenees, or no!"

This proprietary criticism was based on affection, since he had for several months been one of the many among London's eligible bachelors who worshipped at Miss Buchanan's shrine. His infatuation had at first astonished his doting sister, for in the past Galen had invariably given his susceptible heart to the more spectacular beauties among the *ton*. No less baffled were many hopeful parents possessing daughters whose looks were widely acknowledged to be superior, yet whose popularity could not hold a candle to that of The Unattainable, as Miss Buchanan had come to be known. Euphemia was not a beauty. Her eyes admittedly were unusually fine, and of a rare deep-blue lit by the sparkle of a resolute and somewhat mischievous disposition. But her hair, although silky and luxuriant, was of an unfortunate hue; a trifle more gold, and she would have numbered another asset, but the gold was too touched with titian, and in the sunlight her head glowed, as one matron had sniffed, "like a copper kettle!" She was, besides being much too tall, further cursed by high cheekbones, a firm chin, and a generous mouth that robbed her face of the soft and helpless look so much admired in young females. As though this were not bad enough, she had a disconcerting tendency to fix one with a level and interested gaze, rather than employing the fluttering lashes and shy upward glances that were The Thing. A sense of humour she was not always able to control, coupled with her occasional outspokenness, had oft times plunged her into disgrace. Always, she made a recovery from such lapses and, oddly enough, emerged more popular than ever. A great favourite with the embassy set and the military men, she had rejected many offers for her hand. But since she refused her suitors with unfailing charm, managing to free them from any sense of embarrassment, they remained her staunch friends, and new offers continued to come her way, despite the fact that she had now reached the perilous age of two and twenty.

"For heavens sake!" cried the exasperated Miss Hilby, tugging at her brother's sleeve. "The poor girl is beside herself with fear. Do you not see how pale she is?"

"Does look a trifle hagged," observed Galen judiciously. "Though why Leith's news should—" He stopped. The Colonel's dark head was lowered to murmur something to those about him. At once many concerned faces turned to Euphemia, and a path was opened through the quieting crowd. "Oh . . . gad!" groaned Hilby. "You don't suppose poor old Buchanan has stuck his spoon in the wall?" He locked horrified glances with his sister, then began his own struggle to reach Miss Buchanan.

The object of his concern, reaching downward as Leith limped towards her, was speedily restored to the floor. He took both her hands and held them firmly, saying in his gentlest voice, "How fortunate that I found you here, lovely one. May I steal you away somewhere, so that we can talk for a moment?"

I must not faint, thought Euphemia numbly. I am a soldier's daughter. If the news is very bad, I must be brave. She heard herself asking if Leith's wound was of a serious nature, and his light response that it was "just a shell splinter, but they want a man here to look at it." She was deeply fond of him and knew a sense of relief for his sake, but could say no more and seemed quite incapable of movement. A stillness had fallen over the ballroom, and it seemed that all eyes were upon her. Gripping his hands very tightly, she cried, "Oh, Tristram, tell me, I beg you! Is . . . is my brother—"

A smile curved his mouth, and his gaze slipped past her. Suddenly, a hand came from behind to cover her eyes. She jumped, her heart leaping into her throat, as she removed that concealing clasp and turned around.

A lieutenant stood there. His curling sandy hair seemed almost dark now by reason of his pallor. His beautifully shaped lips smiled, although the blue eyes were strained, the young face drawn and haggard. He also wore full regimentals embellished by the buff collar and silver lace of the fighting 52nd. But if some among the crowd thought that Sir Simon Buchanan (despite the face that his right arm reposed interestingly in a sling) was quite cast into the shade by the dashing Colonel beside him, Euphemia saw only her brother's loved face, and her heart was so full, she could not completely muffle the sob that broke from her as her arms went out to him. Buchanan, his own emotions weakened by illness, turned a little to protect his wounded shoulder, and gathered her close in his left arm, bowing his face against her fragrant hair.

The silence deepened, and many the lady who had to press lacy handkerchief to tearful eyes, many the gentleman who blinked and uttered a concealing cough.

Galen Hilby, making his apologetic way through the quiet gathering, came up beside Euphemia, shook Leith's hand briefly, and gripping Buchanan's left shoulder said kindly, "Come, my dear fellow. I fancy you and Mia would welcome a few moments alone."

Euphemia stepped back, dashed her tears away, sniffed audibly, and proclaimed in a shaken voice, "I am not crying. Really, I am not. But . . ." Still holding her brother's hand, she looked up into his tired eyes and said, "Oh, my dear, how *glad* I am to see you. And, how very, very proud." And as she spoke, her other hand went out to be met and held by Leith's.

They presented a dramatic tableau, had any of them but been aware of it, the two fine young soldiers, the tall, vibrant girl, and the emotions of the crowd broke loose. Vaille, springing to the statue, waved one arm and shouted, "Hip . . . hip . . ."

The "hurrah" rocked the rafters—or would have, had there been any.

"So, here I am," smiled Buchanan, comfortably relaxed on the sofa in the luxurious anteroom, "alive and well. Though how you could have known I had been brought down is more than I can guess."

"Of course, it is," nodded his sister, refilling his glass and carrying it to him. "For you are, after all, a mere man." She allowed her fingers to rest for the briefest moment on his hair, then crossed to sit in the armchair, where she might more easily watch him as he sprawled there, long legs stretched out before him. He looked very ill, she thought, wherefore, of course, she assured him he looked splendid and said another silent prayer of gratitude because he was alive. And longing to hurry him home and settle him into bed, she knew she must not, that he was a fighting man, accustomed to hardship, and would think her wits to let did she too obviously coddle him. Thus, for a respectable interval, she allowed him to talk proudly of their fine victory, of the wonder of being at last over the Pyrenees, of the invincibility of the mighty Wellington, and of the fact that he had been personally visited by that great man as he lay in the farmhouse they had appropriated for the wounded.

Euphemia had toiled in, and wept many nights away over, some of those farmhouses and fought to keep her voice steady as she expressed the hope that Wellington had escaped unscathed. "Yes, thank God!" answered Buchanan fervently. "For lord knows, Mia, what we would do without him!"

"We shall not have to do so. The 'Finger of Providence' rests upon him, so he once told me. He believes that, with all his heart."

"Then I pray he is right. Oh, incidentally, he sent his regards to you."

"*Incidentally!* He never did! Simon, you are hoaxing me!"

"Devil a bit of it. Told me you was a most striking young lady, and he hopes when I come back, I'll bring you with me."

A coldness touched her at the words, ". . . when I come back . . ."

"Amusing, ain't it?" he said quietly. "He never said, 'Bring your lovely wife, Buchanan.' Only 'bring your striking sister.'" He had been twirling his glass, looking down into the amber liquid. Now he raised his head and with a wry smile met her eyes, toasted her silently, and drank.

Euphemia bit her lip, and a knife turned in her heart. Simon, the dearest, kindest, most valiant of men, should have gone straight to the arms of a loving wife. Instead of which—

"Why do you stay at the New House?" he asked lightly. "I'd fancied you ensconced in Grosvenor Square. Ernestine said she had invited you."

It had always been thus. The great house on Hill Street was the New House because the foundation had been laid in 1740, whereas the central block of Buchanan Court, their country seat in Bedfordshire, dated to 1495. Buchanan Court suited Lady Simon. The New House did not, and the spoiled beauty had pouted, stormed at, and teased her doting bridegroom until two years ago he had purchased a fashionable, enormous, and enormously costly mansion on Grosvenor Square. Euphemia had received no invitation to share her sister-in-law's "loneliness"—nor would she have accepted had such a courtesy been extended. Therefore, she kept her lashes down, for once avoiding Buchanan's searching gaze, as she folded a careful pleat in the cream satin ball gown that draped gracefully about her. "Oh," she shrugged, "Grosvenor Square is too grand for me."

"Is it? How long since you saw my wife, Mia?"

"Well, she's down at the Court, you know, and it has been so very cold, I've not cared to journey to Bedfordshire." How subdued he looked, poor dear. She should tell him, of course, but this was not the time. And so she stood, gladly postponing her bitter news, and urged, "Now come along, you must to bed, for you will be tired, love, and—"

"You are very good," he said gravely. "But I have been to Grosvenor Square, Mia. I know."

She murmured a helpless. "Oh," and, clenching her hands, wished she might instead throttle the life from the tiny darkhaired girl with the petulant mouth, the perfect little nose, the enormous pansy eyes, who went by the name of Ernestine, Lady Buchanan.

"I understand," Buchanan said in that quiet, expressionless tone, "that I am to be congratulated." He put down his glass, turned his head on the back of the sofa and, looking at her, smiled faintly. "Ain't you going to congratulate me?"

"Oh . . . *Simon!*" She choked over the words and flew to kneel at his side, clasp his drooping hand and hold it tightly. "I am so sorry! I should have written and warned you, but—it seemed . . . I just could not!"

"I understand. Have you . . . er—seen him?"

She shook her head, her lips quivering.

"My third. She has called him William, I hear." A pucker appeared between his brows. "After whom, I wonder . . ." His sister remaining silent, he stared blankly at his glass for a moment, then drew a hand across his eyes and muttered half to himself, "I wish they did resemble me, you know."

Euphemia knew then how very tired he was, or, close as they were, he would never have voiced so betraying a remark. "Belinda does, dear," she reminded huskily.

He sat straighter at once, his eyes brightening. "Yes, by gad! I must go down and see the little lass. Is she well? Tina has that good nurse still, I—" He had forgotten his injury in his eagerness, and leaned forward too sharply. He broke off with a gasp, then finished a rather uneven, "I . . . trust."

Euphemia stood at once. "Belinda is healthy as a horse, which is more than I can say for her papa! You, sir, shall go nowhere until you have spent at least the next three days allowing your doting sister to pamper, cosset, and altogether ruin you with kindness!"

Euphemia's blissful expectations of keeping her favourite brother beside her for three days were exceeded beyond her wildest dreams. Exhausted by the journey home and shattered by the news that had greeted him, Buchanan suffered a setback; the shoulder refused to mend properly, and two weeks later the deities at the Horse Guards were still withholding their consent for his return to active duty. He came home from the most recent of his medical examinations with the word that his leave had been extended to January, at least. Euphemia was elated, but he viewed her joy glumly, for, although he knew he was not in fit condition to get back into action, he fretted against the wound that kept him in England while his comrades of the Light Division were in the thick of the fighting.

Tristram Leith visited the New House before his own return to France and, as usual, renewed his offer for Euphemia's hand. Buchanan, who wholeheartedly approved Leith's suit, was not excluded from the proceedings and urged his sister not to accept such a great gudgeon for a husband, even did he go down on his knees. Grinning broadly through Leith's warnings of a horrid end, he complained that the children of such a union must dwarf their poor, averaged-sized uncle. Euphemia considered her large suitor curiously and, with a pronounced lack of the blushes and shy posturing the situation justly warranted, enquired if he *would* propose upon his knees. Ever the gallant, Leith at once made a great show of dusting the immaculate floor and dropping his handkerchief upon it, and she stopped him in the nick of time, by asking whether the life of a country squire would really suit him.

"Country . . . s-squire" he echoed, dismay written clearly upon his handsome features. "Oh, dash it, Mia, you would not wish me to resign my commission?"

Such a prospect would have delighted her, but she was not the type to attempt to remodel the man she chose and thus merely pointed out, "But you have such a delightful estate in Berkshire. And only think of how happy your Papa would be did you settle down at Cloudhills and provide him with all the peace of the country, broken only by the patter of little feet, to brighten his declining years."

How she had managed to keep a straight face while she said this, she did not know. Leith's mercurial sire had once been described by the Countess Lieven as "the most confirmed here-and-thereian" of that lady's acquaintance and would have fainted had such a prospect been painted for him. Wherefore, Buchanan gave a whoop of mirth, and it was a full minute before Leith was sufficiently recovered to gasp out the shaken observation that Mia would never do so frightful a thing to a "poor gentleman!"

Euphemia burst into her delightful ripple of laughter and confirmed this, adding a fond, "Nor to you, my dear Leith. For although you are quite definitely a matrimonial prize of the first stare and such as no lady in possession of her faculties would refuse, we would not suit at all, you know."

He protested this verdict in a lighthearted fashion that concealed his total devotion and, finding her amused but unmoved, sighed disconsolately, "Alas, The Unattainable remains so! I warn you, Fair One, I shall try again."

"On the day you come to me in smock and gaiters, Tristram," she smiled, "I may take your proposal seriously. But—"

The thought of the dashing Colonel thus clad sent Buchanan into hysterics, and soon they were all enjoying a merry half hour of their customary easy raillery. But Leith's laughing eyes saw more than they appeared to, and he left Hill Street secure in the knowledge that if his admired Euphemia was not yet ready to wed him, neither had she given her heart to any other.

Sir Simon, however, took a less amiable view of the matter, and the moment Leith's fiery chestnut stallion had pranced, danced, jumped, and sidled his high-bred way around the corner, he went shivering back into the house and proceeded to take his sister to task for rejecting so unexceptionable a suitor. "Indeed, Mia," he said severely, warming his hands at the fire, "you must be all about in your attic! London positively bulges with young ladies who would swoon with joy did Leith so much as glance in their direction."

"You know," she mused thoughtfully, "you are right." Buchanan's hopes rose, and she went on, "I seem to recall that the mere sight of him in his full-dress uniform once sent Miss Bridges to the boards in a dead faint."

Her mischievous smile won a stormy reception, her brother advising her that Alice Bridges had ever been a silly goose. "But you are not," he went on, "and must certainly be aware of how splendid a fellow he is."

"He is indeed. Though not always to his subalterns, I hear. And—"

"I have yet to hear Leith rage at his officers or his men, unless they did something damn ridiculous!"

"—And," she resumed, serenely ignoring his bristling defensiveness, "is not in love with me, my dear. Oh, he thinks he is, I grant you. Or . . ." Her smooth brow wrinkled, "Or is it, I wonder, that he feels we are such very good friends, and I might make him an agreeable wife. He was impressed, you know, when I accompanied Papa on his last campaign." Her brother's eyes saddened at this reference to the so-missed gentleman who had been their father, and she went on quickly, "But neither am I in love with Tris, though I *do* love him— never doubt it."

"What a romantic," he teased. "And do you mean to wait

17

for the one and only man in the world who can claim your heart? Terribly bourgeois, m'dear!"

"Poor Simon, to think you have nurtured a bourgeois sister to your bosom all these years and never known it."

"Oh, have I not! You and your poems and romances! How well I remember Miss Springhall grieving lest you become a bluestocking!"

"Yes, and peeping into my books herself, so soon as she fancied me asleep! But it was in one of those books that I came across a little rhyme . . ." She rarely experienced shyness with this loved brother, but now she looked down at the hands folded in her lap, and rather diffidently recited. " 'Riches or beauty shall ne'er win me. Gentil and strong my love must be.' " Meeting his eyes then, she found them grave and without the mockery she had half expected and, with a faint heightening of the colour in her cheeks, added, "It is very old, of course, but . . . it fairly describes the man for whom I wait."

He settled into the nearest chair and, knowing that she was deadly serious, pointed out gently, "And fairly describes Leith. On all counts. Is it possible, little puss, that you love him and are as yet not aware of it?"

"When I meet the man who will claim my heart," she answered, looking at him in her level way, "I think I shall know him at once."

She probably would, he thought. And having a shrewd idea of how deep was Leith's *tendre* for her, experienced a pang of regret. "What if you should not find this peerless individual?"

"Why, then I shall die a maid. For I mean to be quite sure, you see, that I will love as deeply as I am loved." She had spoken lightly, thinking of Tristram, but had no sooner uttered the words than she could have bitten her tongue, knowing how Simon would interpret her remark. She was correct.

"Admirable," he said slowly. "God knows, I only wish I—" He checked, frowned, and finished, "—wish I may be allowed to give you away."

She managed a bright, *"Certainement,"* and moved to poke up the fire and conceal her distress. Simon had visited Buchanan Court twice since his return. On the first occasion he had come home almost feverishly cheerful and told her that Belinda was adorable and his wife looking lovely as ever. He had not stayed, he explained airily, because the house was so dashed full of people he scarcely knew, he'd decided he would recuperate more rapidly in Town. The second visit had been at the beginning of the week, and he had as yet said nothing of it. "I should not ask, I know," she said, still turned away from him. "But—what do you mean to do?"

Buchanan leaned back in his chair, staring through the window at the gray November skies and the frost that still clung to the rooftops across the street. He had no wish to discuss it. He wished only to return to the fighting—to forget himself and his troubles amid the hardships, the incredible camaraderie, and the wild excitement of battle. But Euphemia must be told the truth, and so, with slow reluctance, he said, "I believe when I first went down, I . . . disappointed her. For an instant, when she came into the drawing room, she looked at me—" He bit his lip. "She said what a surprise to see me, when she had supposed the new arrival was someone come to . . . to tell her she was widowed."

Euphemia blenched and for a moment did not trust herself to speak.

"On Tuesday," he went on quietly, "I asked her for a divorce."

Contrary to his expectation of an appalled protest, his sister gave a cry of delight and spun around. "Oh! I am so glad! If she could say such a thing as that, I would think she'd welcome a divorce!"

He smiled the faint, twisted smile that hurt her and shrugged, "She has no fancy to become notorious, it seems."

"Oh! Has she not!"

"Her *affaires de coeur* are, so she tells me, conducted with tact and discretion. Meanwhile, she likes her title, and Buchanan Court, and the house on the Square. And she likes the allowance I make her."

Euphemia moved closer to him, flinging out one hand in her agitation. "Then in the name of God—stop it! Sell the house! And divorce *her*! Heaven knows you have grounds enough!"

"Lord, how I wish it were that simple!" Buchanan's head bowed onto one clenched fist, and he groaned, "I cannot! If you but *knew* how many nights I have lain awake . . . cursing my folly!"

"No, no, love," she cried, coming swiftly to kneel beside his chair. "How shall you blame yourself? Tina was so very beautiful. Even now, wherever she goes, people stare as though—"

"Yes. I know. And have you seen her when she rides in the barouche with Johnny on one side of her and Belinda on the other, both in velvet and lace, and her gown and bonnet to match? She looks holy almost! A dream of motherhood such as would cause Lawrence to dash madly for easel and palette. Whilst I—" He gave a despairing gesture.

"You? A splendid military record! A spotless reputation!"

"Would to God it were! Oh, Mia! You have the veriest clodpole for a brother!" He drew a hand across his eyes distractedly, and Euphemia waited, a small crease between her brows, and apprehension tightening her nerves.

"That first summer you and Papa were in Spain," he said at length. "I contracted a stupid fever. Do you recall? I came home—totally unexpectedly—and found Tina with ... with James Garvey."

"Good God! The Nonpareil? The same Garvey who is so close a friend of the Regent?"

"The same. It was my first intimation that my lovely bride was not the pure saint I had supposed." For a moment his eyes were very sad. Then, as if recalling himself, he went on, "At all events, I threw Garvey from the house. Bodily. He was enraged and swore he'd call me to book, but never did. Tina and I quarrelled bitterly, and I took the children—Belinda was four then, and John, two—and brought them here. Mrs. Craft hired a nursemaid who was—young ... and ..." His eyes flickered and fell, and he went on haltingly, "She was a taking little thing. And I was angry, and lonely. No excuse, of course, but ..." He stole a look at his sister's face and, finding only compassion there, groaned, "How could I have been so stupid? One of the maids told Ernestine's abigail that I had installed my particular in the house. With my children! Tina came at once, like an avenging angel. She brought her solicitor and— and the *curate*! You should have seen her—she was superb. Outraged purity, personified. The betrayed wife ... the grieving mother. I could do nothing. I had no legal proof of her behavior, whereas she had a witness ready to swear to mine."

Momentarily aghast, Euphemia made a swift recovery and exclaimed, "But surely this is ridiculous. Ernestine has borne three children, only one of which is your own! If *that* were to be made public ... !"

"I had leaves, don't forget. Whatever I suspect, I can prove nothing. And I'll admit, Tina has been very discreet."

"Discreet!" she snorted. "Yet Wellington himself intimated—"

"Nothing that could be construed to be any more than a partiality for you." He stood, paced restlessly to the fireplace and, leaning his left hand on the mantle, muttered, "Even so, what a lovely mess it would be, eh? *Her* revelations of my 'sordid depravity.' *My* accusations of her adultery. Good God! Papa would turn in his grave! And the children, poor mites, would be marked forever!"

Aching for him, she asked, "Does she threaten to drag it all into the public eye?"

"Only if I persist in asking for a divorce. Can you not picture her in court? Fixing a judge with those lovely eyes. Letting her mouth droop in that helpless way she has? I would be made to seem a fine villain! And does she persuade Garvey to bring influence to bear against me through Prinny, as she says he will gladly do, I will be in worse case, and likely have to resign my commission. We would be ostracized. Can you imagine the effect upon the family? Great Aunt Lucasta . . . ?" He shuddered. "And my brothers. And—you especially. Even did you find your 'gentil and strong' love, he'd not marry into so shocking a family!"

"Much I would care for that!" she cried loyally. "For was he so easily put off, he'd not be the right one." But she was taking inventory and it was not a pleasant task. One by one she counted off aunts and uncles who might be counted on for an outraged reaction. As to their immediate family, Robert, who was at Eton would likely think it a great lark, but Gerald . . . She shrank a little. In his first year at Cambridge, sensitive, shy, and vulnerable, Gerald would be horrified. She felt crushed and defeated and forebore to mention their sister Mary, whose husband was newly ordained. Helplessly, she asked, "Is there someone else you care for?"

He shook his head, but a bleak look came into his eyes, and, searching that pale, wistful face, she cried, "Oh, *mon pauvre!* you still love her?"

He tried to look nonchalant, failed miserably and, walking to the window, said in a tormented voice, "I think I despise her. I *know* I do. But . . . when I see her . . . She is so damnably beautiful, and I remember those first months . . ." For a moment he was silent, then muttered heavily, "Did I not tell you, Mia? You have the veriest clodpole for a brother."

❧ *Chapter 2* ❧

Buchanan looked up from the copy of the *Gazette* that was propped against the marmalade dish and, with a lift of the brows, enquired, "Whom do we know in Kent?"

"Not *in* Kent, dear," said Euphemia patiently. She waved a scented sheet of paper at him. "You were not listening. Aunt Lucasta writes to invite us to Meadow Abbey for Christmas."

"Meadow Abbey ain't in Kent," he pointed out sapiently. "I can see you need a change of scene, poor girl. Been in Town too long. You're getting windmills in your attic!"

She laughed. "I admit that. No, Simon, do pray forget the newspaper for a moment and pay heed to your addle-brained sister. Should you purely loathe spending Christmas with Great Aunt Lucasta?"

He considered this carefully. It would be a change of scene for both of them. On the other hand, it was a long way, and the winter unusually cold. "What about the boys? And Mary, and that prosy fellow she married?"

"Gerald and Robert can go straight from school, and Mary has already accepted. Oh, Simon, it *would* be nice, do you not think? The Abbey is such a lovely old place, and Aunt Lucasta sets a magnificent table."

It was a telling stroke. "Yes, she does," he agreed. "But—it ain't in—"

"Kent!" cried Euphemia, starting to her feet.

Although startled by such vehemence, Buchanan also stood politely. His surprise was heightened as a small boy tore across the breakfast room to halt before Euphemia like a well-trained horse that strains at the bit, yet knows it dare not take one step further.

Euphemia bent to smile into that glowing face and pull the

boy into a hug that was crushingly returned. "Welcome home!" she said gaily. Then, detaching his clutch from her skirts, took him by the shoulders and, turning him, added, "Simon, this is my page. Kent, you must make your bow to my brother, Lieutenant Sir Simon Buchanan."

Utterly astonished, Buchanan responded to the mystifying hint of warning in her eyes and, bestowing his charming smile upon the boy, said, "How do you do, young fella? You'd best take off that scarf. It's warm in here."

The grey eyes became huge in the child's thin, peaked face. Having obediently unwound the scarf from about his neck, he bobbed a nervous bow and retreated a step toward Euphemia's skirts, the unblinking and awed stare still riveted to Sir Simon.

"Kent has been down in Surrey," said Euphemia. "Mrs. Craft took him to her son's farm."

Baffled, he said, "How er—nice. Did you like the farm, Kent?"

A nod was his only reply.

"He loves animals," explained Euphemia, and again the boy nodded.

"Well, that's splendid." The wide stare was beginning to disconcert Buchanan and, wondering what in the deuce his sister wanted with a page, and why she should treat him as though he were a long-lost brother, he enquired, "What kind of animals did you find at Mr. Craft's farm?"

A painful flush spread up the finely boned features until it reached the thick, light hair. Euphemia reached to the sideboard, took up a tablet and pencil and placed it on the table beside the boy.

Kent wrenched his eyes from Buchanan to look up at her appealingly. She smiled encouragement. "Sir Simon will understand. Show him how clever you are."

The pleading eyes fell, the lips trembled, but obediently, one thin hand took up the pencil and with painful care printed, "Cow. Dux. Chikens."

Over that downbent head, Buchanan met his sister's anxious gaze and, his kind heart touched, said, "By George! Is that a fact? Regular Noah's Ark! Have you seen the wild beasts at the Exchange?"

The child had proffered his report with his head bowed. At these magical words, however, the eager eyes fairly leapt to search the man's face. Tears glistened on the long curling lashes, and Buchanan wondered whether that shame had been occasioned by the obvious lack of education or the fact that he was mute.

"Kent? Are you in? Oh! You naughty boy!" Mrs. Craft appeared in the doorway, her plump, usually good-natured face pink with chagrin. "How dare you rush in here and interrupt Miss Buchanan and Sir Simon! I do apologize, Miss. He ran from the hack before I could——" She checked, for the effect of her words had been disastrous. Kent was cowering back, one arm flung up as if to ward off a blow, while panting sounds of terror issued from his white lips.

"The devil!" Buchanan expostulated. "What have you been doing to the poor child, Mia?"

His sister, however, had already dropped to one knee, and was murmuring, "It is quite all right. Do not be frightened. Nobody is going to beat you."

"Beat him!" exclaimed the distressed housekeeper. "I never had no such thought! Poor little fellow!" She bustled forward to slip an arm about the small, shrinking form and, with motherly caresses and soothing reassurances, led him away.

Buchanan pulled out Euphemia's chair for her and resumed his own place. Picking up a piece of toast, he demanded, "What the deuce was all that about? I vow, Mia, no sooner is my back turned than you're at it again! Who is it this time? Some crossing sweep or link boy I shall be required to find a place for? Now dashed if my coffee ain't cold!"

Despite these grumbles, there was no anger in his face and, undeceived, Euphemia poured out the offending coffee and, refilling his cup, said, "He was a climbing boy and tumbled down the library chimney while I visited my sister at the Rectory. He had no real name apparently, and since I found him in Kent, that seemed as good as any other."

Taking his cup, he frowned, "A climbing boy. Poor brat! That devilish custom must be stopped. Should have been stopped years since."

"Indeed it should. How I pray that the men who allow such wicked torture of innocents are reincarnated as just such helpless victims of our 'civilization'! I wish you might have seen the child, Simon. I was never more shocked. He huddled there in the corner of the fireplace like a living skeleton, covered with soot, and fairly sobbing with terror. But when I made towards him, he fainted dead away."

"And so you bathed and cared for him, and have taken him

under your wing," he said. But his eyes were approving, for all his teasing words. "What did his master say?"

"A great deal. And Roger, of course, 'supported' me by folding his hands and murmuring that the 'law is the law and one must not interfere with the way of things for all is planned and ordained,' or some such fustian!"

Buchanan snorted. "Prosy bore! How Mary ever came to wed such a sanctimonious do-noth—" He closed his lips over the rest of that remark, and then grinned, "I'll wager *you* took care of friend sweep!"

"I told him I had little doubt but that the boy was stolen, and as my brother-in-law had said, the law is the law and we would send for the Watch at once and have the case investigated. The child's feet were most horribly burned, and his poor little back bruised and cut from beatings, while from the way his bones stuck out one might suppose he'd not eaten for months! It was all I could do not to take my sunshade to that wicked man's sides! And so I told him!"

"And he fled—incontinent? You should have been with us at the Rhune!"

"Oh, *I* did not chase him off," she said demurely. "Rather, I set the dogs on the fellow."

"What, those two ancient Danes? They can scarce totter about."

"No, but they do bark and growl so beautifully." She laughed outright. "The villain turned as white as the child was black, and ran like a hare!"

"How I should love to have seen it! But I'll lay odds our Roger was most perturbed."

"Yes. So I apologized, listened attentively to his advice to put the boy in a foundling home, and instead brought him here. That was only ten days before you came home. I sent him down to Surrey hoping we could get some meat on his poor bones, and also because he had become almost doglike in his devotion to me. I'd hoped it would . . ." She hesitated.

"Enlarge his horizons? Ain't. He looks at you as if you was the Goddess of the Dawn." Buchanan's blue eyes twinkled. "And he's not the only one. I—"

"I intend to teach him to read and write," Euphemia interposed hurriedly. "You can see he's already made progress, and he is so eager to learn. How sad that the poor boy is quite unable to speak."

"So, what are my orders? A tiger? Good old Ted Ridgley might—"

"No! I have seen Lord Ridgley drive! If you do not object, dear, I mean to keep him here, and perhaps educate him sufficiently that he could train for a valet."

Buchanan pursed his lips. "Lofty aspirations for a lad without a name."

Her brows lifted at this, as did her firm chin, but before she could speak, he threw up one hand and conceded, "I surrender! I know that look too well! Unless I mistake it, our Kent is already fated to valet Prinny someday. At the very least!"

Buchanan withdrew his gaze from the wintry scene beyond the carriage windows and his thoughts from the 52nd, and turned to his sister, muffled in her fur-lined pelisse, the hood drawn up even inside the luxurious vehicle. "I beg your pardon? What cannot you like?"

"Kent sitting up there on the box with Neeley," repeated Euphemia. "He must be utterly chilled and is so very frail."

"Frail? Devil a bit of it! The boy's all sinewy steel. I vow, Mia, after a day with him at the Exeter Exchange, I thought I'd be obliged to take myself to the nearest surgeon! Even Old Hookey don't run us that hard! Why, damme if I ever had a chance to get cool, let alone cold! And it was freezing!"

Since her brother had returned from that expedition with Kent's hand confidently tucked in his, and the pair of them with eyes aglow and cheeks rosy, she was undismayed and said smilingly, "You have worked wonders with him." She thought, And how we shall miss you when you go back . . . But pushing that grim spectre away, asked, "How old is he, would you suppose?"

"Who knows? Climbing boys are usually so stunted it would be difficult to hazard a guess. To judge from his size, had he not been working long in the chimneys, he might be six or seven. Otherwise, he could be as old as twelve." They were silent for a moment, occupied with their thoughts. Then he said, "I'm glad you kept him, Mia. I like the boy. He's surprisingly mannerly. Have you remarked how he eats? Almost finicking, he is so dainty about it."

"Yes, and never pushes himself forward, or behaves in a crude way. There is good blood in him, I do believe."

"I fancy you have tried to question him about his past?"

"Many times. But it is quite hopeless, except—I went to

26

visit Sir Giles Breckenridge in Town. Sir Giles and Deirdre and I fell into a discussion of the war, and I suddenly realized that Kent had wandered off and was staring at the big canvas of the gypsy encampment. You recall it, I've no doubt." Her brother, no art lover, merely wrinkled his brow dubiously, and she went on. "Well, at all events, Kent held my hand very tightly and kept pointing up at the painting. He seemed so agitated, poor mite, I can only think that at one time he may have lived with gypsies."

"Stolen, beyond doubting," he nodded soberly. "And they sold him for a climbing boy." A gust of wind rocked the carriage, and, glancing out at the starkly unclad trees and bleak countryside, he muttered, "Jove, it's a good thing I decided to leave yesterday! Had we tried to journey next week, I doubt we would have reached Bath in time for Easter! Looks like it is about to snow, drat it!"

He quite expected this observation to trigger a request that Kent be brought inside, which he had begun to think would be justified. To his surprise, however, his sister asked absently, "Where is Dominer?"

"Domino?" He stared at her. "Does Aunt Lucasta plan a masquerade, then? Good lord, I cannot abide such frippery—"

"I said *Dominer*, silly! The estate."

"Oh, you mean Hawkhurst's place. About ten miles this side of Bath." Curious, he asked, "Why?"

"Have you ever seen it?"

"Papa took me there once, when I was a boy. There was a fête or some such thing. As I recall, it is absolutely magnificent. Everything they say of it." He frowned and, a chill light dawning in his eyes, asked, "*You* have not been there, I trust?"

The unfamiliar tone brought her head around to him. "Good gracious, if it is as lovely as you say, I'd think you would want me to see it."

"I had best not catch you within ten miles of the place!" he growled. "Fellow's got the worst reputation I ever heard of! Downright shocking!"

"A rake?" Her eyes sparkled, but, noting that his mouth had settled into the grim line that came so seldom to his pleasant countenance despite his personal troubles, she was intrigued and said chidingly, "Now, Simon, I never knew you to be strait-laced. And you must certainly be aware I am perfectly capable of taking care of myself."

"More than a rake, Mia."

27

"A traitor? A-a bluebeard? Oh, *pray* do not be fusty! Tell me! Has he murdered seven wives and tossed their bodies to the dogs? Or—Good gracious, dearest! I spoke in jest, merely."

"It is no jest. But I collect I had best tell you what I know of it, before you decide you may rearrange *his* life for him!" Buchanan's frown lingered, and, waiting with interest, Euphemia forgot the frigid temperatures and decided that Hawkhurst must be a real scoundrel.

"You will not remember Blanche Spaulding, I fancy," he began slowly. "Devilish pretty girl. Fair as an angel, with great green eyes, and the softest, sweetest voice you might ever wish to hear. She was the undisputed Toast about . . . Well, it was when I was still up at Cambridge—must be seven or eight years ago. At all events, every Buck in Town was after her, although she was practically portionless. Why she chose Hawkhurst none of us could understand. Oh, he was popular enough, then, and I'll admit, a fine sportsman. But never much for looks, and Blanche was not the type to marry a man's wealth. Still, he wooed and won her and took her to Dominer, and she was seldom in Town after that. A year later, I heard she had presented him with an heir. I'd have thought no more about it, but one night I dined with Timothy van Lindsay—one of your more ardent beaux!" He grinned as Euphemia smiled archly, and went on, "Tim chanced to mention that rumours were rife about the Hawkhursts. Ugly little whispers that he ill-treated her; certainly, he was known to have taken a very high-flyer under his protection. I thought it most sad, for Blanche had been such a lovely little creature, but it soon slipped my mind again. The whole thing broke like a mine blast at the time I came home with that fever. I can only think Hawkhurst had become ripe for Bedlam. From what I gather, he had been conducting a running feud with a neighbour, a jolly good chap, Lord Gains, who was used to be one of his oldest friends. One night, Gains rode over to Dominer to demand an accounting. They quarrelled fiercely, and instead of calling the fellow out like a gentleman, Hawkhurst tossed some kind of acid in his face!"

Euphemia gave a gasp. "How despicable!"

"Wasn't it! Blinded Gains in one eye."

"Good heavens! They went out, of course?"

"Can't say . . ." His brows furrowed thoughtfully. "I never heard of it."

"Even so, how did this affect your lovely Blanche?"

"From what I heard, when she ventured to reproach her husband for such revolting behaviour, he knocked her down. The poor girl probably thought him quite crazed, for she fled the house that very night, with her child and her maid. It's said Hawkhurst chased her half across the Continent. Nobody really knows what happened, save that catch her he did, in the south of France. And that very day her chaise went off the road and into the sea."

Appalled, Euphemia asked, "Was she killed?"

Buchanan nodded glumly. "And her little boy. Hawkhurst came home. He wouldn't admit it, of course, but everyone knows. The chaise, you see, had been tampered with. The Préfet de Police of the area made it known that he was sure foul play had been done, and they say Hawkhurst got away barely ahead of a mob eager to exact justice for the little lady."

Euphemia was silent for a moment, her lively imagination re-creating the tragic episode. "I can scarce believe," she muttered, "that such monsters walk the earth. Why, he should have been hanged! Though, were it up to me, I'd have ordered him drawn and quartered, besides! That poor girl . . . how utterly terrified she must have been for her baby!"

"What vexes me so," growled Buchanan, "is that no one would help her. Since she died Hawkhurst has become a positively slavering rake, though he never goes near Town, of course. Likely be run out on a rail, did he try it! So now you can see why I will not have you near that place."

"Yes. Though . . . we could see the house from a distance, could we not?"

He said a grudging, "I suppose so. It is on a hill, as I recall. Why? Have you an insatiable craving to see what a monster looks like?"

"Heavens—no! But, well, Kent so loves to look through my *Guide to the West Country*, and he especially admires Dominer. It would be so nice for him to see the actual estate." She watched Simon's disapproving frown anxiously. "Is Hawkhurst *always* in residence? Might he not have gone away for the holidays?"

"Matter of fact, by the oddest coincidence, I saw his curricle in Reading last night. Drives fine cattle, I'll say that for him."

"*Curricle!* In this weather? His poor groom!"

"Told you he belongs in Bedlam. Even so, Mia, he owns the land for miles around. I cannot like you to set foot on it!"

"Then I promise not to leave the carriage! Oh, I should so

29

like to see the house, and it would take us only a little way from our road. Please, dear?"

Buchanan argued, fumed, and struggled. And in the end, of course, he pulled on the check string and lowered the window to call to Neeley. Settling back again, his teeth chattering with cold, he murmured a disgusted, "W-W-Women!"

"Oh, but the countryside is heavenly!" exclaimed Euphemia, admiring rolling hills that fringed a patchwork of neatly hedged meadows spread out below them. "How unjust that so evil a man should own it all."

Buchanan, his cheek pressed against the window, said, "And more unjust that we are followed! If it is your Bluebeard, my girl . . ."

"You do not really think so? Heavens! Tell Neeley to turn around!"

"What, on this blasted narrow track, with a sheer drop three feet from the wheels? Devil I will! Besides . . ." He opened the window and, squinting into the icy air, hurriedly drew back. "Perhaps I was mistaken. He may have turned off, for there is no one in sight now, and—"

There came a sudden thunderous roar. Euphemia's eyes widened in fright and Neeley's voice rang out in a shriek. Buchanan glanced to the left, snatched his sister into his arms, then they were flung down as a great shock hit the coach. The breath smashed from her lungs, Euphemia did not even have time to scream . . .

Papa's batman had left the tent flap open again, most assuredly he had, for the air was full of dust, and the endless Spanish wind . . . was . . . Euphemia opened her eyes. For an instant nothing was clearly distinguishable. Then she saw a light floating above her. She frowned at it in puzzlement, and gradually it resolved itself into a window. But what in the world was the carriage window doing up there . . . ? Her head hurt, and dust was everywhere. It was hard to think, and harder to breathe. But that was not because of the dust. Something was across her throat. She reached up and pulling away an arm, turned to discover Simon, huddled and unconscious beside her, his white face resting on the right-hand windows. With a sob of fear, she remembered. There must have been a landslide—or perhaps a tree had fallen. "Simon!" she choked. Her brother gave no sign of life. Her head throbbing, she struggled to sit up, and the carriage rocked alarmingly. What was it he had said just before the accident? ". . . a sheer drop three feet from the wheels . . ." My God! she thought. Are we hanging over the edge? Moving cautiously, she managed to touch his face. It was warm. He was alive still, but perhaps his shoulder was hurt again. She tried to kneel and gave a little gasp of terror as once more the carriage lurched. Why did Neeley not come to help them? Oh, if only Simon had not sent her maids and his valet on ahead of them! And—

"This is no time to essay a quadrille, ma'am."

Her heart jumped despite that calm and lazy drawl. A man was looking down at her through the left-hand window that now was so crazily situated in the air. An arresting face, lean, and with deep clefts between the brows and beside the thin nostrils. He was very dark, the loosely curling hair touched at the temples with grey, and Euphemia had a brief impression of kind eyes, a high-bridged nose, a well-shaped mouth just now curving to a smile, and a strong chin.

"If you will stay quiet a minute or two, we shall have you clear," he said, and vanished. She heard his deep voice issuing crisp orders.

Then another man called, "The horses must've broke loose and bolted, sir. No sign of 'em. Will I unhitch one of the greys?"

"No, you fool. How would you get him over that damned great mess? Run to the house and bring men. And send a groom for Dr. Archer. I said—*run!* Manners! Get over here and help me set some boulders on these wheels—and fast, before the wind beats us!"

Kent! thought Euphemia, and started up only to shrink back as the carriage heaved terrifyingly.

"Madam!" He was at the window again, a glitter in the eyes that she now saw were a remarkably fine, clear grey. The drawl was gone as he said sternly, "If you will refrain from hopping about in there, we may yet—"

"But . . . the boy—" she began.

His keen gaze flashed to Buchanan. "—will stand a better chance of recovering do you not dance the pair of you down the cliff!" he interposed curtly and was gone.

"Wait!"

But he did not wait, and a faint moan escaped her brother just then, as he stirred, provoking an exasperated, "Oh, damn the woman!" from outside.

31

"Lie still, dearest," said Euphemia urgently. "Simon, are you much hurt?"

His eyes opened dazedly. He raised his head, and she could have wept her relief because, although his cheek and forehead were cut, his eye was unhurt. "What . . . ?" he muttered. And then, in a clearer voice, "Mia! My God! Are you—" Frantic, he got an elbow beneath him and started up, but at once his face twisted with pain, a choked gasp cut off his words, and he slumped down again. Euphemia's half-screamed, *"Simon!"* returned their rescuer's face to the window.

"All right, ma'am. Let us have you out. Are you injured?"

He was wrestling with the door, and when she had replied that she was not at all hurt, he grumbled an impatient, "Manners? Where in the deuce are you?" The door swung suddenly upward, then fell open with a crash. Euphemia's heart leapt into her throat, but this time there was no resultant rocking from the carriage.

"Everything's right and tight," said the stranger, giving her an engaging grin as he reached for her hands. "Can you manage? Lots of room for dancing out here. I'm sure you shall like it . . . better. Up you come!"

His grip was very strong, and she was hoisted to sit on the side of the carriage while he jumped down. He reached up, smiling that warm quirkish smile, and she leaned to him and was lifted to the ground.

"My brother!" she gasped. "He's newly home from the Nivelle, and—"

"Is he, by God!" He swung back onto the carriage side once more. "Wounded . . . ? Where?"

"His right shoulder. And I fear he has hurt it again."

"Wouldn't be surprised." He disappeared into the interior, his voice coming muffled to her. "You sit down, ma'am, and we—"

"And there is a boy!" she called.

His head reappeared, and he scanned her tautly. "Not on the box, was he?"

"Yes." She glanced around a scene of chaotic devastation. Great heaps of rocks, dirt, and smashed shrubbery spoke of the fury of the landslide. A liveried groom was bent above a sprawled shape, and she said anxiously, "Neeley! Is he . . . ?"

"Lucky to be alive, ma'am. Minor damage." He climbed out and with a supple leap was beside her. "Your brother don't

32

seem too bad. But—I fear that the boy may have gone over the side."

Euphemia followed his frowning gaze and swayed, a sickness sweeping over her. The carriage lay at the very brink of the road, the boot hanging out over the drop. Only a small tree, now horizontally leaning in space, had saved them from going straight down, but they undoubtedly would have been at the foot of the cliff by now, but for the heavy boulders that were piled on the right wheels. She started for the edge, and at once a firm hand was upon her arm. She flashed an irritated look at her rescuer, mildly surprised to find that she had to look up at him, although he was not so tall as Leith. He accompanied her without comment, however, only tightening his hold when she stood at the brink. Instead of the gradual slope she had so hoped to find, she looked down a perpendicular wall to tree-tops far below. There was no sign of Kent . . .

"Steady," said that deep voice. "Perhaps he . . . was . . ." She heard the hiss of indrawn breath and, glancing up, saw his narrowed eyes fixed to the right. Looking there also, she threw a hand to her mouth, at once relieved and terrified. The sheer wall bowed outward at that point, and from beneath the outcropping could be glimpsed what appeared to be the roots of a bush. And clinging to those roots, two small, white hands! She sobbed, "Oh . . . my dear God!"

"Why in the devil didn't he shout?" the man grumbled, already shrugging out of his many-caped driving coat and a peerlessly cut jacket. "Is he mute?"

"Yes."

He shot an astonished glance at her, then shouted, "Manners!" and, as the groom sped towards them, drawled "I dare not fancy myself so blessed that you've a rope in your carriage, ma'am?"

She confirmed this pessimism, and Manners, a dark, impassive-featured, slender man, came up and said coolly, "Sir?"

"Cut the reins from the greys. Fast."

Manners was gone.

Looking down at the small, desperately gripping hands and the petrifying drop below them, Euphemia opened her mouth to call encouragement.

Strong fingers clamped ruthlessly over her lips. "No sympathy, for Lord's sake! If the boy loves you, that very love may weaken him." He withdrew his hand. "What's his name?"

However irked she might be by such arrogance, she could not but accept the wisdom of his words, and replied, "Kent."

"Hey, there Kent!" he shouted, tossing his jacket aside. "I'm coming down after you. If you let go before I get there—I'll blister your rump!" He slanted a faint grin at Euphemia. "Your pardon, ma'am. Oh, good man! And already tied." He tugged at the thin leathers Manners handed him and nodded his approval, then came to the edge and played the impromptu rope downward. "Not long enough. Dammit! Ma'am, I'll essay that climb, but a fly I am not. Your pelisse, by your leave." It was off in a flash, and Euphemia fighting against shivering from both cold and apprehension, as he used his pocket knife to slash it into four strips. He tied knots dextrously and tested them hard but, still not satisfied, proceeded to rend his coat in like fashion. When the last strip was tied, he muttered, "That should suffice." He secured one end of the rope about his lean middle, his eyes searching about. His horses would have been invaluable, but the great mound of earth and rubble completely blocked the road. Close at hand, a downed tree offered an upthrusting splintered, but solid-looking, branch. "Manners." He pointed. "Use that." He thrust the rope at his groom and strode towards the rim.

Euphemia's heart was thundering. The leather looked so thin, and her pelisse and his coat bulky and unreliable. Two lives would depend upon that clumsy line. Manners, echoing her thoughts, said a worried, "Mr. Garret, I—"

His employer was already sitting with his legs over the edge. "Blast your eyes, hasten!" he commanded, but his brilliant grin flashed an appreciation of the solicitude. The groom shook his head, took up the slack, and looped the rope about the branch, holding the free end firmly. "Play it out evenly, now," cautioned Mr. Garret. He swung around, gripped the edge with both hands for a second, then lowered himself.

Euphemia's breathing seemed to stop. The dark head swung perilously beneath her, but she saw that he was leaning against the rope, bracing himself with his feet as he backed down. He seemed, she thought gratefully, to know what he was about. The wind was blowing the fine cambric of the white shirt, and she noted absently the breadth of the shoulders and the ripple of the muscles. He must be half frozen, but he was a splendid athlete, no doubt of that. He was also solidly powerful; Manners, more slenderly built, would never have been able to haul him up! She turned back, intending to offer her help, and was greatly relieved to see Neeley, battered and bloody, but assisting in the playing out of the rope. Peering anxiously over the edge, she could still see Kent's hands, and then Garret, far down on the outcropping, roared, "More, for God's Sake! About six feet! Hurry!"

She relayed the information to the men at the tree and saw the rope slacken. Too fast! she thought and, sure enough, heard a blistering outburst of cursing from beneath the outcropping.

"Hold up now!" shouted Mr. Garret, and she waved an imperative summons to Manners. She could not see either man or child, and there was no sound for a few seconds. Then she heard the rumble of Garret's voice, followed by a sudden sharp crack, a shout, and the rope became taut. She whispered, "My God . . . My God!"

A considerably breathless voice restored her heartbeat. "Haul . . . away!"

The men hauled obediently, and the leather became appallingly taut. It must not snap . . . it *must* not! Shaking with cold and anxiety, her head splitting, Euphemia peered downward. Mr. Garret's wind-tossed hair came first into view, and she saw that he was trying to ease the pressure on the rope by again half-walking. She saw also, with a great surge of thankfulness, that he held Kent, not on his back, as she would have supposed, but clinging around his neck, so that the man's arms were an added protection about him.

Her relief was short-lived. The rope seemed to slip backward a little, and she saw Garret flash a tense glance upward. One of the seams in the coat was unravelling! Before her horrified eyes, the garment, still several feet below the edge, began to pull apart. Momentarily frozen with terror, she heard Mr. Garret's harsh, "Take him! Quick!" He was holding the boy upright, the small feet on his chest, the hands reaching to her. Without an instant's hesitation she flung herself flat and stretched down her arms. She could just barely feel Kent's fingertips. Garret managed another step. She heard a ripping sound, but she had those frail hands fast gripped now. A startled cry rang out, and the boy was a dead weight. She thought anguishedly, It broke! That brave man is dead! But then, beyond Kent's white terror-stricken face, she saw that by some mighty effort Mr. Garret, freed of the encumbrance of the boy, had managed to grab the parting rope just above the ripped fabric and clung, with both hands, to the leather strap.

Kent was astoundingly heavy, and for once she was glad to

be tall and strong. She pulled with all her might but with little success, until strong hands came to aid her, and Neeley was dragging Kent over the rim. She saw Mr. Garret, climbing hand over hand up the rope. Sitting up, she took the shuddering child in her arms, and he clung to her, sobbing in silent hysteria.

Neeley was reaching down again. "Jolly well done, sir!" he cried, and Mr. Garret hove into view and seconds later was sitting close by, head down, panting heavily.

Only then did Euphemia recall that her brother still lay hurt and alone. Gently, she put Kent aside, clambered to her feet, and tottered towards the carriage. Vaguely, she knew that Manners was bending over his employer, and that Neeley was comforting the boy. She was weeping now, feeling sick from the reaction, and her head hurt so. The landscape began to blur and waver before her eyes. I cannot faint yet, she thought doggedly. A strong arm was supporting her, and she leaned gratefully against a white shirt, saw it spotted with crimson and glanced up to discover Mr. Garret beside her, an ugly laceration above his right eye. He had, she thought numbly, very fine eyes, the grey emphasized by a dark band around the outer rim of the iris . . .

Her last sensation was of being swept up and held like a child in his arms. She had not been lifted so in years . . . he must be very strong. She felt perfectly safe . . .

❧ Chapter 3 ❧

"Of course I intend to lay her upon a bed! Had you the ornamental water in mind?"

The words were uttered in a low but irked tone, and interrupted Euphemia's comfortable doze. She did not quite hear the words the woman spoke but was amused by the snorted vehemence of the male voice. "D'ye take me for a gapeseed? Be assured I know it. But her brother's with her and—"

Simon! Euphemia's eyes shot open. She was not in the rocking coach as she'd drowsily supposed. Instead, she was being carried through a room redolent with the smell of burning logs and lit by a warm, glowing light. Above her was a high and splendidly plastered ceiling. She realized that her head had fallen back, and raising it a little saw a very long and wide hall, charmingly furnished, and decorated throughout in shades of blue, gold, and cream.

"So you are awake," said Mr. Garret in a gentler fashion. "Parsley!"

That commanding shout sent Euphemia's hand to her aching brow.

"You've a fine lump," he nodded. "My apologies!" And in a fierce whisper, "Aunt Carlotta, *where* is that blasted idiot of a butler?"

"He is attending to the bedrooms. Now pray do not be provoked. You yourself told the maids they might go to help decorate the Church Hall."

Mr. Garret now turned into a huge circular central area, this floored with exquisite parquetry and decorated in a continuation of the main theme. Brocaded blue and cream draperies, tied back by gold-tasselled cords, hung at the many windows; giant double doors at the left apparently constituted the main entrance, and from the centre of the room a graceful staircase spiralled upwards.

Awed, Euphemia murmured, "I would like to be put down, if you please."

"So you shall," he whispered, his eyes glinting at her. "Upon a bed. And why in the devil couldn't Mrs. Henderson attend to the bedrooms?"

Still a little muddled, Euphemia was about to tell him she was not acquainted with a Mrs. Henderson when the woman answered, "Because she is preparing bandages and medical supplies and heating water."

"Good God! One might suppose I have not a maid or lackey left!"

"They are—"

"Never mind." He started up the stairs, paused, and, half-turning, drawled, "Is Colley here yet?"

For the first time, Euphemia had a clear view of the lady who followed them. Of middle age and with black, neatly banded hair under a beautiful lace cap, she wore a mulberry wool gown trimmed with black velvet. She was excessively thin, the skin of the fine-boned face having an almost stretched look. Her eyes were dark and lustrous, but just now filled with resentment, as she looked at the man above her and said with a defiant lift of her chin, "He is expected."

"So is the Messiah," he snorted and continued on his way.

Euphemia fixed him with her most daunting frown. "I do not wish to be laid down upon a bed. I wish to see my brother and Kent. Are they all right?"

"Your brother is being carried here." Mr. Garret paused again on the curve of the stairs and leaned against the railing for an instant. "Gad, you are no lightweight, ma'am!"

Ignoring this unkind observation, she gasped, "Carried? He is not—"

"Knocked out of time. Nothing worse than that shoulder, I think, so do not fret. But he insisted upon remaining staunchly beside you until he folded up like a dropped marionette." The grim smile he flashed at her held none of the warmth or kindness she had found in it at the landslide and, with a sudden chill of apprehension, she said, "I have not . . . introduced myself. I am—"

"I know who you are. And now you've exactly the same look as your bacon-brained brother."

"My brother, sir," frowned Euphemia, as he again strode upward, "is—"

"Is quite convinced I have carried you here so as to lock you in the nearest bedchamber and rape you."

She gave a gasp and, hearing a shocked cry ring out from below, knew at last who carried her. "You . . ." she stammered, filled with an illogical sense of crushing disappointment, "you are—"

"Garret Thorndyke Hawkhurst," he announced, his chin lifting and the thin nostrils flaring a little. He glanced down when she made no comment, his heavy lids drooping over the grey eyes in an expression of mocking hauteur she was soon to identify with him. "What—ain't you going to swoon?"

"Miss Buchanan," intervened the lady he had referred to as "Aunt Carlotta," "I most humbly apologize for my nephew's unforgivable language. His sense of humour is atrocious!"

He uttered a subdued grunt, and at that moment they reached the first floor. A door flew open, and a man called, "In here, sir. We have all in readiness."

Hawkhurst strode into a magnificent bedchamber, boasting a great luxurious bed with the silken sheets turned down and rich curtains tied back at the posts. He bent to set his burden very gently on the bed, but for an instant seemed to lose his balance, and braced himself with one hand on the velvet coverlet.

Euphemia realized belatedly that he looked pale and, glancing from that scratched hand to the bloodied forehead, said, "I fear you were hurt when the rope dropped so fast."

He made no response, still leaning over her, his eyes fixed on her face in a searching intensity. She thought, This man murdered his wife and child and threw acid in the face of his friend ... And instinctively, recoiled. At once his expression changed, his lip curled, and the scorn returned to his eyes, full measure.

"Are you all right, Mr. Garret?" An impressive gentleman with thinning brown hair and a thickening waistline, presumably the butler, took Hawkhurst's arm and peered at him anxiously.

"Of course, I am all right." He straightened. "Have they brought Buchanan in yet? Or the child?"

His aunt, who was instructing one maid to pour hot water into the bathtub before the fire, and another to "bring the posset now," spun around and stared in horror. "A *child*? In *this* house?"

The faintest flush appeared on Hawkhurst's cheeks. "Unfortunately. But we'll see our guests on their way at first light." A gleam lit his eyes, and he added, "Sooner, does Buchanan have his way."

"They are both here, sir," the butler murmured. "Mrs. Henderson is with the little boy."

Euphemia restrained the comely maid who bent to speak to her, and asked anxiously, "Is my brother badly hurt?"

The butler darted a look at his master. "My staff have their limitations, ma'am," drawled that gentleman. "Among 'em, my butler is not a physician. But we've a splendid fellow in Down Buttery. He will be far better equipped to answer your questions." He lifted one autocratic hand as her lips parted, and went on, his boredom very apparent, "Meanwhile, whatever else I may be, I have not lately murdered the child of a guest. So by all means set your mind at rest and allow my servants to restore you." He bowed, started away, then turned back again, frowning, "Devil take me, I've lived in this wilderness too long! My aunt, Lady Carlotta Bryce, Miss Euphemia

Buchanan." And he added with an amused grin, "Colonel Sir Army Buck's daughter."

Surprised both by his knowledge of Armstrong Buchanan's nickname and by Lady Bryce's obvious astonishment, Euphemia shook the dainty hand that was extended and, as Hawkhurst prepared to leave, called, "One moment, if you please, sir."

He swung back, one dark brow lifting in haughty condescension.

"Whatever else I may be," she said gravely, "I've not lately neglected to thank a very brave gentleman who saved my life, and nigh lost his own, rescuing my page."

She saw surprise come into his eyes and knew he had assumed Kent to be a relation. Then he grinned and bowed theatrically.

"Mia! Are you all right?" Buchanan stood clinging to the doorjamb, a dramatic figure with his white, bloodstreaked face and eyes desperate with fear as they flashed from Euphemia to their reluctant host.

" 'Course she ain't," mocked Hawkhurst rudely. "In *my* lair? Come now, Buchanan, you know better than that!"

"Most ridiculous damned-nonsense I ever heard of!" The stocky, grey-haired physician who had been peremptorily summoned from Down Buttery glared at Sir Simon, sprawled on a blue and white striped sofa in this elegant small salon, and demanded, "Why in the devil could you not be laid down upon a bed like any normal, rational gentleman?"

It was the last straw. Frustrated because he had been forced to permit Mia being carried into this evil house, fretted by the knowledge that his hurt was exacerbated and his recovery thereby further delayed, humiliated by the awareness that he was under considerable obligation to a man he despised, and in a good deal of pain, Buchanan was in a foul temper and answered with a rudeness normally foreign to him. "Because no 'normal, rational gentleman' would be seen dead in this house, Dr. Archer! Besides which, my unwed sister is in my charge, and were I to lie down upon a bed, I might be so ill-advised as to fall asleep and thus leave her defenceless!"

Archer stiffened. His bushy eyebrows drew together, and the deep-set brown eyes below them fairly shot sparks. He hauled over a small table and slammed his leather bag onto it. "Positively overset with gratitude, ain't you?"

Buchanan reddened and, wishing he might retract his remarks, said wearily, "I intend to properly thank Mr. Hawkhurst. I am aware I stand indebted to the man."

"Charmingly said. Your manners, I presume, grow on one." Archer flung open his bag.

"Pray do not put yourself to any great effort in my behalf," said Buchanan. "I mean to leave here just as soon as my sister is recovered."

The shirt beneath the injured man's cravat was wet and crimson and, unbuttoning it, the doctor smiled grimly. "Do you? I wish I may see it."

"And I wish I may see the last of you, sir!" Buchanan wrenched himself upward, sank his teeth into his underlip, and sagged back again.

Archer heard the faint gasp and saw sweat start on the pallid brow. The boy was in no state to be rational, and, irritated for having allowed himself to become so angry, he at once became angrier, and roared, "Hawk! Parsley! Mrs. *Hen* . . . derson . . . !" No response being forthcoming, he returned his attention to his unhappy patient and growled, "So you intend to repay your rescuer by forcing me to work on you in here, and likely ruin his pretty sofa."

"To the . . . contrary, sir. I have not the least desire to . . . impose upon your time," quoth Buchanan, indomitable but very white of lip. "All I ask is that you . . . tie it up and let me reimburse you . . . and be on my way."

Archer ignored him and cut away the sodden dressing, and after a brief but unpleasant interval announced that a bone chip was coming out. "Just as well. Ain't healing properly. What you get when you consult those puffed-up fools in London. Sooner go to a native witchdoctor! Have to open it."

Buchanan's feeble protestations were brushed aside. Another series of roars for assistance made him jump, and the physician marched to tug fruitlessly on the bellrope, then returned, muttering, "Whole blasted army of servants hovering about 'til you need one! Weather's awful. You want to go by yourself, that's your bread and butter. But the child certainly cannot travel."

"Kent? Was he hurt then? I had thought—"

"That he would be dead were it not for your despised host? Had you? Hmnnn. I'd not have guessed it." Archer met the blaze of those blue eyes levelly, then rummaged in his bag

41

and brought forth a small but vicious-looking knife and several bottles.

Incensed beyond endurance, Buchanan hauled himself upward. Archer pushed him back and observed with a marked lack of sympathy that he'd thought, "our gallant military heroes feared nothing."

"Not an ill-mannered . . . country doctor at all . . . events!" flared Buchanan.

"I am most dreadfully sorry Dr. Hal," called a soft voice from the doorway. "But I fear we are rather short of maids this afternoon. They are gone to help decorate the Church, you see, and the two we have left are preparing guest rooms and assisting Mrs. Henderson. Hawk has taken most of the men to help with his team and see if they can clear the road."

"Stephanie? Come in, my dear." The doctor's gruff bark was suddenly gentled, and he bent lower to hiss at the still fuming Buchanan. "Hawkhurst's sister, and she loves him, so I'll thank you to keep a civil tongue in your head!" He ignored the spluttering wrath this adjuration provoked, laid a pad over the wound, and turned to smile at the girl who moved towards them. "Will you be so kind, Stephie, as to give me your assistance here? Oh, for God's sake, man! Miss Hawkhurst's seen a male chest before! She's a splendid nurse. Helped me at the village last winter when the wind took the roof off the Parish Hall and two of the walls collapsed. I'll need a glass of water too, m'dear. A fine set-to that was, with better than thirty men, women, and children hurt, ladies fainting in all directions, and our brave girl here, working like a da—er, like a ministering angel. Some hot water now if you please. Oh, by the bye, Miss Hawkhurst, this gallant is Lieutenant Sir Simon Buchanan, come home with a mangled shoulder from that fool Wellington's caperings. Well, do not gobble, sir! You have just been introduced to a lady."

His ferocious glare challenged the seething Buchanan, who somehow overcame his fury at this maligning of the superb Wellington and uttered a polite, if uneven, response. Beyond his first horrified glance, he had tried not to look at the female who quietly assisted the volatile doctor in laying out the horrendous articles of torture with which he was all too well acquainted. During Archer's monologue, however, he had slanted a shy glance at her and discovered a slight, young woman of average height, with light-brown hair fashioned into fat braided coils behind her ears. Her fair complexion was just now rather

42

pink, doubtless from maidenly embarrassment, but he thought clinically that she had little to recommend her in the way of looks, seeming utterly colourless in her plain, dove-grey gown. Her hands, however, were slender and beautifully shaped, with long tapering fingers, and she moved them with smooth grace as she pursued her tasks. He was watching them when she glanced up. Her hazel eyes were large and well-opened, holding a calm, gentle expression, but encountering his, the pale lashes fluttered down at once, and the colour in her cheeks deepened.

Archer, meanwhile, had finished his preparations and was stripping off his jacket. "You'd best find an old sheet, Stephie," he said. "Hawk will take a dim view of my spoiling his sofa, and Sir Lancelot here refuses a bed in this nefarious pile."

Miss Hawkhurst slanted a faintly reproachful glance at Buchanan's scarlet countenance, and left them, walking with smooth, unaffected gait, to the door.

"B-by God!" Buchanan burst out when she was gone. "*Had* you to say that?"

Measuring pale liquid into a glass, Archer muttered, "She is a gracious girl, and I sought to spare her the mortification of having an offer of hospitality flung back in her teeth."

"Flung . . . back— Now, damn your eyes, sir! What d'ye take me for?"

Archer thrust the glass at him. "I take you, sir, for a self-righteous, stubborn young ass. But—I could be wrong. Drink it all down."

Buchanan forgot his rage as he peered uneasily into the glass. "What is it—laudanum?"

"Would you believe me did I tell you it was?" Archer's lip curled. He bent closer and hissed dramatically. "It is really oil of vitriol! We also arrange landslides every Tuesday morning and have a secret and well-filled cemetery in the basement!"

It would have been so simple to explain that he was one of those unfortunates totally unable to tolerate the drug, but by this time Buchanan was too enraged to be logical. He ground his teeth and said an icy, "Thank you. No!"

"Good God! A Spartan!" Archer gave a snort of ridicule and set the glass aside as Miss Hawkhurst returned, carrying a steaming bowl and with a sheet over her arm. With unexpected gentleness the physician assisted Buchanan to raise himself so that the sheet might be slipped under him. "I shall have to sit down to work," he grumbled. "Not a customary position. I will try not to allow my hand to slip very far, I promise you."

"Doctor Hal!" The girl's words held a gentle reproach.

Buchanan found her concerned gaze full on him. She had, he noted then, the kindest eyes he'd ever seen. His shoulder was pure torment, but he felt comforted and managed a smile. "It was my fault, ma'am. I was rude."

"I'll own I've little patience with stupidity," rumbled the doctor.

Miss Hawkhurst shook her head at him and said with a reassuring, "No matter what he *says*, Sir Simon, you are in the best possible hands."

Archer grinned and took up his glittering little blade. The faint colour receded from Buchanan's face. Suddenly, he looked very young and helpless, and, knowing he was suffering miserably, the doctor's mood softened. "You've seen one of these before, I collect. Miss Hawkhurst will endeavour to hold you, but if you'd a single grain of sense you'd take the laudanum."

"It will not be necessary to hold me. I shall manage," Buchanan asserted, his muscles cramping into knots as the blade came closer.

Archer shrugged and bent forward. "For about two seconds," he estimated cynically.

He had reckoned without the dogged courage of his patient. Buchanan lasted for ten.

The fire was sending out a pleasant warmth now, and seated in the deep chair beside it, Euphemia listened drowsily to Kent's deep, steady breathing. He was asleep at last, poor child. Winding the sash tassels of her borrowed dressing gown into a braid, she glanced around the bedchamber which had been assigned to him. The small room was lit only by the flickering flames of the fire and one candle, placed on a table far from the bed, but even by this dim light, luxury was manifested in thick carpets, tasteful furnishings, and rich appointments. Such a very lovely house, even as Simon had told her.

Thought of her brother brought a pang of guilt. She could only hope he would give her the most severe setdown of her life, as she so richly deserved. Had it not been for her insistence that they see Dominer, none of this would have happened, and he would not at this very moment be enduring heaven knows what misery at the doctor's hands. She consoled herself with the recollection that Hawkhurst had said Archer was "splendid." He had certainly seemed gentle and efficient when examining Kent, although his manner towards her had been rather dour. He'd told her the lump on her head was not serious, but that she should at once go to bed and get a good long sleep. He had started, in fact, to summon a maid to watch the child. Perhaps it was her refusal to leave Kent which had prompted that swift look of anger—perhaps he thought her afraid to go to her bedchamber. She had certainly not intended to imply a mistrust of the man who had rescued them, but on the other hand, Dr. Archer must be aware that she had cause for unease. She was an unwed lady, and should word ever leak out that she had spent the night here—even with Simon in the adjoining bedchamber—her reputation must be sadly tarnished.

Her mouth tightened a little as she recalled what Simon had told her of Blanche Hawkhurst. She would wedge a chair under the latch of the door to the corridor, that was certain! At once she was ashamed of the thought. Why must everything be so illogical? That their gallant rescuer should also prove to be a savage murderer was scarcely to be believed. In her mind's eye she could see him on that sheer cliff face, whipped by the wind, handing Kent up to her, his only apparent concern being that the child might be saved before the rope broke. Her every instinct told her that here was a most gallant gentleman, unhesitatingly risking the ultimate penalty for his valour. When he had later swept her into his arms, she had experienced the oddest sense of . . . what? Trust? She sighed. Misplaced, evidently, for Simon was not the man to exaggerate. There was only one answer: her usually unerring judgment had failed for once. The decision depressed her, and she was almost relieved when a threshing movement from the bed sent her springing up, only to gasp to the protest of sore muscles and move less precipitately to the boy.

Kent's small fair head tossed against the pillows, and his thin hands tore at the eiderdown. She leaned to take them in her own firm clasp, and the big eyes opened, frantic with fear. He flung himself into her arms and clung to her, panting and shuddering, and she hugged him close, murmuring that he was safe now, that everything was all right, until at last he quieted, and she was able to lay him back down. Poor little boy, she thought, stroking his hair fondly. The fear began to fade from his eyes. He smiled his blinding smile of gratitude and, when she urged him to go to sleep, closed his eyes obediently. She began to move back, but at once his hand tightened around her wrist, and he started up in new panic. "I shall not leave you," she promised gently.

Nonetheless, he watched anxiously as she returned to the chair, and for the next quarter hour would open his eyes from time to time, to assure himself that she was there.

A few moments after his deep and regular breathing told her he slept again, the door was cautiously opened to admit Lady Bryce, who came with swift and silent tread into the room. Euphemia stood to greet her and ask anxiously for word of her brother. "Dr. Archer is with him now, my dear," said her ladyship. She went over to feel Kent's forehead, then pursed her lips and shook her head worriedly. Returning to Euphemia, she said. "How very sad. But we will not despair. He may recover. And you must get to your bed at once. Why ever was a maid not sent to stay with him?" She made her graceful way towards the bellrope, but Euphemia placed a detaining hand upon her arm. "You are too kind, ma'am," she smiled. "But I have promised to stay."

"Pho! What silliness! We all have obligations to our servants, but you must not let him get the upper hand. And children *will* try us, you know."

This seemed to be rather in conflict with her earlier disquieting remark, but Euphemia merely answered, "Yes, I agree. But he has had a terrible shock and is an excessively nervous child, so I must keep my word."

"Nervous? At *his* age?" Lady Bryce gave a little titter. "Lud! It is easy to see how simply it would be to take advantage of so kind a mistress. But you must be kind to me also, Miss Buchanan. Do you come downstairs tomorrow morning looking even a trifle hagged, my nephew will be angry, and—Oh, dear. Now you will think him vicious, which he is not, I promise you, whatever you may have heard to the contrary. Hawkhurst does have a trace, the *teensiest* trifle of a temper, I grant you. And when he is angered, alas, I always am the one who—Well, what I mean to say is, he will not listen, however I may assure him I begged you to rest."

"Then I shall rest now and hope you will bear me company for a while," Euphemia smiled in her pleasant way and settled herself into the chair again. "Your nephew saved us, ma'am, did you know it? It was most gallant, and I am deeply indebted to him."

"Good gracious me! Never tell our Hawkhurst you feel indebted!" That thin little laugh rang out, and one delicate hand patted her wrist. "The naughty fellow would assuredly contrive to collect that debt. And it would be dreadful to upset your poor brother at such a time." Her ladyship bestowed herself in the larger armchair and went on in her soft, well modulated voice, "You cannot guess how very pleased we are—my sister-in-law and I, at least—to have visitors. I am perfectly sure you cannot like to be here, and who could blame you! Nor would we have wished you should suffer so horrible an experience, but . . ." With a wistful smile she sighed, "We do get so lonely, and—I will not dissemble—no one comes here any more. Not from London, at all events."

Her kind heart touched, Euphemia said, "What a great pity, ma'am. I will admit I have heard rumours, but it has been my experience that rumours tend to grow out of all proportion to actual fact."

"*Dear* Miss Buchanan! You express my own feelings exactly, for had I believed all that was said, *nothing* would have induced me to bring my own dear son to dwell under this roof. But, alas, I was ever of a trusting and gullible nature." She shook her head regretfully.

Euphemia blinked and, suspecting she was being drawn into very murky waters, attempted a change of subject. "I heard Mr. Hawkhurst mention someone named—Colley, is it, ma'am?"

"My only son." The dark eyes were lit with pride. "Coleridge is near twenty, though it don't seem possible. And the dearest, most handsome, and obliging-natured youth one would ever wish to meet." She gave an apologetic little laugh. "How naughty in me to puff off my own son, but he will be here soon, and you may judge for yourself. At least, I *pray* it will be soon." Her expression grew troubled, and the fine hands wrung nervously. "Hawk becomes *so* enraged if he is a little late."

"I see. Something of a martinet, is he, ma'am?" Euphemia smiled at her. "My Papa used to be the same, and demanded my brothers toe the line. How they smarted under it—yet loved him dearly."

"Why, there you have it exactly, Miss Buchanan. Colley admires his cousin so, I vow it is pathetic! And *strives* to please him. And he should, of course, for he is Hawkhurst's heir now that his own sweet son is gone. But alas, he can do nothing right, poor boy! Oh, enough! I must not burden you with our

47

troubles. Tell me the latest *on dits* of Town, I do implore you, for I positively hunger for news of the *ton*!"

It was a request Euphemia would have hoped could be delayed until the next day, but, stifling her weariness, she obliged, passing along tidbits she sensed would gratify the lady and being rewarded by such eager questions and comments, such delighted little spurts of laughter, the she was again conscious of pity and asked, "Do you always stay at Dominer, ma'am? Or have you perhaps a house in Town?"

"Oh, if I only had! Life is strange, is it not? When I was . . . much younger than you, my dear, my parents rejected the suitor I hoped to wed, for they judged him possessed of inadequate fortune and his prospects poor. So they married me to Bryce instead. And now, the man *I* had chosen is an ambassador and leads so gay and carefree a life, while my poor Bryce gamed away his fortune within five years of our marriage and had drunk himself into the grave within another five, leaving me to fend for my children as best I might." She dabbed at her eyes with a lacy handkerchief and finished brokenly. "And none—to lend a helping . . . hand!"

"How dreadful! Were you sister to Mr. Hawkhurst's Papa, ma'am?"

"No. To his mother. I am a Thorndyke, Miss Buchanan, which is why my son was named Hawkhurst's heir. Dominer, you see, has belonged to the Thorndykes since 1760, and I, need not tell you . . ."

She need not, for Euphemia was well acquainted with the romantic story of how Dominer had come into possession of the Thorndykes. Nonetheless, for the next half hour she did little more than listen politely and insert an occasional suitable comment, while Lady Bryce chattered on. She was apprised of Dominer's past glories, of the Public Days, the crowds and the excitement that had been terribly annoying, yet so jolly. And no longer allowed by the present master of the house, alas. Not that anyone would come, save for lovers of the macabre—which would be ghastly! Even her own married daughter dared not come here, for Bertha had married a Kingsdale, "and they are *so* high in the instep! I'll say this, her husband don't harp on our . . . disgrace. But—his Mama!" As to young Lord Coleridge Bryce, he was up at Oxford, but had been rusticated (through no fault of his own!). This circumstance was a terrible worry to his obviously doting parent, since Hawkhurst was "forever hammering at the boy to buy a pair of colours. Not," she sighed, "that I have anything against the Army. A splendid career. For some. Your own Papa was military, was he not? And—dead, poor man . . ."

And so it went, until at length her ladyship scolded gently that Miss Buchanan looked very, very tired and simply must not chatter any longer. She would, she announced, go and supervise the placing of a warming pan between her sheets, since the housekeeper, although efficient enough, was a trifle lax when it came to such little acts of consideration.

In the silence that followed the closing of the door, Euphemia gazed thoughtfully into the fire. She had been not a little shocked by so frank and unrestrained a flood of confidences, especially upon such short acquaintance. But perhaps this was unkind, for the poor woman was certainly very lonely and just as certainly delighted by the advent of visitors. On the other hand, although she felt a very real sympathy, Euphemia was not without common sense. Despite Lady Bryce's assertion that none had lent her a helping hand, she was obviously dwelling on Hawkhurst's charity. Someone must be paying her son's expenses at Oxford, expenses Euphemia knew from experience could be very high, even if the young man was quiet and studiously inclined. Furthermore, one might suppose a lady in desperate financial straits would find it necessary to sew her own garments or even sell her jewels, yet Lady Bryce had worn a gown of costly fabric, and, unless she was a most skilled needlewoman, it had been created for her by an expert couturier. A very fine diamond had glittered upon one hand and a ruby on the other, while the double rope of pearls about her throat had been real, to judge from the gems that had gleamed in the clasp. It would appear that she had much for which to thank her nephew. And yet . . . Euphemia frowned. Was it merely that she as so bone weary she was not thinking clearly, or had she been painted a picture of cruel tyranny? Not once had Lady Bryce spoken of Hawkhurst disparagingly—not openly, at least. Yet, by means of half-finished sentences or hastily amended remarks, she had implied an existence riddled with fear, not for herself, but for her son. Young Lord Coleridge, it would seem, did not suit his cousin's notion of an heir; in fact, his gentle manners, sensitivity, and unwillingness to embrace a military career were all an affront to Mr. Garret Hawkhurst. The fact that his cousin should wish him to enter the military began, thought Euphemia uneasily, to take on an ominous significance.

Chapter 4

Lieutenant Sir Simon Buchanan sighed and, opening his eyes, saw beyond the hand that waved hartshorn under his nose a plain but worried face and a pair of speaking hazel eyes. "Poor young man," said this disembodied apparition gently. "Are you feeling better now?"

"If he ain't," growled Archer, "he damned well should be!"

"I am indeed," Buchanan affirmed faintly. And with a twinge of unease added, "I trust I was not a nuisance."

"You were very brave," said Miss Hawkhurst, in her shy fashion.

"Brave enough to warrant something more heartening than that lavender water you slopped over him, Stephie!" The doctor grinned and thrust a full wineglass into his patient's rather shaky hand.

"*Stephanie!*" The shriek made Buchanan's hand shake even more violently, causing him to choke and splash some excellent cognac onto the fresh bandages Dr. Archer had just secured across his chest.

A plump, untidy figure rushed into the room, a lady with a wealth of rather doubtful red hair that seemed determined to escape both cap and hairpins, giving her a decidedly wild appearance. She wore a very large robe of dark blue velvet, the hem of which looked as though it had been stitched in place by several seamstresses, each having a different eye for length. From the basket in her hand, silks, a pair of scissors, a thimble, and a paper pattern tumbled, one after another, for as she came, she constantly tripped over her uneven hem with a resultant hop, skip, and stagger that caused Buchanan to view her with considerable astonishment.

"You are in here!" gasped the newcomer redundantly, her

pale blue eyes starting out in alarm. "With a strange gentleman who is—" She tripped, dropped the basket altogether, clutched for a chair which toppled into an occasional table, sending a bowl of mint confections hurtling across the carpet, and, righting herself, finished, "Whoops! Unclad!"

"Oh, my God!" moaned Archer, *sotto voce.*

"Aunt Dora," smiled Stephanie fondly.

Scrambling to his feet, Buchanan swayed and uttered a horror-stricken, "I r-really . . . am not . . ."

"Good heavens! Do not stand! Poor, poor soul! I heard a gallant soldier-man had come amongst us!" The lady rushed to his side imploring, "Sit down, I do entreat! Stephanie! Do not look, dear child! Avert your eyes!" And flinging up one arm dramatically, she sent two hairpins flying, one of which splashed into Buchanan's wine. "Sometimes," she intoned, "too hot the eye of heaven shines!"

Archer turned away with a muffled snort, and "Aunt Dora" lowered her arm and said with a dubious, "Hmmm. That may not quite fit the situation, do you think, Stephie?" Her cheeks very pink, Miss Hawkhurst murmured that the quotation was very nice. "All right," said the newcomer, seemingly cheered. "Now off with you!" and fairly swept her niece from the room, closing the door after her and leaning back against it, quite out of breath from her efforts.

"My boy," breathed the doctor, whose opinion of his patient had escalated considerably during his surgery, "you are about to meet a *rara avis.* Gird up thy loins—else you'll not survive the encounter!"

"There!" gasped the *rara avis,* with pleased satisfaction. "Well, now . . ." And forward she came again, with that eager gait that was somewhere between hare and hounds, and, having all but toppled in the scared Buchanan's arms, beamed down at him. "How may we help? What needs to be done, Harold? Name it! I am here!"

She was very much here, as a consequence of which Buchanan drew as few breaths as possible, yet felt half-strangled, so pervadingly acrid was the lady's perfume. His expression brought an appreciative gleam to the physician's eye. "Allow me," Archer volunteered. "Mrs. Dora Graham, Lieutenant Sir Simon Buchanan. No, begad! Sit still, sir!"

"Please do! Oh, *please* do!" said Mrs. Graham, her plump hands fluttering as she lurched over a curtsey. "Are you Army Buck's boy? Ah, I see you are. Where's his shirt, Harold? Oh dear . . . cannot wear *that*! Send for a maid. Oh, never mind! You are *slow*, Harold. *Slow!* One might suppose you were growing old!" Trotting sideways towards the bellrope, she half turned to flash the doctor a saucy smile, tripped over a footstool and fell with a squeal onto an occasional chair.

Beginning to grin, Buchanan again started up and was again pushed back as Archer strode past to restore the lady to her feet. Archer sighed, "Dora, how you have possibly managed to survive is a source of constant amazement to me. I vow you will rush and tear and fall and crash through life—and outlive the rest of us by fifty years!"

"Oh, I do hope you are mistaken," she said cheerfully, striving to restore order to her flying hair and leaving it wilder than ever. "I should purely despise to be left all alone with no friends around me. Did you know your Papa proposed to me? No—not *your* Papa, Harold! Good gracious, I should only have been . . . What are you saying? I'm not *that* old! Now where was I? Oh—the bell, of course." She trotted towards the pull, gave it a solid tug and let go so abruptly that it rebounded into the air, the tasselled end becoming entangled in a wall sconce. She frowned at it. "Foolish thing. I cannot get you down, you know."

Archer turned away, his eyes rolling ceiling-ward.

"You were acquainted with my father, ma'am?" asked Buchanan eagerly.

"Indeed, I was." She came hurrying back, just barely missing the footstool the doctor whipped from her erratic path. "What a devil he was, to be sure! Did he ever tell you about the time in Paris when my chair broke and he and the toothpick designer fell into the Seine? No, of course, he would not, for that was when he had that delicious opera dancer under his protection, and—"

"Dora!" the doctor admonished, although his eyes danced with mirth.

She giggled. "Oh, I always forget that we ladies are not supposed to know such things. But, in truth I—Oh, my dear young man, you look so pale. Drink up! Drink up!"

"Yes, *do* drink up," urged Archer fiendishly.

Buchanan raised his glass, encountered the hairpin, and froze for only an instant before nobly sipping his wine.

"A true hero," murmured the doctor, pulling up a chair for Mrs. Graham.

She sank into it. "We must get you to your bed at once.

That is very good cognac, you know. Does it not suit your taste? Poor fellow, I should enjoy a teensy sip, Harold dear."

Archer crossed to pour her a glass even while teasing her that sister Bryce would not like to see her take brandy.

Mrs. Graham slanted a guilty glance towards the door. "No, but she is not here, is she? So I may be as naughty as I wish." She gave a merry little laugh. "Oh dear! I should not have said that. Ah, thank you, Harold. Wherever is the maid, I wonder. Poor Sir Simon, you must be freezing. Put his jacket around him, Harold. No, I shall do it. Oh my now I've spilled wine on you. Never mind, we can clean you up in no—"

"*Whatever* are you doing, Dora?"

In the act of putting down her depleted glass, Mrs. Graham gave a small gasp and swung around, "I—er—only came to help, Carlotta," she stammered guiltily.

Lady Bryce paused on the threshold and, surveying the havoc, pressed a hand to her cheek. "Alas! So I see. Which is precisely why I requested you should not do so." Her gaze came to rest on her sister-in-law's wineglass and lingered pointedly. "What a pity . . . Poor dear, I do not doubt you *meant* well."

Mrs. Graham blushed and moved back. Buchanan met her eyes and smiled warmly, and she gave him a look of such pathetic gratitude that he was reminded of the devoted but disastrous spaniel puppy he had once owned.

My lady had been followed by two maids to whom she turned and said sweetly, "Please try to set some of this frightful chaos to rights. It is so upsetting for an invalid."

Buchanan was far more upset by the curious and sympathetic stares of the maids and pulled his jacket tighter, as Dr. Archer, his face completely wooden, performed brisk introductions. Lady Bryce extended her hand. "Poor Sir Simon, I do apologize for all this. How *very* foolish you must fancy us."

He fancied a good deal, but he was feeling a little steadier now and, having already come to his feet once more, negotiated a clumsy left-handed handshake and assured her he was most grateful.

"Despite what you might be pardoned for imagining," she said with a deprecating little laugh, "this is not quite a madhouse. So soon as you are able, you shall be assisted to your room, which—I know you would wish—adjoins that of your sister." The doctor tossed her an irritated frown, and serenely unabashed she observed that, "One must be truthful, you know, my dear Hal."

One of the maids was sent running in search of a suitable dressing gown, and, when this was brought, my lady personally assisted Buchanan to don the garment, constantly admonishing him to have a care, yet her movements were so brisk that the doctor intervened to demand his patient be allowed to get to his bed before he was again reduced to a state of total collapse.

Supported by Dr. Archer, Sir Simon was conveyed into the magnificence of the Great Hall. As the door closed behind them, he heard Lady Bryce say in her gentle fashion, "My dear foolish Dora, *whatever* are we to do about your hair? And—that perfectly frightful scent . . . ?"

A soft scratching at the door awoke Euphemia. Kent was fast asleep, and the clock on the mantle indicated that only an hour had passed since Lady Bryce had left. She limped stiffly over to the door and discovered her brother, clad in a long, quilted, black dressing gown that brought an appreciative sparkle to her eyes.

"Let me in quickly!" he urged. "That molten physician believes me tucked into my bed!"

"As you should be, Machiavelli!" she said softly, drawing him into the room nonetheless. "Are you—" And she stopped. He had been silhouetted against the lighted hallway, and she'd not seen the sling that again supported his arm. She led him to the chair she had just vacated and, occupying the other one, searched his face. His grin was bright as ever, but the weary look about the eyes confirmed her fears, and she asked a compassionate, "Was it very bad, dearest?"

"Lord, no. But a fine bumble broth we've cropped into, eh?"

It was typical that he should not reproach her now that they really were involved, and, just as typically, she admitted, "All my fault, I *am* sorry!"

"Stuff! Who could have guessed the whole blasted hillside would choose just that moment to give way? I cannot like it though, Mia. When we get back to civilization you're not to breathe a word to anyone that we came here. Wouldn't do your reputation any good, y'know, however we explained it away."

"I might not have a reputation to be concerned about, had it not been for our Bluebeard," she pointed out, a pucker disturbing her smooth brow. "What do you make of him, love?"

"*Make* of him? Gad! All I want is to make *away* from him! I'll admit we stand indebted to the man, but did you mark his face? Even harder than I recollect. And that chin! I'll go bail he'd balk at nothing!"

"He certainly did not balk at risking his life for Kent," she said quietly. "Though why he should take so desperate a chance to help someone he'd never seen and yet savagely murder his own son . . ." She gave a shrug of bafflement. "Simon, are you *sure*? Was it ever really proven?"

Buchanan frowned a little. "Do not be blinded to what he is, Mia. I recall he was used to have a way about him that charmed the ladies— God knows why. What's all this about Kent?" He glanced to the bed anxiously. "Not in very bad case, is he?"

"Scraped, and badly bruised, and terribly frightened, poor little fellow. But the doctor says that, does he stay free of fever, we should be able to leave tomorrow." She recounted what had transpired on the hillside, omitting nothing, nor yet embellishing her tale. Knowing her, Buchanan was more impressed than he would have cared to admit and, when she finished, gave a low whistle. "By George! I can see why you would be at *Point Non Plus*! Don't add up at all, does it?" He moved uncomfortably as he spoke, and the throat of the dressing gown parted a little.

"You said it was not very bad!" cried Euphemia, catching a glimpse of thick white bandages, "It looks—"

He grinned boyishly. "Oh, no! Do not go into the boughs! I've had enough ladies fluttering over me! What with mints all over the carpet, hairpins in my cognac, chastised bell pulls, and young damsels viewing my nakedness—"

"Good God! What on earth . . . ?"

He chuckled, and told her, succeeding in so lightly sketching the scene of his ordeal that she was reduced to soft but helpless laughter. "You know, Mia, I could not help but like Miss Hawkhurst, though she's a poor little dab of a female. And I felt sorry for the fat lady, Mrs. Graham, even if she has . . ." He hesitated and finished rather guiltily, ". . . quite an—er—air about her, on top of all else."

Intrigued, Euphemia echoed, "You mean she uses a poor scent?"

"A hunting pack might love it. But, Jove! Do you feel obliged to repay Hawkhurst, your service might be to persuade the lady to abandon that eau de dry rot, or whatever it—" He checked as a soft knock sounded at the door.

"Oh, dear," sighed Euphemia. "I pray it is not Lady Bryce."

In response to her call however, it was not her ladyship but their host who entered. He was dressed for dinner, his cravat a masterpiece, and a jacket of dark blue superfine hugging his wide shoulders like a glove and bringing a gleam of admiration to Buchanan's eyes. The ugly graze on his forehead was surrounded by a blackening bruise, but he looked alert and well rested. Raising a jewelled quizzing glass, he turned it lazily from brother to sister and drawled, "Safety in numbers?"

Buchanan had risen and now said formally, "We are deeply indebted to you, sir. In behalf of my sister and the boy, I would like to—"

"Oh, stubble it, for God's sake! I merely came to discover how the child goes on and to tell you that we have retrieved your cattle, relatively undamaged. We'll search for the rest of your luggage in the morning."

Buchanan bowed and persisted with polite if cold hauteur. "I am ever more in your debt, Mr. Hawkhurst. I owe you not only my own life, but—"

"Are you always so winningly warm towards your rescuers?" Hawkhurst laughed and with hands on hips asked, "Or is this charming demeanour reserved for Foul Fiends such as I?"

Despite himself, Buchanan's lips twitched, but he retained his aloof manner as he completed his proper expression of thanks.

Hawkhurst offered a slight, dismissing wave of the hand in response to it all and, flashing an amused glance at Euphemia, met an answering sparkle in her deep-blue eyes that banished his smile. For a moment he stared at her rather blankly, then said, "Are you feeling well enough to travel, ma'am?"

Shocked, she managed to ask calmly, "Tonight, sir?"

Buchanan's shoulder throbbed; he felt alarmingly weak and was so weary he could scarcely make conversation, but he would have died sooner than admit it, and snapped a frigid, "Does Mr. Hawkhurst prefer that we leave tonight, my dear, then we shall, of course, do so."

Hawkhurst said mockingly, "Mr. Hawkhurst prefers that you light the lamp."

There was a touch of steel under the lazy drawl, and reacting instinctively, Buchanan started to obey, then flushed and stood very still. Hawkhurst uttered a soft chuckle, and

56

Buchanan's mortification deepened. Well acquainted with that mulish look upon her brother's face, Euphemia quickly lit the lamp. Hawkhurst strolled over to the bed, placed a hand very lightly on Kent's forehead, and scanned the child narrowly. Turning back to them, he murmured, "I wish you may leave. But I confess myself a coward and shall not risk Archer's wrath."

Buchanan looked ready to explode with indignation, but Euphemia, who had been absently contemplating Hawkhurst's thick, and artfully tumbled hair, now asked a swift, "Not fever, surely?"

"He is very warm, ma'am, and I'd wager is in no condition to—"

The door again opened, and Lady Bryce drifted in. She also had changed her dress and was elegant in a gown of rose-pink crepe with a fine diamond choker about her throat. When she saw the group gathered in the bedchamber, she gave a scandalized gasp. "Hawkhurst! Are you run mad? And the girl in her nightrail!"

"No, is she?" He turned his quizzing glass interestedly upon Euphemia as if seeing her for the first time. "So she is, by Jove! And I, alas, thwarted by the presence of her admirable brother." He sighed and, allowing the glass to swing from its black velvet riband, shook his head reproachfully at Buchanan.

Euphemia's attempt to hold back a gurgle of laughter was not quite successful, but her brother's face remained set and grim. Infuriated by Hawkhurst's raillery, Lady Bryce drew herself up. "Most amusing," she observed scathingly. "And I quite apprehend that Miss Buchanan is accustomed to continental manners, but I do assure you that such—"

"No, pray do not moralize at me, dear Aunt," he smiled. "You will have me in a quake, and you know I am long past saving. Place your confidence rather in this intrepid young officer, and draw comfort from the fact that the lady is known to be—ah—'Unattainable' and thus doubly safe—for tonight, at least, since I've guests arriving momentarily." Euphemia had again to stifle a smile, but my lady's face took on an aghast expression. "Guests . . . ?" she said feebly. "But, Garret, you can *not*!"

"Put them off at the last minute, d'you mean, ma'am? You are perfectly right, and I understand your reluctance since you so enjoy company."

"Not *that* kind of company!" she flashed, forgetting her manners. "I would not be seen—"

"My dear, of course you would not," he intervened gently, the wave of his glass indicating the company she appeared to have overlooked. "You are so busy these days, planning your Musicale."

She flushed and bit her lip but determined to fight to the death in the cause of virginal innocence, said pleadingly, "We have a sick child, and Miss Buchanan to consider. And Sir Simon—"

"Yes, how very remiss in me. Buchanan, do you feel up to the rig, you are most welcome to join my little . . . party. We shall be merrymaking in the North Wing, where we will disturb no one. And another gentleman would not come amiss." Hawkhurst's head was thrown back a little, his eyelids drooping over eyes that held an amused challenge.

Buchanan replied levelly, "Under the circumstances, sir, I must decline."

"Sir Simon is hurt!" Lady Bryce exclaimed, patently horrified. "Is it not bad enough he must remain here protecting his sister? You should be—"

"I am truly grateful for your solicitude," Euphemia interposed, noting the polar glint that was at last creeping into Hawkhurst's eyes. "But, I fear—"

"And small wonder!" my lady deliberately misinterpreted. "Well, you may set your fears at rest, my dear Miss Buchanan. Your dinner shall be brought to you on a tray, and since you do not trust our maids, I personally shall sit up with your page. He will be perfectly safe with me, for I have reared children of my own and am, were truth to be told, far better qualified than you, my dear, to nurse an ailing child."

The thought of Kent awakening after so nerve-wracking an experience to encounter the doubtful comfort of Lady Bryce's presence troubled Euphemia, and yet she could not gracefully refuse after the barbed wording of that offer. She glanced helplessly to Hawkhurst.

"Your humanity, Aunt," he murmured idly, "never fails to astound me. I shall advise your languishing offspring he must come about without your aid."

"Colley?" she gasped, one hand flying to her throat. "He is here?" He nodded and, in a sharpened tone, she demanded, "What has he to 'come about' from? What have you done to him?"

58

"Exactly," he sighed, giving her a bored smile, "what you might expect, dear ma'am."

Lady Bryce's eyes glittered. She closed her lips with a great effort over a blistering denunciation and without another word marched to the door.

Her nephew moved swiftly to open it and bow her from the room. Swinging the door closed, he settled his shoulders against it and remarked, "Sir Simon, had you the brains you were born with, you'd already be betwixt the sheets. If you do not soon retire, I shall have Archer berating me because you've gone off into another swoon."

Both words and manner further inflamed Buchanan. Euphemia, however, was startled and went to take her brother's arm and gaze up at him anxiously. Yearning to smash the mockery from his host's features, Sir Simon managed to say with a semblance of calm, "I was a trifle knocked up, but . . . a country doctor, Mia."

"I'll wager," drawled Hawkhurst, a sudden flash in his eyes, "our 'country doctor' was more skilled than any your almighty Wellington provided!"

Buchanan's jaw tightened. In a very quiet voice he enquired, "You have some quarrel with Lord Wellington, sir?"

"I have some quarrel with your pride," Hawkhurst sighed and, smothering a yawn, added, "It fairly exhausts me."

Buchanan gritted his teeth and took a pace forward. Hawkhurst raised one hand in a graceful fencing gesture and, with a sudden and unexpectedly warm grin, said, "But I admire it. And your Hookey friend, also. Now, instead of calling me out, admit rather that, although Hal Archer may have hurt you like the devil, your wound is easier now."

Thoroughly disconcerted by the abrupt transformation, Buchanan halted. He had the uncomfortable feeling that he had been acting like a fool and, embarrassed, stammered, "Why . . . y-yes. That is true. And I—er—did not mean to sound ungrateful. He was most skilled, despite his uncertain temperament. And Miss Hawkhurst was incredibly kind."

"Oh, my sister's one in a thousand." Hawkhurst reached into an inside pocket and withdrew a small but deadly-looking pistol. "I had intended to offer this to *your* sister. But, since you obviously mean to stand guard over her all night . . ." Those veiled grey eyes flickered appraisingly up and down Euphemia. "Not that I blame you. She's a devilish fine-looking girl."

"You become," rasped Buchanan, rigid again, "offensive, Mr. Hawkhurst."

"Do I? Then the more reason for this." Hawkhurst proffered the weapon with a flourish. Pale with anger, Buchanan stood motionless. Hawkhurst put up his brows and surveyed him with wicked enjoyment. Euphemia stepped swiftly between them, took the weapon, and, holding her breath, slipped her finger through the trigger guard and essayed the spin that Harry Smith had taught her in Spain.

"By . . . God . . . !" breathed Hawkhurst, admiringly.

"Be warned, sir," she said with feigned severity and then, laughter leaping into her eyes, asked, "Are you not terrified?"

"Do you know how to fire it?"

"I outshot Lord Jeremy Bolster in a match at Fuentes de Onoro."

He bowed low and straightening, one hand held over his heart, admitted, "Ma'am, I acknowledge myself terrified." With a twinkle, he added, "And here I'd fancied the shoe quite on the other foot."

"Oh, no," said Euphemia gravely. "I have three brothers, you see, and am thus well accustomed to little boys who think it fun to be naughty."

Buchanan, looking from one to the other, was rendered speechless.

His stunned eyes never leaving her face, Hawkhurst murmured, "Well, that properly drove me against the ropes!" and with a bow, left them, closing the door softly behind him.

Sir Simon flung his good arm about his sister and whirled her around. "*Romped*, by Jupiter!" he exulted. "You properly vanquished our Bluebeard, Mia!"

Euphemia smiled. But she thought, I wonder . . .

Mrs. Graham came to Kent's room soon after Hawkhurst's departure and offered to help with the "poor little page." Euphemia took an immediate liking to the untidy lady and, promising her brother she would now retire, sent him weaving off to his room, so exhausted he could barely set one foot before the other. Mrs. Graham observed happily that it was "just like dear Army" to have such delightful children and launched into a vignette about the gallant Colonel that left his daughter weak with laughter. She realized gratefully that this aunt was a very different proposition to the other, and when she left Kent's bedside, it was without a qualm.

In her room she was delighted to find that one of her valises had been recovered, for her own nightgown was laid upon the bed, and a middle-aged, buxom abigail was in the process of hanging her favourite riding habit in the press. Her name, she said, was Piper, but would Miss mind called her Ellie, for she felt "that embarrassed" to be called Piper. However named, she was the soul of kindness, her concern over Euphemia's stiff movements resulting in her insistence that she massage her charge with a liniment that left Euphemia tingling all over and her aches and pain so much lessened that she fell asleep before Ellie could give her the powder Dr. Archer had prescribed. Her last drowsy memory was of the abigail closing the curtains around the great bed.

"W-won't-move a step! P'fer t'talk out here! Free blasted country, ain't it?"

The words were slurred and had not been spoken very loudly, but Euphemia was blessed with sharp hearing, and she was awake at once. For an instant she could not think where she was, but then a deeper voice said something she did not catch. Hawkhurst's cynical countenance sprang into her mind's eye, and she sat up, listening.

"Know it," the first and decidedly drunken speaker proclaimed. "M-mother told me all-l-l 'bout it. Prob'ly sound 'sleep by now, 'tall events, so no reason you should get so up in th'boughs. You cannot force me to go inside!"

So this must be Lady Bryce's "languishing offspring." Moved by curiosity, Euphemia drew back the curtains and slipped from the bed. The heavy drapes were wide, as she had requested, and she crept cautiously towards the lighter square of the windows, shrugging into her dressing gown.

"Do not dare use that tone to me, you wretched puppy! Were you not well foxed, I'd show you what I can force you to! Get inside at once! I'll not—"

" 'f you s'anxious to go inside—why was you standing 'bout, leering up at . . . her windows? Good fer goose, is—"

"Damn you! Will you keep your voice down!"

Through the lace undercurtains, Euphemia saw a half moon shining fitfully between racing clouds, revealing a wide terrace edged by a low balustrade, and with shallow steps leading downward. She caught a glimpse of tree-dotted lawns, flower beds, statuary, and the gleam of ornamental water, but her attention held on the two men below her. Hawkhurst and a tall, slender youth who gave no appearance of being cowed as he

61

swayed before his cousin's rage. She could not see his features, but discerned that his hair was lighter than his mother's and that he either had almost no neck at all, or wore a jacket with grossly exaggerated shoulders. Grateful that she had required Ellie to open the casements slightly, she leaned nearer. She did not quite hear what the boy muttered, but the tone was defiant, and Hawkhurst, his voice low and restrained, rasped, "While you are under my guardianship, my lord, you'll do as I say! You were *not* with the Fortescues, for I saw them in Reading, and—"

"Spying on me, coz?"

The slim figure swayed. Hawkhurst's hand shot out to grip the cravat, and Bryce was wrenched forward. "Do I ever judge it necessary to spy on you, bantling, I'll sooner kick you all the way to the Horse Guards—where *they* may succeed in making a man of you! Meanwhile, I've no need to resort to such means. I know damned well you were with young Gains!"

"M'friends are my own!" the boy retaliated, struggling vainly to free himself from his cousin's firm grip. "Y'ar'not—"

"I cannot but marvel that Max Gains allows *my* cousin within a mile of his precious brother!" Hawkhurst released the youth so abruptly that he staggered.

"Lord Gains, at least, d-don't int'fere with Chilton's friends!"

"Does he not? Perhaps, since Chilton had sufficient gumption to serve his country, he has some—"

"Y'think I'm 'fraid!" Bryce put in savagely. "Well—ain't! Not 'fraid of getting killed—which is what y'want."

Euphemia caught her breath. There was a moment's total silence, through which Hawkhurst stood as if frozen.

"No! Hawk!" There was sudden anguish in the young voice. "I d-din't mean—"

"Well, I *do* mean," Hawkhurst overrode icily, "to ensure that Dominer shall never fall into the hands of a dainty, effeminate milksop!"

Bryce swore. His fist clenched and swung upward, only to be caught in a grip that made him gasp. "And, furthermore, Colley," his cousin went on, "do you *ever* take my match bays again, without my leave, I am liable to strangle you without waiting for Boney to take you out of the line of succession!" He flung the boy's arm down and started away, but Bryce caught at his sleeve and said humbly, I . . . I did ask, Hawk. And you made no answer. I thought—"

"Devil, you did! Your question warranted no answer. God knows I've told you often enough! I collect you took 'em to show off to Chilton."

"Yes. And—Max was abs'lutely wild about 'em. Said they was th'finest he ever saw."

"Max knows his cattle." Hawkhurst was silent a moment, then asked, "How does Chilton go on? Do they mean to operate again?"

Bryce seemed to take heart from this enquiry, stern though it was. "Well, they must, y'know. He cannot rejoin his regiment with that stupid ball in his side. But . . . oh, Hawk, I do 'pologize. I *didn't* mean it. It's just—Well, Chilton don't dare come and ask you, but—he'd dearly love to . . . to buy your bays."

Hawkhurst snorted and said drily, "I'll lay odds he would!"

"He's really a very good fellow, y'know. He don't—er—hold it 'gainst you . . . I mean—'cause of Max's face."

"Then he's a gutless fribble!" Hawkhurst exploded. "43rd, or no! What's his line of reasoning? All's fair in love and acid? God! You may tell your silly sainted Light Bob that, were my bays twenty years old, sway-backed, half blind, and went with a shuffle, I'd not sell 'em to him for thirty thousand! Furthermore, I've seen him drive, and he's damnably cow-handed!"

"Cow-handed! Why, of all the—"

Hawkhurst shook one finger under his cousin's nose. "And you may further advise your good friends at Chant House that, do I find that flea-ridden hound of theirs in my drawing room again, I'll send home his head *à la* John the Baptist!"

"Hawk! You never would! Sampson's a good old boy! Hawk . . ." Bryce reached forth one appealing hand, but his cousin was stalking off. The hand lowered. Once more Hawkhurst's name was spoken in a wistful half-whisper. Then Bryce turned also, put both hands into his pockets and, with shoulders slumped, made his unsteady way in the opposite direction until he vanished into the shadows at the incurving end of the great house that was called the North Wing.

Euphemia became aware that she was shivering and flew back to snuggle under the blankets. She frowned into the darkness, thinking over what she had heard. There were, she thought, faults on both sides. Hawkhurst's, for attempting to force the boy into a career he did not wish—not every man was suited for military life. On the other hand, Bryce had been very drunk, and she could well imagine Simon's reaction if

63

Gerald had commandeered his horses without a by-your-leave. She decided, however, that the balance of guilt lay with Hawkhurst. It was obvious that Bryce admired him. Even in the dark she had seen that the careless and oddly attractive style Hawkhurst's man achieved, with his thick locks had been copied by his cousin. A little understanding, a grain of tact, and the boy would be butter in his hands.

She closed her eyes. The man was arrogant and autocratic. Worse, although he had rendered them a service for which she must always be grateful, to the list of his crimes had been added another. He was cruel to animals, and that he would make good his threat against the unfortunate Sampson she had not the slightest doubt. Not that it was any of her affair. Resolutely, she put Garret Thorndyke Hawkhurst out of her mind.

And fell asleep, wondering why he had been "leering" up at her window . . .

❧ *Chapter 5* ❧

The following morning dawned bitterly cold, but the skies were clear, and pale winter sunshine flooded into Euphemia's bedchamber. Never a late sleeper, she had been abed for almost twelve hours. Upon awakening, she rang for an abigail, then arose and made her somewhat stiff way to the windows. By daylight, the grounds of Dominer were even more impressive, so that she gave a soft cry of admiration and stood there, just drinking it all in.

Ellie arrived with a tray of hot chocolate and much concern for her charge. Sir Simon, she imparted, had already gone downstairs. The family would take breakfast at ten o'clock, but there was no one expecting Miss to go down, and she would fetch up a tray. Euphemia refused this kindness, but accepted the abigail's assistance with her toilette and found her very obliging and with a real skill at hair arrangement. Half an hour later, hurrying into the hall in her new cream muslin, with a yellow shawl draped about her shoulders, she slowed her steps involuntarily. Last evening she had been too tired to notice very much, but this morning she could not but be charmed both by the beautiful plan of the great house and the exquisite taste of the appointments. Her feet sank into thick Aubusson carpets laid upon floors that gleamed richly. Here and there, splendid porcelain and crystal were displayed on old chests or tables that were, of themselves, so beautifully wrought she could not refrain from inspecting them more closely. The walls were hung with magnificent oils, mostly landscapes or still lifes, but with an occasional family portrait amongst them, and several proud suits of armour, in excellent states of preservation, stood about impressively. So much beauty, she thought. If only Simon and Kent had not been subjected to such danger, she must be glad she had been able to see it all.

Proceeding to her destination, she found Kent's bedchamber and slipped inside. A comely young maid was seated beside the window, mending tablecloths. She stood and bobbed a curtsey as Euphemia entered. The little boy was still sleeping, she said. Mrs. Graham had gone to bed at six o'clock, but Mrs. Henderson, the housekeeper, would come up shortly, being that she was a fine nurse.

Euphemia thanked her and trod softly over to the bed. The child was deep in slumber, his thin cheeks flushed. His forehead felt hot and dry, and, recalling what Hawkhurst had said, she left strict instructions that she was to be called at once if Kent awoke. Returning to the hall, she tried to convince herself that she was worrying needlessly. He was probably simply recovering from exhaustion, on top of which he may very well have caught a cold.

She closed the door gently and stood for a moment, her hand still upon the latch, staring blindly at a splash of sunlight on the carpet.

"Do not grieve, dear ma'am. He will soon be well again. Dr. Archer is really superb, you know."

The gentle voice caused her to look up at once, and, like her brother before her, she thought, What very kind eyes. Miss Stephanie Hawkhurst was wearing a shapeless beige wool gown this morning, and a shawl, beautifully embroidered in shades of cream, gold, and rust, was fastened to her bodice with a handsome antique brooch. Smiling, Euphemia put out her hand. "You must be Miss Hawkhurst. I am very beholden to you for your care of my brother. He has had an unpleasant time of it since he was wounded."

"How do you do?" A soft hand clasped her own briefly, and an unexpected twinkle danced into the hazel eyes, as Miss Hawkhurst murmured, "Army Buck's daughter. Will you accompany me downstairs? I had thought to have breakfast served to you in your room, for I am sure you must be very tired still."

"Not at all. I slept like a log, in fact. And I see Mrs. Graham has been telling you of my dear Papa."

Dismayed, Miss Hawkhurst said, "Oh, nothing to his discredit, I do assure you!"

"Too late, my dear!" Euphemia slipped a hand in her arm and said in her friendly way, "Your aunt already told me a tale about my father, some of which I'd suspected, and all of which I found delightful!"

Miss Hawkhurst breathed a sigh of relief. "Thank goodness you are not stuffy! I was afraid from what Hawk said—" She felt her companion stiffen and added hurriedly, "Oh, dear! Only that you was a fine figure of a girl, able to snare any— er—that is . . . Well, you know," she floundered, "I am not clever, or in the least fashionable, and I do not know how to . . . to—"

"Go about catching a husband?" asked Euphemia, smiling, but with a glitter in her fine eyes that would have at once alerted her friends. "Well, if your brother told you I am still able to snare offers, even at my age . . ."

"Oh, he did!" said Miss Hawkhurst, disastrously eager to make amends.

"Ah. Why then he was right." Euphemia's teeth were a trifle more noticeable than usual as she uttered that confirmation. "Did he also tell you, perhaps, that I followed the drum with my father and have a wide acquaintanceship among the military set?"

"Oh, is that what he meant by 'military rattles'? I thought . . . Is something wrong?"

"By . . . no means." Euphemia's titter was uncharacteristically shrill. "Only, I trust he does not think me too set up in my own conceit."

"I am sure he does not. In fact, he admires you, for I heard him tell Dr. Archer you did not want for sense and were probably waiting until you found one who had come ..." Her innocent brow puckered. "Something about socks."

"Hose?" gasped Euphemia. "Hosed ... and shod?"

"That's it! Someone who has come hosed and shod into the world. Does that mean a soldier, Miss Buchanan?"

Fortunately, they had by now come to the head of the stairs, and Euphemia's dazed expression and sudden clutch at the magnificently carven railing were easily explained away. "Not ... exactly ..." she uttered. So he took her for a fortune-hunter, the abominable wretch! "My, but your lovely home quite ... overwhelms me." And, by the time they had reached the ground floor, she had regained her aplomb, outwardly, at least.

Miss Hawkhurst led her across the splendour of the Great Hall and into a cherry breakfast parlour, where were gathered Dr. Archer, Buchanan, Lady Bryce, and a young exquisite who could only be Lord Coleridge Bryce. Euphemia, who had gained no very clear picture of him by moonlight, was astonished to find, instead of the sulky boy she had expected, an open-faced youth with fair skin and hair, a chin faintly reminiscent of his cousin's, and a wide, shyly smiling mouth. The gentlemen stood as they entered. Dr. Archer drew out a chair for Euphemia, Bryce performed that office for Miss Hawkhurst, and Buchanan told his sister that she looked a bit more "The Thing" this morning.

"Dear Miss Buchanan," gushed Lady Bryce, "you have not met my son."

Lord Coleridge's rather jerky bow and bashful response warmed Euphemia towards him, though it also brought the fear he would cut his cheek on his extremely high shirt points. However bosky he may have been the previous evening, he gave little sign of it now, only a slight puffiness under the eyes betraying him. He bore little resemblance to his mother, and not until her gaze rested on Miss Hawkhurst, did Euphemia see the family likeness. He had the same hazel eyes as the girl and the same rather thin face and long beautiful hands. Lady Bryce watched him with the clear hope he would say something clever. He slid one finger under the fearsome convolutions of his neckcloth, fumbled with one of the several fobs and seals at his waist, and observed that the heavy rains of last month must have caused the landslide.

"That's what Garret said," Miss Hawkhurst agreed in her

gentle voice. "He went up there again this morning, with Manners and two of the grooms."

Lady Bryce arched her brows. "Did he now? I am amazed the poor fellow could manage it. He had such a time with his guests last night. He don't like it when they over-indulge, Miss Buchanan. I'd not have you think he condones such behaviour, for he *always* tells me afterwards that he is sorry they are so—er—rowdy."

Bryce, staring fixedly at his napkin, said, "I did not hear any rowdiness last night, Mama."

"But how should you, dear boy? You were long abed. But *I* was disturbed. Not that it matters about me, of course, and I am accustomed to it ... But, to think of Miss Buchanan and Sir Simon, and that poor, poor child! It was unforgiveable, and so I told your cousin this morning. They were shouting under my windows at two of the clock, and, had I not feared I might take a cold—you know how prone I am to germs, dear Doctor Archer—I should have got up from my bed and opened the window to quiet them."

Euphemia accepted a crumpet from the tray the butler offered, and he poured her coffee. Inwardly amazed that such a conversation should take place before the servants, she watched Bryce from under her lashes. He had aspirations to dandyism, all right; those shirt points and the grotesquely padded shoulders of his jacket attested to that. His head sank a little lower, but he said nothing. Hawkhurst very obviously had not betrayed him, and she could guess how that knowledge must mortify the boy.

She found Dr. Archer observing her, a speculative expression in his deep eyes. "You are early abroad, sir," she smiled.

"Stayed the night. My people know where to find me should the need arise. I'd have to check your brother's shoulder this morning at all events, and I want to look in on the boy. He's a frail little fellow."

She had encountered his type before, and the very quietness of his manner alarmed her. "Yes. I thought him a trifle feverish just now."

No die-away airs here, he thought. And, gad, what a fine lass! Far above mere prettiness! If he were only ten years younger ... or twenty ... Those great blue eyes were questioning him. And she was the type to want it straight out. "Inflammation of the lungs," he said bluntly.

Miss Hawkhurst gave a little cry of dismay. Euphemia

paled, for, although she had guessed Kent was sick, she'd not expected this. She reached out her hand instinctively, and Buchanan leaned to take it firmly and ask a quiet, "Serious?"

"Of course, it is serious!" cried Lady Bryce. "It carried off my poor sister in only six days, and——"

"Well, it will not carry off the boy," Archer interpolated, his gaze still on Euphemia. "He became thoroughly chilled hanging onto that branch, I don't doubt, but Hawk had the good sense to get him into a hot tub at once, and I think we've caught it quickly enough." Curiosity touched his eyes. "Fond of your little page, ain't you, Miss Buchanan? Well, he'll get good care here, I do assure you. But you'll not be able to move him for a week or two."

Euphemia exchanged a troubled glance with her brother.

"You must stay here," said Lady Bryce, her mind planning busily. "The boy would pine away without you."

Buchanan thought that very likely, and his heart sank at the prospect of being compelled to remain in this house of infamy. He was too well bred, however, not to be shamed at once by such a graceless reaction. Not only had Hawkhurst saved his life, it also was beyond doubting that every hospitality would be extended to them. Irked with himself, he smiled ruefully at Miss Hawkhurst. "I fear that would be a dreadful imposition."

"No, but it would be our very great pleasure, Sir Simon." The girl blushed as she spoke, and, thanking her, Euphemia thought abstractedly that Stephanie Hawkhurst was more taking than she had at first realized. That braided hair, however, which would be charming on a vibrant beauty like Deirdre Breckenridge, was too severe for so pale a countenance, and her lashes were a light gold that became invisible save when the light chanced to touch them, giving her eyes a naked look. A softer coiffure, a subtle use of cosmetics might——

"I will send Neeley to Meadow Abbey," said Buchanan. "Would you wish me to write Great Aunt Lucasta a note, Mia?"

Euphemia said she would write directly after breakfast, since she did not want Simon to use his right arm. She wondered what Hawkhurst would think of his new development. Last evening he had said, "I wish you may leave . . ." Well, if he became obnoxious, they would simply *have* to leave.

"Oh! What a lovely change it will be for us to have house guests!" exclaimed Lady Bryce, clasping her hands theatrically. "However reluctant they may be! Only think, Miss Buchanan!

You will very likely be here for my Musicale! It is only ten days distant. And meanwhile, we shall do all we can to make your stay here, if not exciting, at least not ... unpleasant. I do trust my Fifi pleased you? I can tell she arranged your hair, for it looks very well today."

From the corner of her eye, Euphemia saw a quirk tug at the corners of Simon's lips. And she says it all with such an innocent smile, she marvelled. "You are too kind, ma'am. I had expert assistance indeed, but the abigail who waited on me is called Ellie."

"Ellie?" Lady Bryce turned a shocked gaze upon her niece. "Oh, Stephie! How could you have blundered so? I distinctly told you to send Fifi to Miss Buchanan, for our simple country girls would never do for a lady who has travelled so much about the world! Really, I cannot think what dear Miss Buchanan must think of us!"

Blushing fierily, Miss Hawkhurst looked with dismay from her aunt to their guest, and Euphemia interjected lightly. "No, no, please! I cannot imagine anyone having been more perfect, for I ached so, and she applied a lotion to my bruises that has made me feel like new."

"Only listen, Stephanie," purred my lady, patting her niece's hand. "For your sake, Miss Buchanan is so good as to overcome her natural reluctance to speak of so personal a matter. How much it will help you to be exposed to such sophistication." She turned to Euphemia, who was beginning to think herself quite a scarlet woman, and lamented in a lower but all too audible voice. "Poor child, shut away here—what chance has she to learn how to go on? I have so pleaded with Hawkhurst to give her a London season, but he will not hear of it! No, do not defend him, Stephanie! It is very naughty of him, for the years pass by so quickly, and, before we know it, all your brilliant potential will be suffocated until you become just another drab little country dowd!"

"Good God, Mama!" Bryce protested unhappily. "You embarrass poor Stephie to death! Let be!"

"Silly boy!" His parent slapped his wrist playfully. "My dearest niece knows very well I have only her best interests at heart!"

Her "dearest niece" was all too crushingly aware of her total lack of any "brilliant potential" and, knowing that she was already "a drab little country dowd," kept her tearful eyes downcast, praying the earth might open and swallow her, her heated cheeks adding to her despair.

Euphemia could have positively scratched the odious woman. Long ago, Tristram Leith had once laughed that his adored Mia could charm even gruff old General Picton into languishing at her feet, and now, revealing nothing of her vexation, she murmured a thoughtful, "Do you know, ma'am, I believe you have the right of it. Miss Hawkhurst has been hiding her light under a bushel. But with very little effort I think she might surprise us all." She leaned forward and, placing her hand over the fingers clenched so tightly upon an inoffensive teaspoon, smiled, "My dear, will you do as your clever aunt suggests and have a cose with me this afternoon? I am sure we will find much to chatter about, though I do not promise to reveal all the witchcraft by which large and ordinary girls such as I wring offers from helpless gentlemen!"

Buchanan laughed, and young Bryce threw her a look of warm gratitude, while Archer grunted and regarded Lady Bryce with sardonic triumph.

Miss Hawkhurst, striving to speak, could not, but her eyes conveyed her thanks so humbly that Euphemia knew she could easily learn to love this gentle girl.

Whatever plans Euphemia cherished for the beautification of Miss Stephanie Hawkhurst were destined to be postponed. Even as Lord Coleridge prepared to conduct them on a tour of the great house, a lackey came running to say that the little page was most distressed, and could Dr. Archer please come at once. Hastening upstairs after him, Euphemia found Kent tossing frenziedly, his blurred gaze turning to her with pathetic relief. The doctor's manner became so kindly that terror struck into her heart. He left, promising to send medicines, warning her the boy must get worse before he got better, and arming her with instructions on how to cope with possible emergencies. He had no sooner departed than the housekeeper bustled into the room. The neat, plump little Scotswoman proved a far cry from the disinterested individual Lady Bryce's casual remarks had implied. Nell Henderson was a pillar of strength, possessed of a kindly disposition, a merry good humour, and a knowledge of nursing that proved invaluable. She popped into the room regularly throughout that long morning, and at half past one, when the ailing child at last fell asleep, Euphemia yielded to her persuasions, returned to her bedchamber, and, having washed and changed clothes, went down to luncheon.

Only Mrs. Graham and her stifling "perfume" awaited her in the smaller dining room. Mr. Hawkhurst, it developed, seldom ate lunch. In preparation for the Musicale, Lady Bryce had gone shopping in Bath, and Miss Hawkhurst had gone into Bristol on a long-planned visit to her old governess. Sir Simon, said Mrs. Graham, surreptitiously retrieving a scallop she had contrived to send darting into her saucer, had handed my lady a letter addressed to his great aunt, and, while she shopped, Lady Bryce's coachman would deliver it to that renowned grand dame. Euphemia said worriedly that she trusted Simon had not irritated his shoulder, but Mrs. Graham refuted this. "My sister took with her a groom and footman, her abigail, a coachman and two outriders, but Colley decided to ride part of the way beside her carriage, and your brother felt well enough to accompany him, my dear."

"What?" exclaimed Euphemia, thunderstruck. "He never did!"

"But, yes. They took the curricle. I saw them, leave."

"If that is not the outside of enough! Simon had no business riding out in this weather, and with his wound so troublesome!"

"As I tried to warn him. But did you ever know the man who would admit himself not quite up to par when another fellow was inviting him to go somewhere?" She signed and added, " 'For his friend he toiled and tried. For his friend he fought and died . . .' " Euphemia blinked at her incredulously, and Mrs. Graham tilted her untidy head and mused, "Oh, my, that doesn't sound very encouraging, does it?"

"Who wrote it?"

"Why I haven't the vaguest idea. But never mind about that. Eat up, dear Miss Buchanan. May I call you Euphemia? I did know your Papa so well. And you must call me 'Dora.' No, I insist! Drat these scallops! How elusive they are! There goes another!"

It was an erratic meal at best, but after a while one grew accustomed to the heavy aroma, and Dora's conversation was so merrily idiotic that Euphemia found it difficult to be downhearted. It was as well she was enabled to forget her worries, for, when she went back upstairs, Kent was awake, coughing incessantly and in much discomfort. All she and Mrs. Henderson could do was to bathe that hot little body and see to it that the medicines were administered as the doctor had prescribed. Soon, Dora came up to "take a turn with the poor fellow" and succeeded in so fascinating him with her tale of a frog who developed an insatiable craving for bonbons that he was quiet for some time. As the afternoon waned, however, he became more and more distressed, and it was not until he dropped into an exhausted slumber just before six o'clock that Euphemia again felt able to leave him.

She went downstairs in time to see Bryce and her brother come in from the rear of the house. Simon was laughing, but he looked tired and very cold, and she could have shaken him.

Wearing a superb frieze riding coat, Hawkhurst strode through the front doors. He pulled off his gloves and, handing them to the footman, frowned and told Bryce with a flashing look of irritation that he should have had more sense than to take Sir Simon out driving on such a bitter day.

Bryce ventured an anxious enquiry, to which Buchanan responded that he had thoroughly enjoyed it, adding a diversionary, "How's your page, Mia?"

"Not at all improved, I fear. Dr. Archer is coming this evening, thank heaven."

At this point two lackeys carried in some battered but recognizable pieces of luggage. Hawkhurst apologized that, although he and his men had spent most of the day at or near the scene of the accident, this was all they had been able to retrieve. One of the portmanteaux had split open, but the losses appeared negligible, and fortunately, Euphemia's jewel case proved to be intact.

Climbing the stairs again, her relief at the recovery of her jewels was marred by the fact that Simon sneezed twice. This so wrenched his shoulder that, when she remonstrated with him, he requested irritably that she kindly not maudle over him, and that he felt splendid. Knowing him and his rare ill-humours, she restrained a cutting comment and feared the worst.

By morning, having spent a frightening night with Kent, her fears were realized. Simon remained in bed, stricken with a very bad cold. With typical male perversity, having allowed not a whimper to escape him when a heavy lead musket ball had smashed his shoulder, nor once complained through the agonizing weeks that had followed, he was now the complete invalid, sneezing, snuffling, groaning, and calling down maledictions upon a malignant Fate, while never once admitting that his own folly had brought about his condition. Much as she loved her brother, Euphemia found herself quite out of charity with him and informed him roundly that he should be spanked for such irresponsible behaviour.

Hawkhurst was no less incensed with Bryce, and that young man, having received a royal set-down at his guardian's hands, hurriedly took himself off and remained least in sight for the next several days.

Those days were trying indeed for Euphemia. Simon was genuinely ill, and, despite her irritation with him, she was obliged to divide her time between the sickrooms, dreading lest his cold worsen into pneumonia or his wound become inflamed by reason of his violent sneezes. Kent, meanwhile, grew worse, the harsh, racking cough convulsing his small body, and his fever mounting. Mrs. Graham, Ellie, and the invincible housekeeper were reinforced by an endless succession of maids in caring for the two invalids, but, despite their devotion, Euphemia was the only one who could calm the child, and as time wore on she scarcely dared relinquish his burning little hand, but what the hollowed eyes would fly open in a terrified seeking for her.

Shortly after two o'clock on the third night, he became so weak that she was sure the end was near. Thoroughly frightened, she roused Ellie, who was dozing in the chair, then ran downstairs in search of Hawkhurst. Candles still burned in the library, but the pleasant room was empty. She was about to pull the bellrope and despatch a servant to wake him when she heard voices outside. Drawing her shawl closer about her, she stepped onto the terrace. A chaise with the door wide stood upon the front drive. Two young gentlemen, decidedly inebriated, clung to each other as they viewed Hawkhurst's laughing and clumsy attempts to lift a reluctant beauty into the vehicle. He placed her upon the step, but was staggered as she launched herself into his arms again with a shriek of hilarity. "Not so loud!" he urged. "We've a sick child in the house!"

His inamorata fairly squeaked her astonishment, and one of the gentlemen hiccoughed, "Ch-child? *You*? Wha' th' deuce? Did y'lovely Blanche bring y'brat back t'haunt you, Gary?" It was an ill-judged remark, and the effect on Hawkhurst was startling. He abandoned the lady and turned on his foxed friend like a fury, one fist whipping back.

At any other time, Euphemia would have immediately retreated. Now, illogically angered that he should be thus occupied when she so needed him, she ran forward, calling his name. That lethal fist dropped, and he spun around, an expression of dismay crossing his flushed face as he beheld her. Striding forward then, he took the hands she stretched out and searched her pale, tired face. The moment she felt that strong clasp, she felt comforted, a sensation that deepened when he said with quiet authority, "Go back inside at once. I'll bring Hal."

His voice was only slightly slurred, and she thought thankfully that he was not so drunk as to be stupid. His friends were, however, and stared in total, befuddled silence as she ran, shivering, back into the house. Climbing the stairs, she wished Hawkhurst had sent a groom to Down Buttery. He would likely have difficulty retaining his seat, much less be able to ride faster than a walk. Moments later, she heard a thunder of hooves upon the drive, and was contrarily appalled by such headlong speed. The moon was dim tonight, and to ride so fast was to invite disaster. She sat bathing Kent's burning face, counting the minutes, and praying that Hawkhurst's recklessness might not result in his being carried home a corpse.

She had supposed the journey to Down Buttery and back would take the better part of an hour, but he must have ridden like the wind indeed, for within thirty minutes she heard the rumble of wheels outside. Soon, quick footsteps sounded in the hall, and Dr. Archer hurried into the room, followed by Hawkhurst, who moved to wait silently in a distant corner. The doctor nodded to the worried Ellie, threw Euphemia a smile, and questioned her softly as he made his examination. When he finished, he turned on her in mock outrage and grumbled that the boy had taken a decided turn for the better. Euphemia was both overjoyed and mortified, but Archer stilled her rather shaken apologies by saying she had done splendidly and that now she could safely rest, having given him the opportunity to enjoy some of Hawk's excellent brandy.

Thus reminded of her host's efforts, Euphemia turned to thank him. She was too late, however. Hawkhurst had quietly slipped away.

The following morning, Buchanan felt much improved. Not only was his cold relieved; his shoulder was easier than it had been since he was hit. A few more days like this, he thought with elation, and he would be able to rejoin his regiment. He breakfasted in bed and allowed Bailey, Hawkhurst's imperturbable valet, to shave him and assist with his toilet. Then, in high spirits, save for the unwelcome notion that he had been a nuisance at a most trying time, he went off in search of some way to make amends. A shy maid advised him that Mrs. Graham was still sleeping, that Miss Euphemia, poor dear soul, had taken to her bed at dawn, that Miss Stephanie was come home again and somewhere about, and that my Lady Bryce and Mr. Hawkhurst's secretary were in the small gold salon upstairs, planning the Musicale.

Feeling decidedly *de trop*, Buchanan proceeded down the stairs. Lord Bryce, clad in an enormously caped riding coat, with hat, whip, and gloves in one hand, was crossing the hall. At Buchanan's hail, he halted and beamed upward. He went considerably in awe of the Lieutenant's military prowess, but despite this and the difference in their ages, a deep liking had sprung up between them. He told Buchanan he looked "in jolly good point" today, and that they would have to throw some dice later on. Guessing that Bryce meant to ride over to Chant House to visit Chilton Gains, Buchanan hopefully offered to bear him company. Bryce turned quite pale and began to stammer his way through an involved morass of excuses. Hawkhurst had very obviously put the fear of God into him, and, having no wish to cause him further embarrassment, Buchanan politely remembered that he really must write some letters and watched rather wistfully as Bryce all but heaved a sigh of relief and fled the premises.

Hawkhurst was Sir Simon's next quarry and was run to earth in the library, half-sitting against the reference table, one booted leg swinging and a grim expression on his face as he stared down at a letter he held. He wore riding dress and was as usual quietly elegant. Surveying the cut of the bottle green jacket, the fit of the buckskins, the impeccably tied neckcloth, and the absence of any jewelry save for his large signet ring, Buchanan wondered that Colley, so obviously admiring his cousin, did not look and learn.

Hawkhurst's head lifted at his approach. For an instant he stared unseeingly. Then, recovering himself, he came to his feet and offered his felicitations upon his guest's improved state of health.

"Yes, well, that's why I came. To thank you, sir. You've been dashed decent about it all, and I'm truly sorry, for we've been a confounded pest, I've no doubt!"

"I am quite sure of it," murmured Hawkhurst and, noting

the immediate upward toss of that sandy head, chuckled, "I meant—that I'm sure you are sorry, and with no cause, for it has been our pleasure. Egad, Buchanan, do you go through life so curst hot at hand, I wonder you've survived this long!"

"Well, you damned well deliberately provoke me!"

"I apologize. I prefer your rage to such abject gratitude, I admit."

The twinkle in the grey eyes was irresistible. Buchanan grinned and was at once invited to play a game of billiards. How could one hold a grudge under these circumstances? He decided one could not, accepted with delight, and they spent a pleasant hour together, at the end of which time he had lost approximately seventy-eight thousand pounds (fortunately all represented by buttons!). Hawkhurst played a skilful game, his movements carelessly graceful, yet containing the odd suggestion of leashed power that epitomized him. He was every inch the aristocrat and unfailingly the courteous host, and, scanning him surreptitiously from time to time, Simon knew a touch of uncertainty. *Did* rumour speak truly? Was this man who had so courageously rescued Kent also capable of having murdered his wife and their child? The lined face, the heavy brows and jut of the chin, the firm mouth, all bespoke an individual one would not lightly cross; certainly, a potential for ruthlessness hovered in the cold grey eyes. The trouble was that they were not always cold, nor was the mouth consistently set into that thin, uncompromising line. When Hawkhurst laughed, as he did occasionally during their game, the ice vanished, the eyes sparkled, and the harsh face underwent such a transformation that Buchanan was shocked into remembering that years ago he had from a distance actually admired the fellow—and even more shocking, that Hawkhurst was only four years older than himself!

Their game was interrupted when a large, neatly clad, and shrewd-eyed individual appeared in the doorway, made his bow, and announced, "The horses is ready, sir." Hawkhurst sighed and put down his cue. "What a merciless tyrant you are, Paul."

The large man grinned and said he would wait in the kitchen. Hawkhurst turned to Buchanan and offered his apologies, saying wryly that his bailiff was extremely demanding. He begged that Sir Simon proceed exactly as though he were in his own home, then started for the door but, with his hand

77

on the latch, turned about to asked interestedly, "And what is your verdict, Buchanan?"

Buchanan stared at him.

Hawkhurst put up his brows. "What, no conclusion? And after all those sidelong glances . . . all that frowning deliberation! My poor fellow, how very vexing for you! Allow me to be of assistance. I am innocent! Pure as the driven snow! There, now you may be at ease for the remainder of your stay."

And, with a cynical grin, an infuriatingly mocking bow, he was gone.

❧ *Chapter 6* ❧

When Buchanan recovered sufficiently that he was able to restrain the impulse to stalk the nearest footman and strangle him, he decided that he might as well get to his letters. He caught a glimpse of Miss Hawkhurst in the hall and brightened, but she ran quickly up the stairs, almost as though seeking to avoid him. He went into the library, where he spent a great deal of time sharpening a pen, while thinking of a dozen people he should, but did not care to, write to. He was reprieved when Lady Bryce buttonholed him and desired he take luncheon with her and her niece. Like any basically healthy young man, he was always ready to enjoy a meal, and he was also eager to hear of Miss Hawkhurst's journey and what news she had of the war. Therefore, he willingly took his place beside Lady Bryce in the small dining room and thanked her for having taken the trouble to deliver his letter to his great aunt personally. She at once launched into a rapturous account of what a delightful cose she had enjoyed with her "dear friend" Lucasta. Murmuring a polite response Buchanan was reminded of the extremely irate letter he had yesterday received from the hand of her "dear friend's" groom. "You wretched boy!" Great Aunt Lucasta had commenced, not mincing her words. "How *could* you have allowed that *odious* Carlotta Bryce to come to my house? I have been obliged to invent an involved tale to explain her presence, for, allow the gabblemongers to know where you are now domiciled, I will *not*! And does *she* spread the tale (ingratiating hornet that she is!), I shall deny it!" The missive had gone on at great length, bemoaning the fate that had flung them in the way of the evil Garret Hawkhurst, and concluded with the warning that, page or no page, did Simon not remove his sister from "that den of infamy" within another week at the latest, his poor aunt would have to set aside her preparations for the holidays, in order to come for them! Even Hawkhurst's suave hauteur, thought Buchanan, must crumble before the full flood of Lady Lucasta's famous tongue. Which, under the circumstances, would not do! No, he simply must ensure that they arrive at Meadow Abbey well before his aunt's patience expired. And certainly before the much vaunted Musicale—a sure fate worse than death!

He was diverted from his thoughts by the advent of a maid, who conveyed Miss Hawkhurst's regrets, but she was fatigued of her long drive and begged they would excuse her. Buchanan was disappointed, and his feeling that the girl was seeking to avoid him deepened.

At half past two o'clock, Buchanan's elbow slipped off the arm of the chair in the library and woke him. He had settled down to think about the next letter he would write and must have dozed off. He stretched, took up his solitary effort, and wandered into the hall to deposit it in the jade salver for delivery to the post office. Yawning, his idle gaze encountered the stern stare of a splendid gentleman in periwig and laces. The portrait was beautifully preserved, and the frame a work of art in itself and, reminded he had not yet visited the gallery, he made his way up the spiral staircase and thence to the sweep of stairs that led to the top floor. To his left lay the game room and servants' quarters. He turned right, past more guest rooms and salons, until the corridor curved into the South Wing and approached the gallery. The floors here were especially fine, the rich parquetry embellished with many cabinets and screens, all in the oriental motif. The gallery doors stood open, and beside them an exquisite chinoiserie clock occupied a corner that echoed the chinoiserie design, even the flooring having been inlaid so as to continue those elegant lines. Impressed, Buchanan wandered into a long, wide room, graced here and there by thick rugs and brightened by recessed bays through which pale sunlight traced the latticework of dormer windows onto the boards. Richly carved credenzas and chests held bouquets of chrysanthemum and fern. And along the walls an impressive array of Thorndykes and Hawkhursts looked down upon the visitor with varying degrees of calm, amusement, or condescension.

Buchanan wandered among this august assemblage with mild interest until he came to the portrait of a dark young man with high-peaked brows and a lean face mainly remarkable for a pair of speaking grey eyes and a wide and whimsical mouth, both of which features put him in remind of their host. Thick hair tied in at the nape of the neck and foaming Brussels lace at throat and wrists proclaimed an age of elegance now, alas, lost to the world. Buchanan leaned closer and read on the gold plaque, "Christopher Valentine Thorndyke—Fourth Earl of Aynsworth."

Staring upwards, conscious of an odd feeling of liking for the man, he was startled by a small clatter. He turned about and saw a spool rolling towards him from one of the bays, the thread jerking as though desperate hands strove to retrieve it. Buchanan swept it up and, winding it carefully, walked after that leaping strand. He suspected the identity of the lady he would find in the bay and was not disappointed. Miss Hawkhurst, clad in a plain green gown and with a shawl about her shoulders, was sitting in the window seat. She all but shrank as he strolled towards her, still rewinding the thread. He offered his spool in silence, and she stood to accept it, a swift flood of colour coming painfully into her cheeks and sending her pale lashes fluttering downward.

"Why," he asked gently, "do I frighten you so?"

Her colour fled, and, dropping the spool into her workbasket, she said, "Oh, no. You do not. At all. But I like to work up here, for the light is good, and I—I like to be alone."

It was cold in the room, for the fires were not lit, and her finger had been like ice. Undeceived, he touched her elbow. "Please do not be afraid of me. Can you believe I mean harm to someone as good—as gentle, as you?"

The downbent head flew up, the big eyes wide with earnestness. "*No!* Never! It is only that . . . that Aunt says—" She bit her lip and was silent.

"Your Aunt Carlotta?" He might have known! "What does the lady say? That I am of shocking repute, and you must not—"

She smiled wanly. "She thinks you splendid, of course. But your sister offered to . . . that is . . . she wants to . . . to teach me how to . . . to . . ."

"To make yourself into the beauty no man in his right mind could resist," he finished kindly.

"She is so good," she gulped. "To be willing to help me try to be . . . a little less plain and—and dowdy, than I am."

"Oh, what fustian!" He took her hand in his friendly way and said an encouraging, "My sister is a very sweet soul, Miss Hawkhurst, but the world's busiest arranger. I vow she arranged the lives of so many people in Spain that her victims are known as 'Mia's Mandates'!" A twinkle crept into her shy eyes, and he nodded, "Truly. You may ask anyone! Untold couples who live blissfully in the delusion they found one another of their own ingenuity are wed only by reason of her cunning machinations!" A rich little gurgle of merriment resulting, he squeezed her hand slightly and, releasing it, persisted, "Now to what, precisely, does Aunty object?"

The flush on her cheeks heightened, which made her look unsuspectedly attractive, he thought. But not looking away now, she said quietly, "She says, do I try to be—er, to put on—airs, you must believe I am . . . I . . ." But she was too well bred to bring herself to say it, and her gaze flickered and fell again.

"What?" gasped Buchanan. And with a peal of laughter, said, "Setting your cap—for *me*? Throwing out lures? Oh, that's rich!"

She flinched and stepped away, head bowed. And cursing his clumsiness, he moved closer behind her and said, "But, dear lady, how could this be? I am safely wed. And with three hopeful children."

A small gasp broke the silence that followed. For an instant Miss Hawkhurst was rigidly still. Then she turned a rather pale face to him and said gaily, "You . . . are?"

He nodded. "So your aunt cannot accuse you of such naughty mischief."

"She . . . she most assuredly cannot."

"I think we must confound her, you and I. You may let Mia play her little games, if that is your wish, for you are safe with me, and, if you wait until some *eligible* young gentleman is here, Aunty may then really contrive to throw a rub in your way. When she is convinced you have totally ensnared me, we shall tell her all her suspicions are for nought, and by that time you will be the rage of four counties, at the very least!"

Her laugh was sweetly musical, if somewhat breathless. "Oh, thank you, sir! You and your dear sister are just . . . too kind."

"I cannot deny it. Wherefore, I am lonely and neglected, and your sewing can wait, can it not? Come now, and tell me who was this very fine young gentleman."

He led her to the portrait, and looking up, her eyes softened. "Lord Christopher. Is he not handsome? He was the first Thorndyke to own Dominer, and my great-grandfather on Mama's side. And here . . ." she moved to the portrait beside that of Lord Aynsworth, "is his lady wife."

Following, Buchanan viewed a lovely young woman with coppery golden ringlets and eyes of a rich green, long and wide, and filled with an inner happiness that the artist had in some magical fashion captured on the canvas. "Leonie, Countess of Aynsworth," he read, and murmured, "She looks as though she were thinking of something very beloved."

"Probably her husband. My Grandpapa says they were the happiest couple he ever knew. In love all their lives."

A wistful smile touched her eyes, and watching her, he said, "I expect, someday, you will find such a love."

"I pray so, but to how many is given such a very great gift?"

The smile died from Buchanan's eyes. For one brief year he had thought to have possessed such a gift and dreamed it would last forever. But the bubble had burst, leaving nothing but this painful yearning for the might-have-been. He looked up and, finding her concerned gaze upon him, asked brightly, "Should you care to go for a ride? Oh, do say you will. Would Hawkhurst object, do you think?"

"Most decidedly. As would I. Dominer has harmed you enough, Sir Simon. I will not be a party to your being made ill again."

She spoke in her usual soft fashion, but there was a firm set to her chin, and he realized in some surprise that beneath her shyness dwelt a resolute spirit. "If you would care for it," she suggested, "I should instead be most pleased to show you over the house and the conservatory."

He agreed only after extracting a promise that, if he was

obedient today, she would ride with him tomorrow. Then, he proffered his left arm, Stephanie smiled and lightly rested her hand upon it, and they commenced the tour.

By the end of the week Kent was beginning to exhaust his nurses with his reviving energy. Always sweet-natured and easy to manage, he nonetheless contrived to be up and walking did they for an instant relax their vigilance and was frequently discovered kneeling among the cushions of the window bay, gazing out across the frosty gardens.

Returning to the sickroom after luncheon one cold, gray afternoon, Euphemia was astounded to find Hawkhurst sprawled in an armchair, long booted legs outthrust and crossed at the ankles, chin resting upon interlaced fingers as he frowned at the small patient. Kent, absorbed by something, was sitting up in bed. He threw her a quick, loving smile, then bent to his task once more. Intrigued, Euphemia trod closer. "What is it?"

Hawkhurst pulled his lean form erect and shrugged a bored, "Crayons, and a picture to copy. Come."

She glanced at him interrogatively.

"You are pale and hagged," he imparted with cool candour. "And I wish to speak with you. I shall take you for a drive in the curricle."

"Thank you. But—no." How swift the narrowing of the eyes, the upward toss of the head, the haughty droop of the eyelids. Her confrontations with him had been few these past eight days, for she had usually been too busy with the child to go downstairs to dine, and when she had put in an appearance, Hawkhurst had been off somewhere, consorting with his ragtag friends, she supposed. But whatever he was, he had saved their lives and offered a most generous hospitality. "If I may," she said, "I would prefer to ride. Have you a suitable mount for a lady, sir?"

"By the time you are changed, your steed will await you. And," he added dryly, "probably be exhausted by the wait!"

She responded to that challenge, of course, and with Ellie's assistance changed into her habit and in a very short time took up her fur-lined pelisse and gloves and hurried to the stairs. Halfway down she paused as a roar of rage sounded from the music room. To her astonishment, a very large and ugly dog, somewhere between a bloodhound and a wolf, shot into the hall, sent rugs flying as it scrabbled wildly on the polished floors, and floundered with total ungainliness into the dining

83

room. Hawkhurst, face flushed, raced into view. "Where in the devil did that miserable brute go?" he snarled.

"Brute . . . ?" echoed Euphemia innocently, pulling on one of her gloves.

"The Gains mongrel!" He marched to the library and flung the door wide. "I'll have its ears, by God!"

"It must be very well trained."

He darted a black scowl at her.

"To be able to unlatch a closed door," she smiled.

"That worthless flea-carrier, madam," he observed acidly, "has, for some ridiculous reason, a predilection for lumbering five miles across my preserves and creating havoc wherever it lays its clumsy feet. It tears down young trees, uproots plants and shrubs, jumps into the ornamental water and devours all the confounded goldfish! And having performed these acts of vandalism, it adds insult to injury by trailing its mud, slime, and vermin across my rugs! I *warned* Gains! And by heaven, I shall—"

A loud crash sounded from the dining room. With a triumphant cry, he sprinted across the hall. Her heart in her mouth, Euphemia followed. A shout, a thud, and she jumped aside in the nick of time as The Flea-Carrier, tongue lolling, ears back, tail high, panted past and gamboled disastrously towards the kitchen. A muffled groan made Euphemia's nerves jump. She hurried into the dining room. Hawkhurst lay sprawled on his back on the floor. With a little gasp of fear, she sped to kneel beside him. He looked dazed and oddly youthful and tried to raise his head, but it fell back, and he gasped out, "Damnable . . . brute. Ran between my . . . legs."

"Are you hurt?" she asked, battling the urge to laugh.

" 'How . . .' " he quoted faintly, " 'are the mighty . . . fallen . . . in the midst of—' "

It was too much. She broke into a peal of laughter. Lying there, the breath knocked out of him, Hawkhurst wheezed along with her. He came to one elbow, grinning up into her merry face, until he saw beyond her a small crowd of servants with an awed disbelief on every countenance. "Are you all blind as well as deaf?" he demanded, well knowing what had brought about those amazed expressions. "That blasted hound of the Gains has been at its depredations again! Get it the devil off our grounds!"

The doorway cleared in a flash. Hawkhurst clambered to his feet and, taking Euphemia's elbow, assisted her to rise. Her eyes slipped past him. The exquisite Han Dynasty vase from the corner display cabinet lay in fragments on the floor. Following her horrified gaze, Hawkhurst groaned and muttered something under his breath. The oath was not quite inaudible, but she could scarcely blame him.

"My goodness!" Euphemia patted the glossy neck of the big black horse admiringly. "He is magnificent! Wherever did you get him?"

"Gift from a friend," said Hawkhurst. "He's called Sarabande, and you'd do well not to stroke him when Manners ain't holding his head. A bit inclined to be playful."

"So I see." She stepped back as the black danced, his eyes rolling to her. "My, but he's full of spirit. How I should love to try him."

"He's not broke to side saddle, ma'am. Nor ever likely to be, for I need no more lives on my conscience!" His eyes were grim suddenly. "Now, may I throw you up!"

She rested her booted foot in his cupped hands, and he tossed her easily into the saddle, then mounted Sarabande and led the way from the yard at a sedate trot. Once in the open the black strained and fidgeted, fighting his iron hand. Hawkhurst's jaw set, and Euphemia smothered a smile and murmured, "My, how invigorating this is."

He slanted a suspicious glance at her, saw the dimple beside her mouth, and chuckled. "If you will pardon me a moment, I'll take some of the edges off . . ."

He was away, leaning forward in the saddle, the great horse stretching out in a thundering gallop. Euphemia looked after him appreciatively. He had a splendid seat. She suspected, however, that it would take more than a moment to cool the fire in that spirited animal, and it had been a long time since she'd enjoyed a gallop. She kinked her heels home, and the mare's ears pricked up eagerly.

Thus it was that Garret Hawkhurst, setting Sarabande at a low wall which concealed the stream beyond it, landed neatly on the far side, allowed the black to gallop a short distance, and, swinging back, was in time to witness Miss Buchanan soar over wall and stream and canter towards him. "Oh, well done!" he exclaimed impulsively, but as she came up with him, frowned, "And very foolish!"

"Yes," admitted Euphemia, flushed and breathless. "I'd no

idea the stream was beyond. Fortunately the mare did. How is she called?"

"Fiddle," he said rudely and, seeing her brows arch, explained mischievously, "Because after a while she tends to become diverted by such mundane items as grass and shrubs."

She laughed and drew her hood a little closer. Heavy clouds were gathering, and together was the smell of snow in the air. She wondered suddenly if they would reach Meadow Abbey in time for Christmas—exactly two weeks away.

"Too cold for you, ma'am?" asked Hawkhurst.

"Not as cold as I would have been in your curricle, thank you, sir."

"Oh, I'd have bundled you up. And I begin to think you'd have been safer."

"Indeed?" she said indignantly. "I'll have you know that—" But she saw his lips twitch and finished in a milder tone. "I collect you would have driven at a snail's pace."

"But, of course."

"From what I have heard, Mr. Hawkhurst—"

"I make no doubt of what you have heard!" His eyes pure ice now, he went on, "If you will turn about, ma'am—"

"I shall not," she intervened coolly. "And, as I was about to say, I have heard you—ride, Mr. Hawkhurst. On the night you went for Dr. Archer, I was quite sure you would be borne home, slain."

A slow flush darkened his cheeks as he met her level gaze. "My apologies. I thought you referred to another matter. However, I was three parts drunk that night and probably rode with very little of common sense."

"And I suppose you will say you were three parts drunk when you came to our rescue." His gloved hand made a short gesture of dismissal, but she went on, "It is quite useless, dear sir. I have every intention to thank you for all you have done. And—"

"Your brother has thanked me. It only half killed him, I gather. And now, if you will kindly turn about, Miss Buchanan . . ."

He had spoken roughly. She sensed that he was trying to put her off-stride and, wondering why, protested, "But we only just came out!"

Hawkhurst's movement was very fast. Before she had a chance to resist, he gripped the bridle, and her mare was turned. Unaccustomed to such high-handed methods, her eyes flashed fire.

He shrugged. "You have been here nigh two weeks and not yet properly seen the exterior of my home."

She looked up eagerly and was speechless. They had been riding steadily uphill and, from the elevation whereon they now sat their horses, were able to view Dominer, spread magnificently on its own hill below them. The red brick mansion, a uniform three storeys, was built in a wide semicircle, the north and south wings reaching backward, and the ground floor widening at the centre of the house, front and rear, to accommodate the full circle of the Great Hall. The white columns of a portico dignified this central curve, and the enormous double doors and all the wood trim were also white. The terrace was edged by a low balustrade, opening to steps that led up to the entrance. Extensive pleasure gardens were threaded by paved walks, dotted with benches and statuary, and shaded by tastefully placed trees and shrubs. The flowerbeds were bare now, the ornamental water, both front and rear, edged with ice, and the fountains not in operation, but Euphemia could picture it all in the springtime, and murmured softly, "I had heard how very lovely it was."

He made no answer, and, glancing up, she found him watching her. She was seldom discomfited, but something about that piercing scrutiny set her pulse to fluttering. The frozen breath of the wind ruffled the fur that edged her hood, but her shiver was not for that chill touch.

"Thank you," he said, slightly frowning.

She was flustered and, attempting to conceal it, looked about her and remarked, "Oh, what a very pretty bridge that is! May we ride that way?"

"We may not. The bridge is being rebuilt and is unsafe." He saw her brows lift a little at his gruff tone and went on, "Come now, it's too cold to sit here and since you enjoy a gallop . . ."

He led the way at a spanking pace, up the hill and across a stretch of turf, avoiding the icy paths. The mare was taxed to the utmost, but Euphemia was sure Hawkhurst had held the big black in, and the stallion was scarcely blowing when he was reined back to a canter, and then to a walk.

"You ride very well," Hawkhurst acknowledged. "Learned in Spain, did you? I heard you were right up with the best of 'em when they forded the rivers over there."

She glanced at him in some surprise, wondering how much

else he knew of her. "Yes. But you did not bring me out here to talk of Spain, did you?"

He smiled rather sardonically at this direct approach and guided her down a slope, then followed the winding route of a stream. Sarabande snorted and sidled at the rustle of a patch of reeds and shied when a flock of fieldfares soared raucously upward a short distance away, but, ignoring these idiosyncrasies, Hawkhurst said mildly, "My sister has taken a great liking to you, ma'am."

Euphemia, who had been admiring his superb horsemanship, thought, Aha! So that's it! and replied, "A liking I return, I do assure you. She is the dearest girl and has been of so much help with poor little Kent. Indeed, it seems that each time I turn around there is something else for which I must thank you."

She had hoped that this would irritate him away from the subject, and sure enough one of his hands lifted in that autocratic gesture of impatience. "Nonsense. I am only sorry you had so terrifying an experience," his eyes turned to her thoughtfully, "while on my land."

Euphemia answered his unspoken question at once. "We were trespassing, I know. Dominer is featured in my guidebook, you see, and, since we would pass through Down Buttery on our way to Bath, I begged my brother to let us detour just a little way so that we might actually see it."

"I'll warrant you had to beg hard," he said cynically. "Buchanan's no admirer of architecture. Nor of me."

"To the contrary. He told me Dominer was magnificent." A small frown came into her eyes. "And you must think him a sad case if you fancy him ungrateful for all you have done. The way you went down that cliff after the boy was—"

"Damned foolish," he intervened curtly and, seeing her mouth opening, added a hurried, "Speaking of the boy, may I ask why he is called only Kent? Is he a foundling?"

"Very much so. I found him in my sister's chimney." He directed a curious glance at her, and she recounted the sad story. By the time she finished, he looked very grim indeed. "Poor little devil," he muttered. "No wonder he's mute. Probably scared half to death. It happens to some of our men who are in the worst of the fighting, you know. I've a good friend, in fact, who may never be able to speak again."

"You—you *could* not mean Lord Jeremy Bolster?"

Hawkhurst had been staring rather blankly at his horse's

ears, but the incredulity in her tone brought a glint of anger to his eyes, and he snapped, "Yes. But pray do not let the secret out—it would quite ruin the poor fellow! Now, as to my sister. I am told you intend to . . . er, make a beauty out of her."

He was not pleased, that was very obvious. Making a recovery from her astonishment that he could number so fine a young man as Bolster among his friends, Euphemia began, "I merely hoped to—"

"Gild the lily?" he sneered rudely. "Why? Not all men like painted, perfumed, and posturing females."

Flabbergasted, she fought to remain outwardly calm, even while wondering how that arrogant face would look with claw marks down it. "Nor had I intended to make her into a replica of myself, sir," she riposted, with saintly humility.

Briefly, he looked taken aback, but refusing to acknowledge that his deliberate insult had been flung back in his teeth, he compounded the felony. "I am glad to hear it. Stephanie is happy and has no need to cultivate a lot of foolish affectations to no purpose."

For an instant Euphemia could scarce believe she had heard him aright. Then, she was fairly dizzied with rage. *Never* had she met such a crude barbarian! "Foolish affectations" indeed! She clung to the memory that he had saved their lives and was thus enabled not to betray the anger that she sensed would gratify him. Entering the lists with grace, but with her lance poised, she murmured, "Ah, but *is* she happy?"

"The devil! Why would she not be?" He flung out one arm in an irked gesture that startled Sarabande into a sideways leap, a dance, two bucks, and a whirligig. Euphemia clapped her hands and laughed aloud. Hawkhurst rode it out in magnificent style, but was flushed and tight of lip when at last he reined the black to her side. Perhaps because he knew her mirth well-warranted, he snarled, "I collect country life would seem dull to someone who has jauntered about the world as you have done, ma'am. But I assure you my sister desires no such flibbertigibbet existence. She is a shy, quiet bookworm. You were charitable enough to describe her 'beautiful.' That, she ain't! She has far more important attributes—a heart of gold, and the disposition of an angel. If some bright young Buck could only see beyond the end of his nose, he'd grab her up fast!" Really furious now, Euphemia attempted to respond, but up went his hand again, and, looking down at her as from Mount Olympus, he decreed, "She would no more fit into that frippery round of empty-headed entertainments and empty-headed people in London Town, than—"

"Stuff, sir!" she flashed, goaded beyond endurance. "Oh, you may scowl and droop your haughty eyes at me if you must! I shall have my say! Your sister, Mr. Hawkhurst, is a young and lovely girl. She should be happily shopping with friends for fashionable gowns and bonnets and ribands and reticules, and all the little pieces of prettiness you, I have no doubt, designate 'nonsense,' but that are dear to the heart of any lady! And had she the disposition of a saint and the face of a goddess, much good would it do her so long as she is cooped up here all year round! How may she meet her 'bright young Buck,' sir? I've seen few callers since we came. And *none* any gentleman would wish to introduce to a loved sister! Stephanie *should* be going to balls and routs and parties and 'frippery entertainments,' meeting other young people, and eligible young men!"

"Well ... she ... shall ... *not!*" he grated between his teeth.

"Indeed? Then what *is* your intention for her, dare I ask? To keep her hidden away so as to share a lonely old age with you?"

He froze, whitened, and reached out to seize her bridle, once more pulling the mare to a halt. His eyes glittering, he rasped, "You certainly speak your mind, Miss Buchanan!"

The black minced and pranced, and suddenly their mounts were close together. Hawkhurst's scraped forehead was almost healed now, the bruises faded, but his sudden pallor accentuated them, reminding her of the accident. Perhaps it was the aftermath of her anger that was causing her to tremble in so odd a way, but she was shocked as much by the depth of that anger as by her unforgivable outburst. "Yes," she said meekly, "I am famous for my hasty tongue. I know that was unpardonable, but—forgive me, I beg you." His lips remained set in that tight, harsh line. She placed one hand on his arm and smiled up into those glinting eyes, and the rage faded from them. For one brief second she thought to see a very different expression, but then the lids drooped, and, drawing away, he started onward, saying coldly, "Very well, Madam All-Wise, what would you have me do?"

"Allow me to ... to show her how to dress her hair more becomingly," she said, still strangely shaken. "And perhaps, if there is time, she could come into Bath with me, and we could shop a little and find her—"

"Oh, spare me!" Hawkhurst was riding slightly ahead now, since the path had narrowed, and over his shoulder said a bored, "Never bother with an itemized list, ma'am! I'm all too well acquainted with the lures you ladies throw out to catch yourselves a husband."

Euphemia usually found it downright child's play to wrap gentlemen around her little finger and certainly had never in all her days been blatantly insulted. He was unique! But he'd not get the best of her this easily. "I am very sure you are," she said sweetly. "In fact, dear sir, I pray you will enlighten me, for there is so much I've yet to learn."

The path widening again, he waited for her to come up with him, his eyes searching her face narrowly. "From all I hear, you have rejected more offers than most of our acknowledged Toasts."

Euphemia was convinced now that he sought to come to cuffs with her and that her well-meant interference with his sister had thoroughly enraged him. Her demure silence did not improve his mood appreciably, for he added a sneering, "What's the difficulty, ma'am? Has no mere man measured up to your expectations?"

It would not, she thought, be quite polite to take off one's boot and cast it into a gentleman's teeth. She was very tempted to tell him that she hoped to snare one who had come "hosed and shod" into the world, but to do so would be to betray Stephanie's confidence, so instead she sighed, "Alas, that is true. The man of my heart did not offer for me."

Hawkhurst was taken completely off his stride. Horrified, he sought frantically for something to say that would mitigate his savage attack. But she looked so very saintly that suspicion seized him, and, albeit uncertainly, he said, "And I suppose this paragon is some fashionable fribble, appropriately tall, dark, and handsome?"

"Yes, he is." She heard a disgusted snort and, beginning to enjoy herself, appended outrageously, "And so dashing in his uniform!"

"Oh? A Gentleman's Son, no doubt? How those military rattles dazzle the ladies in their scarlet!"

"True. But my admired gentleman did not wear a scarlet coat."

"Oh? A rifleman?"

"A naval officer. And, much decorated." (He would be *vastly* decorated! He would have every decoration known to man!) "He served with Lord Nelson."

There was silence. Euphemia stole a glance from under her lashes and could have screamed with mirth at his awed expression.

"Did he, by George! And—his name? Or, perhaps I presume?"

"Not at all. His name is Algernon Montmorency . . . Vane—" She met his eyes as she sought about mentally and encountered a totally unexpected twinkle.

". . . Glorious!" he suggested.

She had to choke back an instinctive laugh and finished, "Vane-Armstrong."

"Poor fellow!" He clicked his tongue. "What a mouthful! And, his title?"

He meant to check his *Peerage*—the wretch! "Oh, none! But, from a very fine old family, as you doubtless know. So, will you not help me, Mr. Hawkhurst?"

Watching her, he echoed rather vaguely, "*Help* you?"

"You said you were well acquainted with . . . lures I might throw out."

His eyes sharpened and held very steadily on hers for a space. She could not know how her blue eyes sparkled, nor how rosy were her cheeks. With a small start, he said, "Oh Lord, there are millions of 'em, I don't doubt. I've had millions flung at me, it seems. You'd not believe, Miss Buchanan, the lengths to which some of these fortune-hunting wenches will go. I've had 'em 'lose their way' and be 'compelled' to walk to Dominer for aid. Or 'need repairs' to their carriages, and we were 'the closest house.' And all this in the face of my . . . ah, lurid reputation, you'll mind. Ain't nothing can dim the lure of gold, is there, ma'am? Do you know, I had one saucy puss arrive positively dripping with diamonds—all rented, I suspect. And purely to impress me with the fact that she was as rich, if not more so, than me! Jove! I'd not be surprised to have such a hussy drive her carriage clean off the road—did she believe 'twould gain her entrance to Dominer."

The words were as deliberate as they were vulgar, and his hard eyes challenged her. Euphemia found it difficult to draw breath, but managed, "Is . . . that so? Well, you have given me much to think on, Mr. Hawkhurst. I do thank you!"

The colour in his cheeks deepened. Very abruptly, he swung

Sarabande away. "Our tongues travel faster than our mounts!" he called. "Come, ma'am." and he galloped on and around a stand of young trees.

"Bluebeard!" Euphemia hissed after his lithely swaying back. "Overbearing! Odious! Conceit-ridden, puffed up *gudgeon!*"

And, wheeling Fiddle, she rode deliberately in the opposite direction and into the Home Wood.

❧ *Chapter* 7 ❧

For a time, Euphemia was so enraged that she saw only Hawkhurst's smirking countenance and hard, cold eyes. So he fancied her dropping the handkerchief, did he? By heaven, but he must credit her with superhuman powers to have arranged that horrible landslide! He surely could not believe that she would have risked Kent's life in so reckless a fashion, even *had* the slide been contrived, which was of itself nonsensical. Perhaps he thought it merely happenstance, that she and Simon had ridden onto his lands intending to "arrange a breakdown," only to be caught in a real disaster. How *dare* he! And as if any lady of quality would throw herself at so wretched an individual. It was probably all a hum! "Ain't nothing can dim the lure of gold, is there, ma'am?" Oh, but he was hateful! If what he said was truth indeed, the type of women he had attracted must be the very dregs. Her teeth gritted. And he apparently believed her to be one of those dregs!

She rode on, fuming, until there came the insidious recollection of him lying sprawled on the floor of the dining room, winded and helpless, yet with his eyes laughing into hers as he gasped out his quotation. Simon, she knew, would have said he was a good sportsman at that moment. Increasingly, Mr. Garret Hawkhurst seemed to be two men, totally unlike: the one gallant, haunted by tragedy, yet still possessing a warm, rich sense of humour; the other hard, cruel, and capable of—She bit her lip. No! Even at his worst, she could no longer judge Hawkhurst capable of murdering a woman or a child. Seeking about for a key to the puzzle, she reflected that emergencies tend to bring out the best in certain individuals. Some of the wildest, most rabble-rousing womanizers under her father's command had been the most high-couraged fighters when battle was joined. Hawkhurst must be such a man. The emergency was over, and so he had reverted to type. She nodded her satisfaction with the theory. Still, she was deeply indebted and would repay him. By helping his sweet sister. However, he must be set down for his abominable rudeness in trying to chase her away before she could do so. Now, how might that best be accomplished? The calculating expression in her eyes remained for a little while, but gradually a smile replaced it.

She glanced up. Her smile died, and she gave a shocked gasp. She must have been lost in thought for much longer than she had realized, as she had evidently come a good distance. The gently rolling hills and dimpling valleys had been superseded by wooded slopes and sudden sharp little ravines, unsuitable country for riding—especially for a lady, unaccompanied. She wheeled Fiddle about. In that same instant a large hare flashed under the mare's nose. The quiet was shattered by a deafening explosion. Fiddle screamed with fright and reared madly. Euphemia had to exert every ounce of her horsemanship to keep from being thrown. When at last she was able to lean forward and stroke the sweating mare, a quiet voice murmured, "Splendidly done, ma'am. My compliments!"

A gentleman wearing a leather hunting jacket, top boots and buckskins stood watching her with admiration. He carried a gun finely inlaid with mother-of-pearl over one arm and a game-bag lay on the ground beside him. "I almost shot you, I'm afraid," he apologized. "I am most dreadfully sorry. I can see that would have been a terrible loss for this tired old world."

She liked him at once. He looked to be a year or two older than Simon, about thirty, she would guess. His hair, worn somewhat longer than the current fashion, was a crisp brown. The face was square and strong, but with a well-shaped mouth and laugh lines at the sides of the brown eyes. And, noting that one of those eyes lacked the twinkle that shone so warmly in the other and that the skin below it was puckered as though it had been burned, she said, with a smile, "You must be Lord Gains. Good gracious, but I have come a long way! Shall you have me seized by your keepers for trespassing?"

She reached down as she spoke, and he came at once to shake her hand. "An excellent notion! How you would brighten my house, Miss Buchanan." Her brows arched her amusement at this, and, thinking her even more attractive than he had heard, he stepped back and explained, "My brother told me you were Hawk's guest. And Leith has spoken of you often. Can you spare me a moment? Or do I detain you?"

Mildly surprised by his use of Hawkhurst's nickname, she allowed him to lift her down, and he took the reins, leaving his gun and the game-bag propped against a tree as he walked on beside her.

"You know Tristram Leith?" she asked.

"Yes. Very well. We are old friends, which makes it a bit—er, awkward for him, I'm afraid. Tris has told me he intended to offer for you again. Dare I presume to ask if he was accepted?"

She was a little taken aback but, meeting his laughing glance, could not be angry and replied, "Leith is one of my very dearest friends. I really do not think I could get along without that friendship."

Gains shook his head. "Poor fellow. Then there's still hope for the rest of us, I take it?"

"Heavens! You make your mind up swiftly, my lord!"

"He who hesitates," he grinned. "Shall you mind adding a one-eyed man to your legion of admirers? My left orb is blind, you know."

"Yes. I have heard of it, and have often wondered . . ." She frowned. "Forgive me; I've a dreadful tongue, as I've lately been reminded."

He noted the sudden frown in her eyes and asked a shrewd, "Hawkhurst? Ah, I could wish you did not stay at Dominer."

"My brother is with me, my lord."

"Oh. Well, I'd not meant to imply—" He smiled in response to her questioning look and said, "Do not believe everything you hear of him, Miss Buchanan. He's not quite as black as he's painted."

Such magnanimity from one who had suffered so cruelly at Hawkhurst's hands utterly overwhelmed her, and she stared at him, recovering her voice at last to stammer, "How very generous of you to say so. I can scarce believe any man could be so forgiving. Or have I been misinformed perhaps? I was told that Hawkhurst . . . er—"

"Did this?" He gestured toward his eye. "Yes. But it was—" He rephrased, with a small shrug. "Some of the things I said to him were quite unforgivable."

"Then one would think a gentleman should have called you out. Or perhaps—Oh dear! There I go again! And the subject must be painful to you."

"Not now. Nor have we faced one another in a pearly dawn at twenty yards, if that is what you mean." His light manner evaporated and he said with a touch of grimness, "Though it is, I fear, only a matter of time. And does he continue to abuse my dog, that time may be extremely brief."

It seemed to Euphemia that the time for their confrontation had been four years back—and over a matter of far greater moment than Hawkhurst's threats against a canine interloper. But she could imagine Simon's horror were she to comment to that effect and therefore said with a smile, "I shall have to bear witness, sir, to the fact that today Sampson struck the first blow."

They had come out onto a high, rolling heath, with a spectacular view of the countryside beyond, and Gains halted, facing her in dismay. "What? That stupid animal never trotted all the way over there again?"

"I fear he did. And raced jubilantly through the house, scattering rugs, breaking Han vases, and leaving the master flat on his back."

"Good . . . God! Not that superb vase in the dining room? The Admiral gave it to him. Oh, but this is frightful."

Euphemia eyed him curiously. "You know a good deal about your mortal enemy, sir. May I ask who is 'the Admiral'?"

"Admiral Lord Johnathan Wetherby—Hawkhurst's grandfather and a fierce, magnificent old warrior who remains, thank heaven, very much my friend. Hawk idolizes him, with good reason. But Wetherby's seldom at Dominer since . . . er . . . these days, so may not notice the absence of the vase does he come this year. As for my knowledge of the family, Hawk and I grew up together, a long time ago, as it seems now." He looked sad all at once, then brightened. "If you will look down the slope to your left, Miss Buchanan, you'll see my home. Small, compared to Dominer, but my brother and I would be overjoyed to welcome you. Will you come and take a dish of tea with us? I've a splendid housekeeper who would not leave your side for an instant, did you consent."

Euphemia admired Chant House, a sprawling Tudor edifice set in a spacious park dotted with great old oak trees. She thanked Lord Gains for his invitation and liked him the more for the fact that he made no attempt to argue with her refusal. His offer had been a mere courtesy, of course, for they both knew her unchaperoned presence in the home of two young bachelors would be unthinkable, and that this very conversation was, in fact, quite improper. Therefore, having also refused his offer to get a mount and escort her, she listened carefully to his directions, promised to ride this way again with her brother at the earliest opportunity, and sent Fiddle picking her dainty way down the slope towards the east and Dominer.

The clouds were darker than ever now, and the air so cold her breath hung upon it like little clouds, while Fiddle blew white smoke as she cantered along. Euphemia was only vaguely aware of cold, clouds, or Fiddle, however, for her thoughts were on Maximilian Gains, his gentle courtesy, and the gallantry that enabled him to speak of his enemy with comparative objectivity. He was, she decided, a most remarkable young man, and she at once popped him into the small group of her favourites, which included such gallants as Jeremy Bolster, John Colborne, Harry Redmond, and Tristram Leith. It would be a great pity, she thought, if Gains and Hawkhurst were to meet on the field of honour, for, although they looked to be much the same age and each in splendid physical condition, she could not but think that Gains would have little chance against Hawkhurst's cold ferocity. It was remarkable, really, that they had not fought, for surely—

She had been riding along in the lee of a hill and, having come to the end of its sheltering bulk, rode out into the wind at the same instant as a horseman galloped around the curve. Fiddle let out a terrified whinny and shied. For the second time that day, Euphemia had to call up all her skill to quiet the chestnut. When at last she succeeded, she found the new arrival sitting his horse while staring at her with unblinking stillness. An extremely well-favoured gentleman, this. Slim and tall, he was richly clad in a brown greatcoat that must have all of ten capes, the furred collar buttoned high about his finely moulded chin, and a furred beaver clapped at a jaunty angle over curls that shone like gold even under the threatening winter skies. He was mounted on a showy hack, very long of tail

97

and rolling of eye, whose bay coat shone almost as brightly as did his owner's hair. But Euphemia, wise in the ways of men and horses, found the gentleman's brown eyes rather too large, his mouth, although perfectly curved, too full and sensuous, and his horse entirely too quivery of nerves and a shade too short in the back for all his show and bluster.

Thus, for an instant, each took stock of the other, and the man's recondite look gave way to admiration, as his dark eyes flickered from Euphemia's hood to the shapely boot that peeped from beneath her habit. Off came his beaver with a flourish, down went the golden head, in a bow remarkable for its grace, in view of the cavorting bundle of nerves he bestrode. "Well met, Madam Juno," he said in a pleasant, well-modulated voice. "Are you just arrived? I pray so, for our dull evenings will be brightened if that is the case."

"You are newly come to Dominer, sir?" she countered smoothly, conscious of a fervent hope this was not so.

"Dominer? No, by Jove! Ah, but you jest, ma'am, for no lady such as yourself would sojourn at so wicked a spot! Allow me to introduce myself. I am John Knowles-Shefford, of Shefford's Den in Yorkshire." Again his bow was profound, but his questioningly upraised brows won only a cool smile and the response that, did he journey to "the wicked spot," her identity would be made known to him.

Briefly, he looked genuinely taken aback, and she realized that he was older than the five and twenty she had at first guessed, perhaps by as much as a decade. He recovered himself and began to pour out apologies, ending his humble pleas for her forgiveness with, "Ah, fair Juno, must you abandon me in this wilderness?"

Impatient with his verbosity, yet amused nonetheless, she teased, "You are scarce two miles from Chant House, sir. I would suppose your chances of reaching it safely to be excellent."

His eyes swung in the direction she indicated. "Yes, but Max is a dull dog, and it is lonely there. What, will you be away then? Your name, lovely one, I beg you! At least give me leave to call upon you in Town—But, no, alas! You mean to leave me, disconsolate and drear."

"Drear?" she laughed. "But, really sir!" She bade him good day, not unkindly, and with a kick of her heels sent Fiddle off towards Dominer once more.

The man she had left sat unmoving for a few minutes,

watching her ride from sight. And as he watched, the foolish smile vanished from his face, leaving it with another expression—an expression that would have caused Euphemia much disquiet.

Daylight had faded now, and, while one of the lackeys lighted the candles, another moved about the pleasant salon, shutting out the cold dusk by drawing the thick, red-velvet draperies. With his frowning gaze upon this innocent individual, Hawkhurst twirled the wine in his glass impatiently and said a curt, "Of course, I am not angered!" He glanced to Buchanan, standing beside him, saw the laughter that danced in the blue eyes, and grumbled, "But, by God! I scoured that freezing damned wood for better than an hour with my grooms, and—" He checked as his guest strove not too successfully to look contrite and finished with a wry grin, "Is your sister always so headstrong and impetuous, sir?"

"Usually," murmured Buchanan, "only when extremely vexed."

"Indeed?" The dark head immediately jerked higher. "Well, she'd absolutely no reason to—" But Hawkhurst paused, flushed, and looked away. "Oh," he grunted, then took a sip of cognac and asked, "How does the boy go on?"

"So far as I am aware, nothing has befallen him in the last half-hour."

In a total departure from his usual assured manner, Hawkhurst looked even more discomfited, and faltered, "I . . . I only dropped in for a minute or two, and—"

"And left him smothered with books, pictures, magazines, and that knife of yours that must drive the maids insane," grinned Buchanan.

"No, but I showed him how to use it. He'll not hurt himself, I do assure you. He has quite a knack for—"

A crash in the hall was followed by a moan, a ripple of feminine amusement, and a deeper male laugh. The door opened to admit Dora Graham, her plump face apprehensive, followed by a smiling Stephanie, and Coleridge Bryce. At the sight of that gentleman, the enquiry on Hawkhurst's lips died, and Buchanan had to stifle a chuckle. Bryce was awesome in a maroon-velvet coat, the shoulders of which were padded to the point of being absurd. His shirt points were so high that, were he to turn his head unguardedly, he must risk impaling an eyeball, and wide-legged grey trousers, caught in at the ankles, did nothing to mitigate the outlandishness of his appearance. After one scorching scan, Hawkhurst ignored him and escorted his aunt to a chair. He held his breath for a moment against her perfume, but then said nobly, "How dashing you look, dear lady."

"I dashed a vase, love," she confessed remorsefully and, slanting a hopeful look at him, added, "but it really did not have the best of lines, Garret. Quite dull, actually."

He smiled into her anxious eyes. "Then I thank you for ridding me of it."

Mrs. Graham heaved a sigh of relief and told him he was the dearest boy. She really did look well this evening, in a gown of grey velvet trimmed with blue beads and with her hair quite neatly arranged. Stephanie's attempt to look her best had been less successful. The pale blue linen made her look washed out; the high, round neck and large bishop sleeves were too matronly for a young girl, and the beautiful shawl she carried loosely across her elbows, being mainly embroidered in shades of pink, white and red, quarreled with her gown. Buchanan, who had looked up eagerly at the sound of her voice, noticed neither unbecoming shades nor ugly sleeves, however, but, as he drew a chair closer to the fire for her, thought only what a very pleasant person she was.

The butler filled Mrs. Graham's glass from an elaborately handpainted Oriental decanter. She sipped appreciatively, sighed that she was so relieved to hear Miss Buchanan had at last come safely home, and, sublimely unaware of the sharp glance that flashed between her nephew and Buchanan, imparted, "The countryside hereabouts can be quite dangerous, dear Sir Simon, if one is unfamiliar with it."

"Mia is a magnificent rider, ma'am. Lord Wellington once remarked she is the only lady he knows who might be able to handle Copenhagen."

"Did he so?" All interest, she leaned forward, at once dislodging a comb from her hair. She made a clutch for it, and the fringes of her shawl floated into her wine. "Alas!" she mourned whimsically, "*Why* must I be such a clumsy creature?" Buchanan at once retrieving the comb, she reached out to take it. "Thank you, dear boy! Whoops! There goes my hankie!"

The "dear boy" again came to the rescue, bowed, but dared not take another breath. Whoever concocted that cloying perfume of hers should be shot! He moved back, managing not to betray his aversion, but then found Stephanie's eyes upon him, so alight with michievous understanding that he was almost undone.

Hawkhurst, meanwhile, had wandered over to where Bryce stood a short distance from the fire. "And a poppy-flowered waistcoat!" he murmured ironically. "The icing on the cake! Tell me, Colley, does our redoubtable Miss Buchanan mean to make a beauty out of you, also?"

"I knew you would laugh!" Coleridge reddened. "If you must know, Hawk, these trousers are all the crack up at Oxford. Brought 'em down with me!"

"So *that* is why you were rusticated! Egad! Cannot say I blame the Dean!"

His lordship's rustication had stemmed from quite another cause, and one he had no intention of divulging. His jaw setting stubbornly, he retaliated, "Were it a *scarlet* jacket you would approve! But because I've a flair for art, you mock and sneer and—"

"Flair for dandyism, more like! Now hear me well, my lad. I shall not embarrass you by demanding that you immediately go and remove that ridiculous collection of horrors with which you have chosen to deface yourself. But do you ever come down to dinner wearing it again, I shall personally eject you!"

Coleridge felt impaled by that grey stare. Hawk meant it, all right. And seeking vainly for some devastatingly sophisticated retort, he was obliged to fall back upon the ages-old response of oppressed youth, "*Why* must you persist in treating me as though I were still a child in leading strings?"

"The answer to that," said Hawkhurst acidly, "is too obvious to require utterance." And he strolled to his aunt's side, leaving Bryce trembling with passion.

Since all of this had been conducted in very low tones, and since Dora had chattered merrily throughout, several times bringing Buchanan and her niece to laughter, it appeared to have escaped notice. Buchanan, however, could guess what had transpired and, eyeing Hawkhurst admiringly, wondered who was the genius who tailored him. The dark-brown jacket was very plain, save for brown-velvet rolled revers, but fit like a second skin. His cream-brocade waistcoat and fawn pantaloons were impeccable, and his only affectations were his signet ring and a fine topaz in his cravat. Beside his quiet elegance, Bryce with his fobs and seals, and rings, a snuffbox held in one hand and his handkerchief in the other, looked a total buffoon.

Pondering thus, Buchanan became aware that Miss Hawkhurst watched him. They had spent much time together during the past few days and had become so comfortably at ease that formalities had been abandoned, and they were more like lifelong friends than comparative strangers. He drew his chair a little closer and pointed out in a low voice, "Colley has good stuff in him, Miss Stephie. He'll likely develop into a splendid fellow."

"I am sure of it. I do hope your own brothers appreciate having so understanding a gentleman as the head of the family."

He grinned. "Doubt they ever give me a thought, save when they are in need of the ready! Gerald—he's at Cambridge, you know—has his head full of schemes to right the world's wrongs, while Robert, the young demon, yearns to turn back the clock to the naughty and infinitely more appealing days of our grandfathers."

She gave an appreciative little laugh. "And you are so kind and doubtless indulge them terribly. Tell me, does Gerald affect the fashions my cousin Bryce admires?"

The very thought of his brother making such a cake of himself was sufficient to arouse Buchanan's ire. "He most certainly does not! Why, if I ever caught him so much . . . as . . ." He broke off. Stephanie's head had tilted, and her eyes were bright with mirth. He glanced to Hawkhurst and smiled ruefully. "You wretch! You trapped me neatly! And how did you know I was entertaining such critical thoughts of your brother, pray?"

She lowered her lashes and, her smile fading, murmured, "You have . . . very expressive eyes, and—"

"Oh, my! Am I so late, then? I *do* apologize. The cook was apoplectic when I was obliged to tell him to set dinner back an hour!" Lady Bryce swept into the room, impressive in a purple lace robe over a pale lavender slip. Tall plumes swayed in her velvet turban, and a fine amethyst-and-pearl necklace was spread across her bosom. "I have kept everyone waiting, I perceive," she sighed, as she surveyed the ladies and the three young men who had stood at her coming. "How very, *very* bad mannered in me!"

Feeling about an inch tall, Buchanan stammered, "I am afraid my sister is not here yet, ma'am."

"The prerogative of a guest," said Hawkhurst. He motioned to the butler to leave and, pulling a chair closer to the fire, urged, "Do sit down, Aunt Carlotta. You are all gooseflesh."

She cast him a resentful glance, but seated herself. Her son, dutifully bringing her some lemonade, filled her vision for the first time. She gave him a small shriek and almost dropped her glass. "Good *heavens*! What on earth are you wear—"

"Impressive, is it not?" Hawkhurst interposed, occupying a chair between her and Dora. "I have told Colley that I do not feel his shoulders require so exaggerated a style, but these new fashions are all the rage at the University, and the young Bucks must try 'em."

The awkward moment passed. Coleridge breathed a sigh of relief and shot a grateful glance at his cousin. Lady Bryce was very willing to drop so embarrassing a subject and launched into an animadversion upon how furious the cook had been, and the general impertinence of servants these days, only to stop in mid-sentence, her mouth widening into an expression of mingled awe and incredulity.

Buchanan followed her gaze and was as one turned to stone. Hawkhurst, equally astounded, sprang to his feet, while Bryce, in the act of refilling his aunt's glass, glanced up and froze.

Euphemia's arrival having been every bit as spectacular as she had hoped, she paused in the doorway, one hand upon the frame, surveying the silenced gathering with an arch smile. "Am I . . ." she enquired throatily, ". . . late?"

A total stillness answered her. She moved with a decidedly sinuous glide across the floor.

"Good . . . God!" breathed Buchanan, tottering to his feet.

"Good . . . evening, ma'am," said Hawkhurst in a strangled voice and advanced to greet her.

She extended her hand. It was not easy, but she managed it. She was fairly covered with jewels. In addition to the diamond choker clasped about her throat, she wore a triple strand of large pearls and an opal pendant. A great ruby brooch was pinned to one shoulder of her décolleté, pale-orange, silk gown, and on the other a fine emerald pin clashed wickedly. The tiara in her hair, of diamonds and sapphires, was "complimented" by shoulder-length pearl and ruby earrings that sparkled and flashed as she turned her head provocatively. Every one of her fingers was beringed, sapphires vying with amethysts, diamonds, opals, and emeralds. From wrist to elbow, both arms were weighted down. There were bracelets of gold, jade, and silver; cunningly wrought gold filigree encrusted with glittering gems; loops of pearls, and, next to a splendid ruby bangle, one of garnets. The overall effect was as blinding as it was vulgar.

Having opened her fan, Lady Bryce plied it very slowly, staring in open-mouthed astonishment.

Aghast, Buchanan started forward. A slender hand touched his arm, and he looked down into a face aglow with mischief. "Were *you* . . . party to . . . ?" he gestured feebly towards his sister.

Stephanie nodded and whispered, "I had to borrow most of it, but I did not dream how delicious it would look."

Hawkhurst, bowing over Euphemia's hand, choked, "I can scarce find . . . room to . . . to kiss it, ma'am."

"Then at least hold it up," she murmured. "I think my poor arm is about to break!"

With a muffled snort, he pressed a kiss into her palm and, straightening, his eyes full of laughter, threw up one hand and acknowledged, "A hit! Bravo!"

"Is that all you can say?" she demanded indignantly. "Are you not thoroughly lured?"

"I am," he gulped, "utterly undone. I—I bow, ma'am! Piqued, repiqued, and capotted! I own it!"

"Colley!" shrieked Lady Bryce.

Coleridge jumped, looked down, and groaned, "Oh, my Lord!"

Dora peered over the side of her chair and, shaking her head, sent a small shower of hairpins into the puddle of Madeira. "Whatta waste . . . Wha' drefful waste!"

Bryce ran for the bellrope.

Recovering sufficiently to escort Euphemia to a chair, Hawkhurst bowed her into it. "I think," he said, *sotto voce*, "it will stand the weight."

"How very ungallant of you, sir," she tittered, rapping his strong hand lightly with her opal-studded fan. And, crossing one knee outrageously over the other, thus revealed her bare feet clad in gold Grecian sandals. On three of her toes, diamond rings winked in the light of the candles, as she swung her foot.

Hawkhurst let out such a whoop of laughter as his family had not heard issue from his lips for five long years. Staggering to the side, he collapsed into an armchair and lay back, wracked with mirth.

His Aunt Carlotta frowned from his disgracefully abandoned display to the disgusting vulgarity seated beside her. His Aunt Dora laughed merrily with him. His cousin Bryce, a delighted grin curving his mouth, observed him with new hope, and Buchanan, holding the hand an hilarious Stephanie had involuntarily extended, watched his sister in bewildered amusement.

Triumphant, Euphemia was also somewhat disconcerted. It was, she thought, remarkable that laughter could so completely change a grim, acid-tongued cynic into a warm, likeable, and rather devastatingly attractive man.

The notes of the harp hung like liquid drops upon the air, faded, and were gone. The applause rang out, and Euphemia, divested of her finery, jumped to her feet, clapping wholeheartedly. Whatever her failings, Carlotta Bryce played like an angel. Looking up as she straightened the instrument, her ladyship was flushed with pleasure, and the eager audience crowded in around her, full of acclaim and requests for more.

Hawkhurst wandered across the music room to perch on the arm of his sister's chair and place one long finger under her chin, lifting her face. He had never before seen her so radiant. However she had managed it, Miss Buchanan had changed the shy child into quite a taking little thing. "Happy?" he smiled.

"Oh, yes! Is it not lovely for us to have such pleasant company? How I wish they could stay for the holidays!" A shadow touched her bright eyes, but she said quickly, "Well, they are here now, at all events." Her brother was silent, and, scanning his expressionless features, she asked, "You are not angry? I mean, Euphemia told us how you had teased her. And indeed, to hear you laugh so, was wonderful."

"A fine spoil-sport you think me," he chided. "I deserved it and must only admire so excellent a set-down." He flashed a glance to where the candlelight was making Miss Buchanan's head into a shimmer of gold, as she bent to compliment his aunt, then averted his eyes hurriedly. "She is a scamp, but a very delightful one. However, were I her brother—"

"But," she interposed gently, "you are *not* her . . . brother."

A small pulse beat suddenly at his temple, and one hand clenched, but his drawl was lazy as ever. "I have been thinking that perhaps you should have a Season, little cabbage. I have supposed you to be happy here and thought you did not wish—"

"That is not true, Gary," she again interrupted.

He stiffened, a wary light coming into his eyes. He well knew that this quiet, calm girl missed nothing of what went on about her. And because he had long feared her perception, he was silent, waiting.

"You thought," she corrected in her soft little voice, "that I would be made to suffer because of your reputation. That I would be humiliated. You sought to spare me that. Oh, yes, I knew it, my dear." She reached out her hand to him, and, taking it, he bent suddenly to press it to his lips. "And I *was* content." Her eyes lifted from his crisp, dark hair to gaze sadly across the room at two other heads now close together, one having glowing coppery ringlets, and the other slightly curling hair of the paler hue that is called "sandy."

Hawkhurst straightened, but before he could comment she went on, "I have no longing for a Season. All I could ever want from life is . . . here." But her eyes evaded her brother's while a slight flush touched her pale cheeks.

A woman, seeing that look, would have at once taken warning. But, for all his scandalous *affaires*, Hawkhurst was still a mere man and said slowly, "Yet I begin to think you are missing a good deal. You should be shopping for the . . . er, ribands and trinkets and pretty things you women so delight in."

She smiled at him lovingly. "And what of you?" His eyes became veiled at once, and she tightened her grip on his hand. "Oh, Gary dear, how much longer? Surely he has got over it? Surely you could tell—"

"No!" The exclamation was harsh; something very like despair flashed briefly in his eyes, then was banished. She had drawn back in dismay, and he patted her hand and murmured, "My apologies, Stephie, but you do not understand." He stood. "I'm going up to see the boy. We will talk of this again." And he left her, his tall figure moving swiftly to the door before the others had taken their places to await his aunt's next rendition.

He found Kent still awake and was greeted by the boy leaping up in bed to thrust a small carving at him. He sat on the side of the bed and turned the wooden bear curiously, reminded of something . . . "This is very good," he murmured absently. "I knew you had a knack for it." A cool hand pushed at his brow in an attempt to smooth the lines away. He grinned and was dazzled by the answering smile that lit the small, peaked face. "Looked a grump, did I? So will Mrs. Henderson, when her maids have to clean up all these shavings! I'll be lucky if she don't cut up stiff with me! Now you lie down, sir-rah! And I shall endeavour to tidy up this mess."

He commandeered a wastebasket and began to brush the wood shavings across the coverlet. Kent snuggled down obediently and grinned as, after the fashion of such perverse objects, the shavings bounced more back than forwards, only a few falling into the basket. Hawkhurst grunted, seized the coverlet, and attempted to shake off the debris. Wood chips flew in all directions. Small, mirthful gasps were coming from the invalid. Flashing him a frustrated glance, Hawkhurst strove once more.

"Here!" Soft but capable hands removed his grip. He knew at once who it was, and his heart quickened to find that vivid face so close to his own. "Hello," he drawled. "Still 'luring,' ma'am?"

"Hold the basket," said Euphemia coolly, "and stop."

He watched her flip the remnants deftly into the basket he held and said with fine boredom, "Stop . . . what?"

"You know very well." She straightened, in her eyes a warmth that devastated him. "Now, if you will be so kind as to restore this to the corner. And you, young man," she bent fondly over the merry-eyed child, "should be asleep. Where is the abigail?"

Hawkhurst, replacing the wastebasket, offered over his shoulder, "Gone to fetch some hot milk."

"So you had to come in and thoroughly wake him," she scolded gently.

"Wherefore I shall now depart, very properly set-down." He bowed, strode to the door, and turned back to wink at the boy. "Becoming accustomed to it," he said wryly.

The gallery was icy cold and very dark but held no terrors for Stephanie, who enjoyed robust good health despite her slender frame and pale complexion. She walked to the south window and gazed unseeingly over the wintry scene lit by a new moon. The snow had been very light, and was already vanishing, but she could not remember it ever having been quite this cold in December.

He was married. "Safely wed and with three hopeful children." And, from a small remark Euphemia had dropped in the bedchamber this evening, his wife was very beautiful. She would be, of course. While she herself . . . how had Aunt Carlotta phrased it? "Another drab little country dowd . . ." The moon swam suddenly, and she closed her eyes, feeling the tears slip down her cheeks and knowing herself a hopeless fool, and hopelessly lost.

"Thought I'd find you up here!"

She gave a gasp, and one hand flew to wipe frantically at those betraying streaks.

"It's much too cold for you to—Hey! What's all this about?"

He stood before her, his angelic blue eyes peering at her anxiously. He was everything she had ever hoped to find in a gentleman—kind, gallant, sensitive, and—oh, so very good-looking. She tried not to imagine him in all the glory of his regimentals and, more devastatingly, recalled him sprawled on that sofa, Dr. Archer working over his poor shoulder, and never a sound from his lips until his dear head had sagged back, the eyes closing, and his face so deathly white. And because such thoughts made her heartache unbearable and the tears beyond controlling, she swung away and pressed both hands to her mouth, fighting desperately to hold back the sobs.

"Now this will never do," said Buchanan, quite forgetting that weeping women horrified him. "Has that ca—er, has your aunt been railing at you again?"

Stephanie could not speak, but her shoulders shook, and stepping closer, Buchanan drew out his large handkerchief. That wretched woman had done this, and just when the poor little chit was commencing to look so happy—she'd been positively aglow this evening. How anyone could distress so sweetly-natured a girl was beyond understanding. If it was up to him, that sharp-tongued harpy would be given a scold she'd recall for many a year to come! He dabbed gently at the wet cheeks, murmuring consolingly, "Never let her wound you, Miss Stephie. She probably don't mean it, y'know. Cannot help but feel sorry for poor old Bryce, must have led a dog's life." He checked as her tragic eyes blinked at him, and a smile flickered valiantly through the tears. Poor little thing! He knew a strong compulsion to take her in his arms and comfort her but, deciding in the nick of time that this might be constituted improper, said instead, "Now, what did she say? I'll lay you odds—I mean, I don't suppose it was near as bad as you think."

She smiled in earnest at these kind but clumsy efforts and lied, "It was my—brother."

Buchanan was surprised. It had seemed to him that Hawk fairly doted on the chit.

"He wants to give me a . . . a proper come-out. And I . . ." She gestured helplessly.

A come-out? The man must be all about in his attic! Her name would close every door, and as for vouchers to Almacks—never! He would have to have a careful word or two with Garret Hawkhurst. "I can readily see why," he lied kindly. "But—do you not wish it?"

"No, oh, no!" She turned away again and said brokenly, "How should I know how to go on . . . with all those—those beauties, and debutantes? I would look a . . . perfect fool."

She'd look a damn sight more desirable than the rest of 'em put together! he thought staunchly. She'd make some lucky man a gentle, devoted, loving wife, and she'd a sight more sense than most. She'd be dashed good with children too, for he had seen her several times with Kent, always so tender and sweetly patient. Her head was bending lower, and, comprehending that despite his busy thoughts he had said nothing, he responded impulsively. "You'd be splendid, and the man who looked twice at anyone else must be a regular chawbacon—Er, well, what I mean is—"

She faced him, laughing shakily. "How very kind you are, Sir Simon."

Buchanan again dried her tears with care, and told her she was not to worry. "Mia will manage everything."

Stephanie nodded, but her teeth bit hard at her underlip. This, she thought miserably, was one thing even Mia could not manage!

❧ *Chapter 8* ❧

Hawkhurst did not put in an appearance at the breakfast table, and Euphemia found herself with only Coleridge Bryce for company. The boy looked glum, and her efforts to cheer him met with brief smiles, followed by a clouding of his hazel eyes and a stifled sigh. Euphemia left him to his thoughts for a while, then said casually, "Oh, I must tell you, I met your friend Gains while I was riding yesterday, my lord, and—"

"I wish you will call me Colley, ma'am. All my friends do. But I'd not thought Chilton would ride in this weather. He's been a trifle down pin."

She expressed her regrets and explained it was Maximilian Gains she had encountered. "He seemed a most pleasant gentleman."

"That's like Max." Genuine regret was in his pleasant face. "He is the very best of fellows. He and Hawk was inseparable as boys, you know, and I think Max might . . . If only . . . But, Hawk cannot—" He ceased this disjointed utterance and said apologetically, "You will be thinking me a fine idiot for spilling the wine in that foolish way last evening. But, Jove! you surprised me, ma'am!"

"I suspect I surprised everyone," she smiled. "And I wish you will call me Euphemia, or Mia. Indeed, I feel almost like one of the family."

"How I wish you were! Hawk is like another man since you came. And as for Stephie! Why, only last night Hawk marvelled at the change you have wrought in her. She is becoming positively pretty!" He reddened, and gasped, "Oh! Not that she was plain before! I did not mean—"

"Of course, you did not." He looked horrified, and, liking him the more for it, she thought, How little he resembles his Mama. "To tell you the truth, Colley, I have not yet discussed fashions and such with Stephanie. You are very fond of her, are you not?"

"Oh, well, she's a jolly good sport. None of your missish airs and vapours, you know. Two years ago I was tossed heels over head near the old ruins and fractured my leg. Awful mess, but Stephie stopped the bleeding, covered me with her own cloak, for it was coming on to rain, and rode for help—just like any fellow!"

Stifling a smile at this boyish endorsement, Euphemia admitted she was not surprised. "She is the dearest girl. The kind who would always be ready with sympathy and understanding."

"Yes." He sighed and said wistfully, "If only Hawk would be—" Again biting back his unguarded words, he took another muffin, only to become even redder in the face as he encountered the half-eaten one already on his plate. His embarrassed glance at Euphemia met with such a merry chuckle that he could only shrug and say a rueful, "Lord, what a clodpole I am!"

"No, no. Merely troubled. And if I dare presume to guess— you do not wish a pair of colours, is that it?"

"Hawk thinks I am afraid, but I'm not! Indeed, I would love to go, for I think it would be grand to fight with such fine fellows as Richard Saxon and Leith and Colborne. You know them all, I fancy?"

"Very well. And a young man could find no finer inspiration than to look to any one of them. But, if you do not wish a military career, surely your cousin would agree to another? A diplomatist perhaps? Or—have you given any thought to the law?"

"Oh, yes. Hawk would be delighted did I choose such a course," he nodded bitterly. " 'Tis only my own choice disgusts him. He says it is unmanly nonsense, that I claim an interest merely to keep from being packed off to Spain. But do not, I beg of you, speak for me, for it would but serve to make him despise me even more!"

He looked so dejected that she leaned closer and said earnestly, "Surely your cousin would not be so unkind as to—" She broke off as Colley's horrified gaze lifted and, turning, was dismayed to see Hawkhurst standing in the open doorway.

He had obviously come in from riding, for his hair was windblown and his whip still under his arm. His face was a mask of rage, his eyes murderous slits.

Strolling to the table, he drawled, "Inciting the troops to riot again, Miss Buchanan . . . ?"

A hump under the bedclothes, Stephanie yawned, "Nine o'clock? Is something wrong?"

"Wake up, you lazy girl!" laughed Euphemia, ruthlessly pulling back the comforter. "This is my day to incite the troops, so you may as well be next!" She paused, and for an instant her brow puckered, as she recalled poor Colley's frantic attempts to explain the situation and Hawkhurst's white-lipped fury. Odd, but she was perfectly sure that rage was directed neither at her nor his cousin, and had in fact been provoked by something that had occurred earlier, something a great deal more serious. She became aware that Stephanie had slipped back into slumber and, tugging at the blankets, cried, "I vow you are just like Simon, half asleep until after breakfast! *Do* hurry, Stephie! I can spare you only an hour or so, for Dr. Archer will be here at eleven. Your room is warm as toast, and here is your faithful Kathy with all the fal-lals I asked her to fetch. Up, you lazy girl! Up!"

Thus it was that the befuddled Stephanie was whisked through the business of bathing, helped into her underclothes and petticoat, a kimona wrapped about her, a sheet bound tightly about her throat, and herself seated at her dressing table—all before she had time to draw a breath, or so it seemed.

"Set Miss Stephanie's chocolate there, if you please," requested Euphemia, flashing her friendly smile at the apprehensive maid, "and brush out her hair whilst I sharpen my scissors."

Kathy touched the long, rippling silk of Stephanie's thick tresses and uttered a little cry. "Oh, Miss! You never mean to cut it short? Mr. Garret will be that *vexed*!"

Eyeing the shining blades with equal unease, Stephanie demurred, "Mia, perhaps . . . we should not."

Euphemia sighed, "It is a pity, I grant you, but—yes. I am sure! Be brave, love. You may always purchase a wig!"

Kathy squealed in horror and turned away, only to be commanded to stop being such a featherwit, and heat the curling tongs at once.

Feeling very pleased with herself, Euphemia hummed cheerfully as she made her way along the corridor. She started down the stairs, then checked. The fireboy had told her that Blanche Hawkhurst's portrait was to be hung today, as it always was, in case the Admiral should chance to honour Dominer with a visit at this festive season. Curious, she turned back and climbed the second flight of stairs.

The doors to the gallery were wide, and two lackeys, directed by the butler, were positioning a very large portrait in the centre of the long room. Euphemia glanced about her admiringly. What a splendid old place it was, and fortunate, indeed, the lady who would occupy it as Mrs. Garret Hawkhurst . . . She was at once shocked by this trend of thought. Poor Blanche Hawkhurst had been far from fortunate!

The lackeys marched dignifiedly past, and the butler stopped beside her, his pudgy hands clasped as he asked in his formal manner if he might be of any service. "I came to see Mrs.

Hawkhurst," she confided frankly. "Do you really think Lord Wetherby will come, Parsley?"

Accompanying her back along the gallery, the butler replied that he doubted it. "The Admiral has only been here three times since Mrs. Hawkhurst died, Miss. He never has got over the shock, you see." The interest in her eyes, which he thought among the most handsome he had ever seen, led him on. Mr. Garret would not like it, he knew. Nonetheless . . . "She was the apple of the old gentleman's eye. But—perhaps I should tell you that . . ."

Euphemia, who had been gazing up at a most formidable looking old lady, turned to him enquiringly, "Yes, Parsley?"

"Well, er—" He paused and, losing his nerve, gulped, "My name, Miss, is Ponsonby."

It was not what he had intended to say, Euphemia was sure of it. Drat the man! Still, she was sufficiently shocked to exclaim, "Oh, my goodness! How very rag-mannered you must think me!"

"Not at all," he reassured hurriedly. "It is a childish nickname, and sometimes Mr. Garret forgets."

"Well, I think it insupportable! You have every right to insist . . ." His affectionate smile and slow shake of the head stopped her. "But you are too fond of him for that, I see," she nodded.

"I have known him since he was a sad little boy in short coats," replied Ponsonby, who had not failed to note the new light in his master's eyes of late. "And, if I may say so, Mr. Garret grew into the most high-couraged youth, the most loyal and—and truly gallant young man it has ever been my privilege to serve!"

Having made such an emotional declaration, he looked embarrassed and uncomfortable, but his sincerity was beyond doubting, and, impressed, Euphemia said slowly, "I see that I understated the case. You are more than fond of him."

"A great deal more, Miss," he mumbled, very red in the face. He gestured upwards. "This is Mrs. Hawkhurst. And little Avery, rest his soul."

Euphemia tore her gaze from his honest features, looked up, and stood transfixed. Simon's description of Blanche Hawkhurst had been, if anything, inadequate. A vision looked down from the canvas, a young woman, seated in a rose arbour, a small boy clutching at her skirts. Her hair was a cloud of gold, with two sleek ringlets dropping onto one snowy shoulder. Pale green eyes, long and well open, were fringed by thick, dark lashes; a perfect little mouth pouted slightly in an expression that was reminiscent of Simon's wife; and the dimpled chin was uptilted in a faintly challenging fashion. Yet, all in all, the perfect oval of the face was exquisitely lovely, the flawless complexion and delicate nose enhancing a beauty that certainly must have had all London at her feet. Euphemia let out the breath she had been unconsciously holding in check and glanced to the child. He looked to be about three years old, an adorable little boy, as fair as his lovely mother, but with a twinkle in the grey eyes and a suspicion of stubbornness about the chin that, even at that early age, spoke of his sire. "Oh . . ." she murmured regretfully, "how very sad."

"Sad indeed," agreed a gruff voice at her elbow.

It was Archer's voice, and, glancing around, she discovered that Ponsonby had gone and the doctor now stood beside her. "You knew her, sir?" she asked.

"I did." She scanned his strong face curiously, and he went on, still gazing at that angelic face. "She was the loveliest woman I ever saw."

"Very lovely. No wonder Hawkhurst pursued her so desperately."

He uttered a loud and mocking snort of laughter, saw Euphemia's mouth droop a little with surprise, and thought it a most pretty sight. "Hawk pursued his son, ma'am!" he explained. "And has been like a soul lost in some bleak wilderness ever since his death. The boy had given back to him all the joy Blanche destroyed. He was Hawk's world, his life, his every hope for the future. When I hear fools whisper that Avery died by his father's plotting—By heaven! I could throttle 'em with my bare hands!"

Euphemia's heart had, for some reason, commenced to beat very rapidly during this little speech. "But . . . but," she stammered, "why has he refused to tell what happened?"

"Pride, partly. He's a surfeit of that, I'll admit. Anger, too, that any dared so accuse him. But I'll tell you this, Miss Euphemia, had Garret Hawkhurst to have chosen between his own death by the slowest, most hideous means the mind of a man can devise, or that child's life—he would unhesitatingly have sacrificed himself! I don't blame him for turning his back on the Society that named him murderer! The *haut ton*, ma'am? I've a better name for 'em, but cannot use it before such as yourself! And worse than any of 'em is the man who brought it all about!" He turned, hands gripped behind him, and, stalking to a portrait on the opposite wall, nodded at it vengefully. "Here's your culprit! Here's the blind, proud, unrelenting, maggot-witted bacon brain who caused it!"

Euphemia's eyes were already scanning that other portrait: a naval officer in full-dress uniform, cockaded hat under one arm, the other hand resting upon the stone parapet of a balcony, with far beyond him the shadowed outlines of a harbour and many great ships. A tall, sparse gentleman, with thick hair tied in at the nape of the neck, a high forehead, a beak of a nose, fierce dark eyes, a thin mouth and proud chin. The face of an eagle, she thought. One who would demand instant obedience and unwavering loyalty.

"Impressive, ain't he?" sneered Archer, his eyes on the girl's awed face.

"Very. They say he may come here."

"Well, I hope to God he don't! He only comes to turn the knife in Hawk. And succeeds, damn him!"

She turned at that and said in her forthright way, "You should not talk to me like this, you know." He scowled, but said nothing, and she smiled. "But I hope you will not let that weigh with you."

He chuckled and, encouraged by the twinkle in her eyes, extended his arm. Euphemia took it, and he escorted her slowly along the gallery, much as if they were out for a morning stroll.

"We owe Mr. Hawkhurst a great deal," she pointed out. "Perhaps, did I know his story, I might repay him somewhat by—"

"By countering some of the gossip?" Archer shook his head. "Cannot. I've tried. People believe what they wish to believe and would liefer hear bad of a man than good. Besides, all Hawk will say is he had no hand in killing them. Ain't enough, don't y'see. As to how it all started . . ." He sighed, brow furrowed and eyes reminiscent. "Well, it was a race. The most stupid, murderous steeplechase, and all London agog and betting crazy. Hawk was near seven years old when his Papa rode and led all the way—to the last water jump. They carried him home on a hurdle. Back broke. He died the next day. It was all so blasted nonsensical! So wags the world and its follies . . . His wife Cordelia had been a great beauty in her day, but she was a frail woman. She adored her husband and, when he was killed, her heart went with him. She lacked the strength to go on living for the sake of her children and quite literally grieved herself into her grave."

"Oh, the poor soul," Euphemia murmured, her warm heart touched.

Archer grunted unsympathetically. "Oh, the poor children! The two older girls were placed in a seminary. Stephanie was a babe in arms and went to her Aunt Dora, but the Admiral held Dora incapable of rearing a boy and acceded to his daughter-in-law's wish that her cousin take him. Her admired Wilberforce." He swore under his breath. "Vanity, thy name is Wilberforce!"

"He was a dandy?"

"He was—what you would call today, a 'Top o' the Trees'! All coats and cravats and every sporting venture, every bit o' muslin, every gaming table in Town! That selfish young blade had no time for a heartbroken little boy. He put Garret in the care of a tutor, pocketed the funds the Admiral supplied, and promptly forgot the boy. And the tutor! Now, *there* was a rare individual! Or at least," a fiercer look glittered in his eyes, "I *pray* they're rare! The slimy type who bow and smile and simper to the Quality—and hate their—er, insides! Such was the man friend Wilberforce selected, wherefore young Garret endured over a year of pure hell at his hands. A housemaid saved him. Garret had tried to run away, and the tutor's revenge was more than she could abide. She risked her entire future, went to the Admiral's lodgings and told his man all about it. Wetherby was expected home the following day, and he moved fast, I'll say that much. Hawk was out of the house within an hour of his return, and the housemaid (now our Nell Henderson, by the way) with him. I heard that when Wetherby first laid eyes on the boy he was so enraged, he knocked Wilberforce right off his feet. I hope it's truth! At all events, from a nightmare of inhumanity, Garret found himself in a dream world where he was not only once again decently treated, but affection was lavished on him. You can guess the rest; he idolized the man who'd rescued him. From that day to this, did Wetherby ask for his heart on a plate, he would have it!"

Archer paused and, while Euphemia waited quietly, stared out of one of the recessed bays. "All went well for a few years. Until 'friendship' entered the picture. Our Admiral wasn't much given to making 'em. Friends, I mean—not pictures! But he had one, a fine young fellow he'd met at Harrow.

They went all through their school and university days together, he and Spaulding, and finally, both fell in love with the same girl. Spaulding won and wed the lady. I don't think Wetherby ever got over that first love, but he eventually married, and I gather it was a moderately happy match. Anyway, the two families remained close friends. The Wetherbys had a son, Garret's Papa, and two daughters of whom our Mrs. Graham is the only one now living. The Spauldings had only one son, who later fathered Blanche. And Blanche grew to be the image of Wetherby's great love, by now gone to her reward. The Admiral doted on the girl. Her Papa was killed at Assaye, and, when her grandpapa died, she and her mother lived very frugally until Wetherby stepped in and moved them into a charming house he owns just off Grosvenor Square. Blanche soon became the Rage—a great Toast. I needn't tell you that it was Wetherby's dream his grandson should wed her. Garret resisted at first, for he had no *tendre* for her. I think he suspected that there was little of character behind that beautiful face. To the old man, however, Blanche was the embodiment of everything he had loved and lost. She wasn't. She was weak and foolish and insanely in love with a fellow named Robert Mount. A handsome young devil, but not a feather to fly with!"

"Good heavens! Did Hawkhurst know she loved another man?"

"Not then, more's the pity. And to have seen her with the Admiral you'd have thought her downright saintly, she was so loving and devoted."

"So . . . he married her," murmured Euphemia, "only to please his benefactor."

Archer nodded dourly. "And thereby destroyed her, himself, and their child! Fool that he was! But I still hold that the man responsible was—Why, you young rascal! What the deuce d'ye mean by cavorting about when I said you must lie on the sofa and be quiet?"

A small hand was tugging urgently at Euphemia's skirt. She looked down into Kent's face, aglow with excitement as he pointed towards the hall. He was dressed and looked much better at last, but the doctor was perfectly right, for the air in this room was much too cold for him.

"I rather gather," she said with a merry twinkle, "that I am summoned." She put out her hand. "Thank you, doctor. For our . . . discussion."

He took her hand, patted it gently, and grinned, "Call it—an investment, dear lady."

Walking towards the stairs with the excited boy hopping along beside her, Euphemia pondered Archer's last remark. ". . . an investment . . ."? Did he mean because of her promised effort to refute the gossip about Hawkhurst? He had opened her eyes to a good deal, and she had no least doubt but that he had spoken truthfully. Still, there was the matter of Gains. No one would ever forgive Hawk for so savagely disfiguring his neighbour, even if—

She was surprised at this point to discover that she was being urged not down the second flight of stairs to the ground floor, but along the landing towards the rooms occupied by the family. She looked at Kent wonderingly, but he nodded his fair head, beaming up at her and continuing to pull at her hand.

At the far end of the corridor, two maids were peering through a half-open door. They turned at Euphemia's approach and, the elder of their pair proving to be Ellie, hurried to her. "Oh, Miss! I know Master Kent didn't mean to be naughty but—if Mr. Garret comes there will be *such* a bobbery! Me and Cissy's scared to go in, and don't dare to call one of the footmen, for then Mr. Garret would be sure to hear of it!"

Really alarmed now, Euphemia swept past the maids and pushed the door wide.

The luxurious bedchamber was graced by three tall windows with plumply cushioned windowseats. Large, deep chairs, and a sturdy leathern sofa flanked a great fireplace, and to one side was a fine old desk of glowing cherrywood with a tapestry-covered chair before it. Against one wall stood a well-stocked gun cabinet, and there were several bookcases crammed with volumes. Yet all of these things registered only dimly in her mind, for to the far right of the room stood an enormous canopied bed, the red brocade curtains tied back to reveal a decidedly uninvited occupant who sprawled comfortably upon the eiderdown, his unlovely head resting on the pillow as though it had been placed there especially in his behalf.

"*Sampson!*" gasped Euphemia.

"And—Lord Gains be such a *nice* gentleman!" whimpered Cissy.

Kent ran to stroke that massive head fondly and grinned back at Euphemia.

"The dog was waiting outside the kitchen door," Ellie supplied. "And when the little fellow see him, I 'spect he thought he lived here, so he let him in. They runned all over! Me and Cissy's been straightening up the rugs and the stuff they knocked over. But Master Kent can't make him get off! Mr. Garret's out with Sir Simon, but they'll be back any minute, and the master's . . ." She glanced at Kent's now uneasy countenance and finished carefully, "He's not in a very happy frame o'mind, Miss."

The recollection of Hawkhurst's black rage at the breakfast table sent Euphemia's eyes flashing to the gun cabinet. "Kent! Get him down from there!"

Obediently, the child seized the hound by the throat and pulled manfully. Sampson opened one eye, licked his hand, then went back to sleep.

Euphemia nerved herself, stepped inside, her heart racing at such flagrant impropriety, and entered the fray. She cajoled, scolded, and threatened—in vain. The two maids began to moan and wring their hands. "Quiet!" she hissed. "We mustn't attract attention! Sampson, you stupid great elephant, do you *wish* to be shot? Come down this instant, sir!"

Sampson regarded her with tolerant amusement, lolled his tongue, turned onto his back and stretched, then allowed his legs to droop in a most impolite abandonment. Euphemia's frustrated moan faded into a gasp as she heard Hawkhurst's distinctive voice raised in a shout for "Parsley!"

"Oh, my God!" she ejaculated. "Come and help me, quickly!" The maids, however, craven in the face of peril, had deserted. Her knees turned to water. How *ghastly* if she was found in here! But she could not allow the foolish animal to be slain. "Kent, run and find something he might like to play with!"

The child ran to the dressing table and returned bearing a riding crop with an intricately carven grip inlaid with mother-of-pearl. He gave the insouciant hound a prod in the ribs with this. Sampson half opened one eye and was transformed into a maelstrom of energy; legs writhed, back twisted, ears flapped, and tail wagged furiously. He stood on the bed, then launched himself for the "stick," landing with a crash against a chest of drawers, thus sending two candelabra and a clock toppling.

"Good! Now, hurry!" cried Euphemia, running for the door.

It was too late. Hawkhurst's voice, raised in irritation, was already in the hall. With a stifled sob, Euphemia drew back. Heavy brocade curtains, matching those of the bed hangings, closed off what appeared to be a dressing room. Pushing Kent before her, and with Sampson bouncing along, flourishing the crop that now resided between his jaws, she made a dart for it, swung the draperies closed behind her and, finding a heavy door also, pushed it to, praying it might not squeak. It did not, but before she could latch it, the hall door burst open and she shrank back.

". . . damned well ruined is what drives me into the boughs!" Hawkhurst was exclaiming. "If a man cannot shoot straight with a Manton, he's no business owning one!"

"I wish you will not treat it with such levity, Mr. Garret!" protested the agitated voice of Mr. Bailey. "It is my opinion the Constable should be summoned. You might well have—"

"Stuff! Where's my riding crop?" Euphemia threw a hand to her mouth, her heart thundering as she heard the clatter of articles moved by impatient hands. "Dammitall, Bailey! I collect I've left it in the stables. My head is full of windmills these days!"

Sure that he would next look in the dressing room, Euphemia hove a sigh of relief as he grumbled on, with Bailey making small placating remarks. It was probably a brief respite at best, however, and she would positively die of mortification if he discovered them in here! A grinding sound brought her startled gaze downward. Sampson was single-mindedly devouring his prize, while Kent, kneeling beside him, watched his efforts with admiration. It was doubtful that the crop could be wrested away without considerable commotion, and she dared not risk latching the door. Retreat was the only answer. She glanced swiftly around the dressing room. A tall mahogany chest held a clutter of male articles, several letters, and a miniature of a dark-haired woman with a sensitive mouth, and eyes of the same clear grey as those of Hawkhurst, his mother, beyond doubting. There was a full-length standing mirror and a recessed area with a clothes-rod, on which were hung the garments he would probably wear for luncheon. A hunting gun was propped against the side of the chest, and a dark blue quilted satin dressing gown was tossed carelessly over a straight-backed chair. Her eyes flickered swiftly over these items and flew to the door at the rear of the small room. She tiptoed to try the latch and could have wept with chagrin. It was locked, and there was no visible key.

". . . might be down in the stables," Hawkhurst was calling. "Oh, and be a good fellow, tell Dr. Archer I'll ride back with him." Bailey's distant voice raised an immediate protest, and Hawkhurst responded, "Devil, I will! Tell him!"

The door was closed, and she gripped her hands in relief. If he intended to ride again he was not likely to change clothes now. But that revolting dog was grinding like a full-fledged grist mill!

Hawkhurst muttered a vexed, "What the . . . hell!"

He must have seen the fallen candelabra and clock. With a flutter of the heart, Euphemia knew that, if he next found dog hairs upon his pillow, they would be undone, for he would certainly initiate a search for the culprit.

Kent tugged at her skirts and peered up at her, his small face anxious. Poor child, she must not frighten him. She forced her pale lips into a smile and bent to whisper, "I do not wish Mr. Hawkhurst to be cross with Sampson, dear, so we shall play a little game of hide and seek. Try to keep him quiet." Intrigued by the game, he nodded, and she draped the large dressing gown over the crouching boy and the busy dog. Sampson raised no protest, and Euphemia's hopes escalated as she heard Hawkhurst stride across the room and open the door. Thank heaven! She eased the dressing room door open and peeped between the curtains.

"Fillman!" he bellowed, then grumbled, "Why don't you answer the bell, damn your ears?" He slammed the door. The draft sent the curtains billowing outward, and, sure she would be seen, Euphemia jumped back. Her elbow struck the door causing it to swing wide and crash against the wall. She barely had time to gasp with fright before two strong hands wrenched the curtains apart.

Hawkhurst towered over her, his face grim and deadly. She could have sunk but stood her ground, her knees shaking and her reeling brain searching frantically for the convincing explanation that did not exist.

Hawkhurst, on the other hand, quite literally sprang back, so obviously flabbergasted that she knew a nervous need to giggle.

"Wh-What . . ." he gulped. "What . . . in the *name* of . . . ?"

Her mouth very dry and her face very red, Euphemia said feebly, "I—I was . . . er—lost."

"Lost?" he echoed, recovering somewhat, although he was pale with shock. "I have encountered many 'lost' people on my estates. But never, I must admit, in my bedchamber!"

"Well, I can understand that would . . . er . . . be so," she stammered, tottering valiantly into the bedchamber. "But . . . I did not quite know . . . that is . . ." She floundered helplessly. What on earth could she say to the man?

His eyes, chips of ice now, slanted from the fallen candelabra and clock to the curtains behind her. "What have you been about?" he demanded suspiciously. "I have been a slowtop again, is that it? And this whole damnable thing was a badly managed scheme to—"

"To do—what?" she countered, indignation banishing fear. "Steal that Rembrandt you have in the gallery? Make off with your twenty-foot tapestry from the dining room? But, of course! I have 'em both. One tucked in my ear and the other up my sleeve! Would you wish to inspect, perhaps . . . ?" And she leaned to him, pulling out her ear lobe in angry mockery.

Her slight movement was accelerated as his hands clamped onto her shoulders and pulled her to him. She was crushed against his chest, and he was bending to her mouth. She did not scream but, even as she struggled, knew that this was scarce to be wondered at. What must he think of her? And he was so terribly strong, she could not break free. Her heart began to leap erratically. His lips were a breath away. A new light was in his eyes, a look of such tenderness that her anger was transformed into a sudden and hitherto unknown terror. Gone was her famed calm in time of crisis, gone the cool courage that had always enabled her to meet whatever Fate flung at her. Out of this debilitating panic came a strangled sob, and, jerking her head from his questing lips, she gasped, "I have none but myself to blame for this crude assault. God knows, I should have had more sense than to investigate a strange sound—in the bedchamber of the most notorious libertine in England!"

For an instant he stood very still. Then he straightened and stepped back, bowing slightly, a twisted smile bringing no trace of mirth to eyes over which the lids once more drooped cynically.

She felt drowned by remorse and reached out to him in an intense need to make amends, but before she could speak a sound penetrated the silence, a sound as of grist being ground between heavy millstones.

Hawkhurst's gaze flashed to the dressing room. "Strange sound, indeed!" he breathed, and sprinted for the curtains. And in that same instant, as though a capricious Fate decreed it, Sampson elected to gallop for freedom, the remnants of the crop carried triumphantly between his jaws, a piece of mother-of-pearl shining atop his muzzle. He caromed into the advancing man, and, caught off balance, Hawkhurst reeled into the wall. Sampson plunged for the door. Quite undismayed to find it shut, he diverted himself by tearing three times around the room, sending rugs, a chair, and a lamp tumbling. He then bounded onto the bed and crouched, panting happily, perfectly ready to participate in whatever game was next offered him. Hawkhurst, less amiably inclined, gave a howl of rage. "Get off my bed! Down, you damnable imp of Satan! Blast your fleas! What's he got there . . . ? My *whip*? By God! But this is too much!" He made a dive for the dressing room and emerged, gun in hands and murder in his eyes.

Euphemia, however, had seized her opportunity. The door stood ajar, and the echoing thump of four large paws, punctuated by an occasional crash, drifted to them.

"Out of my way, woman!" raged Hawkhurst. "How in the devil did that worthless mongrel get in here? By thunder, I'll murder the—"

"Be still!" she admonished sharply. "The child is here."

Infuriated, he swung around to discover Kent, who had crept out from under the dressing gown, and now stood white-faced in the doorway to the dressing room. "Did *you* let that miserable hound in here?" Hawkhurst demanded. "What in the deuce are—" And he broke off, fury fading into consternation.

Kent, his face twitching, shaking his head pleadingly, was shrinking back. Frowning, Hawkhurst started towards him. Euphemia ran to snatch the gun from his hand. He cast her an irked look and strode for the boy. "Kent, now you must certainly—"

But the child, sobbing in his pathetic, soundless fashion, was stumbling ever backward across the dressing room, until the locked door barred his way, until his fumbling hands, pressing frenziedly at the wall, could find no escape. And, accepting the inevitability of his fate, he cringed there, arms flung upward to protect his face, his slender body crouched and shuddering in anticipation of the beating that must follow.

Hawkhurst stared down at him in stark horror. Forgotten now was the dog or the whip that had been his father's. Forgotten, even, the girl and her scorn that had seared him. The years rolled back, and he himself stood thus before the raging tutor, terror making him sweat, and the cane whistling down at him . . . He fell to one knee and adjured softly, "Kent, *never* do that. Not to me, boy."

The voice held a caress, and, reacting to it at once, the child peeped between his shielding arms and found the dark face magically transformed. The mouth curved to a kindly smile, the harsh lines had vanished, and the anger in the cold eyes was replaced by a gentleness such as made the threat of savage reprisal a thing impossible. Daring to breathe again, Kent lowered his arms. Hawkhurst reached out. For a moment the boy stared wonderingly, then with a thankful gasp, threw himself into those strong arms, to be enfolded and held firm and safe against a corduroy-clad shoulder.

Blinded by tears, Euphemia crept away and left them together. And, running to her room, for one of the few times in her life, she lay on her bed and wept with total abandonment. When at last the paroxysm ended, she lay there limp and exhausted, breathing in great shuddering gasps, and bewildered by her own hysteria. She sniffed, sat up, and, drying her tears, took herself firmly in hand. How ridiculous to behave in this missish way. There was no reason to tremble so, nor to feel so frightened and lost. Whatever was the matter with her? Hawkhurst would understand now why she had ventured into his bedchamber. He surely would not take her for the wanton he had evidently assumed her to be when first he found her there. He would soon apologize for having seized her so brutally . . . so tenderly . . .

Unaccountably, her eyes grew dim again, her throat tightened painfully, and with the memory of his stricken eyes tormenting her, she thought achingly, Oh, I *wish* I had not spoken so!

❧ *Chapter 9* ❧

Mrs. Graham would not be comforted. In a highly agitated state, the little lady gestured dramatically all along the upstairs corridor. Her sister-in-law, she mourned, would be furious, and there was not a bit of use to pretend innocence, for she never had been any good at dissembling, and Carlotta would know in a trice that she had been aware of the scheme.

"But, you *were* innocent, Dora," Euphemia smiled. "Now pray do not worry so. Hawk—hurst must like his new sister. And if *he* likes her, Lady Bryce will not dare to scold you."

Apparently unaware of that swiftly corrected slip, Dora merely heaved an apprehensive sigh. In an attempt to change the subject, Euphemia commented on what a fine young man Coleridge appeared to be and asked if his cousin really meant to force him into the army.

They had by this time come to the Great Hall and started toward the gold lounge where the family had lately formed the habit of meeting before luncheon. "I doubt he would force Colley to go," said Mrs. Graham. "But, he would like him to buy a pair of colours, for he is afraid, I think, that . . ."

"That his own reputation may ruin Coleridge?" asked Euphemia.

"Why, how well you have come to know us in these few days, my dear." Dora made a convulsive grab at her tumbling crocheted shawl, and then paused to try and disentangle it from the holly branches in the great Chinese urn beside the music room. "Yes, partly that. And partly—well, Hawk was in the military, and—"

The rest of her words were lost upon Euphemia, who could almost hear a sneering voice say, "How those military rattles dazzle the ladies . . ." Why on earth would he make so contemptuous a remark if he himself had worn a scarlet coat? Baffled, she said, "He was? Why, I'd no idea. What was his regiment?"

"Oh, my . . . Now, was it the 52nd? Or was that poor Harry Redmond? No, I think it was the 43rd. Or was that Colborne?"

"Redmond was a Light Bob, ma'am. And had Mr. Hawkhurst served with John Colborne, I would have met him, I do believe—or heard tell of him."

"Oh, but this was several years ago, child. Gary fought in a battle, I know. Bustle or hustle, something or other. It was soon after his wife and son were . . . er—And so he bought a pair of colours and went. I was sure he would be killed, as he hoped to be, the poor soul."

A pang pierced Euphemia. "You must mean Bussaco," she said in a shaken voice. "Goodness, but you are trapped. Allow me to help. Was he wounded?"

"No. Is it not always the way? His friends said he was in the very thickest of the fighting, but not so much as a scratch. Such a disappointment it must have been! But then he was needed here, and the Admiral demanded he come home. He has often spoken of how splendid his comrades were, and I think that is why he wants Colley to join up. He hopes it will make a man of him."

"Lord Bryce *is* a man," frowned Euphemia, finally extricating the shawl. "We cannot all be the same type you know, dear ma'am. Nor have the same interests. Your nephew should really—"

"No more an accident than Prinny is a postulant! I tell you, Buck, it was a deliberate attempt at murder!"

The familiar male voice held Euphemia rigid with astonishment.

Dora clapped her hands. "Thank goodness! We have more company. Carlotta will be happy! Ah, you have freed me, my dear!" She flung her shawl exuberantly about her, then, pulling down the end that had whipped about her mouth, cried, " 'Free as nature first made man, ere laws of . . .' Now how does that go? 'Ere laws of serving people'—or something, 'began.' " And, with a whimsical giggle, she trotted and tripped her way into the lounge.

Following, Euphemia saw two young men standing beside the fire. One was Simon, and at the sight of the other her heart gave a leap of joy. "Leith!" She moved swiftly to greet this good friend, and with a glad cry he strode to take her outstretched hands, press each to his lips, and scan her, eyes bright with adoration. "What a *very* great pleasure to find you here, Mia!"

"A pleasure shared," she said warmly and, tugging at the unfamiliar blue of his sleeve, asked, "A promotion? Are you now one of the great man's 'family'?"

"He's deserted for a confounded staff officer!" laughed Buchanan. "Dreadful!"

"I think it splendid! And indeed Wellington could have done no better! But—how surprised I am to see you *here*. Are you acquainted with Hawkhurst, Tris?"

"Scandalous, ain't it?" drawled a cynical voice.

Euphemia glanced to the side and could have sank, as Hawkhurst, who had been sprawled in a wing chair by the window, stood lazily.

Leith's shrewd eyes flashed from one to the other. Euphemia's cheeks were scarlet. He had seldom seen her off-stride, but now her customary poise, her ability to smooth over the most awkward of moments, seemed to have deserted her. Inwardly troubled, he bowed in his gallant way over Dora's hand, then dropped a kiss upon her cheek in the manner of a very old friend, answering her eager questions with the regretful news that he could stay a very short time. He'd come with dispatches to the Horse Guards, must return to France in the morning, and had detoured here for only a very brief visit.

"And will not tell us any news," fretted Buchanan, "until we are all at luncheon!"

"Savage!" Euphemia chastised, making an outward recovery, although her heart still pounded unevenly. "Tell us only this—have we lost any good friends?"

She had expected that he would at once set her fears at rest, but momentarily he looked grim, and she exchanged a swift glance with her brother. More welcoming cries interrupted their discussion, as Bryce and his mother entered. Leith seized the young man's hand in a firm grip, pounded briefly at his shoulder, then whirled the Lady Carlotta off her little feet and planted a healthy kiss on one warmly blushing cheek. "Rogue!" she laughed happily. "Oh, how very glad I am to see you again! And looking splendidly, as usual, though I think you would do better to stay with your red uniform my dear, much more dashing than that dull blue! Do you overnight?"

"Just a hasty drop-in, I'm afraid," he said fondly, flashing an amused glance at Buchanan's hilarity as he set her down.

"And never," his dark eyes turned to Euphemia, "more pleased than to find the lady I mean to make my wife visiting you also."

Bryce looked surprised. Euphemia blushed and felt a surge of irritation. Dora shot a troubled look at Hawkhurst's still face, and Carlotta, her eyes frankly dubious, scanned the tall girl without appreciable rapture and murmured, "Dear me . . . another surprise."

"A magnificent one!" Coleridge said with real enthusiasm.

"Well, you crusty old misogynist?" grinned Leith. "What have you to say to that?"

Hawkhurst had wandered over to the window and stood with his back to them, but he turned with a bored smile and shrugged, "I wish you happy, of course. And for myself, I wish my lunch. Can we go in? Or are we all—? Ah, I see that my sister is not yet—" And he broke off, staring at the girl who had come shyly through the door to pause on the threshold.

Stephanie's pale hair that had been bland in those thick braids had come to life, and the glow of the firelight danced among the short curls clustering about her ears. The fullness of those curls broke and softened the rather long line of her face. Her pale brows and lashes had been very subtly darkened, and the eyes that had been so nondescript as to elude notice had gained new depth and brilliance. She would never be a Toast, but Euphemia had spoken truly: her light was no longer hidden under a bushel. However shyly, Stephanie glowed, the added colour in her cheeks, the pale golden gown, and the amber velvet riband about her hair, transforming a somewhat insipid girl into a most attractive young lady.

"Good . . . God . . . !" gasped Bryce.

"By Jove!" Leith exclaimed in delight. "Euphemia, my beautiful, have a care! Do you not set the date, you're liable to find me in the toils of this enchantress!"

Stephanie's dismayed glance at her new friend discovered such an amused look that she relaxed again and laughed down at Leith who had fallen to one knee to clasp her hand and kiss it. "Behold me at your feet, you vision," he grinned and, standing, added, "Egad, Stephie, the last time I came you were a shy schoolroom miss. Now, look at you! A Beauty, no less!"

"Faithless wretch!" scolded Euphemia.

"He's right, though, dashed if he ain't!" Coleridge Bryce

crossed to give his cousin an impulsive and rare hug. "You look much better, Stephie. Don't she, Mama?"

"Very pretty," Lady Bryce acknowledged. "Indeed, how even our clever Miss Buchanan could achieve such miraculous—"

"Absolutely beautiful!" interposed her sister-in-law quickly. "I shall embroider you a new shawl, Stephanie. I've a piece of silk very close to that shade of amber. It will look delightfully."

Leith's eyes had returned to Euphemia, only to find her watching Hawkhurst, a faintly challenging smile on her lips, but her eyes anxious. And, noting how studiously that individual avoided her gaze, his unease was heightened.

Stephanie, meanwhile, having thanked her aunt for the kind offer and, being a little flustered by reason of all this attention, turned to her brother. "Gary . . . ? You are not vexed?"

"I bow to our so adept modiste," he said, throwing Euphemia a slight bow, though his glance barely flickered in her direction. "And also, I claim the right to lead our Beauty in to luncheon."

Although he was longing to claim Euphemia, Leith's manners would not allow it, and he escorted Lady Bryce. Buchanan was not loath to escort Dora, whose gaiety and good nature he felt compensated for her unfortunate taste in scent, and Coleridge offered Euphemia his arm with so gallant a flourish that she was able to laugh despite a heavy-heartedness that was as unusual as it was confusing.

When they were all seated around the table, Leith was at last badgered into informing them that Wellington had scored again. Another splendid victory, the Battle of St. Pierre had been won against apparently hopeless odds. Cheers rang out at this, and everyone sprang up, while Hawkhurst, his face flushed and boyish, proposed a toast: "To Lord Wellington, and our magnificent fighting men who will soon drive Boney back where he belongs!"

"Do tell us of it, Leith," Buchanan urged as they resumed their places. "Has the rain stopped over there?"

"It rains like the Flood still. And old Soult caught us fairly at the Nive, which was so blasted overflowing the Beau had to split us into two sections. But he felt we would prevail, and we did, by God!"

When the servants had withdrawn, Hawkhurst murmured, "Casualties . . . ? Or can you speak of it?"

"Unbelievable." Leigh's face darkened. "Worst I ever saw.

'Auld Grog Willie' had every member of his staff downed, one way or another. Never fear, Hawk, Colborne's unhurt, and looks quite himself again, though he carries that shoulder a trifle crooked these days." He turned rather reluctantly to Euphemia, who was striving not to look astonished yet again. "I'm sorry, lovely one, but . . . your admirer, Ian McTavish of the 92nd. And Johnny Wentby of the Gloucesters—you'll recall old John, Hawk? Bob Grimsby, who wrote that ode about your eyes, Mia, and—"

She said on a choked sob, "Dead . . . ? All—dead?"

"McTavish, I'm afraid. And right gallantly. Wentby also. Grimsby lost his leg, but might pull through. And indeed, war is no game for children. You of all people know that, m'dear."

"But you play at it as though it were!" sniffed Lady Bryce, who had also been fond of the dauntless Major McTavish. "All your riding and hunting and careering about over there . . . as though you'd not a . . . care in the world!" She wiped at her eyes, quite forgetting to be dainty about it.

Euphemia was so shattered she was finding it difficult to maintain her composure. Leith went on talking easily, turning the conversation to lighter aspects of Wellington's brilliant advance and, as he did so, unobtrusively placed one hand over Euphemia's small fist, tight clenched on the tablecloth. Hawkhurst noted that kindly gesture, the easy assurance with which it was accomplished, and the grateful, if quivering, smile that was bestowed upon Leith in return. For a moment he stared rather blankly at his good friend. Then he concentrated on his plate and for the balance of the meal said very little.

The contribution he might have made to the conversation was not missed. Leith, a superb raconteur, soon had them all in whoops with his tales. Carlotta, who very obviously doted on him, was happier than Euphemia had ever seen her, and Dora, her rich sense of humour easily aroused, laughed until the tears slipped down her round cheeks.

Through it all, not once did Stephanie appear to glance in the direction of Lieutenant Sir Simon Buchanan. And, through it all, the troubled eyes of that young gentleman rarely left her face.

"So here you are! What luck! I feared I'd not find you alone." Leith strode across the music room to join Euphemia, who was leafing through a pile of music.

"I have promised to sing at the rectory party tonight," she smiled as he pulled a chair close beside her. "You come with us, I hope?"

"I wish I might, but I must be at the Horse Guards first thing in the morning, and the weather looks a bit grim. Mia, I simply must talk with you. Can I persuade you to join me for a gallop before I leave?"

She would not have refused him under any circumstances, for always the dread that she might never see him again haunted her. But the thought of a ride today was doubly welcome, and she stood eagerly. "Lovely! I will go and change. I promise to be very quick."

"Oh, I know that," he said cheerfully, accompanying her into the hall. "You are famous for not keeping a gentleman waiting above three hours whilst you change your bonnet."

"Wretch!" she laughed. "Own up, Leith. That very quality is what won your heart, is it not?"

"But, of course. Above all else I demand promptitude in my wife!" The words were as light as ever, but there was a wistful quality to his smile, and Euphemia's eyes wavered. "You run along," he urged, "and I'll ask Hawk for the loan of a couple of hacks. I wonder where he's disappeared to. He was with the boy after luncheon, but—Oh, there they are."

Curious, Euphemia followed him into the library where Hawkhurst and Kent had their heads together over a fine old book of wild animal engravings. Kent's small face was aglow with happiness. He threw her a beaming smile and pointed to the book. She admired it dutifully, her heart warming towards the man for his kindness. Leith meantime had begged the loan of two horses, and Hawkhurst was already crossing to the bellrope. "Had you to ask, bacon brain? I'll tell the grooms to saddle them for you immediately. But you'll not ride Sarabande, and so I warn you."

"Graceless villain," Leith chuckled.

"Dare I beg, sir," Euphemia asked teasingly, "for a mount with a little more spirit than the gentle mare you allotted to me the last time I rode?"

She had turned her most winning smile upon their host, in the hope that this might constitute a start toward repairing the gulf between them. Her effort was lost.

Two eyes of solid ice regarded her as from a great height. "I fear, Miss Buchanan," he drawled, "that you shall have to let me be the best judge of my undoubtedly poor selection of cattle."

Leith threw him an astonished look. Euphemia, feeling as though she had been struck, dropped a curtsey and, her cheeks flaming, murmured, "I am most truly set down, Mr. Hawkhurst."

Ignoring her, he fixed the Colonel with a stern stare. "I may, I am assured, rely upon your discretion, Leith?"

Euphemia could not hold back her gasp of indignation and was reminded of his own total lack of discretion, not only with regard to his innumerable birds of paradise, but in his attempt to force his attentions on her that very morning! Leith, who had never so much as hugged her, seemed momentarily struck to silence by the implication. Then he murmured a wooden, "You may," and, with a somewhat stiff smile, ushered her from the room.

Seething, Euphemia walked beside him to the stairs, mounted the first step, then whirled to look down at him. The handsome face was raised to her, the dark brows lifted enquiringly. How *dared* such as Garret Hawkhurst cast an aspersion upon the character of this thoroughly honourable young man! Furious, she exclaimed, "Tristram, I am sorry! He is . . . he is absolutely impossible! How dare he speak to you so!"

He blinked a little in the face of such vehemence, then, a wistful grin curving his fine mouth, said, "No, but Hawk is within his rights, Mia. He *is* responsible for your safety while you are here, you know."

"The deuce he is!" she flared hotly. "Oh, I know I should not use such terms, but, really, that man is—is the outside of enough!"

And turning, she ran lightly up the stairs, leaving Leith to gaze after her, his dark eyes unwontedly sombre.

Euphemia seated herself at the dressing table and took up her hairbrush, wondering vaguely why Ellie should have looked so worried because she had said she was going riding. She began to brush her hair, her thoughts refusing to leave Hawkhurst. She found it difficult to hold her anger and sighed, recalling what Ponsonby had said of him: ". . . the most high-couraged youth, the most loyal and truly gallant young man . . ." A frown puckered her smooth brow, and she thought with a surge of irritation, The most vexing collection of contradictions!

Ponsonby was prejudiced, of course. Only this morning Lady Bryce had complained that Hawk allowed the servants to take advantage of him, and not only overpaid them outrageously but was forever coddling them, heedless of how this might inconvenience the family. For example, this evening they were all to be allowed to go to the Christmas party at the rectory. Euphemia sighed and wished that, now dear Leith was come, she would feel a little less miserable.

". . . with *him*, Miss?"

She glanced up, realized that she must seem a total featherwit and, feeling her face burn, enquired, "Your pardon, Ellie? I fear I was wool-gathering."

"I said, you ain't never going riding . . . with . . ." The abigail faltered into silence before the sudden chill in the usually kind blue eyes.

"Mr. Hawkhurst," Euphemia said levelly, "is having the horses saddled at this moment, I believe."

Ellie gave a muffled grown and, tearing nervously at her frilled apron, persisted, "Oh, Miss, you been so . . . so good to me. I know I shouldn't say nothing, but—Oh, Miss! He didn't ought to let you ride with him!"

Anger brought the glitter of ice into Euphemia's eyes. She had become fond of Ellie, but the woman was not a lifelong servant, and for a relative stranger to be so presumptive was unpardonable. "You have some objection to Colonel Leith?" she said frigidly.

To her surprise relief flooded the abigail's broad features. "Oh, thank goodness! I thought as ye was going with Mr. Garret, ma'am."

"Indeed?" The rage that swept Euphemia now made her previous vexation seem trite. She stood and, with chin high and manner regal, said, "You will, I feel sure, explain that disloyal remark."

Ellie shrank away a pace, then bowed her head into her hands and burst into tears. "I shoulda knowed," she wept. "Mr. Garret . . . bean't the type to . . . to put a lady's life in danger. I shoulda knowed. It *was* disloyal!"

Euphemia's knees turned to melted butter. She was vaguely aware of sinking onto the bench and of feeling terribly cold. Like the pieces of a nightmare jigsaw puzzle, she saw again Hawkhurst clinging to the end of that makeshift rope on the cliffside; herself and Kent, hiding in the dressing room and Hawk grumbling, ". . . if a man cannot shoot straight with a

Manton ..." to which Mr. Bailey had said anxiously that the Constable should have been summoned; and finally, Leith, as she had first heard him today, "... I tell you, Buck, it was a deliberate attempt at murder ... !"

"My dear God," she whispered. "Someone means to kill him!"

"Yes, Miss," mourned Ellie, wiping her eyes with her apron. "This morning the ball went right through his new hat. Manners said, instead of seeking cover, Mr. Garret rode straight at the place where the shot had come from, but the man was too far ahead. He dropped his gun, but Mr. Manners says they don't know whose it is. Hogwaddle, Miss! We all of us knows! It be Lord Gains! Small wonder that his lordship should hold a grudge, I suppose, but he should call Mr. Garret out, like a gentleman. Not keep at him like this."

Very pale, Euphemia asked in a far-away voice, "What else has happened?"

"Year before last, he was set on by Mohocks. He was with Colonel Leith, thank goodness, and they give a good account of theirselves. But I heard the Colonel talking to Dr. Archer after they come home, and he said it was no more Mohocks than his sainted Grandmama! 'They was after Gary!' he says. Six months later, the master was sailing, and a leak come in his boat. It was a new boat, Miss, and there must've been a lot of leaks, 'cause it went down like a stone, and if he wasn't a strong swimmer, he'd surely have drowned. That was when we all began to start putting two and two together! When he was in London in the summer, a coping stone fell—missed him by a hair, his aunty said. He pretends it's all just 'accidents,' but he ain't fooling none of *us*!"

Euphemia felt sick and was silent until, realizing Ellie was speaking again, she said, "I'm sorry. What did you say?"

"I said it's wicked to torment a man so, just now and then, so he never knows what's coming. Fair wicked!"

Euphemia walked slowly along the corridor, drawing on her gloves, her riding crop under her arm and her brow furrowed with worry. The shock of learning that Hawkhurst's life was threatened, and with such fiendish persistence, had driven all other considerations from her mind. It could not be Gains! It just *could not* be! Seldom had she been more instantly drawn to a man, and seldom did her judgments prove wrong. Her first impression of Hawk, in fact—She checked, startled to realize that she was beginning to think of him by his nickname and, also, that her cheeks were very warm. Seized by a sudden need to once more view the incredible beauty of Blanche Hawkhurst, she ran up the stairs to the top floor.

She hurried into the gallery, her feet soundless on the thick carpet, and stopped abruptly. Hawkhurst sat on the bench before the central portrait. His head was down-bent, elbows on his knees, and hands loosely clasped between them. No one seeing him thus would have dreamed he did not mourn his wife, for he looked every inch a man crushed by grief. Even as she watched, his shoulders drooped lower, and one hand was drawn across his eyes in a weary gesture. Then, as if impatient with himself, his head came up; his shoulders squared; he stood and, never glancing in her direction, wandered to the far window and leant against the panelled wall, staring out into the gardens.

Euphemia's heart was wrung. He looked so very alone that she had to fight an all but overmastering urge to run and cheer him somehow. But he was a strong man, and her witnessing of his sorrow would merely exacerbate his feelings. Reluctantly, therefore, she turned and walked slowly to the doors. Perhaps Dr. Archer had been mistaken, after all. Perhaps Hawk really had loved Blanche, if only for her beauty. She felt again the unfamiliar urge to weep and wondered if she was turning into a watering pot.

Someone stood before her, and, looking up, she beheld Tristram Leith, a romantic figure in his staff officer's uniform, his eyes very grave as he watched her. She forced a smile and held a finger to her lips. He stepped aside at once and walked beside her to the stairs.

"Whatever must you think of me?" she apologized. "I am truly sorry. Shall we still have time to ride?"

He teased her gently about her tardiness and assured her there was time for a short ride. Leaving the house, however, was like entering the polar regions. Euphemia gave an involuntary gasp, ducking her head against Leith's cloak, and at once he took her arm and said solicitously, "No, it's too cold for you. We'll talk inside."

"Never!" she laughed. "I need this, Tristram. To blow the cobwebs away."

"The cobweb ain't spun that would dare mar you, lovely one. Come then, let's make a dash for it before we freeze solid."

Hand in hand, they ran to the stables and rode out seconds later at a canter that swiftly became a gallop, down the slope and up the far hill.

From the end dormer window of the gallery, two grey eyes watched broodingly until the riders were lost from sight.

"Oh, Leith!" gasped Euphemia, cheeks a'tingle and eyes sparkling. "That was superb! Thank you!" She looked around curiously at the mouldering arches and walls that had been erected long and long ago on this lonely hilltop, and among which Leith had halted to lift her from the saddle. "What is this place?"

"Nobody really knows. It's part of Dominer's Home Farm now, but scholars say it was a temple once and that Druids may have worshipped here. We often came here when we were boys. We used to climb to the top of the tower. It was Hawk's favorite place whenever he craved solitude."

She looked at the great ivy-clad tower that soared at the very brink of the hill. "My heavens! How dreadfully dangerous! Had you fallen—"

"Then I'd not be here to pester you today," he grinned. "But I wish you might see the view from up there. It's superb."

She advised him firmly that she was perfectly satisfied with the view from their present vantage point and seated herself on the handkerchief he spread atop the lower outer wall.

Leith stood beside her, tall and straight, everything a girl could hope for. And watching him, wishing with all her heart that she loved him, she knew she did not, nor ever would, save as a cherished friend.

A dog barked somewhere, deep and baying, and she said anxiously, "Goodness! I do hope that's not Sampson!"

"So you've met that hound, have you? Trust Max to acquire a mongrel who's a natural born clergyman."

She gave a ripple of laughter. "Clergyman? You mean he saves souls?"

"Devil a bit of it. He visits. The sick. And the indigent. And the rich, the poor, the hale, the hearty—and especially, he visits Gary. It's a delight to both of 'em, you know. Don't think they could get along without one another."

Incredulous, she stammered, "But ... Hawkhurst tried to ... to kill him! He said he'd send him back to Gains à la John the Baptist!"

He gave a shout of laughter. "And probably grabbed a pistol

and tore after him howling bloody murder, eh? Lay you odds the gun wasn't loaded. Or if it was, he'd have been unable to get 'the blasted trigger' to work or some such fustian."

"Oh!" she gasped indignantly. "And I swallowed the whole!"

Leith put one booted foot on the wall and, leaning forward, took up her whip and toyed with it absently. "Hawk saved your life, so I hear. And young Kent's, which must have been a shade trying for him, poor old fellow."

"Yes." Her indignation faded. "I had heard he does not care to have children around him. I can understand why."

"It has done him good. I could see it the instant I arrived." Her vivid face was raised in an immediate and eager questioning, and, his heart sinking, Leith said quietly, "Hawk's been like a man frozen these last four years, Mia, a man afraid to live—not daring to love, and so grasping at every straw in a sort of defiant seeking for the happiness he cannot have."

"But, why not? Lives can be rebuilt. Happiness can come again. Even if he loved her so—"

"*Loved* her? Good God! I wonder he didn't strangle her! Oh, I know I should not speak ill of the dead—and Blanche was not an evil lady, do not mistake. In a way, Hawk was better served than poor Simon, for Blanche was not, so far as I am aware, er . . ."

"Generous—with her affections?" Euphemia supplied dryly.

"Right you are. She was just possessed, heart and soul, by another fellow. And she was so besotted she would do whatever he bade her. Blast him!"

"Mount," Euphemia nodded. "Did you know him, Tris?"

"Regrettably. And for a while I hoped she would settle for him. They were much alike, their total selfishness disguised by beauty. But I think Mount really loved Blanche insofar as he was capable of it, and I know she was mad for him. Only . . ." He hesitated as though fearful of betraying a confidence and shrugged, "Well, they would have been penniless. So she married Hawk."

"I heard some of it. But, Leith, you are Hawk's friend, and you have always been as loyal as you could stare. Is there nothing can be done? His Grandpapa surely, could—"

"The Admiral worshipped Blanche," Leith interposed softly. "He holds Garret solely to blame for her death."

Stunned, Euphemia stared at him. So that was what Archer had meant when he'd said Wetherby came to "turn the knife" in Hawk. She'd somehow imagined it was the child the old man reproached him for. "But—but that is so *wrong*! Was he blind? Could he not see what manner of woman . . ." Leith's raised brows brought a hot surge of colour to her cheeks. "I know it is none of my affair," she said hastily. "Indeed, we'll be gone in a day or two, and I doubt shall ever see him again. I came here believing Hawkhurst to be some kind of—of Bluebeard. But he's not, Leith! I have seen him be incredibly brave, and kind, and . . . and gentle. It seems so wrong for those wicked rumours to—"

"Wicked?" he exclaimed, as if surprised. "You do not believe them?"

"Of course not! Good heavens, it must be very obvious that Hawkhurst is not the type to hurt a woman, let alone the child he loved so deeply!"

Leith merely shrugged once more, and, searching his features, she cried anxiously, "Tris? You are not beginning to doubt? You will not turn against him, too? Oh, my dear friend, do not, I implore you. He needs you. He is so terribly alone. I feel sometimes that he is like a prisoner here, trapped by a reputation he does not warrant, but will not deny, and—" Leith was regarding her with a sad, sweet smile, and, rather aghast, she stopped.

"My lovely lady," he murmured, taking one soft ringlet and twining it about his finger. "My pure girl; my brave, warmhearted, dream wife . . ."

A lump rose in Euphemia's throat. He was going to offer again. Why must Fate be so difficult? Why could she not be in love with this fine young man?

"Do not look so grieved," he said. "I am not going to offer—ever again, love. You are free of me, at long last."

"Oh, Leith. Do not . . . do not . . . Or . . . I shall surely cry."

"Never do that. The last thing I would bring you is tears. You should instead give me credit, my dear, for knowing when I am beaten."

She met his eyes then, although her own were a'swim. And seeing the puzzlement in them, he said wistfully, "Poor little girl, you do not know it yourself, do you? Mia, oh, my sweet Mia . . . The blasted rogue don't deserve you, but you love him, you henwit."

Euphemia stared at him blankly. And, cursing himself for a fool, he walked away, ostensibly to secure one of the horses which was pulling free of the shrub to which he had tied it.

Poor Leith, she thought numbly. He was quite mistaken. She did not love at all. She could not. For she had always been perfectly sure that she would know her love at first sight. That she would only have to set eyes on him, and she would know. But—Why was her heart hammering so? Why did her breath flutter in such agitation? Unable to remain still, she rose and walked to the archway, where she stood staring out across the wintry landscape, the pale hills, the bare trees swaying in the wind, the heavy, gathering clouds. And saw instead eyes as grey as those clouds, a face lined by care, hair prematurely touched with frost, and a well-shaped mouth that could be so fierce and harsh, yet curve unexpectedly to laughter or to a tenderness incredible in its sweetness.

And, like a great light, the truth burst upon her, burning away the heavy-heartedness that had so oppressed her these past few days and that she now knew had been occasioned by her struggle against this same truth. She could have spread her arms and danced and shouted with the wonder of it. She *did* love! For all time, for all her days, Garret Thorndyke Hawkhurst was her love! Whether discredited and disgraced, whether held in contempt by all the *haut ton*, or by all the world—she loved him! Radiant, she spun about.

Watching her, grieving, Leith was touched by awe. Never for him had that light shone in her glorious eyes; never had he seen that deep, transforming glow. He walked towards her and put out his arms, and she ran into them, lifting her face. He kissed her on her smooth brow, gently, lovingly. And in farewell.

"You know," he said huskily, "had I ever dreamed he would steal my lady, I'd never have given him that blasted horse. I think I'll just take him back!"

Blinking rather rapidly, Euphemia said. "Home . . . ?"

"Sarabande. I gave him to Hawk when he was foaled. Didn't you know? I always told him it was only a loan, because he was too fine to take to the Peninsula, and if I left him at Cloudhills my Papa would likely bestow him on one of his . . . ah . . ."

"Barques of frailty?" said Euphemia, well acquainted with Leith's irrepressible father.

"Precisely . . . That treacherous rogue! By God, I *shall* take him back!"

Long after Sarabande was out of sight and Leith's groom had entered the chaise and followed his master into the fading afternoon, Euphemia remained by the gatehouse, needing to be alone for a little while, to savour her new-found joy. Darkness fell, and there was no moon, but the bitter cold seemed to sharpen the air, and the stars hung like great jewels, suspended above her. She felt at one with the universe tonight, for the first time in her life, a being complete. And humbled by the wonder of it, she looked up and whispered, "I love, Papa. At last I have found my mate. Do you like him, dearest one? Do you approve? Of course, you do, for he is a man. And I dare believe, a gentleman. You would have asked no finer for me."

She wheeled her mount then and rode slowly back towards the house.

Not until she realized how few of the rooms were lighted did she recall the party at the rectory. With a shocked gasp, she spurred down the slope and into the stable-yard. A slender shape came to meet her. A quiet voice enquired, "Are you all right, Miss? We were worried."

As always, Manners spoke like the well-bred man he was, but there was a trace of censure in the tone. Her chin lifting, Euphemia said, "Then I must at once go and make my apologies for such thoughtlessness. Take her for me, would you, please?"

He obeyed, and she slipped from the saddle and walked away in silence. But suddenly she remembered him at the scene of the accident. He loved Hawk, and therefore she could not be angry with him. He was standing watching her when she turned back. She said softly, "The Colonel returns to France tomorrow, Manners."

"Yes, Miss. He is a splendid gentleman. The master thinks very highly of him. And . . ." A small hesitation, then a rather breathless, "Perhaps, since I know him so well, it would not have been impertinent for me to have offered my congratulations."

So that was why she had been scolded. Stifling a smile, she walked back a few paces. "Not impertinent, perhaps. But most inappropriate."

"Inappropriate, Miss?"

He sounded brighter, and she asked, "Did you tell Mr. Hawkhurst that the Colonel took Sarabande?"

"Not yet, Miss. He'll likely send him back by easy stages tomorrow."

"I doubt it." She heard the startled gasp and went on, "Colonel Leith seemed to feel Mr. Hawkhurst owed him something."

"He . . . he *did*, Miss?"

No mistaking the joyous note in the voice now, and bless the man for all that was implied by his delight. Euphemia again started towards the great sprawl of this beautiful house she had come to love, but a hand was on her arm, and Manners said, "Miss, they've all gone to the rectory."

"Mr. Hawkhurst as well?"

"No, but if I dare be so bold—that is, you must be tired. There's Mrs. Henderson, and one footman. May I ask for dinner to be sent to your room?"

She could not see his face in the darkness, but something was amiss. She murmured her thanks, but refused and hurried to the side door.

The footman who bowed to her in the Great Hall was very young and, in response to her question, allowed that he had, "No h-idea as to where the master might be found."

Euphemia put back her hood, unbuttoned the throat of the pelisse, and handed the garment to him. Taking up the skirt of her habit, she hurried along the hall. How quiet the house was . . . She glanced into drawing room, lounges, salons, library, music room, and the small dining room, all without success. His study, perhaps. She all but ran to that small room, where she knew he retreated when Carlotta sniped at him or Coleridge vexed him.

The door was closed, but she could smell the fragrance of wood burning and, daringly, lifted the latch and entered. Hawkhurst was sprawled in the wing chair by the fire, one booted leg slung carelessly over the arm, the other stretched out before him. A bottle lay on the rug, and his glass, half-full, sagged in his hand. He peered around the side of the chair, his face flushed and aggressive, then came to his feet to stand weaving unsteadily. He had not dressed for dinner and had discarded his jacket; with his dark hair tousled and his cravat loosened, he looked amazingly younger and much less formidable. "Well, well," he said jeeringly, the words only faintly slurred. "Thought you was gone, ma'am. W'all thought you was gone. Others went to th' party without you. Sorry. But . . . they thought—"

"I was gone," she finished gravely. "But I am here, you see, Hawk."

He flinched almost imperceptibly at her use of his nickname, then reached out to grasp the chair with one hand, holding himself steadier. "Yes. Well, you should not be. Private . . . s-study. Don't allow ladies in here. An' 'sides, Leith wouldn't like it."

She longed to kiss the bitterness from his eyes, but said gently, "I can understand your concern. He is your very good friend."

He stiffened and turned slightly from her. "My . . . friend," he muttered to the carpet. "Yes. He is." He swung back and said in a less hostile fashion, "And he does 'deed have my . . . congratulations. He's truly splendid fellow, ma'am. I w-wish you happy."

"Do you?" She moved past him to warm her hands at the fire. "Yet you are frowning again."

He gave a foolish laugh. "Well, that's 'cause . . . I'm li'l bit foxed, y' see." Euphemia turned to regard him in her candid way, and as if in defiance he lifted his glass and drank, blinked very rapidly, and said in a wheezing rasp, "Not . . . not bosky 'zackly, but—"

"You, sir," Euphemia contradicted, "are what my brother would term 'very well to live.' "

"No, no! Ain't. Not really. Shouldn't argue with lady, but . . . but y' shouldn't be here 'lone w'me. Not . . . proper. An' . . . no jacket. Where . . . the devil's m'jacket?"

A faint smile touching her lips, Euphemia rescued that article from the log basket. "A trifle rumpled, I fear. And will not make you less foxed, Hawk."

Again, a tremor ran through him. He turned away, mumbling a low-voiced, "Y'bes' go. I must . . . fairly reek of cognac."

"Yes. You do. And I have bivouacked with an army."

He drew a deep breath and, his head coming up, said, "Well, you'll not bivouac with me, madam."

A gasp escaped Euphemia. The hauteur was back in his reddened eyes, with a vengeance. How dare he say such a thing? And with such total contempt! And yet, what more natural, poor soul? He believed her promised to Tristram Leith, and the moment his friend's back was turned she had come in here to invade his sanctum sanctorum. Only this morning, though it seemed a century ago, he had found her in his bedchamber. She suppressed the furious retort that had sprung to her lips, therefore, and instead said softly, "That remark was unworthy of you, sir. And of me. And I am not—"

The denial of her betrothal to Leith died on her lips as the door burst open unceremoniously to admit Mrs. Henderson. "By George!" Hawkhurst growled. "This is my p-private study, Nell! Y'know perfectly well I don't 'low ladies—"

Her kindly face pale and her voice cracking with terror, the housekeeper interrupted, "He's *here*, sir! Oh, Mr. Garrett! He's *come*! The *Admiral*!"

Hawkhurst positively reeled and reached out to grab the chair back again, while the high colour drained from his face to leave it very white.

"Manners has taken him to his room," Mrs. Henderson went on, wringing her hands distractedly. "He told him you was meeting with your steward, but would be with him directly. Sir, *whatever* shall we do? The house is bare of servants! I've made no special preparations for dinner. And—"

"And I," he said faintly, "am most . . . thoroughly . . . jug bit, Nell. My God! Here's . . . fine pickle!"

"I'll—I'll tell him you had to go out," said Mrs. Henderson bravely, though her voice still shook. "I'll say—"

"Can't do that. Though I thank you for t-trying. He'd leave, don't y'see. And I've not seen him . . . for so—" He put a hand across his eyes, as though striving to force the mists from them and, shaking his head, muttered, " 'F'all th' beastly luck. I shall have to . . . to jus' admit I'm—"

"Mrs. Henderson," Euphemia interjected crisply, "Coffee! Black and strong, and plenty of it! Hawkhurst, go with her to the kitchen; your Grandpapa will not seek you there. A footman of sorts is lurking about. He will help you. You must bathe and change—and drink coffee all the time."

"But, Miss," mourned the housekeeper, turning hopefully to the girl's restoring calm. "There's no water heated for a bath!"

"Cold will be better. Oh, and squeeze some lemons, and make Mr. Hawkhurst drink the juice. Rinse your mouth well, Hawk, and—"

"I'll b-be sick!" he protested. "Cannot stand lemon juice and—"

"Excellent!" Implacably, she urged the woman towards the door. "Hurry, now—and we shall bring the master through this, somehow."

"Oh, bless you, Miss!" gulped the housekeeper, and ran.

"Mia," said Hawkhurst, forgetting protocol in the urgency of the moment, "I'm more grateful than c'n say . . . But I can't leave m'grandfather un-unwelcomed. He'll—"

"*I* shall welcome him. He'll just have to forgive my doing so in this habit instead of a proper gown. Go!"

He wavered towards the door but on the threshold turned back to look at her for a long moment. "Leith," he mumbled, "Leith's the . . . luckiest man I know."

"Yes, for he has purloined your black Arabian, sir!" she flashed, and had the satisfaction of seeing shock appear in his eyes. "*Will* you go? And—trust me! I'll handle him."

The shadow of a smile playing about his lips, he said, "I believe you may, at that."

He left her then, and, watching his reeling stagger along the hall, she shuddered, then called a desperate, "Send Manners to me. I shall be in the drawing room."

He waved a response, almost fell, then stumbled on again.

The fire was still smouldering in the drawing room, and with a sigh of relief Euphemia piled two more logs on the dying blaze, poked at it cautiously, and was rewarded by a sudden flicker of flames. Lighting candles with frantic haste, she thought that the room was a little chill, but having come from a long and undoubtedly cold ride, the Admiral would probably find it warm enough. A beautiful old mirror hung above the credenza on the right wall, and she flew to it, uttering a moan of apprehension as she viewed her wind-blown hair. And she had no comb, for she'd left her reticule in—

She spun around, horror-stricken, as the door opened, then felt limp with relief. "Manners! Thank heaven it's—" She paused. Across his arm the groom carried the new cream brocade gown she had intended to wear on Christmas Day at Aunt Lucasta's. From one hand her best pearls dangled, and comb, hairbrush, and perfume bottle were clutched in the other. "Oh, wonderful!" she exclaimed. "But, is there time?"

"If you're quick, Miss." He shot a conspiratorial smile at her and murmured, "The old gentleman's very angry, I'm afraid. Good thing I opened the door for him instead of that young fool, Strapp. But, he's a stickler for manners, and I thought . . . this dress might be—er, better."

She glanced around. There was no obliging screen in this room.

Manners laid the gown across a blue velvet chair. "I'll leave you and stand guard outside, in case—"

"No! I've no time for modesty now. Turn your back—and for heaven's sake don't let anyone in!" She struggled with buttons and fasteners as he returned to the door and faced it obediently. "The Admiral's preferences, Manners!"

"He likes Spanish cigarillos, Miss. There's a special box in the dining room. I'll get them directly I leave you."

"What about wine?"

"Port. Mr. Hawkhurst keeps a supply of 'seventy-three in the cellars. I know, because Mr. Ponsonby let me try a glass once. I'll basket some. It will be cold enough and should be welcomed, I would think."

"Excellent," gasped Euphemia, muffled under the brocade. Surfacing breathlessly, she asked, "Can Mrs. Henderson muster a decent meal, d'you think? I know men. My Papa was never so vexed as to come from a day on the march and find a poor table."

"Nell says she's some cold chicken and a pig's cheek. There's no time to make a pie, but there's a dish she knows with potatoes and curried meat she says will serve. Miss, can I go? Mr. Hawkhurst—"

Struggling vainly, Euphemia moaned, "Manners, are you wed?"

"Yes, Miss." He grinned at the door panel. "Buttons?"

"Yes. You're a gem! Come, do—and strive never to remember this, or I shall be as disgraced as your master!"

He spun around quickly and, searching her face, saw the mischievous smile as she started forward, his eyes admiring. Her hair was rumpled and coming down, but the pale gown accentuated the rich colour of it, and the pearls made her fair skin seem almost luminous. She might not be a beauty in the

strictest sense of the word, thought Mr. Manners, but by
heaven she was a fine-looking girl!

Euphemia stood before the mirror unabashedly as he fumbled with the four-and-twenty small buttons at the back of her
gown. Plying the hairbrush, she said, "Tell Mrs. Henderson to
be sure to make as many sweets as possible. If she has none,
a trifle—well soaked with wine—should serve. How does your
master go on?"

"When I left just now, he was . . . ah, a trifle indisposed,
Miss."

"The lemons!" exclaimed Euphemia around a mouthful of
hairpins. Manners chuckled, and she said, "Poor soul! Well,
he'll feel better for it. Now, tell me. Has Admiral Wetherby
any pet subjects?"

"I've heard he was devoted to Nelson. And he's an admirer
of a new artist called Constable. One of the few, I think."

"Thank you." She coaxed a ringlet over her shoulder. "Now,
have you told the old gentleman to come in here?"

"I tried, but . . . it's hard to tell him much. I wasn't able to
explain—"

Whatever had not been explained to the Admiral, Euphemia
was not then destined to discover, for a querulous voice was
raised in the hall, demanding, "Where in the *deuce* is everyone? Lottie . . . ? Dora . . . ?"

"Doesn't he know they're at the rectory?" whispered
Euphemia, whipping her hair into place. Manners, wrestling
perspiringly with the last two buttons, groaned, "I had no
chance to tell him, Miss. He was full of complaints from the
moment he alighted from his coach. His man looked—Oh my!
He's coming!"

"Here!" Euphemia swept up her discarded habit and thrust
it at him. In desperate haste she flung some perfume behind
her ears, slipped the bottle into a pot of ferns, and hissed, "Out
the terrace door! Quickly!"

He raced for the curtains, turned back suddenly, drew a fan
from his coat pocket, and tossed it to her. Euphemia caught it
and, collapsing into the nearest chair, gave a gasp of relief that
just as suddenly became a whimper of dismay. She still wore
her riding boots!

The hall door swung open. She whipped her feet back and
stood, as Admiral Lord Johnathan Wetherby strolled into the
drawing room. He was indeed "a stickler for manners," for he
wore knee breeches and a black jacket. This much she saw be-

fore she sank into her curtsey. Straightening, she smiled into eyes as dark and cold as a midwinter night and with a quickening of her pulse knew she faced a formidable adversary. The features of this erect old gentleman were little changed from those in the portrait, only a few lines and the white hair betraying the years that had passed since it was painted. She stood slim and tall before him, unaware that her head was slightly thrown back, as his quizzing glass was lifted and he scanned her with slow deliberation from head to hem. She said nothing, wondering if he suspected her knees were a trifle bent, so as to prevent her confounded boots from showing.

The Admiral was, in fact, thinking that this girl was a cut above Hawk's usual run of doxies. "How very remiss of my grandson," he murmured, "to leave so charming a . . . lady alone."

"Yes," she smiled, having noted the deliberate pause. "Is it not? But I shall not rail at him since he has sent so delightful a . . . gentleman in his stead."

The quizzing glass, which had begun to lower, checked just a trifle, and the dark eyes sharpened. "Since we are faced with the embarrassment of no host, or hostess, to perform introductions, allow me to—"

"But it is not necessary, my lord." Seating herself, feet carefully tucked back, Euphemia added, "I know who you are, you see. And I do believe I shall make you guess my identity."

"Indeed . . . ?" His tone held the barest hint of boredom, but his interest had flared nonetheless. She was a graceful chit, with the poise of a Duchess. Hawk's taste was most decidedly improved. He took the chair she waved him towards—for all the world as though she presided over this house, the brazen jade!—and his eyes lingered with sardonic amusement on the fan she wielded.

Glancing down, Euphemia saw, too late, that Manners had taken up the ruby-encrusted fan that Papa's officers had presented to her last year. Her abigail had packed it by mistake, since it was by far too ornate for a country house. She bit her lip in momentary vexation, then continued to fan herself gently.

"I could scarcely have a notion of your identity, ma'am," he shrugged quellingly. "And that such as yourself could derive any pleasure from chatting to a crusty old sea-dog, I find . . . questionable."

"No, but it will be such a change, for you see I am accustomed to chatting with crusty old military men." Her smile was as sweet, her eyes as level as ever, but amused now, Wetherby suppressed a grin with difficulty. "Military . . ." he said, tilting his head thoughtfully. "You have a father, a brother, on the Peninsula, perhaps?"

"Only a brother now, sir." Briefly, sorrow touched her eyes, and she stifled a sigh as she thought of her beloved father, and a smile at the knowledge of how this interview must have infuriated him.

Manners entered to place the cigarillos and a tinder box at the Admiral's elbow. "Mr. Hawkhurst had bespoken some wine for Lord Wetherby," Euphemia lied softly. "You will not forget, Manners?"

"Your pardon, Miss. I will bring it at once."

"New man, I see," murmured the Admiral, his longing gaze on the cigar box.

Wondering what he would say if he knew he had just been waited on by the head groom, she evaded, "He is very good, but since your grandson is short-handed tonight, sir, I shall have to ask that you prepare your own cigarillo."

He glanced up eagerly. "You do not object, ma'am?"

She gave a little trill of laughter. "Lud, no. In Spain, I—" She stopped and bit her lip, as though she'd let the clue slip unintentionally.

"Aha!" he ejaculated in triumph, opening the beautifully inlaid box. "You betrayed yourself, ma'am! You accompanied your Papa, did you? He was an officer, then!"

"Alas, you are too clever for me, my lord."

He chuckled and, applying flame to tobacco, puffed contentedly, then, leaning back in his chair, asked, "Are you an . . . old friend of my grandson?"

"We have been at Dominer not quite two weeks, sir. In point of fact, we were on our way to Bath for the holidays when our carriage overturned, and Mr. Hawkhurst was so kind as to bring us here."

"How unfortunate. No one injured, I trust?"

"My brother again, a little, poor dear," she said with total innocence. "And my page became very ill un—"

"And now I have you, ma'am!" Wetherby sprang up with a surprisingly quick, lithe movement. "You are Armstrong Buchanan's girl! I heard his daughter had titian hair, and that her brother was come home with a ball through his shoulder. I trust Buchanan sustained no severe set-back?" He was bearing down on her even as he spoke, and she lifted her hand saying a rueful, "Oh, my! How very quick you are!" He laughed delightedly and bowed over her fingers. "Forgive me, my dear. I was disgruntled, and supposed you to be—someone else."

Knowing perfectly well what he had supposed, she smiled, "Of course. I thought perhaps you were a trifle into the hips after a tiresome journey. And my brother is mending so nicely I fear he will be returning to his regiment very soon. For which I have your grandson's magnificent friend, Dr. Archer, to thank." The instant the remark passed her lips, she saw his own tighten and, recalling Archer's hostility, knew it was shared and that she had committed a *faux pas*. Wetherby said nothing, however, and returned to his chair.

Manners slipped back in with a tray of decanters and glasses. The Admiral glanced at Euphemia, and she shook her head. He sniffed of the bouquet when Manners handed him the glass, sipped, and sighed ecstatically. "Hawkhurst keeps a fine cellar. I give him credit for that, at least."

"He has been a splendid host, my lord. Indeed, we are most deeply in his debt."

The old gentleman scanned her thoughtfully. This nice child should not be here. Perhaps she did know what she risked. "I take it," he said with slow reluctance, "that you are aware of my grandson's regrettable reputation, Miss Buchanan?"

"I am, sir. And find it far more regrettable that such wicked slander should be permitted to flourish against so very gallant a gentleman."

The Admiral all but dropped his cigarillo and practically goggled at her. "Your pardon, ma'am? I had thought we were discussing my grandson—Garrett Hawkhurst?"

"Indeed we were. How proud you must be. I am sure my brother will wish to convey his thanks to you also, for, were it not for your grandson, Sir Simon, myself and my page would all be in our graves today."

Lord Wetherby, recovering himself with a visible effort, leaned forward. "Dear lady, I see you have much to tell me. Would you be so good as to begin?"

"I quite fail to see," said Amelia Broadbent, with a wrinkle of her pert little nose, "what is so very remarkable about the fact that Stephanie Hawkhurst has had all her pretty hair cut off and has taken to using cosmetics in the most vulgar fashion!" Raising her own carefully darkened brows, she added, "One might suppose the gentlemen to be a bunch of witless schoolboys, the way they scurry around her!"

"And one more remark like that, child," said her fond parent, smiling upon her fair loveliness with a terrifying expanse of bared teeth, "and you shall be taken home and made to lie down upon your bed with a dose of the elixir prescribed by dear Dr. Beddoes!"

This dire threat sufficed to have Miss Broadbent turn pale and subside behind her fan, albeit sending many a jealous glance at the small crowd gathered around Stephanie in the far corner of the gaily decorated Church Hall.

All evening it had been thus. Upon the arrival of the Hawkhurst party Stephanie had created a near sensation, both ladies and gentlemen pressing in to admire the shy but well-liked girl. There had been a small tussle between Ivor St. Alaban and John Stiles as to which should escort her in to supper. A pointless tussle, since the handsome guest of the Hawkhursts, Lieutenant Sir Simon Buchanan, had claimed that honour. Still, he could not be said to have monopolized his fair prize at the table, and in fact they scarcely exchanged words, each attending politely to the remarks of those about them and paying little heed to one another.

The music struck up, and the young ladies were again overjoyed to note that Sir Simon made no attempt to vie for the pleasure of leading Stephanie through the country dance. Their delight was tempered, however, when the gallant young soldier did not seek any other lady for a partner, instead charming the dowagers and gratifying the gentlemen who sought him out for news of the war. The more mature ladies smiled upon him and extolled his pretty manners. The younger damsels, deciding that he must still be too weakened to dance, thus found him more romantic than ever and sighfully watched him over their fluttering fans.

Stephanie, meanwhile, was torn between triumph and tears. To meet with outright admiration was something entirely new in her experience and could only send her spirits soaring. Yet to be so near the man she loved but not dare to look at him for fear of betraying herself, to long to dance with him and know he would not seek her out, to tremble with the consuming terror that tomorrow, or the next day, he would go away, leaving her life a howling desolation, was to suffer the depths of despair.

Her cousin, leading her from the floor after a country dance, told her with boyish delight that she was become a Toast. "You're the belle of the evening," he imparted generously. "Dashed if I ain't proud of you! Jolly glad Miss Buchanan didn't come, or you'd have been quite cast into the shade, but you're made, Stephie. No doubt of it. You can wed whomsoever you choose now, and must be in—" His glowing laudation faded into silence as, with a murmurous apology, Stephanie fled, leaving him staring after her in utter bafflement for an entire five seconds before the coy glance of Miss Broadhurst ensnared him.

Snatching up her pelisse, Stephanie hurried outside through a rear door and wandered towards the rectory. The night air was bracing, and in a minute or two she dried her tears, told herself sternly that she simply could not go through life in such sodden fashion, and tred down the narrow side steps into the vicar's pleasant garden. A dog barked hysterically somewhere close by, and she was startled when a small shape whisked through a cluster of poles from which untrimmed chrysanthemums still drooped, crashed into the glass frame of a potting shed, and lay in a still and shapeless huddle.

With a cry of sympathy, she ran to kneel beside the little creature, heedless of the dirt that soiled her new dress, or the icy hardness of the ground against her knees. The rabbit was inanimate to her touch, and she gathered it up and held it tenderly, murmuring her distress.

Lord Coleridge had not been the only person to note Stephanie's abrupt departure from the Hall. Young Ivor St. Alaban's eyes lit up as he watched her slip away, and, running a hand through his curly locks and straightening his garishly striped waistcoat, he followed. He had known Stephie Hawkhurst all his life and thought of her as a jolly good girl, shy and quiet, but always willing to make up a group if the numbers were not just right and never one to pout was she left out. Not until tonight, however, had he thought of her as a dashed pretty creature. All the other fellows had noticed her too, more was the pity, but they'd not been as alert as he, fortunately. He had to delay a moment while he sought out his frieze greatcoat, for he was susceptible to the cold and had no wish for his teeth to chatter while he flirted with the girl. At last, however, he stood on the rear terrace, peering out. Stephie was heiress to a considerable fortune, and did he play his cards right—

"St. Alaban, isn't it?"

The cool words brought him spinning around, his youthful face reddening. There could be no mistaking that erect form, nor the proud tilt of the sandy head. "Y-Yes, sir," he stammered. Buchanan had not stayed for a coat. Was he guarding the chit for her brother? Good God! In his enthusiasm he had completely overlooked the hovering menace constituted by so notorious a duellist, a man said to be equally deadly with sword or pistol! He'd best tread softly, for Hawkhurst would kill the man who interfered with his sister as soon as look at him!

"Come out for a breath of air?" asked Buchanan mildly.

"That's r-right. Beastly hot inside, y'know."

"You do look rather flushed. That's the trouble with these gatherings. One tends to become easily ... overheated."

Wishing the ground might open and swallow him, St. Alaban nodded, gulped something incoherent, and beat a hasty retreat into the house, watched by a pair of amused blue eyes.

The boy, thought Buchanan, had pursued his quarry with all the grace of a wild boar. Harmless, probably, but there might be others. He began to wander across the lawn. Stephanie was so innocent and had no knowledge of her charm, which was perhaps her greatest charm. It simply would not occur to her that any man might desire her. He smiled wryly—least of all, a *married* man with three hopeful children! How shocked that pure-souled girl would be did she guess how he had come to regard her. He'd not realized himself at first what was happening. He'd thought her very kind and gentle, and somehow, so easily, he'd begun to add to her merits: her soft, sweet voice, her lilting little laugh and merry humour, her devotion to her family, her unceasing willingness to help Kent with his drawing, or point out birds and plants to him in the gardens. Never a sign of temper or impatience. He sighed. How blessed the man who would win her. And how different his own life might have been, had he found her first. But there was no use repining. He had ruined his life and found his true love too late. He had these few days, at least. He could store up some precious moments against the dark emptiness of the years to come ...

He had reached the steps leading down into the rectory garden and at first thought Stephanie must have gone into the house. And then he saw her. She had fallen! His heart leapt into his throat, and, frantic, he ran to her.

"Stephie! My God! Are you hurt?"

The familiar voice sent arrows through Stephanie's heart.

The terror in that same voice made her tremble with foolish hope. She looked up into the so-loved face bent anxiously above her and said with more pathos than she knew, "Poor little bunny. A dog was chasing it, I think, and I fear it has killed itself. See . . ." She held the little shape up, sadly. "Is it not the dearest thing?"

Her face was touched by the new-risen moon, so that it seemed to him to be encircled as by a halo. "The dearest . . . thing," he breathed, never knowing how his heart was in his worshipful eyes.

But Stephanie saw and mesmerized, clasped the rabbit to her bosom, gazing up at him. "Did you . . . want me?" she asked.

Did he *want* her!

Restored perhaps by the warmth of its tender cushion, the rabbit gave a sudden leap for freedom. It was a small rabbit, but it was frightened and, after the style of such creatures, had powerful hind legs. Wherefore, Stephanie gave a little cry and threw one hand to the torn lace at her bosom.

"Did he hurt you?" Buchanan dropped to his knees also and, drawing her hand away, saw a speck of blood on the white lace. "He cut you! Oh, my dear! We must take you to a doctor! You are—" And he froze, horrifiedly aware that he had pulled back the ripped lace, that he was holding his handkerchief against the scratches upon the sweet curve of her white breast. He whipped his hand away and drew back, head down. "Forgive me! *Forgive* me!" he groaned. "Whatever must you think? I did not mean . . . I . . . I only—"

Her soft hand was upon his lips, staying that shamed utterance, and he could no more have stopped himself from kissing those fingers than have halted the moon in its course. Her forgiving hands were seeking to raise his abased head, and, daring to look up, he saw the light in her eyes—a light that banished all sensations, save love.

"Silly boy," whispered Stephanie yearningly. "Oh, my dearest, silly boy. Did you think I do not . . . know?"

She swayed to him, all eager submission. His arms slipped about her, and her face was uplifted for his kiss.

It was quiet and very cold in the deserted garden, but to the two upon their knees, lip to lip, heart to heart, it might have been balmy as a summer's day, and the air filled with lilting music.

Only one living being viewed this strange behaviour, and he

cared not—and proved it by departing the scene with the flash of a white puff of a tail.

❧ *Chapter 11* ❧

Hawkhurst placed one hand firmly on the latch of the drawing room door, drew a deep breath, and walked inside. His grandfather, head thrown back in a hearty laugh, the stub of a cigarillo in one hand, eyed him with something very like cordiality for a moment, before standing and putting out his hand. "I am glad you could spare the time to say hello, Hawkhurst." His grip was firm and brief, as always. Withdrawing it, he said, "Cannot say your presence was missed, however. Was it, m'dear?"

The old gentleman levelled his guns swiftly, thought Euphemia. And scanning Hawkhurst with the eyes of love, found him pale, but fully in command of himself, his speech unslurred as he smiled, "And I cannot allow you to manoeuvre my guest into so tight a corner, sir. How very good to have you here. May we hope it will be a lengthy visit? If you could spend Christmas with us, it—"

"Quite impossible, I fear. I have already accepted an invitation to join Vaille and the Hilbys. I had intended to overnight with you and leave in the morning. However, now that I have met your most charming guest . . ." Wetherby took up his glass and raised it in a silent toast to Euphemia, his eyes as warm, when they alighted on her, as they were cold when turned upon his grandson.

"I perceive that I owe you a—" Hawkhurst's gaze also turned to her, and his breath was snatched away. No wonder the Admiral was dazzled. She looked magnificent! "—a debt of gratitude, ma'am," he finished with an effort.

Wetherby slanted a shrewd glance at him.

"Not at all," Euphemia answered. "It was my very great pleasure. But if to have acted as your hostess indeed constituted a favour, it must be small indeed beside the debt we owe you, Mr. Hawkhurst."

He bowed, told her she looked very lovely this evening, and moved to refill his grandfather's glass. "Have you heard the news, sir? Another grand victory for Wellington!"

"I have. I was in Waiter's when the word came. Pandemonium! The Church bells are ringing in every town in England—as well they should! But I have had news from this delightful lady that pleases me also, Garret. You saved the life of her page, she tells me. How gratifying, when Fate gives us a chance to mend our fences. Is it not?"

Hawkhurst said nothing. Only the hand that replaced the stopper in the decanter paused for the space of a heartbeat before completing that small task.

Euphemia was relieved when Manners appeared to announce that dinner was served. The Admiral offered his arm at once, but, taking it, she reached for Hawkhurst's arm also, saying laughingly that no lady would be content with one escort when she might have two.

The old gentleman proved a charming dinner companion, and Euphemia flirted with him outrageously, to his obvious gratification. Mrs. Henderson had managed very well, and, although her efforts merely added to the nausea of the master of the house, Euphemia was vastly relieved. Wetherby was certainly enjoying himself, and she began to hope his wrath might wear itself out before the meal was over. Twice, however, he slanted barbs at his grandson, the remarks so carefully worded they would have conveyed nothing to a guest unaware of the tragedy that lay between them. Euphemia, knowing more than either of them guessed, cringed at the acid behind the innocent-seeming words and could well imagine the havoc they wrought upon the apparently calm young man at the head of the table.

"I will tell you, my lord," she said laughingly, when Wetherby commented upon the excellence of the food, "that it was very swiftly and cleverly prepared by Mrs. Henderson. I doubt the Vicar served any better fare."

"We shall soon know," murmured Hawkhurst. "Our party-goers should be returning shortly."

"Oh, dear," she sighed. "I shall be in dark disgrace, I fear."

"In this house?" Wetherby gave a belittling shrug. "We do not even admit the existence of such words, dear lady." His eyes flashed a murderous anger, as he added, "And speaking of words, I must have a few with you, Hawkhurst."

"Whenever you will, sir."

There was a note of strain in the deep voice now, and Euphemia saw a faint gleam beneath the dark hair at his temples. That the Admiral was a stern disciplinarian, she did not doubt. But, however dearly he had loved little Avery, or the grandchild of his lost love, however bitterly Hawk may have disillusioned him, four years was too long to nurse so bitter a rage as this. Wetherby had suffered a more recent provocation, and a major one, obviously. Well, they must not be permitted a long talk now, not with the Admiral marshalling all his forces against a half-disabled adversary. And therefore she sighed plaintively, "I beg you will not linger too long over your port, gentlemen, for I am never in my best voice after ten o'clock."

Hawkhurst shot her a startled glance. The Admiral, turning to her eagerly, asked, "You sing, dear lady?"

"Indifferently well, I fear. But Caro Lamb taught me some little Spanish songs that might interest you." She hesitated and, summoning all her courage, said with a twinkle, "So long as you promise never to tell my brother I sang them for you."

"Capital!" Wetherby beamed. "A promise gladly given. I vow I never dreamed to spend so delightful an evening here. Entirely thanks to your lovely presence. Hawk, you are a blind fool, do you not join the ranks of Miss Buchanan's admirers!"

"I fear those admirers are soon to be shattered," drawled Hawkhurst. "For Miss Buchanan is recently betrothed, I believe."

"Indeed?" The Admiral turned a disappointed gaze upon the girl. "Who is the lucky fellow who has won your heart, may I ask?"

"I rather doubt he is the gentleman your grandson has in mind, sir," she answered demurely. And conscious of Hawkhurst's start, went on, "Colonel Tristram Leith was here today, and——"

"Leith? Now, by heaven, that's a splendid choice! A most valiant young fellow. Hear he's just been appointed to Wellington's staff. By gad, I'd be proud to have him for a grandson, I don't mind telling you!"

You, sir, should be spanked! thought Euphemia. And, not looking at Hawkhurst's blank smile, she said, "Yes, I love Tristram dearly. He is a lifelong friend. But, alas, we would not suit."

Wetherby looked positively thunderstruck. "Not . . . suit?" he gasped. "You rejected *Leith*?"

He made it sound as though she had kicked an Archbishop, and she replied mildly, "Oh, yes. And have done any time these two years. But he knows now that I shall never wed him, for what gentleman wants a lady whose heart is already given?"

From the corner of her eye she saw Hawkhurst's fingers clamp convulsively over a fold of the tablecloth. Then she was standing. The Admiral fairly jumped to assist her. She told him archly, as he bowed her from the room, that she would go to prepare her music and left them alone.

As the doors closed behind her, she leaned back against them with a sigh of relief. She had allowed them barely ten minutes. How she had found the effrontery to do so, she could not guess. Surely the old gentleman could not maul poor Hawk too badly in ten minutes . . . ?

"Well, sir?" demanded Lord Wetherby curtly. "What have you to say to that?" He puffed at his cigarillo, glared at his grandson through the resultant cloud of smoke, and waved it away impatiently.

"I was . . . unlucky at the tables," offered Hawkhurst slowly.

"Unlucky? Man, you were accursed! *Twenty-five thousand pounds?* In *three* months? My God! Are you run quite mad?" Hawkhurst remaining silent, he went on irascibly, "What is it? These endless women of yours? Oh, I heard you'd lured the Rexham girl here, shameless baggage! Her husband should take his whip to her sides—and his pistol to you, sir!"

"No woman comes here unwillingly, Grandfather."

"And no woman stays, eh? Nor could anyone blame 'em!" Hawkhurst's brows flickered slightly, and, hating this, Wetherby said a gruff, "I'm sorry. Whatever was between you and Blanche was your own affair. But . . . I just cannot—"

"Forgive me it? I understand that, sir. But, do you still believe I killed her?"

"How *dare* you ask such a thing?" The Admiral's clenched fist slammed down onto the table, sending walnuts tumbling from the bowl and wine splashing. "Of course I do not believe it! What the devil do you take me for? Not for one instant did I pay heed to such irresponsible scandal-mongering. And, if you cared for me one whit, you would know that!"

The emptiness was struck from his grandson's eyes. His

face twisted as his control broke, and in a rare display of emotion he leaned forward and said hoarsely, "*Care* for you? Sir, you know that I respect and . . . and love you, more than any man living! Do not . . . please—"

"If you loved me," the Admiral interposed with low-voiced bitterness, "you'd not have driven her from you. That you contrived her death is a filthy lie. But that you were indirectly responsible, I know too well. She came to see me just days before she ran from you. Ah, you didn't know that, I see! She showed me the—the bruises . . . the welts you dared to put on her. Lord! I could scarcely believe my own eyes. That sweet, heavenly child." He waited, his eyes pleading for a denial, but the younger man's head was sunk onto his chest, and he was silent. "For that," said Wetherby huskily, "I *never* shall forgive you. However she may have met her death, you drove her to it. And in so doing also destroyed that . . . that very dear and innocent . . . little boy." He turned away, his mouth quivering betrayingly. Hawkhurst's head bowed lower, his teeth driving into his underlip as he fought to regain his control.

"Enough . . . for that," the Admiral decreed. "The past cannot be undone, unfortunately. But the future may be guarded. Do you continue at this rate of reckless debauchery, squandering thousands on your women and at play, even your great inheritance must be gone within five years. Dominer, thank God, is entailed, so that weak-chinned whelp of Lottie's will—"

"Coleridge has chin enough and to spare, sir!" Hawkhurst's head flung upward, a resentful gleam lighting his eyes. "He has stood up to me and given me back as good as he got, I do—"

"Words! Pah! Has he ever bested you with the foils? Has he ever stood up under those famous fists of yours? He is a dandy, sir! An effeminate, dainty do-nothing who lacks the gumption to hie himself over to Spain, and—"

"No, sir! Colley is no coward. Young and striving to find himself, perhaps. A dandy, unfortunately, yes, though I do believe he will outgrow it. But he will not relinquish his plans, no matter how I hammer at him, and—"

"Oh, have done with interrupting me!" his lordship interrupted fiercely. "I came here not to be diverted by your companionship of that nincompoop, but to tell you, flat out, I'll not stand by and see you squander your fortune!"

Hawkhurst said in a quiet, controlled voice, "I am nine

years past coming of age, sir. Your pardon, but what I do with my fortune is my own affair."

"Why, you damned impertinent cub!" Pale with anger, Wetherby was on his feet, both hands flat on the table, as he rasped out, "Do you *dare* to imagine that, because your inheritance comes to you from your mother's house, I've no say in the matter? Fortune or no, it is *my* name and title that will come to you someday! And, though the Hawkhurst fortune cannot compare with the Thorndyke, I take it very ill if you presume to tell me I count for nought in this family!"

"I had no such intent, sir! Truly, I—"

"You had best *not* have! I may be only an old ex-sea dog now, but I've still a name in this country that all your indiscretions cannot mar. *I* honour the Thorndyke name, and, however little it may mean to you, I'll not see you strip both respect *and* fortune from the estate! God knows I've little use for that puppy, Bryce, but there *may* be hope for him, and I'll not stand by and watch you reduce him to inheriting a great house he'll not be able to afford to maintain!" Jabbing one finger at the silenced young man, he barked, "I give you six months, Garret. And that is five months longer than I *should* allow you!"

"And then, sir?"

"Do you continue with this insane folly, much as it would pain me, I shall have no alternative but to judge you . . . mentally incompetent." He heard Hawkhurst's gasp and clenched his fists, forcing himself to continue. "I shall take steps, therefore, to have Belmont certify you as such . . . and remove you from control." Shattered by the stunned white face, the horrified disbelief in the eyes of this young man he could not stop loving in spite of everything, he went on, "These past three years you have frittered away more funds than most men see in a lifetime—but twenty-five thousand in three months? No, sir! That is too much to be dropped at the tables, or charmed from your pockets by your flashy ladybirds! Call an end to it! Or . . . be warned! I shall!"

He snatched up his cigarillo, shoved his chair clear, and, stamping to the door, grated, "Come. I have said what I came to say, and your lovely guest has sufficient backbone to carry out her threat and refuse to sing for us. Now, *there's* the type of girl for you, Hawkhurst! Not that she'd give you a second look, of course, for she's been properly bred up, I don't doubt. Indeed, I wonder that fine brother of hers did not remove her from this notorious den of yours—page or no page!"

He flung the door wide and, having received no answer, glanced back. His grandson was still sprawled at the table, a hand across his eyes. For an instant the old gentleman's shoulders sagged. For an instant his proud head was bowed also, and he submitted to the lash of heartbreak.

Hawkhurst pulled himself together somehow, started around, and saw that dejected figure. A slow, admiring smile curved his lips. It had hurt the dear old fellow to do this. That knowledge strengthened him immeasurably. He turned quickly away and, making quite a noisy procedure of pushing back his chair, faced his now recovered grandparents with his chin as high, his eyes as bored as ever. And, sauntering to his side, thought, ". . . now *there's* the type of girl for you, Hawkhurst . . . Not that she'd give you a second look. . . ."

> "Now if you ask, what did he do
>   In such a situation?
> Why, sirs, he did what you'd do too.
>   And did it with . . . elation!"

Her heart pounding at such daring, Euphemia lifted her hands from the keys of the pianoforte and stole a glance at two astounded faces. They had both looked so strained when first they came in, but perhaps she had gone too far.

The Admiral slapped one hand on his thigh and gave vent to a howl of mirth. Hawkhurst, his brows raised, but laughter brightening his weary eyes, crossed to the piano and murmured, "You brave girl! How often have you sung that piece of naughtiness?"

"Never, I do assure you," she said, looking up at him mischievously. "Buchanan would be most shocked. But, I thought . . . well, you seemed—"

"Yes. You're an angel. It did wonderfully."

His hand came out as if to touch her cheek. His eyes held that special tenderness that made her heart twist painfully, but then the Admiral came to join them, and Hawkhurst drew back.

"By George, ma'am, but you are one in a million!" laughed Wetherby. "Fear not, we shall keep your secret. Our Wellington would enjoy hearing that!"

"Oh, he has, sir. But, not rendered by me, I promise you."

The door flew open, and cries of welcome rang out. As the family hurried in to greet the old gentleman, Euphemia detected love in Dora's eyes, anxiety in those of her sister-in-law, and an affectionate respect on the face of young Coleridge. Stephanie, straightening her hair nervously, looked flushed and quite definitely pretty. And Simon ... Dismay touched her, and she crossed to where he hesitated just inside the door. "Does your shoulder pain you, dear?"

"No, no. I feel perfectly fit, thank you. And do not seek to defend by way of attack, Mia. Where were you? I'll have you know, my girl, that, had it been any but Leith, I'd have been after you with a loaded musket, to say the least of it!"

"Then you would have wasted your shot." She squeezed the hand she held. "Foolish one, did you think I would be so gauche as to elope? Or that Tristram would be so ungallant? He offered again, and I sent him away saddened, which worries me so." Simon's face darkened. He did not like her to dwell on the possibility of casualties, and therefore she went on brightly, "Admiral Wetherby and I have been going on famously, though he's predictable as any volcano."

"So I've heard. Hawkhurst looks a trifle green about the gills. Have they come to blows already?"

"I fear so, though I—Oh dear!"

It was very plain that hostilities had broken out anew. Hawkhurst looked grim, Wetherby appeared about to explode, and Coleridge, very pale, all but trembled.

"Sent *down*?" roared the Admiral. "Why, in God's name? Or dare I hazard a guess? You were defending your cousin's 'reputation,' eh?"

Carlotta threw a shocked look at her son, and the boy reddened to the roots of his hair.

"Is that true, Colley?" Hawkhurst snapped, his face rigid.

Bryce floundered helplessly. "Well, I . . . er—"

"Oh, *no*!" wailed Lady Carlotta. "Is it *never* going to end? How much *more* grief must we all suffer?"

Those awful words seemed to hang on the air through the breathless pause that followed. Longing to scratch her, Euphemia instead slipped back to the piano bench and began softly to play the Spanish ditty she had sung earlier. The Admiral slanted a glance at her, the rageful glitter fading from his eyes. His gaze lowering, he stared, began to grin, then clapped a hand over his mouth. It was too late; all eyes had followed his. Dora went into a peal of mirth, Bryce chortled gleefully, and they were soon all convulsed.

From beneath the rich brocade of Euphemia's stylish gown,

a sturdy riding boot was clearly visible upon the pedal. She had completely forgotten the fact, but it proved heavensent, and her wry explanation that she tended to be forgetful sent Wetherby into new whoops.

Vowing he also was forgetful of his manners, he demanded that Sir Simon be presented and next commanded cheerily that they all gather around the piano "and sing together, as we was used to do!" And thus, very soon the gracious room rang to the happy sounds of music and song, and a merry time they made of it.

Hawkhurst's aching head was not helped by the music, however, and gradually he eased back from the glow cast by candles and firelight and seated himself in a shadowed corner, watching the pleasant scene. Euphemia was hidden from his view by the singers gathered about the piano, and he told himself sternly that it was just as well. She had been a friend, indeed, and, save for her, this evening would have ended very differently. But to allow his interests to wander in that direction must be the very height of folly!

To try to sleep was useless. Euphemia put on her dressing gown and curled up in the windowseat. It was very cold, and she wondered absently if it would snow tomorrow. After such an incredibly crowded day it was astonishing that she was not exhausted, but there was so much to think on. The fiasco with Sampson, Leith . . . *dear* Leith, Stephanie's sweet face, the formidable, yet lovable Admiral Wetherby—and Simon's preoccupation. The kind, patient boy was longing to be gone from here. She was torn between the desire to please him and the dread of leaving Dominer. Above all, to know that Hawk stood in danger was terrifying. If she lost him, so soon after finding him . . . She shivered.

Perhaps she could speak with Maximilian Gains. The man had ample reason for seeking vengeance, but she found it impossible to picture him so mercilessly tormenting an enemy. Unhappily, there were other men who probably had reason to hate Hawkhurst: irate husbands, men who still cherished fond memories of the lovely Blanche, men who—

She stiffened and peered incredulously at a closed chaise that loomed into view like some macabre ghost vehicle, with no clatter of hooves or grating of wheels to accompany its progress. A chill whispered down her spine, and then she saw that the chaise was not on the drive but was being driven across the lawns! She stared, petrified. There was something horribly sinister about the inexorable progress of that silent, slow-moving chaise, creeping upon Dominer in the wee hours of the morning. And, even as she watched, it vanished from the field of her vision.

Staying for neither candle nor slippers, she ran to the door, wrenched it open, and sped wildly along the corridor. A lamp set on a teakwood chest lit her way, and she ran on to the next window. The draperies were closed. Grasping them with hands that trembled, she opened them a crack and peeped out.

The ghost chaise had halted at the far end of the North Wing, and two figures—a tall man and a woman muffled to the ears in cloak and hood—had alighted and were struggling to drag something from inside the vehicle. That they could barely manage their large burden was apparent, and, having at last succeeded in removing it, they bore it with difficulty to the unoccupied section of the great mansion, where Hawk was wont to entertain his "personal friends." Not once during their efforts did the conspirators appear to converse. Their movements were sly and furtive, and it was very apparent that they went in dread of making the slightest sound. At the last instant, as though he sensed that they were watched, the man darted a look up at the windows. The moonlight, pale though it was, struck his face. Euphemia's heart sank. It was the very person she had suspected, yet so hoped it would not be. For the moonlight revealed the tense features of Lord Coleridge Bryce.

Dominer was early astir the following morning, as preparations for the afternoon's Musicale got under way. At nine o'clock, Hawkhurst stood before the window in his aunt's bedchamber, a hand in his pocket, and one shoulder propped against the wall. He frowned into the gardens below him, then turned to meet Carlotta's bland smile and said, "Go to her head? Why should it, ma'am? Stephie's no different now than ever she was."

Carlotta settled back more comfortably against her pillows and, having sipped her chocolate daintily, agreed, "Why, of course she is not, love. And so I said to Dora. 'Then why,' says she in her clever way, 'why do the beaux all cluster round her now? And why was she gone from the party for half the evening (though where I cannot guess) and come back looking downright moonstruck?' Not that *I* would listen to such stuff, you know, Garret. Any more than my dear Colley would listen to those who said such dreadful things about . . . you."

He put up his brows at her mockingly and knew he should pay no heed to her prattling. But Stephie *had* seemed rather jumpy last evening, now that he came to think about it. And there *was* a difference about her of late—an inner light and yet a hint of sorrow, withal. By heaven! If some wet-behind-the-ears young Buck was daring to attempt to fix his interest with her . . .

Carlotta, sorting through her morning pile of correspondence, fluttered a sly glance up at him and, seeing his eyes darkened and his jaw set into that horrid hard look so often turned upon poor Colley, knew she had him and returned smugly to the letter in her hand.

"Was that all you wished to say to me, Aunt?"

"What, dear? Did I ask you to come, then? I do not seem to recall . . . Oh! How clever of you to remind me, for I had quite forgot. Guess! Only *guess* who I met at the rectory last night!" She paused breathlessly and, his eyes holding only that familiar look of polite boredom, did not wait for his response but divulged triumphantly, *"Mrs. Hughes-Dering!"*

"What, old Greg Hughes' sister? How very dull for you! The woman was ever a rabid social climber as I—"

"Social . . . climber!" Carlotta fairly clutched for her vinaigrette and, having revived herself, gasped out, "She is a Leader of Society! A Power to be reckoned with in Town. Or in Bath! All evening I catered to and smiled at and fawned upon the odious old hag. And finally she agreed—yes, she actually *agreed* to come to my Musicale!"

"Good God!" he uttered, aghast.

"Yes," she nodded, misinterpreting his reaction. "I do not doubt that she knows your dear Grandpapa will be there, and the Buchanans also. Such a coup! Though I will admit I all but went down on my knees to her!"

"You did?" he grinned. "A little too much wine, dear Aunt?"

She gave a small shriek and denied that alcohol had ever touched her lips. "Which is more than could be said for my poor sister-in-law! One glass of ratafia, and Dora is positively tipsy."

Hawkhurst's grin widened, for he was well aware of the fine Madeira that filled Dora's pretty Chinese decanter. "You are the essence of virtue," he acknowledged, sauntering towards

the door. "And, if your saintliness will stretch so far as to endure Monica Hughes-Dering for above two minutes, you will
have my admiration, ma'am, if not my company. I shall see
you when the affair is over, and do trust all goes well."

"*Hawkhurst!*" Her scream brought his hand from the
doorlatch as though it had been red hot, and he spun about,
crouching slightly, eyes narrowed, and every inch of his frame
poised for combat. Nothing had changed in the luxurious bedchamber, however, and, straightening, he said an irked, "Gad,
madam! What ails you? I fancied three assassins with drawn
swords at my back!"

"What did you mean?" Carlotta whimpered. "You *do* intend
to come? You must! It is vital! For, if Mrs. Hughes-Dering re-
ceives you, perhaps others will."

"She is far more like to give me the cut direct. The old lady
loathes me, and well you know it. I've no objection to your entertaining her, but I refuse to be set down in my own home!"

Carlotta sat straighter, leaning forward as she launched into
an impassioned plea that he oblige her in "this one teensy instance" and, seeing the steel unyielding in his eyes, pointed out
that he owed it to his poor sister. "For years," she moaned,
"we have lived here as though stranded in a desert oasis. Oh,
I know the local people have taken pity on Stephie, but—
consider, Hawk! If my Musicale is well attended and a success,
we might, we just *might* begin to be accepted again!"

He moved back to the bed and stood frowning down at her.
She looked so desperately anxious, her hands tightly gripped,
her eyes fixed imploringly on him, and his expression softened. "If it is this important to you, my dear, I shall open the
London House, and you can—"

"Oh, can I not! A grand reception we would receive in
Town, with every door closed to us! I would stand no more
chance of getting Stephanie a voucher to Almack's than of being invited to Carlton House!"

"To the contrary." The familiar cynicism slipped back into
his eyes. "You would merely have to affect an abused manner,
and the *ton* would fairly crush you to its bosom! More victims
of my savage infamy! Lord! You'd be so smothered with solicitude, you'd likely become reigning Toasts."

It was a possibility, and she considered it carefully. But, "It
will not serve," she wailed. "Stephanie would die before she'd
permit any criticism of you! Oh, Hawkhurst, this is our one
chance—don't you see?"

"If you believe that, believe also that you will fare a great deal better *sans* my presence!"

"But, no! If you do not attend, Mrs. Hughes-Dering is sure to put it about that you were ashamed to face her."

"Much I care for that. She may think what she chooses. Now, resign yourself, I beg, dear lady. I shall gladly stand the huff, but suffer through a combination of Monica Hughes-Dering *and* the Broadbent girl's cacophonous spasms . . . ?" He gave a snort of repugnance, "Be dashed if I will!" and again trod towards the door.

My lady promptly burst into tears. Hawkhurst lengthened his stride and cravenly wrenched the door open. Her sobs were heartrending. He gritted his teeth and swore softly at the ceiling, but then turned back again. Even the sound of the closing door did not shut off the waterworks, as he'd fervently hoped. Scowling, he retraced his steps until he stood reluctantly beside her. Still she wept, her slender shoulders shaking.

"Oh, for heaven's sake!" he growled. "Madam! Aunt . . . ? Devil take it, you make me out the complete villain!" He sat on the bed, pulled her into his arms and, patting her shoulder, pleaded, "Do not, I beg of you! Do not. Oh, very well, blast it all! I'll pay court to the preposterous woman!"

Dabbing at her eyes and sniffing in a most unladylike fashion, Carlotta blinked up at him and choked, "You—you . . . will? And . . . will be n-nice to her?"

"If you insist." His smile was rueful, but his eyes very kind. She thought suddenly that he really was a charming young man when he chose to be and, wrapping him in a hug, said joyously, "Oh, Garret, thank you! Thank you! We shall see our little girl achieve a brilliant match yet!"

Wiping teardrops from his new jacket as he walked down the hall, Hawkhurst was undeceived. If Carlotta thought of Stephanie at all, it was the least of her concerns. Her main hope was to fight her own way back into the favour of the Society that had rejected them all. His steps slowed. Poor soul, he'd never guessed she missed that life so much. And with a pang he admitted at last that he missed it himself, that to walk into White's and be looked upon without the total revulsion that had greeted his final appearance in that venerable club would be a heady triumph indeed—and, of course, utterly impossible. He sighed. Still, if Carlotta so hungered for it, and if it would make Stephanie happy, the Countess of Carden was loyal still and would help, he was sure. And certainly Tristram's erratic but noble father, Lord Kingston Leith, could be of assistance.

Walking on, his face became grim and hard. Carlotta was right. Stephanie deserved a brilliant match, and would have one. But if some slippery young Buck *was* courting her without daring to have begged his leave . . . may God help him!

❧ *Chapter 12* ☙

"I'd be very much obliged to you, Buck," murmured Coleridge, his eyes upon Stephanie as she stood at the brink of the hill, looking down upon Lord Gains' fine old home. "I shouldn't be above twenty minutes at the outside, but I really must have a word with Chilton. He's not quite up to the knocker since he came home, you know, and I'd . . . er, there's something I've to discuss with him. Quite important."

"You do not really expect him to confess that his brother is seeking to murder your cousin, do you?" asked Buchanan mildly.

Lord Coleridge swung to face him. "The deuce! You knew then?"

"Manners showed me the gun they found. It's a beautiful weapon. Do you think it belongs to Gains?"

"Lord, no! Or I'd not go near them. But Chil is quite fond—that is to say . . . to be honest, he dotes on his brother. And Hawk, well, he's got such a temper, but they're both jolly good fellows, Simon. They simply must not go out! Too well matched you see—suicidal!"

"I understand. Go along with you. I'll take care of Miss Hawkhurst."

With a relieved grin and a murmur of thanks, Coleridge swung into the saddle again. He was down the slope at a speed that made Buchanan gasp, taking the tricky jump over the ditch in neck-or-nothing fashion and galloping on towards the distant house.

Buchanan heard Stephanie move to his side, and her hand slipped into his. "What a rare opportunity, dearest," she said tenderly.

He tightened his clasp on her fingers but without turning muttered, "He trusted me with you. What a treacherous rogue I am become."

Fear, her constant companion these days, chilled her more than the breath of the wind. Buchanan detected her shudder and at once threw her up into the saddle and rode beside her to a copse of trees beside an old boundary wall. When he lifted her down, her arms slipped about his neck. Her face was raised to his, her eyes very soft, but he put her from him and turned away. "Stephie," he said wretchedly, "I . . . I must tell you—"

"I know. Hal Archer says Kent may travel the day after tomorrow. What did you think, my dear? That you would break it to me gently? Oh, Simon! Can such news *ever* be broken gently?"

He said nothing, and she came up behind him to stroke his sleeve and ask with sad longing, "Why do we allow it? Why must we let . . . her . . . ruin our every chance for happiness?" She ran quickly before him and, placing her hands on his chest, said with sudden intensity, "Would she give you a divorce, do you suppose? Hawk is very rich, and I know he would help, for his own wife was much the same type. If we paid her . . . lots . . ."

His expression halted her hopeful utterance, and he shook his head, his lips tight. "Ernestine likes being Lady Simon Buchanan. She likes Buchanan Court and the house I bought her on Grosvenor Square. And she despises notoriety. But, even if she did not, do you fancy me the type of ramshackle ne'er-do-well who would go to your brother and beg to be bought from a marriage?"

He led her to the wall, and they sat close together, huddled against it, out of the wind. Stephanie noted the grim line of Simon's mouth, the eyes that avoided her own so steadily, and, knowing she must fight for her chance at happiness, sighed, "Then we both face a life of loneliness. Only, you at least, have your children."

He said bitterly, "One of whom is my own, I do believe."

Tears came into her eyes. She could not speak, but leaned her cheek against his sleeve in mute sympathy. Buchanan did not dare to look down at that fair head and, staring at the ragged trees, managed to say with assumed lightness, "Now tell me of yourself and your plans for the future."

For a moment she did not move. Then, sitting up and folding her hands in her lap, she answered slowly, "People say I am gentle, Simon. Perhaps what they mean is that I am conformable. I only know I am . . . not very brave."

He scanned her sad, sweet face, the fine curve of the brow, the soft blowing curls, and argued tenderly, "Of course you are. Euphemia says—"

"Dear Euphemia," she interjected and, taking up a small stick, began to poke at the earth with it. "And oh, how I envy her. To have travelled: To have seen far-away places and peoples, and such a diversity of customs."

"You would not be averse to travelling a good deal?" he asked, recalling Ernestine's indignant refusal to accompany him to Spain.

"Good gracious, no! I love England dearly, but I long to see the rest of the world. To be able to do so beside one's love must be—" The stick snapped under her fingers. Casting it away, she said, "That, alas, is denied to me. Some ladies, losing the man they love, find the strength to go on living and perhaps, in time, love again. But I have always known that I would only ever love once."

"Do not," he begged, his voice low with misery. "You will marry."

"No. Not now. Which is sad, because I think I might have made quite a good mother."

Her calmness was beginning to frighten him, and searching her face, he demanded, "What do you mean? Tell me!"

"There is only one answer, for I couldn't endure to grow old and—"

"My dear God! Stephie! What are you saying? You do not . . . you *cannot* mean you . . . you would—"

"Kill myself? No, foolish boy." She reached up to caress lovingly his cheek and murmur, "I shall enter a convent, where I can be of some use, but shall not have to watch other ladies and . . . their children . . . around me."

His face drawn and frantic, he grasped her by the arms. "*No!* You must *not*! There are those for whom it is the perfect answer. But, not you! You were made for loving and cherishing, for motherhood! Stephanie! Promise me, I beg of you. *Promise* me that you will not."

"On the day you leave," she said, in a remote but resolute voice, "I leave also. I could not bear to live on at Dominer. To see the rooms where you once were, the paths we have walked and ridden together." Her voice cracked a little, but she finished, "Never grieve so, my darling. At least my life will not have been lived to no purpose."

He gazed into her eyes for a long moment, then bowed his head into his hands and, wracked with anguish and guilt, knowing there was no way out, no possible solution for them, groaned, "My God! What have I done?"

Stephanie touched his curling hair, love rendering all other considerations of little moment. "You have shown me how beautiful life could be . . ." She paused a second, then, playing her last card, breathed, ". . . how beautiful it *still* might be, if only . . . Simon, beloved . . . Take me with you!"

"What?" His head flung upward and looking at her in stark disbelief, he gasped, "No! And . . . *no!* Never! What manner of crudity do you fancy me?"

Her lips a kiss away, her eyes pools of yearning, she murmured, "I know only what *I* am. If Ernestine loved you, or if you loved her, I would let you go, and if I must die of grief—so be it. But she does *not* love you and has given you only sorrow. Simon, my own, take me with you."

White-faced, appalled, he drew away from her. "You do not know what you ask of me! You cannot realize what our life would be like!"

"Paget did it! He ran off with Wellington's own sister-in-law, when she already had four children! Yet you still respect him!"

"Yes, I do. But was there *ever* such a scandal! The dreadful things that were said of the poor lady in the newspapers! And Hookey for years deprived of one of his finest cavalry officers."

"Yet they survived it! People forgave them—even Wellington. Oh, my love, it is our only hope. Unless—" She scanned him in new anxiety. "Would your career be ruined? Totally?"

"I don't think so. I doubt he'd boot me out, not now. He needs trained officers too badly. And Colborne would stand by me, I know—Devil take it! What am I saying? No, Stephie, I cannot! I love you too much to—Oh, sweetheart, don't you see? Even if I agreed to disgrace you so shamefully, Hawk saved my life! It would be utterly reprehensible!"

"If you really loved me . . ." she faltered, her lips quivering pathetically.

"How can you say that?" He drew her to him and, resting his cheek against her fragrant hair, groaned, "I adore you, heaven help me. And you know it."

"And yet," tears began to creep down her cheeks, ". . . care more about your pride, than whether I must dwell in a convent for the rest of my . . . days."

Tormented, Buchanan's lips silenced those heartbroken words. And when their bittersweet embrace ended, she whispered, "My darling, say you will at least think about it. Promise me!"

He shook his head desperately. Approaching hoofbeats announced the return of Bryce. With a gasp of relief, Buchanan moved back, but Stephanie clung to him, weeping, "Simon, *promise!* Oh, beloved, do not break my poor heart . . . like this."

Lieutenant Sir Simon Buchanan ignored the dictates of his own heart and strove valiantly.

It was a doomed effort.

At about the same moment that Stephanie was working her feminine wiles against the hapless Buchanan, Lady Bryce sang to herself and bustled down the hall for one last check of the music room. Not that she expected to find it one whit changed from the calm tranquillity it had radiated an hour since, but merely to gaze fondly around the gracious chamber, imagining it crowded with her proud and influential guests. The mellow notes of the grandfather clock were striking twelve as she flung open the door, only to check with a strangled squawk and stand as one paralyzed. A veritable sea of greenery met her eyes: potted palms, ferns, and juniper were everywhere, and through a screen of fronds, servants moved busily about. A familiar aroma assailing her nostrils, she found her voice to shriek, "*Dora!* Whatever are you about?"

Hawkhurst, attracted by his aunt's pained yowl, wandered up to grin appreciatively at the verdant panorama. Mrs. Graham hove nervously into view from having placed a large aspidistra plant on a stand beside the harp. Her sudden movement sent the plant toppling, and, wringing her hands as she eyed the debris, she stammered, "I—I was only—"

"Good God! The room looks like a jungle! And . . . what in

the name of—An *unclad male*! In my Musicale? Have you entirely lost your wits?"

"It . . . it's only Adonis. I thought, perhaps—"

"And near lifesize! Oh, I shall suffer a spasm! I know it!"

"Come now, ma'am," said Hawkhurst, turning from his amused contemplation of the luxuriant indoor garden. "I'm sure that at her time of life Mrs. Hughes-Dering has seen an unclad—"

"Hawk . . . hurst . . . !" cried his Aunt Carlotta awfully.

He chuckled, motioned to a lackey, and together they took up the shameless Greek and bore him into the hall, Dora trotting anxiously after them.

"What the devil have you there?" the Admiral enquired, wandering down the stairs, quizzing glass levelled.

"Adonis," grinned Hawkhurst. *"Sans bienséance!"*

"Of course. So . . . ?"

"Aunt Carlotta feels that clothes make the man, sir."

"Do you suppose," began Dora hopefully.

"No, I do not!" Hawkhurst laughed. "My clothes would not suit. And I'll not insult him by swathing him in a sheet!"

"Oh, pray *do* put him down, Garret!" she pleaded, tripping over his foot in her agitation and almost bringing them down, all three.

"Fine-looking chap," said the Admiral, viewing the statue critically. "Where'd you come by him?"

"Lord knows. Miss Buchanan! Hide your eyes, ma'am! This is not fit sight for a single lady!"

Euphemia, wearing a pale-green, long-sleeved gown and with a jade band holding back her ringlets, was such a sight as to bring a softness to his own eyes, however, wherefore he turned his attention to the relocation of Adonis beside a tall display cabinet.

"After the Battle of Fuentes de Oñoro, Mr. Hawkhurst," imparted Euphemia serenely, "I saw—"

"Spare my blushes," he smiled, unable to resist another swift glance at her vivacious countenance.

"By George! Were you at Fuentes, m'dear?" the Admiral asked, advancing upon her eagerly.

"Will someone *please* send some footmen to remove all these plants?" wailed Carlotta from the music room. "I vow our guests shall not be able to see one another in this rain forest!"

"Oh, dear," mourned Dora. "I had thought it looked quite nice."

"So did I, love," Hawkhurst soothed, sending the imperturbable lackey to aid Carlotta. "And besides, no one would have noticed if I fell asleep."

She giggled. "You would not dare! Scoundrel! I must go and help!" She drew back her shoulders and quoted in a voice of martyrdom, " 'Here am I who did the deed. Turn your sword on me.' "

Wetherby rolled exasperated eyes at the ceiling. Hawkhurst shot a meaningful glance at Euphemia, and she immediately slipped her hand in Mrs. Graham's arm and, all but recoiling from the overpowering stench of her "perfume," said, "Dear ma'am, I would like so much to have a small cose with you. Can you spare me a moment or two?"

"Sweet child, I could spare you a month!"

"Does Miss Buchanan intend to stay at Dominer for that length of time," said Wetherby, "nothing will drag me away!"

Euphemia stayed to drop him a curtsey. "You are too kind, sir. But we are promised to my aunt in Bath. And Dr. Archer informs me that Kent may travel on Friday."

The ladies walked away, arms entwined, and the Admiral muttered, "Then I shall plan on leaving also. Ain't often—" The cutting words ceased. His grandson, he perceived, had quite obviously forgotten his existence and was watching the ladies climb the stairs, an unguarded expression on his face that struck the old gentleman mute. He followed that gaze thoughtfully and, after a moment, observed, "She has brought the laughter back into this house." He turned his shrewd eyes back to Hawkhurst. "She is herself like a bright sunbeam. Do you not agree?"

"Sunbeam . . . ?" murmured Hawkhurst, half to himself. "I think of her more as the light from a candle." His voice lowered so that the Admiral had to lean closer to discern the words. "One . . . small candle."

Wetherby purely disliked quotations, if only because his daughter's habit so irritated him, but, searching his memory for the rest of that wise old Chinese maxim, felt a stirring of unease. Did the boy really fancy himself to be "walking forever in darkness"? Hawkhurst flashed a guilty look at him and, realizing he had spoken an inner thought aloud, hurried away, his face reddening.

For a moment the Admiral frowned rather blankly at the

stairs. Then, more troubled than he would have cared to admit, he wandered off in search of Miss Buchanan's page.

"Indeed not." Mrs. Graham's voice was muffled behind the great pile of papers, periodicals, fashion pages, odds and ends of fabric of all shades and sizes, and innumerable lengths of embroidery silk which she had cleared from a chair in her large bedchamber, in order to enable Euphemia to sit down. "Colley is the dearest boy, but—Oh, drat that stuff!" And, having stooped three times to recover one wisp of yarn, she abandoned the entire attempt, allowed the rest of her collection to follow it to the floor, and, dusting off her hands triumphantly, said, "Well, that's all shipshape! Now—" She stepped over the debris, "do sit down, my dear." She wriggled her way into the approximately eight inches of free space on the littered sofa and beamed at her amused guest. "Whatever were we talking about?"

"Colley. He shows a deal of promise, I think, and will doubtless acquit himself well when he inherits Dominer."

"Much he cares for that! The boy would far rather see Hawk happily wed and with sons of his own to inherit the title and estates. All he wants for himself—" Dora bit her lip and said quickly, "How sorry he will be to see you leave, for he has taken quite a fancy to your brother."

"I suspected as much. But to be truthful I would leave with an easier mind did I know who was behind these murderous attacks upon your nephew. I am—we all are—deeply in his debt, ma'am, and for Mr. Hawkhurst to stand in such danger causes me great anxiety. Only last night I thought to see something I could not but think most suspicious." She noted her companion's guilty start, and her heart sank.

"You d-did?" faltered Dora. "Er, what was it?"

"A closed chaise, driven straight across the lawn at dead of night! Never, ma'am, have I seen so furtive a pair! They pulled up by the North Wing and dragged forth . . . a body!"

"Oh, no, no! Indeed, it was not! I—" Dora squeaked with fright, clapped a hand over her lips, sent a cushion and two periodicals tumbling, and was still.

"You?" cried Euphemia, quite cast down by the success of her small trap. "Oh, Dora! Do you dislike Hawk, too?"

"Dislike Hawk? Why, he was the sweetest child, and—Oh dear! Colley will be so cross. I have let the cat out of the bag with a vengeance! Dear girl, will you *promise* to keep our secret?"

Euphemia blinked. It did not sound like a murder plot. "Secret?"

"Come, I will show you. And now I am getting quite excited, for no one has ever caught us before!" She jumped to her feet and, grasping Euphemia by the hand, trotted merrily off, whispering to herself, with her shawl gradually sliding, until Euphemia caught and replaced it.

Along to the end of the corridor they went, up two pairs of stairs, a half-turn to the right and along another hall, colder, but just as impressively furnished as that of the main house. They were in the North Wing now, and suddenly Dora threw a door open. A great dining room stretched before them. Three chandeliers hung in their covers like giant inverted mushrooms from a splendidly carven ceiling; the table, flanked by innumerable chairs, was at least thirty feet long, and enormous mirrors in gilded frames hung between each of the six long windows and above the fireplace. Dora beckoned eagerly and tripped across the slightly dusty parquet floors. A door far at the left side was closed, and she knocked: three spaced hard knocks, and three swift light ones. Fumbling movements could be heard inside, then the door opened to reveal Lord Coleridge clad in a very dirty smock over corduroy breeches. "Wherever have you been?" he grumbled. "I thought—" And he stopped, his face comical in its dismay as he saw Euphemia.

"You were perfectly right," trilled his Aunt merrily. "Miss Buchanan caught us last night. We must throw ourselves on her mercy, for she believes us to have been carrying bodies into the house, Colley, my love!"

She was drawing the girl inside as she spoke, and, with Bryce's shocked *"Bodies?"* ringing in her ears, Euphemia looked around her. She stood in a large anteroom. Sheer curtains at the windows provided privacy, yet allowed the light to pour in. There was very little furniture, only two small armchairs and a table littered with bottles, cans, pots, knives, brushes, and rags. To one side a long bench held a partially painted and ferocious clay dragon, and all about it were many figures and carvings in wood, stone, and clay. On the other side of the room stood several easels, and many canvases were propped against the walls. Between clay and oils, the air positively reeked, and at last Euphemia understood why Dora affected such very strong perfume. "My goodness!" she cried, vastly relieved. "Why, how very clever you both are!"

The conspirators promptly embraced one another. "Me first!" cried Dora like an eager child. "Please may I, Colley?"

He bowed gallantly, and Euphemia was led through the weirdest display she had ever beheld. Dora's art came in all sizes and in every shape imaginable. Exclaiming dutifully over a squidgy blob with two apparent brooms protruding from its middle, Euphemia did not dare attempt to identify it, but her careful remarks were evidently satisfactory, for Dora clasped her hands in an ecstasy of delight. "And which one," she asked breathlessly, ". . . do you like best?"

Euphemia scanned the contorted collection and fixed upon the one object she felt safe with. "The—" she began, nodding to the dragon, but, chancing to catch a glimpse of Colley over his Aunt's shoulder, was saved in the nick of time by his frantic gestures, and corrected hurriedly, "Oh, dear, how difficult it is, for they are all so very interesting. Won't you tell me about . . . this one?"

"Sampson?" laughed Dora, placing a fond hand upon her maligned creation. "So you recognized him, did you! Naughty doggie! On one of his raids, of course!"

"You've certainly caught the spirit of the beast," Euphemia admitted, biting her lips to restrain a grin. "How Lord Gains would like to have this."

"Oh, no! For no one else has ever seen any of it! Save for the one piece I bribed Parsley to pop into the music room."

Euphemia's mind's eye at once engaged in a fast review of the adornments of that charming room. Her uncertainty becoming apparent, Bryce said, "The gentleman who so shocked my mother."

"*Adonis . . . ?*" Euphemia gasped. "But . . . but he's not at all like . . ." She gestured feebly at the grotesques.

"Well, he was one of my earliest efforts," Dora apologized, fortunately misunderstanding the flabbergasted look on the visitor's features. "I do think I've come quite a way since then, if I say so myself. Which I shouldn't, of course. But I can tell you now that what you saw Colley and me hauling up here so 'furtively' in the dead of night was a piece of stone for my new project. Not," her eyes sparkled mischievously, "a body, my love! Did you see this one?" She indicated an apparent banana pierced with many toothpicks. "I was shaping the clay when I sneezed and most of my hairpins fairly whizzed into it, but I do think it adds to the effect, don't you? I simply covered them with clay, you see . . ." Euphemia's eyes were rather misted, and she dared not look at Colley, the mischief in the boy's face having already almost proved her undoing. She was spared commenting on the "effect" as Dora added blithely, "Enough of me! Now, Colley will show you which of us is the *real* artist!"

The youth staunchly denied this, but his aunt had spoken truthfully. In only a moment Euphemia apprehended that here was a great talent. The first work Coleridge shyly presented for inspection was dark: country folk beginning to drift homeward from a fair, the moon high in the sky, and flares being lit in the booths behind them. At first, the people seemed to be indistinguishable from the background, but they gradually materialized to such incredible reality that she could all but reach out and touch them. The next painting was of a storm and a lonely sheepdog herding his flock, with wind blowing the snow into a great vortex about them, the cold seeming to creep from the canvas, and the dog's devotion vividly apparent. Many paintings followed, each seemingly better than the last, until, flushed with pleasure, Coleridge led her to the easel at which he had been working when she arrived. It was a nearly completed portrait of Hawkhurst. The boy had painted it with love, capturing the strength of the man, yet managing also to show the humorous quirk to the shapely lips and the smile in the grey eyes. He had chosen to portray Hawkhurst in his uniform, a Light Dragoon. Euphemia stood entranced, staring and staring, until her eyes grew blurred and the lump in her throat choked her. She did not hear Colley leave, but when she looked up, blinking away her tears, he was gone, and Dora's pudgy little hands were clasped, her face ecstatic. "Oh, my dear," she said tremulously. "You *do* love him! I was sure you did!"

Euphemia tried to speak, but could not, so instead walked into those outreaching arms, and when she had been kissed and urged to the nearest chair, she dried her tears and asked the reason for all the secrecy. "For you both have such really astonishing gifts! Hawkhurst would be so proud!"

"Alas," Dora said ruefully, "I fear he would instead be furious! He never has had anything but scorn for poor Colley's ambitions. And, if he knew I had encouraged him, and spent such a great deal of money upon our hobbies . . . Oh, my!"

"But he could not know how much talent you both possess! If he saw——"

"Oh! I would not dare! Although we do plan to surprise him. Someday. When we are ready."

"You are ready *now*! Oh, Dora, would you have your showing before we leave? I should so love to see Hawk's face! And the Admiral! They will be totally astounded!"

Having said which, she must again be hugged and thanked for her dear kindness and asked suddenly, "Does he know you care for him?"

Euphemia blushed and looked down with a strange new shyness. "I think . . . he does."

"And are you willing to forgive his dark past? His terrible sins, his women, his reputation?"

"I do not believe Hawk has ever—*could* ever—hurt anyone so savagely," she answered defensively. "And as to his women, why, he was cast out by society. Lonely . . . striking back, perhaps."

"Perhaps. For if ever there was a man meant to love and be loved, and instead . . ." Dora heaved a regretful sigh.

"But, if you all knew about her and Mount, why did no one tell the Admiral?"

"We did not know, until it was too late. But when I learned of it, I tried to summon the courage to tell Papa. After the tragedy, he was so heartbroken and so enraged with poor Garret that I actually did manage to write a letter."

"You did? But how splendid! Whatever did Lord Wetherby say?"

Dora gave a helpless little moue. "I never sent it. The old gentleman suffered a seizure, and the physician who attended him obviously held Hawkhurst to blame. The rumours—oh! they were thick and terrible then, I do assure you, and the doctor believed them all. He warned Garret that any more grief, any slightest shock, could prove fatal." She shrugged. "I did not dare post my letter. Hal Archer says Papa is healthy as a horse, and it was likely simple dyspepsia, but Garret idolizes his grandfather and has flatly forbidden any of us to speak of it."

Euphemia said tenderly, "How very typical of him. But what a frightful nightmare it must have been. Was that when his hair began to grey?"

"Yes. And I wonder it is not white as snow! The wicked newspaper articles and insinuations! The way he received the cut direct wherever he went. And all the while he was nigh distracted with grief for dear little Avery. I was quite sure he would wind up in Bedlam, poor soul, and, even though he did not, it has changed him—beyond belief." She paused and went on with slow reluctance, "I . . . must be honest with you, sweet child. I cannot think of any lady better suited to be Garret's bride, and I wish—oh, with all my heart—that you might lead him back to life, and love. But . . ." She shook her head doubtfully.

Catching a flying hairpin, Euphemia stared down at it for a moment, then asked, "You think I have no chance at all? You think he has forgotten how to live, and love?"

"Oh, pray do not mistake. Gary is too much of a man to, er, have given up, er—"

"The companionship of ladies?" prompted Euphemia gravely.

"Exactly so. But he chooses the type of . . . ah . . . lady, who will be easy to discard. I hear he is generous, very generous, to his *chères amies*. But to love again would be to make himself vulnerable, don't you see? So I think he has locked his heart away, poor dear, as if in some impregnable fortress. That he will never again give anyone the chance to hurt him so terribly."

Her heart aching for him, Euphemia was silent but could not suppose it to be truth. Dora, with her highly romantic nature, saw only the carefree youth, his reputation blackened, his life blasted. And, to her gentle soul, the inevitable result must be a shrinking withdrawal from any possible repetition of such heartbreak. Euphemia, more worldly wise, clung to her faith in Hawk's strength. He was not the man to allow one buffet from Fate to shatter him so. However Blanche may have enraged and humiliated him, the only way she had been able to really wound him must have been through his little son. Beyond doubting, that loss must have been searing, but many people had suffered such tragedy, and it had not destroyed them. Perhaps Hawkhurst *was* reluctant to love again, but, if so, it was for some reason other than fear of being hurt.

"Lord Wetherby encourages the little fellow, Simon," Euphemia pointed out as she seated herself in the parlour adjoining her bedchamber. "But as for his own sake, I simply cannot allow Kent to behave as though he were part of the family. Poor little fellow, he is very good and does not mean to overstep the bounds. He is so sensitive and was quite shattered when I spoke to him. Such a problem, is it not?"

"I'm sure you are right," murmured Buchanan absently.

Euphemia glanced at him. He stood with his back towards her, gazing out of the window towards the east and distant London. "Evil creature," she teased. "You've heard not one word of it all. Own up!"

He at once whirled around and begged her pardon. "I fear my thoughts were elsewhere. Please tell me what you said, and I shall be all ears."

"No, no. It was of little import." He was rarely so distracted, however, and with a twinge of guilt she said repentantly, "How thoughtless I am. You were violently opposed to our coming here and yet have not once either given me the scold I warrant or raised the least complaint through all these many delays. You are too good, Simon. But I promise you we shall leave the day after tomorrow." And she had to force a smile to hide the terrible sinking of her spirits.

He stared at her for a moment, then turned back to the window once more and muttered, "I wish you would not place me on so high a pedestal, Mia. Someday you will be forced to admit that I am a most ordinary fellow, with perhaps more than my share of failings."

"Ten times more, in fact! For, although you are occasionally a fairly satisfactory brother, I consider your taste in horses— and women—thoroughly execrable." She had spoken with a laugh in her voice and was dismayed to see his head lower a trifle, while, instead of an indignant response, there was silence. "I shall miss our new friends," she went on hurriedly. "Even Carlotta. And as for Stephanie—Oh, Simon, I am so very grateful to you for squiring her about as you have done. I know it must have been a bother, and—"

"Not at all," he said in a polite, if strained, tone. "She is a . . . a pleasant girl and most sweetly-natured."

"Yes. And you must admit my meddling has been to some purpose. I know it is presumptuous to say, but she *is* prettier with her hair dressed so. Do you not agree?"

"What? Oh, I suppose so." Desperate to change the subject, he swung around. "*Must* we go to that blasted Musicale this afternoon?"

"I fear we must, or Lady Bryce will be very hurt." She stood and crossed to his side, saying contritely, "I am really sorry, love. Because I have found such a great joy here, I completely forgot what a total bore it must be for—"

"You found . . . *what?*" He gripped her shoulders, scanning her face intently. "Do you refer to this beautiful estate? Or your new friends? Or—" And he stopped, astounded by the droop of her lashes, and the blush that strained her cheeks. "Good . . . God! *Hawkhurst?*"

She nodded and admitted with a shy smile, "Your foolish sister, who was so sure she would know her 'gentil and strong' love at first sight. Whereas it was, in fact, almost two weeks before she knew that her heart was given at last."

Stunned, Buchanan released her. "Hawkhurst!" he muttered. "Of all the men you might have had!"

Anxiety seized Euphemia at this, for she loved him dearly, and, if he really objected, it would be dreadful. "Are you terribly shocked, dearest? He is not what people say of him, I know it, for I could not love such a man."

"Has he offered?"

"Of course not! And would never be so wanting for manners, as to do so without first obtaining your approval."

She had the oddest impression that Simon winced, but in the next second he was directing his boyish grin at her and asking, "And if I refused it, should you give him up?"

"I would be . . . very grieved," she evaded worriedly. "But, dearest, you do not really *despise* him, do you?"

He sighed and, sitting down in the windowseat, stretched out his legs and stared at his boots. "No. In fact, I cannot help but be drawn to the fellow. But your way with him would not be easy, you know. People would say—" He gave a little snort of cynicism and, to her utter bewilderment, suddenly burst into a shout of laughter. "What strange tricks Fate plays on us," he said breathlessly, "does she not?"

Euphemia agreed readily, vastly relieved that he had taken it so well, and far more willing to endure his raillery than his anger.

Not until much later did she realize what it was that her brother had actually found so bitterly humorous.

By three o'clock, the music room was commencing to be comfortably filled. Outside the weather was hazy and frigid, to compensate for which Lady Bryce had ordered the fires at each end of the large room banked high, and between the warmth, the congenial company, and the several mild flirtations that were under way, the room fairly hummed with lighthearted talk and laughter.

Superb in a robe of ecru lace over blond satin, Carlotta received her guests in the great hall, her nephew beside her. She was aglow with delight at so splendid a turnout in spite of the inclement weather and almost equally pleased by Hawkhurst's appearance. There was no denying the boy was blessed with a splendid physique: his long-tailed, bottle-green jacket was as if moulded to those broad shoulders; the pale green and cream stripes of his waistcoat could offend none; his cravat, which an awed Colley had advised her was known as the *trône d'amour*, had won several admiring glances from the gentlemen; and those magnificent legs were set off to admiration by pantaloons that might allow him to sit down, were he cautious.

The Reverend James Dunning and his wife passed into the music room, to be followed by the Taylor Mannerings and their pretty daughter, Margaret, whom Carlotta had long known to cherish a *tendre* for Hawk. Incredible as it seemed, almost all those invited had arrived, and when Lord and Lady Paragoy drove up with their party, it wanted only the presence of Mrs. Hughes-Dering to complete Carlotta's triumph.

Pending the arrival of that grande dame, Mr. Ponsonby and his satellites offered hot rum to the gentlemen and hot mulled wine or cider to the ladies. Accepting a glass of wine from the tray, Euphemia declined either cake or biscuit and, turning to the Admiral, murmured that Lady Bryce must be pleased that so many had come, despite the cold.

"They came to see you, of course," he grinned, patting her hand. "As did I."

"Oh, what a rasper!" she teased and, when his bark of laughter had died down, added, "You meant from the start to attend this affair and were probably instrumental in persuading Mrs. Hughes-Dering to come. You want to help Hawkhurst. Come, admit it."

He chuckled. "I'll admit I have no love for musicales, and normally would have set me sails and upped anchor for Timbuctoo. But since I'd to come on—" he frowned suddenly, "—on another matter, it seemed a good opportunity to try and—Oh, devil take the woman! Why did she invite That Quack?"

Dr. Archer came up to introduce his sister. He bowed over Euphemia's hand and shot a look of belligerent defiance at the Admiral. The stare he received in return dripped ice and was even more defiant, being aided by the magnifying lens of a quizzing glass. Miss Archer, a tall, angular spinster, rested shrewd eyes upon Miss Buchanan, took in her glowing good-looks, her frank gaze and humourous mouth, complimented her upon her gown of pale amber crepe trimmed with French beads, and moved on, to advise her brother *sotto voce* that she agreed, "The girl is perfect for Gary."

Coleridge brought over young Ensign Dunning. An awed Ivor St. Alaban joined them, and Euphemia was quite surrounded by gentlemen when at length Mrs. Hughes-Dering made her entrance.

That this entrance should be solitary was dictated by the dimensions of the doorway. Unlike the dining and drawing room, the music room boasted only a single door, and Mrs. Hughes-Dering was so vastly fat that no other person could possibly have traversed it beside her. Euphemia blinked at an enormous royal-blue velvet robe over a slip of only slightly paler blue silk and surmounted by a vast turban, the feathers of which shot out to the sides instead of in the customary erect style. Hawkhurst followed this apparition and directed a glance at Euphemia, his eyes gleaming in response to the astonishment in hers. He drew up a large chair for his charge and, having eased her onto it, remained close by as various of her cronies were graciously received. Euphemia was reminded of nothing so much as her governess telling her of the audiences King

Henry VIII had conducted at Hampton Court and was hard pressed to keep her features sober when Wetherby took her over to make her curtsey to this tyrant of the *ton*. She straightened to find herself transfixed by a pair of beady eyes almost concealed by rolls of fat and, realizing that the small mouth was smiling, returned the smile. "Armstrong Buchanan's gel, eh?" The voice was nasal and high-pitched. "My late husband was well acquainted with your father, m'dear. Though he was Navy. Great friend of Wetherby's." She directed a chill stare at Hawkhurst and added bodingly, ". . . else I would *not* be here."

"But, how charming . . ." said Euphemia. Mrs. Hughes-Dering's beady eyes narrowed to slits, even as Hawkhurst's widened and began to dance with mirth. ". . . that you knew my dear Papa," Euphemia went on smoothly. "You must meet my brother, ma'am. Simon, how pleased you will be. Mrs. Hughes-Dering was a friend of my father."

Ever gallant, Buchanan made his bow and, at once winning the approval of the fearsome lady, enabled Euphemia to be borne off by a quietly hilarious Hawkhurst. "Rascal!" he chuckled, as he conducted her to a chair. "Must you always twist the tails of tigers?"

"It is one of my favourite diversions," she breathed.

Amelia Broadbent, all virginal purity in white velvet and blue ribands, was presented to Euphemia, but Amelia had fixed her soulful gaze upon Sir Simon, and her conversation, though polite, was vague. That the handsome young Lieutenant was wed to some Great Beauty, she was well aware, but he was not under the cat's foot whilst in Wiltshire, and a flirtation with so admirable a gentleman must help her standing enormously. Her hopes rose as she noted that Stephanie Hawkhurst was seated far to the rear of the room, beside the Dunnings. Stephanie wore a gown of soft cream wool trimmed with a fur collar and cuffs, with a fur band holding back her curls. The odious girl seemed prettier than ever, but Mildred Dunning was a compulsive talker, and with luck she'd be trapped there all afternoon.

Mrs. Hughes-Dering concluded her audiences, and the Musicale began. Lady Bryce was the first musician and, being also remarkably talented, enchanted the assemblage with a melodious work by the late young Austrian, Mr. Mozart. Euphemia was delighted by this choice and smiled as she caught her brother's eye. Buchanan, both a music lover and an admirer of Mozart, smiled back at her, but he was not happy. In company with his host, he disliked crowded and overheated rooms, and his discomfort was not helped by his preoccupation with his problems, his spirits swinging from delirious happiness at the prospect of a life with Stephanie to crushing guilt that this must cause her to be disgraced. He was seated in close proximity to a cold-eyed and uncommunicative lady named Mrs. Frittenden, who had brought along her beautiful but sulky little grandson. The child, seated next to Simon, was fidgety and engaged in a continuous, if subdued, whining that he wanted "another cake!" Miss Broadbent's eyelashes were an additional trial, fluttering at him so endlessly that he began to wonder why they did not alleviate the rising temperature.

Hawkhurst rose at last to escort his aunt from the harp amid polite applause, and the next item offered for the delectation of the guests was the voice of Miss Broadbent. Coleridge ushered Amelia and her Mama to the pianoforte, Mrs. Broadbent seating herself, and Amelia standing, looking very pretty and demure as she prepared to sing.

"If you was to ask me," whispered Archer into Euphemia's right ear, "they spelled 'pianoforte' wrong. Should've transposed the 'i' and the 'a.' See if you don't agree after this gem!"

"Shame on you, sir!" she scolded with a twinkle.

"Now God help us all!" whispered the Admiral into her left ear.

Thus doubly warned, she nerved herself.

Through the short pause as Mrs. Broadbent fastidiously arranged her music, Hawkhurst moved back to his seat. He dropped one hand lightly upon a chair back in passing, only to have it grasped by small, sticky fingers. His downward glance encountered a pair of rebellious grey eyes and the meaningful jerk of a curly golden head. He bent lower and, being apprised of the boy's needs, looked enquiringly to Mrs. Frittenden. She beamed upon him thankfully. Buchanan also beamed upon him thankfully. Well, he thought, at least it would remove him from the piercing shrieks that were sure to emanate from Miss Broadbent. He led Master Frittenden from the room, noting that to endure the contact of a small boy's hand was become not quite so harrowing since Kent had arrived in Dominer.

Once in the hall, the child asked, "Do you like all that din, sir?" Hawkhurst beckoned to a hovering lackey and evaded this rudeness by pointing out that many people were fond of singing. "Well, I'm not!" his charge said bluntly. "I think it awful stuff. I did not want to come here, and I don't like it. I want something to eat. Do they not got food in this fudsy old place?"

Hawkhurst surveyed the little darling without rapture and instructed the lackey to "Take this upstairs, and thence to the kitchen where it may vex Mrs. Henderson. And convey to her my apologies—and thanks."

Not unaware he had been dealt with in a disparaging fashion, Master Frittenden opened his mouth to retort, encountered a minatory stare, and thought better of it. The lackey bowed, pierced Master Frittenden with a revolted eye, and ushered him towards the stairs.

Hawkhurst turned to find Ponsonby at his elbow, enquiring if everything was proceeding satisfactorily. "Unfortunately," sighed the master of the house. "I wonder how the deuce my aunt got so many of 'em to brave my lair."

"Perhaps Lord Wetherby took a hand, sir," said the butler woodenly. "He appears eager for the local people to meet the . . . er, Buchanans."

Hawkhurst bent a thoughtful gaze on his devoted retainer, had the satisfaction of seeing the butler's cheeks redden, and advised him that he might be about his business. Somewhat flustered, Ponsonby bowed and departed.

Hawkhurst was about to return to the apparently expiring Miss Broadbent when he discerned a movement amongst the dimness that screened Adonis. A faint quirk tugged at his lips. "Kent!" The movement ceased. "Kent!" he repeated. The boy crawled from his place of concealment and came forward, head down and steps dragging, and, having stopped before the tall man, waited. "Do you like music?" asked Hawkhurst. The small fair head nodded, the eyes flashed up shyly, then were lowered again. Hawkhurst extended an inviting hand. Kent looked from it to the smiling face above him, then drew back. "I am telling you that it is permitted," said Hawkhurst quietly, "if you behave." Kent looked up again and, mindful of the gentle cautioning of his goddess against pushing himself, backed away and shook his head. Hawkhurst frowned, and at once a scared expression crept into the thin face, the right arm began to lift protectively. "Do . . . not . . . dare . . ." breathed Hawkhurst. The arm was lowered. A whimsical grin suddenly illumined Kent's features, and he ran to clutch the man's hand with both his own, head thrown back, and that soundless laugh as clear as though it echoed through the hall. Hawkhurst chuckled and rumpled the thick, straight hair, then took the boy quietly into the music room and installed him in a vacant chair, half-hidden under a potted palm near the door.

After an excruciating interval, a hearty burst of applause heralded the termination of Amelia's offerings. Carlotta stood to announce that, "We simply must call dear Miss Broadbent back again later. And now, Miss Buchanan has agreed to sing some songs for us that she learned whilst on the Peninsula with her late Papa, Colonel Sir Armstrong Buchanan."

A pleased murmur rippled from the captives. Hawkhurst's brows shot up, and he darted an incredulous glance to his grandfather. The Admiral, eyes a'dance, winked. Buchanan escorted his sister to the pianoforte. She seated herself, and her smile flickered around the hopeful audience and lingered for an extra few seconds on Hawkhurst before she began to play. Watching her, he was enchanted, yet could not but be conscious of the stifling heat. Several of the ladies were fanning themselves, and he saw the Reverend Dunning furtively raise a handkerchief to his sweating brow. Euphemia sang three short songs and concluded her performance to the accompaniment of a veritable roar of applause. This time Hawkhurst was at her side before his aunt's rather tardy approach and bent to murmur, "I was disappointed. I thought it would be the ditty you performed for us last evening."

"Odious man," she murmured with her sweetest smile. "I shall save that for the second half of our programme."

"There's more?" He groaned through his own smile as he led her towards the advance of admirers, and, when the crowd closed about her, he went on to open one of the terrace doors slightly.

"Considering your brother is so universally despised . . ." murmured Euphemia, watching the guests mingle amiably about the buffet table in the drawing room.

"Not by his own people," said Stephanie. "They have known him all their lives. And they knew Blanche. Still, had this party been in Town, I doubt one of them would have come."

Euphemia's eyes had turned again to Hawkhurst's dark head, clearly visible above the throng, and, watching her, Stephanie saw the softness come into her face and touched her elbow timidly. "Mia, you rather like Gary, don't you."

It was a statement rather than a question. Euphemia met that anxious regard and said in her forthright way, "If I should be so fortunate as to win an offer, should you object, my dear?"

The big eyes blurred with tears. For a moment an embrace appeared imminent, then Stephanie said a choked, "You cannot know how this . . . eases my mind. If I can think he has found his own happiness I—it would not be—"

A crash followed by a small scream terminated her incoherence. Hawkhurst exchanged an alarmed glance with Coleridge, and both men ran to the music room.

Mrs. Hughes-Dering, seated amid a circle of sycophants while awaiting suitable refreshments to be carried to her, was stroking the head of a large and unlovely latecomer. Coleridge uttered a yelp. Hawkhurst swore under his breath. "Such a *dear* doggy!" gushed the grande dame. "He did not mean to knock over the silly table, did you, precious? Hawkhurst, I'd no idea you were a dog man."

"Logical enough, ma'am," he gritted. "Since I am not. Not with respect to *that* filthy mongrel, at all events." He advanced threateningly.

Assured that powerful forces were backing him, Sampson lolled his tongue and laughed confidently.

"What are you going to do?" demanded the dowager in shrill indignation.

"Put him out. At the very least!"

"Do not *dare* hurt the poor puppy!" Mrs. Hughes-Dering bowed forward, flung out her arms, and crushed the head of the "filthy mongrel" to her vast bosom.

"Er, Hawk . . ." Coleridge tugged uneasily at his cousin's sleeve.

Hawkhurst looked up. He was encircled by outraged faunophiles. Fuming, he rasped, "I warn you, ma'am, does that brute stay in here—"

"If *he* goes," said Mrs. Hughes-Dering regally, "then *I* go, sir!"

A glint of unholy joy lit Hawkhurst's eyes. But at the side of the room, his Aunt Carlotta, pale and horrified, was tearing her handkerchief to shreds. He sighed, bowed, and checked as his nostrils were assailed by a fragrance very different from the ghastly concoction Dora affected, but in its way as offensive since it was all but overpowering in its intensity. Master Frittenden stood beside him, the picture of cherubic innocence. And reeking.

"Good gracious!" gasped Mrs. Hughes-Dering, clapping handkerchief to nostrils. "What is it?"

"Some scent I found," said the boy. "They keep it in the plants in this funny old place. Would you like some, ma'am?" His hand shot out, replete with unstoppered bottle. *Eau de Desiree* splashed. In the nick of time, Hawkhurst intervened, and the bottle was diverted from its dastardly path. "I would suggest to you, my lad," he murmured, soft but grim, "that you go and wash yourself."

"Well, I will not!" glowered Master Frittenden. "And that was mine! Finders keepers!"

Hawkhurst, his palms itching, glanced to the boy's Grandmama and wondered how close a friend she was to Carlotta.

"Eustace!" cooed the lady. "Come. We will go home, for you are tired, sweet angel."

The "sweet angel" turned and, beholding Sampson's tail, moved his shoe purposefully. A strong hand clamped upon his shoulder. "Not in this house," warned Hawkhurst, very low.

"*You* do not like dogs," hissed the boy indignantly. "I heard you say—"

"He is not a dog, he is a pest. I remove pests, but I do not suffer them to be trampled. Even by so charming a lad as yourself." And Eustace was firmly propelled to his grandmother.

"Horrid little savage!" observed Mrs. Hughes-Dering in a stage whisper.

"Why should *I* have to go?" shrieked Eustace, reversing his stand. "They let a *servant* boy come in here with the Quality! Why should *I* be made to leave?"

Hawkhurst scowled his irritation, but Kent slipped from his chair to back against the wall, his scared gaze whipping around the circle of surprised eyes.

"He ain't a servant!" flashed Bryce indignantly.

"Don't dignify it by arguing with the brat!" muttered Hawkhurst, irked.

"He's the red-haired lady's page," yowled Eustace, one ear now firmly in his Grandmama's grip. "I know! The lackey told me! It's not fair!"

"I'd fair the little monster!" rumbled the Admiral.

Hawkhurst stepped over the sprawled mound of Sampson and went towards Kent. He all but collided with Mrs. Frittenden, who stopped abruptly as she dragged her recalcitrant grandson from the room. For an instant she stared down at the cringing page, then she marched onward, Eustace's howls fading as the door was closed behind her.

People began to settle into their seats, and some inspired soul was pounding out a rousing military march. Hawkhurst occupied the chair Kent had vacated, pulled another beside him, pointed the boy into it with a jab of one not-to-be-argued-with finger, and prepared to endure the balance of the Musicale. It was destined to be a far shorter balance than he anticipated.

Euphemia was the saviour at the pianoforte and, their spirits lightened by enjoyment of the preceding little fiasco, the stirring music, the bountiful buffet, and the festive bowls, the guests were now in a very jolly mood. Regrettably, the uninvited guest caught the spirit of the occasion. He heaved himself to his feet and, impervious to the suspicious scrutiny of his reluctant host, began to lump around the room, bestowing his head upon various knees and waiting patiently for it to be caressed. Euphemia, finishing her piece, gave way to Miss Broadbent. Hawkhurst nerved himself.

Whether the lady's first piercing note offended Sampson, or whether he also decided to make a contribution, who shall say? Certainly he jumped when the first high C was so nearly missed. Wandering back to his protectress, he began to sniff interestedly about her voluminous skirts. Hawkhurst, whose gaze had followed Euphemia, saw shock in her eyes as they flashed him a warning. It was too late. By the time he turned his head, Mrs. Hughes-Dering was vying with Miss Broadbent. The twin shrieks were warning enough for Sampson. He ceased his depredations, shot across the room, and left through the same slightly open terrace door by which he had effected his entrance.

It was close to two o'clock. The last of the guests had long since gone, family and friends had retired, and the lackeys were moving softly about the great house, extinguishing candles. Hawkhurst, standing on the terrace, gazed unseeingly at the drifting wreaths of fog that were gradually obscuring the moon, and sighed deeply.

"I wonder," snorted the Admiral from behind him, "you can stand here blithely relaxing, after so infamous an affair!"

Turning to him, a smile lighting his eyes, Hawkhurst said, "A harsh judgment, sir, after Colley and Buck and I chased the misbegotten hound halfway back to Chant House."

"Yes, and whooping with mirth every step," grinned the Admiral. "You made your escape and left me the most unenviable task!"

They both burst into laughter. How long had it been, thought Hawkhurst gratefully, since they had enjoyed such a rapport. "My poor Aunt Carlotta! I only pray she will not remember her fall from grace, in the morning! When we returned, and I heard her recounting that barracks-room story of the Archbishop of Canterbury and the opera dancer, I vow I could scarce believe my ears!"

"It's . . . it's a damned good thing . . ." the admiral gasped, wiping his eyes, "you come when you did and intervened before the *end* of that story! I confess I was quite paralyzed!"

"No more than poor Carlotta," chuckled Hawkhurst. "And I thought Dora would faint! I've not yet been able to come at how it happened, sir. Did old Parsley accidentally give Dora's Madeira to Aunt Carlotta?"

"No, no. Everyone was fussing around Monica Hughes-Dering, and poor Lottie was so shattered, she snatched up the nearest glass and gulped down the contents!" He lapsed into another shout of laughter and went on breathlessly, "The blasted glass was . . . full! Blister me, if I ever saw a woman change so! One thing, the Hughes-Dering woman was so diverted she . . . she quite forgot her own . . . disaster. Lord! What a night! Haven't laughed so much in years, nor was I the only one! Your aunt's Musicale will go down in history, my boy!" Hawkhurst groaned, and the Admiral added, "Never did dream when I left Town I should so enjoy myself. Between my little Stephanie blossoming so, and this infamous party, and that purely delicious Buchanan girl." His eyes very keen, he said, "Speaking of whom, what d'ye intend to do?"

How like the old gentleman to attack when he was completely off guard! Gathering his forces, Hawkhurst put up his brows and said mildly, "Sir . . . ?"

"Don't fence with me, boy! You know what I mean. She's one in a million. Not many men get such a second chance. Though she's totally different to—to Blanche."

Hawkhurst turned his face a little away. "Yes. She most assuredly is."

"Have you approached her brother?"

"No, sir."

"If you do not, you're a damned fool! And do not tell me she's averse to you. Last evening she charmed me into telling

191

her of my friendship with Nelson, and chattered so knowledge-ably of Constable's genius I nigh forgot how curst furious I was with my clod of a grandson. By heaven! Were I only thirty years younger, I'd give you a run for your money, and so I tell you!"

Her cloak gathered about her, Euphemia paused in the door-way and drew back into the darkened library. She had hoped for a moment alone with Hawkhurst, but the Admiral's words had reached her ears, and she waited, listening hopefully.

"I . . . think not, sir," smiled Hawkhurst. "And it is very cold. Perhaps—"

"What in the name of thunder d'you mean?" demanded Wetherby, with a swift resurgence of the anger that had been banished by the day's events. "I'll have you know, sir, that I was not shunned by the fair sex in m'youth! I may not have won myself the notoriety you've managed to achieve but, if you fancy yourself able to have outshone me in my prime, I'll be—"

"I had no such thought, sir," Hawkhurst put in quietly. "I merely meant that I would not have vied with you for the lady. I have no wish to remarry. Now—or ever."

Euphemia experienced a sudden chill that came from neither frost nor fog but did not retreat.

The Admiral barked, "Why?"

"Once was enough."

"What nonsense talk is that? You've an obligation to your name and to all who have carried the names of Thorndyke and Hawkhurst before you! You *must* have an heir!"

"Coleridge is my heir, sir."

"That popinjay? Good God! Did you see those damnable shirt points? And the way he was mooning over the Broadbent girl this afternoon? And her fairly slathering for young Buchanan, the hussy!"

"Sir," said Hawkhurst patiently, "Colley is—"

"Oh, the devil fly away with Colley!" The old gentleman took another pace towards his grandson and, with hands tight-clasped behind him, growled, "On the day you wed Euphemia Buchanan, I will abandon my plans to have the management of your estates taken from you."

In the shadows, Euphemia gave a little gasp.

Hawkhurst said slowly, "That day will never dawn, sir."

"I may be growing old," rasped the Admiral. "But I am not quite blind as yet. I saw the way you looked at her on the stairs this morning. Aye, and at that fiasco this afternoon. You're fairly crazy for the girl!"

Hawkhurst was very still through a short pause. Then, "Very well, sir," he drawled. "Since you force the issue, I find the lady most attractive. But not as my wife."

"*What?* Now damn your eyes! Have you the unmitigated gall to expect that poised, charming, delightful lady of quality will become another of your harem of lightskirts?"

"Not if she don't want to, of course. But you'll certainly not blame me for asking—"

"B-b-blame . . . you?" sputtered Wetherby. "*Blame* you, sir? Were I her brother and you dared to speak to her in such dastardly fashion—I'd not *blame* you! By God, I'd have your miserable heart out! You are a rogue is what you are! An unmitigated rogue! A womanizing gamester, sir! Well, I'm done with you! I leave here first thing in the morning!" He started away, then swung back, so suddenly that he almost surprised the wistfulness in his grandson's eyes. "And, furthermore," he raged, shaking his fist under Hawkhurst's firm chin, "when Sir Simon calls you out—as I hope to heaven he does!—I'll be more than half minded to act as his second! Goodnight, sir! And do you have the dreams you deserve, you'll not sleep an instant!" He stamped into the house, fairly snorting his wrath. And left behind him a man who smiled sadly at the last rather jumbled denunciation, then stood with head bowed, heedless of the cold and the mists that drifted in ever-deepening clouds about him.

It was several minutes before Hawkhurst detected something sweeter than the clammy scent of the fog, so that the hand which rested upon the balustrade tightened spasmodically. "You are up late, ma'am," he observed, not turning towards her.

Euphemia stepped a little closer. "The terrace doors were open." She saw him tense and went on, "I overheard your conversation with Lord Wetherby."

Hawkhurst was silent.

"Well," she said. "I am waiting."

He glanced at her. The hood of her pelisse framed her face with the richness of ermine. Even in the darkness he could see the wide fearless eyes, the intrepid tilt of the chin, and he echoed blankly, "Waiting . . . ?"

"I understand that there is something you intend to ask me."

For a moment he was struck dumb. Then, making a swift

recovery, he drawled, "You've excellent ears, ma'am. Very well. I find you most charming, and I believe you may not be averse to me. Will you be my love? For a while at least?" And taut at such arrogant effrontery, he waited for her to slap him.

"Dear, oh dear!" sighed Euphemia, the hood falling back as she shook her head reprovingly. "That was quite paltry, Garret. You shall have to do a great deal better." He moved back, and she could have laughed aloud at his bewildered expression. "You are supposed to seize me in your arms . . . like this . . . and crush me to your heart." She tightened her arms about him although he made no move to return her embrace, if anything leaning slightly away. "And," she said, her voice beginning to tremble very slightly with the fear that her heart might have misled her, ". . . smother me with kisses." And standing on her toes, she raised her face invitingly.

He stared down at her, eyes almost glazed with astonishment. Euphemia allowed her lashes to droop and her head to fall back a little. It was too much. She felt him tremble, and with a groan he crushed her to him indeed. His lips claimed her own in a hard, long kiss. A blaze of joy and desire swept her, and she returned his embrace until she was breathless and dizzied. Murmuring endearments, Hawkhurst kissed her closed eyelids, her cheek, her throat, and she lay in his arms, enraptured, conscious only of the wish that this moment might last forever. But suddenly he checked, all but pushed her away, and gasped out, "God forgive me! I should be horsewhipped!"

Swaying and breathless, she took his arm. "Why? For loving me?"

"I love 'em all," he said harshly. "Go, for lord's sake! Get to your bed. And . . . let me be!"

"I will not! Hawk, I'm not one of your missish simpering girls straight from the schoolroom. I know what I want! You love me! And I—"

He put a hand across her lips, his narrowed eyes glinting down at her. "Do not! Ah, do not! Don't you understand? Since Blanche died, I have been ostracized. I was damned for her death and for . . . for my son. I *hated* those who dared think that of me! I hated her—for what she was. Most of all, I hated myself for my utter folly in having married a woman I could neither love nor respect. *God*, what folly!"

"Horace says," she faltered, as his hand was removed, " 'mingle some brief folly with your wisdom.' " And remembering the rest of the quotation, did not complete it.

" 'To forget it in due place is sweet,' " he finished bitterly. "But Horace was wrong—or my own folly far from brief. I cannot escape what has happened. I *cannot* forget! And the world would not let me, even if it were possible."

Still clinging to his arm, she moved closer and said huskily, "I will make you forget her, darling, I—"

"You don't know what you are saying!" He took her by the shoulders, shaking her slightly even as his yearning eyes devoured her upturned face. "Look at yourself! Lovely, courageous, sought after, admired. And respected. Girl, girl! Don't you know what *I* would bring you to? Don't you know how cruel the world can be? How people can snipe and sneer and cut you to shreds with their polite savagery? I've wrecked my own life, so be it. But do you think I would allow you to wreck yours? No! Marry someone clean and decent and looked up to. God knows you've the chance for the best of 'em all!"

He meant Leith, of course. But, "I have *found* the best of them all," she said doggedly. "And I don't care what people say of you, my love. No—" She reached up, taking his drawn face between her hands and turning his averted head towards her again. "Do not look away. Listen to me. No matter what anyone says, you were *not* responsible for that accident. What happened between you and Max Gains, I do not know, but I know that I love you and that I could not love an evil man. You pretend to be cold and cynical and base, when you are in fact warm and kind and honourable. Oh, Garret, I—"

"Be still!" He wrenched away with a cry in which pain and grief were mixed, and with a vehemence that struck dread into her heart. "Little fool! You are blinded by gratitude because I was fortunate enough to be of help when you needed it. Just now you heard my grandfather call me a womanizer ... a gamester. Well, I am! And worse! Do you know how many men would shoot me, did they dare to face me? You think I am *not* a rake? My God! You must be blind!"

"You were lonely; grieving. But—"

"But ... it is ... *done!* Regardless of why, my reputation was lived up to! I *became* what they said of me, and I cannot change."

"You *can!* You never really *were* what they said! And you did not become a murderer! If the women came here, it was because they wished to. You have *never* been named in connection with an unwed lady of quality, and—"

"And never shall be!" he flared, again facing her. "Let my

195

having helped you—saved the boy, if you will—be *something* to which I can cling with pride. Do not tempt me into dragging your name through the dirt along with my own! What your fine brother would say, I cannot—"

"Buchanan knows," she interposed softly.

He gave a gasp and stared at her in mute disbelief, then rasped, "And does he also know I am a gambler, ma'am? Does he know I have gone through sixty thousand pounds in the last three years? Twenty-five thousand in these last few months? No, he does not! Do not be hoodwinked, Mia. Those people came here today out of respect for my grandfather, out of pity for my poor aunt, perhaps. They know—and will never let me forget—that, because of me, Blanche is dead. No matter what she was, she is dead. And . . . my son . . ." His voice broke at last, and he jerked his head away.

"I will give you more sons," she breathed, somehow overcoming her dismay at the news of those unbelievable losses at the tables.

He shuddered, then turned his head and looked down at her, his eyes full of pain and helpless longing. Then, he bent and kissed her, very gently this time, a loving kiss, but having in it an element of farewell that terrified her. "My 'small candle,' " he murmured softly. "Perfect, pure, and indeed, Unattainable. No, my very dear, I'll not add *you* to my list of follies."

"Even knowing you will . . . break my heart?" she said, tremblingly aware that he was too strong for her, that at last she had met the man she could not bend to her own will.

He nodded. "Better a broken heart than a lifetime of regret." And he left her standing there, blinded by her tears.

The intentions of both Admiral Lord Wetherby and the Buchanans to leave Dominer the following morning were foiled. During the night the fog had thickened, closing down like a dense blanket over southern England and making a journey of any length out of the question. Euphemia awoke feeling listless and exhausted, for much of the night had been passed in pacing the floor and fighting useless tears. She had waited too long for Hawk to doubt her choice and thus through the hours of darkness had alternated between admiration for his unselfishness and rage that he must be so stupidly proud. By morning, she had decided that, if there was no other course, she would be like Charlotte Hilby, who pursued the man she loved with such quiet but unrelenting persistence that even those who had been initially most opposed to the match were now sighing that they wished Vaille would marry her and be done with it!

Aided by a sympathetic Ellie, Euphemia repaired the ravages of her tears so successfully that, when she entered Kent's room, the boy thought her as lovely as ever. He greeted her with the shy anxiety he had shown since she had warned him against imposing on the Hawkhurst family, but his love for her was unchanged, and he listened attentively as she explained that their departure must be delayed until the fog lifted. "Hopefully, though, we will be able to get away later in the morning," she said, with hollow cheerfulness. His small face fell, and touching the pale hair, she said softly, "You like it here, don't you?"

He ran for his tablet and pencil and, sitting on the bed beside her, printed with painstaking care, "Kent loves him." Euphemia's eyes stung. She had to fight to keep her voice steady as she asked, "Mr. Hawkhurst?" He nodded, his face sad. "He saved your life," she said, blinking rapidly. "He is a—a brave and good man. Why, how nicely you have written that. Have you been practicing?"

He brightened and, taking up his pencil again, wrote proudly, "He helpt me." "Mr. Hawkhurst?" she asked, and the careful pencil spelled out, "Sumtimes. But mostly the Admirable."

"How very kind of Lord Wetherby. We shall thank him before we leave, though I believe he plans to journey with us, for part of the way, at least. I will ask Ellie to come and help pack your things. Is there anything being washed today? We must not—" She checked as the boy held up one hand in the oddly assured manner that sometimes characterized him. He darted away but returned, beaming mischievously, to lift her hands one at a time and place them over her eyes. Euphemia waited, and in a moment something was laid across her knees, and her hands were pulled down.

An old stuffed toy had been presented, a bear, once white, but now grubby from much handling, and with one ear missing, the damage covered with a faded blue patch. One of the servants must have given it to the boy. Watching his bright expectant face, Euphemia took up the bear, said that he looked a splendid old warrior and saw at once the words must have been inspired, so brilliant was the smile he turned upon her. Touched because he was so grateful for the smallest manifestation of kindness, she hugged him and left him gathering together his few possessions.

In the corridor, Admiral Wetherby turned from closing Carlotta's door and raised a warning hand. "Spare yourself, my dear. Lady Bryce indulges in an orgy of repentance. I tried in vain to convince her it was the party of the season. You do but waste your time."

She commended him for his efforts, but said she must try, and went in to see the poor sinner. Wetherby had been right, however, and for half an hour she strove to no effort. While Dora laid cold rags across her aching brow, and Euphemia did everything she might to console her, Carlotta wallowed in her misery and degradation. Not until the door opened to admit Hawkhurst's tall figure was any progress made. With his eyes tired and his cool boredom more marked than usual, he said, "For pity's sake, Aunt, do stop being such a henwit. After a life of total abstention, you must judge God harsh indeed does

He condemn you to hellfire for one small error at a moment of great stress!"

"Garret!" she cried, shocked out of her wailings. "Such language in front of Miss Buchanan!"

He darted an oblique glance at Euphemia, who had risen at his entrance and moved to the window. "The lady has bivouacked with an army," he said dryly. "I doubt she's heard a deal worse than that. And, as for you, love, the *ton* may enjoy a triumph, but they adore a failure. You're likely being sympathized with throughout Wiltshire at this very moment."

"And . . . laughed at!" she gulped, the tears starting again.

"Perhaps. But they were vastly diverted. Furthermore, I've often had a suspicion Monica Hughes-Dering is inclined to favour the decanter. Last evening she positively mellowed and left having called me 'dear boy,' a term she's not used to me in years."

Carlotta put aside the wet rag and sat bolt upright, her eyes brightening. "She did, Garret?"

"She did. So you may celebrate not only the most entertaining party held in the county all year, but the apparent relenting, to some extent at least, of one of my severest critics." He turned from his aunt to Euphemia and, with features composed and emotions chaotic, enquired, "I trust you slept well, Miss Buchanan? I fear your brother will not choose to travel in this murk, however. It would seem you are condemned to remain with us for another day."

"At the least," she corroborated gravely.

For a breathless moment his eyes remained locked with hers, then he turned and, totally unaware of the fact that his Aunt Dora was addressing him, stalked from the room, closing the door softly behind him.

Hawkhurst did not put in an appearance at luncheon on that hushed and clammy afternoon, and the Admiral, in a grim mood, contributed little to the conversation. Dora chattered brightly, her occasional quotations obviously irritating her father. She lapsed into quivering silence each time his irked glance shot at her, but so ebullient was her nature she was soon merrily prattling once more. There could be little doubt that she loved Wetherby yet went in considerable awe of him. Euphemia had become very fond of the cheerful little woman and, despite her own heavy heart, decided she would have a chat with the old gentleman and try to persuade him to a more kindly attitude towards his daughter.

When the meal was concluded, however, Bryce begged a moment alone with her. They went into the music room, and, when the door closed, he diffidently expressed his thanks for her enthusiasm over his paintings.

"It is I should thank you," she said warmly. "But should you not be studying art, Colley?"

He gave a helpless gesture. "My dream, Miss Euphemia, but—"

"Mia," she corrected.

He grinned and went on, "If only Hawk would—That is—" He bit his lip, looked up at her shyly from under his brows, and said in a voice made hoarse by nervousness, "Aunt Dora says that you . . . that Hawk might listen to you. And I—I thought you . . . would . . ."

"Intercede for you? Gladly. But it is only fair to tell you that I have not found your cousin highly persuadable."

"Nor I. The most stubborn man alive, in fact."

"I hope not," murmured Euphemia, "else my task must be difficult indeed."

Misinterpreting her remark, he said anxiously that he did not mean to saddle her with a heavy burden. "If you find him intractable, I beg you will make no attempt to convince him. I'd not have you upset for the world, and Hawk can be," he grimaced, "cutting as the very deuce."

She looked at him thoughtfully. "You should have shown him your work long since, you know. I'm surprised your Mama did not recommend such a course to you."

"Mama ain't an art lover, Miss—er, Mia. She hasn't seen much of my work. And besides, she was afraid—" He hesitated again, then blurted out, "I am so scared he might . . . laugh."

His face was scarlet, and, realizing at last how intense a nature was concealed beneath that boyish charm, she said quietly, "That is unfair, Colley. You have given him no chance."

"I know," he groaned. "And truly, old Hawk is the greatest gun! It's not that I don't *like* him, Mia! He's splendid, whatever people think, but—"

She placed a hand on his sleeve, her smile quieting his remorse. "Of course. I understand. When I speak to him, may I tell him of your 'secret' room?"

"Yes, you—you may. In fact, my Aunt D-Dora and I—Well,

you *did* suggest a showing. And we're getting everything . . . ready." He mopped his perspiring brow. "Oh, egad! What a stupid cawker!"

Euphemia laughed. "No, no. Only tell me where this dragon of yours may be found. I shall seek him out at once."

"Will you? Jove, but you're a good sport! Hawk's in the stables, I expect. Leith sent Sarabande home, and he's looking him over. Loves that black devil."

Outside the fog was still dense, with visibility little more than ten feet. It was so cold that Euphemia wondered the vapours did not freeze solid, but instead they swirled about her unpleasantly as she made her way towards the stables. How typical of Tristram to return the Arabian, in despite his avowed intention to keep him. She recalled now that Hawkhurst had seemed relatively undismayed when she'd broken the news of his abduction. He'd probably known his friend would be above so petty an action.

She heard laughter from the stables and, as she entered, saw Hawkhurst standing before an end stall, caressing Sarabande's proudly tossing head. ". . . devil he did," he was saying. "You might as well tell me, John. I'm not like to blame you for whatever that madman said."

The stocky, middle-aged groom threw a hesitant look at Manners and, receiving a confirmatory nod, answered, "As near as I recollect, sir, he says as how you stole summat as he's been arter fer these two years an' more. So he felt all right in stealin' summat o'yourn."

"Blasted hedgebird! And did he say why he was returning his spoils?"

"Oh, he ain't sent nothin' else, sir. Only the 'oss."

Euphemia caught a glimpse of Hawkhurst's flashing grin, then Manners translated in his quiet way, "The master means, why did he send Sarabande back to us?"

"Ar. Well, now, these is Colonel Leith's words, y'understand, sir. He says, 'Now I come to think on it, he'll likely (meaning you, sir) be too noble to claim the prize wot he won, so he best have the 'oss back arter all.'"

Sudden and unexpected tears stung Euphemia's eyes. Dear Tristram, how well he knew the man she loved. God keep you, my best of friends, she thought and turned away, wiping her eyes.

"I had not heard you come in." Hawkhurst was beside her,

but his cool manner vanished as he saw her sudden rigid dismay. "What is it? What's wrong?"

She pointed to the splendid hunting rifle that lay on the bench. "Is that . . . the Manton you found when you were shot at?"

"Yes. Why?"

It was as if she stood once again in that lonely copse on the land of his enemy. Almost, she could see Maximilian Gains smiling up at her as he set his gun and game-bag aside. She had marked at once the beautiful inlay in the stock and grip of that gun. She felt betrayed and yet still could not believe him capable of such cowardly treachery. Besides, even if he did own the weapon, it need not necessarily follow that he had fired it, and—

Hawkhurst touched her elbow. "You have seen that before, I think, ma'am. Was it on the day you became lost? You rode toward Chant House, I understand, and I believe you said you met someone . . . ?"

"Oh, yes. I met a gentleman," she managed breathlessly. "A most charming gentleman, who . . ." She gave a nervous trill of mirth. "Who at once professed to have fallen in love with me." Hawkhurst's lips tightened, and she plunged on, desperate to divert his suspicion from Gains. "An extreme handsome fellow in his way, but rather too smooth of tongue, and with great eyes almost too large for—" Her words ceased, for Hawkhurst's face had become dark with passion, so that for the first time she feared him and drew back.

"What did this 'extreme handsome fellow' look like?" he hissed, taking her wrist in an iron grip. "Had he dark, curling—" His gaze shifted past her. He pulled himself together, released his hold, and snapped out an irked, "Well?"

With a murmur of apology, Bailey proffered a letter. "I'd not have brought it down, sir, only I chanced to discover it in the pocket of your green jacket and thought if might be important."

Hawkhurst took it, frowned at the superscription, and muttered, "Oh, yes. Ponsonby gave it me last evening. I'd forgot it, I'm afraid."

"It does say 'Urgent,' " the valet murmured. "Rather blurred, but see there, sir."

Hawkhurst peered. "Is that what that is . . . Oh, well. Thank you, Bailey."

The valet bowed and trod his stately way from the premises,

gesturing sharply so that Manners and the groom at once followed.

Hawkhurst broke the seal of his letter and, returning his gaze to Euphemia, said grimly, "You were telling me of this weapon, Mia."

Dare she tell him? *Should* she tell him? It would most assuredly precipitate a duel, and she knew wretchedly that she not only feared for her love but dreaded the thought of Max Gains lying dead at his feet. Her intuitive belief that Gains had not pulled the trigger persisted, but she knew that intuition is not infallible. She would discuss it with Simon; he would know what to do. She put a hand to her temple and murmured, "I wish I could be of more help, but I cannot quite recall."

He frowned, but murmured, "By your leave, ma'am," and began to read his letter. The result was electrifying: his face convulsed as though he had been stabbed. "No!" he groaned. "Oh, God! No!" And he bowed forward, shoulders hunched, and clenched fists beating in maddened frustration at the workbench.

Heart in her throat, Euphemia cried frantically, "Whatever is it?"

He pulled away from the hand she placed upon his sleeve, cast her a look of wild-eyed despair, and, with a sound between groan and sob, ran past her and into the rolling fog.

Distraught, she stared after him. A scrap of paper must have been torn from the letter by his violence and lay at her feet. She snatched it up and read the words that had been penned in so neat a hand:

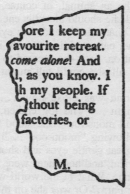

ore I keep my
avourite retreat.
come alone! And
l, as you know. I
h my people. If
thout being
factories, or

M.

Euphemia moaned in fear and bewilderment. However confusing the fragment, one thing was clear. Hawk had gone to meet someone, someone who had the power to command his instant obedience. A creditor perhaps . . . ? Then, with sinking heart, she remembered that Lord Gains' first name was Maximilian. And Gains' rifle had been used against Hawk only three days ago! If her judgment had been wrong and Gains had sent the letter, then Hawk may have gone to meet a man who wanted him dead! And he had gone unarmed! Terror stricken, she started for the house. But the letter had stressed *"come alone . . ."* She paused, torn by indecision. Whatever the threat that was held over him, it must be frightful indeed to so torment that strong man as to bring tears to his eyes.

Even so, no matter what the note had said, he must not walk to his death alone! She picked up the Manton and ran wildly in the direction Hawkhurst had taken.

Half an hour later, chilled to the bone, feet in their thin-soled velvet half-boots bruised and aching, hair straggling down her forehead in wet strands, nose and ears blue with cold, Euphemia had failed to find Hawkhurst, and knew herself hopelessly lost. At first she had thought to hear him ahead of her, but each time, however recklessly she ran, she had met only the ghostly trees, their mournful dripping the one small sound to disturb the smothering silence. Now, once again she heard a sudden crackling, as of someone striding through bracken. It might be an animal, of course, but she dared not call, for God forbid she should alert his enemy. She pressed on in the direction of that brief sound, her eyes peering through the white clouds, her ears straining. If only it were not so cold. Shivering, she went on, until she seemed to have been walking for hours, and for all she could tell might have turned completely around!

But, no! Someone was close now . . . A sudden heavy breathing to her right . . . The fog eddied, and a dark shape loomed up, dim and monstrous. She stood there, shaking with terror. A deep, bellowing "mooo-ooo . . ." rang out, and she could distinguish great gentle eyes and short horns. Her laugh was slightly hysterical, and her knees were shaking so that she could scarce continue. What in the world was a cow doing so far from the Home Farm? Or *was* she on the Home Farm? She started off again, her eyes becoming round with excitement. When Leith had taken her to the hilltop ruins, he'd said they were part of Hawk's Home Farm, and that they'd often come here as boys. The ruins, then, might well be the "favourite retreat" mentioned in the letter! And Gains would certainly be aware of it! She tightened her grip on the gun and hastened on.

A wild shout came from somewhere ahead—a shocked, jerking cry, smothering to a groan, and silence. Euphemia halted, her thundering heart choking her. Then she began to run, calling, "Hawk? Where are you? Hawk?"

But there was no further sound, and in the reckless speed of her going she stumbled, fell, and rolled helplessly down a slope, to fetch up at the foot with a thump that knocked the breath from her. Gasping, she lay there for a moment or two, but then struggled to her knees and groped about for the gun. It was a miracle it had not discharged when she fell. And only then did she think, If it is loaded! "Idiot!" she raged, "stupid imbecile!" But she sought for it, clambering about on her hands and knees until at last she found it.

Sighing with relief, she stood and looked around her. The fog was even thicker in this hollow, pressing in so that she seemed swallowed up in a white and soundless sea. And she had lost her sense of direction entirely! She had no slightest notion of whence had come that despairing cry! Hawk could be lying somewhere—dying! And to attempt to find him might be to in fact walk away! She would fire the gun! She stopped long enough to assure herself that the Manton was indeed loaded, but again was daunted by the realization that, if a would-be murdered was nearby, she might need the shot.

"Hawk!" she cried desperately. And then, in a near scream, "Where are you?"

"Here! Up here."

The voice sounded breathless and was muffled with distance, but she could have wept for joy. He was alive! And she knew now which way to go.

She struggled on and, coming to a hill, clambered upward, heedless of cold, or aching feet, or her ripped, muddy gown, or anything but her need to reach him. At last a glooming bulk rose before her. It was the ancient wall on which dear Tristram had spread his handkerchief for her and dimly, beyond it, soared the great moss-and-ivy-covered tower. She put one hand on the wall and leaned there briefly, her eyes straining to pierce the mists, while she fought to catch her breath. Her call went unanswered, and she began to search the outer ruins, but there was no sign of him. He *must* be here! He *must*! But he was not, and reluctantly, she lifted her eyes to the last hope, the place Leith had said he always retreated to when he craved solitude. There would be no superb view today. Surely he would not have gone up there? "Hawk . . . ?" she cried tremulously. "Are you up on the tower?"

For a moment there was no sound, then the answer came, faint and uneven—and from high above her. "Is that you . . . Mia?"

He *was* on the top! Good God! she thought, I cannot climb up there! But she called, "Yes. Darling, are you all right? Can you come down?"

"I fear not. Don't try to come up here. *Please*. Go and . . . get help."

His voice sounded weak. Her heart twisting, she fairly flew to the tower. It looked dark and crawly inside, but through the gap in the thick rock walls she could dimly discern rough steps leading upward. She clambered through, trying not to think of spiders and bats and other terrifying beasts. The rock stairs were narrow and very deep and wound precariously around the walls to the roof, far above. There was no railing, and at her very first step she almost fell, for the surface was slippery and treacherous from the dampness. Hawkhurst must have heard her frightened gasp, for his voice came at once, sharp with anxiety. "Mia! Do not . . . come! For God's sake! It's too dangerous! Mia . . . don't!"

The words were choked off. She thought she heard a smothered moan, forgetting all about spiders or bats, fought only not to slip. Soon she was at least thirty feet from the littered floor. Her knees shaking, she concentrated fixedly on just the step ahead, not daring to look down, knowing that to fall onto that pile of rock and rubble would be sure death.

She could see daylight above her now and fog writhing down through a crumbling aperture. At first she thought the distance between the final step and the roof would prove insurmountable, but there was a hole in the wall, and, by reaching up and pushing the gun onto the flat roof, she was enabled to grip the edge, put one foot in the hole, and pull herself to the opening. Her wriggling clamber through was not the most graceful act she had ever accomplished, and her skirt, being narrow in the prevailing slim style, promptly ripped, but at last, somehow, she was up and sitting on the edge.

She was on a wide, platform-like structure that in centuries past had certainly been a lookout. The tower, perched as it was at the brink of the hill, must be very high. There were mounds here and there around the edge that might once have been battlements, but, as to a view, she could discern only a billowing sea of fog and still no sign of Hawk's tall figure.

And then she saw him, and her blood seemed turned to ice. He lay sprawled on his side at the very edge of the roof, one arm clinging to the tattered remnants of a turret, the other propping himself amongst the ivy. His white face was turned towards her, and she saw a frantic anxiety in his eyes as she started for him.

"Careful!" he called hoarsely. "There are unsafe places. No, no! To the *right*! Wretched girl, I . . . I *told* you not to come up!"

"Foolish man!" Her eyes alternately seeking safe footing and flashing to him, she asked, "Did you fall, love?" She trod carefully around a hole and was beside him at last, her eyes scanning him for some sign of a wound.

"I'm afraid," he said with a wry smile, "I rather . . . put my foot in it."

Euphemia followed the direction of his nod and gave a sob of horror.

His right leg was caught between knee and ankle by a device half concealed in the ivy—an animal trap, the twin rows of steel teeth deeply sunk into the leather of his top boot, the jaws extending some six inches to either side.

"My dear God!" she gasped, sinking to her knees beside him. "What is it?"

His voice thready, he answered, "I think it's known as a 'bear tamer.' I'll admit, it has . . . tamed me!"

She touched the heavy steel, saw blood seeping through those wicked teeth, and fought panic. "Is your leg broken, do you think?"

"If it is not, it sure as the devil . . . feels like it. Can you get the damnable thing open? I've tried, but . . . cannot quite manage it."

Exploring desperately, she said, "There doesn't seem to be any kind of lever."

"How clever of him. See if you can force it. Have you a knife? Lord! What a stupid question! Perhaps . . . did you hit the spring there, with a rock."

"Oh, Hawk!" She scanned his sweating face in anguish. "It would kill you!"

"Devil, it would!" Incredibly, he managed a strained grin. "But . . . it isn't all that comfortable, so . . . try, if you please."

She *must* try! Heaven knows she'd seen wounds on the battlefield—terrible wounds. But they'd not been on the man she loved. She nerved herself and gripped the steel jaws, wrenching at them with all her might, but to no avail. Her hands came away wet with blood, and, blinking through tears, she saw that Hawkhurst's head was turned away, his fists tight-clenched on the ivy.

"No . . . use," he said unsteadily. "Help me to sit up, can you, Mia?"

She put her arms about him, not daring to look at the dizzying drop that was scant inches away. A shudder went through him, and she heard a choking gasp, but at last he was half-sitting, half-lying against her and muttering, "Good girl. Now, let's have a look . . . here."

She took out her handkerchief and wiped his wet face, and he kissed her hand gratefully. "What a rare creature you are. Please do not be too frightened. I'm not likely to die from . . . this nonsense, you know." He bent forward, peering at his leg. "Egad! Bled all over the place. What a nuisance. I wonder you didn't faint. Ladies . . . always . . ." He had seized the spring as he spoke and, with a mighty effort, heaved at it. Mia, her lips trembling, gripped it also, but their combined strength could not prevail against that heavy coil of steel, and she grabbed for Hawkhurst frantically as he sagged.

He lay lax against her, and she pulled him back from the edge, his total helplessness terrifying her. In only seconds, his long lashes fluttered, comprehension returned to his eyes, and he said ruefully, "Well, that was stupid. Poor girl, I'm a fine hero!"

She pressed a kiss upon his pale brow. "You are splendid, Gary. But I must go and get help."

"Doubt you could find your way . . . in this murk. Come now, we're two sensible people. Mustn't let a stupid piece of steel . . . beat us. If only we'd something to use as a lever."

"The gun! I brought Max Gains' Manton. I can—"

His hand clamped over her wrist as she started up, and despite his hurt his grip was still strong. "*Whose* Manton?"

Her heart jumped. How could she have been so thoughtless? "Never mind! There's no time for that now!"

He released her and watched narrowly, instructing her as she picked her cautious way over the ancient roof to where she had laid the gun. Returning, she asked eagerly, "Can I shoot it open? I'm a good shot. I had to be, in Spain! Just tell me where to aim, and—"

"There is an old Chinese saying," he said, smiling, but gripping his leg painfully. "Dora says it . . . all the time. 'She who shoot gun at steel trap . . . liable to find bullet twixt teeth!'"

"Ricochet." Her shoulders slumped. "Of course. I should have known. Garret, you're bleeding quite dreadfully. Shall I try a tourniquet?"

"Yes. But, please, let's first have another try at my blasted . . . fetter. If you can slip the barrel of the Manton through the jaws and pull down, I can kick at the other side. If we can get the jaws just a little apart, they might spring open. See if it will go through." Obeying, Euphemia strove cautiously and at last succeeded in forcing the steel barrel through the slightly parted teeth beside his leg.

Hawkhurst gave a breathless exclamation of triumph. "Now . . ." He put his left boot heel against the far teeth. "On the count of three, I'll push this side as hard as I can, whilst you pull down with the Manton. Only, you must pull very hard, my sweet. No matter how I swear."

She trembled, but nodded, and gripped the gun butt.

"One . . . two . . . *three!*"

With all her might, she pulled, trying not to think of those teeth deep-sunk into his flesh. It wasn't giving. It wasn't moving but a fraction of an inch. And . . . how could the brave soul endure it?

A sudden ringing clang. A deep groan from Hawkhurst, and he was rolling to the side, to lie face down and limp, but his leg clear at last of those murderous jaws.

Euphemia dropped the rifle and knelt beside him, stroking his tumbled hair, her heart overflowing. For a few seconds he kept his face hidden, but at last one shaking hand reached up feebly to seize her caressing fingers and draw them to his lips.

"My brave love," she gulped. "I must bind your leg. Can you turn?"

He struggled up almost immediately. He was panting, his face drawn, his eyes full of pain, but he asked irrepressibly, "Shall I be . . . allowed to watch you . . . tear your petticoat?"

Euphemia wiped away her tears and sniffed, "You've earned it, dear one." Her petticoat was already torn, and with ruthless hands she was able to rip the flounce away. She handed him the strip, then gingerly explored the crushed boot, cringing as she found that the leather had been driven deep into the wounds. She glanced up at him, and he smiled encouragement. Not a whimper escaping him as she gently pulled the torn boot away, and rolled back the saturated edges of his breeches. The cuts were deep and ugly, the shin bone laid bare, and the calf pulsing blood. Struggling against a sick weakness, she said, "Will you try to move your foot, dearest?"

"Fiend . . . !" he gasped, but set his jaw, and she saw his foot move slightly.

"Then the bone is not broken! The boot must come off, though. I shall have to pull it, I'm afraid, Gary."

"Do so," he warned between gritted teeth, "and I shall very likely strangle you! Just—just tie it up, if you . . . please, Mia."

"Very well." She took up the flounce and tore it in two. "Have you a pencil?"

He groped in his pocket and essayed a twitching grin. "Do you intend to draw up a plan?"

"My plans," she said gently, "are already made, sir, and so I warn you."

His strained smile faded, and he handed her a pencil. She put it behind her ear, and bandaged the wounds tightly, but crimson began to seep through at once. She tied the remaining strip of her petticoat a little below his knee, fashioned a loose knot, and thrust the pencil through it, as the surgeons had taught her in Spain. She was striving desperately to be cool and efficient, as she had been in the old days, but this was her love, and, glancing up at him, she was almost undone. His eyes were blank, but he looked exhausted, his face streaked with perspiration and a bluish tinge about his mouth that she had seen often among the wounded.

"I'm . . . prepared," he nodded. "Do your worst, madam."

Still she hesitated, dreading to hurt him again. Once more that quirkish grin gleamed valiantly, while his voice came like a steadying support through her fears. "You are very brave, if I have neglected to say so."

Her throat tightened, and her eyes were swimming. She wiped them impatiently and began to turn the pencil. Asking a muffled, "Is that all you have to say to me?"

"No . . ." he gasped out. "I . . . adore you, but . . . I shall—shall never—" But he was unable to complete his warning and had hurriedly to avert his face.

Euphemia blinked away new tears and turned the pencil resolutely.

❧ *Chapter 15* ❧

Hawkhurst dampened his handkerchief from a small puddle the
vapours had deposited in a hollow of the roof. Murmuring
words of admiration, he gently wiped mud from Euphemia's
cheek, then took her trembling hands and began to remove his
blood from them. She watched him numbly at first, then pulled
away. "I vow I am wits to let! *You* are the one to be comforted!"

"And have been," he smiled. "Most competently. But you
should not have followed me, my dear. You fell, I think? Have
you hurt yourself?"

"A few bruises only. Oh, Hawk, who did so dreadful a
thing? And why? And why ever would you come up here?"

For a moment he did not answer and then said bleakly, "On
a clear day just to look at the view from this particular spot
is—" He hesitated and said with the shyness of a man unused
to speaking his thoughts, ". . . balm for the soul, I suppose you
might say. I was—I had an appointment to meet someone here.
Someone who knew, if I did not find him, I would climb to the
tower. The trap was covered by ivy and set where I always
stand to look toward the sea. Most . . . unfriendly."

"Unfriendly! How can you jest about so terrible a plot? He
meant you to fall from the edge!"

His thoughts far away, Hawkhurst muttered, "Damnably
clever, for he could thus be miles away at the time of my
death. And yet, it makes no sense . . . for he c-cannot want
m-me . . . d-dead, or . . ." His teeth were chattering so that he
could not continue, and his efforts to stop shivering seemed
merely to aggravate the seizure. Euphemia threw her arms

about him, and he clung to her, despising his weakness but quite unable to control the shudders that racked him.

Euphemia knew that part of this was the reaction, but it was much too cold and exposed up here. She had allowed herself to think that they could wait until help came, but now she faced the fact that it might be hours before they were found. The fog seemed thicker than ever, and it would be much colder, perhaps freezing, after the sun went down. Hawkhurst had lost a deal of blood, and, even for so splendid a physical specimen, a night of exposure after such a horrible ordeal might have tragic consequences. If only he had a greatcoat or she had her pelisse, but they had left in such haste, clad only in the garments they had worn in the house.

"I must be the veriest fool," Hawkhurst drawled, his voice a little steadier, "to terminate this delightful embrace. But I think perhaps we'd best start down, Mia."

The thought of that sheer, slippery stair sent a deeper chill through her, but she stood at once, and by coming first to one knee and then leaning heavily on her, he managed to stand also. He did not betray himself but could not conceal his pallor, and, watching him, Euphemia said a frantic, "Dearest, you cannot! Perhaps I could find . . ." But the fog was quelling, and hope died away.

Hawkhurst nodded, took a step, and reeled drunkenly. It required every once of her strength to keep him from falling, but he gripped her shoulder and mumbled a faint and disjointed, "I'll be . . . all right. It's . . . that gown of yours . . . drives me to distraction."

She looked down. Her dress was ripped from thigh to hem. Incredulous, her gaze flashed up again. Pain was making him breathe in erratic little gasps, but there was a whimsical twinkle in his eyes, nonetheless. This, she thought, was the kind of valour that had so awed her on the Peninsula, the indomitable humour that could sustain a brave man through almost any emergency. She blinked and said huskily, "Alas, my reputation will be quite gone. I shall say you did it, and you will *have* to wed me!"

He laughed, took a step, and gritting his teeth, struggled on.

The worst part of the journey down was for him to come through the hole in the roof and onto the top step, but when at last that painful manoeuvre was accomplished, he turned back to assist Euphemia.

"Do not!" she cried anxiously. "Hawk, you should have let me go first!"

"What, and miss so trim an ankle?"

That he had seen far more than her ankle she was well aware, but she soon knew also why he had refused to let her go first, for despite his brave words he swayed dangerously as he essayed the first step, then leaned weakly against the wet rock wall.

"You cannot walk down," she decreed, peering at his averted profile. "Hawk, sit your way, or you will surely fall!"

"Good gad . . . ma'am . . . I am the head of . . . my house. What of my dignity?"

"I had rather have you humbly alive, than the most dignified corpse in—" A small, cold frog slithered across her foot. She let out an instinctive squeal, moved without volition, and slipped. Terror seized her. So did an arm of iron. She was slammed back against the wall so hard that the breath was beaten from her lungs, and panic overtook her, the courage that had upheld her this long dissolving into a shuddering sob. Hawkhurst, his own knees shaking, knowing how close they had come to tragedy, took up her cold hand and kissed it. "We'll follow your scheme, my brave girl," he said softly. "Farewell to dignity for both of us. Down with you!"

And so, most unheroically, they negotiated that chill and treacherous descent until at last they came to the ground and, having clambered through the choked aperture that had once been a mighty door, stumbled to the outer wall. Here, at last, Hawkhurst's strength gave out, and he sank down, groaning a frustrated curse at his weakness.

"My poor love," Euphemia said, scanning his ashen face and closed eyes with fearful anxiety. "I wonder you could get this far. Hawk, you cannot walk any further. I *must* go and try to find help!"

He caught at her hand and pulled her back as she made to leave him. "No. It's not so cold down here. And Colley may come. We'll wait . . . together."

Cold and trembling, she sat close beside him and, suddenly recalling the shawl pinned about her shoulders, began to unfasten it, intending to wrap it around him. His hand closed about her fingers, and she glanced up. He was leaning wearily against the rock wall, watching her, and in his eyes a light such as she had never before witnessed, and that brought a new humility to her, so full was it of love and reverence. He said nothing but smiled and put out his arm, and she crept within it, snuggling close against him.

"You do love me," she whispered. "I knew it. You cannot deny it now."

"I never said I did not. I said only that I would not marry you."

"Oh. Well then, we can—"

"We most assuredly can *not*!"

The fear that had haunted her ever since she'd seen that fragment of his letter became certainty. Staring blindly at his rumpled cravat, she said, "She's alive, isn't she, Garret? That's why you cannot offer me marriage."

He gave a harsh derisive laugh. "If it were only that simple! I could divorce her. Lord knows she gave me reason."

"Tell me." She moved back and watched him tautly. "It is not because of . . . of your—"

"Reputation? By God, but it is! And even were that all, it would be reason enough!"

"Well, it is not all. Garret, I love you. I have a right to know why happiness is denied me."

He scowled at the tower and muttered, "It is to ensure your happiness that I deny you."

"Then I will wait, however long it takes, until you disabuse your mind of such noble nonsense."

He watched her frowningly and, perhaps because he was weak and in much pain, sighed, "I believe you might, at that. Very well. You may see how hopeless it is." He groped in his pocket, took out the crumpled remains of the letter which had plunged them both into this perilous adventure, and held it out.

The fragment Euphemia had found had been thrust into her pocket. Her heart leaping, she retrieved it, fitted it carefully into place, and read:

My Dear Patron:
    Your payment was adequate, wherefore I keep my word. Dawn tomorrow. At your favourite retreat. We will arrange a meeting. But *come alone*! And please—no plotting! I am no fool, as you know. I shall leave strict instructions with my people. If I do not return by a certain time, and without being followed, Avery will be sold to the factories, or to the mines.

Ever yrs, etc.
Robert M

"*Avery* . . . ?" she breathed, astounded. "Your *son*? Avery is . . . *alive*?"

He nodded dully. "And had I but read that at once last evening, I might have seen him, at last. But I was too late."

"No, my dear one. Never grieve so! Mount had no thought but to kill you. What an evil man! He must be quite mad!"

"Yes, I think he is, now. Perhaps, to an extent, he always was."

"Because of Blanche?"

He gazed at her blankly, and, seeking to spare him as much as possible of that bitter retelling, she said gently, "I know some of it, Garret. Dr. Archer told me why you married her. And that she and Mount loved one another."

"Yes . . ." He looked away again and after a moment of brooding silence said, "I didn't know about that until after Avery was born. When I learned of it, I told her I had no objection to her pursuing her affair with Mount, so long as she was discreet about it." His lip curled. "More folly. I totally underestimated the depth of her passion. Mount was her god. And Mount wanted Dominer even more than she did. You may believe that I saw as little of either of them as I could manage, else I might have realized that fact. At all events, when Avery was two years old, I became very ill. Archer couldn't find the cause, but I grew steadily worse, and he insisted I be moved to his house. My recovery was rapid. Astonishingly so." Euphemia uttered a shocked gasp, and he smiled sardonically. "Hal tried to warn me. There were all kinds of rumors about, he said, odd rumors that I ill-treated my wife and son. Lord knows, I saw Blanche seldom, which might have been construed ill-treatment, but Hal said there was more to it and seemed to suspect some kind of plot. I laughed at him and said it was a lot of melodramatic fustian. And then one evening, Max Gains came over. We'd had a dispute for a long time. A foolishness that began over some trees along the boundary line. I'd cut them down. Max liked them. He never forgave me, and his blunt manner irked me. One word led to another. He always was terribly hot at hand, and I suppose I was, too. I could have ended it all by telling him that the trees had been diseased. But, like a perfect fool, I did not, and it went on until we were on the brink of a duel. This particular evening was extremely sultry, and I'd sent a lackey to bring me a glass of water just before Max arrived. I was alone in the library when Max burst through the terrace doors and started ranting at me about some nonsense that was so utterly unfounded I could only laugh at him. He came at me like a maniac. The glass was in my hand. It seemed so . . . logical to . . ." The words trailed off. He leaned his head back and gripped his leg and was silent.

Eyes wide, she whispered, "You threw it in his face? And . . . it was oil of vitriol?"

"Shall I ever forget how he cried out," he muttered sombrely. "How he stood there . . . clutching his poor face."

"If you . . . had *drunk* it! My God!"

"I sent Manners after Hal," he went on. "Max was half out of his mind with pain, and, as soon as it was possible, Hal took him back to Chant House. I went after that lackey. He was gone, of course. The poor fool had been dazzled by Blanche, and I've no doubt that he would have been branded my murderer had their nasty little scheme succeeded. But I knew better. I knew Hal had been right, and I went tearing upstairs after her. She was ready. She hid behind the door and lost no time in breaking a vase over my head." He smiled bitterly. "She had the gumption to hit hard, I'll say that for her. By the time I came around she had gone and had done her work well. The household was agog with the news that I had tried to kill her because she upbraided me for blinding Max. She had fled for her life, taking her child with her."

Euphemia squeezed his hand comfortingly. "So you went after her."

He nodded. "I should have gone to Max, I suppose, for, when I eventually returned to England, the time was long past when I could have explained anything. But Blanche never had cared a button for Avery. I knew the life he'd have with her. She went to Mount, of course. I chased them over half the Continent and caught up with them four months later in Nice. It was a dark night, and I left my curricle and raced into the pension where they were staying. What Mount had told those people I've no idea, but they behaved as though I were the fiend incarnate. I ran out of patience and started tearing doors open. The proprietor went after the local gendarme, but I saw Blanche and Avery run across the street. I charged downstairs, but two of the waiters held me. I was not to molest *'la très jolie mademoiselle,'* they said. Blanche looked back over her shoulder. She was very frightened." He scowled broodingly. "I collect she thought it logical enough to take Avery away in my own curricle. She didn't know that Mount had seen me arrive and had tampered with the axle . . . She was good with the ribbons, but loved to spring her horses. When the axle parted, the curricle went off the road—and into the sea." He stared blindly into the fog, and Euphemia, scarcely daring to breathe, waited.

"Mount got to the wreckage first. The boy had been thrown clear, but Blanche was killed instantly. He took Avery and told the police later that the child had been lost in the sea. At first, I believed it. Then . . ." He drew one hand across his haggard eyes. "Mount wrote to me. He was quite explicit about what would happen to Avery if I did not follow instructions. He's been blackmailing me ever since."

There was a short silence, Hawkhurst haunted by memory, Euphemia variously horrified and perplexed.

"Garret," she said at last, "could you not have set agents to search for the boy?"

"I had one of the finest men in Europe hunting him for better than a year, but it was as if the earth had opened and swallowed him. All we were able to discover was that he *was* my son, that he was quite recovered from his injuries, and that Mount had him. Then, I received a warning. Diccon, my agent, had come close. If it ever happened again, Avery would die. As it was, I could be assured my interference had resulted in the boy being . . . severely punished. I was powerless. After a while, I recovered some backbone and sent more men. I dared not go myself, for Mount had warned I was watched, and, if I sought them or let one word leak out, Avery would suffer terribly. I told my men that, if they even suspected they had located Mount, they were to do nothing, just let me know at once. But they never again caught up with him. All his demands were handled with painstaking cunning and never twice by the same method. The letter he sent the other day was my first intimation he was even in England."

Euphemia looked at him uncertainly, and Hawkhurst elaborated, "It was left at the Receiving Office in Down Buttery, on the morning you cut my sister's hair."

So that was why he had been so furiously angry. She said slowly, "I see . . . And Mount doesn't want you to marry, for fear you will get yourself an heir."

"More than that. He blames me for Blanche's death. The accident was intended for me, so by his reasoning I am responsible. At first, he used to write me letters describing his treatment of my son." His head lowered, the hand on his knee tightening. "Then, he warned me that, since I had killed his

217

love, I would never be allowed to take a wife. I honestly believe he would murder the boy if I did."

"Oh, Hawk, my poor darling! How awful! But, should you not have told Lord Wetherby? The poor old fellow must grieve so. Surely, if he had some hope . . . ?"

"Good God, no! He worshipped Blanche. To learn what she really was would alone be enough to kill him, for I'm sure he would start to blame himself for the whole mess. Likely worry himself into the grave. And, as for Avery, how he doted on that child! To give him hope, hope that might prove false . . . Mia, had my grandfather been put through what I have had to face these last four years, he would be dead! He may look well, but he's had one seizure, and the doctor said shock or worry would be fatal."

"Yes, dear. But Archer thinks—"

"He *thinks*! But if anything happened to the old gentleman—No! I will not allow it. When I have Avery safe, then, gradually, he shall know the whole. For the time, better he go on despising me. At least, I can have the consolation of knowing he's alive."

Euphemia watched him, her eyes blurring. Small wonder his dark hair was streaked with grey. Small wonder he sometimes was harsh and impatient. Her cherished little poem drifted back into her thoughts: "Riches or beauty will ne'er win me. Gentil and strong my love must be." And with a great surge of tenderness she knew her love was gentil and strong, indeed.

Hawkhurst glanced at her furtively, then turned away, muttering, "Do not look at me so. I am not worthy."

She smiled. "Be still, dear foolish creature, for you have not the faintest notion of how worthy you are. Nor of how very, *very* much I—"

"What the devil is gong on here?"

Euphemia gave a gasp and grabbed for the gun, but Hawkhurst was already swinging the weapon to aim steadily at the man who sat astride the wall, watching them. "Good afternoon, Max," he said ironically. "How charming of you to come."

Lord Gains wore a heavy greatcoat, a muffler was wrapped about his throat, and a curly-brimmed, high-crowned beaver resided at a jaunty angle upon his brown locks. He stared from Hawkhurst's bloodstained bandages to the girl who knelt, dishevelled but protective, beside him and, swinging down from the wall, started towards her. "Good heavens! Dear lady! Are you all right? What—"

"She's perfectly all right," Hawkhurst growled somewhat inaccurately. "And that's far enough, if you please."

Gains halted, his irked gaze flashing to his enemy. "I see you found my gun. Do you now intend to blow my head off with it?"

"Tit for tat!"

"What the devil d'you mean?"

"You know damned well what I mean! And I have every right to shoot a trespasser on my land."

"Why not?" sneered Gains. He gestured towards his face. "Finish the job."

Euphemia looked from one to the other in stark incredulity. Here lay Hawk, battered and hurt; she herself was mud from head to foot, her clothes in rags. And all they could do was wrangle in this idiotic fashion! "My lord," she said determinedly, "this has gone on for much too long, and—"

"I can well believe that! Poor soul!" Gains interposed wickedly. "No gentlewoman would care for *this* situation!" He shrugged out of his greatcoat and, ignoring the levelled Manton, walked over to wrap it about her. "If you will allow me, I shall escort you back to Dominer and send help for—"

"Devil you will!" Hawkhurst snapped. "Perhaps you will be so kind—before you get yourself off my property—to admit that you tried to put a bullet through my head with this!"

Gains' brows lowered. "I'll own I should have done so four years since. But, if you must know, I lost the gun, and—"

Hawkhurst gave a hoot of derisive laughter.

"By Jove!" breathed Gains thunderously. "I must be mad to have let you go on living, you arrogant clod! Well, I shall rectify that as soon as you're on your feet again. Meanwhile, I am on your accursed property seeking my dog, whom you persist on luring here to—"

"*Luring?*" Hawkhurst exploded. "Why, that miserable flea-carrying cur has caused more chaos in my home than a herd of elephants! I'll send you my reckoning, by God! And do I catch him on my land again, I shall—"

"Oh, be still!" cried the indignant Euphemia.

"If you harm one hair of Sampson's head . . ." snarled Gains.

"Who do you take me for? Delilah? I'm not interested in the

hairs on his blasted head! I'll put a ball through his mangy car-
cass, is what—"

"And within that same hour, my seconds will call on you!"

"Oh! How I tremble, my lord!"

"Will ... you ... both ... be ... *quiet!*" shrieked
Euphemia.

Shocked, they stared at her. "I have *never*," she began furiously, "in all my days, seen two grown men behave so—"

A shout from down the hill interrupted her. "Mia? Is that
you? Mia?"

Euphemia gave a cry of joy. "Colley! Oh, thank heaven!"

"You need not have worried, dear lady," said Hawkhurst,
venomous gaze on Gains. "I could've kept him back!"

All but spluttering his wrath, Gains turned from him. "Miss
Buchanan, have I your leave to call upon you while you are in
Bath?"

"No, you have not, damn your impudence," Hawkhurst
blazed. "And how the devil did *you* know she was going to
Bath?"

"Colley!" Euphemia ran eagerly to meet the young exquisite
who jumped the wall with lithe grace, only to pause, stunned
by the scene that met his eyes. "Oh, Colley! I have never been
so glad to see a rational human being in all my life!"

Warmed by his cousin's greatcoat, and with the assistance of
both Gains and Coleridge, Hawkhurst was hoisted into the saddle. Watching Colley swing up behind him and support his
wilting form, Euphemia was amazed not only by the fact that
Gains had been quite willing to help, but that Hawkhurst apparently found nothing odd about that assistance. She could only
conclude that, being a mere practical woman, she was incapable of understanding the rules governing the dangerous game
the two men were playing. Hawkhurst's passivity only went so
far, however. The effort of mounting had exhausted him, and he
was bowed over the horse's mane, but, when Lord Gains insisted that Euphemia ride his grey, he dragged up his head and
demanded caustically, if threadily, that they all stay close together during the ride back to Dominer. Gains lost no time in
delivering a withering rejoinder. Colley, meeting Euphemia's
disbelieving eyes, sighed and gave a rueful shrug.

The journey was necessarily slow, the fog being all but impenetrable now, and the daylight fading so that Euphemia
feared that if they did not somehow find Dominer before dark,

they would be doomed to overnight in the open. Bryce, however, possessed an uncanny sense of direction, and, to her great relief, within half an hour they were met by anxious grooms who ran out from the yard to greet them.

Lord Gains, who had led his horse all the way, lifted Euphemia down. He bade her a kind but brief farewell, shrugged into the coat she insisted upon returning, and rode off, an airy wave of his hand silencing her fervent thanks.

Bryce now took charge. He guided his sagging cousin into the arms of the waiting grooms with near feminine tenderness, sent a stableboy racing to the house to alert the staff and the family, and commanded one man to bring Dr. Archer at once and another to ride to the village for the Constable. Hawkhurst muttered something in apparent protest at this last order, but was ignored as Bryce swung easily from the saddle and steadied him, saying a firm, "We'll carry you, old fellow, and—"

"Not likely!" Hawkhurst peered around uncertainly. "Mia, where are you? Are you . . . all right?"

She was aching with fatigue, but assured him that she was very well. "Now you must let Colley help you, Garret. You are in no condition to walk."

"I'll not be carried . . . in," he muttered stubbornly.

Coleridge swore under his breath, but drew his cousin's arm across his shoulders.

Thus supported by Bryce and Manners, Hawkhurst struggled up the steps and into the side hall. Euphemia was so vexed she could have hit him, but, running ahead to open the door, she was confronted by the Admiral, and one look at the old gentleman's stricken face explained his grandson's attitude.

"Nothing to be concerned about, sir," announced Hawkhurst cheerfully. "Made a blasted fool of myself. But it's not serious."

Wetherby appeared to have been struck dumb. He followed meekly as Hawkhurst was aided into the Great Hall. Lady Bryce hurried around the corner, took one look at her nephew, and fainted dead away. Ponsonby, a maid, and a lackey ran to restore her. Coleridge, his voice crisply authoritative, called to Mrs. Henderson asking that medical supplies be brought to Mr. Garret's room. "Ellie, Miss Buchanan has suffered a bad fall and will need your best care. One of you people find Sir Simon at once, if you please. Manners and I shall carry you upstairs now, Hawk. A chair-hold would be the easiest style, I fancy, Manners."

Hawkhurst was near the end of his tether and raised no demur. He could no longer see anything clearly but managed to keep his head up, determined he would not alarm his grandfather by being so stupid as to faint. On the second step, his determination was overcome. He gave a small sigh, his arms slid from the shoulders of his bearers, and his head rolled back limply.

The Admiral was aghast and, recovering his voice, sprang forward crying an anguished, "Oh, God! Is he—?"

"He'll be right and tight, sir," said Colley breathlessly. "Could you please go on ahead and open the door for us?"

Even through her own anxiety, Euphemia marvelled at the boy. A shout would have brought the omnipresent Bailey to perform this small service and innumerable lackeys and footmen hovered about, eager to assist. The Admiral's face brightened predictably, and he hastened to do as he was asked. Hawkhurst was borne into the great bedchamber. Starting instinctively to follow, Euphemia found an arm slipped about her waist, and the Admiral said kindly, "You may be assured he will be well cared for, my dear. Our Nell Henderson has dealt with worse than this. You look ready to drop. Come now, and perhaps when you are rested, you will tell me what has happened."

She leaned on him gratefully, not until that moment realizing how utterly exhausted she was. By the time they reached her bedchamber, she was trembling as with ague. No sooner had the Admiral left, however, than the door flew open, and a petrified Stephanie ran in to plead for word of her brother. "They will not let me in the room! What was it? Has he met Gains at last?" Euphemia shook her head, but her attempt to reply was foiled as she instead burst into tears and to her horror seemed quite unable to stop weeping. The faithful Ellie swung into action. Miss Hawkhurst was begged to go for a glass of cognac. "Not ratafie, Miss. Your brother's best brandy. Come now, Miss Euphemia, you cuddle up to Ellie and have a good cry. Then we'll get you bathed and popped into a nice warm bed. You're half-froze and half-naked, poor brave soul. Cry, my lamb, cry away."

Euphemia lay drowsing between sleep and waking for a little while. Not until she moved lazily and sore muscles protested, did recollection flood back. She sat up, snatching for the bellrope, and saw her brother hovering at the foot of the bed, watching her anxiously.

"Deuce take me!" he moaned. "Did I wake you, Mia? Ellie will have my ears!"

She reached out to him, and anticipating her question, he came to give her hands a squeeze and smile into her frantic eyes. "He's resting comfortably now. And Archer gives the credit for that entirely to you, for Hawk would have bled to death had you not found him. Colley showed me those ruins this morning. Egad, what a gruesome mess! I could scarcely believe you climbed those steps all the way to the roof. And I give you fair warning, the old gentleman is in a fair way to placing you on a pedestal." He looked grave and added, "Seems to make a habit of it, don't he?"

"Simon, what did Archer say about his leg? He'll not be lamed?"

"He says not, though it took him forever to stitch Hawk back together. Had the very deuce of a time, poor fellow, although Archer gave him laudanum. What none of us could understand is how you happened to find him in that pea soup yesterday afternoon."

"I honestly don't know. I thought I heard him a few times, but—it was dreadful! A nightmare! Did the Constable come?"

"Yes. What a clunch! Weather permitting he means to come again this afternoon." Euphemia slanted a glance to the windows, and he went on, "Yes, it's still quite murky outside and very thick in spots. At this rate, Aunt Lucasta may have to sit down to Christmas dinner with only half the Buchanan contingent represented."

"What a shame," said Euphemia, trying to look disappointed.

He chuckled and tugged at a curl which had escaped her cap. "Not very convincing, sister mine. Are you feeling better this morning? May I ring for your tray?"

She said that she felt stiff, but much better, and declined the tray, wanting to talk with him. He drew up a chair and settled down astride it, facing her over the back. "I do not mean to plague you for details. Colley told us much of it, and you'll have to wade through the rest later, I'm afraid. Just one or two questions, to which I'd like immediate answers, Mia!"

"How very brotherly," she said fondly. "I've some questions of my own."

His eyes were very empty all at once. "Such as . . . ?"

Poor dear. Did he suppose she had not noticed how downcast he had been these past few days? "You first, sir," she said, folding her hands demurely upon the coverlet.

Despite his uneasy conscience, he was amused as always by her assumption of meekness. "Very well. Regardless of the cause, you were alone with the man you love for some time. You are sadly compromised. Does Hawk return your affection?"

She could not know of the softness that came into her eyes, but Buchanan saw it, and his last doubts vanished. "He loves me," she said. "And, oh, Simon, you must have thought him splendid. He was incredibly brave and made no fuss, although that ghastly trap . . . !" She shuddered.

"Yes, I saw it. We brought it back, in fact. How Hawk managed to avoid being thrown to his death I cannot comprehend. Which brings me to my second question. Does he really believe Gains could be so—so devious and savage?"

"Colley is sure Lord Gains was not responsible," she replied, evading his eyes. "I fear that Hawk has many enemies." And hating to deceive him so, she scolded lightly, "You have now exceeded your quota, sirrah, and must submit to *my* inquisition. I notice that you have spent a great deal of time with—" She paused, struck by the way his hands clung so tightly to the chair back and wondering if his wound still troubled him. "—with Coleridge. Have you by any chance met Chilton Gains?"

"Yes." Able to breathe again, the guilty plotter relaxed. "Fine young fellow."

"I rather thought he would be. I've met his brother twice and cannot help but like the man. I do so pray it will not come to a meeting between them, but they are both so terribly hostile."

Buchanan frowned but said nothing. Certainly Gains had sufficient reason to demand a meeting at any time he chose. A duel was not imminent, however. From what Archer had said of Hawk's injuries, he would be unable to walk for a week, at least. He thought, Thank God! and could have sunk from self-loathing.

Sir Simon had much to learn of the stubborn nature of Garret Thorndyke Hawkhurst.

By three o'clock that December afternoon, a breeze had sprung up, and by four the fog was definitely dispersing. Stephanie was laid down upon her bed, having spent much of the night sitting beside her brother, and Buchanan was in the stables, checking over his horses and equipment in preparation for the journey to Bath the following day. In the drawing room a shocked group had gathered to hear Euphemia's account of what had transpired at the ruins. Carlotta and Dora were seated at a card table which had been set up so that they might work on Christmas decorations. Euphemia sat beside the fire, with the Constable, a paunchy, middle-aged gentleman named Mr. Littlejohn, next to her. Kent was kneeling at her feet, listening intently to the proceedings, and the Admiral stood with his back to the hearth and glared at the Constable.

"Most dastardly thing I ever heard of!" he snorted, pulling at his whisker and managing somehow to imply that the entire matter could be laid at Mr. Littlejohn's door. "Murdering Bedlamites running loose through the countryside, assaulting the Quality! Deplorable!"

Mr. Littlejohn appeared to be more concerned over why Miss Buchanan had been "traipsing about in the fog," a concern that drew an outraged snort from Wetherby.

Not altogether accurately, Euphemia explained that, having been confined to the house for some days with a sick child, she had felt the need for a breath of air and had gone out, only to become lost. "I chanced to hear Mr. Hawkhurst calling and managed to find him."

"But whatever was Hawkhurst doing on top of the tower, love?" Dora looked up from the paper chain she was fashioning and said curiously, "He could not have gone up there for the view, you know, for the fog was too thick to see anything."

The Constable, writing painstakingly in his tablet, suspended his endeavours to nod approval and tell her that was "a good point."

"Hawkhurst has for years loved to look at that view." Carlotta set her glass upon the table and thought the contents were not nearly as agreeable as the ratafia which had plunged her into disgrace after the party. "That," she went on absently, "is a well-known fact in the neighbourhood."

The Admiral chomped his jaws with an impatience that was heightened as the Constable, writing busily, muttered, "A . . . well-knowed . . . fack. Still, fack remains as it were a sight odd to look at the view when there wasn't none. And a odder sight. Or a sight odder," he frowned uncertainly, "that any persons would have knowed as he was a'going up on that there tower on that *partickler* afternoon so they could leave that there trap there. Now, you may wonder as how I knows that!" He scanned the baffled group with a portentous eye. "I *knows* as it musta been left fer Mr. Hawkhurst, 'cause no poacher in his right mind would set his traps atop a fifty-foot tower! Less'n he were looking fer to catch a eagle!" He leaned back, smiling around triumphantly, until he met the molten glare levelled at him by the Admiral.

"I would not think," Dora offered sapiently, "that a poacher would use a trap like that for an eagle. Would it not be . . ." she attempted to remove a paper loop from her sticky fingers, ". . . rather large? Eagles have small feet."

Wetherby gave a subdued snarl and gritted his teeth at the chandelier.

"Ar! Very true, ma'am," smiled Mr. Littlejohn. "You got a real head on your shoulders! I don't rightly know what you'd use to catch a eagle, but—"

"God bless it!" roared the exasperated Admiral, "there *are* no damnable eagles hereabouts!"

"Ar," agreed the Constable and added with remarkable sagacity, "No more there bean't any bears neither! And, even if there was, why a trap, I ask you? Fella wants to kill someone, he shoots him, or sticks a knife in him. Don't go leaving no Russian bear tamer lying about on top of a fifty-foot tower on the off-chance his murder-ee, as you might say, would fancy a stroll on top o' said tower to admire the view in the middle of a thick fog! Odd, says I!" and he nodded with ponderous vehemence. "O-d-d . . ."

"Nothing odd about it, Littlejohn," Hawkhurst contradicted from the doorway. "It gave the man a chance to kill me with no risk of incriminating himself."

Euphemia and Dora both sprang to their feet. The Admiral spun around, and Kent rushed to seize Hawkhurst's hand and beam joyously up at him.

"No use, sir," sighed Bryce, helping his cousin into the room. "Couldn't keep him upstairs."

"Oh, Hawk!" worried Euphemia, forgetting herself. "Dr. Archer said—"

"Man's a quack!" proclaimed the Admiral, pleased by her proprietary air. "Sorry, m'dear, but he always was. Don't blame you a bit, Garret. Kent, stop jumping up and down and bring that footstool for Mr. Hawkhurst."

Kent obeyed with alacrity. Bryce eased the invalid into a chair, then bent and, keeping one eye watchfully on his face, lifted the bandaged leg.

Hawkhurst's gaze lingered on Euphemia, and, if he noted that she looked a little wan today, she noted the flicker that touched his eyes as Bryce lowered his foot. Her hand went out to him in an instinctive gesture of sympathy. He smiled and winked at her. Not very much, but seeing it, Dora smiled dreamily and spread glue on her thumb, while Wetherby could have danced a jig and, turning to the Constable, felt almost in charity with him as he declared, "Now you'll get your answers, Littlejohn!"

The Constable's enlightenment was delayed, however. Lady Bryce attempted to lift her glass and let out a cry of vexation when she was unable to do so. There was, it appeared, a crack in Dora's pot of glue. Considerable consternation ensued. Ponsonby and two maids were summoned to rectify the situation, not benefitting from the acid suggestions of Lord Wetherby and Colley's barely contained hilarity.

At length, however, the glass was pried from the table and the gluepot set onto an old chipped saucer. Scarlet with mortification, Dora crept to the rear of the room, and Coleridge sauntered over to help with the paper chain while engaging her in a whispered conversation.

Constable Littlejohn, who had watched the upheavel with a reinforcing of his convictions that most of the Quality were short of a sheet, resumed his questioning. Hawkhurst's lazy drawl was noncommital. He told Littlejohn that he had walked to the tower because "it was too foggy to ride," which infuriated his grandparent as much as it satisfied the good Constable. The rest of his answers were as asinine, but Littlejohn took them all down as though they were pearls of wisdom. Aware that the Admiral was becoming apoplectic, Coleridge concealed his own mirth sufficiently to enquire if the minion of the law would care to see the bear tamer. It transpired that Littlejohn would very much like to see both the "murder wepping" and the glass of home-brewed that was cunningly offered. Bryce led him off and, with a conspiratorial grin at his cousin, closed the door.

"And now," gritted the Admiral, stalking over to frown down at his grandson, "before that cloth-headed gapeseed comes back, let us have some plain speaking, sir! I've been chatting with your grooms, and I hear this is not the first time an attempt has been made on your life. Why was I not told? It was not Gains! For all his justification he'd not resort to such loathly means and is no coward, so do not hand me that farradiddle! I put it to you, Hawkhurst, that I mean to track down this villain, if I must call in Bow Street to do it! In fact, I think I shall send a man off to Town in the morning for that—"

"No, sir!" Hawkhurst sat up very fast, winced sharply, clutched his knee, and subsided, as Kent ran to pat his shoulder comfortingly.

"By Jupiter!" ejaculated Buchanan, wandering in and staring at Hawkhurst in stunned shock. "You're up?"

"Garret!" barked the Admiral testily. "I want some answers, if you please!"

"Well, *I* do *not* please!" Hal Archer surged into the room. "Pon . . . son . . . by!" His howl rattled the glasses. Dora, who had been blowing back a lock of hair that persisted in falling into her eyes, was so startled that she forgot she still held the glue-brush and pushed the curl back with it.

"Archer," fumed the Admiral. "Will you be so kind as to—"

"Your lordship, I will not!" the doctor retaliated, not waiting to learn what the opposition had to say. "In this instance, *I* am at the helm! And I shall do as I dashed well please! Oh, there you are, Ponsonby. Help Mr. Hawkhurst to his room. At once! The sooner he is out of this bedlam, the better!"

The Admiral was so incensed by both interruption and delineation that he found it necessary to follow doctor, butler, and patient up the stairs, vociferously expressing his resentment each step of the way. Kent, slipping in beside his hero, found Ponsonby supporting him on one side and a cane employed on the other. Undaunted, he gripped a corner of Hawkhurst's jacket and thus became a part of the small procession.

Euphemia, meanwhile, moved to the aid of the hapless Dora, and Carlotta proceeded to offer some barbed advice as to the best method by which the glue-brush might be extricated from her relative's locks.

Unnoticed in the confusion, Buchanan and Stephanie drifted quietly away.

Archer's mood had mellowed considerably when he left his patient half an hour later. Encountering two worried young ladies in the hall, he told them that, if Hawk could be chained to his bed so that the stitches might have a chance to hold, the leg would doubtless heal in due course. Euphemia's fears were considerably eased by this news, but to her surprise the usually calm Stephanie questioned the surgeon so exhaustively that he at length advised her not to be a silly goose, for she knew her brother was forged of Toledo steel.

Downstairs, meanwhile, Coleridge and Mrs. Graham were in spirits because the fog had lifted, thus enabling them to drive into Down Buttery for the Broadbents' annual Christmas party, and when Stephanie and Euphemia joined them, Colley urged that they go along. Lady Bryce entered a caveat, saying it must surely be improper to attend a celebration after their dear Garret had been so murderously set upon. Dora's face fell. "I am sure you are right, Lottie," she said wistfully. "We had best not go." Colley looked downcast, but to Euphemia's delight the Admiral intervened. Hawk, he said, would be the last to wish anyone to miss some merrymaking on his account, and he urged that they all go. In the event, only Carlotta, Dora, and Coleridge took his advice. Euphemia pleaded weariness, but actually had no wish to leave Hawkhurst on what would be her last evening in the great house. Buchanan said he had some letters that simply must be attended to, and Stephanie declined on the grounds she wished to spend some time with her dear Euphemia. At the last moment, Colley asked if he might take Kent along. "It will be a little late for him, because there will be dancing half the night after the children's party is over, but it's a grand affair, Mia. All the village children are invited, and he would likely have a fine time. And never worry, they've a large house, and there is sure to be a spot where he can curl up until we leave." Euphemia accepted gratefully. Kent was summoned and, thrown into a fever of excitement, went racing joyously off in search of his coat and hat.

The house was quiet when at last they were gone, and Euphemia was very glad when dinner came to an end. Not only was she extremely conscious of the lack of Hawkhurst's vital presence at the table, but the knowledge she was to leave tomorrow, coupled with the fear that she might never see her love again, weighed heavily upon her spirits. Fortunately, the Admiral was in a high good humour, and his amusing reminiscences of a Christmas he had passed in Bombay brightened the meal until he directed a casual enquiry to Ponsonby as to Hawkhurst's disposition. The butler replied gravely that Constable Littlejohn had been with the master for the last hour and more, whereupon Wetherby rose up like an erupting volcano. "I vow that maggot-wit has settled in like a bulldog," he snorted. "Pray excuse me, for I must kick him downstairs before he wears poor Hawk to a shade!" Saying which, he sailed out with all storm signals flying.

Euphemia and Stephanie left Buchanan to his port, but he joined them very shortly, and a few moments later the Admiral returned. The Constable thought the village blacksmith might be able to shed some light upon the possible owner of the bear tamer. Would they forgive so flagrant a breach of good manners did he accompany Littlejohn into Down Buttery? Implored not to stand on ceremony at such a time, he kissed his granddaughter and told her not to wait up for him, adjured Buchanan not to go rushing off in the morning without allowing him to say his farewells, and winked mischievously at Euphemia. "As for you, dear lady, I've no doubt we shall see *you* often enough after the holidays."

Watching him stride briskly from the room, Euphemia longed to share his confidence. She stifled a sigh and glanced around to find Stephanie watching her. The girl said earnestly, "He is quite right, Mia. We *will* be seeing you. Very often. No matter . . . what happens."

Despite the words, it sounded like an ending. Her voice was uncertain, and tears glittered on her lashes. Not until that moment had Euphemia realized how deeply fond she had become of this gentle girl; nor that her affection was as fully returned. They hugged one another tearfully, then Stephanie mumbled that she simply must go and see Garret and left brother and sister alone.

"Well," said Buchanan brightly. "Ready to be off, love? Great Aunt Lucasta must be in a rare taking. Save for the fog, I've no doubt she would have come with a blaze of trumpets to rescue us from this house of infamy."

Euphemia responded just as light-heartedly, but the deception was pierced, and she was suddenly swept into a fierce and rare hug. Reciprocating, she then leaned back in her brother's arms, looking up at him wonderingly.

He let her go and said with a rather strained laugh, "Sorry, but I just cannot endure to see you so determined to be brave. He *will* come after you, Mia. You are not losing him forever, you know."

Long after Ellie had closed the bed-curtains and left her, those words haunted Euphemia. Would Hawk come after her? Or, as soon as she was gone, would he limp into his curricle and drive to some remote spot where she might never find him? Worse, would he join up once more? Wellington stood in urgent need of experienced cavalry officers, and he would certainly be welcomed. The thought so terrified her that she sat bolt upright in bed, staring with wide and fearful eyes at the bedpost.

It was no use—she was far too distraught to sleep. She swept back the curtains and lit the candle. Half past twelve . . . She took up the book she had selected from the library and wasted an hour reading words that barely broke into the anxieties that crowded her mind. She closed the book at last and set it aside. Perhaps if she had some warm milk she would be able to go to sleep. But to wake Ellie at half past one o'clock seemed unkind. She stepped into her slippers, donned her warm dressing gown, and having ensured that her cap was neatly disposed over her curls, took up her candle and went downstairs.

A lamp, turned down low, still burned beside the massive front doors, but that flickering glow was the only sign of life. She trod softly along the Great Hall, admiring the sweep of the plastered ceiling and the perfect lines of this dear old house that the inspired architect had managed to make both palatial and welcoming. Crossing the central hall, her slipper caught on a fold of the rug, and the heel curled under her foot. She crossed to the long teakwood chest near the front doors, to right matters. A letter lay in the jade salver. Glancing at it as she set down the candle, she saw the superscription: "To Miss Euphemia Buchanan." The printing looked familiar, but why would Simon be so formal, or leave a letter here for her? Curious, she took up the folded paper. Foolish boy, he should have known it would not be given to her until morning, when she would see him anyway. She broke the seal, and read:

My Dearest Mia:

Do you remember our little chat before the Musicale? I told you that I am a very ordinary fellow, and that someday you would have to admit I've more than my share of failings. Best of all sisters, I fear that day has come, for I am seizing my chance for happiness and thereby abandoning you to a most difficult situation.

Perhaps you have already guessed that Stephanie and I are desperately in love.

Euphemia clutched at the table, her heart seeming to stop beating. Blinking dazedly, she read on,

Please believe that I have not lied to her. I am not quite that base. She knows Tina will never give me a divorce, but has consented to elope with me regardless.

"Oh . . . my . . . God!" moaned Euphemia, pressing a hand to her temple. He *could* not! Not Simon? Through a haze of tears, she was able to make out,

I may be kicked out of the 52nd. I don't know. With the help of Leith, and the support (I pray) of John Colborne, I hope to retain some rank. I am not pressed for funds, at least, and Stephanie will never have to know want. I have attempted to explain to her what she *will* have to face, but her regard for me is such that she refuses to be intimidated by that prospect.

Please believe that I deeply regret having to resort to this reprehensible flight. I would by far prefer to meet Hawkhurst on the field of honour, which he would, of course, demand. But I have come to the conclusion that a duel could only make a difficult situation worse. Were either of us killed, all four lives must be wrecked, and what would that serve?

I abandon you, my loved sister. I run like a craven when

my benefactor is crippled and ill. For this, I feel total shame.
But no shame can compare to the joy of having found the
lady I can truly love with all my heart, and who loves me
in return.

I am comforted by the knowledge that love has come to
you also, and that with so fine a gentleman as Hawkhurst to
care for and protect you, someday you may perhaps forgive,

Your unforgivable,
Simon.

How could she have been so blind? Euphemia choked on a
sob and let tears flow unchecked. How could she have been so
foolish as to suppose Simon was being "kind" in escorting
Stephanie? Or think the girl's new radiance was purely the result of her changed appearance? Poor Hawk, so cruelly bedevilled by Fate, must know more sorrow! And whatever could
she find to say to—

"So you could not sleep either, my Unattainable lady."

The deep voice behind her sent her eyes flying open. She
clutched the letter to her bosom, her heart thundering with fear.
If he discovered this, he would go after them, hurt or no!
Nothing, no one on God's earth would stop him! He would
catch them, she had no doubt of it. And Simon would die!

Hawkhurst had seen her start and gently begged pardon for
having alarmed her. Her throat was dry, her lips stiff, but she
must answer! Furtively, she dashed the tears away, swung
around, and, fighting to sound lightly scolding, said, "Garret!
Whatever are we to do with—"

He was leaning on his cane, his face tired and wan. But
hobbling closer he demanded, "What is it? You are white as
death."

The telltale letter concealed beneath a fold in her dressing
gown, she replied, "How should I be otherwise, love? For we
leave here tomorrow."

"I know it," he sighed. "And I wish, with all my heart . . ."
He stopped, his narrowed gaze searching her face in the dimness. Perhaps only the eyes of love would have detected the
gleam on her lashes, but Hawkhurst loved greatly. "You have
been weeping!" His hand shot out to grip hers. "And why do
you tremble so? Here's more than grief! You are petrified! Did
you think I would not know? What is it? What have you there?
Another letter? Gad! It is a deluge! Stop seeking to protect me,
for the love of heaven! Give it me!"

"No!" she gasped, stumbling backward, "It is not—"

But as she twisted away, he groaned, swayed, and grabbed for the table. At once her arms were about him. And as swiftly, he had the letter.

"No!" she sobbed, snatching at it. "Hawk, that was despicable! You tricked me!"

"Of course," he said, straightening and leaning against the table as he held her away with one hand. "I will not have you upset by—" His words trailed off as he saw the superscription, and he started to return the letter, but it unfolded, and, even as she again reached out eagerly, his attention was caught by his sister's name. He frowned, pulled his hand back, and his eyes flashed down the page. "Now, damn his rotten soul!" he gasped. "That *bastard*!" He crumpled the letter, flung it to the floor, and wheeled about.

Galvanized into action, Euphemia sprang after him and caught at his arm. "Hawk! If you love me, I beg of you—"

With a savage wrench he sent her staggering. "Save your breath! Do you think that sweet sister of mine has the slightest idea of what it is like to be *really* scorned? Well, *I* do, by God! And she'll not live that hell whilst I can prevent it! Stay back, Mia!"

But she would not and, sobbing, pleading, clinging to him, contrived at last to grip his cane and, leaping away, sent it spinning across the hall, then sobbed her anguish as he sank, flinching, to one knee.

"Hawk, oh, my darling, I beg . . . I *implore* you! Do not try to get up! Hawk, you will break the stitches! I love you! Hawk, I *love* you! Please, *please*, give them their chance!"

His face convulsed, he came somehow to his feet, reeled to the wall, and tugged the bellrope. "He is not . . . worth . . . your tears," he said breathlessly. "If I have to crawl, I'll not see him drag her down . . . with him. He'll rot in hell first!"

A sleepy footman yawned into the hall, checked, than ran forward.

Euphemia fled. Five minutes later, clad in her warmest habit, her fur-line pelisse flying out behind her, she ran to the back stairs.

Lights gleamed in the stables. The grooms, half clad, were harnessing a magnificent pair of matched greys to a racing curricle. In dressing gown and nightcap, Manners was shouting, "When you're done, turn 'em to the side road!"

One of the grooms checked, staring at him in dismay. "But

it ain't repaired, Mr. Manners. The bridge ain't safe! Mr. Garret wouldn't—"

"Oh, yes, he would! Do as I say, and be ready for the master. I'm going to get dressed. Don't let him leave without me!"

Euphemia ran to intercept him. "Manners! Do you love him?" He halted, staring his incredulity, and she seized his arm, shaking it in her frenzy. "If you would not see him complete the ruin of his life this night, help me in!"

"In . . . the curricle . . . Miss?" he faltered.

"Yes! Oh, Manners, I *know* you love him. *Help* me! I beg of you!"

The grooms were hanging desperately to the heads of the greys who, because of the fog, had been stabled for many days with little exercise. Euphemia ran to the side of the vehicle, and, handing her up, his face pale with anxiety, Manners groaned, "He'll have my hide for this!"

"In here now! Beside me!" she said tersely. "Quickly! Lean forward, so he does not see me!"

Moaning, he did as she commanded. "Miss, are you sure . . . ?"

"I love him too. Do you think I would do this, else?"

Manners snatched off his nightcap with a trembling hand as Hawkhurst limped from the house, pulling on his gloves and leaning on the arm of a befuddled Bailey, who wore a startling red dressing gown over his nightshirt.

"Put the Mantons under the front seat!" rasped Hawkhurst, and, as the valet obeyed, then attempted to fasten the top button of his master's many-caped driving coat, he cried, "Have done! Manners, your hand!" He clambered up, gasped out a pained oath, then ejaculated, "Dammit! Why in the devil are you not dressed? Get down, man! I'll not have pneumonia on my conscience in addition to—" And he checked in sheer, stunned shock as Manners jumped out, thus revealing the white-faced girl who sat there.

"Hell and damnation!" roared Hawkhurst, recovering. "Get down, madam!"

"I will not!" she flashed defiantly.

"Then, by God, I'll put you out!"

He bent towards her. "Stand away!" cried Euphemia and swung the whip she held in a wild, snaking crack over the heads of the horses.

The greys reared, screamed, and plunged. The grooms jumped for their lives. Hawkhurst, caught off balance, grabbed the reins with one hand and the side with the other, and some-how managed to avoid being thrown out. But there was no stopping the team. They bolted, wild with nerves, excitement, and high-bred nonsensicality.

Clinging to the side in heart-stopping terror, for several min-utes Euphemia was sure they must both die. But, sobbing for the breath that was swept from her by the rush of air, she re-alized at last that the grim-faced man beside her, far from at-tempting to slow them, was urging them on, his keen eyes fixed upon the road ahead, his hands sure and firm on the reins.

The quaint old bridge she had once admired was directly ahead: the bridge that was not yet properly repaired! "Hawk!" she screamed. "Stop! You'll kill us!"

"You should've thought of that before!"

She shot a terrified look at him. He had lost his hat when he almost fell at the start. The wind had whipped his hair into a tumbled untidy darkness about his pale face, and he looked wild and unyielding. The bridge shot towards them, the curri-cle looking twice as wide as that narrow span. "Do you feel the need," he shouted, "pray!"

She prayed. A deeper rumble of wheels, a wild jolting, and they were across. From somewhere behind them, she thought to hear a startled yell, fading swiftly into the night.

It was a race against time now. A mad, plunging, reckless nightmare of speed. A scattering of cottages appeared distantly, flew towards them, and were gone. Euphemia's eyelashes were blown back into her eyes, and her hair was whipped about un-til it all came down and screamed out behind her. Her hands clutched at the side until they were numb. Her feet were braced against the front panel, and she wondered how Hawk could brace himself with that injured leg. The curricle rocked around curves and flashed between hedgerows at what seemed impossible speed, but always Hawkhurst's sure hands guided the thundering greys with hair's-breadth precision. And gradu-ally Euphemia's terror gave way to exhilaration. Lips parted, eyes shining, she leaned forward, gazing into the night, watch-ing trees and barns and hayricks loom out of the darkness, shoot at them, and whip past.

They had long since left the Dominer preserves, and now turned onto a main road. A sleepy village hurtled by, and scant moments later another loomed up and was gone. Bishops Can-nings, she thought. Hawkhurst left the road and headed across the country. He must be mad! Surely he'd never dare go through the forest at night? Instead, they bumped onto a road again, and soon a mail coach approached, challenging them for more than its share of the narrow surface. Euphemia shrank, but Hawkhurst, his jaw set, held the greys relentlessly straight. A horn blared stridently, a howl and a stream of curses, wheels that came so close they shaved the hubs of the curricle's wheels. Screams and yells, and the six-in-hand broke into wild, rearing confusion. A harsh laugh from Hawkhurst, and they were clear. Weak in the knees, Euphemia sat and shook. No more traffic now, only the jolt and rumble and pound of their own flight. On and on, until her eyes smarted from the buffeting of the icy wind, and she closed them briefly.

"Hells fire!" shouted Hawkhurst. "Hang on, Mia!"

Startled, she looked up and uttered a choked gasp. To the left was a stand of trees, and on the right, a rockstrewn slope descended to a rushing stream. A tree was down across the road ahead, and beyond it were two mounted men, masked and grim, with pistols levelled.

"Stand!" they bellowed jointly.

"You had to come, woman," Hawkhurst roared. "They must have missed the Night Mail! Get down!"

She stared at him in bewilderment and, torn between pride and horror, knew that he did not mean to stop. His arm shot out. She was seized and flung forward, her nose jamming against her knees, and then every bone in her body was being jolted to pieces; her teeth snapped together; the air was beaten from her lungs as the curricle turned right and headed sharply downward, bouncing and swaying over ruts and rocks. One stumble of the greys, she thought, and they would overturn! A shot rang out, deafening in the quiet night, and then another. Angry shouts blasted her ears with swiftly fading profanity. The jouncing eased, and the wheels were on a level road surface once more.

Euphemia sat up straight, scanning Hawkhurst for any sign of a wound. The moon was brighter now, painting the countryside with its faerie light, and he looked unhurt. She touched her nose, and her suspicions were confirmed.

"Confound you, sir!" she cried furiously. "Now see what you have done!"

He shot an admiring glance at her, then looked again, anxiety stark upon his face. "Oh, egad! Are you all right?"

She leaned against him weakly. "Oh, Garret . . . I am so . . . faint."

Frantic, he pulled back, slowing the team. Then he grunted, "The deuce you are!" and dropped his hands. "Giddap!"

"Hawk, *listen*! Please, at least listen!"

He ignored her, leaning into the wind, holding the reins with one hand while shoving a handkerchief at her with the other. She took it and mopped at her nose. "Lean your head back!" he shouted.

She did and after a minute or two looked up. The horses were not racing as fast now, and she asked, "Where do you suppose they have gone?"

"To Town. Your precious philanderer will need his uniform, his bank, and the Horse Guards."

He was right, of course, and Euphemia's heart sank. It was near inconceivable that her dear brother, so brave and upright, was prepared to subject that sweet girl to the humiliation and degradation that must be her lot wherever they went. But, glancing at the man beside her, she knew she had been willing to risk such disgrace, had even been so bold as to suggest it. Only Hawk, with his iron control, his rigid adherence to the very code that had ruined him, had rejected her.

They were coming into a hamlet, quiet and peaceful in the moonlight. The wheels rattled over the cobbled streets, and Hawkhurst pulled into the yard of The Fox and Hounds and tossed the reins to a sleepy ostler who came stumbling to them. He clambered out painfully, steadied himself, then reached up to her. He looked white and strained, and she refused his aid, jumping lightly down on the other side with a flash of neat ankles. He turned to the ostler. "My blacks. Five guineas if you break your record!"

The ostler's chin sagged. Then he whistled shrilly, and another man ran from the stables, tucking his shirt into his breeches.

Rubbing drowsy eyes, the proprietor stepped out of the inn and was galvanized into action. "Mr. Hawkhurst! This way. What, are you hurt, sir? I'll get my cane for you. Take my arm. This way, ma'am."

The parlour was low-roofed, quaint, and warm. Hawkhurst perched wearily on the edge of a chest, and the proprietor hurried away to call his wife.

"Do you try to abandon me, Garret," warned Euphemia

softly, "I shall scream bloody murder and vow you're carrying me off!"

He was staring sombrely at the dying fire and for a moment appeared not to have heard her, but glanced up suddenly and said, "They should not believe you. I am well known here."

"Then they would most assuredly believe me," she countered. Appreciation brightened his eyes, and his stern mouth quivered for a brief second.

"I should like to tidy my hair and wash," she said.

"You have precisely ten minutes, ma'am."

She knew better. A plump country woman wrapped in a voluminous flannel dressing gown showed her to a pleasant little upstairs bedchamber. She splashed a wet rag over her face, bound up her flying hair so that it looked halfway presentable, and returned in less than five minutes to find Hawkhurst seated on the outside bench, tankard in hand, watching as the ostlers harnessed a fine team of blacks to the curricle. He was slumped against the wall, and she had a fleeting impression of total despair and hopelessness, but he glanced up, saw her coming towards him, and scowled with chagrin. The proprietor followed to hand her a sandwich and a tankard into which she peered uneasily. "What is it?"

"Hemlock!" ground out Hawkhurst.

"Hot toddy, ma'am," the proprietor chuckled and went to his grooms.

"You'd best drink up," said Hawkhurst. "If you insist upon going to an execution, you will need it."

Tears stung Euphemia's eyes, and a pang went through her, but she would not weep. She must be strong if she was somehow to prevail. She took a sip of the toddy and coughed, but it was hot and invigorating. She was mildly surprised that at so terrible a moment she could be ravenously hungry and took several bites of the sandwich before pleading, "Does it mean nothing to you that I love him? Dearest, only think what an impenetrable barrier you will build between us if you persist."

"Your loyalty is commendable. Your judgment questionable. And the barriers between us are already impenetrable, Mia."

"You were not so harsh in the ruins," she said, shamelessly reminding him of his obligation.

He looked at her steadily, but said nothing.

"Oh, Garret, have you no compassion? Simon is—"

"A black-hearted rogue! He was willing enough to accept

my hospitality, even though he despised me! And he repaid me by weaseling himself into the affections of a pure and innocent girl! Oh, I've a couple of cousins, ma'am, I'd give him gladly enough, I assure you! But, Stephanie? No, by God! I'll see the slimy scoundrel dead at my feet, rather!" Her muffled sob tore his heart despite his fierce utterance, but he said with grim implacability, "Were you and I happily wed, Mia—which can never be—I would not be turned aside from this." And he stood, took up the cane the landlord had brought him, and began to hobble towards the curricle.

Euphemia ran to stand before him and reached up to tug at the cape of his coat in desperation. "Garret, please! I love him, just as you love her! You cannot imagine what his life has been with that awful wife of—"

"Oh, can I not!" He flashed bitterly, striving to pull her hands away.

She clung to him tenaciously, gazing into the steely grey eyes with tearful entreaty, having no idea of how bewitching she looked with the moonlight gilding the drops that clung to her lashes. "Garret, my dearest one, do you not yet know what it *really* means to love? To long to be with someone so that each moment apart is an eternity? Every beat of your heart an ache of longing?"

At this the hardness faded from his eyes, to be replaced by a yearning sadness. He threw the cane into the curricle and reached to take her hands and press them to his lips, murmuring, "Yes, God help me, now . . . I know."

"And I also. Darling, think of what you throw away. Think of what our future might be."

He leaned to her. "I adore you," he breathed. "Even with mustard on the end of your pretty nose!" And before she could move, shoved her brutally away.

Euphemia fell, sprawling. Dragging himself painfully into the curricle, Hawkhurst snatched up the reins. But she was nothing if not true to her word. Her voice teacher might have despaired of her singing, but he had at least taught her lung control. Abandoning every instinct of propriety, even as she went down she let out a shriek that brought light flaring into several windows of the old hostelry, while half-clad ostlers and stablehands ran into the yard. She continued in full cry, and her piercing screams, which merely startled the human beings, wrought havoc with the thoroughbreds. For several minutes it was all Hawkhurst could do just to keep the panicked blacks from climbing into the curricle with him.

When at length he swung the whip and sent them streaming out of the yard and onto the road, Euphemia was at his side.

❧ *Chapter 17* ❧

They were rumbling over a hump-backed bridge across the Kennet when Hawkhurst saw the chaise ahead. He grinned savagely and sent the whip hissing out, and the blacks, who had been nursed along for the last two miles, sprang into their harness and were off at a headlong gallop.

"I am amazed," shouted Hawkhurst sardonically. "He took Stephanie's new chaise. I thought he'd help himself to my other racing curricle, at the very least! D'you suppose your noble brother fancied me too knocked up to follow, ma'am?"

Euphemia winced, but said nothing, hanging on for dear life, perceived that Simon must have seen them, because the chaise ahead lurched suddenly and was away at top speed.

Never afterwards would she forget that frenzied race through the night, the total disregard for the irregularities of the road, for common sense or human life. She could well imagine the despair in Simon's heart and the terror that must possess poor Stephanie. As for herself, if Hawk shot her brother, her own life would be finished, for to lose them both must either rob her of all reason or plunge her into a grey world in which there would be nothing left but loneliness. She glanced down, wondering if she could possibly reach the flat and deadly box Bailey had thrust under the seat. But at this speed it must be a hopeless attempt. They were creeping up relentlessly. Poor dear souls, they had no least chance!

And then the chaise slowed and pulled to a stop, and Buchanan jumped down.

Hawkhurst swore under his breath as the curricle went shooting past at such a rate that it was necessary for him to make a wide swinging turn and send the team cantering back.

Tensely, Euphemia waited her chance. When he started out, she would push him and seize the Mantons. It would break her heart to hurt him again, but better that than tragedy for them all.

Hawkhurst reined the team to a halt, turned to her with a weary smile, and suddenly caught her in a merciless grip. She squealed as she was whirled across him and over the side, to be dumped unceremoniously onto the grass at the side of the road. With a reckless leap, he sprang from the curricle, gasped, and clung to the wheel, head down. Strengthened by fury, he stood straight almost immediately, hauled out his Mantons, and with the box under his arm hobbled towards Buchanan, who stood beside the chaise still, Stephanie held close against his heart.

The girl broke free and ran to face her brother. "Gary," she sobbed, wringing her hands in despair. "Simon did not want this. The fault was mine . . . only mine!"

"Fustian! Stand aside!"

Instead, she reached out to him imploringly. "I told him I would . . . enter a convent. I meant it! Gary, dear one . . . I beg of you—"

"I should rather by far see you take the vows than embark on the pretty life he plans for you! I gave you credit for more integrity than this, ma'am!"

Buchanan strode to take Stephanie by the shoulders. He was very pale, but his voice was steady. "I told you this would happen, love. And I cannot say I'm sorry. Allow me now to handle it with some shred of honour." He set her aside and faced Hawkhurst. "I am at your disposal, sir."

"Oh, no . . . no!" sobbed Stephanie.

Euphemia took the distraught girl in her arms, experiencing a feeling of total helplessness. She had done all that it was humanly possible to do. Her brother looked at her with a fond, sad smile, and, despite her love for him, she knew in her heart that Hawk was all too well justified, even as she knew that Stephanie, fighting for her happiness, must have driven Simon to this decision. What a hopeless mess!

Hawkhurst regarded his weeping sister for a moment and, his eyes a glare in his drawn face, grated, "One chance,

Stephanie. Swear you will never see him again, and I'll let the cheating cur live."

Buchanan's head flung upward. "I think," he said angrily, "we have come too far for that, sir!"

"You . . . *think?*" Hawkhurst swung to him fiercely. "I would be well justified in shooting you out of hand! Think on that!"

"Yes, in your place I would feel the same, no doubt. But I shall not give her up, so do not bother to ask."

Hawkhurst nodded. "It will not be necessary for me to slap you, I trust? I despise histronics." He opened the pistol box and offered it, the moonlight gleaming on those beautifully wrought messengers of death. Buchanan selected one, tested the balance and gave a wry smile of appreciation. "Where?"

Hawkhurst glanced around and nodded towards a level patch of turf between two clumps of trees a short distance off the road. Courteously, he enquired if Sir Simon had any objections, to which, just as courteously, Buchanan replied that he had none, and they started off, the girls, arms entwined, following helplessly.

Hawkhurst was paying a bitter price for all this activity and was obliged to slow on the last few yards, which were up a slight rise. As Buchanan passed, he said unevenly, "You had best . . . say your last words to . . . my sister."

"Thank you, but they were all said whilst you were racing your team half a mile down the road and back."

Hawkhurst nodded, tossed a curt command to the girls that they remain here, and accompanied Buchanan onto the turf. Stephanie wept softly. Euphemia was pale and silent, unable to tear her eyes from the two young men who, in time-honoured fashion, now stood back to back.

Slanting a glance to the side, Hawkhurst saw her agonized gaze and thought, This must be goodbye, my dearest love. Either way. And he said softly, "Last chance, Buchanan. Give her up."

"Never. But it was a filthy way to treat you after what you have done for us. I apologize for that."

"Thank you. Twelve paces?"

"Ten, if you please. It's night, and I lack your skill."

"As you wish. I will call."

They began to walk, pistols raised at their sides, while Hawkhurst's calm voice counted off the strides. As they moved apart, Euphemia's eyes shifted from one to the other: Simon, slim and straight and proud, Garret, hobbling painfully without his cane, but by far the deadlier of the two. And watching the erect carriage of his head, despite his uneven gait, her eyes blurred with tears, and her prayers were fast and frantic.

And then, that fateful, heart-stopping word: *"Ten!"*

They turned simultaneously, only Hawkhurst staggered very slightly, then staggered again as the deafening blast of Buchanan's pistol rent the silence.

Euphemia felt frozen, her breath held in check. Beside her, Stephanie gave a small moan and sank to her knees whispering, "My God . . . my God!"

Smoke curled slowly from Buchanan's weapon. Blood was slipping down Hawkhurst's forehead, and he could scarcely see, but his arm held steady, the long wicked barrel of the Manton aimed unerringly at Buchanan's chest. "Give me your word . . . damn you! Don't make me kill you!"

The pistol fell from Buchanan's hand. His head went up a little. He was very white, but he stood in silence, unwavering.

Stephanie was also silent, still upon her knees, watching in horrified fascination. Beside her, Euphemia felt as though they were all suspended like the figures in a cameo on this clear, cold winter's night. The serene moonlight made the scene even more incongruous—Hawk, with his arm so rigidly outstretched, the pistol gleaming in his hand, Simon, bravely waiting for death. She thought a numbed and trite, and only eleven days before Christmas . . .

Hawkhurst's head was less punishing now; he could feel blood cold on his cheek, but the ball had come short of stunning him, and he could see more clearly. He sighted with care. He'd given the sneaking cur every chance, God knows. Euphemia's voice, shaken with grief, echoed devastatingly in his ears: "Do you not yet know what it *really* means to love?" His hand trembled, but it was his duty to protect the ladies of his house. "I told him I would enter a convent . . . Gary, dear one . . . I beg of you." Dammit, he must not fail! Nor must he torture Buchanan, who stood there so staunchly, blast him! He'd chosen his route, hadn't he? He gritted his teeth and fired, the sharp retort shattering the peaceful country quiet. Through the billow of smoke, he saw Buchanan crumple and go down. Stephanie screamed thinly. He lowered his arm and walked away as both girls rushed to that still figure.

Stephanie reached her lover first and dropped to her knees, sobbing out his name.

Kneeling at the other side, Euphemia saw her brother's eyes flicker open. "Good . . . God!" he breathed, incredulous. "Am I not dead?"

Stephanie gave a choked cry and bent to kiss him. Euphemia's eyes dimmed with grateful tears, but ever practical she asked, "Where are you hit, Simon?"

He blinked at her, then sat up, holding his left forearm.

Euphemia drew a great sobbing breath, sent a silent prayer winging to heaven, and managed to request with relative calm that Stephanie run to the chaise and fetch her reticule.

Five minutes later, the flesh wound in his arm bound, and his coat slung about his shoulders, Buchanan walked to the man who leaned against the curricle in a silent waiting. "Did I hurt you badly, sir?"

"Did you try?" Hawkhurst countered in a tone of blasting contempt.

Buchanan bit his lip. "Had you remained still, I'd have missed you entirely."

"My apologies."

Euphemia went to Hawkhurst and with her handkerchief gently wiped the blood from his face. "Thank you!" she whispered. "Oh, Hawk, thank you! I know how easily you might have killed him."

He grunted and said a grim, "Do not expect my blessings, Stephie."

Her lips quivered. "You have . . . mine," she said on a sob.

Gripping his wounded arm, Buchanan said, "Thank you for this, Hawkhurst. I don't feel quite so worthless."

Hawkhurst gave a cynical snort. "Do you not?"

For a long while there had been silence between them. Hawkhurst, apparently busied with his driving, had said not a word in response to Euphemia's two attempts at conversation. Not daring to disturb that frowning concentration again, she occupied herself with her own thoughts. Simon had kissed her lovingly, begging her forgiveness and asking that she journey with them back to London. She had forgiven him, of course, but had refused to go with him, not only because she must await Kent's return but also from a reluctance to leave Hawk so abruptly. Whatever Simon may have thought, he had said only that he would write to her and that he wished her every happiness. Stephanie's parting with her brother had been poignant. Hawkhurst had growled that he prayed she would not come to regret this decision bitterly and turned from her pleading eyes with cold disdain, only to swing around at the last moment, sweep her into a fierce embrace and whisper that she could return at any time, knowing she would be greeted with love. She had clung to him, weeping but overjoyed. Simon had started to put out his hand, then lowered it, a gesture Hawkhurst had apparently been quite unable to see. Watching Simon's painful flush and Hawk's implacable stare, Euphemia had known sorrow for each of them, but since her brother might very well have been lying lifeless on that cold little patch of turf, her overwhelming emotion had been one of thankfulness.

Now she glanced up at the stern features of the man she loved and tried once more. "He will be good to her, dearest," she said softly. "Try not to hate him."

He turned his head and for a moment stared at her blankly. Then, as if comprehension suddenly dawned, ejaculated, "My God! You should not be here!"

"I know," she smiled. "I am properly compromised now." But, despite her outward calm, she was frightened. Several times, on that wild journey here, his demeanour had puzzled her. He had voiced no protest when she had refused to accompany Simon and Stephanie to London, which had surprised her. Instead, he had struggled into the curricle, said not a word when she climbed up beside him, and, until just this moment, behaved as though totally unaware of her presence. He was gripping his knee, and she leaned forward to appropriate the reins. "Foolish boy," she scolded with tender solicitude, "You should have let me drive as I asked. Your leg is paining you."

He drew a bewildered hand across his eyes. "I must be unusually stupid tonight. I cannot seem to think. Give me the reins, Mia."

Unease tightened its hold on her. Rage, scorn, bitter disappointment, she had been prepared for. But this withdrawn confusion was terrifying. He had done his best, he must know that. However much he loved Stephie, he was too strong an individual to be crushed by the knowledge he was beaten—or by fear of his grandfather's inevitable fury. Perhaps . . . Her heart fluttering, she asked, "Have you lost your love for me because of Simon?"

"Yes. Now give me the reins, if you please."

"No! And you tell the most dreadful whiskers, Garret Hawkhurst!"

Instead of simply possessing himself of the ribbons, as he

would normally have done, he leaned back without further argument. "No one need ever know ..." he muttered, half to himself. "Colley can escort you and the boy to Bath, first thing in the morning."

She did not comment, and he sighed and lapsed into morose silence. The curricle moved smoothly along the silver ribbon of the road, while the moon sank lower in the sky, and only the hoofbeats and the distant voice of an owl disturbed the stillness. Euphemia thought Hawkhurst was sleeping but, slanting a glance at him, discovered that although he was slumped against the squabs, his brow was deeply furrowed as he stared ahead. Common sense argued that this was not surprising behaviour. He had been weakened and brutally hurt by that trap. Instead of remaining in his bed as Dr. Archer had demanded, he had suffered a night that would have taxed a well man. He must be in much pain, on top of which he was tormented by the loss of his beloved sister. But intuition would have none of common sense. She had come to think of him as unquenchably indomitable, a man who might reel under Fate's buffets but would always come up fighting. Now he seemed utterly crushed. She drove on, worrying at it, and as the miles passed was plagued by the certainty that something else had happened, something to eclipse even the shock and grief of Stephanie's elopement. Was that what had brought him downstairs at half past one tonight? Or could he, perhaps, have suspected that Stephie and Simon loved one another? Had he been prepared to start after them? But she rejected the notion at once, for his reaction had been one of total shock. Recalling that terrible moment, she shivered and then tensed. When he had snatched Simon's farewell message from her, he had said, "Another letter? Gad! It is a deluge!" A *deluge*? She had the answer now and pulled the team to a standstill. "My darling! You have heard from Mount again!"

He stared at her in amazement, and, seizing his hand and clasping it between both her own, she went on, "What did he say? Is it . . . very bad news?"

"How—" he gasped, thunderstruck, "how could you possibly know?"

"I love you! Have you forgot? *Tell* me!"

His hand lax in hers, he hesitated, then said dully, "I have been permitted to . . . to see my son, Mia."

"*What?*" She searched his face for the elation she should have found there, but he merely looked haggard and very tired, the deep graze left by Simon's bullet a dark bar vanishing into the hairline above his temple. "But *when?*" she demanded. "You have had no visitors at Dominer since the Musicale, and—" His faint, bitter smile alerting her, she stopped, a cold fist closing about her heart, and faltered, "No! Oh, *no!* Eustace?"

"Eustace. Clever, was it not? Mrs. Frittenden—that's not her name, of course—is Mount's aunt, so he says. When he learned of the Musicale, he sent her to Dominer with the boy." "But, how? Had he an invitation?"

"Didn't need one. Their carriage 'broke down' on the way, and the Paragoys were so kind as to take them up, naturally supposing them to be invited guests. When they arrived," he shrugged, "my aunt assumed they were with the Paragoys." Speechless, Euphemia stared at him, and after a small pause he went on in a low, stricken voice, "I underestimated my enemy. He has chosen a revenge far more deadly and destructive than the beatings and starvation he was used to taunt me with. He has taken that—that splendid child and made of him a greedy, spoiled, selfish little . . . crudity." He wrenched his head away and groaned, "Can you imagine the . . . the *man* Mount will make of him? My . . . lord!" He fought for control, regained it, and, glancing at the silent girl, encountered such a wealth of love and sympathy shining through her glistening tears that the ache in his heart was eased. He pulled his shoulders back, and wiping away those tears, kissed her on the brow. "What a night you have had. And how wretched of me to burden you with—"

"With such awful . . . stuff!" she gulped fiercely. She saw his brows go up and, taking his handkerchief, blew her nose, dashed away the remnants of her tears, and averred, "I *never* heard such dreadful nonsense! That little brat is not your son!" A rueful smile touched his eyes, and, desperate to spare him this last bitter blow, she went on recklessly, "How do you know it for truth? Did you recognize him? In the slightest? He was practically a babe when you lost him. Can Mount *prove* that Eustace is your son?"

Hawkhurst took back the reins and started the tired blacks. "I am not a complete flat, you know. When I received the first demand for money, I refused to pay a groat until I had a report from a reputable physician as to Avery's health. The boy was injured in the accident, as you are aware. The attending physician sent me a report—from Rome. It was very explicit and included a complete description of Avery." He saw Euphemia's mouth open and threw up a detaining hand. "Yes, I sent agents to verify the physician's authenticity. Mount and my son had gone, of course, but there is no doubt. It was Avery."

"But *how* can you be so *sure*? Is there any distinguishing mark? A birthmark, or something of the sort?"

To her dismay, he nodded. "When Avery was two, he knocked over a glass. Before his nurse could reach him, he had trod on a fragment and the sole of his foot was badly cut. It became infected and left an odd scar. Our physician, Sir Alec MacKenzie, told me Avery would carry it to his death. In his latest letter, Mount enclosed the doctor's report on Avery's present health. It was from Sir Alec. He is retired now and half crippled by rheumatism. He lives in Wales, but Mount had persuaded the old fellow to examine Avery, explaining he was the boy's 'tutor' and that I had been out of the country for a long time. He knew that nothing would induce Mac to betray me, and that I was aware of that." He smiled at her wanly. "Thorough, eh?"

She blinked, but said with dauntless persistence, "Yes. And clever enough to have copied the scar. Oh, I know that would be cruel, but he is a vengeful and cruel man, love. And you are dealing with a great fortune, and a title. Gary, there are all too many people merciless enough to go to such lengths."

"Yes. But why should he? He has my son, why—"

"Well . . . well, suppose he has not? Suppose—forgive me, dearest, but—suppose Avery had . . . died in that accident? Mount would have been left with nothing! But if he found a similarly featured, grey-eyed child, and had the scar copied—Hawk, it *could* be done! And don't forget, four years had passed since your Dr. MacKenzie had seen Avery. A little boy changes a lot between three and seven . . . and . . ." The words died on her lips; her heartbeat seemed suddenly to suffocate her, and she sat in frozen silence, stunned by the absurd notion that had crept into her mind.

Hawkhurst was silent also, thinking regretfully that she had tried so valiantly to ease his grief, and must now realize how useless it was.

He was mistaken, for Euphemia was in fact shivering with excitement. Dreading lest she be mistaken, she tried to speak calmly, asking, "Why would Mount try to kill you, then? He has blackmailed you very successfully these past four years. One would think he has many profitable years ahead."

It was a point that has puzzled him to no small extent. He said frowningly, "Hatred, perhaps. A madness that could no longer be contained. Perhaps he imagines that, with me out of the way, he can produce Avery, invent some tale to explain it all, and get his hands on the estate. He would have several doctors to back his story, and he took care to see I would not dare confide in anyone." He paused, then went on thoughtfully, "The only thing is, it is such a stupid risk. However plausible his tale, *Avery* would inherit. Mount's share would, at the most, be a reward, and gratitude. Unless he supposes that he would have the boy under his thumb, and through him would get the fortune somehow." He smiled grimly, "In which case, he don't know my Grandpapa very well!"

"Just so!" cried Euphemia, gripping his arm with an excited little pounce. "Hawk, it does not make sense! That fierce old gentleman would see through Mr. Mount's Canterbury tricks before the cat could lick her ear! And even if he did not, by making his move now, Avery would be removed from Mount's influence, for your Grandpapa would certainly send the boy away to school! No! It must be the height of folly for him to act now, when by waiting he could blackmail you for years, until Lord Wetherby is . . . gone, perhaps. Avery would be a young man by then and completely under his control. Oh, darling do you not see? If Mount *is* mad, he would want to prolong your suffering, not shorten it. Unless, he was *forced* to act now . . . Unless . . ." And she stopped her impassioned speech, aware that he was watching her narrowly, and terror stricken lest she build his hopes to no purpose.

Hawkhurst stopped the team. He took up her hand and kissed it. "Go on, my brave girl. Unless—what? Do you think—Dear Heaven! Do you think Mount is become so unstable he means to kill my grandfather too?"

With a stifled sob, she threw herself into his arms. "Garret, I love you so. When I think what you must have felt tonight. To have read that wicked letter from Mount, and only moments later discover that—that Stephanie and Simon had eloped. My poor darling! I *dare* not risk hurting you any more."

Hawkhurst took her shoulders and held her away from him. And, shaking her gently, he said, "You must give me credit for more backbone than that, dear girl. I own I was rather downpin. And my confounded leg is a bit of a nuisance. But, whatever I may have to face, I've come this far. I'll survive."

Wordless, Euphemia put one hand to caress his cheek, and he smiled, "You have restored me, as you seem so able to do, so tell me what you suspect if you please, ma'am. And I shall promise in return never again to throw you out of my curricle."

Her answering smile was tremulous. "Very well. But, first— The landslide that brought me into your life, *was* it an accident? Leith said—"

"Leith! He is on the Peninsula, surrounded by shot and shell, and at the mercy of those two juggernauts who strive against one another. And he worries. About *me*! No, it was an accident, but I'll never convince Tris of that."

"And the Mohocks in Town? Ellie said they near killed you."

"They could have finished the job easily enough, but did not. And no matter what Tristram said, it may have been sheer coincidence."

"What of the shot that went through your hat? And the falling coping stone? And your new boat? All coincidences?"

Puzzled by all this and rather irked that she had been worried by it, he said a rather brusque, "Probably. Who knows?"

Euphemia's heart was beating very fast. She moved back from him and, clasping her hands nervously, said, "Then it is very possible that Mount had no intention of killing you. Not until . . . *after* the Musicale."

He watched her. Waiting.

"Hawk," she quavered, "I once told you why Simon and I first came onto your lands. Do you remember?"

"Why, I believe you said you wanted to have a look at Dominer."

"I did. But—but it was more than that, dearest. I *really* came because . . . I had become so very fond of . . . of Kent, you see."

Hawkhurst stiffened, and the faint of colour that had come back into his cheeks fled, leaving him whiter than before.

"I told you how I found him," Euphemia rushed on, gripping her hands ever more tightly. "That sweet child, half-starved, beaten, abused. And . . . the soles of his feet, so badly burned." She saw his eyes widen at that and went on, "When he started to recover, I surrounded him with books. Yet, so *often*, I would find him gazing at one picture . . . Dominer. I began to be curious and to want to see the estate myself. But—" She bit her lip, then burst out, "Oh, dearest, if Eustace really *is* your child, does it not seem odd to you that Mount would indulge and pamper the son of the man he so hates? Such deliberate destruction of moral integrity would be fiendish, I grant you, but surely too subtle, too lengthy, to afford immediate pleasure to a warped mind? On the other hand, Kent was ... was sold to gypsies. And later, after God knows what misery, sold again, for a climbing boy! A nightmarish slow death for that intelligent, sensitive child! An experience so terrible that he lost all power to speak. And I believe *was* near death when I found him."

Hawkhurst was so horrified he could not move and stared at her for what seemed an eternity while doubt and fear and imagination had their way with him. He had been drawn to the boy from the first ... That piquant, thin little face; those clear eyes and tender mouth. Such a change from the rosy-cheeked, plump little fellow he had lost. Yet the eyes and the colouring were the same. There was the same sweetness of disposition, the same warm affection. He clenched his fists, fighting hope. He must not, *dare* not, dream it to be true. Yet already his heart was hammering uncontrollably. "That Frittenden woman," he muttered, running a hand distractedly through his hair. "I remember now, at the Musicale, she stopped in front of Kent."

"Yes. I saw her. She stared and stared, and then rushed out."

Hawkhurst bowed his head and gripped his throbbing temples. Had she recognized the boy? She might have seen him recently enough to know him.

Echoing his thoughts, Euphemia said tenderly, "Darling, don't you see? If she identified him and told Mount, he would know his game was almost done. I believe that is why he tried to kill you on the tower. He dared not risk your learning the truth. He had to settle for whatever he might be able to pry from your Grandpapa—after you were dead."

Hawkhurst sat up straight. His mouth was dry, his mind spinning. It made sense now. It all made sense! And the boy *did* seem to like him and had settled into Dominer almost as if—A recollection sprang to mind that was like a blow to the heart. He was visibly jolted, and Euphemia demanded frantically, "What? What have you thought of?"

"His ... bear ..." he half whispered. "Dear heaven! Why did I not think ... ? Mia! His *bear*!"

"You saw it? But—oh, did you give it to him? Poor shabby little bear. He loves it so, I think he has hidden it away somewhere for fear it might be taken—"

Hawkhurst gasped and grabbed at the side of the curricle.

For a moment Euphemia feared he would collapse. Then, look-ing up at her, he said in a thread of a voice, "What . . . what kind of . . . bear? A . . . little carven . . . wooden bear?"

"No, but—How odd, I had forgot the wooden bear he carved. And now that you mention it, that little bear had only one ear as—"

A wild cry escaped Hawkhurst. He all but sprang to clutch her arms and shout, "What *kind* of bear?"

"Wh-why, a stuffed bear. Very old and worn. It had been white once, I think, and with one—"

"One ear gone! And . . . did anything . . . conceal . . . the torn place?"

"Yes. A blue patch."

"A . . . blue . . . patch . . ." he whispered. "A *blue patch*!" He pulled her close, crushing her against him, kissing her ju-bilantly, half laughing, half weeping. "My beautiful . . . price-less woman! A *blue patch*! It is true! It *is*, by God! Only one person in this entire world knew where that bear was hidden, Mia. Jerry Bolster gave it to Avery on his second birthday, and he scarcely let it out of his sight afterwards. When the ear came off, Nell Henderson sewed a 'bandage' on for him. Each night, before he went to bed, he would hide his bear in a 'se-cret cave.' When Avery was lost to me, I tore the house apart, but I could not find the bear! Oh, Mia! He is! *Kent is my son!*"

❧ *Chapter 18* ❧

"Almost dawn . . ." Wetherby turned from the window and, letting the heavy curtains fall back once more, stamped across the gold salon to glare at Lady Bryce, who huddled in an arm-chair, clad in dressing gown and cap, with a sodden handker-chief pressed to her mouth. "Almost dawn!" he repeated grimly. "Four hours since I came home to find this house turned topsy turvy and that groom of Hawk's strove to fob me off with one Banbury story after another! Four hours since I had the truth from the caper-wit! And Hawkhurst ain't back yet! What the devil's the boy about? If he don't drag home that sly, wanton little grandaughter of mine, I'll . . . I'll have done with him! Once and for all!"

"My . . . sweet Stephanie . . . !" wailed her ladyship hoarsely. "Oh, how could that wretched boy do such a thing? And him . . . wed . . . and a parent! I *never* trusted his sister, and so I told you, sir! But . . . Buchanan! A war hero!"

"War, pudding!" snarled Wetherby. "These sprigs today don't know what war's all about! Now, when *I* served with Nelson, *there* was action for you! Seventy-four guns and my *Sweet Avenger*, and when we was engaged . . . Ah, but enough of that. Where is your nephew, madam? *That's* what I want to know!"

"Hawkhurst is hurt, my lord," fluttered Carlotta. "You take no consideration of the fact the poor fellow can scarce walk. Not that I have any least expectation he will fail, for he's a savage man when roused. A most dreadful disposition! Heaven help that poor Buchanan boy! He's doubtless lying dead this—"

"I hope he is!" bristled the Admiral. "Conniving libertine! If 'twere me, I'd—" He tensed as a clatter of hooves could be heard on the drive. "They're back! By God! Now we'll see some fireworks!" He ran into the hall, Carlotta tottering after him.

A lackey swung the doors open, and Euphemia hurried inside, cloak flying, hair disarrayed, and eyes filled with anxiety. She stopped at the sight of Admiral Wetherby's grim scowl and Carlotta's tears and said a pleading, "My lord, I know—"

"You have my deepest sympathy, ma'am," snapped Wetherby, "and my admiration that you've the courage to come back here when—" His eyes flashed to Hawkhurst, who limped in, leaning heavily on Ponsonby's arm. Scanning that haggard countenance, relief swept the old gentleman, but he said nothing until the doors had closed out the interested servants. "Well?" he barked, then. "Did you kill the slippery lecher?"

"No, sir. I did not. Where is Kent?"

"Kent?" thundered Wetherby. "Where *should* he be at this hour? A sight more to the point, where is my granddaughter? You cannot tell me you failed to call the rogue out! He caught your head, by the look of it! Downed, is he? Dying, is that it?

Should've stayed until the world was free of him, Hawk. Your pardon, Miss Buchanan! But you young folks today do not—"

"Sir," Hawkhurst intervened impatiently, "Buchanan is neither dead nor dying. He grazed me, and I could not bring myself to kill the man my sister loves. I—"

"You . . . could . . . not . . ." Wetherby's mouth fell open, and he took an uncertain step backward. "Do . . . do you seriously tell me, sir—" His voice rose to an enraged bellow. "Do you *dare* to stand there and tell me you'd a pistol in your fist and lacked the gumption to blow that bigamous damned scoundrel into the hell he warrants?"

Beyond words tired, beyond belief eager, Hawkhurst said, "Sir, I am sorry. I have failed you again. Aunt, is Kent abed?"

"By God, I begin to believe you're a changeling!" opined the Admiral and, ignoring Carlotta's shocked cry, spluttered, "You are the head of your house, and you stand there and mew like a kitten about your sorrow and ask after a page boy? If you did not kill the rapscallion, sir, then what in the hell *did* you do? Kneel to him and offer your sister on a silver platter, with an olive branch clutched between your craven teeth?"

Hawkhurst sighed and drew himself up. "My lord," he said in a voice Wetherby had never before heard, "I have loved and honoured you all my life. The time is long past when you should have been told the truth about my marriage and . . . my son. In a few moments I shall explain everything. But—" One hand was raised in an authoritative gesture that froze the interruption boiling in Wetherby's throat. "For the time being, I must respectfully ask that you be silent." He turned again to his aunt. "Ma'am, will you please go and bring Kent here at once?"

Lady Bryce glanced from her enraged elder relative to her nephew. Hawkhurst looked ready to collapse, yet in his eyes shone a light she'd not seen in years. She felt a tingle of excitement and said, "I cannot, Garret. The St. Alabans brought me home, but Coleridge and Dora elected to stay, despite the advanced hour, and have not yet returned."

Hawkhurst's eyes flashed to the clock on the mantelpiece. The hands indicated a quarter past four o'clock, and anxiety deepened the clefts between his brows.

"Colley said there would be dancing, and they'd likely be late," Euphemia put in. "Don't worry, Hawk. He will take care of the boy. And now—"

"And *now*," the Admiral interposed grimly, "perhaps you

will be so very good, Mr. Hawkhurst, as to explain what in the name of heaven is going on in this madhouse!"

Euphemia slipped quietly away.

At nine o'clock that morning, Euphemia entered the gold salon to find a fire blazing on the hearth but the drapes still closed. Hawkhurst was asleep on a sofa, and the Admiral sat in an armchair, head sunk on his chest, snoring loudly. Ponsonby, in the act of straightening a blanket over his employer, glanced up, and crossed to her side. The gentlemen, he whispered, had been asleep for a few hours. Lord Coleridge had not yet returned, and he had sent Manners into Down Buttery to find him.

Despite their lowered voices, Hawkhurst moved lazily, then his head turned toward them. Euphemia requested that a light breakfast be served in half an hour and, hurrying to the sofa, sank to her knees beside it.

Hawkhurst started up and asked anxiously, "Is Colley come home yet? Have—"

She placed her hand over his lips. "Hush, love. Lord Wetherby is still sleeping. Ponsonby has sent your head groom to the Broadbents, to find Colley." Hawkhurst had lowered his feet to the floor as she spoke, and, noticing how cautiously he moved, she said, "We must have the dressings changed at once, Garret. How does it feel?"

"Much better, thank you," he lied cheerfully and, running a hand over the stubble on his chin, added, "I must look a sight! Your pardon, ma'am."

She smiled. "I have seen—"

"I know. You and your bivouacs." He caressed her cheek and, as she snuggled against his hand, murmured, "My blessed candle, how may I ever thank you for all you have done?"

"Well," she said thoughtfully, sitting back on her heels and joying in the tenderness so clear in his eyes, "since Kent belongs to me, and I've no slightest intention of giving him up, you might—"

"Nothing has changed, Mia," he interposed. "My reputation is no whit less shocking today than before."

"No, but mine is *very* shocking," she pointed out. "I fear the name Buchanan will soon be vilified throughout the length and breadth of England."

An arrested expression came into his eyes, but before he could respond the Admiral spluttered and started to waken.

"Did you tell him?" whispered Euphemia.

"Yes, he was becoming so apoplectic I thought it the lesser of two evils. He took it very well, thank God, but is so damnably humble I can scarce endure it."

Wetherby's first enquiry was, of course, for Kent, but having been informed on that score, he proceeded to call down blessings on Euphemia's head, extolling her rare humanity in having rescued the boy in the first place, her saintly compassion in caring for and protecting him, and her perspicacity in having finally identified him, until she begged for mercy. "For truly, my lord," she smiled, "my part in this was small indeed. Who would not have helped the child in his sorry condition? The one who has borne the heaviest burden has been your grandson."

This well-intentioned remark unleashed a veritable flood of self-recrimination. She could not but assume Wetherby to be a tyrannical monster, a blind, foolish old curmudgeon. And she was right, for he deserved to be flogged and keel-hauled at the very least. He was unworthy of his grandson's regard, let alone his affection. Hawk, on the other hand, was the finest, the bravest, the most exemplary and gallant individual who had ever drawn breath! Having said all of which, the old gentleman stood and began to move towards the door in an attitude of utter dejection.

Flashing a grim look at Euphemia, Hawkhurst limped over to put an arm about Wetherby's bowed shoulders and assured him that nothing could ever mar the regard in which he held him. "Please let us speak no more of the past, but—" His eager glance flashed to the side as the door opened. "Manners! Did you find the boy? Have you brought him back?"

"I found him, sir," the groom imparted breathlessly. "But the children all stayed up very late, watching the dancing. The nursemaid said they are still fast asleep, and to wake Kent would be to wake the others in the room, so she asked that we let him stay a little longer. I hope that was all right, sir? Lord Coleridge has taken Miss Broadbent for an early drive, but Mr. Broadbent's man said his lordship means to go back for Master Kent and will bring him home."

Hawkhurst breathed a sigh of relief and assured the groom he had acted very properly, but the Admiral glowered, "Up all night, dancing! Then goes for an early ride!" He grinned suddenly. "Oh, to be young again!"

In great good humour the two men repaired to their chambers to bathe, shave, and change clothes. Lady Bryce, exhausted by the night's events, was still sleeping, but within half an hour Euphemia, Wetherby, and Hawkhurst sat down to breakfast. It was not an easy meal: The conversation turned mostly upon the joyous recovery of the boy and the chain of events that had led up to this moment, but, despite Hawkhurst's attempts to steer away from the subject, they all thought often of the runaways, and twice the Admiral so far forgot his deep obligation to Euphemia that he launched into a denunciation of her absent brother that made her blush with shame.

They had repaired to the drawing room, and Hawkhurst was telling the Admiral of Kent's wood-carving when Dora trotted into the room, still wearing her cloak and with her bonnet all askew. She took her nephew's outstretched hand and panted, "Say it is not true! Our little Stephanie, gone from us? Nell Henderson just told me. Oh, my poor dear boy! How sorry I am, though I could see it from the start, of course." She accepted the glove Euphemia picked up and restored to her, but dropped it again as she clasped her hands and observed dreamily, "So romantic . . . 'no sooner met but they looked; no sooner looked but they loved; no sooner loved but they sighed; no sooner sighed but—' "

"Good God, Dora! What in the *deuce* are you jabbering at?" rasped the Admiral. "Is Kent come home with you?"

His daughter blushed furiously and stammered something utterly unintelligible.

Bryce strolled in from the stables, still clad in his party finery, and halted to stare around uneasily. "You're a glum-looking lot, I must say!" His eyes narrowed, and with a total change of manner he asked perceptively, "What's wrong?"

Hawkhurst hobbled eagerly toward him. "Where is Kent?"

"Kent? What, ain't he here yet? Lord, but he had such a jolly—"

A cold premonition seized Euphemia, and she came to her feet, the breath fluttering in her throat.

Whitening, Hawkhurst snapped, "How could he be here? What d'you mean?"

"Manners said you was bringing the boy home," said the Admiral hoarsely. "Where in God's name is he?"

Looking from one to the other uneasily, Bryce said, "I cannot guess, but it is nothing to go into the boughs about, I do—"

"Damn you!" grated Hawkhurst, advancing on him, threateningly. *"Tell me! Where is Kent?"*

Dismayed, Coleridge stammered, "Wh-why, some of us went for a drive after the party, for it was a brilliant morning. When we came back, Mrs. Broadbent said the others had decided to start home and would bring Kent, for the boys had struck up quite a friendship. I do not see what—"

"You young block!" roared the Admiral. *"What* others? The Dunnings?"

"N-No, sir. It was an unexpected guest, I gathered. She chanced to drop in and stayed, of course. I am not personally acquainted with the lady, but Mama must be, for she came to her Musicale. Name of Frittenden. You—Oh, gad!" And with a gasp he leapt forward to steady his swaying cousin.

Wetherby, whose face had begun to take on a livid hue, rallied amazingly. Throwing an arm about Hawkhurst, he cried, "The boy's ill! Dora, send one of the grooms for That Quack. Miss Buchanan, some cognac if you please. Sit him down here, Colley. It's all right, Garret. Just rest, dear lad. You're weak as a cat, and small wonder, cavorting about the countryside half the night with that leg not so much as begun to heal! Never you worry, my poor fellow. Colley and I will ride out after that harridan at once. We'll have Avery back here in a pig's whisper!"

Hawkhurst propped himself on one elbow and peered down at his injured leg. "Not that bad, is it, Nell?"

"I only wish as Dr. Archer would come," gulped the housekeeper, leaning over the bed as she gently spread salve on the wounds. "Look how it's swole! And black from ankle to knee! You shouldn't never be up and about, Master Garret, and you knows it! Yet, however can I blame you, when that sweet child . . ." Her words scratched into sobs. Hawkhurst felt tears splattering onto his ankle and, managing to regain the breath her ministrations had snatched away, gasped, "Courage, my Nell. We've weathered this far. We'll get him back." He patted her shoulder and watched Bailey usher her from the room, wishing he could believe his own words.

The valet closed the door and returned to his side. "You will be wanting riding clothes, sir? I doubt we can get a top boot over those bandages."

"Then I'll wear shoes and drive the curricle. Now hurry, man!"

Despite his resolve not to vex his master, by the time the change of raiment had been completed, Bailey was shaken out of his imperturbability and pleaded, "Sir, you cannot! We've already sent every available man out on the search. Can you not rest? You will lose that leg if you go on like this!"

"Sooner my leg," said Hawkhurst quietly, "than my son."

Downstairs he found Euphemia presiding over the tea tray in the drawing room, while acquainting his aunts with details of which they had been unaware. Dora and Carlotta, sitting very close together on the sofa, both stood as he limped over to kiss and comfort them. He turned to Euphemia, and her hand went out to him. Taking it, he said apologetically, "I fear I have allowed myself to behave very badly. I cannot quite re-call what happened. Bailey tells me my grandfather and Colley went after . . . Avery?"

Dora and Carlotta exchanged stricken glances. Euphemia also had seen the faint quiver of Hawkhurst's lips as he spoke his son's name and, knowing he had been pushed to the break-ing point, said in her calm fashion, "Yes. Colley drove the cur-ricle like a Roman gladiator. I only hope they may be able to stop in Down Buttery! And," she tightened her clasp on his hand, "as for your behaviour, Hawk, you have been splendid throughout, but—"

The doors were flung open, and Coleridge entered. Carlotta and Dora clung to one another, trembling. Hawkhurst blenched and stood very straight, like a man braced to receive sentenc-ing. But there was no need for words; the youth's strained ex-pression spoke for him. Hawkhurst turned away, his head bowed. Carlotta uttered a wail and sank into Dora's arms in a flood of tears. Sick at heart, Euphemia slipped her hand through Hawkhurst's arms. He patted her wrist automatically, his fingers like ice, and, without turning, asked in a remote voice, "How much head start . . . has she?"

"A good two hours, I'm afraid," Coleridge said miserably. "No one even noticed which way she went. Oh, Hawk, I am so sorry. I'd give my life not to—"

"I know. It wasn't your fault. Do not blame yourself." Hawkhurst sat down wearily, and Bryce stood before him, wringing and wringing at the hat in his hand and longing to be able to help.

Carlotta's weeping was becoming hysterical. Euphemia summoned Mrs. Henderson, and Dora helped convey her sister-in-law upstairs.

When they were gone, Bryce said frantically, "Hawk, there must be *some* damned thing we can do?"

Hawkhurst leaned his head back against the sofa and closed his eyes for a second, then looked up and asked, "Is my grandfather all right?"

"Yes, and I'd have gone with him and Hal had I thought—"

"Archer?" Euphemia interposed. "Lord Wetherby went somewhere with Dr. Archer?"

He nodded. "We met him in Down Buttery. The Admiral apologized to him so humbly I think the poor man was more appalled than by all the ranting and raving. When he learned the whole, nothing would do but that they both go rushing off in Archer's gig, for the old gentleman is convinced Mrs. Frittenden will take the London Road."

"I doubt it. The roads will be clogged with holiday traffic." Hawkhurst stared blindly at the fireplace. Two hours ... He gave a little gesture of hopelessness and muttered, "She might have gone to the West coast or to Scotland, or Wales. Or she might be safely hidden away. I'll warrant they'll have vanished into thin air, as they did before. And she ran while I sat here ... like a total clod ... and ate breakfast!"

Euphemia and Bryce exchanged glances of helpless frustration, but neither spoke.

"She will take my little son back to that merciless hound," Hawkhurst said dully. "And if they sell him ... to a sweep again ..." He shrank and bowed his head into hands that shook.

Bryce swung abruptly away and paced to stand staring out at the morning that was again becoming bleak and grey, the brief sunshine hidden by heavy overcast. Euphemia put one hand on her lover's shoulder, struggled to muffle her sobs, and strove vainly to come up with some helpful suggestion.

"*Hound!*" Coleridge exploded. He spun around. "You have it, by Jupiter!"

Euphemia watched him with a rebirth of hope. Hawkhurst raised tormented eyes and waited.

Coleridge strode to drop to one knee and grip Hawkhurst's clenched fist. "Sampson!" he beamed. "Your 'filthy mongrel' has the best nose in all Christendom! If anyone can smell out our Kent—or Avery, I should say—it is old Sampson!"

For a breathless moment, Hawkhurst stared at him. Then, taking his hand between his trembling ones, he half whispered, "Sampson ... ? Colley, do you really think ..."

"Yes, by Jove! I saw him at work once when Chil was training him to retrieve. He hid a riding crop—*miles* from the main house! Old Sampson went straight to it! The brute thought it great fun, but I was never more impressed!"

Hawkhurst drew a deep shuddering breath. "It's a slim hope. But, by God, it's better than no hope at all!" He stood, Coleridge eagerly helping him up. "Colley," he said, his voice crisp and sure once more, "tell the grooms I want the chestnuts and the blue curricle. And send Bailey here, if you will."

With a whoop, Coleridge sprinted from the room.

Hawkhurst took Euphemia by the hands and looked down into her eyes.

She thought with a pang, Oh, he looks so ill! But she was truly a soldier's daughter and said only, "May I come?"

"No, my dear. Not this time."

Bailey, who must have been waiting close by, hovered in the doorway and coughed discreetly. Hawkhurst looked over his shoulder. "My coat, hat, and a brace of loaded pistols, Ralph. And Master Kent's nightshirt. Hurry, please!"

Marvelling that he was still able to rally against so desperate a challenge, Euphemia said, "Darling, surely Gains will not refuse?"

"It don't signify, for I mean to have his flea-carrier. But, more than that, I mean to find Mount." His jaw set, and into his narrowed eyes came a gleam that appalled her. "And when I do," he said very softly, "I shall kill him, Mia."

She was silent, fearing for his life if he should face his enemy in this weakened state, and for his sanity if he did not.

Hawkhurst's expression changed then. He tilted her face, his eyes becoming very tender. "I am a man of no reputation," he murmured, "a rake and womanizer, my Unattainable one. But, I fear I have an even worse flaw, for . . . I am becoming selfish."

Hurrying in with two holstered pistols in one hand and a drab driving coat slung over his arm, Bailey heard the last few words, and his face lit up. Coleridge followed, buckling a sword belt about his slim waist.

Shrugging into the coat, Hawkhurst glanced at his cousin. "This will be a fight, Colley. I can feel it in my bones. I'd not have you hurt, boy."

"And I am not a boy." The hazel eyes were steady and aglow with excitement, the gentle mouth set into a stern line. "I go with you, Hawk. Or behind you. Either way."

Hawkhurst grinned. "Good man. Come then, we shall go and beg, borrow, or steal Max Gains' flea-carrier!"

"*Who* did you say?" Lord Maximilian Gains looked up incredulously from the Spanish doubloon he had been inspecting, while his brother, who had been reading before the fire, sprang to his feet, the book tumbling.

Before the footman could repeat his extraordinary announcement, there was a scuffling in the hall, an outraged shout of, "You cannot go in there, sir! My lord! Have a care!" and the door to the study was flung wide, the lackey staggering as he was shoved aside.

Gains dropped his magnifying glass, whipped open a drawer in the desk, and snatched up a fine silver-mounted pistol. "What the *devil* do you mean by this, sir?" he demanded, aiming the weapon unerringly.

"Max, I need your help," said Hawkhurst, his right hand lifting slightly to the menace of that long barrel. "Please, if you—"

"My . . . help . . . ? Why, damn your impertinence! If that ain't the—"

"Sir," Coleridge interjected, "it is a matter of life and death!"

"You're right there, by George! And if you do not get your philandering kinsman off my property, it will be *his* death we—"

"Max, I *beg* of you!" Hawkhurst pleaded. "I will meet you whenever and wherever you choose. But this is for my son. If you would but listen, I—"

"You treacherous, lying dog! Avery has been dead these four years! And you've no other son—unless it's one of the many you have sired on the wrong side of the blanket!"

Chilton Gains, a tall thin young man with brown hair, gentle eyes, and a face worn by extended illness, had been watching Hawkhurst intently, and now remarked, "Perhaps we should listen to what he has to say, Max."

Again, the door burst open. The butler and two footmen, armed to the teeth, stood with weapons levelled at the intruders, their grim expressions bespeaking their willingness to fire if need be.

"Remove Mr. Hawkhurst from the premises," grated his lordship unrelentingly.

His men moved forward.

"I will go," said Hawkhurst. "But not without Sampson. I'll fight you now, Max, to the death, if I must. But I want that mongrel!"

"You . . . want . . . what?" Gains flung up a detaining hand, and his men halted, looking equally astonished. "But you loathe my—Aha! You plan to shoot him, eh? What's he done this time? Bitten you, I trust!"

"Sir," said Coleridge earnestly. "Robert Mount has stolen Hawk's son. We had only just found the boy!"

Gains had never known Coleridge to be anything but the soul of honour. Taken aback, he stared his bewilderment. His pale face intrigued, Chilton said, "Mr. Hawkhurst, will you not sit down and tell us how we may be of service?"

"Service!" howled Gains, making a recovery. "Are you short of a sheet? Haven't you seen how he served *me*?"

"Yes," nodded his brother, quite unintimidated. "And wondered often why you never called him out for it. Now we shall perhaps hear the truth of the matter. A bargain, Mr. Hawkhurst?"

Chafing at the delay, Hawkhurst frowned, but agreed, "A bargain."

"Very well." Lord Gains dismissed his men, waved his visitors to chairs, and sat behind his desk, a glint of excitement lighting his brown eyes. "I hope I am a fair-minded man. Let us hear your lies."

Hawkhurst remained standing, leaning on his cane and fixing him with a steady gaze. *"Did* you arrange that landslide, or fire at me from ambush?"

"What?" His lordship flushed darkly and grabbed for the pistol he had just laid down on the desk. In a wild spring, Chilton was first, however, and snatched the weapon away. "Villain!" Gains raged, jumping to his feet and shaking his fist at Hawkhurst. "I've no need to plot and lurk about! Had I wished you dead, I'd have called you out four miserable years since!"

"But did not. Why? Because you loved my wife? Because you and she had a more than passing fancy?"

Gains was stunned into silence. The choleric hue faded from his face. He drew back and turned away and, after a tense pause, ejaculated in a stifled voice, "Damn you! So, you knew."

"Of course. Blanche told me."

Gains flung around, staring his incredulity, and Hawkhurst

264

added dryly, "My apologies, Max. But, it was all part of the scheme, you see. Mount hoped I would call you out."

"You . . . lie! He worshipped her! And I—"

"Loved her?" Hawkhurst's cynical gaze held very steady, and before it Gains' shocked eyes fell. "I rather thought you did," Hawkhurst said in a kinder voice. "I knew it must have been a consuming passion for you to, as you thought, betray me."

Gains winced, walked over to the fire and, staring down at the blazing logs, muttered, "I thought she was . . . a saint. She seemed to love me. I swear I . . . I never meant to—" He turned suddenly and faced Hawkhurst fully. "I have never felt so utterly worthless. You were my closest friend. Later, I could not entirely blame you . . . for what you did. I fancied I had deserved it."

"Probably you did," nodded Hawkhurst. "But did you also fancy it my habit to fritter away my spare time by standing about clutching a glass of vitriol?"

"Why, I supposed you had been intending to clean something, or—"

"I had, to the contrary, been intending to drink it!"

Bryce's gasp joined two others. Hawkhurst went on, "I believed it to be water, you see." He sat down and added wryly, "Blanche arranged it for me."

Gains paled. Chilton swore under his breath. Coleridge's jaw dropped, and he stared in total horror.

"You had best," sighed Hawkhurst, "hear the rest of it . . ."

Five minutes later, he finished and stared fixedly at his outstretched legs. Gains, perched on the edge of the desk, watched him, aghast, and the two younger men exchanged shocked glances.

"I suppose I always knew it was something like that," Gains muttered at last. "But I couldn't bear to admit I'd just been a tool. Nor did I dream Avery was alive. Of all the foul, murderous ploys!" He sprang up. "Chilton, the bell! Hawk, can you forgive me?"

Hawkhurst struggled to his feet, hand outthrust and eyes eager. Gains moved forward but did not take his hand, saying instead, "I'll not let you borrow my hound, though." Hawkhurst's arm dropped, and Gains went on, "Unless you allow me to come with you."

Hawkhurst grinned. They gripped hands in a firm, lingering clasp that wiped away four years of bitterness, then, together, moved to the door. Chilton winked at Bryce, and they followed.

"Brownlee!" shouted his lordship in the hall. "Where's that confounded dog of mine?"

"The last time I saw him, m'lud," returned the butler, aware to the last syllable of what had transpired in the study, "he was asleep on your lordship's bed."

Chilton Gains rode back to the curricle through the thickening murk of the fog, and Hawkhurst leaned forward to ask, "Where in the devil are we?"

"Approaching the southwest side of Bristol, I believe, sir. My brother's having the deuce of a time to hold Sampson now. Can you credit the good old hound dragging us all this way?"

Gripping his knee painfully, Hawkhurst admitted, "I bless his every flea if he has brought us to my son. But how do you go on, Chilton? I hear you've brought a musket ball home with you."

The young man gave a deprecating shrug. "A confounded nuisance that ties me here when I should be with my Regiment. Not that it causes me much bother, you know."

Scanning the pale face and strained blue eyes, Hawkhurst nodded gravely. "I'm glad to hear it. You might tell your brother to have a care. I'd not wish his ravening brute to warn Mount of our arrival."

Chilton nodded and rode ahead again, his upright figure blurring as the mists closed about him. Hawkhurst turned to Colley. "He should not have come. That side is troublesome." His cousin merely surveying him with a judicially elevated eyebrow, he smiled faintly. "I don't like this. Bristol—ships, Colley. If Sampson has led us truly, I fear Avery may be destined for a cabin boy this time."

They had been driving for hours, Sampson's eager progress delayed by side excursions into various thickets and riverbanks which seemingly held Avery behind every bush and tree, each one of which required the dog's personal attention. Twice, they had been diverted into chases after rabbits, and the third detour, which proved to have been inspired by the prowls of an indignant black cat, had provoked Hawkhurst to growl that he could not conceive how Sampson had "gone straight to" a concealed riding crop, over more than a mile of land presumably similarly infested with delicious distractions.

The light was almost gone now, and as they entered the suburbs, flambeaux began to glow through the misty gloom. Chilton once again waved Avery's nightshirt under Sampson's nose, and the dog pranced off untiringly, threading his way through ever-deteriorating neighbourhoods until they were among noisome slums clustered about great warehouses. It was bitterly cold, and there were few people about, but occasionally they passed some hurrying individual, head tucked down into collar or scarf, hands deep thrust into pockets in an effort to keep warm. Once they were all but halted by a raucous group of seafaring men with flashily dressed, bold-eyed women hanging on their arms. The luxurious curricle and the two mounted men, one holding a leash at the end of which strained the great dog, attracted immediate attention. The women screeched mockingly, and the men shouted crude comments at the "nobs wot's come among us." Surreptitiously, Hawkhurst checked his pistols and saw his cousin's slim hand drop to his sword hilt when an arrogant lout lurched towards Sampson, only to leap back as the dog sprang eagerly to meet him. Gains spurred to a canter, Coleridge whipped up the team, and the unlovely crew jumped for safety, their profane resentment soon swallowed up by the fog.

Sampson's excitement was growing, his nose busier than ever as they turned down a narrow, furtive alley. A place of slimy cobblestones this, with refuse odorous in the kennels, and rundown, old half-timbered buildings leaning over the narrow thoroughfare, their dirty windows draped with sacking or stained and ragged curtains, close drawn as though to shield whatever went on in those rank interiors. Soon the lane curved, the buildings to the left ceased, and in their stead a railing guarded the edge of a steep bank. Below the bank, another road surface paralleled the street they travelled and, beyond it, loomed the dim outline of the docks.

Sniffing about frantically, Sampson raced ahead, paused, retraced his steps, turned back yet again, and stopped, baying madly at a tavern, the most decrepit, villainous old place Hawkhurst had ever laid eyes on. The multiple peaks of the roof sagged crookedly; chimneys leaned at precarious angles; the weathered siding was warped and stained with age; the windows were boarded; and a heavy chain secured the scarred front door. The sinister structure was a perfect setting for an individual having so unsavoury a reputation as Mr. Robert Mount, and Hawkhurst breathed an impassioned but silent prayer that Sampson had not failed them, that somewhere inside, little Avery was captive—but alive.

Peering at the faded sign that hung listlessly from a rusted iron bracket, Gains muttered, " 'The White Rose.' Huh! 'The Weed Patch,' more like!"

"What a gruesome hole," Coleridge agreed, but with his artist's eyes noting every detail of the old building. "Can you imagine the wicked history of it?"

Chilton was busily engaged in rewarding Sampson with pieces of cheese he had carried in his pocket. He told his pet proudly that he was "a jolly good dog," and Sampson wagged his tail and sought hopefully for any dropped crumbs.

Reining back, Gains bent towards Hawkhurst. "Don't give up, old fellow. It looks empty, but—"

"But is not," said Hawkhurst softly. "I saw a gleam of light from a side window, and the place fairly reeks of ale."

His voice held a note of suppressed excitement. Bryce marvelled at his control, but felt also a pang of dread. What if poor Hawk was doomed to another disappointment? A man could only stand so much, even this dauntless man! His cousin rightly interpreted that troubled gaze and cuffed him gently. "Don't be a cawker. I'm all right." He pointed to the lower street. "Max, we should go down there, I think. We'll be less obvious, yet close enough to keep an eye on the place."

Accordingly, they made their way along to a cut through the bank and, reaching the lower level, swung back again towards The White Rose. As they approached, it appeared they were not the only ones interested in that establishment, for a small, sinewy-looking individual stood on tiptoe, gripping the railing and peering at the tavern. Either the man was deaf, or the fog muffled their coming, for he did not seem to hear them drive up and only at the last instant turned a startled face, then darted away. Obedient to his brother's shout, Chilton sent his mare galloping in pursuit. Sampson tore free enthusiastically and followed with much flapping of ears and with legs that flew erratically. The small man sobbed with fear as the dog came at him and cringed against the bank, throwing an arm across his throat and whimpering, "Call 'im orf, mate! Don't let 'im savage me, melor'! I didn't do nuthink!"

Chilton spoke sternly to Sampson, who cavorted about the captive, his friendly ungainliness so misinterpreted that, by the time he had been herded back to the curricle, the little man was quaking with terror. He snatched off a grimy knitted cap, and a spate of pleas burst from him that Hawkhurst terminated with the lift of one gloved hand. "Why did you watch that verminous place?" he demanded.

The man started and peered into the stern, aristocratic face. "Sir . . . ? Ain't I see you somewhere afore? Wasn't you with General Craufurd's Light Division at Bussaco?"

Hawkhurst leaned forward. "I was. And you?"

The man drew himself up. "Draper, sir. Sergeant Robert. 43rd. I knowed I'd seen you. Friend o' my Captain Redmond, wasn't you?" His face saddened. "Him what was killed at Rodrigo."

"If you mean Captain Sir Harry Redmond," said Hawkhurst. "He was found alive, sergeant. They brought him home. He's not quite recovered, but—" He paused. The leathery features were twitching, the eyes bright with tears. "Cor!" gulped the sergeant. "I wasn't never so glad to hear nuthing! Never!"

Hawkhurst reached out at once and only then noticed that Draper's right hand was gone. "Lieutenant Garret Hawkhurst," he said and, as a gleaming steel hook came up, smiled and shook it. "Kicked you out, did they?"

"Yus, sir. I come home, and me brother took me in, me not being good fer much no more. Me right hand, y'see, sir. But Bill's been jugbit frequent lately, account o' his sweetheart up and married a man milliner. He ain't been home now fer four nights. A cove told me he went in that Satan's pot, and many a man's been shanghaied from there, so I been keeping me ogles on it—not that it's done me a particle o' good. Poor Bill's off to the Indies by this time, I reckon. But sometimes they waits fer a ship, and I thought p'raps I could catch 'em at it and spring him free."

"Have you reported this to the authorities, sergeant?" asked Gains.

Draper gave a scornful snort. "Ain't no authorities fer the likes o' me, sir. The ships masters need crews, and the Watch—such as we got, which ain't much—turns t'other way."

Hawkhurst dismounted with care, the little man hastening to aid him. The night's activities, plus the long, jouncing ride, had done his leg no good at all, and the pain was becoming exhausting, but he asked intently, "Have you ever been inside the tavern, Draper?"

Gains added, "Mr. Hawkhurst's son has been stolen. We think he's there."

"Then Gawd help 'im! A little tyke, eh? A cabin boy they'll

mark him fer. Lucky if he comes through the fust voyage alive. And as to have I been in there, yus, I have. And I don't mind telling you, it fair give me the shakes. You has t'go in the back way. The Watch closed 'em down twice, but they only bolt up the front door and give a wink at the back."

"Where would they have my son, d'you think? In the cellar?"

Draper shook his head. "Too many rats, sir, and the ships' masters don't like their crews brung on board fulla bites. Upstairs is more like it. The ground floor's all give over to kitchens and the tap, and there's a parlour o'sorts where you can get summat to eat—if y'aint' too partickler about the rats and roaches having a nibble afore ye!"

"Charming," said Gains dryly. "Do we venture this menu, Hawk?"

Hawkhurst, who would have given all he possessed for a sound leg at this point, smiled and checked his pistols.

"Don't do it, sir," said Draper. "You wouldn't last two minutes, not none o' ye. A fine bunch o' rum touches up there. Make me look like a pure angel, they do! Though, there *is* gents o' sorts wot goes in reg'lar."

Hawkhurst seized his shoulder. "A tall man, sergeant? A handsome scoundrel with brown curling hair and unusually large eyes?"

Draper thought a second, then shook his head decisively. "No, sir. The only gentry cove wot I'd call handsome has yeller hair. Now *he* come, 'long about three s'arternoon. They druv inter the back, so I couldn't see whether there was a boy with him, but I did see a lady."

Colley interpolated eagerly, "Hawk, Mia told me about an odd chap she met when she was lost that day. She said he had rather too much charm, but was extremely good-looking and had yellow curls!"

Hawkhurst's breath hissed through his teeth. Watching him, Gains said, "It fits, Hawk. All but the hair. Dye, perhaps . . . ?"

Hawkhurst nodded. The same excitement that had always possessed him before his regiment went into action was making his pulse race. The throbbing misery in his leg was quite forgotten. He knew somehow that he would face Mount tonight—at last! Exultant, he turned to the curious Draper. "Sergeant, if you will help us, there'll be a place on my staff for you."

"Sir," said Draper, with a quiet dignity, "I'd help you no

matter wot! I seen you in action at Bussaco. You only got t'tell me wot you wants me to do."

❧ *Chapter* 19 ❧

The air inside The White Rose was foul with the odours of smoke and ale and unwashed bodies and so hot that Hawkhurst could scarcely abide the heavy motheaten blanket he wore, a hole cut in the centre to enable this unlovely garment to slip over his head. A large, sagging-brimmed old hat shaded his features, and he leaned gratefully on the heavy crutch that Sergeant Draper had also miraculously procured. Not half an hour had passed from the time they'd sent the little man off on his errands until he had returned with "suitable clothing" for the three of them. Hawkhurst glanced at Coleridge, who had entered the tavern beside him, and could barely restrain a chuckle. His dandified nephew, a patch over one eye, hair matted with bacon grease and straggling around his dirty face, was clad in a filthy coat that hung in tatters about him and breeches that had made the young exquisite blench as he'd slipped them over his own immaculate garments.

Their disreputable appearance had won them little attention as they made their way to the tap. Hawkhurst's quick eyes had at once noticed a door on the far side of the low-roofed, smoky room that must, he thought, give onto a hall. They procured two tankards of ale, and by means of shoving Colley repeatedly in an apparent argument, Hawkhurst had gradually manoeuvred them close to this door. They now slouched against the wall, mumbling in quarrelsome fashion to one another and awaiting the arrival of Gains, whom they had left attempting to pacify Chilton, incensed because he had been delegated to remain with the curricle.

Draper reeled past, raised his tankard in apparently drunken recognition, and hissed. "Door aside you, sir. Stairs at the end o' the hall. I'll try and stop anyone who looks like follerin'," and went on.

Glancing about from beneath the brim of his hat, Hawkhurst saw no sign of Mount, but a more unwholesome lot he'd seldom beheld. Voices were coarse, conversation profane, eyes hard, and manners belligerent. An occasional howl of laughter would greet some rank joke, and sometimes a snatch of song emerged from the din. Here were the very dregs of the waterfront, the veneer of civilization thin indeed. He saw not one face upon which he would care to turn his back and spotted several slippery-eyed fellows he'd have laid odds were rank riders, at the very least!

"Hawk," breathed Coleridge in awe, "I'm sure that big fellow by the tap is the rogue who held me up on Hampstead Heath last spring!"

"Pray he don't recognize you!" advised Hawkhurst and nudged him warningly. A husky and decidedly foxed man, his crossed eyes wavering from one of them to the other, lurched up and demanded to know where was the borde as was owed him. Hawkhurst growled an admonition to "stow his whids," advised he'd had too much strip-me-naked, and cursed him gutturally, whereupon the opportunist retreated.

"By Jove!" grinned an admiring Colley. "What's a borde?"

"A shilling. And I wish to God someone would start a brawl so we can—"

A wild commotion erupted beside the door, shouts and curses and guffaws of laughter. "Devil take it!" groaned Hawkhurst. "It's Sampson! He'll draw attention to us, confound him!"

"Let the pup in, dang ye!" snarled a large, bloated individual, shoving the man who strove to eject the hound.

"Gains!" whispered Coleridge.

His lordship was resplendent in a tattered old rifleman's jacket, a cap worn back to front, his features barely visible behind the tangled hair that hung over his eyes. Ignoring his aggressive critic, he continued to push at Sampson. The bloated one promptly back-handed him, so that he staggered, causing a coster to spill his ale. The coster howled his wrath and swung his tankard at the peer. Gains ducked with commendable alacrity, and the bloated one took the ale full in his red face. The taproom became a mass of flying fists, breaking glass, and plunging bodies, while shrieks, howls, and shouts increased the din.

Delighted by this diversion, Hawkhurst cried, "Now!" swung the door open and limped into a dark, cold hall, Coleridge close on his heels. The heavy door closed behind them, shutting off an astonishing amount of the uproar, and a narrow hall stretched out starkly, lighted only by the candle on a rickety table beside a flight of uncarpeted stairs. Hawkhurst tucked the crutch under his arm and leaning on Bryce managed to hobble his way upward. The treads squeaked and groaned under them, but at last they reached the top and a corridor that led towards the front of the tavern. Breathing hard, Hawkhurst counted six doors, all closed. He tried the greasy handle of the first room to his right, and a man grumbled a demand to be left in peace. Coleridge opened the left-hand door and peered into a bedchamber to be rewarded by a feminine screech and the crash of a glass against the door he hurriedly swung shut. And then, from the far end of that dank hall came a shout of mocking male laughter and a woman's voice, cultured but indignant, "But, Bobby darling, you *promised* I should have a ruby!"

Hawkhurst stood immobile, the years rolling back as a deep, velvety voice said, "Greedy little doxy! That's all you think of! Were I penniless, you'd be back to Everett without so much as a farewell kiss!"

A primal glow began to burn in Hawkhurst's eyes, and one word hissed softly through his gritted teeth. "Mount!"

"But you are not penniless, love," the woman cajoled. "And as soon as you get rid of the brat, we can—"

" 'Ere! Wot you two doin' up there?"

The rough challenge came from the stairs. Swinging around, Hawkhurst was in time to see Colley level a ruffian who charged at them, but another followed, his howls causing a door to the right to burst open, disgorging several burly louts and revealing a brightly lit room and two women with painted faces and gaudy gowns who ran eagerly to watch the excitement. Hawkhurst swung his crutch and discovered it to be a fearsome weapon as his first opponent, a veritable giant, was struck on the jaw, sailed backward over the railing, and thence, noisily down the stairs. A bull-necked, grinning bully replaced him, muscular arms eagerly outstretched. Vaguely aware that Colley was fighting like a Trojan at his back, Hawkhurst lunged with the crutch as though it were a sword. The bully jumped clear, seized the crutch and wrenched it away. At once,

Hawkhurst sprang to ram home a solid right to the lowest button of the dirty waistcoat. His grin vanished, the bully jack-knifed and lay on the boards, gasping like a landed trout. The women started to screech lustily; Hawkhurst started for the door. It slammed, and he heard a key turn in the lock.

Colley was striving heroically, but a narrow-featured individual had crept up the stairs and was in the process of levelling a pistol at his back. Belatedly recalling that he also carried a pistol, Hawkhurst whipped it from his pocket and fired from the hip, having no time to aim properly. The retort was cacophonous in the confined space. He was mildly astonished to see the would-be assassin drop his weapon and clutch a smashed wrist.

Light flooded along the dim hall as the end door was flung wide. Robert Mount (better known to Euphemia as John Knowles-Shefford), clad in a brown velvet lounge jacket and light beige pantaloons, the lamplight gleaming on his golden curls, stood in the aperture, a woman peeping over his shoulder.

Hawkhurst tore blanket and hat away and leapt forward, an inarticulate snarl of rage escaping him.

Mount gave a shocked cry, flung the glass he held at the onrushing man, and sprang back, whipping the door to, but Hawkhurst's shoulder smashed it open. He caught a glimpse of an incongruously elegant parlour, richly draped and carpeted and graciously furnished, and of a beautiful woman, clad in a flowing blue silk gown and running clear of his maddened charge.

Never one for hand-to-hand combat, Mount wrenched open the drawer of a walnut escritoire. Hawkhurst launched himself across it. Mount jumped back, holding a small pistol, but the toppling escritoire slammed against him, and he went down, Hawkhurst crashing onto him. Still gripping the pistol, Mount swung it upward. Hawkhurst, his fingers having barely locked around the throat of his enemy, was forced to abandon his hold so as to smash the weapon away. At once Mount drove a fist against his jaw, twisted free, snatched up a marble clock, and swiped it at Hawkhurst's head. Dizzied, but coming to his knees, Hawkhurst ducked. The clock caught him a glancing blow, starting the cut above his temple to bleed copiously again. For an instant he could see only wheeling lights, but pain was a distant thing which must not be heeded. Mount was already on his feet, and he was after him like a tiger. Frantic with fear, Mount caught up a chair and flailed it in a vicious arc. Hawkhurst swung clear, and it flew on across the room to miss the woman by inches, drawing a terrified shriek from her.

"Stand and fight, you cowardly rat!" roared Hawkhurst.

Mount, however, dodged desperately, heaving whatever he could lay hands on at his enemy. Pursuing him grimly, Hawkhurst was aware of a continuing uproar in the corridor and knew that a battle royal was under way out there. Colley was acquitting himself well. Mount had backed into a corner, and, triumphant, Hawkhurst started forward. A heavy tread sounded behind him, and something smashed into his back, beating the breath from his lungs. He went down hard, the shock sending pain lancing through his leg from ankle to thigh, but to relax was death, and so he rolled, started up doggedly—and froze.

His cheek grazed, and his curls sadly disarranged, the shoulder of his jacket ripped out, Mount yet grinned his triumph. One hand was tightly twisted in Kent's hair; the other again held the pistol which he waved tauntingly, so that at the end of each wave the muzzle ruffled the fair hair of the boy's temple. "Excellently done, Japhet," he wheezed, and Hawkhurst saw that the large individual Colley had recognized as a member of the High Toby stood smirking at him, a leg of the shattered escritoire gripped in one beefy hand. So that was what had brought him down. Panting, he fought his way to his feet, his eyes drinking in his son. The boy's fine hands were bound before him, and a bruise at the side of his mouth accentuated his extreme pallor. Yet he did not weep; his eyes instead fixed upon Hawkhurst with an expression varying between adoration and anxiety. Hawkhurst summoned a grin and winked encouragement. The highwayman gave a mocking laugh and rammed the improvised club into his ribs, staggering him. Enraged, Hawkhurst crouched, fists clenched, poised for battle, and the large man advanced willingly.

"No, no, Japhet," Mount chuckled. "Rather, go and stop all the clamour before we have the Watch here! As for you, Hawk, I admire you. No, but really I do! Look at him, Anne. He is as close to indestructible as any man I've met."

"Despite your efforts to the contrary, eh, Robert?" Hawkhurst's head tossed back, and the look of boredom Mount had never been able to tolerate was very pronounced.

"But I had no intention of killing you, dear Garret. Not for a long time yet. Do you refer to my little games with Mohocks and other commodities, plus your former friend's hunting gun?" He shrugged slyly, "One must have *some* fun, after all. And you'd come off so damnably easy. I knew I must be sensible, of course, but there were times when I simply could not restrain my desire to . . . ah, make your life a little more, shall we say—uncomfortable? I had intended to kill you worrying, and paying, until my son was a few years older. Oh, yes, Eustace is my own—and it seemed poetic justice that he should inherit Dominer." He sighed. "But this . . ." His merciless hand shook Kent's head savagely, ". . . complicated matters. How you ever found him, I cannot know, but I am now compelled to call a halt to the game. Sad. For you have not paid nearly enough for the death of my love!" He grinned and tightened his grip so that Kent's mouth twisted with pain.

The anguish on that small face roused Hawkhurst to a rage he could scarcely contain. Watching him, Mount chuckled, but his mirth was short-lived. Kent brought his heel crunching down onto his tormentor's slippered toe. Mount let out a yowl and sent the boy hurtling across the room. It was all Hawkhurst needed. He rocketed forward and seized the pistol. Mount swore and hung on like grim death. From the corner of his eye Hawkhurst saw the woman run forward, an upraised dagger glittering. Dismay seized him. Perhaps, he thought desperately, even if she stabbed him he might be able to put an end to Mount. The knife whipped down, and his back muscles tightened in anticipation of the thrust. A shout died in a shocking cry; he caught a glimpse of Colley staggering back and falling to his knees as the woman fled from the room. Abandoning his hold on the pistol, Hawkhurst chopped savagely for the throat. Mount squawked, and his grip loosened; the pistol clattered down, and he crumpled, dragging Hawkhurst with him as he caromed into a chair. They went down in a tangle, the wrenching fall leaving Hawkhurst sickened with pain. Mount's hands fastened in a choking hold around his throat. Instinctively, he swung up his arms, somehow succeeded in breaking that grip, and with all his failing strength drove a short jab at the classic jaw. Mount grunted, sagged, and lay unmoving.

Sobbing for breath, Hawkhurst rolled over and dragged himself to his feet. "Get . . . up, you poor . . . lunatic."

Mount was perfectly still. Hawkhurst limped towards the fallen pistol. He flashed an anxious look at Colley, who was crouched on his knees, head down, with blood trickling from the hand that clutched his arm.

Watching from under his lashes, Mount timed it nicely, and kicked out hard.

White hot agony seared through Hawkhurst's leg, and a strangled cry was torn from him. He had no recollection of falling, but found himself sprawled on the carpet, waves of nausea blinding him and reducing Mount's cackling glee to unintelligible echoes. As from a great distance, he saw the pistol and groped towards it, but another hand snatched it up.

"Watch, dear friend," Mount jeered, all his hatred in that sibilant gloating. "Watch, while I pay you in full!" And the pistol swung slowly until it pointed not at the man, but at the terrified child huddled in the far corner.

"No . . . !" groaned Hawkhurst. "Not the boy! *Mount*, for the love of God . . ." He fought frenziedly to stand, but could only crawl, his agonized gaze on that deadly pistol.

"Look, Hawk," Mount giggled and aimed carefully.

Hawkhurst managed to get his left foot under him, but his attempt to stand reduced the room to a shimmering grey blur, and he was down again, Mount's cackling laughter echoing in his ears. He raised his head and saw Avery pressed against the wall, his terrified little face so very white. Tearing at the rug, fighting madly to drag his failing body up, his fingers encountered something solidly heavy. The clock Mount had smashed at him. He grabbed it.

"Mount!"

In immediate response to that changed tone, Mount spun. Hawkhurst threw the clock with all his might. It struck the pistol barrel in the same instant Mount pulled the trigger. The weapon was slammed upward, and the explosion, sharp and shattering, was followed by the bloom of smoke. Through that screen, Hawkhurst saw Mount topple. It was very apparent that he would never get up.

Panting, Hawkhurst sagged forward, bracing himself on his hands, eyes closed and head hanging in exhaustion.

"Well, if that don't beat the Dutch! Do stop playing about, Hawk!"

Dazedly, he peered upward. Lord Gains, one eye blackened, a swelling contusion across his cheek, scanned him indignantly. "Food's terrible here," he imparted, hauling him to his feet. "Be damned if I'll stay!"

Sobbing silently, Avery flew across the room, and Hawkhurst snatched him close and hugged him, eyes blurring with tears of thankfulness. But, trying to walk, he would have fallen save for Gains' ready arm, and his lordship said very gently, "It would help Mr. Hawkhurst if you would walk, young fella." Avery clambered down instantly and grabbed Hawkhurst's right arm supportively with his bound hands.

Draper came in, surprisingly holding up a battered and sagging Chilton, and Coleridge was struggling to his knees.

Gains scanned his brother tautly. "Damned fool! Can you navigate?"

"I've got him, sir," said Draper, eyes widening as he saw Mount's sprawled body. "You help Mr. Hawkhurst. No, over here! Hell's loose down below. We'll never get out that way! Quick! Quick now! There's a side stair somewhere about— likely that flash cove's private entrance." He led them to the rear door, opened it hopefully, and sure enough it gave onto a rickety balcony.

The sudden transition into the freezing cold cleared Hawkhurst's muddled brain. He was being guided to stairs and, as he stumbled wrackingly downward, called, "Colley? Are you all right?"

"Perfectly fine . . . Hawk," gasped his cousin staunchly. "But . . . but Chil ain't very good."

"Best . . . damned fight I was . . . ever in," Chilton groaned, barely able to set one foot before the other.

Somehow, they were down and clear of the insanity that was The White Rose. Even as the little party reeled and staggered away, a window exploded outward and a man's body hurtled through. Dark figures were thumping down the stairs. A hoarse voice shouted, "Murder! Stop 'em!" And two ruffians raced after them. Sampson, inexplicably delayed, gladly joined the game now, pranced down the steps and between the legs of the man in the lead. With a surprised yell, he went down; his cohort tumbled over him, and the chase ended abruptly.

Draper ran ahead and brought up the curricle, the horses tied on behind. The casualties were boosted inside; Gains climbed into the saddle of one horse, and Draper mounted the other.

"Hawk," said his lordship, putting the reins into his hand, "your leg's leaking, I know, but it will have to wait until we're away. Then we shall stop and tend to the three of you poor cripples. Can you drive, old fellow?"

The words came as from a great distance to Hawkhurst. His back ached viciously, his head pounded, and his leg was pure torment. And he could have sung for joy because, huddled on his lap, the small body pressing against him was his son! " 'Course can ... drive!" he said, faint but indignant. "Lead on!"

The fog swirled around them as they started off. The cold was bitter and the night very dark. For quite some time, as they went, they could hear from the old tavern, the crashes, shouts, and screams of battle.

Ears up and tail wagging, Sampson led the victors towards home.

Dominer was ablaze all through that foggy evening and far into the night. Flares were set at intervals of ten feet all along the drivepath for some distance up the estate road, and grooms patrolled with lanterns as far as the London-Bath Road, hoping to encounter the curricle. Inside, the drawing room was bright with candles, the glow as cheery as the faces of those gathered there were glum.

Euphemia, hands folded in her lap, was very pale, but she waited quietly, fears held in check. None of them had enjoyed very much sleep, and, although they had rested in the afternoon, they were all tired, but no one thought of bed. Surprisingly, Lady Bryce had shed her die-away airs and was a pillar of strength, comforting Dora, keeping the Admiral well-plied with the cigarillos she loathed, and doing whatever she might to ease the tensions of this interminable vigil.

At two o'clock, Ponsonby carried the tea tray in for a second time, followed by Mrs. Henderson, bearing platters piled with little cakes, hot scones, and biscuits. Her eyes on the slow creep of the clock's hands, Euphemia scarcely noted their arrival. Hawk had been gone more than twelve hours ...

The Admiral stirred the tea Carlotta handed him and, leaning back without tasting it, said suddenly, "Do you know what I was thinking? How the little fellow used to like me to tell him of Trafalgar." His voice cracked, and he puffed on his cigarillo, so that he all but disappeared in the resultant cloud of smoke.

"I have been thinking the same, sir," said Euphemia. "And of how many people would be enchanted by your reminiscences. You should set it all down, you know. Not only from the historical sense, for I am sure that will be done for years to come, but for the little human incidents you have told me of. I feel sure it must be a great success."

"Do you now?" He stubbed out the cigarillo and took up his cup again. "By George, it's an idea! Would give me something to do."

"Do you know what *I* have been thinking?" Dora murmured. "I have been thinking of how dreadful it would be—at such a time as this—to be alone. Not to have loved ones near. Thank heaven we have each other, for fear is such a terrible thing." She sighed mistily. " 'Fear has many eyes and can see things underground.' "

"Well, we *have* got each other, dear," soothed Carlotta, nobly overlooking the fact that Dora's tea was spilling into her lap.

" 'Course we do!" said the Admiral hearteningly. "Though," he scowled, "I wish my little Stephie was—" He glanced at Euphemia, coughed, and was silent while they all drank their tea and thought their thoughts, and the moments ticked slowly away.

Hawk, thought Euphemia, come back! Oh, my love, come back to me.

"*What* things?" growled Wetherby, fixing Dora with an irritated frown.

"Th-things . . . Papa?" she stammered nervously, dropping her spoon.

"What the deuce d'ye mean, 'see things underground'? What kind of nonsense is that? I've been scared in my time—am just now, I don't mind admitting—but I never went snooping about under cabbages and turnips! See things underground, indeed! What kind of slowtop would make such a blasted idiotic remark?"

"I . . . I believe it was Cervantes," she gulped.

"Might've known it would be some hare-brained foreigner! Well, I'll tell you what, Dora, anyone goes peeping about under roots and such is liable to be put away, and so—" He checked, eyes flashing to the door. "Did you hear—?"

Euphemia was already on her feet, her heart pounding madly as a distant barking came nearer. The teacup she held began to jiggle on the saucer.

A commotion in the hall erupted into a chorus of shouts, then a cheer, and the door burst open. Sampson galloped into the room, leapt across the table, sending the teapot flying, and jumped onto the Admiral's lap, licking his face ecstatically. Wetherby's rageful howl following her, Euphemia ran to the hall.

A battered, bloody, exhausted little cavalcade was staggering into the house. Chilton Gains, hanging weakly on the arms of his brother and a small man she had never before seen. Colley, Ponsonby supporting him as he tottered along, his face very pale, but his eyes alight with triumph. And behind them, the man for whom she sought so frantically, borne along by Manners and a footman, the right leg of his breeches crimson from knee to ankle, his eyes glazed, but beside him, a bruised and very dirty small boy who left his side to rush and hug her, then fly into the outstretched arms of the Admiral.

Weeping at last, Euphemia said and choked, "Hawk! Oh . . . my dear!"

He reached out and, as she ran forward, took her hand, while Manners beamed upon them both. "We got . . . him back, Mia!" Hawkhurst whispered radiantly. "Praise God! We got him . . . back!"

Euphemia settled herself against the squabs of the luxurious carriage, and Manners tucked the fur rug solicitously about her, put up the steps, and closed the door. Lord Wetherby, having assured himself she was comfortable, pulled a rug over his own knees, for it was freezing, and traces of fog again hung in the air on this Christmas morning. Euphemia waved happily to the many loved ones gathered at the windows of Meadow Abbey to bid her farewell. The carriage lurched and then began to move up the drive. She tucked her hands back into her ermine muff and turned to the Admiral. "Oh, sir! How very kind in you to come and fetch me. It was lovely to be with my family, of course, but I have been so very anxious! How is . . . everyone? And little Kent, I mean Avery? And, oh, forgive me, but I've been away so long, and—"

"A week!" he laughed. "Only a week since your dragon of an aunt came breathing her fire and fury and kidnapped you away from us! She seemed more cordial today, I must say. Though I'd no notion as to what kind of reception I'd meet, calling for you on Christmas morning! Poor taste, I'll own."

"Oh, no, but they have all forgiven me," she said happily. "When I told them the full story of Garret and—everything, my dear sister was moved to tears, and even Aunt Lucasta was . . ." She blushed prettily and lowered her eyes. "Was willing to let me visit Dominer, in case someone should chance to invite me. Oh, dear sir! Do tell me! Hawk was so very ill when I left!"

"But we sent messages every day," he said, his eyes twinkling into her anxious ones. "Did you not—"

"Yes, yes. But all you said was that everyone was recovering nicely, and I was afraid—He was so terribly weak, and if he did not stay abed . . ."

"Now, now, never worry so. I'll confess when first I saw that leg I was sure he must lose it, but thanks to That Qua—er, Hal Archer, he's doing famously. He's up and about again, though on a very restricted basis, and complains that we all watch him like so many wardens, Avery in particular."

"How is the dear little fellow? I have missed him so. Has Garret told him yet?"

"The boy is happy as a lark, and a joy to everyone. Hawk was so kind as to allow us all to be present when he told Avery the truth of his birth. He stood there like a little soldier, but with tears streaming down his cheeks, then fairly jumped into his father's arms. Er . . . I'll confess . . ." he cleared his throat, "we were all rather overcome. Bless him, he is the dearest, most warm-hearted little fellow." He blinked, took up her gloved hand and, patting it, said gruffly, "How I can ever thank you is quite beyond my imagination. You have restored the sunlight to some very shadowed lives, Mia. I—"

Euphemia leaned suddenly to plant a kiss on his cheek. The old gentleman became red as fire and, to cover his confusion, launched into an account of the recent events at Dominer. The Gains brothers were still their honoured guests, he said, since Archer had requested that Chilton remain under Mrs. Henderson's care until he was improved. "Poor lad, he should have stayed with the horses, as Max instructed him. But he's a high-couraged boy, and I collect there was no holding him once he heard the uproar. However, he goes along well enough, and I believe has enjoyed all the festivities. Oh, there have been some changes, my dear. The truth has leaked out about Hawk and Blanche. Lord knows how, unless the servants got hold of the details in some way. At all events, we've been fairly inundated with callers. Folks who had conveniently forgotten that Dominer ever existed are suddenly beating a path to the door and falling over themselves with affability. Disgusting! But Carlotta is in seventh heaven, of course."

Delighted by this news, Euphemia said that very likely they would soon have newspaper people posting out from London. "Then you shall be in all the papers, and Hawk will be furious, but will be truly forgiven so that . . . he . . ." Her words trailed off. "Good gracious, sir! Have I offended you? Or have the newspapers already printed something?"

He nodded, eyebrows jutting. "They have. Blasted long-noses! But not about Hawk . . . exactly."

She stared, then said a small, "Oh, dear. Simon?"

"Yes. They don't mention names, but—Egad, how that scurrilous crew loves a bit of gossip to chew over! The *ton*, they said, was agog to hear of the elopement of a certain wounded officer, newly returned from the Peninsula to join his wife and family, and a young lady of gentle birth, whose brother, Mr. G—H—was himself a few years back involved in a shocking scandal. Faugh!"

"And—and did they mention the duel, sir?"

"Hinted at it. Hawk wasn't pleased, as you may guess, and vows to go into Town and twist the writer's nose for him, so soon as he's able."

Euphemia sighed, hoping that this would not cost Simon his commission, but drawing solace from the thought that the wise Colonel John Colborne knew his General and would await the most opportune moment before approaching Wellington in the matter.

They chattered on as the miles were eaten up by the steady plodding of the horses. The air was frigid, and a scattering of snowflakes began to fall from the dark skies, but the Admiral wore a warm scarf tied over his head beneath his beaver, and Euphemia's knitted cap, edged with ermine, flattered her bright colouring and rosy cheeks, so that he thought her truly the loveliest girl he had ever known. Save one . . . perhaps.

At last they were clear of the Home Wood, and there below them lay the great house, so beautiful, and yet so warm and welcoming that Euphemia's heart constricted at the sight of it. Smoke curled from the chimneys, candlelight brightened the windows, and on the terrace a bundled-up small boy and a very large hound clad in a blanket-coat, waited. Down the hill they went, and, starting up the rise, the groom blew up a blast on the yard of tin. The dog sprang up, and boy and hound advanced towards the carriage so exuberantly that it would have been difficult to determine which of them did the most jumping. Euphemia desired his lordship to instruct Manners to halt. Wetherby pulled on the check string, and the carriage slowed and stopped. The footman let down the steps, and she was outside, embracing the ecstatic child, while the dog gave every indication of total insanity.

They walked towards the house together, and a familiar figure came onto the terrace to meet them. A man who limped and leaned upon a cane, but whose dark head was held very erect. Euphemia's heart turned over. Vaguely, she heard Wetherby call Avery, and then Hawkhurst stood before her. Pulse racing, she waited to be seized and kissed and worshipped. Instead, scanning her face intently, he took her hand, then bent and pressed it to his lips and, straightening, merely whispered, "Mia . . ."

"Hawk . . ." she said tenderly.

Watching from the carriage windows, the Admiral was less restrained. "Stupid young gapeseed!" he snorted.

§ Chapter 20 ¾

It was snowing steadily by the time the yule-log was borne in by Max Gains, Coleridge (albeit he tugged at it with one hand since the other was still carried in a sling), a radiant Avery, and the Admiral, behaving as though he were seventeen rather than seventy. They were escorted, of course, and Sampson chose to regard the log as a thing alive and entertained himself by making short little rushes at it, barking hysterically, and then galloping three times around the bearers.

The drawing room, decorated with holly and golden bells, was warm of air and warmer with happiness when they gathered there in late afternoon. Lady Carlotta played for them, and Euphemia sang, and then they all sang together, Avery, resplendent in his best suit of brown velvet, waving his arms happily in time with their music. Hal Archer and his sister arrived, eyes bright, and cheeks rosy with cold, and shortly thereafter Ponsonby carried in the wassail-bowl and all the servants joined in the traditional toasting of the head of the house, his son, grandfather, and company. The Christmas boxes were handed out, and the golden moments slipped past, the great room ringing with talk and laughter until day melted into early evening and gradually the servants went their ways, some few remaining to close the curtains.

Euphemia was happy, her happiness shadowed only when she thought of Simon and Stephanie. How they must be longing for home and families, and how very much they were missed.

Dinner was served at six o'clock, a noble feast laid upon a table bright with garlands. The first course was dealt with lightly, and, when the remove was carried in, Hawkhurst carved roast suckling pig, roast beef, and venison, then deferred the honour to his grandfather, while he sat looking joyously around at the faces of his love, his newly found son, family and friends, keeping his eyes resolutely from the two chairs at the end of the table that were empty tonight.

The second remove had been brought in when Sampson, who had been lying in the Great Hall thoughtfully contemplating the legs of Adonis, suddenly hove himself up and burst into full-throated warning. Euphemia laid down her knife and fork and felt an odd shiver chase down her spine. Ponsonby slipped quietly from the room, to return a moment later, obviously agitated, and hasten to murmur in Hawkhurst's ear. Euphemia saw the loved face pale, the smile vanish from the grey eyes, the brows drawn into a thunderous scowl. And she trembled.

"Who the devil is it?" demanded the Admiral testily. "Tell 'em we're eating our Christmas dinner, for lord's sake!"

Hawkhurst, however, had already put down his napkin and reached for his cane. A lackey sprang to pull back his chair, and he stood. "If you will all please excuse—" he began.

Euphemia gave a gasp. In the open doorway, tall and very dashing in his regimentals, but with his wistful gaze fixed upon her, stood her brother.

"By ... God!" exploded Wetherby, his chair going over with a crash as he leapt to his feet. "Of all the unmitigated gall!"

Euphemia ran to throw her arms around Simon. He stooped to kiss her, then set her aside and faced Hawkhurst's flint-eyed fury. "Sir," he said timidly, "I do most humbly beg your pardon for having come. But, your sister—"

"Is Stephanie ill?"

"She grieves for you all," said Buchanan, and added in hesitant fashion, "I would not have come. But . . . it is Christmas, and . . . I hoped—"

"A trifle late to remember that!" barked the Admiral.

"I regret, Sir Simon," said Hawkhurst, his eyelids at their haughtiest, "that I must ask you to leave. Indeed, your effrontery in coming here passes all understanding."

Dora pressed her handkerchief to suddenly swimming eyes, and Carlotta seized Colley's hand, her lips quivering.

"I am very aware of that," Buchanan admitted. "But I *had* to tell you, Hawkhurst. And—" his gaze flashed around that hitherto merry table, "and the rest of those she loves, and the one I love." He smiled down at Euphemia, but with sorrow lurking at the back of his blue eyes. "The newspapers, as you know, had quite a field day with the news of my elopement."

"And did that make you proud, sir?" snarled the Admiral.

"It did not make my *wife* proud, my lord. She was, in fact, outraged. It would, it appears, have been perfectly convenable for *her* to have acted in such a way. But for *me* to have done so, caused her great embarrassment."

"Simon!" Euphemia exclaimed, holding his hand very tightly. "Ernestine has agreed to give you a divorce!"

"Yes! She has, by Jove! And, what is more, says she will wed Admiral Sir Hugh Larchdale!"

"What?" Wetherby was practically apoplectic. "Hugh must be all about in his upper works! Splendid fellow! But must be old enough to be her—" He paused and added thoughtfully, "Devilish plump in the pockets, come to think on it."

"Wherefore," said Buchanan, "I humbly beg permission, Mr. Hawkhurst, for the honour of your sister's hand in marriage."

"Beg . . . *permission*? Why damme! You put the cart before the horse, you curst young reprobate!" Striding around the table, the Admiral's eyes alighted on his stern-faced grandson, and he checked and waited in silence.

"Lord Wetherby is perfectly correct," said Hawkhurst woodenly. "Your request is considerably belated, Buchanan."

Sir Simon reddened, but persisted earnestly, "Yet your approval—er, I mean, your permission, and forgiveness, would make me the happiest man alive, sir."

"And me . . . the very happiest girl," quoth a small and shaking voice from the hall.

Hawkhurst whirled around. Sobs and muffled exclamations were torn from his aunts.

Stephanie peeped around the door jamb, wearing cloak and mittens, and with her hood fallen back from her fair curls. She looked rather astoundingly lovely, her hazel eyes poignant with pleading.

Hawkhurst said nothing, regarding her with unyielding disapproval.

"I know I had no right to come," she said bravely, "but— Oh! My heavens! *Gary!* Dear one, you are ill! And . . . Colley! Whatever—"

She started to run to him, her own hopes forgotten in her anxiety, then remembered her disgrace and shrank back.

That gesture was too much for Hawkhurst. He tossed his cane aside and held out his arms. "Come here, you . . . wicked wench," he choked.

With a stifled sob, she sped to him. Everyone was standing then, hurrying to embrace and welcome the miscreants, every heart full.

Hugging his sister close, blinking rapidly, Hawkhurst reached around her and thrust out his hand. His own eyes suspiciously bright, Buchanan gripped it hard, and the happy crowd closed in about them.

The gothic letters of the sign were large, colourful, and impeccably executed and read: "Please Follow the Guide." The first footman bore it as though it had been a royal banner and led the little procession along the hall. Candle sconces and lamps lit their way, but the air was chill in the North Wing, and Wetherby grumbled that he was dashed if he could see why they'd had to leave the warm drawing room and traipse half a mile to be blasted well frozen!

Leaning to Euphemia's ear, Hawkhurst murmured, "What do you know of this, my Unattainable Plotter?"

"I know how to 'follow the guide,' " she answered evasively and was relieved to see Coleridge appear in the ballroom doorway, wearing his paint-spattered smock over his evening dress. Hawkhurst's brow darkened at the sight of such a garment, however, and the Admiral's whiskers bristled alarmingly.

Well aware of these reactions, Coleridge was pale and nervous but bowed to his guests, assuring them the fires were lit and that it was warmer inside.

"And smellier!" Wetherby gave a snort and wrinkled his nose. "Gad! What is that awful aroma? Smells like Dora's

287

'perfume'! Now, what the deuce? Are we to see an entertainment, then?"

A long line was stretched across the centre of the brightly lit room. Hung with sheets, it formed an impromptu curtain, held up at intervals by lackeys, two of whom, having dipped liberally into the wassail-bowl, looked as though they needed to be held up themselves.

Colley had slipped away and now fumbled through the curtains to stand flushed and laughing before his small audience. "Mrs. Dora Graham and Lord Coleridge Bryce," he announced bravely, then bit his lip in a new flood of nervousness and, his colour fading, gulped, "are p-proud to welcome you to ... to their first ... showing."

The lackeys allowed the curtain to drop to the floor, then whisked it away.

Hawkhurst stood in stunned silence, gripping his cane very tightly as he stared at the *objets d'art* so carefully arranged for their inspection, and the only sound in the room was Wetherby's awed, "By ... thunder!"

Unable to endure the suspense, Coleridge moved to slip a hand onto his cousin's shoulder. "Hawk, please do not be angry."

"Angry ... !" breathed Hawkhurst, scarcely able to tear his eyes from the various canvases. And, putting up his own hand to cover those talented fingers, he said a gruff, "I will very likely *murder* you! How *dared* you allow me to believe you a mere dabbler?"

Dora tottered dangerously amongst the exhibits and stammered, "I-I *do* so wish someone would ... c-come and look."

With cries of delight, they did so. One large canvas in the very centre of the display was covered, but each of the other items received their full share of admiring attention, so that the two artists revelled in the compliments lavished upon them.

Slightly apprehensive, Euphemia watched the Admiral, who was curiously examining the "banana" into which Dora had sneezed her hairpins. "Half Moon Island ..." he breathed in awe. "And all the dead palm trees ... ! By Jove, Dora! I never thought you was attending when I told you of the place! What talent! Bless me if you ain't such a total feather-wit, after all!" And he reduced his daughter to tears by taking her hand and kissing it proudly.

"And only look!" cried Carlotta, taking up the "squidge" with the two brooms, "It is that ridiculous bonnet Mrs.

Hughes-Dering wore to Lucinda Carden's garden party last summer! Dora! What a quiz you are to be sure!"

Dora laughed happily, but concerned, Euphemia drew her aside and whispered, "Dora, I hope you don't mind ... I mean—"

"Sweet child, never worry!" the little woman rhapsodized. "Only think, *anyone* can create an Adonis, but I fashion nice *friendly* shapes, and each person can see something different in them! Oh, is it not delicious?"

Euphemia agreed that it was and hugged her. For the next half-hour and more the two artists happily accepted the unfeigned admiration of their guests. Hawkhurst, demanding the right to kiss his clever aunt, and braving a veritable storm of teardrops to do so, then turned to Coleridge. The youth watched him tautly, and for an instant they stood thus, eye to eye, then Hawkhurst said a low voiced, "Colley, did you think I would mock ... this?"

Bryce's flush darkened, and his lashes lowered.

"Of course, he did not," said Lady Bryce. "Although you *have* made fun of his aspirations this year and more, you must own it, Garret." Hawkhurst flinched, and Carlotta added an injured, "Colley, my love, you might at least have told your Mama!"

"Clever young scoundrel," said the Admiral, his eyes glowing with pride. "What's under the sheet?"

"His very finest work!" Dora proclaimed. "Show them, dear boy, and I think you should sit down again, Garret."

Hawkhurst seated himself obediently. Coleridge fumbled with the sheet that covered his canvas and, worried by the inscrutable look on his cousin's face, said with blushingly painful shyness, "This ... is a gift for someone I have ever honoured. And ... loved."

He removed the covering with one swift movement. Amid the shouts of admiration, Euphemia heard Hawkhurst's hissing intake of breath. The portrait was even more magnificent now that it was completed, and, gazing at it, she rejoiced with pride in both the man so sensitively captured on the canvas and Colley's great talent.

"Devil take it!" gasped the Admiral. "The lad's a master!"

Quite unable to speak, Hawkhurst stretched out one hand. Coleridge came to grip it strongly and reiterate his plea that Hawk not be angry. "I wanted only to be sure I had something worth showing you. If you still wish me to go to Spain, I—"

"Wretched ... cub," Hawkhurst muttered unevenly. "You shall go, well enough! You shall go with me to see Joseph Turner. We'll take this to him and ask what he thinks you should do."

White as death, Coleridge gasped, "T-Turner ... ? Do you ... know ... *Turner*?"

"Well, if he don't, I do!" The Admiral marched up to clap him on the back. "Burn me if I didn't take you for a mutton-headed cawker! I've never been more pleased to admit my error! By Jove! *What* a Christmas this has been!" He glanced to the side, and his bright eyes softened. "Come along in, you rascal! What are you doing up at this hour?"

Avery, clad in nightshirt and dressing gown and holding the battered old bear in his arms, came timidly around the door. His questioning eyes met his father's, a great beaming smile spread across the small face, and he ran to lay his bear upon Hawkhurst's knees and slip his hand into Euphemia's ready clasp.

"What were you about?" Hawkhurst forced his gaze from the boy and took up the bear. "Tucking him into his secret place for the night?"

Avery nodded.

"Poor old bear. I cannot recall his name. It was an odd kind of name. Avery called him after someone we know, Miss Buchanan. Now, whoever was it?" He pondered thoughtfully, while his son watched him with eyes brimful of love and laughter. "Something like ... cushion ... or quilt, but that cannot be right. Bolster ... ? I *think* it was Bolster?"

Avery giggled hugely. "Feather, Papa!" he corrected joyfully. "Feather!"

An hour later, Euphemia closed the drawing room doors quietly upon the rapturous occupants and wandered thoughtfully along the hall. Surely there had never been so happy a group as shared Dominer this Christmas night. Surely, never had there been such an outpouring of joy as had greeted little Avery's spoken words. When the tears and laughter and embraces were done, the Admiral had asked that Hawkhurst lead them in prayers of thanksgiving. Garret's dear voice had been hoarse with emotion, his fervent words near drowned by Dora's sobs.

Avery, too overwrought for many questions, was now fast asleep. Hawkhurst had slipped away, partly, she thought, because he was exhausted, and partly, she suspected, to reassure himself that the son he had been parted from for so long was truly safe in his own bed.

Euphemia sighed a little and, coming to the stairs, encountered Ponsonby, who bowed and (being nobody's fool) enquired whether he should serve tea at ten as usual, adding, "The fog seems to be coming up again, Miss."

"Then perhaps you should ask Mrs. Henderson to have rooms prepared for the Archers. Set tea back until half-past ten, if you will. Oh, and Ponsonby, have you seen Mr. Hawkhurst?"

His eyes benevolent, he murmured, "In the gallery, Miss."

"Thank you. And, a very merry Christmas, Ponsonby."

"Thank you, Miss. It has, indeed, been a *very* merry Christmas."

Euphemia smiled at him and hurried up the stairs. A candle flickered at the centre of the gallery, and she realized with a pang that Hawkhurst sat on the bench before Blanche's portrait. She hesitated a second but, upon moving quietly towards him, saw that the large canvas had been taken down. He started up, reaching for his cane, but she slipped swiftly onto the bench beside him, and he sat back again.

"Are you quite done up?" she asked anxiously. "It must have been thoroughly exhausting for you."

He smiled faintly. "Can one be done up by happiness, I wonder?" Euphemia made no answer, and he said, "I feel rather awed, in fact. So much has been given me. I've a whole new life, Miss Buchanan. And I'm not at all sure I've a right to it."

How formal he sounded. A small pang touched Euphemia. He had indeed a whole new life. One in which, perhaps, there would be no room for her . . . She folded her hands meekly in her lap and was silent.

After a moment, he muttered thoughtfully, "I think I shall hang my new portrait here. What do you say, Miss Buchanan?"

She shot an oblique glance at him. "I have no right to venture an opinion, Mr. Hawkhurst. But, if I had, would say a most definite *no*!"

He turned his head to her with that familiar lazy smile that made her yearn to be enfolded in his arms. "It *is* rather flattering, of course, but—"

"Very," she agreed mischievously. "Still, were the choice

mine, I would say it must go downstairs. In the Great Hall, near the front doors."

"Good God! Would you frighten away all my newly discovered friends?"

"Perhaps it would be a bit daunting, at that, but—Oh, Hawk, is it not splendid? How very proud you must be."

The smile in his eyes faded, and his head lowered. "To the contrary. I was never in my life so ashamed. How savage I must have been to them, that they should hide such incredible talents . . . for fear I would . . . laugh."

So that was why he had come here alone. She said, a little crease between her brows, "Fustian! Those were Carlotta's words. Hawk, she doesn't mean it. She cannot help it, I think. Why, the very reason they worked so hard was in the hope they might please you."

"And have, God bless 'em! When I think of all the secrecy . . . how they must have had to connive and smuggle their supplies into the house."

"At dead of night," she nodded.

Startled, he gasped, "Never say so!"

"I saw them." She gave her musical ripple of laughter. "I thought they had murdered you and were hiding your corpse!"

"And you supposed I had warranted such a fate, no?"

"Oh, *assurément!*"

"Wretched girl!" To emphasize this denunciation, he caught her hand and pressed it to his lips.

"Foolish boy." She touched his crisp hair tenderly. "Instead of grieving because you were, perhaps, a tiny bit impatient with Colley, think rather of the love that went into that exquisite portrait. For he captured more of the splendid man that you are than any stranger could have done."

He turned her hand, kissed the soft palm, and lifting his head revealed an expression that sent shivers up her spine, so that she murmured rather breathlessly, "It is most improper that you should . . . kiss my hand while we are all alone here, Mr. Hawkhurst."

"Most. But no one need ever know of your lapse, Miss Buchanan."

Despite the gravity of his words a quirk tugged at his mouth, seeing which she was emboldened to remark softly, "Once upon a time, you said you were becoming . . . selfish."

"So I did." He wound a gleaming ringlet around one finger

with much concentration. "Because I was going to ask if you would sing that little Spanish ditty for us again."

"Oh! What a whisker! You know perfectly well—" She broke off.

"What do I know, ma'am?" he asked, with difficulty suppressing a smile.

"Why," she said, smoothing her gown with precision, "that I shall be three-and-twenty in March. I shall have to start wearing a cap."

He gave a muffled snort. "I am sure it will become you delightfully."

"Garret . . . Hawkhurst!" she bit out between white teeth.

"Miss . . . Buchanan . . ." he murmured, moving closer to her. "Have I not told you, many times, that I am not worthy?"

"Yes. But I am willing to overlook that fact."

"Thank you. And that I am a quite notorious rake. And have even been named—libertine?"

"True. But even so, I wore all my jewels—and most of your family's—to lure you. Was it all for nought, sir?"

He laughed. "Do I dare to think of it, I am lost! But you would be so much better served, my blessed candle, to wed good old Leith. Who is gallant, and honourable, and very handsome."

But now, his every word was a caress, his eyes worshipping her so that she swayed to him yearningly. His arms went around her, and he kissed her until she lay lax and sighful and blissfully content, against his heart.

"I suppose," she mused, "I shall have to consider Leith, then. For I *do* dislike caps."

He tilted her chin a little, so that he could more easily kiss her left eyelid, and, with her shivers becoming ever more delicious, Euphemia heard that deep voice, so husky now, say, "In that case, perhaps it would be expedient to ask you, my dearest, darling girl, if you would be so incredibly foolish as to accept the hand and the heart . . . and the name of a completely unworthy ex-rake—but *never*, I do believe, libertine! Who will, as God be his judge, give you no cause to regret such a decision. Oh, Mia, my Unattainable love . . . Will you—"

She pulled down his head and silenced his words with her lips. And, when at last he straightened and murmurously demanded an answer to his unfinished question, she said only, "Odious man . . ."

"Agreed," he nodded, a tender smile lighting his eyes. "But why?"

"Because," she sighed, "I shall quite miss being known as 'The Unattainable.'"

He chuckled and bent lower. "Then I must strive to console you."

"It may," she warned, "take years."

Curiously, Garret Thorndyke Hawkhurst did not appear to be put into a quake by such a prospect and did, in fact, commence his task at once.

The
Noblest
Frailty

for Abbie

"And love's the noblest frailty
of the mind . . ."

                    JOHN DRYDEN
"The Indian Emperor," II, ii.

❧ *Chapter* 1 ❧

Miss Yolande Drummond was almost two and twenty. She was a remarkably pretty girl, with abundant hair of that rich shade known as chestnut, wide green eyes, and a very fair complexion that, so long as she guarded it from the destructive rays of the sun, seldom threw out a freckle. Her features were dainty, her voice had a husky quality the gentlemen found enchanting, her figure was slender but nicely curved, and she was blessed with a gentle and conformable disposition. She was widely held to be a Fair, and might well have been an accredited Toast save for the fact that before she was out of leading strings it had been decided she should wed her distant cousin, Alain Devenish. Mr. Devenish being possessed of a singularly jealous nature, a fiery temperament, and breath-taking good looks, the gentlemen were given pause by the two former qualities, plunged into despair by the latter, and reluctantly decided that anything more serious than a mild flirtation with the delectable Yolande was a waste of time.

That Miss Drummond had reached so perilous an age without having married surprised a few people who were not well acquainted with her prospective bridegroom. Close friends shrugged off this circumstance, however. Alain Devenish was, they pointed out, a bit of a rascal. Although barely three years Yolande's senior, he had racked up the dubious distinction of having been expelled from Harrow, sent down from Cambridge, asked to resign his regiment and, more recently, been involved in some kind of very unsavoury affair concerning the powerful Monsieur Claude Sanguinet, as a result of which he had barely escaped France with his life. Only the fact that his birth was impeccable, his charm infectious, and his kindness legendary had saved him from social ostracism, but however popular he might be, few blamed Miss Drummond for waiting until her tempestuous beau settled down a trifle.

On a bright morning in early May, Miss Drummond presented a picture to gladden the heart of any man as she stood on the rear terrace of Park Parapine, gazing out over the pleasure gardens and park of her ancestral home. She was clad in a pearl-grey riding habit that fitted her slim shapeliness to perfection. White lace foamed at her throat, and white velvet ribbons were tied in a large bow at the back of her saucy little grey hat. The prospect she viewed was also fair: Beyond the sweep of lawns and flower gardens, the Home Wood presented a verdant border ranging from the tender yellow tints of new leaves to the dark stateliness of evergreens. The air was sweet with the fragrance of blossoms; here and there chestnut trees flaunted their colourful gowns to mingle with the shyer blooms of apple and plums, and lilacs rose richly against a cloudless sky.

Yet, despite all this beauty, Miss Drummond's smooth brow was marred by the suggestion of a pucker, and her lovely eyes were troubled. The sense that she was no longer alone caused her to turn enquiringly, and she discovered that her mother stood watching her.

"Good morning, my love." Lady Louisa smiled, offering a smooth cheek for her daughter's kiss. "Had you a nice ride? A foolish question, no? On such a glorious morning, how could it have been otherwise?"

Yolande loved her mother deeply, but that charming lady's ability to read her thoughts was sometimes alarming, and now she said evasively, "Glorious indeed, especially after so much rain. How pretty you look, Mama. A new dress? That shade of rose so becomes you."

"Besides which, it is a colour you dare not wear," her mother replied, "so I need not fear to discover you have 'borrowed' it."

Yolande laughed. "If I do—very occasionally—borrow your gowns, you have no one to blame but yourself, dearest. What other girl has a mother so youthful and slender she might well be taken for a sister?"

The compliment was well-founded. Lady Louisa had never been a beauty, but had, in her youth, been said to possess "a pleasing countenance," her appeal springing from an innate kindness, rather than from her looks. At five and forty, however, she outshone many a former Toast, for her hair, although an indeterminate shade of brown, had not begun to grey, her skin was clear and unwrinkled, and her merry disposition kept her as young in heart as in appearance. She was also a shrewd woman and, suspecting that she was being guided from an unwanted subject, said mischievously, "Oh, what a rasper! I must beware, for such tactics usually presage an outlandish plea I cannot then resist. What is it, my love? Are you going to tell me you have thrown dear Alain over in favour of some wholly ineligible young man?"

Yolande's smile faltered. She turned back to her contemplation of the horizon and said slowly, "No, Mama. Of course I have not. I know how you and my father have always wished the match."

Lady Louisa's hands clasped rather tightly, and for a moment she was silent. When she spoke, however, it was to ask in a mild way, "Never say you have set the date at last? Devenish must be floating back to Aspenhill!"

"I . . . er— Actually . . ." Yolande bit her lip. "Oh—we had a small difference of—of opinion."

"I see." Lady Louisa did not see. Were she twenty-five years younger, she thought, and Devenish had smiled her way, Sir Martin might have had a formidable competitor for her hand. As it was, the prospect of having such a son-in-law delighted her, and her husband's heart was quite set on it. He and Colonel Alastair Tyndale had been bosom bows since their schooldays, and it was well known that the Colonel's orphaned nephew, to whom he stood guardian, was his sole heir. Tyndale was not a man of great wealth, but the Park Parapine lands matched with those of his Aspenhill and that the two great estates should be merged by this marriage was the dream of both men.

Doting on her husband, Lady Louisa was in full accord with his wishes in the matter, but she also loved her daughter and therefore said gently, "Dearest, you *do* wish to marry Alain?"

Yolande's lashes drooped, and the colour in the smooth cheeks was heightened. "I—suppose I do," she answered, concentrating upon drawing the thong of her riding whip through her gloved hand.

"You—*suppose?* Good God! Do *not* you know?"

Yolande sighed and asked rather wistfully, "Did *you* know, Mama?"

"Indeed I did! I had never met your papa, of course, although I had seen him everywhere. I was scarce out of the schoolroom when I was told he had offered and your grandpapa had accepted." She smiled reminiscently, her anxieties forgotten for a moment. "I shall never forget when I was brought into the saloon and Papa took my hand and gave it to Sir Martin. I was so frightened, but his hand was shaking harder than mine, and it gave me the courage to peep at him. And when I saw the smile in his eyes . . ." She sighed again, then, meeting her daughter's intent regard, imparted, "My heart was lost in that one moment."

"Oh. And—have you never had—doubts? None at all?"

"Good gracious!" thought my lady, but said serenely, "Never. Oh, there have been times I might cheerfully have boiled him in oil, of course. Men can be so incredibly provoking. But he still has my heart, and I would do anything in my power to keep him happy. You must own he is a splendid gentleman, Yolande. And if you had but seen him when he was a young man . . ."

Yolande smiled. The portrait of her father that had been painted upon his attaining his majority still hung in the great hall of the house, so that she had a fairly accurate idea of how he had looked at four and twenty. He was a handsome man then, as now, although nowhere near as good-looking as Alain. It was easy to understand why Mama had fallen so completely in love with him. If only the same feelings were—A soft touch on her wrist roused her from her reverie.

"Dear child," said Lady Louisa in her gentlest voice, "if you do not love Devenish, we will tell Papa. I am sure he would not wish—"

"Oh, no, no! I would not for the world— I *do* love Dev. He is the very dearest boy. It is only . . . that—"

"The years have a way of slipping by rather fast, you know, Yolande. If you love him, I would have thought—" Lady Louisa did not finish that sentence, but added, "He is *sans reproche* in so far as Family is concerned. And a more handsome young man one could not wish to meet."

"Very true. But—but he is so *wild*, Mama! Only think of that fiasco at Cambridge."

"Yes. Though I vow I cannot remember why he was sent down."

"It was for putting glue on the soles of the Proctor's shoes. The poor man took up so much rubble when they went for their morning run, that he tripped and broke his ankle."

"Dreadful!" said my lady, sternly repressing a smile. "But Devenish was honest enough to confess, no?"

"Oh, he is the soul of honour, who could doubt it? But—on the other hand—consider the whole picture, Mama. Expelled from Harrow; sent down from University; asked to resign his regiment—and then there was that frightful business in which he became involved last year with Tristram Leith and the Frenchman. What it was all about I have never been able to discover, save that one has only to mention it and all the gentlemen become like clams, so it must have been very dreadful. One schoolboy prank after another! Do you know, I sometimes fear he will never grow up, for he is just like a naughty little boy!"

"Oh, just. I wonder you could still love the vexing fellow. He must be sternly guided by his lady, no?"

Yolande looked up, met the smile in the kind hazel eyes, and said with a small, wry shrug, "Perhaps. But—my fear is, Mama, that I am, myself, not always very wise."

My lady's heart sank. Still, she persisted gently. "You have numbered his faults, but he has much to recommend him, do you not agree?"

"Yes, of course I do. I could say off a long list of good points. Only, he is so very . . . unlover-like." Yolande slanted a shy glance at her mother and, blushing, stammered, "You will—will fancy me very foolish, I fear. But Alain has never once wrote me a love note, or vowed his devotion, or—or behaved like a man deeply attached." Having said which, she cast down her eyes in much confusion and turned her head so that her dark blush might not be seen.

Briefly, Lady Louisa was silent. How irksome, she thought, not to have foreseen such a development. She should have suspected it, Lord knows, for being a loving and concerned parent she was well aware of the many novels her elder daughter carried home from the various lending libraries. Certainly, a girl who shed tears over the pitfalls confronting Mrs. Radclyffe's much-tried heroines, and who had often fallen asleep at night with Lord Byron's poems still held in her hands, would find Devenish's breezy big-brother manner unfulfilling.

She gave her daughter a quick hug. "Of course I do not think it foolish!" she declared staunchly. "I *do* think it most perverse of Fate to have made Alain so extreme handsome, and have given him so intrepid and dauntless a nature, only to then dump him in this modern age of ours!" Yolande turned curious eyes upon her and, encouraged, she continued, "Your cousin should rather have lived in the days when England was overrun with bold knights. He was meant to ride with lance in hand, and dragons lurking at every bend of his road through life!"

"Alain?" said Yolande, awed. "Heavens! I had never thought of him in such a light."

"Perhaps because you have grown up together. I do assure you, however, that many other young ladies see him in *just* that light!" And wisely not belabouring the point, my lady went on, "Is it not typical that so dashing a figure should have no slightest vestige of the romantical in his outlook, whereas, beneath the stodgy exterior of some dull, lumpish young man, might burn a soul ablaze with romantic notions?"

Yolande smiled and nodded, and her gaze returned to the view, which she saw not at all. There followed a small, companionable silence, through which Lady Louisa watched her daughter hopefully. Her hopes were dashed.

"If only," Yolande murmured, "he had a steadier, less volatile temperament."

"Less volatile?" Sir Martin slapped one hand against his muscular thigh and gave a crack of laughter. "When did our flighty miss remark that, ma'am? This morning? She's known the boy all her days and only now is discovering he is no milksop?"

Lady Louisa put down the embroidery she had taken up several times during their conversation, and absently regarded her husband, outlined against the window of her private parlour. A big man who enjoyed the life of country squire and found town a dead bore, Sir Martin carried his years well. His colouring was slightly florid since he tended to burn in sun and wind rather than become tanned, but he was in splendid physical condition, his auburn hair still waving luxuriantly, the grey at the temples lending him dignity. His green eyes were only a little less keen than they had been when he was wed, and his countenance was so well featured that Yolande was flattered when her resemblance to her sire was remarked upon.

Neatly folding her embroidery, my lady asked mildly, "If Yolande was to reject Devenish, my love, should you be horribly disappointed?"

"Not *marry* him?" He frowned, all the laughter gone from his eyes.

"Oh, dear," murmured his lady.

"Why the deuce should she not marry him?" he demanded, a testy edge to his voice. "They have been promised since she was in the nursery, practically."

"True. But he has not offered. Formally, that is."

"Blast it all, why should he do so bird-witted a thing, when it has been taken for granted these eighteen years and more!"

"Exactly so." She sighed, taking up the embroidery she had reduced to a neat square and shaking it out once more. "Perhaps that is the whole trouble. I should have thought of it."

Sir Martin departed on the first of several tours about the room, during which he animadverted bitterly upon the frivolity, thoughtlessness, and ingratitude of one's children. Never, he declared, would he have so vexed *his* parents. Especially when they had been nothing but good to him. It was a sorry world when youth today was so insensitive, so selfish. "Devenish," he said, passing his meekly sewing wife on his third lap, "is a splendid young fellow, of impeccable lineage."

"So I told her, Sir Martin."

"He has looks, charm, and a generally sunny disposition. The girls are fairly crazy over him. He owns a magnificent estate in Gloucestershire and will take control of a respectable fortune in a month or so, to say nothing of Aspenhill, for Alastair Tyndale is not like to wed at his age. Does *he* know about this nonsense, I wonder? Good gad! He would be heartbroken! All our days we've planned that the estates would be joined. What a splendid heritage to be whistled down the wind only because some silly chit decides Devenish is—what was it she said? Volatile? Volatile, indeed! The boy's high-spirited as any colt, is all. He's been in a few scrapes, I grant you, but conducted himself very well in that damned mess in Brittany last year, and by what young Leith says, is pluck to the backbone."

"Yes, dear. But—" She looked up at him and asked gravely, "Could you compel Yolande to marry a man she does not love?"

"*Love?* Good God, madam! People of our order do not marry for love!"

Her ladyship said simply, "I did."

Sir Martin stared at her, snorted, stamped up and down, put his hands behind him, and stared at her again. Then, with a wry laugh he marched to sit down beside her, removed the embroidery and tossed it ruthlessly over his shoulder, and took his wife in his arms.

After a moment, Lady Louisa pulled back, straightened her demure lace cap, and said a trifle breathlessly, "Now, Martin! Pray be sensible."

"I am being sensible," he argued, dropping a kiss on the hand he still held. "You know very well, Louisa, that when you look at me in just that way, it always makes me feel—"

"Then I'll not look at you at all, sir," she said primly, withdrawing her hand, but submitting when it was promptly reclaimed. "Now, I have been thinking ever since I spoke with Yolande this morning, and I have a plan which I hope may work. Yolande must not marry Devenish only to please us, my dear."

He scowled. "Why not? Chances are that once they are wed she will settle down and be perfectly content."

"Oh, yes, that is very possible. And nothing would be more delightful than for her to discover she really is in love with Dev. But—suppose she should find to the contrary? She is scarcely the type to take a lover. And even if—" My lady paused, eyeing her husband with disfavour as he exploded into a hearty laugh.

"Apologies, m'dear," he said, patting her hand. "But I was just picturing Devenish's reaction to such a triangle." He chuckled again, "Lord! Can you not imagine that young volcano? Yolande may not know her own heart, but Dev has no such reservations. Yolande is his world. He would tear the man limb from limb!"

"He would, indeed. And I believe you are right, he worships her. What a pity he does not tell her so."

"*Tell* her so? Oh, gad! You ladies and your romantical vapourings! Dev comes over every day, don't he? He takes her riding, brings her gifts. Why only yesterday he—"

"He brought her that fox kit he found! A pretty gift! Not only did it keep Yolande up all night with its yelping, but it was full of fleas and bit one of the maids when she chanced to step on it while she was making the bed. She fell into strong hysterics and the kit raced out, with the cat in hot pursuit, throwing the entire house into an uproar!" Regarding her amused spouse with indignation, Lady Louisa said, "But you prove my point, Sir Martin. Alain has no more notion of how to treat the girl he loves than a Clydesdale knows how to dance a quadrille! And thus, I think—" She waited out another howl of laughter from her lord, who was fond of Clydesdale horses and could envision the scene she had suggested. "I think," she resumed severely, while he wiped his eyes, "that we should send Yolande to visit her grandpapa."

"What—in Ayrshire?"

"Since my own papa has gone to Paris, my love, I scarcely think such a journey appropriate."

"But why journey at all? Oh—do you think the old fellow might banish some of her silly megrims?"

"I think it is a very true saying that 'Absence makes the heart grow fonder,' and Mr. Alain Devenish has been taking your daughter entirely too much for granted."

"Well, if it's absence you want, m'dear, she could go to your sister in Town for a month or two. Don't have to travel all that way up to Scotland."

"I think she does have to," said Lady Louisa thoughtfully. "She must be far away. Where Devenish is not like to follow."

Despite his rantings, Sir Martin doted on his pretty daughter, but at this, he said with a slow smile, "I own no property on the moon, my love."

"To the moon, sir?" Mr. Alain Devenish blinked down into the cold blue eyes of the man who leaned back in the big chair behind the desk, and, running one finger around his elaborately tied neckcloth that suddenly seemed too tight, protested, "No, really, Uncle! I've not been gone *that* long, surely?"

Colonel Alastair Tyndale rested his elbows on the arms of his chair and regarded his nephew over interlocked hands. Twenty years separated the two men, and few, seeing them together, would imagine them to be related. Devenish was slender and not above average height, with curling blond hair, intensely blue eyes, and features almost too delicately carven for a man. Tyndale was tall and broad with a loose-limbed, athletic body, and a head of thick brown hair beginning to grey at the temples. His nose was strong, his chin a fierce jut, and his mouth a thin, uncompromising line. Only in the eyes was there a similarity, and that very slight and not so much a matter of shape or colouring as of expression. The eyes of both men were seldom without a humorous twinkle, and if in Devenish that twinkle could in a flash become a glare of rage, in his uncle it could as swiftly be replaced by inexorable purpose, a determination approaching ruthlessness.

"You have been gone," sighed the Colonel, drawing a rather battered timepiece from the pocket of his waistcoat and consulting it, "precisely eight hours and forty-five minutes. You doubtless forgot I had expressly requested that you return to Aspenhill by three o'clock so as to meet Lord Westhaven."

As always when his guardian was displeased, Devenish began to experience the unease that had afflicted numerous junior officers quaking before Tyndale during his years in India. Despite the fact that he and his late mother's younger brother were often at loggerheads, however, Devenish was fond of his uncle and chagrined by the knowledge that he had once again disappointed him. He took a turn about the pleasant, panelled room and stood frowning out across the lawns of this house wherein so much of his young life had been spent. "I was at Park Parapine, sir," he offered.

"So I had presumed. It was my understanding that you were to accompany Yolande on an early ride. One can but hope that the length of that—er, ride, indicates a satisfactory resolution of your—ah, problems."

"Lord!" muttered Devenish, under his breath. He swung about and returned to toss his slender body into a deep chair beside the desk and divulge that he had not spent the entire day riding. "I chanced to run into Harland," he said. "I think the old boy's lonely, now that Lucian is off honeymooning. Nothing would do but that I go over to Hollow Hill with him. He's leaving for Paris next week." He shrugged. "I forgot the time. And Westhaven." Flashing a contrite glance at Tyndale, he added, "Did I cause you to be embarrassed? My apologies, sir, but—I really have no interest in politics, you know."

"It would be enlightening to learn," the Colonel sighed, straightening a paper on his desk, "what *does* interest you. Besides Yolande Drummond."

Devenish flushed, his lips tightening with resentment, but he said nothing.

"From your demeanour," Tyndale went on, "I have to infer that my cousin's child has once again refused to set a date for your wedding."

The tone had not been unkind, but Devenish squirmed. "She says," he imparted indignantly, "that I am a here-and-thereian."

The shadow of a smile crept into the Colonel's blue eyes. "She is not without justification, would you say?"

"What, because I found University a dead bore? Because I did not—er, take to the military, or—"

"You were *sent down*," Tyndale intervened, his voice suddenly holding a touch of steel, "because you played a childish prank upon the Proctor. You were *obliged* to leave the army because of just such another prank. Had you failed in your studies, having tried your best; had you been asked to resign your commission because of some blockheaded military injustice, I could better have understood matters. You are five and twenty, Alain. In two months it will be time for my guardianship to end, and for you to take over the reins at Devencourt. It is past time you had moved back there. Oh, I know why you have not done so—my estates chance to march with those of the Drummonds. But your lands stand in need of an owner—a resident owner."

"There is no cause for me to remain here now," Devenish grunted.

A frown twitched at Tyndale's brows. "Good God!" he exclaimed. "Never say Yolande has cried off?"

"Lord, no! Never that, sir! But she has made it clear I must change my ways before—" Devenish broke off. "Oh, blast! I shouldn't have said there was no cause for me to stay. What a clunch I am!" He leaned forward in his chair and, with the smile that had ensnared many a hopeful lady, said earnestly, "You know I am more than grateful, sir. You know I've no wish to leave *you!*"

Tyndale's grim features were lit by an answering warmth. "Thank you, Alain. And *you* know I've no wish to scold you. God knows, your conduct last summer in the Sanguinet affair made me very proud. Incidentally, have you heard from Leith? Is there any further word on the Frenchman?"

"I am in touch with Tristram, of course, sir. He feels that Sanguinet remains a menace to England. Somewhere—God knows where—he's up to his tricks. And—when we least expect it . . ." He scowled. "His scheme to kidnap the Regent was damnably clever, but if he strikes again, Tristram thinks it will be with men. An all-out thrust for power." His blue eyes ablaze, he drove one fist into his palm. "Now, *there's* something I would be interested in, by Jove! I hope to God I'm about when the Frenchman does play his cards!"

"I cannot think he will do anything so unwise. He would have to be a complete lunatic to persist with plans about which he must know the authorities have been warned."

"He *is* a lunatic! I believe he has some miserable scheme to take over where Bonaparte left off. He knows our warnings were laughed at. He knows Tristram was as good as cashiered and that both he and his bride are in deep disgrace. Oh, Sanguinet will not give up, I do assure you, sir. He will merely contrive again."

"If he contrives, lad, it may be to your doom. He is a vindictive man. Have a care."

Devenish's blithe response that he was sure Monsieur Claude Sanguinet had more weighty matters on his mind than personal vengeance incurred Tyndale's displeasure. The Colonel embarked upon a lengthy discourse regarding the menace of the ambitious and wealthy Frenchman. At the close, Devenish said meekly that he would write out his will and carry a pistol the next time he left the estate.

Tyndale stared with suspicion at his nephew's angelic innocence and grunted, "Very good. Meantime, I've a task for you. A pleasant one, I hope."

"A task? For the military, sir?"

"Nothing so impressive." Tyndale stood and marched around the desk to perch against the edge. Reaching back, he took up a rumpled paper and glanced at the closely written lines that filled the page. "Westhaven brought me this letter. It appears to have had a rough journey, arriving at length in his hands and he was kind enough to deliver it whilst he was here. It concens your Canadian cousin."

Devenish glanced at the tattered letter curiously. "I was not aware I *had* a Canadian cousin."

"No? Yet you will, I feel sure, recall that I had a brother, Jonas."

"Oh, the firebrand who had to leave the country! Because of a duel of some sort, was it not?"

The Colonel's eyes clouded. He said broodingly, "We are none of us a very stable lot, I fear. But Jonas was rather more than wild. I have not gone into details before, because there seemed little likelihood we would ever see him again. Indeed, we will not, for he is dead, so I learn."

"Oh, I am sorry, sir. Were you fond of him?"

"I was deeply fond of him—as I was fond of your own father. It seems that his wife died a few years back, in childbed perhaps, for he has left a son, and the boy is on his way here to visit the land of his forebears."

A revolting suspicion had taken possession of Devenish's mind. Eyeing his uncle warily, he asked, "A boy, sir? Did *he* write that letter?"

"No." Tyndale replaced the sheet on his desk and explained, "It was written by Jonas's solicitor begging that we receive the little fellow and do all in our power to assist him. In what way, I could not determine, for the page is very travel-stained and some of the words were obliterated. I expect the poor child will find England strange and terrifying, as would anyone arriving orphaned and friendless in a new land. Therefore, I wish that you will—"

"Me?" With a sort of leap, Devenish rose. "Good God, sir! I know nought of children. And as for a brat who likely comes complete with leathern fringes and a furred cap . . . ! Uncle Alastair! How can you even think—"

Tyndale stood up straight and, from his superior height, smiled into his nephew's aghast eyes. "You underestimate yourself, Alain. If you are capable of having aided Tristram Leith to outwit and outmanœuvre one of the most dangerous madmen of our time, you are certainly capable of handling a backwoods child. Now, I have other matters requiring my attention, and must beg that you excuse me." He lifted one hand as his nephew attempted a remonstrance, and returning to sit at his desk, said gently, "We will talk at dinner, Alain."

Devenish hesitated. The old fellow was devilish grumpy today. Probably the news of his brother's death had upset him, which was natural enough. What a clodcrusher, not to have thought of it! He murmured, "I am very sorry, sir. About my Uncle Jonas, I mean. I'll be only too glad to help the boy."

Tyndale voiced his thanks, but did not look up from the papers he was scanning. Devenish crept to the door and closed it softly behind him.

The instant he was alone the Colonel threw down the papers and sank his head into his hands. "Good God!" he whispered. "Perhaps I should tell him the truth *now*, and be done with it!" For a long while he stared, haggard-eyed, at the quill pen, turning the problem over in his mind. But in the end he decided his initial plan must be followed. "I will wait," he thought, "until he meets the child. It would be just like the young rascal to become deeply attached to the boy. Then, it will not be so hard to tell him."

From having known Mr. Alain Devenish since he was in short coats, none of the Drummonds fancied he would fall into a decline by reason of Yolande's scold. However, since he had announced at the conclusion of that unhappy interview that he meant to go on a walking tour, Yolande was mildly surprised to see him coming cantering up the rear drivepath the following afternoon. She had been gainfully employed for the previous quarter-hour in assisting her Aunt Arabella to unravel a piece of knitting and, glancing up, said a not displeased, "Oh, it's Devenish."

Mrs. Drummond uttered a despairing little wail. "But it cannot be, for you quite distinctly told me he was going away! Alas, so it is! And now he will take you from me so that I shall never finish this jacket for your dear papa! You are so *very* clever at understanding complex instructions, Yolande. And I—as usual—am such a dunce."

A small, bird-like woman, Mrs. Arabella Drummond had been married when scarcely out of the schoolroom to Sir Martin's elder brother, Paul. She had early wilted before her husband's forceful personality, deferring to him in all things, and upon his sudden death on the hunting field at the age of two and thirty had fallen into a deep decline from which for a time it had been feared she would never recover. Lady Louisa had insisted on caring for the childless widow, and had nursed her so well that Arabella soon regained her health. The prospect of living alone in the Dower House had appalled her, however, and she had implored Sir Martin to be allowed to stay at Park Parapine, just until she was over the shock of her bereavement. She was not an invigorating companion, and her brother-in-law not only considered her a dead bore but marvelled often through the following years that his wife could endure so lachrymose a personality. His occasional efforts to dislodge her had invariably brought on an attack of the vapours, or palpitations, or a resumption of Mrs. Drummond's famous "weak spells," so that still the Dower House remained unoccupied.

Her aunt having been a fixture in the house for as long as she could remember, Yolande could not imagine Park Parapine without her and, although quite often she contemplated deliciously fiendish acts of retribution upon her vexing relative, she was nonetheless fond of her and said, with her kind smile, "You most certainly are not a dunce! You knit very evenly, dear, and if you will just be sure you do not turn to the wrong page of your instruction papers, all will be well."

Mrs. Drummond was little encouraged by these remarks. She hove a deep sigh and allowed the garment she held to fall into her lap, folding her hands upon it and saying mournfully, "I try so hard. And this time I really did think I might succeed. I own I fancied it odd to have that strange bump suddenly appearing in the middle of the back of your papa's jacket, but then I thought it was to allow for the width of the shoulders."

"No, dear," said Yolande, noting how cautiously Devenish swung from the saddle and thinking that his leg must trouble him, still. "It was for the heel of a sock."

Mrs. Drummond moaned. "You will be thinking I should have known," she sighed, becoming even more dejected. "But how could I, when I never have attempted a jacket before? You will recall the bedsocks I made for your mama last Christmas? Those were nice, were they not?"

Yolande had a clear picture of her father wiping tears of mirth from his eyes in Mama's parlour, when first Lady Louisa had tried on her new bedsocks. "They're big enough . . . for two men— and a boy!" he had choked. Struggling to preserve her countenance, Yolande assured her aunt that the bedsocks had been charming, and finished, "Pray excuse me, ma'am. I must go and welcome Dev."

She made her escape and found Devenish in the garden, holding a basket that her mother was filling with early flowers. Lady Louisa, wearing a becoming broad-brimmed straw bonnet, was saying, ". . . even just a few blooms will so brighten a room, especially if one is not feeling quite the thing. Oh, hello, my love! Here is Devenish come to visit you, and I have been telling him about little Rosemary."

Yolande smiled upon her suitor and gave him her hand. "Good afternoon, Dev. Is Rosemary still poorly, Mama? I had thought she just ate too many cheese tarts yesterday."

"I wish you may be right." Lady Louisa placed a daisy in the basket. "But Nurse says she is feverish. I do hope she is not sickening for one of those endless childhood ailments." And with a worried smile, a nod to Devenish, and a caution that her daughter stay out of the sun, she took the basket and made her graceful way into the house.

Yolande turned to Devenish and succeeded in releasing the hand he had firmly retained during her mother's remarks. "Really, Dev!" she scolded primly.

He grinned at her. "Still in a pucker, are you?"

"*Me!* You were the one went riding off yesterday like a thundercloud!"

A spark came into his eyes, but he had determined not to quarrel with her and, with an extravagant gesture, invited, "Madam—will you perambulate with me?"

She slipped her hand in his arm and they began to walk amongst the flower beds together. She knew that he watched her, but managed to appear unconscious of that fact, pausing to admire various blooms as they strolled along. "Only look at the poppies," she said. "Miller has such a sure touch and always knows just what will thrive in just which spot. Are they not a picture?"

His immediate, "Not so pretty a picture as you," shocked her. She must, she realized, have really alarmed him yesterday. The awareness that he was trying very hard to please, in some perverse way dismayed her, and she whirled away from him so that they were standing back to back. "Since you admire me so," she teased, "tell me, sir, what am I wearing?"

"Why—a dress of course, sweet henwit."

"Describe it."

Devenish groaned. "Oh, gad! It is—er, blue, I think. Yes. Blue!"

"And has it a ruffle? Are the sleeves long, or short?"

"Thunder and— What the deuce has that to say to the purpose?"

"You don't know!"

He gritted his teeth. " 'Course I do. Blast it! There is—ah, no ruffle. And the sleeves are those fat little things you women wear."

"You mean puff, I presume, Mr. Devenish?"

"My apologies, Miss Drummond! Yes. Puff."

"And have I a necklace today? Or ribbons in my hair?"

He was sure there had been no ribbons, so said triumphantly, "You wear a necklace. A blue necklace. To match your eyes."

"Oh!" With a cry of chagrin, Yolande spun to face him. She wore a gown of palest green muslin, the deeply scooped neckline having a demure inset white yoke laced together with matching green ribbons. The sleeves were tiny little puffs, as he had said, nor did she wear ribbons in her rich tresses. Horrifyingly, about her white throat was a necklace of jade beads. Which emphasized the green of her eyes.

"Oh— Lord!" Devenish clutched his fair curls in despair. "I am sunk quite beneath reproach!"

"Be assured of it! I could have forgiven you the colour of the dress, and my necklace, but—have you known me all my life and never noticed that my eyes are green?"

"I am the complete gudgeon," he admitted, peering at her from under his hand. "You would be perfectly right to reject me entirely."

She hesitated, but the mischievous quirk beside his lips brought a frown to her brows, and she tossed her head and started off alone. Devenish hastened to come up with her. "Yolande—for heaven's sake! I do not see what difference—"

"Oh, do you not!" She halted, the better to glare up at him. "Considering, Alain, that you are so deep in love with me—"

"Dash it all! You know I am!"

"I know nothing of the kind! Does a gentleman truly care for a lady, he most certainly knows the colour of her eyes!"

"Yes—and I do, now."

She sniffed and started off again, and Devenish said with disastrous honesty, "It is only that I've known you so long, I simply did not notice."

"Not ... *notice* ... ?" She turned back, frowning in that way he thought particularly delicious. "I will have you know, Devenish, that there have been odes writ to my eyes." The twinkle that came into his own deeply blue eyes vexed her into adding a defiant and rather inaccurate, "Dozens!"

"Oho! What a whisker! Only show me two and I shall rush home and write one myself!"

"How exceeding generous! But I would not so tax your abilities for words. Thank you *very* much, just the same!" Flushed, her head held high and haughty, she walked away, raging. And in a little while, finding that he did not follow, uttered a muted, "Huh!" and paced on. But she was deeply fond of him and gradually it dawned on her that they had been quarrelling like two foolish children, rather than lovers. The knowledge troubled her, as she had often been troubled of late, and she glanced back. Devenish was standing where she had left him, staring at the ground, hands thrust into his pockets. A pang that was as much remorse as sympathy went through her, and she retraced her steps, pausing before him.

The bowed, fair head was raised. The humour had left his face, and for a moment they stood looking at one another in a shared and yet subtly disparate distress.

Devenish stretched out one hand. "Yolande, my apologies. Truly, I did not mean to vex you. But—what *do* you want of me?"

"I do not know." She sighed and with a wry little shrug put her hand into his. "I—I suppose I want you to be more steady. To have a purpose in life, and not be always rushing off, helter-skelter."

They began to walk again, and Devenish said defensively, "I do not rush off! My uncle kicked me out when I was obliged to resign my commission, and—"

"You do! You know you do, Alain. Only look at—well, to-day, for example. You said you were off on a walking tour."

"And so I was."

"You did not walk to Park Parapine, you rode!"

"Oh, don't be a widgeon, Yolande! I changed my mind, is all."

She shook her head at him, then asked curiously, "Why? I thought you had really meant to go."

They had come to a stone bench, one of several grouped about a fountain, and she sat down. Devenish rested one booted foot on the bench and leaned forward. "I did, but—" His brow darkened. "Of all the bird-witted starts! I've to play nursemaid to some puling infant of a cousin I never even saw!"

Yolande stared into his indignant face, then broke into a sil-very gurgle of laughter. "*You?* Oh, no! Who is it?"

"A Colonial." He took down his foot, dusted the bench carelessly and inefficiently with his riding whip, and sat beside her. "Some Canadian brat."

"But—how can that be? I thought I knew all the children in the family. Am I related to him?"

"Must be, I imagine. He is the son of my deceased Uncle Jonas."

Her eyes widening, Yolande breathed, "What, the black sheep? Oh, how fascinating! I must tell Mama. Now, let me see. The child is your uncle's son. And my aunt on Papa's side of the family married a cousin of your mother, so that makes me . . ." Her brow furrowed. "Oh dear, I do get bewildered by these family relationships."

"It will be much simpler when we are shackled," he pointed out. "You will be his cousin, too."

"Shackled! How I despise that odious expression!"

"Egad, how you take me up. Very well—united in the bonds of holy matrimony."

"Thank you. When is he coming? Or have you to go to Canada, Dev?"

"Hey! Would that not be famous?" Eyes alight, he said ea-gerly, "A great continent to be civilized. A whole new land to be cultivated and—"

She intervened dryly, "You have a great *estate* to be culti-vated," and then, seeing the grimness come into his face, added, "You never have told me why you do not like Deven-court."

At once, he grinned boyishly. "Because there is nothing to tell, madam. I positively dote on the place. But I can scarce toddle off and leave the Old Nunks, now can I? Poor fellow would likely fall into a deep decline were he deprived of my scintillating companionship and left lone and lorn."

"But he will not be lone and lorn. Your little cousin will be here. Oh, Dev!" She tightened her clasp on his arm. "Mama will be *so* titillated! When does he arrive?"

"Any day, I collect. Uncle Alastair wants me to take charge of him and get him settled down. If he stays, I fancy he'll be off to school so soon as he's old enough."

"Stays? Dev, is he to stay with you? At Aspenhill?"

"Well I fancy he is. Dash it all, Yolande, the brat's an orphan. Cannot very well have a Tyndale on the Parish—now can we?"

She laughed, but then said in her warm-hearted fashion, "Poor little fellow. How strange everything will seem to him. *Do* let us go and tell Mama. Dev, I can scarce wait to see the child!"

❧ *Chapter 2* ❧

Mrs. Arabella Drummond carefully replaced the luxurious furred pelisse in its large box, folded the silver paper over it, and took the lid Yolande handed her. It was a trifle difficult to put this back on, for the landaulette, although very well sprung, jolted erratically over the rutted surface of the lane. "I really think it a sad extravagance," mourned Mrs. Drummond, as she tied the string about the box. "Likely Rosemary will be better in plenty of time for your mama to accompany you, and you won't need me at all. What a waste!" She shook her head over the new pelisse, and sighed heavily.

"But it looked so nice on you dear," said Yolande, squeezing her arm encouragingly. "Besides, even if you do not come to Scotland you need a nice warm pelisse. You feel the cold so in the wintertime."

Mrs. Drummond wiped away a tear. "Oh, I do, and how kind of you to remember that, dear child. But were I not required to chaperone you on your travels, I could not have allowed your papa to purchase so costly a garment for little me."

"Well, do not worry about it now." Yolande looked up at blue skies, flying white clouds, the lacy branches of trees overhead, and the tall hedgerows that hemmed in the open carriage on either side. "Is it not a glorious morning?"

"It is indeed," agreed Mrs. Drummond, but added lugubriously, "I wonder if we shall have any sight of the sun whilst we are in Scotland. I do trust the weather is not too inclement. Rain is so lowering."

"It has been several years since last I visited my grandfather," said Yolande, struggling to remain cheerful. "But it seems to me that the weather at that time was delightful, and when I came home Arthur said it had rained in Sussex almost the entire time we were away."

"Dear Arthur," murmured Mrs. Drummond. "I pray for him every night. Only think how wonderful it will be does he come safely home."

Yolande blinked at her. "Good heavens! Why ever should he not? The war is over now. Arthur is unhurt and, to judge from his letters, does not find service with the Army of Occupation an unpleasant task."

"No, for he never has been one to complain. However miserably he may be circumstanced. And only think, my love, your poor brother was deep in that horrid fight at—er—"

"San Sebastian."

"Yes. Such a frightful ordeal! And then—that hideous Waterloo."

"Yet came through both unscathed, Aunt."

"Exactly so! And is it not just like Fate, that having lived through such murderous encounters, a man may slip on a cobblestone, or trip on a stair, and—when 'tis least expected—" She broke off with a shriek.

Yolande had a brief impression of a horseman hurtling over the hedgerow to land directly in their path. The horses neighed shrilly, the coachman shouted, the landaulette lurched, swerved, and plunged into the ditch. Clutching desperately at the side, Yolande caught a glimpse of Aunt Arabella sailing into a clump of lupins. She thought they would surely overturn, but with a muddled sense of surprise discovered that the team was still running. The landaulette bounded and rocked. The wheels hit the lane once more, and the vehicle fairly flew along. For a moment Yolande was too stunned to notice anything more than that they were moving very fast. Then, with a gasp of horror she saw that Tom Bates no longer occupied the driver's seat. She was alone in the vehicle! Her teeth jolted together as the wheels hit a deep rut and the landaulette bounced into the air. Still clinging to the side, she leaned as far forward as she dared, but the reins were far out of reach, trailing in the dirt beneath the pounding hooves of the thoroughly panicked team.

The rush of air past her face had already torn the bonnet from her head, and the curls, which her maid had styled into a pretty tumbling about her face, had whipped free and were blowing wildly. She gave a gasp of fear as they shot around a bend in the lane. Two elderly gentlemen, taking an equally elderly spaniel for a dignified stroll, glanced around, saw disaster bearing down upon them and, with surprisingly agile leaps, followed the spaniel into the ditch. The team rushed past and passed also the turn that led to Park Parapine. A scant mile ahead was the approach to the busy London Road. To enter that crowded highway at this speed could only mean death. With a sob of terror, Yolande peered ahead. Her only chance was to find a clear patch of grass and leap from the speeding carriage. But there was no clear patch of grass, only the hedgerows flashing past in a dark blur, and the ditch beside the road that was at best rutted and uneven, and in places strewn with rocks and fallen branches.

Fighting for the breath that the wind snatched away, she screamed, "Whoa! Whoa!" But her voice, shrill with fear, served only to further alarm the terrified animals. With flying manes, rolling eyes, and pounding hooves, they galloped ever faster along the narrow lane. Far ahead now, Yolande could glimpse the signpost pointing to the highway. Once they reached it, there would be no possibility of stopping in time. She would be doomed! Her horrified eyes fastened on that fateful sign. The pointing finger seemed to leap towards her. She could see the letters. Beyond now were the shapes of wains and lumbering wagons; the swifter passage of a mail or stagecoach . . . "God!" she sobbed faintly. "Oh—my dear . . . God . . . ! Help me!"

The thunder of hooves seemed to deepen until it filled her

ears. Then, she saw with a thrill of hope that a horse raced alongside. A tall grey horse with an unlovely hammer-head, eyes starting, and gaping mouth foam-flecked. But it was gaining slowly. It was level. Surely the man bent low over the pommel could not hope to stop the maddened team? But just the knowledge that someone was trying to help comforted her. She caught a glimpse of a grim face, light brown hair, whipped back by the wind, and broad shoulders. But—dear heaven! The signpost was here! And past! Even above the rattle of wheels and the beat of twelve racing hooves, Yolande could hear the sudden frantic clamour of a coachman's horn.

The man on the grey horse leaned far over and with reckless daring grabbed for the trailing reins. Squealing, the panicked bay beside him swerved. The landaulette rocked perilously. The would-be rescuer was all but torn from the saddle, and fought to right himself. Yolande sobbed. "He cannot regain his seat now," she thought. "He will fall and be killed . . . with me!"

But somehow he managed to drag himself up. Again leaning to the side, he kicked his feet free of the stirrups, his narrowed eyes judging the distance, then launched himself at the bay. Incredibly, his gloved hands caught the harness. A lithe twist, and he was astride the terrified horse. Another instant and he had recovered the reins.

Yolande clung to the seat of the landaulette, numbed, and too afraid even to pray, for the London Road was dead ahead.

A stagecoach driver, his scared gaze on the runaways, was heaving at the reins, cursing the carter ahead of him and the stream of traffic to his right.

The man astride the bay made no effort to halt the team. Instead, he bent forward, gripping the reins with one hand, stroking the foam-splattered neck with the other.

The stagecoach seemed to leap at them. A welter of sound—shouts, wheels, neighing, snorting horses—filled Yolande's ears. The carter glanced back over his shoulder and saw the flying team and the rocking carriage. His eyes rounded with shock. He cracked his whip belatedly, with the result that his frightened horses promptly plunged off the road. In the same instant, Yolande's would-be rescuer succeeded in turning the team. They raced along beside the welter of traffic, but now the carter's heavy wagon was directly in their path. To have been so close to safety only to be faced with death again brought a choking sob from Yolande. Tears blinded her and she closed her eyes. She heard a male voice screaming profanities and a keening squeal as the wheels of the landaulette scraped those of the wagon. The wild, headlong gallop went on, but the seconds dragged past and there was no shattering crash, no hideous shock.

Opening her eyes a crack, she saw trees about them again. The cacophonous roar of traffic had faded. He had turned the team! Somehow, he had avoided the carter and the tragedy that had seemed so inevitable.

She knew a great surge of relief and at once also experienced an almost debilitating weakness. With an effort she relinquished her grip on the side of the landaulette. Her fingers were white and cramped, and she was temporarily unable to straighten them.

The horses slowed and stopped, and the gentleman who had mastered them swung from the back of the bay and strode to the vehicle. "Are you all right, ma'am?" he asked, scanning Yolande's white face anxiously.

He looked to be about eight and twenty. His hair was windblown and untidy about his tanned face. It was a strong face with a jut of a chin and a Roman nose that had evidently at sometime been broken. The mouth was wide and well shaped, the brow high and intelligent. A pleasant-looking person, she thought vaguely, whose best feature was a pair of long, well open grey eyes under shaggy brows. He had asked her a question, but she could not seem to reply. Concern came into the grey eyes. They were decidedly nice eyes, she confirmed, and very kind. She closed her own, and quietly fainted.

Something icy cold splashed into Yolande's face. She sat up, gasping.

"No! Please lie back, ma'am."

She was sitting on the rug from the landaulette, which had been spread out in the field beyond the lane. Her rescuer knelt beside her, water dripping from the handkerchief he held as he watched her with fearful anxiety.

"Oh, dear," said Yolande. "You have lost your hat, I'm afraid."

He bent to slip an arm gingerly about her shoulders. "It is of no importance," he declared in a deep, slow drawl, gently pulling her back down.

She struggled, protesting, "I do not want to lie down!"

Nonetheless, she was lowered to the rug. "Ladies who

faint," he said firmly, "should always lie flat for a time, otherwise they become sick."

"You are very determined, sir!" She frowned a little. "And I do not faint. Usually. This is my first time, in fact."

A gleam of amusement crept into his eyes. "The more reason you should obey me, ma'am. I have had some experience, for my mama suffered from poor health and fainted frequently." He raised one hand to quiet her attempted response. "You are exceedingly pale. I do trust you are not hurt, or badly bruised?"

"Oh!" she gasped, memory returning with a rush. "What nonsense I am talking! You saved my life!"

"Having first very stupidly endangered it," he said gravely, sitting down facing her and resting one arm across a drawn-up knee.

"You? *You* were the idiot who came leaping into the lane?"

He inclined his head. "Idiot, indeed. I wish I might deny it. I cannot tell you how sorry I am. I'd no idea there was a lane—thought it was just a hedge."

Incredulous, she stared at him. "But—you *must* have known! You are certainly aware that hedgerows—" And she stopped, the wry lift of his brows alerting her. Aside from a hint of the military about the cut of his coat, he was dressed as one might expect of a well-bred young man out riding. There was nothing of the dandy about him; his shirt points were not exaggeratedly high, his cravat was, if anything, rather carelessly tied, and the dark blue jacket that hugged his broad shoulders did not give one the impression that two strong men had struggled for half an hour so as to insert him into it. His light brown hair was a little longer than was the current fashion and, although it showed a slight tendency to wave, it was neither curled nor had it been brushed into one of the currently popular styles. A typical enough young Briton, yet—there was the faintest suggestion of an accent in his speech.

The grin that curved his mouth widened. "You've rumbled me," he chuckled.

"I—am not sure," she said hesitantly. "Are you—American, perhaps?"

"No, ma'am. I come from Upper Canada. Just landed at Dover yesterday. I haven't been astride a horse for—er, several months, so started off bright and early this morning."

"Oh! What a coincidence! I should like to sit up now, if you please, for I am not hurt and not at all dizzy. Thank you."

Yolande freed her hand from his strong clasp and turned slightly, straightening her gown. "I am expecting a cousin to arrive from your country. Were there any little boys sailing with you, sir?"

"If there were, ma'am, I was not so fortunate as to have met any." He added a rueful, "I chance to be one of those unfortunates who cannot tolerate water travel. I trust that will not give you a disgust of me."

"If it did," she said with a flash of dimples, "I should not know with whom I am disgusted."

"Oh, egad! What a simpleton I am! Please know that Craig Winters is humbly and most apologetically at your service, Miss—er . . . ?" His gaze slanted to her left hand and was thwarted by the mitten she wore.

Yolande smiled. "It *is* Miss—Drummond. Yolande Drummond. My father is Sir Martin Drummond of Park Parapine. And I can sympathize with you about ocean travel, Mr. Winters, for I've another cousin who becomes violently ill if only crossing our little English Channel, though to look at him you would fancy him quite above such miseries."

How straightforward she was, he thought. No missish airs and feigned shyness because she was alone with a stranger. And had the good Lord ever created a more exquisite little creature? "I suspect," he ventured, "that you have a great many cousins and brothers, and such."

The deep eyes were steady and held an expression that made her feel unaccustomedly flustered, but she managed a teasing, "Why, yes. Everybody does, you know."

His smile held a trace of wistfulness. She asked curiously, "Have not you, sir?"

"To say truth, ma'am, I—"

A rapid drumming of hooves along the lane ceased abruptly, and Alain Devenish burst through a break in the hedgerow and ran towards them. "Yolande!" he cried, his face pale and strained. "Good God! You are hurt!"

"She is unharmed, sir," said Winters, standing with the fluid ease of the athlete. "I must—"

"Who the devil asked you?" gritted Devenish, glaring briefly at him and dropping to one knee beside Yolande. "My dearest girl! Are you all right? Mrs. Drummond said you were as good as killed. I have been fairly beside myself!"

"Oh, heavens!" Guilt-ridden, Yolande gasped, "I had quite

forgot the poor soul, and the last I saw of her, she was flying through the air into some lupins."

Immediately diverted, Devenish grinned. "No, was she? I'll wager she was complaining all the way! Never fret, love, she's bruised and shaken, but no bones broken." He turned a suspicious stare upon Winters. "By Jove! Could I but lay my hands on the looby who jumped his horse over that hedgerow . . ."

"I should explain," began Yolande.

"That looby is right here," Winters drawled.

"What?" Leaping up, his hot temper flaring, Devenish raged, "You damnable hedgebird!" He at once regretted his choice of words, especially when he saw the responsive twinkle that came into the other man's eyes. "You'll answer to me for this atrocity!" he said, one hand lifting purposefully.

"No!" Yolande scrambled up and gripped his upraised wrist. "Alain, if you will but—"

"I'll slaughter any swine who endangers your sweet life!" he snarled.

Winters sobered. He glanced from Yolande's pale, anxious face to this astonishingly handsome young firebrand, and the hopes that had bloomed so suddenly, faded. "I quite understand your concern, sir," he said earnestly. "I can only beg you will accept my—"

"Well, do not, because I won't, damn your eyes! What the devil d'you mean by jumping your stupid hack onto a lady's carriage? Are you—"

"If you think—" Winters began, with the trace of a frown.

"He saved my life!" intervened Yolande, tugging at Devenish's arm. "He was superb! If—"

"If he hadn't pranced over the hedge, there wouldn't have been no cause to save your life! It's good that he did so, of course, but that don't excuse it! Fella must be disguised!" He glanced down at Yolande and appended a contrite, "Poor girl, you look worn to a shade."

"And shall be conveyed home at once," Winters declared, his own gaze lingering on Yolande.

Devenish noted that appreciative look. "Miss Drummond," he gritted, pacing a step closer to the much taller and more sturdily built Winters, "will *assuredly* be conveyed to her home. By me. And you, sir, will convey yourself off! And be damned glad I've the lady to care for, else I would undertake to beat some sense into your feeble brain!"

Winters' mouth tightened. "You would do well to temper your language before a lady, sir."

Devenish spluttered and his fist clenched.

Quickly turning her back on Winters, Yolande placed one small hand on her volatile cousin's arm. "Please do take me home, Alain, for I feel quite poorly."

His rage was forgotten at once. "Of course—what a gudgeon I am! Lean on me, m'dear. Or perhaps I should carry you? Very well—this way, then . . ."

He guided her tenderly to the break in the hedge.

Winters watched them go, then stooped, gathered up the rug, and followed.

In the lane, Devenish assisted Yolande into the landaulette. Silently, Winters offered the rug. Devenish snatched it fiercely, then turned back to his charge. He tucked the rug carefully about her. Suddenly very weary, Yolande settled back, content to be fussed over. "Rest and be comfortable, my sweet life," he murmured. "I shall have you safe home in jig time." He hastened to tie his horse on behind the carriage, passing Winters, who had located his tall grey and stood watching. "Should I ever come up with you again, sir," said Devenish in a low, grim voice, "I will call you to book for this day's work."

Winters swung into the saddle and returned no answer. This mercurial young man was obviously deeply attached to the lady. Still, she had said she was a miss. Nor had she indicated a betrothal. He had learnt her name; it should be a simple matter to discover her direction. But not today.

Devenish had mounted to the driver's seat of the landaulette, moving in rather a slow fashion for such a slim and dynamic gentleman. He stopped only to assure himself that his charge was comfortably disposed, then took up the reins and, without another glance at Winters, urged the weary team onward.

For a moment the Canadian sat looking thoughtfully after them. Then he leaned to stroke the neck of his horse and said fondly, "You old fool, you can still outrun anything on four legs." The grey turned to peer back at him, seemingly just as fondly. "Come on." Winters grinned. "Up and at 'em! We still might find the silly place."

He glanced up at the sun, squinting a little to that brightness, then turned the grey through the break in the hedge and across the field to the west.

* * *

For the third time since Yolande had been tenderly ushered to her bed, Mrs. Drummond had recourse to her vinaigrette. "No matter how he rode to her rescue," she gasped out faintly, "that dreadful foreigner might as easily have brought about the deaths of us all! Indeed, I wonder I yet live, for I vow I must be black and blue from head to toe!"

Devenish, seated in a chair in the bright saloon, eyed the reclining victim uneasily. Sir Martin, less impressed, said tartly, "Then you should be laid down upon your bed, ma'am. I'm sure I do not know why you must persist in lying here on a sofa, when you could be resting comfortably, above stairs!"

Mrs. Drummond rested a look of long-suffering martyrdom upon her unfeeling brother-in-law. "I refused," she sighed nobly, "to add to my dear Louisa's burdens. As though she had not enough to bear with little Rosemary deep in the throes of a putrid throat—which could very easily turn into rheumatic fever, you know—and now—"

"Nonsense!" snapped Sir Martin, rising. "The child is perfectly healthy and there ain't no cause for all your doom and gloom, Arabella! I'll thank you not to alarm her ladyship with such megrims!"

Struggling to hide a grin, Devenish stood also. Mrs. Drummond was not at all amused. She said an aggrieved, "As you say, dear sir. But even so, Louisa will scarce be able to accompany Yolande on her journey. If the poor child is *able* to undertake such a long—"

All but snarling his irritation, Sir Martin interrupted, "Your pardon, ma'am. You are clearly in sorry case, and since you refuse to go upstairs where you belong, we will leave you in peace. Come, Devenish."

He strode out before the resentful lady could utter another word, and stamped along the hall to the book room, muttering fierce animadversions upon distempered freaks and blasted idiotic martyrs. The last thing either he or his spouse had wished was that Devenish learn that Yolande was removing to Scotland for the summer. The boy would most certainly have pricked up his ears at the blathering Arabella's indiscreet remarks, so now he must be warned off. An unpleasant task!

"Blast the woman!" he growled, ushering his prospective son-in-law into the room and slamming the door behind him. "Why my lady wife tolerates her I shall never—" He caught himself up, took a deep breath, and, hopeful of turning Devenish's attention, occupied a wing chair and indicated another. "Sit down, my boy, and tell me more of this Winters fellow. From what Yolande says, he must be a jolly fine horseman. That was no mean jump, and how he managed to transfer from his own mount to a bolting team is more than I have been able to come at. Did you see it?"

Devenish himself was too keen a sportsman to find anything unusual in Sir Martin's apparent admiration for the man who had jeopardized his daughter's life. "I did not, but I saw his horse, sir, and a more unlovely brute I've seldom beheld. You'd doubt he had the ability to set one hoof before the next."

"Is that so? Bit of a dark horse, what?"

"Like his owner! They were undoubtedly seeking the nearest circus so as to exhibit their tricks!"

"Oho!" Sir Martin's eyes widened. "From Yolande's manner I had thought him a gentleman."

Devenish shrugged. "A Colonial."

"Really? We don't see many of them hereabouts. I heard the Beau had one on his staff. Fine chap. De-something. Got himself killed, poor fellow. DeWitt—was it?"

"Oh, you mean DeLancey, sir. Yes, he was American—killed at Waterloo. This chap is Canadian. An insolent devil."

Sir Martin decided he had done the trick and that it was safe to now call the discussion to a halt. He said, "Well, I am sure you put him in his place, eh?" Standing, he put out his hand. "You'll forgive me, Dev, but I'd best get upstairs and see how Yolande goes on."

Devenish stood reluctantly, and the two men shook hands. "Of course. But—"

"My regards to Alastair," Sir Martin said hurriedly. "You must come and take your mutton with us. Er, in a week or so, when we've quieted down a trifle."

"Thank you, sir. Is Yolande going away?"

The bedevilled father ground his teeth, but answered brightly, "Not today, at all events." He swung the door open. "As to the future, who can tell? These ladies of ours change their minds every time the wind blows from a different quarter. I remember once . . ."

His memories lasted until the safety of the main staircase was reached, at which point he clapped his balked companion on the shoulder, said heartily that there was no call to show him out since he'd run tame at Park Parapine since he was breeched, and made his escape up the stairs.

Devenish watched that retreat broodingly. "Humbugged, by

God!" he breathed. Every law of proper behaviour dictated that he politely accept his dismissal. He had spent most of his life, however, breaking laws of proper behaviour. He therefore set his classic jaw, turned on his heel, and marched back to the saloon. There, he tapped gently on the door, waited through a sudden scurry of movement inside, and turned the handle.

A little flushed, Mrs. Drummond lay as before, save that the quilt which had been laid over her was considerably rumpled, and on the air hung the distinct aroma of peaches. Devenish darted an amused glance to the teakwood credenza. A jade bowl held some grapes from the succession houses, but there was no sign of a peach. He thought, "Aunty nipped over there and found something to sustain her, the crafty rascal!" But he said, with appropriate if insincere gravity, "I came to see how you go along, ma'am. You suffered a very nasty fall."

Just as insincerely, Mrs. Drummond murmured, "Dear Devenish. How very kind. I expect I shall—come through . . . somehow. . . ."

It was a superb performance, he thought, and said wickedly, "Gad, ma'am! You are become so pale. May I bring you a morsel of food? A glass of wine, perhaps? A little sustenance might—"

"No, no!" She shuddered, wrapping the peach pit in her handkerchief under the shield of the quilt. "The merest thought of food nauseates me! But you have a kind heart. Pray sit down. Not everyone does, you know."

He hesitated. "If you prefer that I stand . . ."

"No," she giggled coyly. "I meant—not everyone has a kind heart."

He smiled and seated himself, prepared to guide the conversation to the questions he burned to utter. He was doomed. On the brink of extinction though she might be, Mrs. Drummond expounded at length on the evils attendant upon allowing foreigners to cavort unchecked through Britain, the terrible ills that had befallen several ladies of her acquaintance following accidents far less severe than the nightmare she had just experienced, and her belief that "this Winters man" was in reality an escaped lunatic. "No one in possession of his faculties," she stated unequivocally, "would have attempted such a jump, let alone failed to consider that a vehicle might be travelling along the lane, and although I grant you it is not as well travelled as it was in my dear husband's day, for then there was a far jollier life here— Oh, but you should have seen the balls and the boat parties and garden fêtes! I well remember those grand times!" She chose not to remember that her "dear husband" was known to have all but bankrupted the estates, so that his brother had been obliged to wage a desperate struggle to restore Park Parapine to solvency. She became so busied with her reminiscences, however, that she forgot the initial trend of her remarks and eventually paused in a little confusion.

It was the opportunity for which Devenish had been waiting with concealed but fuming impatience. "It must have been grand indeed, ma'am," he inserted swiftly. "And as for the fiasco today, I am more than thankful for your concern. But surely, Yolande will not attempt a journey—under the circumstances?"

"I do trust she will not," his foil replied, portentously. "She was quite knocked up, did you not think? She is a brave girl, and people fancy her stronger than she is, but to go all the way to Scotland so soon after a dreadful accident would be most unwise, and so I shall tell her mama. Dear Lady Louisa is not the one, despite *other* counsel, to dismiss as merest frippery the opinions held by family members." This vengeful theme pleased her, and she rattled on happily for some moments, slanting such veiled but slanderous barbs at her absent brother-in-law that she felt triumphant and was much more in charity with him by the time she had exhausted the topic.

Devenish waited politely, but did not attend her and, as soon as was decently possible, escaped. He rode home at a less neck-or-nothing rate of speed than was his usual habit, restraining his beautiful black mare's occasional spirited attempts to break into a gallop. His hand on the rein was, in fact, so unwontedly heavy that twice she rolled an indignant eye at him. Of this, also, he was unaware. He rode along lost in thought, his expression grave. For Mr. Alain Devenish was an unhappy man. Mrs. Drummond's volubility had apprised him of the fact that his chosen bride, aware that she was soon to depart on a long journey, had not only shown no slightest concern about being parted from him for a protracted period, but had failed to notify him of her impending removal. Further, her parents, with whom he had always stood on the best of terms, appeared to be part of what he could only judge to be a conspiracy of silence.

Frowning, he recalled his most recent disagreement (it could scarcely be rated a quarrel) with Yolande. For as long as he could remember he had taken it for granted— He grunted impatiently; well, not *taken it for granted*, exactly, but certainly *anticipated* that they would wed. The two families were so close; Arthur and John and little Rosemary were almost like brothers and sister to him. And he and Yolande had always been such fine friends. She had not, in fact, begun to grow skittish and flighty and argumentative until first he started to speak of setting the date for their marriage. She was a lovely and sought-after debutante, and as such had the usual share of cow-eyed admirers, but he was willing to swear she cared for none of them and was merely, womanlike, being just a little, and quite charmingly, coquettish, before settling down to domesticity. He sighed wistfully. He had been more shaken than he would have cared to admit when she had told him with that suddenly troubled look that *he* was not ready to settle down. Such fustian! He was five and twenty, deeply in love with his lady, and had—as she herself had pointed out—an estate in Gloucestershire that had been too long neglected. Devencourt. His lips tightened. The haunted manor. It was ridiculous, but his childish feeling about the house persisted. His earliest memories were of a great estate standing deserted and lonely in the vastness of its own grounds. An estate crying out for its owner, seeking to entrap him into remaining there until he also became deserted and alone. . . . How foolish that such juvenile imaginings still caused him to avoid his heritage. Yet even now, he could not discuss his reaction to Devencourt; not with anyone. Especially not with Yolande! Still, she was quite in the wrong of it when she named him a here-and-thereian. Not so! He'd had his fill of adventuring, with Tristram Leith last year. He'd been lucky to escape France with his life, and if Claude Sanguinet had had his way, would not have done so. No, when he was wed he would be quite content to settle down to a peaceful and respectable existence divided between town and country, with nothing more exciting to anticipate than the arrival of two or three little Devenishes.

He shifted uneasily in the saddle. Sounded devilish dull. . . . He dismissed the thought hurriedly. The bitter fact was that he was being treated by the Drummonds as though he were a complete stranger! Was it possible that they had received a more flattering offer for Yolande's hand? Surely not! But he glared angrily at Miss Farthing's ears and thought that it would serve them right if Yolande rejected him only to choose some rank ineligible—such as that curst circus acrobat this morning! Blasted encroaching mushroom! The way the fellow had looked at her was alone cause enough to have grassed him! For all his mercurial temperament, however, Devenish was a fine sportsman, and it had already come to him that he had been less than fair to Mr. Winters. The fellow had meant no harm with that splendid jump; he had afterwards most certainly saved Yolande's life and been given precious little credit for it.

He shrugged his shoulders. The Canadian was far away by this time. The thing now was to get back to Aspenhill as quickly as possible and discover whether his Tyrant had also been aware of Yolande's proposed jaunt to Scotland. By God, if *that* wouldn't be the outside of enough!

He touched his spurred heels gently to Miss Farthing's sides, and she sprang eagerly into a gallop that took them rapidly across lush meadow and through shady copse until they reached the last hill beyond which sprawled the Tyndale preserves and the welcome of Aspenhill.

❦ *Chapter 3* ❧

Colonel Alastair Tyndale looked up in mild surprise when his nephew unceremoniously flung open the study door and strode in. Leaning back in his chair, Tyndale laid down the letter he had been reading and said, "I'm glad you came back, Dev. Your—"

"I was at Park Parapine," Devenish interpolated. "Sir, did you know that Yolande is going away?"

The Colonel pushed back his chair and came to his feet, standing very straight so that although the desk was between them, Devenish had to look up at him. "We can discuss that, together with your—ah—unfortunate manners, later," he said. "I must tell you that your cousin has arrived."

"Oh. Well, can the brat wait awhile, sir? What I would like to know is—"

"And," Tyndale continued inexorably, "had you not burst in here at such a rate, you might have noticed that he is sitting behind you."

"Eh?" Devenish swung around to meet his small and unwanted cousin. "I say, I apologize if—" The words died abruptly. He gasped, "The devil!"

The Canadian who sprawled in the chair behind the door may have been unwanted. Small, he was not. Mr. Craig Winters' long, booted legs were outstretched, his chin propped on the knuckles of one hand, while his amused eyes took in Devenish's stark horror. He came lazily to his feet and drawled, "The Colonial looby—at your service, cousin ..." His bow was deep, flourishing, and decidedly mocking.

Devenish spun to face his uncle. "Sir! This is a confounded hoax! This beastly fellow ain't a little boy! Nor is he related to us!"

The Colonel's keen blue eyes drifted from tall, derisive Canadian to slender, fuming Englishman. "I see," he said dryly, "that you two have met." He moved towards the door. "Come, gentlemen."

"Uncle!" flared Devenish, his comely face flushed. "Be damned if I'll—"

"Colonel," drawled Winters, his accent very pronounced, "maybe I'd best get on my—"

"We will talk," said Tyndale arctically, "over luncheon." He opened the door. "You will both be so good as to join me in the breakfast parlour as soon as you've put off your riding clothes. Ah—there you are, Truscott. Where have we put Mr. Tyndale?"

Winters' heavy brows twitched into a frown. The butler, customarily suave and seldom at a loss, was apparently not at his best today. "Mr.—Mr. Tyndale, sir?" he echoed.

"My nephew. Mr. Craig Winters Tyndale. Wake up, man!"

"M—my apologies, sir. Mr. er—Tyndale, is in the blue guest suite." He turned glazed eyes to Winters and bowed. "May I show you the way, sir?"

"You may not," the Colonel intervened. "Devenish, take your cousin to his room, if you please. I want a word with Truscott."

"With pleasure, sir," lied Devenish. Ascending the stairs beside his new kinsman, and bound by the dictates of good manners, he added, "I collect you stand in need of the services of a valet, so—"

"Oh, no. Thank you for so kind an offer. But I sent my man ahead of me. He's here now."

Devenish raised one bored eyebrow. "Indeed?"

Had he put a quizzing glass to his eye and leisurely surveyed his cousin through it, he could scarcely have more clearly implied his scepticism.

That mischievous twinkle again lit the Canadian's eyes. "We Colonials do have *some* of the social graces." He glanced up. "Everything in now, Monty?"

Devenish lifted his scornful gaze to discover the doubtful merits of this "social grace." Scorn was routed. It was, in fact, all he could do to restrain his jaw from dropping to half-mast. The man who stood on the landing, with one hand lightly resting on the banister, was tall and with a suggestion about him of the panther. His long hair was blue-black, tied in at the nape of his neck, and very straight. The skin that stretched over lean cheeks had a coppery glow, and his eyes were unfathomable pools of jet. He wore a tunic and trousers of soft leather that were as if moulded to his lithe form, and on his feet were intricately beaded moccasins. He met his employer's laughing gaze, and his features softened imperceptibly. Not into a smile, exactly, but a semblance of one that was a brief flash of gleaming white against his dark face. "Everything in," he confirmed in a deep rumble of a voice. "You come."

Lips quirking, Tyndale threw a quick glance at his paralyzed relation and went on up the stairs.

For almost a minute, Devenish did not move. A distant shout of laughter roused him from his trance. He tottered to the landing. "Now—by Jove!" he breathed, his eyes stunned. "Now—by Jove!"

An hour later, Colonel Tyndale blew a cloud of smoke into the air and, with an appreciative eye, regarded the cheroot he held. "A very good brand, Craig," he acknowledged. "From your native land?"

"No, sir. They're—er, from Spain, actually. Glad they please you."

Devenish coughed rather pointedly and waved smoke from his vicinity.

"Alain don't smoke," advised Tyndale. "It's a filthy habit, I will admit."

"Oh, absolutely," Winters agreed affably. "Good you don't allow it, sir. Perhaps, when he's older . . ."

Bristling, Devenish grated, "What the deuce d'you mean by that? I'm as old as are you, you blasted circus clown! And furthermore—"

Tyndale lifted a restraining hand. "Peace, gentlemen. Peace! I have heard you both out and, unless one of you is bending the truth a trifle, it must be apparent that Craig acted unwisely, but did his best to atone, and that you, Alain, behaved with your usual calm, good judgment and comforted Yolande."

"Oh, very well," Devenish muttered, reddening. "I'll own I may perhaps have neglected to properly thank you, Winters, for acting as fast as you did to rescue my lady, but—"

"Your—ah, lady . . . ?" breathed Winters. "You and Miss Drummond are promised, then?"

"From the cradle." Eyes narrowed and deadly, Devenish went on, "Furthermore, I warn you, here and now, that—"

"I feel sure," put in Alastair Tyndale, "I need not remind you, Dev, that your cousin is—my guest."

His fists clenching, Devenish choked back his angry words and sat seething for a moment. "If Mr. Winters is indeed our kinsman, sir," he exploded, "why don't he use his rightful name?"

"My apologies, Craig," said Tyndale regretfully. "I'd not intended to be so blunt, but since the question has been raised . . ."

His head very erect, Winters answered, "I understood it was one of my grandfather's stipulations, sir. That if he paid my father's way to Canada, the family name would not be used."

Devenish uttered a barely audible snort. Winters turned suddenly glinting eyes to stare at him unblinkingly.

The Colonel, frowning at the upcurling smoke from his cheroot, pointed out, "That stipulation did not apply to you. The—the indiscretions of your sire are not part of your inheritance. I believe it would be appropriate for you to use your correct name."

Without removing his gaze from Devenish's bland hauteur, Winters said gently, "Your pardon, Uncle. But I have no wish to change."

"My regrets, nephew. But it is *my* wish that you do so," said the Colonel, just as gently.

Here, Winters shifted his attention to the older man, a troubled uncertainty in his eyes. "I have no intent to distress you, sir. Were I to change my name, it would be to take your own, I assume."

"Tyndale. Of course. What had you supposed?"

Winters shrugged. "I wasn't just sure. You Englishmen seem to change your names at the drop of a hat." He glanced at Devenish. "So long as it's Tyndale, I'll settle for that."

"Will you, by God!" raged Devenish. "And I suppose had it been *my* name, that wouldn't have been good enough for your backwoods clodhop—"

"That will do!" The Colonel's voice cut like a sabre through the tirade. "I suggest you apologize, sir!"

Devenish's blazing eyes fell. He was behaving badly, his awareness of which fact did little to mitigate his loathing of his tall cousin. "Yes," he mumbled. "Quite right." And forcing his eyes upwards, met an unexpected glare in the grey gaze across the table. "Apologize, Win—Tyndale."

The glare faded into a grin. The Canadian drawled, "Thank you."

"Still, it might be better," said the Colonel, "did you find someone else to accompany you, Craig. I wish I might go, but I am—er, detained here by—by a matter that I cannot postpone just now."

"Think nothing of it, sir. I've done a little pathfinding through the mountains of Upper Canada. It should be simple enough for me to find my way round this little island."

From the corner of his eye Colonel Tyndale saw Devenish's lips parting, and said a fast, "It might be less simple than you think. The British countryside has a way of confusing people." He turned to Devenish. "Your cousin means to have a look at his property, Alain."

With sublime indifference, Devenish said, "Property? Some distance from here?" And he thought, "I hope it's in Siberia!"

The Colonel put out his cheroot and murmured, "I took you there once, when you were a little shaver—perhaps you recall . . . ?"

A sudden sense of déjà vu seized Devenish. He frowned. "I do seem to remember something. A gloomy old place, no? I think I loathed it."

Winters had been admiring an unusual scarabæus ring the Colonel wore, and so it was that he noticed the strong hand tighten convulsively about the stem of the wineglass. Curious, he glanced at his uncle and would have sworn he saw sweat beading the man's upper lip before the Colonel turned away.

Devenish had also seen. He leaned to slip a hand onto the

old man's arm and asked with a swift anxiety that betrayed his affection, "Are you all right, sir?"

"Perfectly, thank you." Nonetheless, Tyndale's hand trembled slightly as he took a last sip of his port. "Shall we adjourn to the terrace? Or have you something planned, Alain?"

The Tyrant was looking fairly pulled. With a twinge of guilt, Devenish wondered if his own hasty temper was the cause. He managed somehow to smile at the usurper. "As a matter of fact, I was hoping Winters would let me have a look at his horse."

"Yes, by gad!" exclaimed the Colonel, brightening. "And that reminds me, Craig. From all I hear, you must be a superb horseman. How ever did you manage to change mounts at full gallop? I'd give something to have seen it!"

Winters coloured. "I was practically raised on a horse, sir."

"Your papa taught you to ride? He was a grand sportsman, God rest him!"

Something at the back of the grey eyes became blank. "No, sir. Matter of fact, an Iroquois Indian taught me."

"I say!" exclaimed Devenish, immediately intrigued. "How dashed splendid! You said the horse was Spanish-bred. Imported, I gather. Did you bring him over with you?"

Winters' gaze shifted to his plate. "Er—yes," he said.

"Come in, Mama," called Yolande, looking up from the pile of notes and invitations spread out on her quilt. "I am wide awake, and would have got up hours since, save that I decided to indulge myself."

"Very rightly, my love," nodded her ladyship, closing the door and crossing the sunny bedchamber. She kissed her daughter, scanned her face with the knowing eyes of motherhood, and perched on the side of the bed. "I am so glad the sun came out for you. We have had such a wretched spring. Now tell me, should we call in the doctor? Be honest."

"Oh, absolutely not, I thank you. I feel perfectly well."

"Wonderful. And how grateful we must be to Mr. Winters. It was very naughty of him to jump the hedge, of course. But I could not help but dwell on the accident last night. You know how things always seem so dreadful during the hours of darkness! And I thought how much worse it might have been. Only think, it might have been Herbert Glick, for example. Not that I wish to imply a criticism of poor Glick," she added with a guilty dimple. "But—oh, dearest, can you not picture him galloping to your rescue as did Mr. Winters?"

Both ladies succumbed to the deliciousness of the picture thus conjured up, and laughed merrily.

Yolande gurgled, "I cannot imagine him jumping the hedge in the first place, Mama. And had he done so, he would most certainly have parted company with his horse and landed beneath the hooves of our team!" She took up an invitation and said, "A masquerade at Greenwings—oh, what a pity I must refuse. Has—anyone called? I cannot guess how I came to sleep the day away."

"Oh, can you not? I can! You were thoroughly shaken, poor lamb! Yes, Devenish stayed a little while after you was gone up to bed. He was beside himself, naturally." She sighed. "Your papa was so vexed, for Aunt let fall a remark about your stay in Scotland."

"Oh, dear! How unfortunate! Whatever did Dev have to say?"

"He tried to worm the whole out of Papa, as you might expect, so soon as they were alone. Papa says he tried very hard to turn his train of thought, and for a time believed he had succeeded, but Alain harked back to the subject, and your father was obliged to be quite devious."

"Bother! Now he will come and take me to task for not having told him! He must have been very angry, for already he considered me his personal property."

"He did seem angry, I grant you. But I thought his rage was directed at Mr. Winters. Your aunt, I fear, has taken that young man in strong aversion. Do tell me, love—what was he like? Handsome?"

Yolande thought for a moment. "No. Not handsome, though any man would seem plain if compared to Dev. He is certainly not unpleasant to look at, and has the nicest grey eyes. His build is sturdier than Alain's and I would suppose him to be a fine sportsman, for he moves with much grace. But I had the impression he is a little pulled. There was a—a sort of tiredness about his eyes that made me wonder if—" She looked up and found her mama watching her with brows slightly elevated, and felt her cheeks become hot. "Good gracious, Mama! What are you thinking? I have but seen the man once!"

Lady Louisa smiled and remarked that she wished she had seen Mr. Winters once—if only to thank him.

"I wish someone had," said Yolande regretfully, "for I am

very sure I failed to do so. I have a vague recollection, in fact, of ignoring him completely and driving away without so much as a glance in his direction."

"Perfectly understandable. Has the young man any sensibilities at all, he will have found nothing to marvel at—save that you were able to speak at such a time, when most girls would have swooned away!"

The door opened. Peattie, Yolande's abigail, waddled her stout way across the room and deposited a charming bouquet of spring flowers on her mistress's lap. "From a Mr. Winters, Miss Yolande," she announced, broad features wreathed in a grin.

"How—er, pretty!" stammered Yolande, her heart giving a quite unfamiliar leap.

"The gentleman must still be in the vicinity," murmured Lady Louisa, watching her daughter's pink countenance with a touch of unease.

"The flowers was sent over from a flower shop in Bexhill," Peattie volunteered and, crossing to her ladyship, murmured, "The boy who brought 'em said they was ordered by a gentleman what's staying at Aspenhill, milady."

Lady Louisa's unease increased. "Did he now? Thank you, Peattie. Miss Yolande will ring when she needs you."

"Mama?" said Yolande, as the maid closed the door. "Are you provoked because Mr. Winters sent the flowers?"

Her mother started, looked at her rather blankly for a moment, then smiled. "Of course not, you silly goose. What does he have to say?"

"That he means to call this afternoon in order to apologize to Papa for the accident. And that if his unforgivable recklessness has not given me a distaste for him, he will beg to see me for a moment or two." She gave a mischievous giggle. "Prettily said, eh, Mama?"

"And very pretty flowers." My lady touched the waxy petals of a tulip. "Shall you receive him, Yolande?"

"No. For you object, I see. Oh, never speak me a farradiddle, dearest. Something troubles you, I know, for you seldom frown."

"Was I doing so?" My lady put up one white hand to wipe away the frown. "What a shrewd little puss! However, I do not object. It is only ... Yolande, you are quite *sure* his name is Winters?"

"Yes. Positive. Do you know his family, perhaps?"

"No. At least— It just seemed rather odd that he should be staying with Alain and the Colonel, and I wondered— But that is foolishness, of course."

"At Aspenhill?" Yolande exclaimed, not having heard the exchange with Peattie. "Why, how very strange. I had fancied he and Alain took one another in the strongest aversion."

The trouble returned to Lady Louisa's eyes, full measure. "Oh, dear," she muttered. "How very difficult that will be for poor Alastair!"

There was, among the saloons at Park Parapine, one rather smaller than the rest, and decorated throughout in shades of gold and cream. Cream brocade covered the dainty chairs and the Louis XIV sofa; cream velvet draperies were tied back by ropes of braided gold silk; and the fine Aubusson carpets were of cream, gold, and brown. It was to this saloon that Yolande repaired shortly after half-past two o'clock, by some happy circumstance clad in a robe of palest gold linen, opening below the high waist to reveal a paler gold silk slip. Her glowing curls were piled high on her head, the fine tendrils that curled down beside her ears emphasizing the faultless delicacy of her skin. For jewellery she wore the topaz necklace and matching topaz ring presented to her by Alastair Tyndale on the occasion of her twenty-first birthday, and a zephyr shawl of white with gold threads was draped across her elbows.

A very old embroidery frame stood in a well-lighted spot between two windows, a straight-backed chair before it. Yolande made her way to open the sewing box beside the chair, and spread several strands of embroidery floss across the inner tray, ready for use. She then seated herself (making sure that her draperies were gracefully disposed), and took up the needle that had been neatly tucked into the stretched linen.

It was here that her visitor found her, when a superior being in powder and satin ushered him to the saloon shortly after three o'clock. Pausing on the threshold, Mr. Winters gazed at the lady bending so gracefully over her needlework, and knew that never had he seen a more beautiful sight.

Yolande glanced up in pretty surprise and saw him standing tall and straight in the doorway, his head slightly to one side, watching her with an expression that took her breath away. She forgot affectation and came to greet him, holding out one hand in welcome. Winters strode to take it. For a moment, tongue-tied, he simply held her hand, looking down into her eyes with that faint, tender smile still lingering in his own. Then, he bowed and kissed her fingers lightly. "It was most kind in you to receive me, ma'am," he said in his quiet, lazy drawl. "You cannot know how relieved I am to see you so well recovered. I was fairly terrified when you were driven away yesterday, looking so very shaken. Can you ever forgive me for having brought it all about?"

Yolande was finding it difficult to regain her breath, and she made a business of taking up the fan that hung from her wrist. "Far from chiding you, sir," she said, opening the fan and studying the hand-painted parchment as though she'd not seen it a hundred times before, "I must crave your pardon for failing to properly thank you. Had you not galloped after me so gallantly, I am quite sure I should have perished."

Shattered, he bowed his head. "And I the cause of such a tragedy! My God! It would have been past bearing!"

"And did not happen, so never blame yourself. The flowers are lovely. Thank you so much." She glanced to the door, wondering what Mama could be thinking, to allow her to be alone with this young man. "Pray sit down, Mr. Winters," she invited, indicating one of the gold chairs. "I understand you make a stay with Colonel Tyndale. We are related, you know."

He waited until she had seated herself on the sofa, then occupied the designated chair. "Yes. And we also are related, Miss Drummond."

With a surprised arch of the brows, she asked, "You and I, Mr. Winters?"

"Apparently, ma'am. You see, for—er, various reasons, I did not use my full name when first we met. Winters was my mother's name. I am Craig Winters Tyndale."

The fan shut with a snap. "*You . . . ?*" she gasped. "But—but—" Mirth overcame her, and she relapsed into a flood of laughter. Daintily wiping away tears, she apologized. "Oh, whatever must you think of me! How dreadfully rag-mannered! I do beg pardon, Mr.—er, Tyndale."

"Please do not," he said, delighted at having caused her to be amused. "Indeed, I could not be more pleased than to discover I have such enchanting relatives."

She had decided he was shy and bashful, but at this was startled into looking straight into his eyes, which she had guarded against doing. Her gaze was locked with his, and once more that heart-stopping breathlessness dizzied her.

Mr. Craig Winters Tyndale said nothing. There was not the need.

At the same moment, Lady Louisa sat beside her husband in the book room, as stunned as was her daughter, though for a very different reason. "It is as I feared, then!" Agitated, she placed one hand on Sir Martin's wrist, as though for support.

He took up that small hand and, finding the fingers cold as ice, squeezed them reassuringly, then returned his attention to Alastair Tyndale, who stood before the fireplace, staring down at the large brass Chinese dragon which occupied the hearth when the fire was not lit. "Alastair," he said, and paused to clear his throat. "Alastair, does Devenish know? Have you never so much as given him a hint?"

Tyndale passed a weary hand across his eyes. "Never."

The Drummonds exchanged worried glances. Lady Louisa said, "But, you do *mean* to tell him? Surely, now. Especially *now*!"

He said wryly, "It is for that very reason, Louisa, that I *dare* not tell him now! He believes I am upset solely because of the news of my brother's death. I've no need to remind you of how kind-hearted the dear fellow is. He was all eagerness to help, and more than willing to deliver a letter to my solicitor in Tunbridge Wells. He even invited Craig to accompany him. Not very heartily, but he *did* invite him. I succeeded in convincing him that Craig and I had much family business to discuss. Had he suspected we meant to come here . . ." He shook his head bodingly.

"And you say there was instant antipathy?" muttered Sir Martin. "How very strange."

Frightened, his lady scanned his grave features, then uttered a bracing, "Not so strange, surely, Drummond? Two healthy young male animals, snarling at one another over a lovely female."

"Perhaps." The Colonel nodded, accustomed to her frank ways. "Indeed, I pray you may be right. But—if Yolande is attracted to Craig—" He stopped.

"Lord!" Sir Martin muttered, half under his breath. "Add that to all the rest . . . !"

Colonel Tyndale eyed him apprehensively. "What do you think, my dear?" he asked, turning to Lady Louisa. "You, of all people, know how Yolande's heart is engaged. Is she in love with Devenish?"

My lady bit her lip. "She loves him, I know," she said haltingly. "She always has, but— Oh, *why* did Craig have to arrive at this particular time!"

"I see. We have an undecided heart, have we?" Tyndale said with reluctance. "I suspected as much. And what of young Craig? They've only just met, of course, but—I've a suspicion the lad received a leveller."

"Pshaw!" scoffed Sir Martin. "Love at first sight? I never believed in it! Attraction perhaps, but nothing lasting. Not in the wink of an eye! Fairy-tale nonsense! Do you not agree, my love?"

Again, Lady Louisa hesitated. "I feel sure you are right, Drummond," she said quietly. But she avoided the Colonel's searching gaze, and his heart sank. "Nonetheless," she went on, "I cannot but think it would be best, Alastair, did Alain know the truth. If there is already antagonism between them . . . It would be so dreadful if . . ."

Colonel Tyndale stared in silence at the brass dragon. Lady Louisa did not complete her sentence, and Sir Martin looked from one to the other of them gloomily.

"Aye," the Colonel sighed, at length. "You are probably in the right of it, Louisa. But . . . heaven help me! How shall I tell him . . . ?"

Yolande started as her name was uttered in a shrill, horrified screech. "Aunt!" she gasped, wrenching her eyes from Mr. Craig Winters Tyndale. "How you startled me! Whatever are you doing up and about?"

"Why, I crept from my bed so as to let out Socrates, for with little Rosemary so ill I would not dream of requiring anyone to come to *my* aid." Mrs. Drummond gathered her voluminous dressing gown closer about her and, looking at the tall young man who had risen respectfully upon her entrance, said, "Thank goodness I *did* come, dear Yolande. How shocking that you have been abandoned!"

Craig blinked. Flushed with irritation, Yolande responded, "Scarcely abandoned in my own home, Aunt. You will have noticed the door is wide, and Mama will be here directly, I am sure."

"I only arrived a few minutes ago, ma'am," said Craig, colouring up. "At least," he turned a betrayingly warm smile on Yolande, "I—er, *think* it was a few minutes ago."

A dimple appeared briefly and, he thought, adorably, in her

smooth cheek, but Mrs. Drummond moaned. He moved at once to her side. "May I assist you to a chair, ma'am? You do not look—"

A small fox terrier, quite old and very fat, tottered into the room and, upon perceiving this enormous individual reaching for his mistress, gave vent to a piercing spate of barking, rushed forward, and dealt Craig a hearty nip on the ankle.

The Canadian exclaimed an involuntary "Ow!" and stepped back hurriedly.

"Socrates!" scolded Yolande.

"Dear little fellow," cooed Mrs. Drummond, bending to gather up her snarling pet. "He was only protecting his mama, wasn't you, love?"

Tyndale bestowed a smouldering look upon the "dear little fellow." Hastening to him, Yolande asked a concerned, "Did he hurt you?"

A tall grey-haired woman in a flowing grey gown and snowy white apron hurried into the room. "Is my lady here, miss? Oh! Excuse me, sir!"

"Nurse," said Yolande anxiously, "is Miss Rosemary not improved at all?"

"The fever gets higher, miss, no matter what I do. I fear she is sickening for something. There is the beginning of a rash, and—"

"Oh! My heavens!" wailed Mrs. Drummond, sinking dramatically into the nearest chair. "*Never* say it is the smallpox!"

Entering in time to hear those dread words, Lady Louisa blanched and clutched at the door-frame. "Smallpox? God in Heaven! Nurse—it isn't—?"

"Of course not, Mama," said Yolande, crossing to support her. "Aunt Arabella misunderstood."

"Oh, that poor . . . sweet, child!" cried Mrs. Drummond, a handkerchief pressed to tearful eyes.

Nurse, having slanted a disgusted look at these histrionics, vouchsafed that she could not tell what ailed Miss Rosemary, but she doubted it was the smallpox.

"Nonetheless, I must go to her," said Lady Louisa. "Yolande, pray ask your papa to send a groom at once for Dr. Jester."

Craig had moved quietly back to stand out of the way beside the mantel and now came forward, saying with an apologetic smile that he would take his leave and would gladly relay the message to Sir Martin.

"Oh, dear!" Yolande exclaimed. "I have sadly neglected you, cousin! How is your poor ankle?"

Mrs. Drummond's recovery was astonishing. *"Cousin?"* she bristled.

"What happened to his ankle?" asked Lady Louisa, distractedly.

"Socrates bit him," Yolande supplied. "Horrid creature!"

"Mr. Winters may have brought great suffering upon us," Mrs. Drummond said smugly, "but you really should not refer to him in such terms, my love."

Craig grinned at this excellent shot, but Yolande was not amused. She blushed scarlet and turned to her aunt with such anger that Lady Louisa intervened with a vexed, "Really, Arabella! Cousin Craig, my apologies, but—"

"But you must be wishing me at Jericho!" He took her hand, patted it sympathetically, and said his farewells. His smile included Mrs. Drummond and Nurse, in addition to the brief but meaningful seconds during which it rested upon Yolande. Then he was gone.

An hour later, wandering onto the front porch in search of his wife, Sir Martin found her staring after the doctor's departing gig. "Are you coming in, m'dear?" he enquired. "Not worrying over a simple case of measles, surely?"

"What? Oh, no, of course not, Drummond. Though the poor child is so wretchedly uncomfortable. Yolande is with her, which she will very much like, you know."

He nodded, closed the door, and walked across the hall beside her. After a pause, Lady Louisa sighed. "She was right. He really does have very nice eyes."

My lady was in the habit of occasionally speaking her thoughts aloud, sometimes to the complete mystification of her listeners. For once, however, her apparently irrelevant remark did not confuse Sir Martin. He was perfectly aware she did not refer to Dr. Jester.

Two days later, clad in a dark green fitted coat that closed to the waist with large brass buttons, Yolande tied the grosgrain ribbons of her bonnet beneath her chin, surveyed her reflection critically in her standing mirror, and turned to the bed to take up her muff. "I cannot be easy in my mind about leaving you with Rosemary ill," she worried. "Mama—perhaps I should stay."

"And be the cause of a full-fledged duel?" Lady Louisa

handed her an urn-shaped reticule of green velvet, embellished with pale green beads. "How very pretty this is. And goes with your coat and bonnet so nicely."

"Thank you. Mama, you do not really think . . . ?"

My lady smiled into her daughter's aghast eyes, and sat down on the bed. "I think it would be as well for neither young gentleman to see you just at the moment. You look awfully fetching, dear. Come now, never be so worried, I was only teasing. They are likely the best of friends by now."

"I doubt that," Yolande sighed, pulling on one small leather glove. "Mr. Glick said that when he stopped to visit the Colonel yesterday, Alain was in a tearing rage because he had discovered that Cousin Craig had come here whilst he was in Tunbridge Wells?"

"Herbert Glick!" said my lady, with uncharacteristic impatience. "The poor moonling! He likely exaggerated the matter out of all proportion. I should forget all about it, were I you."

Considerably troubled, Yolande argued, "Mama, I *cannot* forget about it. I am—most fond of—of both of them."

Lady Louisa shook her head. She did not say anything, however, but sat staring down at her clasped hands, her expression so pensive that Yolande went and sat beside her. "Dearest, why have I the feeling that you and Papa, and Uncle Alastair too, are terribly upset? Is it because of my—my procrastinating? Shall I set the wedding date before I leave? If it will put your minds at ease, I will gladly do so."

Her ladyship reached up to touch that loved and lovely face and say with a wistful smile, "Fate is very strange at times."

"Oh, *dear* Mama! What is it? I have never seen you so!"

My lady summoned her brightest smile. "Then I must be behaving in a very silly fashion. Now—your papa would like to speak with you for just a moment." Forestalling Yolande's next question, she said, "And—no, it has nothing to do with Rosemary, I promise you. It is just . . . it is something you should have been told of, long ago. Only—well, we never thought it would come to this, do you see?"

"I am frightened," said Yolande, a shiver creeping down her spine. "Is it very dreadful, Mama?"

Again, Lady Louisa looked down at her hands. They were gripped very tightly. She unfolded them. "I fear," she said, a tremor in her gentle voice, "that it really *is*—rather dreadful, Yolande."

Chapter 4

The morning was misty, lacking any trace of the warm sunshine of the past two balmy days. There was a smell of rain on the cool air and, as if glum in the face of more damp weather, even the birds seemed disinclined to sing, so that a deep silence lay over the lush and pleasant swell of the South Downs.

A large hare came hopping up the slope and at the summit stopped, suddenly very stiff and still, ears upright and nostrils twitching as it stared back the way it had come. It darted away then, moving so fast that it was only a tan blur against the rich grasses, swiftly vanishing. And in its wake came the sound that had frightened the small, wild creature. A muffled tremor that at first barely disturbed the air, growing to a distant throbbing, a rhythmic beat swelling ever louder until it became a rapid tattoo of iron-shod hooves racing headlong through the quiet morning. Up over the rise they came, neck and neck, the ungainly grey gelding, the sleek black mare, the riders flushed and breathless, leaning forward in the saddles, fair men both, but one much fairer than the other, and both heads bare, for the wind had long since snatched their hats, and neither would stop to reclaim them. A thunder of sound, creak of leather and jingle of spurs and harness; the earthshaking pound of hooves, the snorting breath of striving horses. A buffet of wind at their passing. And they were gone, plunging down the slope, the grey gaining a little as they started up the other side.

They were out on the Downland now. A long hedge rose ahead, and Devenish grinned and glanced at his cousin as Craig bent lower. Lord, he thought, but the man could ride! And with a widening of that impudent grin he knew the Canadian would have to ride like a centaur to take this jump unawares. He leaned forward, patting the mare's sweating neck, preparing her with hand and voice.

Tyndale, narrowed eyes fixed on the hedge, was sure this time there was no lane, for there was not another hedge beyond, that he could see. "Come on, Lazzy!" he cried, and felt the great muscles tense beneath him as the grey shot into the air. Too late, he saw the gleam of water below and knew that the jump was too wide. The grey snorted with fear, landed with a mighty splash, and fell. Tyndale flew over his head and landed hard on the bank.

Laughing, as Miss Farthing landed neatly on the far side, Devenish glanced back. His laughter died. He swore, reined back, and swung the mare in a wide circle, dismounting in a flying leap. He staggered, gripped his right leg and swore at some length as he limped to his cousin, who lay sprawled at the water's edge.

Thus it was that a moment or two later, Tyndale blinked into a pair of disembodied blue eyes that gradually became part of features that were almost too beautiful for a man, but set into an expression of grim ferocity. "Jove," he breathed, with an unsteady grin. Then, in sharp anxiety, "Is Lazzy . . . ?"

"Scraped one knee. No, lie down, you gudgeon! It's nothing serious."

"Poor old fellow."

"Yes," grunted Devenish, furious with himself. "I should have thought of that." His cousin slanted an amused glance at him, and he flushed and reached down. "Here."

Tyndale disdained the proffered aid, and sat up.

"Why the deuce," exploded Devenish, "did you not slow down? You surely must realize you ain't familiar with the lay of the land?"

"I also realize that because I am a stranger does not make you responsible for me," Craig answered calmly, his eyes fixed on his grey.

"Don't be so damned patronizing!"

Tyndale said nothing, but the cool stare shifted to Devenish, whose flush deepened. "Blast you!" he fumed. "I suppose I should have warned you. I knew you could not hope to negotiate such a jump." His angry gaze fell away. "It was—it was poor sportsmanship. I apologize."

It had obviously been a painful admission, thought Tyndale. But it had been made. "Thank you," he said gravely. "But I do not very often take a toss."

At once those fierce eyes lifted to glare at him. "It is very well to brag, cousin. But had you broken your neck, only think of my position. There'd be the devil to pay and no pitch hot, for everyone would say I had done it deliberately because I dislike you."

Tyndale smiled faintly. "I'd not have cared overmuch for such a development, I admit." He reached up.

Devenish stared.

Tyndale's eyes glinted. He said without expression, "Give me a hand, will you?"

Relieved, Devenish obliged, and Tyndale moved rather erratically to his grey. The big horse nuzzled him affectionately, and, watching as he bent to inspect the damaged knee, Devenish asked curiously, "What is it that you call him?"

"Lazzy. Short for Lazarus because he—after a fashion—rose from the dead." He felt the hock carefully, hove a sigh of relief, straightened, and reeled unsteadily.

"How?" persisted Devenish.

"Eh? Oh, there was a sort of a battle. At the edge of a rapids. Between Monty and me."

Awed, Devenish asked, "You mean, he was after your scalp? That sort of battle?"

Tyndale's mouth twitched. "That sort."

Waiting in vain, Devenish burst out. "Well? Go on, blast it!"

"Monty's mare had just foaled. We caromed into her and scared her so that she plunged about and the foal went over the edge and into the river. Monty and I were a bit—er, done up. So it took both of us to haul him out. When we managed it, Monty insisted the foal was mine and there was another—ah, discussion. We wound up having to doctor one another because the foal began trying to die. Between one thing and another . . . well, we've been together ever since. All three of us."

There was more to it, Devenish suspected. The Iroquois had exuded pride, yet he served Tyndale and was very obviously devoted to him. "Is that where you got that beast of a scar?" he asked. "I wonder you're still breathing."

Tyndale stiffened and his hand flew to his throat. His neckcloth had been removed and his shirt unbuttoned. Buttoning it, he evaded, "It has been said that I'm devilish hard to snuff. Speaking of which—I will concede you the race."

Devenish gave a gasp. "The devil! Did you think I was really trying?"

"To win?"

"To snuff you."

"Were you?"

"I should, by God! If only for that bacon-brained remark!" He stamped to the black, swung into the saddle, and demanded furiously, "Do you seriously think I would deliberately endanger another man's life over a stupid race?"

Interested, Tyndale inquired, "Why *would* you deliberately endanger another man's life?"

"Dash it all!" snarled Devenish, setting his mare to capering. "I did not deliberately— That is, I had thought it would—I—I—Oh, hell and the devil confound you!" And he cantered away until he was out of sight.

Craig chuckled. "Lord, what a fire-eater!" He found his neckcloth and replaced it, then mounted and bent forward to stroke the grey's neck. "I hope we can find our way home, friend, else—" He broke off as rapid hoofbeats announced his cousin's return. Hair windblown, cheeks flushed, and eyes shooting sparks of wrath, Devenish came up at the gallop and, as if there had been no pause, gritted, "Furthermore, since I did *not* win, or if I had it would have been by cheating—"

"Cheating, coz?" Tyndale demurred mildly. "I would not say you cheated—exactly."

Devenish fixed him with a baleful eye. "We will call it a tie. Satisfactory?"

"Oh, perfectly."

They started off, side by side, Devenish stiff, Tyndale relaxed. After a few moments, Tyndale enquired, "What do you do, cousin?"

"*Do?* What the deuce do you mean '*do*'? A gentleman don't *do* anything."

"My apologies. Not being a gentleman, I didn't understand."

"Oh, Lord," groaned Devenish. "*Now* what fustian are you about? Of course you're a gentleman. You're a Tyndale, ain't you?"

"I'll admit that. But—I do not think I'll be a gentleman. Thanks just the same."

"Don't think you'll . . . !" gasped Devenish. "You *are* short of a sheet! Damme if you ain't!"

"Why? Because I don't choose to be a gentleman?" Tyndale laughed. "Gad, Dev, I couldn't abide it! The life of a do-nothing would drive me straight into the boughs! I'd a sight liefer be a coal-heaver!"

"Yes, and probably should be! And do not call me Dev! Only my friends call me that!" He thought, "Cousin's almost more than I can bear!" and added irritably, "Besides, I had not meant *nothing* exactly."

"Oh, I should have guessed. You've likely just come down from University, correct, er, Mr. Devenish?"

Turning in the saddle the better to direct a hard stare at that bland smile, Devenish refuted, "Incorrect. I was sent down."

"Wrong again, alas. Perhaps I had better have addressed you as Lieutenant Devenish?"

Gritting his teeth, Devenish imparted, "I was obliged to sell out of the military. Damn near cashiered. Does that satisfy you?"

"By all means. If it satisfied you, I've no quarrel with it."

"*Satisfies* me? Why, you Colonial clod-crusher! Is there no end to your impudence?"

Tyndale threw back his head and gave a shout of laughter. "My apologies, Sir Cousin."

"Do you know ..." Devenish pulled his mount to a halt, and glowered at his tormenter. "I have been wondering of whom you put me in mind, and now I know. It is Leith, by God."

Briefly, Tyndale looked startled. Then he muttered, "Leith. Oh, yes. Colonel Tristram Leith. A proper dirty dish, eh?"

The amusement that had begun to creep into Devenish's eyes, vanished. He sat straighter. "Your pardon?"

"I said I had heard of Leith. What you people over here would call a wrong 'un, no?"

Devenish swung one leg across the saddle and slid to the ground. There was no trace of temperament about him now, but an icy coldness that, had he known his kinsman better, would have warned Tyndale. "Will you favour me by dismounting for a moment," he invited with a smile.

Tyndale obliged.

Eyes of blue ice fixed themselves upon his face. Stripping off his gloves, Devenish murmured, "You are likely at least a stone heavier than I, Tyndale. On the other hand, you just suffered a bad fall. That should, I think, even the odds." He flung his gloves into his cousin's startled countenance. "Put up your fists, you damned scaly gabblemonger!"

"Hey! Wait! I only—"

Devenish jumped forward and with surprising power landed

an open-handed blow to the jaw. Dancing back again, he shouted, "Fight, curse you!"

Sighing, Tyndale took off his own gloves, tossed them aside, and crouched.

The battle was short-lived, but interesting. Never had two men fought in more diverse styles. His eyes ablaze with excitement, Devenish feinted, shifted, leapt in to unleash a lightning fist, and danced out of reach again. Tyndale, shoulders hunched, eyes watchful, moved very little, as unflustered by his cousin's antics as Devenish was elated. And somehow, as fast as Devenish undeniably was, as lethal the blows that he aimed, at the end of five minutes, there was not a mark on either man, but while Tyndale was as calm and easily breathing as at the start, Devenish was slowing noticeably, his face paler, his movements less springy, some of his enthusiasm replaced by grimness. "Fight, you churlish clod!" he raged. "Do not just stand there like a lump! Fight!"

Tyndale smiled, but did not reply. And it was borne in on Devenish that when the bigger man did move, it was with amazing efficiency, his tall figure swaying easily and never more than was necessary to elude the blows flying at him. Tiring, Devenish's fists lowered, his shoulders slumped. He was breathing distressfully and, watching him, Tyndale dropped his guard a little. In that instant, Devenish sprang. His right rammed home to the jaw. Tyndale staggered and, hurt at last, retaliated immediately and instinctively. . . .

Flat on his back, Devenish smiled up at blurred skies. "Beautiful . . ." he sighed.

Standing over him, Tyndale asked, "Are you much damaged, Sir Cousin?"

"I beg leave . . . to tell you that . . . I shall lie here until my head rejoins . . . the rest of me and . . . be damned t' you."

Tyndale grinned and sat down also, feeling his jaw experimentally.

"Let us have no more of your . . . Canterbury tales," Devenish exhorted. "I know blasted well I scarce laid a fist on you."

"One. Whereby I seem to have several loose teeth."

"No, truly?" Devenish rolled onto his side and, supporting his cheek on one hand, said gleefully, "Egad, but I did mark you a little, at that! Coz—where in the name of all that's wonderful did you learn that left jab?"

"Oh, I sort of—er, developed it. With help. Here and—and

353

there." Tyndale saw Devenish's mouth opening for an indignant retort and added a hasty, "Though why you attacked me so viciously is more than I can comprehend."

Reminded, Devenish sat up, clutched his head, and uttered a trifle thickly, "I do not suffer my friends to . . . to be slandered, in my hearing."

"Leith? But, from what I have heard, he's not worthy of—"

"Tristram Leith," Devenish stated deliberately, "happens to be one of my closest friends. And whatever you may have heard, quite apart from being as far removed from a rogue as it is possible for a man to be, he is a valiant and honourable gentleman. I owe him my life."

Tyndale stared at him. "Then surely it ain't proper that you should so dislike the fellow."

"Dislike *Leith*? Are you mad? I do not dislike him!"

"But—you distinctly said that I reminded you of him."

Frowning into the innocent grey eyes, Devenish declared, "Even Leith has a few mannerisms that are irksome."

"And those you detect in me, eh, sir? Heigh-ho. Life is a sorry thing!" He drew out his handkerchief and handed it over. "Your mouth is bleeding."

Devenish accepted the handkerchief and dabbed at his mouth. Tyndale helped him to his feet.

Setting one foot into the stirrup, Devenish muttered, "Coalheaver, indeed!"

Tyndale laughed.

As the horses passed through the gate at the eastern end of the meadow, and entered the lane, a pink nose and then the rest of a large hare emerged with caution from beneath the hedgerow. For a moment it paused there, very stiff and still, nostrils twitching and ears erect, staring after the departing humans. The sound of Tyndale's laugh had not fallen unpleasantly on its ears, and, reassured, the wild creature proceeded busily about his tasks.

Colonel Alastair Tyndale stood before the hearth of the book room, one booted foot on the gleaming brass fender, and brooding gaze on the flames. He had heard his nephews ride in some half-hour previously and, by means of a casual remark dropped to his omniscient butler, had culled the information that there looked to have been "some sort of dispute." His gaze lifted to the two neatly folded sheets of parchment that lay on the mantelpiece. When those letters were read, the very obvious and mutual dislike between the young men might well harden into all-out hatred, even before he—

The door swung open and Devenish entered, saying in his pleasant voice, "Good afternoon, sir."

Following, Craig offered the hope that they had not kept the Colonel waiting.

Alastair regarded them gravely. They had changed for luncheon and each in his own way was impressive. Craig wore a jacket of maroon that hugged his broad shoulders admirably, and if his neckcloth was less than expertly tied, his pantaloons displayed excellent legs, and his lack of jewellery did not earn him any censure in his uncle's eyes. Devenish, his curls carelessly tumbled, wore a navy blue coat of superfine, his neckcloth was a work of art, and although he lacked his cousin's powerful figure, his physique was in perfect proportion to his size.

Despite the fact that the morning had darkened, no candles were as yet lit in the room, but as the two men moved rather hesitantly towards him, Colonel Tyndale noted the darkening bruise along Craig's jaw, and Alain's puffy and split lip, and his own jaw hardened. He made no comment, however, waving to the sideboard, and suggesting they help themselves from the tray of decanters which the butler had left. "Before we go in to luncheon," he added when they all were seated around the fire, "there is something I must say to you." In silence, he handed a letter to each man.

Glancing at the superscription, Devenish muttered, "Yolande! What the deuce? Good God! Sir, it's not little Rosemary?"

The Colonel shook his head. "I doubt it. But read it—then we will talk."

To a point, the letters were similar, Yolande informing her cousins that she had departed for Scotland and would spend the summer at her grandfather's home in Ayrshire. The closing paragraphs, however, were quite different.

Craig's letter ended:

I am most pleased that I was given the opportunity to meet you, and I take this opportunity to once again express my thanks for your gallant efforts in my behalf. You will, I am assured, have returned to Canada by the time I come back to Sussex. I wish you Godspeed in your long journey.

Although we have been acquainted for so short a time, I

think you may be interested to know that I expect to be married this year, and thus, by the time we meet again shall probably no longer sign myself,

Yr. affectionate cousin,
Yolande Drummond

Devenish, meanwhile, read:

Papa has only now told me the true facts concerning your father's tragic death. I was never more shocked. As you know, I have always deplored violence, and I send you my sincerest sympathies, dear Dev. I can only beg you to allow the past to remain so.

On a happier note, I mean to discuss our formal betrothal with my grandfather and, in the event that nothing untoward occurs by the time I return to Sussex, and if it is still your wish, I think we should at that time fix upon a date for the wedding. Until then, I remain,

Yr. affectionate cousin,
Yolande

His lady's willingness to pick a date for their wedding had the effect of lifting a great weight from Devenish's spirits. It was silly, of course, but lately he had been haunted by the fear that although she was undeniably fond of him, she meant to cry off. That terrifying spectre could now be banished forever, thank the Lord! He thought absently that he must buy a ring for the sweet chit; and that it would never do for her to jaunter about the countryside without his escort. The reference to his father's death shadowed his joy, however. He had always understood that Stuart Devenish had died as the result of a fall, and that the shock had caused his wife to miscarry and soon follow both her husband and stillborn child to the grave. A most frightful tragedy for two young lives to have been so suddenly ended, and a third never quite begun. But why Yolande should have been upset by it at this late date was as inexplicable as her remark anent allowing "the past to remain so."

Baffled, he glanced up, and was further disconcerted to find both his cousin and his uncle watching him.

Craig, his own hopes shattered, asked quietly, "Have I to offer you my congratulations, coz?"

"No law says you must, but I'll accept 'em, with thanks. Sir"—he turned blithely to the Colonel—"since Craig has proven to be out of leading strings and does not stand in need of my aid, with your permission I shall go and instruct my man to pack a valise."

"But you have *not* my permission."

Devenish had already started to the door and he swung around saying a surprised, "What? But, sir, you surely understand that I must go and—"

"And pester your betrothed? I see no reason for it."

The tone was unwontedly harsh. Taken aback, Devenish said, "Pester her? Why—no, I hope I will not—"

"I am informed on the best authority that Yolande is escorted by three outriders, is followed by her maid and personal groom, and accompanied by Mrs. Arabella."

"Oh, no! That prosing antidote? And if Aunty took her revolting animal along, poor Yolande will be driven to distraction, I must—"

"Learn to refrain from speaking disparagingly of a lady?" snapped his uncle.

Again shocked by that unfamiliarly cold voice, Devenish flushed scarlet. "I did not mean— That is, I intended no— Oh, gad, sir! You know very well that the woman is insupportable."

"To the contrary. I know that whatever her small failings, she is devoted to her niece. Now, have you by any chance forgot there was more to Yolande's letter than the matter of your betrothal?"

Stunned, Devenish returned to his chair. "No, sir. My apologies."

Colonel Tyndale thought, "Dammit, there was no call to hurt the boy!" And knowing his harshness was born of a dread of the next few minutes, he drew a hand across his brow and muttered, "I'm sorry if I spoke with unnecessary heat, Dev. But Yolande had told me part of what she intended to write, and I'll own I don't relish telling you of it."

Much embarrassed, Craig came to his feet. "You will be wishing for your privacy, sir. I am the one should go. Besides, I've a long journey before me and might as well get started."

"Journey?" echoed Devenish suspiciously. "To where, may I ask?"

"Why, it seems I have inherited my father's home in Ayrshire. I hope I may find it, but—"

"You mean Castle Tyndale?" Devenish sprang up, his eyes sparkling. "The devil? That's less than ten miles from Steep

Drummond! And I suppose you'd no idea you would be following the same route as my lady, had you?"

Craig's head tilted back a fraction, and his eyelids assumed a bored droop. "Since you appear to be betrothed to the lady, I fail to see your concern. No gentleman could approach her under such circumstances."

"No *gentleman!*" flared Devenish. "Why, you slippery Captain Sharp, you'll not pursue her while *I* live to prevent it! If you really seek your blasted inheritance, I'll ride with you, and let me tell you——"

"You—will—do—no—such—thing!" thundered the Colonel, standing and suddenly looking to be seven feet tall. "Sit down! Both of you!"

When his two dismayed nephews had complied, he went to the sideboard, fortified himself with a glass of cognac, and strode back to the mantel, blinking a little because of the unaccustomed haste with which he had swallowed the strong liquor. For a moment he stood there, swirling the brandy in his glass and frowning down at it. "You will not like what I have to tell you," he said slowly. "It should have been told long since, but from the contents of your solicitor's letter, Craig, I collect you have never been informed, and I'll own I have kept the truth from you, Alain." He looked deliberately from one apprehensive young face to the other, and sighed. "You were aware that my brother and sister were twins," he began. "I suppose of the two of us boys, I resembled my father more closely. I was the stolid plodder, while Jonas was handsome and light-hearted, but with the devil's own temper—always into some mischief or other. Despite our different natures, we were deeply attached, but between Esme, your mother, Dev, and Jonas, Craig's father, there was a bond such as I have seldom seen between brother and sister."

Devenish said, "I knew they were twins, of course. And I believe you said they looked alike."

"Very much. Your mama was a singularly beautiful girl. I remember . . ." The Colonel frowned, his eyes becoming remote and sad. "I remember Jonas bragging that with her looks his twin would wed no less than a duke, and even he would scarce be good enough for her!"

"Instead of which," Devenish put in, "she married the younger son of an impoverished house. Her twin must not have thought much of my papa, eh, sir?"

Alastair's sombre gaze drifted to him. "Jonas was furious,

and did all in his power to prevent the match. He even appealed to my father, but by that time—" He shrugged. "He was such a wild young rascal. He had already been out twice, and was obliged to flee the country and stay abroad for six months as a consequence of one of those meetings."

"Killed his man, did he, sir?" asked Devenish, his eyes sparkling. "By thunder, but he must have been a dynamic fellow! I wish I might have seen a likeness of him."

Craig threw a faintly bored glance at him. The Colonel, vexed by the interruption, said, "You would have, save that my father had every trace of Jonas destroyed, or so he thought. Esme kept a miniature of him, and after her death I acquired it." He walked to the small table beside his chair and opened the drawer. "I intend to bequeath it to you, Craig. But I will ask that you allow me to keep it until my death." He looked down at the small painting with wistful eyes, then held it out.

Craig glanced at it, his own eyes enigmatic. "I have a larger one in Canada. Thank you, sir."

The Colonel's brows lifted slightly, but without comment he handed the miniature to Devenish.

The result was a breathless exclamation. Paling, Devenish gazed down at a man that, save for the style of dress, might have been himself. The fair curling hair, the wideset deep blue eyes alight with laughing impudence, the straight nose and sensitive mouth were almost identical. Only in the set of the chin was there a difference; Devenish's inclined to be more square than that of his long-dead uncle. "The resemblance," he gasped, "is—is—"

"Uncanny." The Colonel nodded, retrieving the miniature and gazing at it. "I told you they were twins, and you take after your mama, rest her soul." He glanced at Craig, wondering if the boy might resent that close resemblance, but the strong face was without expression.

Devenish asked, "Sir, what happened? If the attachment between my mother and her twin was as deep as you say, I would have thought Uncle Jonas could have influenced her against the marriage."

"Do not imagine that he did not try." Tyndale replaced the miniature in the drawer and closed it, but remained standing, hands linked behind him, facing these two so dissimilar young men, and dreading what he must tell them. "Perhaps the most ironic thing about it," he went on, "was that Jonas had introduced them, for all through school and University, Stuart

Devenish was his dearest friend. Jonas reproached himself bitterly for that, but it was too late; Esme adored her brother, but she had her share of spirit and determination, and nothing would sway her from Stuart. She told me once that the instant she laid eyes on him, her heart was given. And I am very sure it was the same with him. They delayed their wedding, hoping Jonas would come home for the ceremony, but he refused, and they were married in his absence. A year later, Alain was born. Jonas was still in Belgium. When he did return he seemed less vindictive towards Stuart. It was not his way to hold a grudge, for he was all fury one minute and sweet contrition the next, so I began to hope the breach might be mended. During Jonas's absence, Stuart's elder brother had been killed in a racing accident and Stuart had inherited Devencourt, the family's country seat in Gloucestershire. My dear sister delighted in the house, but she had never forgotten our happy days in Scotland, and it was there that you were born, Alain. You were at Castle Tyndale again when you were nearing your first birthday, and when Jonas came back from Belgium I told him I meant to journey to Ayrshire for the occasion. I could scarce have been more pleased when he agreed to accompany me."

He paused, smiling nostalgically. "Shall I ever forget that reunion? Stuart had been deeply troubled by the quarrel and was more than willing to let bygones be bygones, but I'll own I was a little apprehensive. My father was ailing, and was at that time dwelling in Cornwall because of the milder climate. He had already announced the disposition of his estates. Because of his impatience with his heir, Aspenhill, which should by rights have gone to Jonas, had been deeded over to me, and Jonas was the legal owner of Castle Tyndale. As a result, he had every right to demand that Stuart leave. However, he marked the resemblance immediately he saw you, Alain, and when he learned they had named you after him, he was so proud it was—I see I have surprised you, Craig. Your cousin is called Alain Jonas Devenish, you were unaware, eh? Your own middle name is Winters, you said?"

Craig drawled with a touch of irony, "To be precise, sir, Craig Stuart Winters Tyndale."

"Now—by thunder!" muttered the Colonel. "So the affection held true—in spite of everything."

Eager to hear the rest of the story, Devenish prompted, "Not so unusual, surely? They had been friends in childhood and were now brothers-in-law. But something occurred to disturb this truce, did it, sir?"

Behind his back, the Colonel's hands tightened. "Yes. The castle. Ah, you may well look surprised, but Jonas was possessed of odd fancies at times. He had always disliked the place, and had told me on several occasions that he never would live there, and that our father had given it to him out of malice because it was haunted; as indeed, legend has it. He could not be easy there, and once—God! Why did I not heed him?—he said he felt the Sword of Damocles poised above his head, and he had best get back to town before it fell!"

He was silent, lips tightly gripped together, eyes gazing into a past that only he could see. Watching him, Craig saw the gleam of sweat on the high forehead, and his own inner apprehension deepened.

"About a week after the birthday party," the Colonel resumed, "Esme became slightly unwell. She was increasing, and at first none of us was too much concerned. It was just a cold, she said. But she was slow to recover. Jonas blamed the climate and asked Stuart if he could take Esme back to Town. In point of fact, I doubt his fears were justified. It was cold, but it was a dry cold, lacking London's penetrating dampness, and it was my impression that my sister throve in the place. Jonas, however, became more and more worried."

"Was my father not concerned at all, sir?" Devenish asked curiously.

"He was willing that Esme should come back to Town. He worshipped her and would have done anything she desired. But Esme wanted her child to be born in Scotland. As I said, she was a strong-minded girl, and she only laughed at what she called Jonas's 'fey fancies.' As the weeks went by, Jonas grew more and more irked by Stuart's refusal to order his wife to leave Castle Tyndale, and I must admit I also was becoming anxious for Esme's welfare. Jonas began to sneer that Stuart dwelt under the cat's foot—that sort of nonsensical talk. It was I think inspired partly by worry for your mama, Dev, and partly by his own fear of the castle. Fortunately, Stuart's disposition was amiable, and he could usually tease Jonas out of his dismals. But one day . . ."

Again he paused. The room was hushed, and the soft rain which had begun to fall sounded very loud as it pattered against the window. The cousins exchanged an uneasy glance, already half guessing what was to come.

"Stuart," the Colonel said heavily, "loved the sea, and it was his habit to go up to the battlements every day, weather permitting, and look out over the cliffs. He was there one afternoon when Jonas came to me in great agitation, saying that Esme had fainted in her dressing room, and that with or without her consent he intended to take her down to London at once and place her under the care of a most excellent physician. I was alarmed, naturally, and I made haste to my sister's room, while Jonas went rushing in search of Stuart. I found Esme laid down upon her bed, with her woman fussing over her. I could hear Jonas and Stuart shouting. I remember thinking, 'My God! What a time to quarrel with poor little Esme lying here so ill!' and I started up to the battlements to try to quiet them."

His voice shredded, and when he resumed his tale, he spoke in so low a tone that his hearers were obliged to lean forward to hear him. "There is," he said, "a side stair that winds up around the northwest tower. And there are occasional windows . . . narrow, and very deep." He turned abruptly, to stand with head down and shoulders hunched. "I see it . . . still . . . So terrible. A sudden—darkness, passing the window. And this—this awful, despairing scream . . ."

White as death, Devenish sprang up. "God in heaven! Sir—what are you saying? Was my father—*murdered?*"

For an interminable moment, the Colonel did not answer. Surreptitiously, he dragged his handkerchief from his pocket and wiped it across his face. With a deep, quivering breath, he turned to face them again, his lean features drawn and haggard. "We found Jonas lying in a dead faint on the battlements. For two days he was as one in a daze; quite unable to tell us what had happened. When he at last could speak of it, he admitted he had flown into a passion and warned Stuart he would hold him personally responsible if anything happened to Esme. Stuart, it seems, turned on him at last, and demanded he cease frightening his sister with his morbid imaginings." The Colonel sighed. "I knew Jonas so well. It would have taken no more to inflame him."

"And because—because of that perfectly justifiable remark," gasped Devenish, "he flung my father from the parapet?"

"He swore he did not. He said he struck Stuart with his open hand only, and at once repented the blow, but that Stuart leapt back, stumbled, and fell."

His fists clenched, Devenish admitted reluctantly, "I suppose that—could be so."

The Colonel said nothing.

Watching him tensely, Craig probed, "There is more, I think, sir?"

"How I wish there were not," groaned the Colonel. "Some of the men Jonas had set to clearing debris from the beach saw Stuart fall. They insisted he had not stumbled, but that they had distinctly seen him hurtle backward as though violently pushed. That he had, in fact, been struck with such force he'd had no chance to catch at the battlements or attempt to save himself, but had soared straight back and down, to his death."

His face set into a grim mask, Devenish fought rage and horror, to ask brusquely, "But the battlements are crenellated, are they not?"

"True, lad. But the crenels atop Castle Tyndale reach to the floor." The Colonel glanced at Craig. "A crenel is the space between the merlons atop battlements. In many instances, the crenels are constructed a few feet from the floor."

"But at Castle Tyndale," Devenish rasped, "they have no lower wall. My poor father had not even that slight chance of saving himself."

The Colonel pointed out miserably, "It would not have helped, Dev."

Devenish swore and turned a contorted face to his cousin. The Colonel was also watching Craig, and he was startled when the bowed head was raised to reveal the cheeks streaked with tears. "I wish," the Canadian said painfully, "I only wish to God—I had *known.*"

"Well, *I* know!" Devenish stood and glared down at him. "From the first moment I saw you, I loathed you! I thought it was because you had hurt Yolande. And later, I supposed it was because of the way you ogled her! But it goes far deeper! Your miserable wretch of a father murdered mine! And the hatred between us is—"

Craig had also come to his feet, his expression only a little less enraged than that of his cousin. "Foul-mouthed clod! What proof have you of his guilt?"

"It was proven long ago! Murder, cousin! Murder most hideous! And I swear that I—"

"*Be still!* Both of you!"

Colonel Tyndale's cry knifed across that savage room. Devenish flung around to face him, rebellion written clearly in his face. Craig started and drew a hand across his wet brow.

"By your leave—*gentlemen,*" the Colonel said angrily, "I

will finish my unhappy tale and be done with it!" The cousins remaining silent, he went on, "Within two months of the tragedy, my beloved sister suffered a miscarriage and died. The doctor tried to ease the blow by saying she would have died in childbed at all events. It was untrue. Esme had lost all will to live. When Stuart was killed, her heart broke. The most ... pitiful thing was that"—his voice became husky with emotion again—"that she blamed *herself*! That sweet, gentle child who was born to love and to be loved. If she had not wed in the face of Jonas' opposition, she used to cry, if she had only obeyed him—none of it would have happened. But that was not the truth of it!"

He paced to stand before Devenish and glare at him until his nephew recoiled a step, his own fury giving way to consternation. "The crime—if such it was," the Colonel grated, "grew from my brother's ungovernable temper! And be warned, Dev! *I will not* stand by and see it happen again! So help me, God, I swear it!"

Devenish said a cautious, "Surely, you are confused, sir! It was Stuart Devenish, *my* father, who was foully murdered. It is Craig on whom your wrath—"

"No! It is very apparent to me that Craig has little of Jonas in him. *You* are the one has inherited that unpredictable temperament!" He jabbed a finger at his aghast nephew and accused, "You—as I told you at the start—take after your mama. My brother's twin. In you, I see again his undisciplined impetuosity, his fierce pride and swift rages. I have struggled these twenty years and more to break you of those tendencies. I have watched irresponsibility drive you from one disaster to the next. I'll not now stand by and see you exact vengeance upon your innocent cousin! No, by God! Sooner would I have you clapped up in Bedlam!"

Devenish gasped and, shaking his head speechlessly, shrank away until he stood against the wall, staring with stricken eyes at this relentless stranger he had known so many years, and knew not at all. "But—but, Uncle," he faltered, "you know— you *must* know that I never deliberately— I mean, a few practical jokes, I—I admit. But I would not—intentionally—really hurt anyone, save in self-defence."

"No more, I doubt," Craig's quiet drawl intervened, "did my father."

Two distraught faces jerked towards him. The Colonel exclaimed, "You knew all of this?"

"I would to God I had! I might have understood him better. I might even have been able to help him."

Colonel Tyndale stepped closer. Devenish did not move, but demanded, "Then what do you mean?"

Craig looked from one to the other, and asked hesitantly, "How old—do you suppose me to be?"

Watching the Canadian narrowly, the Colonel said, "Three and twenty, though I'll own you appear older."

"I am twenty-eight."

"That's not possible!" flared Devenish. "Unless—" With a surprising degree of eagerness, he asked, "Do you tell us you are adopted? That you were my uncle's stepson, perhaps?"

"No. I do not say that. You remarked, sir, that my father was obliged to flee the country because of a duel, just before his twin married Stuart Devenish. My mother was the cause of that duel."

"Was she, by thunder!" breathed the Colonel. "He knew her—*then?*"

"She was his wife."

"That is not possible, by God! Jonas may have been ramshackle, but he'd not—I cannot believe that he—" The Colonel checked, scowled, drew a bewildered hand across his brow, and groaned. "He *would!* Devil take him! I loved the young fool, but . . . he would! And yet—why the secrecy? Was she—your pardon, boy, I mean no disrespect but—was she—"

"Rankly ineligible?" With a prideful smile, Craig said, "She was fair as the morning, my father used to say. A tall, softly spoken, serene lady. The daughter of a—Yankee merchant." He heard a muffled exclamation from Colonel Tyndale and went on scornfully, "She was everything any man could ask in a wife, but my father knew well what his family would think. The daughter of a foreigner. Worse, a foreigner engaged in trade. No background; no title; no ancient name! He was already in deep disgrace. It was more than he dared do to acknowledge his marriage at that time; his father would have cut him off without a penny. Always, he hoped to redeem himself. He used to tell my mother that if he could win the old gentleman over, he would broach the marriage to him, gradually, and that once my grandfather met Mama, and me, he would have to acknowledge us."

"But . . ." faltered the Colonel, "the—duel . . . ?"

"A rascally acquaintance of my father's discovered that Mama was, as he thought, Papa's mistress. My mother had been sent to Paris for 'a European finish' prior to wedding a wealthy man of her father's choosing. The aunt to whom she was entrusted knew of the marriage, but had agreed to keep it secret." He frowned, and said thoughtfully, "I think she was not very wise. Be that as it may, this rascal threatened blackmail. When Father threw him out, he came to England. My mother was beside herself with fear. She was sure the old gentleman would disown him, and if they were both cut off, she did not know how we could live. Her terror enraged my father. He followed the man to England and, before he could speak with Grandfather, called him out and shot him. It was a fair fight, sir. You may remember that my father was wounded in the encounter?"

"Yes, I . . . good heavens!" said the Colonel, still amazed by these disclosures. "Then—you must have been . . . three years old when Alain was born?"

"About that, sir."

"All very interesting," put in Devenish, brusquely, "but I'm damned if I see what it has to do with your belief that he was innocent of my father's murder."

"After we went to Canada," Craig explained, "he was a man tormented. Often I heard my mother striving to comfort him. The truth was kept from me, but I did know that he had been forbidden ever to return to England, or even to use his family name, and as boys will, I imagined all manner of terrible crimes lurked in his past. Mama knew, but she never spoke of it to me. I watched my father age long before his time. Always, he was homesick and flayed by conscience. I suppose it proved more than the poor man could bear. He took refuge in drink, and I—all prideful intolerance—despised him for it. The lower he sank, the deeper was my mother's grief, and the more I—May God forgive me! If only I had known!"

The Colonel shook his head. "You were not to blame, boy. Do not scourge yourself."

"I could have been more understanding," Craig muttered. "He had so many fine qualities, I should have reasoned that—" He cut off that useless grieving and drew his shoulders back. "In some things, we do not get a second chance, do we, sir?"

"No," the Colonel sighed. "Is this why you feel Jonas was innocent? Guilty men can be flayed by conscience too, you know."

"True. But once, in one of his bad moments, I heard him tell my mother repeatedly that he was not guilty of something. I knew from his manner that it must have been something very bad." He hesitated, as if reluctant to continue, then added, "I do not know how it was in his youth, but all my life I found him a deeply religious man. I—I confess that it disgusted me. To see him in his cups on Saturday night, and at church first thing on Sunday. I did not—understand. But I do know that he believed in God, and felt that there is another life beyond this one. I was in the room when he lay dying, and the Vicar asked him to repent his sins. My father roused and said, quite proudly, 'The worst sin of which I was ever accused, I did not commit.' "

Craig paused, looked into his uncle's intent face, and said earnestly, "I suppose, naïve though I was, I loved my father, and could not bear to see him—as he became. But, I *did* know him, sir. And I know he would not have lied at such a moment. I will take my oath that my father did not intentionally cause his brother's death, Devenish—" He stopped. Devenish was gone.

&s *Chapter 5* &s

"I can only beg of you," said Mrs. Arabella Drummond, absently stroking the dog who sprawled beside her on the rocking carriage seat, "to put the matter quite out of your mind. I believe Dr. Jester to be a very fine man. You will recall, my love, that when I took that horrid chill last winter, he was so obliging as to come to the house in the middle of a most frightful storm."

Her nerves rather strained, Yolande pointed out, "He thought you had the pneumonia."

"Yes." Her aunt giggled. "It was naughty of Sullivan to give him that impression, though she was motivated by loyalty to me, you know, and I am sure that as a physician and healer, he must only have been glad I had instead nothing worse than a cold. I think I must have been *close* to pneumonia, however, for I suffered so that poor Sullivan thought it would put a period to me. But Dr. Jester's medicine—though it tasted ghastly! I wonder why medicine must always taste ghastly . . . ? Not that that is either here or there, of course. The medicine was most efficacious, and I particularly recall that the doctor was not in the least irked, in spite of being so young a man, and having drove such a distance. And only think, my naughty boy bit him when he came up to my bed!" She pulled the fox terrier's ear, and cooed, "*What* a scamp you are, to be sure!"

Socrates opened one eye and peered around to discover if it was time to eat. Disappointed, he lay down his head and went back to sleep.

Her attention having wandered, Yolande made no comment. Mrs. Drummond slipped her hand into her muff once more, tilted her head, and frowned. "I do not think that was quite the point I had meant to make."

"We were speaking of Rosemary," said Yolande, stifling a yawn.

"So we were. And although you may think Jester is young and inexperienced, and only a country doctor after all, for I agree he is not to be thought of in the same breath as Lord Belmont, still, I do not doubt his ability to recognize measles when he sees it. It was so silly of Nurse to frighten us all by saying it might be the Pox! Why, I knew very well that could not be, for I distinctly recall that when I was a child . . ."

Again, Yolande's attention drifted. The journey had been slow and although they had left Park Parapine before noon, they had not yet reached Tunbridge Wells. The carriage was cumbersome and not speedy at best, and their stops at various stages to change teams did not, it would seem, coincide with the needs of Socrates, thus making it necessary that more stops be undertaken. At this rate, it would take well over a week to reach Grandpapa's great house. That prospect did not particularly distress her, but she felt oddly heavy-hearted, probably because of leaving her friends and family; or perhaps because Aunt Arabella was not a very enlivening companion. She closed her ears to that lady's unending stream of chatter and at once her thoughts flashed to her new cousin. They did so of late with a frequency that was most disquieting. Therefore, instead of resolutely striving to oust him from her mind, she decided to assess the matter. Dispassionately. And thus reduce it to the proportions it deserved.

Mr. Craig Winters Tyndale, she concluded, had little to recommend him. Aside from his gallantry in having come to her rescue, and the fact that he was a superb horseman, he had a fine athletic figure, an excellent leg, and a pair of shoulders that would probably cause most tailors to exclaim with joy. But, even were Devenish not so well featured as to cast any other man into the shade, Mr. Tyndale could not be termed handsome. She thrust away the image of a pair of long-lashed grey eyes and hastened to the next point in her evaluation. Tyndale was of a more reserved nature than his ebullient cousin. He was also, to a great extent, an unknown quantity; why, one did not even know where the Colonial gentleman had gone to school! As for fortune, Papa had said he could aspire to a modest competence left him by the grandfather he had never met, and an estate in Scotland, dominated by a castle that had stood lonely, and largely unoccupied, since Stuart Devenish's tragic death there. She had never been inside the castle, but she had seen it often and it had always seemed to her to be a fairy-tale place, soaring as it did at the cliff edge, its conical towers rising high above the battlements and sometimes the only parts visible above the mists that drifted in from the sea. She sighed dreamily. What a romantic setting for a deeply in love couple starting their married—

Shocked by a sudden awareness of such impractical digressions, she returned to her clinical appraisal. Cousin Craig had burst into her life like a comet. A rather blinding comet, although one had to face the fact that her initial attraction to him had been founded in gratitude and admiration. (Hadn't it?) She frowned at an inoffensive hayrick they were passing. She *was* attracted to him. And that was perfectly dreadful and must not be encouraged! Much as she might yearn for romance, she was not a foolish girl. She was bound by invisible but very real ties to a man she had known all her life. Devenish was not vastly wealthy, but he had inherited the respectable fortune his papa had not lived to enjoy. He owned a large and beautiful, if somewhat neglected, estate in Gloucestershire that could, with very little effort, become a showplace. He was both loved and approved of by her parents, to whom the match represented the culmination of years of joyous anticipation. Mrs. Alain Devenish . . . Her eyes softened. Dear Dev; so staunch and fearless for all his harum-scarum ways. How many girls adored him? How many men thought him the best of good fellows? And he was! Despite his swift temper and fierce jealousies, he loved her with all his honest heart, and would care for and cherish her all her life. If she allowed him. And if, being such a romantic figure (as Mama had pointed out), he had no thought of romance, why it was a small fault surely. If one truly loved a man.

A pair of fine grey eyes again played havoc with her precise common sense. Eyes so full of tenderness . . . She thought in desperation, "Very well, dear sir. If intrude you must—what have *you* to offer me?"

The answer was immediate. An inevitable duel between him and Devenish, with consequences that could not be less than disastrous for all concerned. More tragedy for Colonel Alastair, and the dear man had already known too much of tragedy. Grief for her parents, who hoped she would make not only a good match but one that would not be tainted by scandal. And as for herself, removal from the family she loved and the only way of life she knew; a new home which, despite her romantical imaginings, actually consisted of a mouldering castle perched on a cliff and (understandably!) rumoured to be haunted; and a future in which loneliness and poverty went hand in hand. She had a mental picture of herself, a bucket in one hand and a mop in the other, toiling at an endless flight of clammy stone stairs, while Craig dug turnips from the stony ground, preparatory to entertaining Grandpapa to dinner. Horrors! she thought, shuddering.

"Why, you naughty little puss! Here have I been prosing on and on, and I do believe you've attended me for not one single minute!"

Seldom had Yolande been more relieved to be wrenched back to the here and now. She sat up straighter and turned a repentant face. "Oh, but I assure you, Aunt, I heard all you said. I do apologize for allowing my attention to wander, but—er, it is this black chaise that comes up so quickly behind us. I have been watching it reflected in the brass of the lamps. Do you suppose the driver means to pass? He seems very impatient."

Mrs. Drummond turned to the window. "Good heavens! I trust he has not that intent, for the road is much too narrow. But—oh, my! Indeed, it seems he does mean— A gentleman, driving his own chaise. No! He must not! Oh, sir! Stay, I beg!" These dramatics were accompanied by alarmed little gestures, culminating in a desperate flapping of her muff at the approaching driver, who paid her not the least heed, but as he drew level, glanced with sardonic amusement into the carriage.

The glance became an intent stare. He removed his tall beaver and bowed his dark head with patent admiration.

Yolande ignored him, and the chaise shot past, pulling in before them just barely in time to avoid the Royal Mail that thundered around the bend of the road and made its stentorian way southwards.

"How very rag-mannered," Mrs. Drummond exclaimed with justifiable indignation. "Did you know him, Yolande?" And, contradictorily, "He doffed his hat to us. Such pretty curls. I was ever fond of a dark-haired gentleman, and especially one so well favoured. He looked familiar. I wonder who he can be."

"Now how can this be, dear Aunt?" Yolande teased. "The gentleman is one of Prinny's particular cronies and was, until her recent betrothal, most assiduous in his pursuit of Lisette Van Lindsay."

"What? That high-in-the-instep creature? I vow I was never more amused than to hear she is to wed Justin Strand. I can scarce wait to meet her starched-up mama and offer my felicitations. Everyone *knows* the poor girl was as good as sold to that nobody on account of her papa's debts. Ah! Now I have it! Our Mr. Impatience is no less than Mr. James Garvey, no? A most desirable *parti* for any lady of the *ton*, and if I dare be so bold as to venture my humble opinion, my love, a far more appropriate suitor for you than young Devenish. And I will own I could not like the way Mr. Winters, or Tyndale, or however one is now supposed to address him, was looking at you when I came upon you both in the small saloon the other day. Not that there could be anything to *that*, of course, for the man is beyond the pale, entirely. Nonetheless, dearest, I must caution you against ever giving cause to be thought fast." She glanced to each side as though eager dowagers clung to the exterior of the carriage, ears straining to hear what went on inside. "I know your dear mama," she said, for once picking up the threads of her monologue where she had left them, "has done all in her power to instruct you, but—"

A stormy light had begun to gather in Yolande's green eyes, so that it was perhaps fortunate that Socrates chose this moment to sit up and by means of a series of piercing yelps, yowls, and shrieks, make known his desire to alight. Mrs. Drummond sighed that she also would appreciate a respite from this eternal driving, and since Yolande was beginning to feel the pangs of hunger, it was decided to stop for luncheon at a charming old posting house called The Little Nut Tree that lay just ahead.

Mine host hurried onto the front steps of the thatch-roofed structure to greet so luxurious a carriage, and when he perceived the three outriders and liveried coachman and groom, his eyes lit up. The arrival of the second carriage which conveyed the luggage and the abigails of the ladies, brought visions of enormous largesse, and mine host was happy indeed.

The Little Nut Tree was a welcoming establishment that shone with cleanliness. The ladies were shown to a bright chamber under the eaves, where they refreshed themselves before going down to the private parlour where Yolande had required that a light luncheon be served. At the foot of the stairs, the host awaited them, all apologies. His good wife, quite unbeknownst to himself, had already promised the parlour to another traveller. It was unforgivable, beyond words distressing, but the coffee room was unoccupied at the moment. There was a pleasant corner from which the ladies could observe the gardens, and he would see to it that they were not in any way disturbed during their luncheon.

At this point, a cool voice intervened, "Nonsense, host. I am acquainted with these ladies."

Yolande turned to encounter a pair of eyes as green as her own that smiled down at her. "Mr. Garvey," she murmured, inclining her head slightly and holding out her hand. "I believe you have not the acquaintance of my aunt. Mrs. Drummond, allow me to present Mr. James Garvey. The gentleman who swept past us at such a rate a little while ago."

Mr. Garvey was delighted to meet Mrs. Drummond, and made her an impressive bow. He was, he vowed, devastated to think that he might have startled two such lovely ladies by driving very fast along the highway. It was his habit; admittedly reckless. And as for their being compelled to dine in the coffee room, such a thing was not to be thought of. Save for his servants, he was travelling alone, and they would be granting a solitary gentleman a great favour would they consent to share the parlour with him.

Yolande hesitated. She knew Mr. Garvey only slightly, but they moved in the same circles, and she had from time to time attended functions at which he was also a guest. No one could deny that he was of the first stare: His birth was impeccable, his close friendship with the Prince opened useful doors to him, he was extremely good-looking, still a bachelor at five and thirty, and his fortune far from contemptible. Indeed, one wondered that the Van Lindsay family, in dire financial straits, had not jumped at the chance when he had shown an interest in their daughter. The fact that they had instead chosen a wealthy young man of dubious lineage had puzzled Yolande, and she had wondered at the time if some whispers anent Mr. Garvey's reputation were well founded. Mrs. Drummond suffered no such qualms. She was charmed by his smile and what she later described as a most insinuating address, and she signified in a lengthy speech that they would be very willing to accept Mr. Garvey's generous offer since a common coffee room was not a proper place for Miss Drummond of Park Parapine to sit down to luncheon.

Yolande waited patiently through the ponderous monologue. Looking up, she found Mr. Garvey watching her with an understanding twinkle in his eyes. She had known from the start, of course, that her aunt was not going to be an altogether salubrious companion, and it occurred to her that their having met up with this polished gentleman might not be such a bad thing, after all.

With hands loosely clasped between his knees and head down bent, Alain Devenish sat on the bench in the shrubbery and contemplated a very small yellow caterpillar that was busily engaged in inching its way up a strand of grass. He had known there was tragedy in the early deaths of his parents, but he'd not dreamed how stark that tragedy was, nor that it had touched so many lives. He was not a young man much given to introspection, being quite willing to travel whatever path Fate offered, and accepting good-humouredly, if not resignedly, any buffets that came his way. He was not insensitive, however, and his heart was wrung by the picture of his young and lovely mother grieving herself into an early grave following the loss of her husband. "Poor little soul," he thought, and could not but wonder how his life might have been changed had she lived. The influence of a gentle lady might have softened his nature. Perhaps he would not now be scorned as a person of "undisciplined impetuosity and swift rages." He flinched a little. Devilish accurate with his lances was the Old Nunks.

His tiny acquaintance had by this time found its way to the

top of the strand of grass, and stopped. "Now what are you going to do, foolish creature?" Devenish enquired. "There is nothing for it but to go down again. Had you a single brain in your head, you would know that!" The caterpillar paid him no heed. Probably, he decided, because it had *no* brains in its head. It was better off in such a deprived state. If one had brains, one cared about people. And just when one least expected it—just when one might, in fact, have felt in need of a little sympathy and support—those same people turned on one like angry serpents. "I have struggled these twenty years and more . . . I have watched your irresponsibility drive you from one disaster to the next . . ." The fair head ducked lower. It was true, of course. And Uncle Alastair had been angry before. Very angry. But had not glared with such a look—a look almost of . . . contempt. . . .

"He loves you, you know."

Devenish frowned at the quiet drawl. Not looking up, he growled, "I came out here to get away from you."

"I know." Craig settled his shoulders against a convenient birch tree and folding his arms, said, "Still I must talk with you."

Devenish sneered, "I wonder you dare. Are you forgetting that I have inherited your father's murderous inclinations?"

"That is not possible."

"Devil it ain't! You saw the likeness the moment we met. At the time I thought it was impudence when you stared so. But it was shock, was it not?" He had brought a frown to those controlled features and, bitterly hurt, wanting only to hurt in turn, laughed. "Was you afraid, cousin? Did you fear I might seek vengeance for my youthful, slaughtered father, my heartbroken mother?"

"No."

"I'd be within my rights, by God, but I would! Yet—you heard him. *You* have the taint of murder in your veins. But *I* am the one from whom people will shrink in horror! I am the one who is—his greatest trial!" He swung his head away, but Craig noted how his hand gripped the bench until the knuckles gleamed white. And with sudden and unexpected sympathy, he offered, "He has cared for you for twenty years; naturally, he—"

"I need no reminders of that, damn you!" Devenish jerked around to reveal a haggard face and eyes that blazed. "You likely think me too selfish to be aware of my uncle's self-sacrifice, eh?"

"Yes."

"Well, blast your smuggery, I am *not* unaware! I have disappointed him a hundred times—and worried him twice that often, belike. But I'll repay him, never doubt it! He is growing old, but his old age will not be lonely, I do assure you."

"Nonsense!"

With a swift, fluid movement, Devenish came to his feet. "Your *pardon*?"

"He is not old. I doubt he's much past forty."

"Five and forty, if you must know, Master Impudence."

"And have you never noticed, my Lord Arrogance, how fine looking a man he is? What he needs is a loving wife—not a repentant would-be martyr."

For a moment Devenish was so taken aback that hurt and rage left him and he stared his astonishment. Then, *"M-marry?"* he gasped. "Uncle *Alastair*? Damme, but you *are* wits to let! I might have known you sought me out to mouth some such fustian!"

"Aye, you might!" Pushing himself away from the tree, Craig said a disgusted, "And I might have known you were too set up in your own conceit to listen to aught that did not concern your all-important self!"

Devenish seized his arm. "Confound you! I'll make you eat those words!"

"Yap, puppydog," Craig taunted.

Devenish's fist swung up. Craig's hand flashed to catch his wrist. For an instant they stood there, eye to blazing eye, the Canadian's fair young might straining to hold back the Englishman's slighter but powerful arm. And then, with a sweep, Craig released his grip and moved back.

"Do you see now? D'ye see how easy it would be? I came out here to bid you farewell, and only look at us! Another moment and—"

"And you would have done—what? Murdered me?"

"Did *you* mean to kill *me*? Think, man! Did you?"

"Don't be so blasted ridiculous! Pummel your cloddish head, perhaps. No more. For Lord's sake, Tyndale, do you really believe I've murder in mind?"

"No more than I believe my father had. But this morning when you attacked me—"

"Dash it all, did you fancy your life in danger then?"

375

"No. But when you tricked me and I grassed you, you went down mighty hard, cousin. Suppose your head had hit a rock? With what lies between us, who would have believed I did not deliberately put a period to you?"

Devenish avoided that earnest gaze and said an uneasy, "Very few people know what lies between us."

"It would all come out, certainly. And what would that do to your uncle?" After a brief silence, Craig went on, "I came to tell you that I am leaving. While I am in Scotland, I mean to find out whatever I may about the death of your father. And I swear—so long as I live, should we ever meet again, no matter how you may provoke me, I'll never raise my hand against you!"

For a long moment they stared at one another in a silent measuring, both faces grim until a twinkle dawned in Devenish's eyes. He said, irrepressibly, "How relieved I am. I shall be safe."

Tyndale's lips tightened. "Goodbye, then. I mean to leave at once. I have already sent Montelongo ahead with my chaise and luggage."

Devenish nodded. Craig started off, hesitated, then turned back. "We will not meet again, cousin. Will you not at least say goodbye to me?"

"No need," said Devenish cheerfully, coming up with him. "I ride with you."

"You—*what?* In spite of all I have said, you still think I pursue Cousin Yolande?"

"No. But since you raise the question, I'll have no interference in that quarter."

"Naturally. Unless the lady should—er—change her mind. After all, no formal announcement has yet been made, so she is not irrevocably bound."

"*Bound?* Why, you insolent bumpkin, I—" Devenish burst into a laugh. "Off we go again! Lord, it will be a miracle do we not come to blows before the day is out. But by hedge or stile, I go with you. I mean to prove to my uncle that, however aggravating you may be, I can rise above such petty annoyances. That I can control my—ah—natural instincts and travel beside you, turning the other cheek to your boorish ways and smug fatuities, and maintaining always my usual calm dignity."

Tyndale demonstrated how aggravating he could be. He gave a shout of laughter.

* * *

"What a perfectly lovely morning," said Yolande from beneath the protection of her sunshade. "I am so glad you suggested that we walk back to the hotel after church."

Mr. James Garvey directed a glance from the vibrant blooms of the gardens through which they strolled on this balmy Sunday, to the lovely face of the lady beside him, framed as it was in a very dainty high-poked bonnet of cream straw, with pale blue velvet ribbons that tied demurely under her dimpled chin. "I had at first thought we might go for an early ride," he said. "But then I supposed you have had sufficient of riding."

She smiled up at him. "I have indeed. You are a most thoughtful escort, sir."

"It has been my very great pleasure, ma'am. Indeed, I am most gratified you do not visit relations along your way, else I should be sent packing, I do not doubt."

"As a matter of fact, we had intended to, but—" She checked and said a careful, "It is—er—imperative that we reach Ayrshire as quickly as possible, and you know how it is with family—you stop to visit for just a little while, and perhaps have dinner, but they are so eager to entertain you that a week passes in a twinkling. Papa decided it was best that we travel straight on."

"And most fortunate for me."

She blushed prettily. "I am assured you will find a way to contradict me, sir, but I cannot continue to take you out of your way."

"I should not presume to contradict so lovely a lady, but will point out, rather, that since I also am bound for Scotland, I would certainly travel the Great North Road."

"Yes, but you must have noted, Mr. Garvey, that we do not make rapid progress. You could travel much faster alone."

"And much less happily!" He drew her to a halt. "Miss Drummond, am I encroaching? These past three days have been a delight for me, but I pray you believe that you have only to say the word and I will leave you in peace."

Yolande scanned the anxious features of this most eligible bachelor and could only like what she saw. Rumour had it . . . But rumour was so often based on petty jealousy. He had been more than kind and, while openly admiring, had not once stepped beyond the bounds of good manners. Aunt Arabella was captivated, for Mr. Garvey spared no effort to show her every attention, never—as was so often the case with gentlemen—granting the older lady the barest of civilities while attempting to ingratiate himself with the younger.

"Our journey must have been a great deal more tedious without your many kindnesses, sir," she said. "For instance, our dinner last night and the play were both so enjoyable."

"You are too kind. I had feared the farce might offend your aunt—it was a little broad. But the play was well done, I thought."

Mrs. Drummond had privately expressed herself as considerably scandalized, but Yolande, no mean judge of character, had suspected that both her aunt and Mr. Garvey had by far preferred the rather naughty comedy of the farce to the melodrama of *The Milkmaid's Secret—or—A Tattered Tinker.* She kept these conclusions to herself, however, continuing to chat easily with Mr. Garvey as they made their way along the sun-dappled paths of the little park and thence to thoroughfares busy with open carriages, their elegantly garbed occupants out for a Sunday drive. Several people recognized her companion and waved a greeting. He was very well acquainted, naturally, thought Yolande, and wondered again why he was going to so much trouble to escort two ladies he scarcely knew. Early in their journeying he had said that he was bound for Stirling, but Aunt Arabella had remarked in private that the gentleman was obviously bewitched, and that she would not be in the least surprised did he persist in escorting them all the way to Steep Drummond. Yolande was too level-headed to believe this suave Corinthian was exactly bewitched. It was said sufficient handkerchiefs had been dropped for him that he would stand knee-deep in them were they all gathered around him at once. Still, he was evidently willing to slow his own progress, and she had been sincere when she'd thanked him for relieving the tedium of their journey. His cheerful presence had done much to divert Aunt Arabella's tiresome chatter and had enabled Yolande to relegate her own perplexities to a far corner of her mind—at least during the hours of daylight.

The afternoon was growing warm by the time their walk was concluded, and Mr. Garvey was handing Yolande up the front steps of their hotel when the diminutive and ferocious boy who served him as tiger approached. He was, as always, very smart in his scarlet-and-gold livery, but Mr. Garvey eyed him with just the trace of a frown. The boy, he ruefully admitted to Yolande, had been bred up in the gutter and, despite all his own efforts, still used such language as must shock any gently nurtured lady. Despite this unenthused reception, the tiger knuckled his brow and bestowed a meaningful look on his employer.

"I collect," sighed Mr. Garvey, "you have got into some mischief from which I am now expected to extricate you. Is it something you can manage to convey without offence to the ears of Miss Drummond?"

The tiger glanced at Yolande and hung his head.

Mr. Garvey nodded. "As I suspected. I fear I must investigate at once, ma'am. If I know this rascal I am quite likely to find the town beadle awaiting with a warrant for my immediate arrest! May I have the honour of escorting you down to dinner? Six o'clock? Or is that too countrified?"

Yolande said that six o'clock would be just right, favoured both Mr. Garvey and his tiger, who bore the droll name of Lion, with one of her brightest smiles, and made her way to the suite she shared with her aunt.

"Here I am at last, dear," she said, opening the door to the parlour that separated their rooms. "Have I been—" She checked, and stood motionless on the threshold.

Two young man had sprung up at her entrance. Two men dissimilar in everything save their fair colouring and something indefinable that she had not quite been able to place. Her wide gaze dwelling a shade longer on the taller of the pair, she gasped, "Alain . . . ! And—Craig! What on earth . . . ?"

"Discovered you was here, my fair." Devenish beamed, striding over to claim her hand and drop a proprietary kiss on her brow.

"B-but," she said unsteadily, freeing her hand so as to extend it to Tyndale, "how? That is— I thought—" Her hand being taken and bowed over, she was struck by some invisible lightning bolt and so unnerved that she at once summoned a fierce frown and levelled it at the unfortunate Devenish.

"Oh, but this is too bad of you, Alain. You know full well my parents wished me to be free from all entanglements so that I might—"

"Entanglements, is it?" he protested with righteous indignation. "Now, see here, Yolande, I ain't no entanglement! I've come rushing here purely so as to escort you—"

Striving to appear collected, when he was in fact badly shaken, Craig drawled, "I thought you were escorting *me*!"

"Yes, but Yolande is so much prettier." Yolande was also obviously astounded by this apparently amicable exchange, and

Devenish grinned, swung the door to, and imparted, "Ain't no need for you to be in a pucker lest I slaughter our Colonial bumpkin, coz. We have declared a truce. Now why in the world would you do so shatter-brained a thing as to journey to Scotland for the summer?"

"I do not see that it should be judged shatter-brained if I visit my grandpapa." Yolande removed her lacy shawl as she spoke and, Craig, being closest, at once took it from her.

Devenish leapt forward and all but tore the reticule from her hand. "You did not tell me you meant to go!" he complained, with a fierce scowl at Craig.

"No. Nor do I need an escort, Dev."

" 'Course you need an escort! A single lady jauntering about—"

Mrs. Drummond made an entrance at this point, hurrying from her bedchamber, proclaiming that she had sent Sullivan out with "him," and that he would soon feel better. She gave a little squeak of surprise when she saw Yolande. "Oh! You are come back, love. Did you have a nice walk? Was not the sermon inspiring this morning?" She cast a stern glance at the gentlemen. " 'Vengeance is mine, saith the Lord!' "

Happily misinterpreting the quotation, Devenish soothed, "Do not get up into the boughs, ma'am. Tyndale's becoming accustomed to it."

Puzzled, Yolande asked, "Accustomed to what?"

"Good old Socrates went after some Canadian beef again. Aunt Arabella had to struggle to restrain him."

"Oh, my goodness! That wretched little beast!" Yolande moved to sit beside her aunt on the rather faded sofa. "You really should keep him on a lead, Aunt Arabella."

"No, but it was famous," Devenish exclaimed, blithely ignoring the thoughtful gaze Craig turned upon him. "That was how we discovered you was here."

Mrs. Drummond said a surprised, "You did not know? But I had supposed you were seeking to come up with us."

"No, ma'am." Tyndale settled himself against a side table. "Devenish guides me to my inheritance. At least, he says that is what he's about."

"Your inheritance . . . ? Surely you never mean that horrid old haunted castle on the edge of the cliffs?"

"Aunt!" gasped Yolande, her apologetic glance flying to Craig's impassive features. "What a thing to say!"

"It is truth, after all," said Devenish, suddenly grim. "I understand you have been put in possession of all the hideous facts, Yolande?"

"I marvel that you two gentlemen can be so convivial," Mrs. Drummond interposed. "Now in *my* young days—"

"I am delighted you are so *civilized*," Yolande interjected swiftly. And in a desperate attempt to change the subject, "Only think, Aunt, we shall now have *six* escorts!"

"If the arrival of your cousins does not discourage our charming gallant," Mrs. Drummond pouted.

Devenish and Tyndale exchanged taut glances. "Gallant?" Tyndale murmured.

"What—has some impertinent fellow been annoying you?" asked Devenish, bristling.

Mrs. Drummond tittered. "*Annoying?* An odd way to describe a gentleman who is all consideration. Quite, in fact, the most courteous and charming man I have met this twelve-month and more!" Her sharp eyes rested fixedly on Tyndale as she spoke, and he reddened and looked away.

Devenish experienced an odd surge of resentment. His unwanted cousin was a clod, and Lord knows he had reason to detest the fellow, but—he *was* family. With a hauteur that startled Tyndale and astonished Yolande, he said, "Then I'm obliged to him. Perhaps I may have the name and direction of this paragon?"

For a second, Mrs. Drummond fancied it had been the Colonel who spoke and she was shocked into silence.

Yolande said, "His direction is here, for he stays at the hotel. I fancy you are already acquainted, Alain, for he is very highly regarded and you may see him everywhere. He is Mr. James Garvey, and I—"

Devenish, who had disposed himself with careless grace upon an arm of the sofa, uttered a muffled exclamation and shot to his feet. "*Garvey?* By God! Why the deuce is *that* loose fish hanging about you?"

Mrs. Drummond uttered a shriek and clapped protecting hands over her ears. Yolande frowned upon her suitor. Intrigued, Tyndale waited.

With no more than a rageful look at Mrs. Drummond, Devenish started for the door.

"Wait!" Yolande ran to stand before him. "Whatever is wrong? Mr. Garvey is the best of good *ton*!"

"Much you know about it! Stand aside, miss!"

"No! Are you run quite mad, Dev? Mr. Garvey is a close friend of the Prince, and—"

"Which of itself should tell you something! Move, I say!"

"I shall *not* move!" She leaned back against the door, barring her seething suitor's way, her eyes flashing with rare anger. "Devenish, I warn you! Do you embarrass me with your unsufferable jealousy, do you insult a gentleman who has been all that is helpful and conciliating—"

"I'll conciliate the b—" Devenish gritted his teeth as Mrs. Drummond again squealed.

Yolande threw a frantic glance at Tyndale. "Cousin Craig! He is insupportable! You must see that!"

"I do, indeed, ma'am," he drawled with his slow smile.

"Oh, do you? Damn you!" snarled Devenish.

A moan arose from Mrs. Drummond.

"Then—stop him!" Yolande implored.

Craig said gently, "Your wish is my command. At any other time. But now, I think it would be best that you should stand aside, Cousin Yolande."

"So much for your promises and declarations!" Her temper thoroughly aroused, Yolande did not pause to reflect that the only promises and declarations that had passed between them had been silent ones, conveyed by the eyes.

Devenish fired up at once. "So you've made promises and declarations, have you? You'll answer to me for that treachery, bumpkin! Yolande—blast it all! Move aside!"

"Profanity will not move me!" she declared, assuming an Early Christian Martyr pose that must have made the great Sarah Siddons envious.

"In that case," he said, grimly determined, "I'll go out the window."

He strode across the room. Knowing him to be quite capable of doing just that, Yolande uttered a shriek and ran after him. He eluded her by means of a lithe spring over the sofa, drawing a faint yelp from Mrs. Drummond, and was to the door and in the hall in a flash.

Callously ignoring her aunt, who was flapping a handkerchief feebly at her face, Yolande ran wildly after Devenish. "Do *not*! Alain! If you do, I *never* will speak to you again!"

"Silly chit!" Devenish shouted, racing down the stairs.

Distraught, Yolande turned and pounced upon Craig. "Stop him! Oh, you *must* stop him! This is utterly disgraceful! I shall be humiliated beyond bearing. Can you not see that he is crazed with jealousy? And—poor Mr. Garvey has done nothing! Nothing!"

"From what I have heard, cousin, Mr. Garvey has traits you could not be expected to—"

"Why do you not help me?" She tugged at him distractedly. "*Do* something!"

He took up her hand and kissed it gently. "Do not worry so. I very much doubt it will come to a duel."

Sudden tears blinded Yolande. Frightened by the unfamiliar emotions stirring in her heart, she took refuge in anger. "A duel! Oh, you are just as bad as Devenish! I think you both utter—utter *boors*! I had sooner be escorted by—by warthogs! And so you may tell Dev!"

The corners of his mouth twitched suspiciously. "I suppose," he sighed, "it's no great distance from a clod to a warthog. Very well—I will go and try to keep Devenish from throttling your beau ideal."

"Oh! He is not! How dare you!"

Craig looked at her affronted beauty with a rueful smile, bowed, and left.

Mrs. Drummond who had viewed the exchange with interest, soothed, "Never fear, my love. Dear Mr. Garvey will be quite capable of defending himself against those two uncouth creatures."

Yolande choked out, "Oh—Aunt!" and burst into tears.

❧ *Chapter 6* ❧

"One thing," said Devenish savagely, sauntering back across the cobbled stableyard, "according to the ostler, the silly court card will be back before evening, and you may depend on it I shall soon nip in the bud any plans he may have to escort Yolande in to dinner."

Tyndale glanced curiously at his cousin's set scowl. "Is he?"

"Taking her in to dinner? Doubtless he thinks so. It is perfectly obvious that he has made a strong bid to engage her affections, which only proves what a ramshackle cawker he is! Only a few weeks back he was in a passion because Justin Strand is to wed Lisette Van Lindsay."

"And this Garvey admired the lady?"

"Fairly slathering for her."

"Hmmm. He would appear to make a fast recover. However, you misunderstood my initial question. What I meant was, is this Garvey a silly court card? Yolande seems to rate him high."

"He's a damn slippery customer is what he is! Trust a woman to see no further than a handsome face!"

Tyndale shot him an amused glance.

Devenish growled, "Do not dare say it!" and stamped in through the door a boy ran to swing open.

Chuckling, Tyndale tossed the boy a coin and followed his cousin into the cool and fragrant hall. Devenish sniffed. "Ale. By gad, but it tempts me and I've no wish to go upstairs, at all events."

Tyndale accompanied him into the dim old tap and they occupied settles on either side of an oak table that was dark with years. Tyndale called an order for a jug of ale. Turning back, he was met by a cold stare and lifted one eyebrow enquiringly. "Are you still raging about my alleged promises and declarations?"

"I shall take your word as a gentleman that you did no more than offer any service you might to my lady. Nonetheless, I wonder that you do not gallop above stairs and charm her with the news I could not find Garvey."

Tyndale smiled thoughtfully. "She was not encouraging."

"So I should hope!"

"She said, in fact, that she would sooner be escorted by— warthogs!"

"Did she now. Er—plural . . . ?"

"Decidedly plural."

Awed, Devenish murmured, "By . . . Jove!" Then broke into a shout of laughter. "What a termagant she can be! But it only adds spice to her charm, bless her! I shall have to spruce up a bit for dinner and try to mend my fences, if— Oh, my God!" He directed a dismayed gaze at Tyndale: "This morning we sent Monty on to Northampton with the chaise and all our luggage! Damn! I shall have to send a groom after him!"

A message having been despatched to the stables, the two men settled down to enjoy their ale. Sighing his appreciation, Tyndale set down the tankard and asked, "How is our friend Garvey, a . . . er, slippery customer?"

"Why, he's supposed to be such a bosom bow of Prinny's, ain't he? Oh, Lord! I keep forgetting you don't know anyone! Well, he is. But—" Devenish glanced around the empty tap.

Tyndale said an amused, "State secrets, cousin?"

Devenish met his eyes gravely. "After a fashion. I mean to tell you some of it, because there's just the barest chance Garvey may have seen me and made himself least in sight. If that is so, I'd not put it past him to—" He frowned. "Never mind. But one of us must be here to keep an eye on Yolande."

This was a side of his cousin he'd not seen before. Intrigued, Tyndale leaned forward. "Has he 'done a deed whereat valour will weep'?"

"So you did go to school! I am all admiration."

"And I am all ears."

"You had better be part discretion. I'll have your word you won't repeat any of this, Tyndale."

"You have it." There could be no doubt but that Devenish was deadly serious. Impressed by this calm stranger, Tyndale begged, "Please go on. He's more than silly, I take it."

"I judge him by the company he keeps. You will remember our earlier discussion regarding Tristram Leith? As I told you, Tris is a grand fellow. He was at Waterloo and rather badly mauled. An English lady named Rachel Strand found and tended him, and he fell head over ears into love with her. Unfortunately, it turned out she was already promised. To a Frenchman. A quiet little fellow named Claude Sanguinet, richer than Golden Ball, up to his eyebrows in international intrigues, and as safe to annoy as any Bengal tiger."

Tyndale's brows went up. "And—Leith annoyed him?"

"Considerably. Tristram was shattered, you see, when he fancied Miss Strand lost to him." His gaze becoming reminiscent, Devenish went on, "At about that same time, my governor and I having had—er, a slight misunderstanding, I was drifting about Sussex. Tristram came back to England, and we met and joined forces. I won't go into the details—suffice it to say that Tris discovered his lady's betrothed, this Sanguinet fellow, was up to some very dirty work indeed. A scheme that threatened the safety, perhaps the very life, of our Fair Florizel."

"The Regent?" Tyndale whistled softly. "The plot thickens. Did Miss Strand know of all this?"

"Not a glimmer. And when Leith realized what she was getting mixed up in, he went to her home to warn her. Unfortunately, Miss Strand had already gone to Brittany for her betrothal ball."

"I doubt that would stop him," muttered Tyndale. "He followed, eh?"

"We both did. I—" Devenish checked and, scanning his cousin's faintly amused expression with a suspicious frown, demanded, "See here—do you know Leith?"

Tyndale blinked at him. "How the devil could a simple Colonial be acquainted with Colonel the Honourable Tristram Leith?"

"I suppose not, but—Hey! I didn't say he was a Colonel! Nor an Honourable, neither!"

"Did you not? Gracious me. Told you I've heard about him. He's quite famous, after all. Do go on, Sir Coz."

Devenish regarded him dubiously. There had been some talk, of course, despite the Horse Guards' struggles to keep everything quiet, and there was no knowing how many people Tyndale may have met before he'd come to Aspenhill.

The picture of interested innocence, Tyndale prompted, "You were saying that Leith followed his lady to Brittany, and that you accompanied him."

"Yes." Devenish nodded, still frowning. "And never in all my days have I seen a chateau so beautiful as Sanguinet's, nor one filled with a more unsavoury lot of guests. We had walked into a veritable hornets' nest of intrigue, and had our hands full getting the girl and her sister out of it, I can tell you!"

"But you did get them out? How? Come on, coz! You're leaving out all the meat of the tale."

"It is too long a story for me to relate now. The point is . . ." Devenish paused, all this chatter having increased his thirst. He attended to the matter, set down his tankard and resumed. "The point is, my clod, that in amongst that nasty little clutch of ruthless, scheming connivers was our own James Garvey, Esquire. The Regent's bosom bow."

"Now was he, by God!" breathed Tyndale. "And what did you and Leith do about that nasty little gathering?"

His eyes dancing, Devenish said with choirboy meekness,

"Do about it? Why, we enjoyed a dish of Bohea with Sanguinet, pointed our toes in a stylish quadrille, and toddled back home with the ladies."

"Damn you, cousin! I want the truth of it."

"So do a lot of others." Devenish grinned but shook his head and said firmly, "No, really, Tyndale, I've told you the only part that need concern you, and enough that you should understand why I take a very dim view of our dandified Buck."

"I can, indeed. But—no! For Lord's sake, you cannot leave me in this puzzle! Did you not warn the Horse Guards, the Foreign Office?"

Devenish stared at the tankard he turned slowly on the table, and said dryly, "We did. Wherefore Leith is no longer a Colonel." He looked up and met his cousin's incredulous stare. "True. He was—er, it was politely suggested that he resign his commission."

"The devil!"

"Precisely. Our Monsieur Claude Sanguinet is a *very* powerful gentleman!" He glanced around again and, although there was no other within earshot, murmured, "And you will not forget you gave me your word?"

"Of course not. But we must keep Garvey away from Yolande."

"I mean to. But, just in case—" Devenish broke off as a groom came in, peered through the dim room, then wandered over to their table.

"Beg pardin, sirs," he said, touching his cap respectfully. "Be ye the gents as was wishful to look at Sir Aubrey Suffield's team, s'arternoon?"

"Wrong gents," replied Tyndale with his pleasant smile.

His blue eyes alight with excitement, Devenish asked, "*Suffield*, did you say? Sir Aubrey is never selling those bays of his? To whom?"

The groom shrugged. "I dunno, sir. He said the gents would be waiting in the tap. I thought as it was you. I'd best see if I can find my proper party." He begged their pardon again, and departed.

Afire with eagerness, Devenish jumped up. "What a bit of luck!"

Standing also, Tyndale asked, "You know this Suffield?"

"Everyone does. Except you, of course. He's a regular Top Sawyer! A member of the Four Horse Club. Drives to an inch.

No man living is a keener judge of horseflesh. I'll wager its Lucian St. Clair who's after those bays! I just may steal a march on him!"

Starting into the hall, they encountered Mrs. Drummond, a leashed Socrates panting along beside her.

"Well, gentlemen," she sniffed. "And did you find poor Mr. Garvey? Does the poor soul lie out under the sun somewhere, with a broken head?"

"Good God!" muttered Devenish, *sotto voce*.

"He was gone out, ma'am," imparted Tyndale, accompanying the lady to the stairs.

"One can but hope that by the time he returns, you both will have thought better of your violent inclinations. Come, Socrates! Mama's little boy can manage these stairs, surely? Up we go!"

"Mama's little boy" struggled up the first step, planted his front paws on the second, and waited. Grinning broadly, Devenish leaned against the wall.

Ever courteous, Tyndale asked if he might be of some service.

Mrs. Drummond eyed him without appreciable gratitude. "Well," she said grudgingly, "perhaps you may, at that. The poor darling ate rather too much nuncheon, I fear, and he is a trifle feeble these days."

Mindful of his earlier encounters with "darling," Tyndale asked uneasily, "Should you wish me to carry him, ma'am?"

"No. He does not like to be taken up. He is too proud, aren't you, my love? He only needs a helping hand, poor fellow. If you would be so kind as to just give his little rumpty a lift up each step, he can be spared embarrassment, and I expect we shall go on nicely."

This declaration brought tears of appreciation to Devenish's eyes. Enjoying himself hugely, he waited. Socrates, still maintaining his stance, turned his head and watched Tyndale's cautious approach, a glint in his beady eyes.

Tyndale liked dogs, but this particular animal he would sooner have shown his boot than a "helping hand." Nonetheless, Mrs. Drummond was Yolande's aunt. . . . He bent, therefore, and with one eye on the dog's still sharp set of fangs, supplied the required boost. The stairs were long and winding, and Socrates' progress was not rapid. Several interested onlookers gathered, sniggering. Under other circumstances, Devenish would have howled his mirth, but as it was, he clapped a hand over his mouth and succeeded for the most part in stifling his hilarity. Tyndale sensed that his subjugation was being observed by appreciative eyes. He darted a mortified glance downward. As a result, his boost was too precipitate.

"Oh!" wailed Mrs. Drummond. "You made him hurt his dear little nose."

Socrates was less vocal. His head darted around and he gave the hand that helped him a good nip.

Tyndale jerked his hand back and clutched it, his narrowed eyes registering his wrath. Socrates hopped nimbly up the three remaining stairs and stood at the top, grinning his defiance. Devenish, wiping tears from his eyes, fled.

"Did he nip you a little?" asked Mrs. Drummond. "Oh, see that—it is scarcely bleeding at all. If you will just twist your handkerchief around it, I will bathe it for you. Come along, little rascal! Much you care for all the bother your poor mama is put to!"

Ten minutes later, his injury having been bathed, sprinkled with basilicum powder and not very neatly bandaged, Tyndale strode along the hall, lips tight and eyes glittering with mortification. He could only pray that he might not encounter any of those people who had witnessed that ridiculous scene upon the stairs. The very thought made him grind his teeth, and to add to his chagrin, despite having made a complete cake of himself, he had not been rewarded by even a glimpse of the delectable Yolande. Mrs. Drummond had said accusingly that her niece was laid down upon her bed, resting, and much upset by the actions of her cousins. And, glorying in her grievance, she had expounded at great length on the peculiar manners and morals of today's young people, so that by the time her ministrations were completed he had been both irritated and eager to make his escape. He gripped his right wrist; his hand felt bruised to the bone and smarted like the deuce. That blasted little cur had caught him fairly. And it served him right. It was pointless to yearn for a last sight of Yolande. She was hopelessly beyond his reach; the sooner he accepted that fact, the less miserable he could be. He sighed and ran lightly downstairs.

The stableyard was deserted at this drowsy hour of the afternoon, and he crossed it briskly. In certain quarters he was accounted quite a judge of horseflesh, and he was every bit as eager as his cousin to see Suffield's famous team. He slowed his steps as he entered the couch house, narrowing his eyes to adjust to the dimness. Someone called, "Over here, sir!" and he started towards a stall where he could discern a gentleman engaged in inspecting the teeth of a horse. Too tall for Devenish, he thought.

A soft footfall behind him brought with it the sense of danger, sudden and strong, and he reacted with an instinctive swing around. He was too late. He did not feel the blow that struck him down; rather, it seemed that the gloom was rent by a searing explosion. He had a brief, confused thought that one of poor Whynyates' rockets had found him. . . .

Mr. James Garvey, resplendent in a jacket of maroon Bath suiting and a cravat that had caused Yolande to wish that her brother John (an aspiring dandy) might see it, frowned thoughtfully at his empty plate. "I fear I must disagree with you, my dear lady," he said. "Rackety, Devenish may be, but as your niece says, it does seem a trifle odd that he and his cousin should have departed with word to none." He looked with grave sympathy into Yolande's anxious eyes. How very pretty she was in that misty green evening gown, and how wisely she had chosen to wear no jewellery, allowing the eye to dwell undistracted upon her fair skin. She was not as lovely as his adored Lisette, of course, but very pretty indeed. And useful, for anyone chancing to see him on his northward journey could now read nothing more into it than that he escorted two ladies. Perfectly innocuous. And with the threat that Devenish constituted now happily removed, he could proceed to his destination with perfect equanimity. "You said, I believe," he murmured, "that you last saw your cousins early in the afternoon?"

Yolande nodded. "Soon after we returned from church. I will own I was a trifle annoyed by—by a small disagreement, but I had not thought they would just leave." She added worriedly, "It is so unlike Devenish."

"Perhaps the Canadian fellow was upset because Socrates bit him," said Mrs. Drummond, off-handedly.

"I doubt that, Aunt Arabella. He did not seem angry when I arrived home from church."

"Oh, that's right! I had forgot that time."

"Good heavens! Never say it happened again?"

"While you were resting, my love. I brought Mr. Tyndale, for somehow I cannot endure to call him 'nephew,' or Craig, he seems so—so *alien*! Where was I? Oh, yes—I fetched him up here and tended him, though it was not a bad bite at all, and soon stopped bleeding."

"*Bleeding!* Oh, Aunt Arabella! I wish you had not brought Socrates! He has the most horrid disposition."

At once firing up in defence of her pet, Mrs. Drummond wailed, "How *can* you blame it on my poor doggie? If truth be told, Mr. Tyndale brought it on himself, for had he not hurt Socrates' little nose, the dear pet would not have bitten the clumsy creature!"

"Craig hurt Socrates?" gasped Yolande, considerably taken aback. "But—but, why?"

"You may well ask, though I'm sure it is all of a piece. He is, after all, from a wild frontier, and obviously more accustomed to deal with savages than civilized ladies and gentlemen. Only think of how he almost brought about your own death, my dear."

"Did he, by thunder?" ejaculated Mr. Garvey, straightening in his chair. "It would seem that you are well rid of the fellow, Miss Drummond."

Irked, Yolande said, "It is not quite as it sounds, sir. There was an accident, true, but Mr. Tyndale rescued me from it most gallantly."

"Oh, *very* gallantly, I am sure!" said Mrs. Drummond, huffily. "And not a thought for *me*, lying senseless in a ditch! It's a wonder my neck was not broke, and indeed I still suffer so many aches and pains that I feel sure it will be found I have taken some grievous inner hurt!"

"Of course Craig thought of you!" Yolande flared hotly. "We both did! I am assured he would never have left you had there not been others to aid you, whereas I was helpless, with the team bolting as they were. I truly am sorry you were so badly shaken, Aunt, but Craig—"

"No, no, never apologize, dear love," Mrs. Drummond inserted in honeyed tones, but with her eyes sparkling. "Indeed, I can but marvel at the forbearance that leads you to intercede for the crude fellow. Under the circumstances."

Flushed with vexation, and looking, or so thought James Garvey, exceedingly lovely, Yolande fell into the trap. "Circumstances? What circumstances? The circumstance that having unwittingly endangered my life, Cousin Craig proceeded very bravely to save it?"

"Why—no, dearest," purred her aunt with sublime innocence. "I had meant simply the circumstance of your being promised to dear Alain Devenish. And the Colonial being so obviously—however presumptuously—enamoured of you!"

Thoroughly angered, Yolande prepared to retaliate with the remark that since she *was* to wed Devenish and that Craig was aware of the fact, her defence of him was as devoid of interest as it was impartial. But she could not speak the words and, tongue-tied, her face flaming, she knew why. Her feelings for Craig Tyndale could, under no circumstances, be described as being devoid of interest.

Mrs. Drummond had little use for Alain Devenish, but she was aware that he was a peerless suitor if compared to his Canadian cousin. Triumphant, she smiled a faint but smug smile through a brief, pregnant pause.

Hiding amusement, Mr. Garvey reached out to place his well-manicured fingers over Mrs. Drummond's hand, lying upon the tablecloth. "Poor little lady," he soothed gently. "How worried your niece must have been for your sake. And how pleased I am that you have effected such a remarkable recovery, so that I may beg you will both accompany me this evening. It would seem there is to be a lecture in the Parish Hall upon the words of Lawrence and a young fellow called Constable. I am no connoisseur of the arts, but I understand the paintings of several local artists will also be on display, and it might prove an entertainment to suit the sensibilities of such gentle ladies as yourselves."

Mrs. Drummond was pleased to accept. Turning to the quiet Yolande, Mr. Garvey gave her a surreptitious grin so full of mischief that her disturbed heart was eased. "You are too kind to us, sir," she protested gratefully.

He shook his head and said with perfect, if oblique, honesty, "Miss Drummond, you cannot know what it means to me to be allowed to keep such charming company."

"Such graciousness," sighed Mrs. Drummond, as she climbed the stairs to prepare for the outing. "Such an air! Oh, Yolande, how it would gladden my heart to see you wed so perfect a gentleman as Mr. Garvey."

Yolande scarcely heard her. "I wonder," she muttered, "wherever they can be."

Mrs. Drummond tossed her head. "If I know anything at all in the matter," she said tartly, "they are likely carousing in some tavern in an intoxicated condition, and will awaken with fearful headaches, wishing themselves dead!"

* * *

Fervently wishing himself dead, Alain Devenish dragged his unco-operative body out of the ditch and again sprawled, face down, at the side of the lane, too nauseated to move another inch. He had, he told himself fuzzily, probably felt worse in his life. He could not remember when. His head ached dully, he felt wretchedly ill, and his leg was pounding so that he clutched at it miserably. Dimly, he was nudged by a sense of urgency; of something vital he must accomplish with the least possible delay, and obedient to that spur he struggled upwards, fighting the nausea until it overwhelmed him and he sank down and was very sick. For a while he lay still, not thinking at all, drenched in a cold sweat and lacking the strength of a newborn kitten. But gradually he began to feel less limp and, after what seemed a very long time, he crept slowly to his knees and thence to his feet. The lane, the dark loom of hedges, the violet skies of evening, tilted slowly to the right. He closed his eyes, gritted his teeth, and hung on. When he peeped through his lashes once more, the countryside had righted itself. His first few steps were uncertain, but in a little while he was going along less erratically. Still, it was several more minutes before he began to wonder why he was here, and where "here" was.

Puzzled, he slowed, then stopped. A large badger, very wet, trotted busily into the lane, paused to shake itself, then froze, petrified, as it saw the human so near to it. There was water nearby, then, thought Devenish. The badger watched, undecided as to whether a retreat or an attack was indicated. Devenish started to bow, thought better of it, and said softly, "Good evening, Mr. Badger. Alain Devenish at your service." The badger abandoned its deliberations and waited fearlessly. Devenish put it in possession of the fact that he had been properly hornswoggled. "I was," he advised, "half suffocated, drugged, and tossed into a ditch. And let me tell you, sir, that if the party I suspect of this dastardly crime was in truth responsible, it is a miracle I yet live!" The badger took a few unhurried steps. "Off to your club, eh?" said Devenish. "Then, if you've no objection, I do believe I shall avail myself of your bath." The badger paused, twitched its long whiskers, and went upon its way.

Devenish watched it, a faint smile lurking about his mouth, then turned aside, crossed the ditch, found a break in the hedgerow and emerged into a wide meadow that sloped downwards to a distant gleam that was the river. Starting thitherward with quickening step, he tensed and stopped. *Yolande!* His lovely little lady was at the mercy of that miserable libertine, Garvey! Trusting him! Supposing him to be—what was it she'd said? "All that is conciliating!" He thought, "*Conciliating!* My God!" He must get to her, and as fast as may be! But starting off, he again checked, the sense that he was followed bringing a recollection of the vicious assault in the stable. He swung around, ready for battle, his keen eyes scanning the quiet loom of the hedge. But there was no movement this time; no rush of dark forms, no sickly-smelling rag to be clapped over his nostrils with the resultant and immediate weakness that had been so swiftly followed by unconsciousness. Perhaps it was only the badger, who had decided to come this way after all. He resumed his route. "Not too sociable creatures, badgers," he advised a field mouse as it scampered past. "But far more decent," he went on, his usually humorous mouth settling into a stern line, "than many of us who walk on two legs!"

The evening air was sweet with the scents of damp earth and honeysuckle, and vibrant with the small, myriad voices of the night dwellers; the warning call of an owl, the pattering progress of some water rat or mole, countless chirps and rustlings that ceased abruptly as Devenish approached the river. Coming to the bank, he sat down, pulled off boots and stockings, divested himself of coat, cravat, and shirt, rolled up his breeches, and stepped gingerly into the water. He gasped and danced a little to that icy immersion, but waded deeper, bent, and with the aid of his handkerchief managed to wash himself quite well. The cold water took his breath but set his skin to tingling and his head began to throb less viciously. When he felt sufficiently cleansed, he trod rapidly up the bank, and then stood very still, listening.

The sounds of the night had resumed when he'd begun to take off his clothes, but now all was very silent. The breathless hush was of itself a warning. He thought, "So I was right the first time!"

"You might as well have taked off the lot," said a clear, childish voice. "You're all over wetness."

Devenish, who had jumped at the first word, now continued up the bank, peering at the small, dark outline beside his discarded garments. "Who the deuce are you?" he enquired, then hopped as he trod on a sharp pebble and added an exasperated, "Dammitall!"

The small figure backed away.

"My apologies. No—do not go away," Devenish pleaded. "What are you doing out alone after dark like this? You should be laid down upon your bed."

"Never mind about me," said the child with surprising firmness. "I may be all of my ownness. But I is not touched in the upper works."

Devenish was beginning to shiver. "N-no more than I. Are you a boy?"

"'Course. What are you going to dry on?"

"My shirt." He took it up and began to scrub vigorously. "It will dry as I go along. And because a fellow bathes in the river, don't mean he's a looby."

"Anyone what puts his whole self—or most of it—into the river at night, is crazy. But it ain't 'cause of that I thought it. I heered you talking to the badger."

Beginning to feel a little warmer, Devenish laughed, pulled the shirt briskly back and forth across his shoulders, then shook it out and began to put it on. "So you were watching, were you? I thought someone was. As for the badger—well, when a fellow's alone he talks to all manner of things. I didn't frighten him, you know."

"I know. You got Rat Paws."

"I've—what?"

The child shrank back behind one protectively upflung arm. "Don't ye clout me! Oh, don't you never clout me!"

"Curse and confound it!" fumed Devenish. "I'm not going to hit you. Put your blasted arm down at once!"

With slow caution that guarding arm was lowered. A scared voice whimpered, "Lor', but you get so cross, so quick! I be afeared!"

Devenish winced. Even from this unknown child! "My wretched temper," he muttered contritely. "I'm sorry, boy. Now, tell me why you made that revol—er, that unkind remark about my hands." He held out one slim, neatly manicured member and peered at it by the light of the rising half-moon. "They ain't that bad, surely?"

"Rat Paws don't mean *hands*! Cor!" the scorn was apparent. "Don't you know *nothink*? It means as you understand the little people. Animals."

"Does it, by Jove!" Devenish pulled on his jacket. "Well, I'll be dashed! Rat Paws, eh? And how did you know, my elf, that I've a way with animals?"

The child sighed and shook his head at this inexplicable obtuseness. "Because of the badger, 'course," he explained patiently. "He would've either runned off or gived you a good bite if you didn't have the Rat Paws. Not many does. I don't. But I seen it before. Among the Folk."

"Aha!" Devenish felt in his pockets. "So you're a gypsy lad, are you?"

The child sprang up and crouched, hissing furiously. "Go on! Count it! Count it! See if I cares! I didn't prig nothink!"

"I doubt there was anything to prig. Someone was before you, I fear."

The boy sniffed and sat down with the unaffected, loose-limbed slump of childhood. "I bean't surprised. You deserve it for being indecent."

"Good God!" Devenish abandoned his hopeful but doomed search for any kind of cash or pawnable item still remaining about his person. "*Now* what are you accusing me of? Because I took off my shirt? Did it offend you to look upon my nakedness, Master Virtuous, you should have continued about your probably nefarious pursuits!"

There was a brief pause, then the boy remarked thoughtfully, "I don't know what all them jawbreakers means. But I heered you say the badger he was more decent than what you is. And badgers are not always nice."

Devenish chuckled. "Well, that wasn't quite what I meant. Now, sirrah, I think I shall walk with you so far as your cottage—or do you dwell in a caravan, perhaps? Anyway, I'll see you safe home. Which way? And by the by, where are we?" The small stocking-capped head turned to him with incredulity. "I was robbed in St. Albans," he explained, "and thrown in a ditch not far away from here, but I've no least idea where I am."

"Lawks! A rank rider?" The boy moved a step closer and looked around uneasily.

"Something like that." Devenish dropped a reassuring hand onto a very frail shoulder. "Never fear, laddie. He's far off by this time."

"I hopes as how he is. We're on the outside of Cricklade."

Devenish knit his brows. "Oh, then that's the Thames, is it? Jove! I've a school friend lives nearby, just past Tewkesbury."

"Tewkesbury!" The boy gave a muffled snort and began to move off. "It's this way. There's a sign at the crossroads."

Following, Devenish scanned him narrowly. How thin he was, poor shrimp. Likely half-starved, and although he moved

396

along well, his stride was short and cautious as he picked his way across the meadow. It was too dark to see the face and, beyond noting how peaked it seemed, the eyes dark shadows in that pale oval, Devenish had no clear impression of his looks. There was an inconsistency about his speech that was intriguing. Although he used cant terms and his grammar was atrocious, the h's and g's were largely intact, and just now he had said with surprising precision, "badgers are not always nice." Odd. Recalling his last succinct exclamation, Devenish enquired, "What's wrong with Tewkesbury?"

"Nought. Be ye going to walk?"

"*Touché!* I suppose . . ." he frowned, "I've no choice." And then, resenting a scornful "Hah!" he demanded, "And why should that disgust you?"

" 'Cause you be a nob. And nobs don't walk better'n thirty miles."

"Surprising as it may seem to you, young sir," said Devenish loftily, "I have been on the padding lay before. Now then"—he indicated the row of shabby cottages they were approaching—"is this where you live?" The boy nodded and led the way to a gate that drooped in a picket fence sadly lacking paint.

Devenish closed the gate behind him, waved cheerily, and went on his way. "Strange little duck," he mused, then glanced back curiously. It was stranger that a gypsy should live in a cottage, but perhaps the child's parents had tired of the nomadic life. At all events, it was none of his bread and butter. But, by gad! when he and Yolande set up their nursery the children would not be permitted to wander about the countryside after dark! Yolande . . . His eyes softened to a surge of tenderness. God love her sweet soul, already he missed her damnably! He squared his shoulders. "Tewkesbury. Thirty miles. Lord!"

He stepped out briskly and soon came to the fork in the land, the signpost pointing south to Swindon, and northwest to the Cotswolds, beyond which lay Tewkesbury and the home of Valentine Montclair. Perhaps he might advance faster by retreating, for Swindon, on horseback at least, was not far from the Leith's country seat, Cloudhills, where he could be sure of a warm welcome and the loan of a chaise and pair, even if Tristram was from home. But he *had* no horse, and Cloudhills was as far as Tewkesbury and in the wrong blasted direction! He'd never visited Montclair's country place, but Val had been a fine fellow at Harrow, and would most certainly do all he might to aid a former schoolmate.

Not until he had walked a long way did it occur to him that Craig might be the villain who'd had him abducted, so that he might dishonourably pursue his cousin's lady without fear of interruption. He halted, scowling, but almost immediately grinned and shook his head. Never. Tyndale, whatever else he might be, was a gentleman.

The gentleman in question was at that very moment lowering himself to the ground, having accomplished which, he stretched out his long legs and leaned back against the stone wall, closing his eyes. The cut above his right temple had stopped bleeding, but the blow must have jarred halfway down his spine, and each hair on his head seemed to throb. He had not the remotest idea of where he was, but considering England was such a tiny island, it was amazing he'd not walked clear across it. The lanes went on and on, one succeeding another, the occasional signposts all too often extending invitations from towns he'd never heard of, and only his small knowledge of celestial navigation enabling him to constantly head north. He sighed. He'd endured worse pain than that which he now suffered, but, Jupiter, he'd be glad to be rid of it! Still, he mustn't lounge here for long. If what Devenish had said was true, and as far-fetched as it seemed, Dev was not the kind to lie, then the beautiful Yolande was in real peril. A man who would betray his country was capable of any villainy. Tyndale sighed again. He was so very tired. He could not guess at the hour, and his watch was gone, along with his ring. He didn't mind the watch so much, but the ring had belonged to his father and carried the family crest. Blast those . . . misbegotten . . .

He awoke shivering and soaked. More rain! It was a wonder this little island stayed afloat! He knew he'd slept only a short while, but it was very cold now, and the rain becoming a downpour. He struggled up and trudged through the puddles, concentrating on Yolande's lovely eyes, and the proud rage that had flashed in them so adorably yesterday. . . . Or was it yesterday? Gad, but he was cold, and to add to his misery, a chill wind was rising, cutting icily through his wet clothes. A gate banged to a sudden gust. His teeth beginning to chatter, Tyndale drew his jacket closer, tucked his hands under his arms, and kept moving. A flickering glow of lightning illumined a cluster of distant, dilapidated farm buildings. The gate slammed again and he saw that it was not a gate, but the door to a small shed located only a few yards from the lane. Part of the farm, no doubt, but hidden from it by a stand of trees. He halted and scrutinized the shed with interest. A glance at the house verified that not a light shone. They would certainly be asleep at this hour. He scaled the low wall in a quick leap and again searched the gloom for irate men, or dogs. He'd had enough truck with dogs to last him for a while. But all was quiet, save for the depressing beat of the rain. He crept to the swinging door and peered inside. A toolshed, having among all the muddy impedimenta, a pile of dry sacks.

Five minutes later, the shed door tight closed, his head comfortably settled on two of the folded sacks and the rest disposed over him, Tyndale smiled into the darkness. It was not the Clarendon, precisely, but it was no worse (a sight better!) than many a night he'd passed with Timothy Van Lindsay and his maniacs. Thunder bellowed, closer this time, and lightning shone through the many cracks in the dusty old shed. Tyndale grinned and yawned sleepily. "Just like Spain," he thought. "Good old . . . Tim . . ."

Devenish awoke to the touch of watery fingers creeping down his neck. He swore and sat up. The roof of the barn had a large hole, this flaw revealed by the glare of lightning. "A fine thing!" he snorted indignantly. The two cats who had curled themselves up beside him opened yellow eyes to blink through the gloom. *"Madame et Monsieur,"* he said, "I regret the necessity to disturb you, but—" The light words ceased, and he stared in stark shock at a fourth inhabitant of the old barn. A small figure, cuddled so close against his back that he'd not seen it when he awoke. "Well, here's a fine start!" he exclaimed. "Who the deuce asked you to attach your—" He ceased to speak as lightning flashed again. His breath was held for an instant, then released in a slow hiss. He'd noted a lantern hung on a nail against the wall, but had made no attempt to light it for fear of betraying his presence. Now, he stood cautiously, groped his way to it and was lucky enough to discover a tinderbox lying on the workbench. When he had ignited the wick, he turned the flame very low and tiptoed to the intruder, lying just as before and breathing with deep, soft regularity. He bent, and held the lantern closer. The shirt was too large for the child, the breeches tattered, and the thin sandals frayed, but it was not these that widened Devenish's eyes. During the night, the stocking cap had shifted and a strand of hair had escaped. A long, dark, curling strand. He uttered a faint moan, reached down, and gently pulled the cap away. Thick, dark, matted curls tumbled down. "Oh, my God!" he groaned. "A female!"

She had not been as fast asleep as he supposed. The long curling lashes flew open. Great eyes at once becoming wild with terror gazed up at him. The pale lips opened in a scream the more horrifying because it was soundless, and she sprang up. Devenish put down the lantern hurriedly, and leapt after her. He caught her at the door; a small, writhing madness.

"No!" she sobbed. "Oh, no! Let me be! Gawd! Let me be!" And between sobs and cries and entreaties, came a thin keening shriek that he swiftly muffled.

"Quiet!" he hissed. "I will not harm you, child! Just be quiet, or we'll be put out in the rain, to say the least of it!"

He glanced down when she ceased to struggle. Her eyes were half closed, the thin features like paper. "Egad! Am I suffocating you?" he gasped, removing his hand.

"Let . . . me . . . be," she whispered threadily. "Do not—oh, do not touch me!"

She looked on the verge of a swoon. What in heaven's name would he do if she committed so dreadful a thing? He released her hurriedly. "Just *please* do not scream," he implored.

She did not scream, but she swayed, an awful moaning escaping her. In a burst of sympathy, Devenish forgot her plea, put an arm about her bony little shoulders, and led her back to the pile of straw and the two cats. "Sit here," he urged, drawing her down beside him. "There—that's better. Poor creature. Was it a nightmare? I've had a few of them m'self."

Those haunted eyes watched him with a sort of dulled pleading, and he smiled his kindest smile and added, "I will not touch you. Promise."

Still looking straight at him, she began to weep; a helpless, undisguised sobbing that smote him to the heart, but when he edged back, horrified, the thin claw of a hand came out to clutch his own, and she gulped, "And—and you ain't like—like Akim . . . or Benjo?"

"I most certainly hope not, if they affect a little girl in this way." A frown crept into his eyes. He asked in a different tone, "Is that why you ran away? From Akim and Benjo?" The tangled, greasy curls bounced as she nodded, and teardrops splattered. Devenish's jaw set. "Are they little boys?"

She shook her head. "Men. And I be eleven—I think."

Eleven. She looked no more than seven or eight. . . . Dreading the answer he might receive, he asked, "What did they do?"

"They started to . . . to look at me." Crimson swept over the pinched cheeks, and she threw grubby hands up to cover her eyes. "And—and one day Benjo catched me washing of myself in the stream. He took hold of my hair when I tried to cover up myself. And—and he laughed and said . . . he said they'd get a good price for me soon, from . . ."

"From whom?"

"From . . . Oh! From one of the *Flash Houses!*" Her eyes, agonized, were fixed on him, and Devenish gritted his teeth over the oaths that surged into his throat. By thunder, but was there anything lower than some men? He'd never been in a Flash House, but he'd heard of those hellish traps in which girls scarcely having known childhood were forced into prostitution and kept thereafter more or less permanently drunk to ensure they continued their trade; a trade from which they reaped only the benefits of food and warmth while their soulless procuress grew rich and fat at the expense of their degradation. Boys fared little better in those dens of vice: if they refused to steal and deliver up their spoils, they were cast out into the street, penniless, where the chances were that they would be hauled off to gaol, flogged, and thrown into the streets once more to begin the whole vicious circle over again.

A small cold hand creeping into his own recalled Devenish from his bitter thoughts. The child was watching him beseechingly. He looked into the tear-streaked face of this helpless piece of jetsam caught in a relentless tide that must only lead to— Cutting off that terrible strain of reasoning, he demanded harshly, "What is your name? Have you no parents?"

"They call me Tabby. And I don't know about me mother or father. I was stole."

He looked at her clinically. Her hair was very dark, but he saw now that her skin was extremely pale beneath the dirt, and her eyes, although dark also, had flecks of hazel in them. She was a dirty, wretched, plain little girl, all skin and bone, but he saw the same promise in her thin form that Akim and Benjo must have seen, and his rage at those crude spoilers grew. Forcing himself to speak calmly, he asked, "Why Tabby?"

" 'Cause I scratched 'em when they tried to touch me like—like Akim did once. And they said I was a wildcat, and after that they all laughed, and teased me, and—and called me all kinds of horrid, ugly things. I hates 'em all." The bony fists clenched. She repeated through her teeth, "I *hates* 'em! So I didn't say nothink, but last night when Akim's mort was asleep and Akim and Benjo was drunk, I creeped away. And I'm *never* going back!" Her angry flush died away, her lips began to tremble pathetically, and her eyes blinked up at him, aswim with tears. "You won't make me go? Oh, please—*please!*" She knelt, cowering before him, hands upstretched in supplication. "I'll do anything! I'll cook for you and scrub your floors when you get some. And when I grows up in a year or two, if you likes me a bit, I'll—"

Devenish gave a gasp and pulled her to her feet. "Hush! Poor child. Now, sit properly and do not even think such things."

Trembling, she whispered, "It would be better, sir . . . than a Flash House, but— Oh! Now I've gone and made you cross again! You do get very awful cross, mister . . ."

"Devenish. Alain Devenish, at your service, madame!" He rose and swept her the most stately bow of which he was capable with his leg throbbing so. The child was delighted, laughter returned to her eyes, and her hands clapped joyously. "Now," said Devenish, "we must find a name for you, for Tabby I will not tolerate."

"A name? A new name? Oh, sir—do that mean as you will keep me?" And she clasped her hands before her thin breast with such an intensity of hope that he feared to hear those fragile bones snap.

"I cannot keep you, child," he pointed out gently. "It wouldn't be proper, for I've no lady wife to care for you, but—"

Undismayed, she said, "Well, if you don't got a wife, you prob'ly have a—"

"No! I have not one of those, either! Now—what am I to call you?" He ran through his mind the names of every lady he could recall. "It must be a pretty name . . ."

She said timidly, "If I was to think of a speshly lovely name, p'raps *then* you might keep me?"

"No. But I shall see to it that you've a decent chance in life. One of my aunts, or cousins—some kind lady will take you in, and perhaps train you for her abigail. Would you like that?"

The child tried to answer, but could not. And to his horror, flung herself down and began to kiss his muddy boots.

"Good God!" he gasped, again hauling her up. "Never do such things!"

She dragged one torn sleeve across her small nose, and sniffed, "I can't help it. You be so good to I. Does you like 'Josie'?"

He said dubiously, "Josie? Why? Do you like it?"

"I don't know." She shrugged. "It—sort of comes into my head sometimes."

Devenish had been considering the merits of Antonia but—"Well, it's better than Tabby!" he said. "Very well, Josie it shall be." He looked about as a sudden flash was followed by a great rumbling bump of thunder. "Josie Storm! How's that?"

"Lovely!" The newly christened Miss Storm hugged herself ecstatically. "I feel new all over! Josie Storm . . . *oooh!*"

❧ *Chapter 7* ❧

"I was sure they would be here for breakfast, Aunt," said Yolande, her worried glance travelling for the hundredth time around the emptying coffee room of the hotel. "I wonder if we should not send one of the outriders in search of them? Or perhaps call in the constable?"

"Yes, and a pretty figure we should cut when they were discovered roistering in some ale house!" her aunt sniffed. "The host told you, my love, that neither Devenish nor Tyndale—or whatever he calls himself—signed the guest register."

"No, but they stabled their horses here, and they were still here when we retired, for I sent Peattie downstairs to enquire. You know how Dev loves that mare. And Craig values Lazzy most highly."

"Goodness only knows why, for a more unattractive beast I

seldom beheld. Oh, mercy, here is dear Mr. Garvey! Perhaps he can set your mind at ease."

James Garvey, looking very well in a dark brown riding coat and buckskins, came to join them, his grave "May I have the honour?" drawing an immediate and dramatic "Oh, *pray* do, sir!" from Mrs. Drummond, and a welcoming smile from her niece. His polite enquiries as to their night's rest were brushed aside, Yolande replying almost impatiently, "Very nice, I thank you. Mr. Garvey, have you seen anything of my cousins Devenish and Tyndale? I hope you will not think me foolish, but I am becoming most anxious for them."

He rested an appreciative gaze upon her. "Your concern does you credit, dear lady. As does your gown. Dare I be so bold as to remark how pleasingly that shade of peach becomes you?"

Irritated by what she considered a pointless digression, Yolande was also struck by the thought that Dev would have said carelessly that her dress was orange, if she'd asked him, and Tyndale would probably merely have observed that she looked charmingly. She smiled politely, but decided she would soon find Mr. Garvey's suave manners a dead bore. Yet—how kindly he was regarding her, and only think how willingly he had spared them from what must otherwise have been a dull journey. "What a wretched, ungrateful girl I am!" she thought penitently.

Her aunt had willingly jumped into the pause resulting from Yolande's brief hesitation and was exclaiming over Mr. Garvey's unending kindnesses. As soon as she paused to draw breath, Yolande cut into this welter of gratitude. "I echo my aunt's sentiments, sir," she said warmly. "You have been too good."

He looked a little solemn then. "I do have some news," he said with marked reluctance. "I trust it will not distress you. The head ostler tells me that your cousins have departed, ma'am. They came to the stable late last night, apparently, claimed their mounts, paid their shot, and rode out."

Stunned, Yolande stared at him. She had, she knew, been out of reason cross with both of them. But could Dev have been so offended he would leave in such a way? Would Craig take himself off without so much as a farewell—a note, at least? A pang pierced her heart, and suddenly she felt miserable and betrayed.

"Typical!" snorted Mrs. Drummond. "It would be asking

too much of you, dear Mr. Garvey, to enquire if they left a *billet-doux* at the desk, perhaps?"

"I did so, ma'am. That is, I asked of the clerk. There was nothing."

Mrs. Drummond cast her niece a smug "I told you so!" look.

Yolande pulled herself together. "How foolish in me to have worried," she said, striving not altogether successfully to sound lightly amused. "Well, dear, you were very right to tease me. I expect Sullivan has given Socrates his exercise by this time, so perhaps we should collect our cloaks and be upon our way."

Sadly in need of a shave, and looking considerably tattered and weather-stained, Devenish lay back against the tree trunk and sighed beatifically. "How strange it is," he mused, "that a dinner of bread and cheese eaten in town would be plain fare, but bread and cheese eaten under a tree is always so dashed magnificent."

Bathed in the golden rays of the late afternoon sun, Josie scratched her head and regarded her protector doubtfully. "Does that mean as ye liked it?"

"Nectar of the Gods!" sighed Devenish. He stood and reached down to help her up. "We've still far to go. Are you tired? We've come a long way today."

"I be a better walker'n you," she said pertly. "Though you're padding better'n what you did last night. Has you got blisters? Them boots is pretty, but they don't look like walkers."

Devenish peered ruefully at his top boots. "They're not. But I shall do, never fear. *En avant, mon enfant!*"

"*Très bien, monsieur,*" giggled Josie.

Devenish, who had been about to explain what he'd said, caught her skinny shoulder and pulled her to a halt. "*What,*" he breathed, "did you say?"

"Nothing bad! Not nothing bad, sir! Oh, don't be cross again! You was talking French, wasn't you?"

"Why—yes. Do you know what I said? What it means?"

"It means 'let's go on' or something, don't it?"

Marvelling, he released his hold and nodded. "What did you answer? In English, that is."

"Very well, sir." He didn't seem cross. Reassured, she tilted her head to one side and watched him curiously. "Why? Does you hate all Frogs, like Akim and Benjo does?"

Starting on again, but still regarding her askance, he said, "Gad, no. I merely wonder, my small conundrum, how it is that your English is appalling, yet you know French. Where did you learn it?"

"Don't remember." Her brow wrinkled, but at length she concluded, "Prob'ly heered a body say it. And my English ain't—what you said. I speak good. Even Akim and—"

"I know. Akim and Benjo. But I doubt they are authorities, elf. We must improve your grammar are you to obtain suitable employment."

She stared at him. "But—she's dead. And even if she wasn't, I don't see why you'd want to mess about with *her* to get me a sittyation."

At first puzzled, Devenish eventually comprehended. "*Grammar*, Josie," he explained laughingly. "It means your use—or misuse—of English."

"Oh." She flushed scarlet. "All right. Go on, then."

"Me? Good God, no! I do not excel in that line myself. But when we reach Tewkesbury—"

"Tomorrow," she inserted, pulling a face.

"Oh, no. I think we can do better than that. If a carter chances by, I shall bribe him into taking on two paying customers."

Josie looked regretfully at his jacket, now bereft of two of its three handsome silver buttons. "You shouldn't have let that tinker gull you out of both them pretty buttons for his bread and cheese. He likely thought you was a proper pigeon for milking. And 'sides, carters isn't s'posed to give rides."

"Listen to Miss Prim." He grinned. "I doubt your sensibilities will be offended, however, for this road seems to attract very little traffic. Still, if one ventures this way I mean to try him, for I'm in a hurry, Miss Josie. I must get myself hooves or wheels—preferably both—as soon as may be."

The child smiled but said nothing, and Devenish's concern returned to his adored Yolande. Whatever must she have thought of his absence? In view of their earlier disagreement and his confounded temper, it was all too likely she supposed him to have ridden off in a huff. He scowled and thrust his hands deeper into his pockets, and the threat of James Garvey heightened his worries so that he did not notice that the afternoon was growing colder and the skies becoming heavy with clouds. Not until a gust of wind cut chillingly through his fine linen shirt was he recalled to the present. He glanced down and saw the child's head bowed, and her feet scuffing wearily at the damp surface of the lane. Contrite, he exclaimed, "What a clod I am!" and dropped to one knee, reaching back invitingly. "Come aboard, madam."

She looked at his shoulders with longing. "No. Thankee, but you'm tired. And your feet hurt, too. I can tell."

"Nonsense," he lied. "You, m'dear, are in the company of a former military man. Why, when I was in the army we used to tramp about all day long—sometimes half the night—just to keep our Colonel amused. This is nothing. Come now—don't dawdle about!"

He waved his arms imperatively, and with a giggle she ran to clamber onto his back. He stood, his arms cradling her bony legs. She was heavy as a bushel of feathers, poor mite. "Gad!" he groaned. "What a lump!"

She laughed and said gratefully, "Oh, this is such fun, and I be warmer already!"

Devenish warned, "You realize, m'dear, that I shall want my own turn at piggyback?"

Another merry little laugh greeted this sally, but she pointed out that he was not going so fast with her on his back.

"Remorseless taskmaster!" He broke into a run, but soon had to slow again.

After a little while, Josie asked, "Be she pretty, your lady?"

"Very pretty."

"Is that why you want to marriage her?"

He smiled, Yolande's vivid loveliness very clear before his eyes. "Not entirely. I've wanted her for my wife for as long as I can remember. She is kind as well as pretty. And she has a happy nature and a quick, merry laugh. She is generous and charming, and—oh, all the things a man wants in the lady he marries."

"Oh." A thoughtful pause, and then, "Mr. Dev, why does some gents have wifes and some have—"

He said hastily, "It's—er, all according to—ah— Well, a gentleman usually—"

He was reprieved from this quagmire as they came around a bend in the lane and Josie interrupted in a scared voice, "Mr. Dev, what are those people doing?"

A burst of shouting broke from a group of burly men engaged in dragging a struggling individual across the field a short distance ahead. Devenish halted and moved into the shade of the hedge. They looked a rough lot and he'd no wish for the child to witness a brawl. A roar of laughter arose and, with it, the body of their victim, soaring into the air to fall heavily onto the muddy lane.

"The deuce!" exclaimed Devenish.

A bullet head appeared over the top of the hedge as the unfortunate sprawling in the dirt commenced a feeble attempt to rise. "That'll do fer'ee," quoth the farmer, grinning from ear to ear. "Next time as ye fix fer to trespass in some 'un's shed, ye best ask perlite-like, fust!" And to the accompaniment of another roar of laughter, his head was withdrawn and the loud voices began to diminish.

"Oh, the poor cove!" cried Josie pityingly. She slid from Devenish's hold and scampered along the lane, her ragged breeches flapping.

Following, Devenish quickened his pace as the man in the road turned on his side, got one elbow under him, and lifted a blood-streaked fair head.

"Well I'll be—Tyndale!" said Devenish.

"Give us your hanky, Mr. Dev," Josie demanded, kneeling beside the victim and extending an imperious hand. Receiving this grubby article, she began to wipe carefully at Tyndale's battered features.

Her patient managed to sit up, and leaning back on both hands peered blurrily at her. "Dev . . . ?" he said, bewildered.

"Over here, you clunch." Devenish bent over him. "Lord, what a mess! Did they run the cows over you?" And, as Josie gently parted his cousin's thick hair, he added, "The devil! Who did that?"

"An admirer . . . in the hotel stable. I thought perhaps you . . ." Tyndale flinched back from Josie's busy hands.

"You would, blast you!" snapped Devenish, considerably irked, and forgetting that he had cherished the same suspicion of his kinsman.

"Try not to wriggle, please, sir," said Josie. "There's a perishing great splinter here."

An amused gleam lit Tyndale's strained eyes, but Devenish groaned, "Josie! For heaven's sake, child, you must not use such terms."

She bit her lip and threw him an anguished look.

Tyndale asked, rather faintly, "Who is my small angel of mercy?"

Josie gave a quick, firm tug, and a little whimper of sympathy. Tyndale's eyes became slightly glassy, and a whiteness under his eyes intensified, but he made no sound.

"You'm brave," she told him, touching his cheek gently. "And I'm new today. I was Tabby, but now I be Josie Storm. When I grows up I going to be Mr. Dev's—"

"Abigail!" yelped Devenish, and then fumed. "And remove that damned smirk from your face, or I'll shove this hunk of wood back in your thick skull! Josie is going to be *trained* for an abigail is what I mean!"

"You should not swear," scolded the "angel of mercy." "And if I had a friend what was so big and strong and brave, I wouldn't shout at him like what you does."

Devenish scowled. "He ain't a friend. He's my cousin."

"Cousin! I thought relayatives liked one another." She added, "I never had no cousins or nothing."

Devenish stared at her small, wistful face, flashed an uncomfortable look at the grinning Tyndale, and had the grace to redden. "Enjoy your gloating," he grunted. "That's not going to stop, Josie. Give me the handkerchief."

She turned away, holding it apart. "*I* know how!" she declared loftily. "I done it for Akim's mort when he hit her with a gin bottle."

"Did you, my God!" Impressed, Tyndale lowered his head so that she might more easily perform her task.

She folded the handkerchief, by now considerably the worse for wear, into a diagonal strip, tied it around his brow, then inspected her handiwork critically. "It ain't high enough," she admitted, "but at least it will keep the bleedings out of your eyes."

Tyndale assured her that it was splendid, and thanked her for her efforts. Devenish slipped a hand under his arm. "Can you stand? Good man. Up with you."

Tyndale swayed, but the rain was beginning to come down now, the air was chill, and Devenish's supporting arm enabled him to remain upright until the dizziness passed.

"He should rest," said Josie, indignantly.

"No—thank you, Miss Josie, but—I shall go on nicely," Tyndale gasped.

And so on they went.

The rain proved of short duration. The wind blew the clouds apart and, unexpectedly, the lowering sun shone benignly upon the odd little trio, the two battered young men, and the child, tattered and dirty but, after the fashion of youth, now skipping merrily beside her new friends, her weariness forgotten.

As Devenish expected, his questioning elicited the information that Tyndale's capture had been accomplished shortly after his own, the main difference being that his cousin had been more crudely struck down. "I rather fancy," he growled, "that they had only enough of that revolting ether for me."

"Likely you're right." Tyndale said slowly, "They seem to have gone to no little pains to separate us. I wonder why."

"Perhaps they wanted us to be further delayed in searching for one another. They wasn't to know we—er, would not give a hoot."

Tyndale was briefly silent. "I didn't mean quite that. I collect you fancy Garvey was behind it?"

"I don't *fancy*, cousin! I know da—er, dashed well he was!"

"But—why? Do you think he was that desperately smitten with Yolande?"

"Well, I'd like to know why the devil he would not be! Yolande is—Yolande!"

"I'll not argue that point. But did you not mention that he was, until recently, deep in love with another lady?"

"The Van Lindsay. An accredited Toast. What I may have failed to mention is that rumour has it he's under the hatches."

Tyndale stiffened. "And the Van Lindsay was an heiress? I understood you to say the family was in Dun territory."

"True. But there is a grandmama who's as full of lettuce as she is full of years, and who dotes on the girl." His eyes grim, Devenish growled, "That hound lost her, so now pursues a lady of greater fortune! There's no knowing how desperate he may be, but he travels with an expensive set; Carlton House, no less! And if he does mean to snare Yolande, I pose a double threat. Not only am I known to be betrothed to the lady, but I could tell her much that Garvey would prefer she remain unaware of."

Tyndale nodded. "It is motive enough, and yet—I still cannot fathom the attacks upon us. At most, Garvey will only buy himself a few days in which to ingratiate himself. He surely realizes you will rumble him, and will tell Yolande when—" He broke off. "By Jupiter! You never think . . ."

"That we were supposed to have been dished?" Devenish gave a cynical snort. "I'd not put it past the rogue!" He lengthened his pace. "Now perhaps you can appreciate why I am so anxious to come up with them! Can you walk a shade faster, cousin? I appreciate you ain't in the habit of marching, but—"

It was as much as Tyndale could do to set one foot before the other, to conceal which, he said laughingly, "Not like you dashing Hyde Park soldiers, eh?"

The more infuriated because it was truth, Devenish whirled to face him. "Now, damn your impudence, I'd like to know what *you* did that was so blasted much more useful."

Tyndale shrugged. "Not my war, cousin."

"No," gritted Devenish, contemptuously. "And I can well believe that even if it had been, you'd not risk your precious hide to—"

Slipping between them, her pointed little face set into a daunting frown, Josie demanded, "Why don't you both dub your mummers! Blessed if ever I see such a pair of shagbags!" She glared up at Devenish, whose face was a study in disbelief. "You ain't no better than a windy wallets, and he—" She turned about to fix angry eyes on the startled Tyndale. "He's too top lofty to admit he's in queer stirrups!"

Tyndale laughed unsteadily, but staggered even as he laughed. Jumping to steady him, Devenish fumed, "And you, my girl, should have your mouth washed out! Dammit, Tyndale—if you cannot walk, why in the deuce did you not say so?"

"Can . . ." Tyndale muttered. "I'm just as eager to reach . . . Yolande as are you. It's—it's just . . . this blasted head, is all."

"And those yokels gave you more rough handling. What in the world did you do to rate such treatment?"

Leaning on him, despite his reluctance to do so, Tyndale tottered on and said wryly, "Well, it was raining, and I came upon a snug toolshed by the road and made myself comfortable. Woke up to find a dashed blunderbuss aimed at my head, and the farmer and his sons mad as fire because I'd trespassed."

"Mad as fire! It was likely a trap. I was once caught in just such a shabby scheme. They put you to work, I collect?"

"I never worked so hard in my life! That mean old curmudgeon even berated his daughter for bringing me a drink of water. This afternoon, old Nimms, the farmer, came out and watched me, guzzling at a tankard of ale, and laughing while I dug every weed and rock from the most miserable field you ever saw."

"What—did they not even give you a crust, or a hunk of cheese?"

"No, and there was all the time the most mouth-watering smell of the stew his poor wife was cooking. When I asked him if there was some way I could work for a meal, he thought it hilarious, but I finally talked him into allowing me to instruct his sons in fencing."

Devenish said a surprised "You fence?"

"A ... er, a little. I told old Nimms I was accounted not paltry in the art, and he said in his crude way that he thought there was little of art in a man's protecting himself. At all events, I was allowed to go into the kitchen and eat, after which largesse I commenced my first lesson." He was feeling steadier and relinquished his grip on his cousin. "Thank you. I can go on now."

"Good. How did your lesson go on? From the look of those louts I'd have thought they'd scarcely know point from grip!"

"Very shrewd of you. They didn't." Tyndale drawled wryly, "Our problem, it developed, was with communication rather than skill. My fine farmer had apparently not thought I referred to fencing with foils."

"With swords? A first lesson? Fella must be queer in his attic!"

"Not with swords."

Devenish frowned. "Then—what the deuce else could—" Comprehension dawned. *"Fencing?"* He grinned, in huge delight. "No, not really! With—*wood?"*

"My good Nimms," Tyndale sighed, "had once seen a picture of an Italian villa surrounded by an ornate fence he particularly admired. He thought I would know of some simple and inexpensive way to build it, and—Now, blast you, Dev!"

"Sorry," wheezed Devenish, wiping his eyes. "So—so when he discovered you'd hoodwinked him, he was—put out, eh?"

"Hoodwinked him? I didn't hoodwink the clod! At least, not intentionally. Much chance I had of convincing him of it!"

"So I should think. What did he say?"

"That he was going to push my face in the dirt and step on it."

"Whereupon," said Devenish, his hilarity fading, "you attempted to show him the error of his ways?"

"Correct. The trouble was he had three stalwart sons. No brains, you understand, but muscles—and to spare."

"And so ... ?"

"And so—they pushed my face into the dirt, and Nimms demanded I admit to being a lying, cheating Captain Sharp. My response, alas, did not please; besides which I had managed to deal him a bloody nose during our little tussle. His sons proceeded to pick me up and run my head against a fence post a few times. So I would know what a fence was, they said. You saw the last act."

"Well, I think it was plain horrid!" Josie said indignantly. "Four to one! They was cowards, sir!"

"Dashed unsporting!" Devenish frowned from his cousin's rueful smile to the blood that slowly crept down to stain the handkerchief about his head. "They must have known you was already hurt."

"From what I saw of the Nimms clan, coz, I rather fancy that would have added spice to their enjoyment."

"Would it! Well, it occurs to me that the family honour has been sullied. And we cannot have that, now can we?" Devenish halted, lost in thought, while his companions watched him wonderingly. "Nothing for it," he said, looking up with a grin. "We must go back."

"Back!" echoed Tyndale. "But—why? Even together we couldn't hope to—"

"Oh, I do not propose to take on the Nimmses. Not—ah, exactly. After all, they did not play fair, so we have a little more—er—scope."

He looked, thought Tyndale, like a small, mischievous boy. "What do you mean to do?" he asked.

Devenish regretfully inspected his last remaining silver button. "Part with this." He wrenched it off. "I had meant to use it to bribe a carter. Still, honour must be served. Josie, my elf, do you recall that last village we trudged through? Do you fancy we can reach it by nightfall?"

She nodded. "If Mr. Craig can walk so far. Oh, what fun it would be! I wonder if the man with the performing bear be there still."

Tyndale, whose eyes had widened during this innocent revelation, turned to his cousin. "Devenish, you never mean to . . . ?" he breathed in awe.

Devenish chuckled. "Don't I just"

It was very cold that night and, although it did not rain, the men of the Nimms family were not without optimism as they advanced in a roseate dawn towards the toolshed.

Edgar, the eldest, was inclined to temper hope with reason, however. "It ain't likely as we'd catch another noddicock this quick," he pointed out in a hoarse whisper. "We should've never let that big cove go, Pa. He could've finished the west field by now."

"Ar," the patriarch agreed. "I were a sight rash there, son. Still, by the time we was done, he wasn't good fer much. And ye can never tell. With all this ragtag soldiery creeping about the roads, we might— Hey! Look there! The door be shut so tight as any drum. What'd I tell'ee? We do have hired ourselves another volunteer!"

Exultant, the four big men bore down upon their cunning trap, never dreaming that they were watched by four pairs of eyes, each alight with anticipation.

Farmer Nimms tightened his grip on the serviceable cudgel he carried. "Ready, lads?" he hissed, one hand on the door. His sons grinned and nodded. Movement could be heard from within the toolshed. "Sounds like another big'un," gloated the good farmer, and his sons brandished their clubs, eager for the fray.

Swinging the door wide, Farmer Nimms stepped inside. "You worthless scum!" he roared. "Get—"

The movements in the shed became more pronounced. A strange voice rose in irate protest. The voice of Farmer Nimms also rose. To a shriek. He left his shed far more hurriedly than he had entered it. So hurriedly, in fact, that he ploughed into the three stalwart offspring who pressed in behind him. The fame of the Nimmses had spread far and wide, and it would have been difficult to determine whether they were best known for their truculence, their dishonest dealings, or the brutality they visited upon the unfortunates they caught in their strategically placed toolshed. They took care never to engage in a fair fight, with the result that it had been many a day since they had been bested. They were bested now. The trespasser looming in the doorway was enough to strike fear into the heart of any reasonable man. The bear was extremely large, brown, and annoyed. It reared onto its hind legs, toppling the toolshed in the process, and letting out another roar of displeasure.

Filial affection went by the board. Trapped by the burly figures of his nearest and dearest, Farmer Nimms damned them for knock-in-the-cradles and fought tooth and nail for freedom. Hurled back, the brothers caught sight of the monster looming above them. None of them could seem to move quite fast

enough and in their frenzy they collided. Their shrieking profanities did little to improve the temper of the bear, who had
taken a very dim view of the toolshed, but had been mollified
by the pot of honey Devenish had had the foresight to provide,
and into which the good farmer had been so unwise as to put
his foot. Since Nimms did not seem inclined to stop and remove the honey pot from his boot, the bear saw his prize being
made off with, and sprang in hot pursuit.

Thus it was that Harry Oakes, the apothecary, driving his
pony and trap on an early call, beheld such a cavalcade as was
to delight the patrons of The Duck and Drake for months to
come. Farmer Nimms was well out in front, head and elbows
back, legs pumping vigorously, albeit the handicap of a strange
pot wrapped around one foot. Behind him, racing at a good
rate of speed, were his three boys, their squeals of terror rival-
ling his own. Next came a large and angry bear (causing Mr.
Oakes to turn hurriedly into the trees), and bringing up the
rear, a lean individual who waved a long chain while imploring
Bruin to stop "like a good boy!"

Not until the procession was fading into the morning mists
did Mr. Oaks discover that others had witnessed it. Two young
men and a little girl lay in the ditch beside the toppled Nimms
toolshed. He was unable to get any sense from them, however,
for they were equally overcome, their howls and sobs of laughter having reduced them to near-imbecility and a complete inability to either stand or converse intelligently.

Mr. Oaks abandoned his attempts to communicate and
joined in their hilarity.

Despite the relatively fair weather, the progress of Yolande's
party was slow. This was in part due to the habits of Socrates,
and in part due to the habits of his owner, who could never be
convinced of the benefits to be derived from an early start.
Mrs. Drummond was of the opinion that none but commoners
ventured abroad before noon, and it was only by dint of long
and patient representations that Yolande was able to prevail
upon the lady to take her breakfast at "the heathen hour" of
nine o'clock.

Two days after leaving St. Albans, Mr. Garvey was still escorting them, a circumstance for which Yolande could only be
grateful. All her protests that they delayed him were waved
aside, and when she again pointed out that he should be travelling eastwards to Stirling, he said he merely altered his plans

so as to take the westerly loop on his way north instead of on the way back down to London. "For I have an aged pensioner dwelling in Kilmarnock," he averred suavely. "A devoted old fellow I am promised to visit. I can deliver you and your aunt to Castle Drummond, continue to Kilmarnock and take the Glasgow road east to Stirling. I gave my friends no definite date for my arrival, so you see, dear lady, your worries are quite without foundation."

If Yolande's concerns were unjustified in that sense, they also appeared unwarranted in another. Mr. Garvey was charming, and his assistance of real value, yet there was something about the gentleman she could not like. She had made up her mind therefore, that if she saw signs of his having developed a *tendre* for her, she would be firm in refusing his escort. It soon became obvious, however, to herself if not to her aunt, that he actually derived much more pleasure from the company of the elder lady than from that of her niece. Since the two of them shared both a wide acquaintanceship among the *ton*, and an inclination to gossip, they were in no time at all the very best of friends, chattering away the miles in convivial, if scandalous, fashion, and thus allowing Yolande to indulge her own thoughts in peace.

Those thoughts were far from peaceful, however. Try as she would, she could not banish her anxiety concerning her cousins. However irresponsible Devenish might be judged, she had never had the slightest doubt of his devotion and, while it was true that she had been very cross with him in St. Albans, he was scarcely the man to be easily daunted. As for Craig . . . Her heart gave that odd little jolt that any thought of him seemed to precipitate. She glanced guiltily at her aunt, sitting beside her in the carriage, and was startled to find that lady's enquiring gaze fixed upon her.

"My apologies, dear ma'am," she said hastily, having a vague recollection of some half-heard remark. "I fear I was wool-gathering."

"So I imagined, dear child," her aunt agreed in a faintly martyred voice. "I was urging dear Mr. Garvey to instruct the coachman to make a small detour. I should so much like to see the new construction at the school, should not you? And since we pass this way so seldom . . ."

Yolande blinked, striving to gather her scattered thoughts. "School?"

"We are coming into Rugby, ma'am," volunteered Mr. Garvey with a kindly smile.

Yolande glanced out at the lush, rolling countryside. "Oh—yes, indeed. So we are. But why should we detour? We have no relations at the school, Aunt Bella, have we?"

"Not presently, but you know that all four of your Aunt Cecily's boys came here. I have not seen the new structure Hakewill designed. The school was rebuilt about seven years ago, Mr. Garvey," she added, turning a warm smile upon their companion, "and my brother-in-law tells me the work was most attractively accomplished."

"I am sure you are right, dear," said Yolande. "But perhaps we might stop here on the way home. I am eager to reach Steep Drummond."

"Oh, but this rushing and tearing about is so exhausting," panted Mrs. Drummond. "I do not complain, for it is not my place. But Mr. Garvey *told* you that Devenish and that Canadian person had turned back, so you need not worry so."

Yolande blushed to think that her distress had been so shrewdly noted and interpreted, but she persisted, "Perhaps they did, at first. But Dev is a very stubborn young man, as you should certainly be aware, Aunt. And Craig is eager to see his inheritance, besides which—"

"Besides which, he was behaving like any love-struck moonling from the moment he saw *you*!" Arabella gave a shrill little titter. "You would scarce credit the impertinence of the fellow, dear Mr. Garvey. No sooner had he all but put us in our graves, then he must come to Park Parapine, trying to ingratiate himself with Sir Martin! I wonder my brother did not at once show the door to the presumptuous upstart, rather than—"

Her own rare temper flaring, Yolande exclaimed, "I think you must forget that Craig Tyndale is my cousin, ma'am, else you would not designate one of our family a presumptuous upstart! Nor can I suppose Mr. Garvey to be in the slightest interested in such matters."

Mr. Garvey's well-shaped brows lifted in faint amusement. Mrs. Drummond, however, stared at her niece in astonishment, clapped a handkerchief to her eyes, and dissolved into tears.

Aghast, Yolande strove to mend matters; a long struggle that ended, of course, with her agreeing that they should detour to see the famous boys' school.

Mr. Hakewill's architectural designs had yielded impressive

results, and Mrs. Drummond and Mr. Garvey were vociferous
in their admiration of the new buildings. Yolande wandered
about reacting politely to their remarks. Inwardly, however, she
was as disinterested as she was disturbed. To have lost her
temper with an older lady was very bad. And even worse, she
had done so in front of a comparative stranger! She *never* lost
her temper. Well, almost never. She would not have done it, of
course, save for the fact that she was so worried about her two
suitors. Guilt struck again and her cheeks flamed. Craig was
not her suitor! "And neither is he a presumptuous upstart!" she
thought with a flare of irritation. He might be a Colonial, and
perhaps he had a shocking blot on his name, and a sad want
of fortune, but . . . She sighed, seeing again the concern in his
grey eyes as he had bent over her while she lay on the rug after the accident; feeling again the firm clasp of his hands as he
made her lie down when she had striven to rise. Such strong
hands and yet, so gentle . . .

"Wake up, dearest!"

Yolande started. Her aunt and Mr. Garvey were watching
her smilingly. Good gracious! She had drifted off again, like
some silly thimblewit! Whatever was wrong with her intellect?

"I declare," said Mrs. Drummond, "one would fancy you
fairly enamoured of that door, for you have looked at it this
age, and with such *tenderness*!"

Mr. Garvey chuckled. "I think your niece's thoughts were
not with the door, dear lady."

"Clever rascal," trilled Mrs. Drummond, giving him a playful tap with her fan. "And you are perfectly right, of course.
My dear niece is enchanted! 'Absence, that common cure
of love' did not prevail. Alas. Yet—oh, to be young—and in
love . . . !"

Yolande could have sunk. She was rescued when Mr. Garvey proceeded to recount an amusing episode of his schooldays, but walking along, her emotions were chaotic. Had she
really been gazing tenderly at a door? If so, she had no least
recollection of what it had looked like. "Oh, to be young and
in love . . ." What stuff, when she had only been thinking
of . . . Craig. An even sharper pang of guilt made her squirm.
Despite her procrastinations she knew very well that she would
eventually marry dear Dev, just as he knew it. To allow her
thoughts to wander to another gentleman in so foolish a way
was wickedly disloyal.

Raising her eyes she found that Mr. Garvey was watching

her with faint curiosity. He must think her a thorough widgeon!
She forced a smile, but her cheeks were so hot she knew they
must be scarlet.

❧ *Chapter 8* ❧

Far into the morning, Devenish and Tyndale were still chor-
tling over the rout of the Nimmses. The day lived up to its
early promise and by mid-afternoon the sun was so hot that the
small pilgrimage began to slow. The men took turns carrying
Josie until she complained that she was quite able to walk and
didn't want to be "babied."

"Why not?" laughed Devenish, setting her down and inwardly relieved to do so. "You *are* a baby"—he ruffled her
tangled hair—"and must be coddled."

She scowled at him ferociously. "I is not! You think I'll be
a great nuisance, but I knows how to take care of myself and
I don't need carrying! You just see if I don't walk so good as
what you and Mr. Craig does!"

She ran out ahead, defiance in every line of her. "Revolting
grammar!" called Devenish, teasingly.

"What the deuce are you going to do with her?" asked
Craig.

"Lord knows. Gad! I keep thinking of how old Nimms shot
out of that shed! It was worth the loss of our funds, damme if
it wasn't!"

"Yes." Craig grinned. "The family honour is restored."

Devenish sobered. "In part, at least," he said pointedly.

Reddening, Craig was silent, but after a while he chuckled.
"How in the world you were able to control that bear is quite
beyond me!"

"Nothing to it. I've got the Rat Paws, you see."

"The—*what?*"

"Josie says it means I've a way with animals. I do, as a matter of fact, and it stood us in good stead today, I'll allow. I wonder if poor old Schultz ever got his bear back? His legs were going a mile a minute the last time we saw him."

They went on, talking more or less companionably, but progressing ever more slowly, and not noticing when Josie dropped back to walk with them, and gradually fell behind.

"Jove," sighed Tyndale, drawing a sleeve across his perspiring brow, "I didn't think it ever got hot in England. Have we far to go, yet?"

"Eight or nine miles, at least. I only hope Val is not from home. He's a dashed good fellow, but—his family!" Devenish grimaced. "His brother's a decent sort, but he has a cousin I'd as soon—"

A shrill scream cut off his words. Whirling, he caught a glimpse of Josie, her hair clutched in a large, grimy fist. From the corner of his eye he saw just such another fist clutching a whizzing branch. He ducked, but the branch caught him across the base of the neck and for a little while he saw nothing but wheeling lights.

He aroused to a scuffling sound; an irregular thudding, short heavy breathing, and an occasional gasped-out curse. A dark shape shot past. Not quite sure of what to do, Devenish gathered that he was missing a jolly good brawl. How it chanced that he was lying down, he could not remember, but he commenced a dogged struggle to get to his feet.

A crowd was involved in violent dispute. "Yoicks!" croaked Devenish, and launched himself into the fray. The crowd thinned, and he blinked and found that Tyndale was battling two men whose head scarves and swarthy countenances proclaimed them gypsies. Even as his vision cleared, a knife was plunged at Tyndale's back. Devenish jumped into action and sent the weapon spinning off.

Tyndale panted, "Thanks . . . coz!"

The knife wielder however, was indignant, and Devenish blocked a hamlike retaliatory fist. "Akim and Benjo, I take it?" he shouted.

"And—Rollo," said Tyndale, jerking his head to the side and a heavily built man sprawled on the grassy verge.

"You took our—Tabby!" snarled Tyndale's opponent, his dark face twisted with passion.

"Yus, and we'll 'ave the law on yer!" shouted his comrade, rushing Devenish, who dodged adroitly.

"Good . . . idea!" Tyndale feinted, then drove home a shattering jab that staggered his sinewy adversary. "We might discover from whom you stole her!"

Patently offended by such tactics, the gypsies abandoned talk in favour of a concentration upon the business at hand. The recumbent member of the trio also surged back into the fray. It was a short but fierce struggle. Tyndale, as Devenish noted with admiration, was a splendid man with his fives, but he was not at the top of his form and was tiring visibly. The impromptu bandage had already been dislodged and the cut over his temple was bleeding so that he was compelled to wipe hurriedly at his eyes. Devenish grassed his man with a well-aimed right, but was sent sprawling by the third gypsy, who had timed the attack nicely. Winded, Devenish cried out as a heavy boot rammed home. Tyndale saw the kick that had savaged him and with a shout of rage leapt astride his cousin. He would have little chance alone, Devenish thought dazedly, and if they were bested, these ruffians would take the child. He fought to rise. She must not end her days in a Flash House, poor mite! She *must* not! He got to his knees, but was unable to stand, so threw himself at the legs of the tall Rollo, and clung doggedly. It was all the chance Tyndale needed. With one blindingly fast uppercut he sent Akim to join Benjo, turned in time to see Devenish crumple again and, seething, drove a fist into Rollo's midsection, then finished him with a powerful chopping blow to the back of the neck.

Hobbling to his cousin, he wheezed, "You . . . all right . . . ?"

"Quite," gasped Devenish, clutching his leg. "Good scrap . . . what?"

A small, weeping shape hurtled at them. Frantic hands reached out to stroke back Devenish's tumbled hair. "I thinked ye was . . . cross with me!" gulped the child. "And then Benjo got me and—and I thinked I was going to be . . . sold to the Flash House, surely! Oh, Mr. Dev! You won't never let 'em take me? Don't let 'em! Promise Josie you won't!"

He sat up and pulled her into a hug. "Silly elf," he said gruffly. Her arms flew around his neck and, sobbing, she pressed tight against him. Over her shoulder, he said, "I rather fancy you saved me from getting my ribs . . . stove in, cousin."

"And you—diverted the knife that would have split . . . my wishbone."

It was said so reluctantly that Devenish flared, "I collect you would prefer I had not?"

"No, but . . ." Tyndale hesitated, frowning.

Devenish burst into a breathless laugh. "A trifle awkward, eh?"

"A trifle."

"No matter. We're even, at all events." Devenish put the clinging child from him. "Come, Miss Storm." He gave her hair a slight tug. "There's work to be done. I think our friends yonder would be the better without their boots. Can you pull 'em off?"

She dashed her tears away with the heel of one grubby hand, smiled tremulously, and flew to do his bidding. Tyndale helped him to his feet and, as soon as the boots were removed from the unlovely trio, the two men and the child set forth once more, each carrying a pair of the purloined articles.

For a space they were silent, all three, Tyndale seeming to ache from head to toe, and Devenish's limp becoming ever more pronounced until Tyndale halted and said, "Friend Rollo dealt you a leveller, did he not?"

Snatching back the hand that was unobtrusively gripping his right thigh, Devenish said brightly, "Pooh! Fustian! I shall do nicely."

"He was limping 'fore Rollo kicked him," Josie put in anxiously. "Don't he allus?"

"No, child. Dev, let me have a look."

"Certainly not!" Devenish threw up a restraining hand as Tyndale stepped closer. "I am a most private type and will suffer no one to inspect my—er—limbs."

Tyndale glanced at Josie.

"I seen legs before," she revealed scornfully. "And once I see Akim's—"

"Never mind!" said Devenish, retreating. "No, really, cousin, what do you take me for? Some kind of Spartan slowtop? If there was anything could be done, I'd have yelled for help long since."

"And old injury?" asked Tyndale.

"Yes. Rollo's boot chanced to find it, is all."

"The war? Oh, no—you said you did not get to the Peninsula."

"True. This was another kind of battle. I suppose it was one of the details you complained I left out, when I told you how Tristram Leith and I got the girls away from the chateau in Dinan."

They started to walk on again, and Tyndale asked curiously, "What kind of 'detail'? A pistol ball?"

"Crossbow bolt." Tyndale's jaw dropped, and Devenish said wryly, "Our Frenchman has a taste for medieval weapons."

"Does he, by thunder! Then we had best—"

Her small face sharp with fear, Josie warned shrilly, "Some 'un be coming!"

Devenish pulled her behind him and both men turned to face the cart that came rattling up.

Clinging to Devenish's jacket, Josie gave a sudden glad cry. "Tinker Sam! Oh, Tinker Sam!" She ran to greet the newcomer. "It be me! Tabby!"

The cart halted. A round-faced, round-eyed, friendly-looking little man exclaimed, "Tabby? Why—so it do be! And two gents what look, as they say, very much the worse fer wear. There's a tale here, I do expect. And one thing as I loves is a tale. So—come aboard, gents and missy. Where be ye bound fer?"

"Hallelujah!" breathed Devenish.

"And amen," agreed Tyndale.

More practically, Josie said. "Tewkesbury. In exchange for three pair of smelly boots!"

With an eye to his own affairs, Mr. Garvey so charmed Arabella Drummond that for the next two days she was induced to rise very much earlier than was her usual custom, with the result that they reached Leeds in good time. Mr. Garvey directed the coachman to a fine posting house just south of the city and procured excellent accommodations. Having ordered up and enjoyed a superb dinner with his two weary charges, he then accompanied Yolande while she took Socrates for a brief outing in the gardens. He returned her safely to her bedchamber, and took himself off to his own room.

Opening the door, he froze. A lamp burned beside the curtained window, and the wing chair was occupied. The gentleman seated there had a fine head of neatly curled dark hair untouched by grey; his build was slight, his age indeterminate, and his elegance considerable. He raised a pair of warm brown eyes from the pages of the periodical he was idly scanning, and revealed features that were good, if not remarkable. "Do pray come in, my dear James," he murmured in French. "One never knows who might pass by."

Garvey hurriedly swung the door shut, advanced into the

423

room to toss hat and gloves on the bed, and demanded, "Are you mad? If we were seen together! *Up here!*"

The Frenchman shrugged. "Yet you were on your way to see me—is it not so?"

Garvey's cloak followed hat and gloves, and he drew a chair closer to his unexpected visitor. "Yes. But I was incredibly fortunate in chancing upon an excellent means of explaining my journey, Claude, and—"

Monsieur Claude Sanguinet smiled. His soft voice and gentle manner were at odds with the fact that he was held by many knowledgeable men to be one of the most dangerous plotters in Europe. Garvey, knowing him very well indeed, knew that smile also and quavered into silence.

"Ah," said the Frenchman, laying the periodical aside. "But I think it must be that you are unaware of something, *mon ami.* Namely, that your—er, 'excellent means' chances to be betrothed to an old and so dear friend of ours, one Monsieur Alain Devenish."

"No, but I *am* aware," Garvey asserted eagerly. "And you must be very pleased, Claude. I have disposed of him!"

Sanguinet rested his elbow on the chair arm, and his chin upon the fingers of one slender white hand. He murmured, "Then I am of a surety indebted to you, my dear James. Dare I ask how this—necessity—has been accomplished?"

Garvey glanced to the closed door and lowered his voice. "That rogue of a tiger of mine hired some ruffians to abduct him, carry him away, and put a period to him." He grinned triumphantly. "You can count yourself avenged for—" In the nick of time he stopped himself from saying "for Devenish having kicked you last year!" Monsieur Sanguinet did not care to be reminded of embarrassments. Therefore, he finished, "for his interference."

"But, how charming. And what a great pity it is that your, ah, hirelings bungled the job, my dear."

Garvey's jaw dropped. "But they did not! They could not have! Devenish would have been hot after us if—"

"They appear to have decided," purred Sanguinet, "that the penalty for murdering two aristocrats was too great. At all events, I have it on the most reliable authority that our intrepid friend and his cousin are on their way north at this very moment. I fancy they mean to stay at Longhills, near Malvern. I discover that Devenish has a friend whose country seat is located there."

Dismayed, Garvey muttered, "Longhills? Oh, Montclair's place. I am acquainted with his cousin, Junius Trent."

One of Sanguinet's brows arched. "Is important, this?" He shrugged smiling sweetly.

Garvey reddened and retreated into bluster. "Now, damn those bucolic clods! They took my gold and left the business undone! By thunder, but—"

Sanguinet waved his hand in a gracefully arresting gesture. "But, as is usual, I must do the thing myself."

Staring at him, Garvey went to the round table before the window, and unstoppered a decanter. "You . . . ?" he echoed, disbelievingly. "You, personally, will—"

"You are ridiculous, James, do you know? Ah, thank you. I wondered if ever I was to be offered refreshment. As you should surmise, I shall be the—how you say?—master-mind. My hands I do not foul. Dear Monsieur Devenish has dwelt on borrowed time these many months. It was not my intention to attend to him as yet. However, once again he is drawn into my orbit, and this time with *très* convenient the cousin. Do you know aught, my dear James, of Devenish's Canadian cousin?"

Sipping his wine, Garvey proceeded to occupy the other chair and replied, "Only that he comes at a curst inopportune time! They mean to go to *Castle Tyndale*, Claude. Did you know *that*?"

"But of course. I know everything." Sanguinet chuckled suddenly. "And do you know, James, our fine Colonial's arrival may be most fortuitous. Almost one might say Fate plays into our hands. With a little manipulation, perhaps, a *soupçon*, merely, our task yet may be very tidily accomplished, and all explained away for us." He raised his glass. "How sadly puzzled you look, James. Trust me. I really think that this time I have our Devenish in a quite delightful trap. Let us drink to its closing with finality. For do you know, if this foolish Englishman should elude me once more, I believe I might be . . . most vexed."

His manner was as languid, his smile as gentle, as ever, but the glow in the brown eyes contained a red shade that sent a chill down Garvey's spine. He lifted his own glass and said hurriedly, "To our dear friend."

Sanguinet nodded. "And his cousin, James. We must not forget the so charming Colonial cousin!"

* * *

Longhills was a beautiful estate, the great Tudor house being situated on a rolling knoll that commanded a fine view of its extensive park, meadows, woods, and rich pastureland dotted with fat brown cows and threaded by the gentle curve and gleam of the river. The travellers received a hearty welcome from the Honourable Valentine Montclair, a slight dark young man to whom Tyndale warmed at once. That his cousin's old school friend was a man of great wealth and social position was obvious, but there was no trace of height in his manner, which was quiet and so unassuming as to be almost humble. However surprised Montclair may have been to have three tattered and disreputable-appearing visitors thrust upon him, he evinced no sign of anything but delight. A considerably less delighted butler was commanded to provide suitable changes of clothing for the new guests, a frigid-mannered housekeeper was required to prepare suitable apartments, and the great house became a bustling beehive of activity as water was heated, linens allocated, and the cook apprised of the need to adjust his dinner plans. Upon learning that his guests had been obliged to abandon their horses in St. Albans, Montclair sent two grooms riding southward with instructions to reclaim the animals and take them to Castle Tyndale by easy stages.

Upstairs, a kindly abigail took charge of Josie. The child was bathed, her hair brushed until it shone, and an old flannel nightdress was hurriedly cut down to more or less fit her. When he himself had bathed, shaved, and donned the clothes Montclair had somehow conjured up, Devenish went in search of Josie and was slightly nonplussed to discover that her bedchamber was quite small and cheerless. She, however, considered the accommodations little short of palatial, and confided to Devenish that she'd not have dreamed she ever would occupy so lovely a bedchamber. She sighed ecstatically, "Never in all me kip!"

Devenish bade her good-night and returned to the quarters he shared with Tyndale. He found his cousin brushing his hair before the standing mirror, clad in rich, if ill-fitting garments, and looking much more civilized than when he had left him. Watching the Canadian thoughtfully, Devenish perched on the arm of a chair and wondered why the housekeeper had found it necessary that they share this bedchamber and the small adjoining parlour. Certainly, the rooms were luxurious, but it did seem odd that in so enormous a house they might not have been assigned individual apartments.

As if reading his thoughts, Tyndale said with his slow smile, "Have you the impression that Montclair is not the master of this house? I think I'd not trade places with him for all his wealth!"

"Nor I, poor devil! His aunt and that old curmudgeon of a husband of hers rule Val with a rod of iron. And if you think our arrangement miserly, coz, you should see what Josie has been offered."

"Well, it's a sight better than any of us had last night. What d'you mean to do with her, by the bye?"

"God knows. I fancy Yolande will have some solution. Or Lady Louisa."

At this point, the door opened and Montclair enquired if they were comfortably bestowed. Coming into the room, he was very obviously taken aback to discover they shared it, but not wishing to cause a commotion, Devenish lied that they had requested the arrangement because his cousin walked in his sleep. Tyndale concealed his indignation admirably. Montclair's dark eyes glinted with anger, but he kept himself in hand. His aunt, Lady Marcia Trent, had returned from visiting in the village, and would join them for dinner. "She is," he said, "eager to meet you, Tyndale. It seems she is acquainted with poor Lady De Lancey, who has often spoken of you."

"Oh," said Tyndale, slanting an oblique glance at his cousin.

"De Lancey?" Devenish repeated. "Wasn't he that American fellow who was Wellington's Quartermaster General at Waterloo?"

Montclair nodded. "Splendid chap. He was killed, you know, and only been married—what was it, Tyndale? A few days?"

"A little over two weeks when he died, I think. A terrible tragedy." It was a tragedy that had touched him closely, so that Tyndale forgot himself and said broodingly, "Poor Magdalene . . . but he died in her arms—she has that, at least." He sighed, sat down, and began to wrestle with his boots.

Staring at him in stark astonishment, Devenish exploded, "The devil! How do *you* know?"

"Er . . . well," said Tyndale awkwardly. "It, er—"

"Of course he knows," Montclair interposed in no little bewilderment. "Who should know better? He was *there*, you gudgeon! Damn near stuck his spoon in the wall as a result, and only—"

"There . . . ?" breathed Devenish. "Tyndale was—at *Waterloo?"*

Montclair stared from one to the other. "Well, of course! He used the name Winters then, but he was a major with the—"

"A . . . *Major* . . . ?" Soaring rage banished Devenish's stunned expression. "Why, you dirty . . . lying . . . bastard!" With a howl, he leapt for his cousin. Tyndale's chair went over and they were down a flurry of arms and legs, while Montclair gave a whoop and sprang clear.

"Miserable *cheat!*" Devenish snarled, locking his hands about Tyndale's throat. "So it wasn't *your war*, eh?"

"Dev! Now, Dev!" Tyndale laughed, tearing at Devenish's wrists. "I never said—"

"No, damn you! But you gave me to—ow!—to understand that—"

"Well—let be! You were so blasted ready to—to believe me a worthless clod, that—"

"Good gracious!" A clear feminine voice cut through the uproar. Sitting astride Tyndale, Devenish jerked his head around, then scrambled to his feet, running a hasty hand through his dishevelled locks.

Lady Marcia Trent stood on the threshold, a tall young exquisite holding the door for her. Tall herself, and angularly elegant, my lady's face had a pinched look, the thin nostrils and tight, small mouth not softened by icy blue eyes, prominent cheekbones, and a pointed chin. Montclair presented his friends with a marked lack of apology for their antics. Nonetheless, as they went down to dine, Lady Trent was soon chattering happily with Tyndale. Her son, Junius, was not so amiable, his sardonic stare repeatedly wandering from one to the other of their unexpected guests while he made few attempts to contribute to the conversation. This was not a cause for dismay, however, since it developed that his mother's notion of "a pleasant cose with the gallant Major" consisted of her complete domination of the conversation, her piercing voice overriding the efforts of any so bold as to attempt a side topic, and only her son daring to interrupt her occasionally.

These tactics neither disturbed nor bored Tyndale. He was very tired and quite content to let the odious woman prose on while he murmured appropriate responses and allowed his own thoughts to wander. Inevitably, they wandered in one direction. He had hitherto known little of affairs of the heart and, although he longed for a loving wife and children, he had begun to fear that either his nature was cold, or his standards too high, for never had he met the lady who could awaken in him any more than a sense of liking or admiration. Until a certain morning in a lane in Sussex. Until he'd seen Miss Yolande Drummond. . . . Yolande, beautiful, sweet and proud, and dainty and brave, and desirable. His sleeping heart was awake and with a vengeance, but what a bitter twist of Fate that of all the girls he had ever met, he must fall desperately in love with a lady who was hopelessly beyond his reach. Not only was she promised, but she was to wed a man who had just this afternoon turned aside the knife that might have killed him! A man who had every right to despise him, and who would likely have been considered justified to have looked the other way rather than saving his life. Not that it made much difference, for no gentleman could pursue a lady already promised. Besides, even had she been free as air, his chances would doubtless have been nil. That lovely and desirable girl would certainly not be permitted to marry a man whose name was so horribly besmirched.

He must, he thought drearily, put her out of his mind. Difficult, if he stayed at Castle Tyndale, for Devenish had said that Steep Drummond was only ten miles distant. To run the risk that occasionally in the empty years to come he would see her—as Mrs. Alain Devenish—was too daunting a prospect to contemplate. No, it would not do. He must strive to clear his father's name, and then either go back to Canada or settle somewhere at a safe distance from his adored but forbidden lady.

He was very quiet for the balance of the evening, and despite his weariness, slept fitfully.

They left Longhills early the following morning, Devenish and Josie occupying the chaise Montclair had insisted they borrow, and Tyndale riding a magnificent blood mare. Their host accompanied them to the northernmost border of his far-flung preserves, then watched rather wistfully as they left him, Devenish turning back to wave and promise the chaise and horses would be well cared for and promptly returned.

Montclair called, "Keep them, old fellow, until my grooms come with your own horses. They can bring back my cattle then."

"Right you are!" Devenish lifted the reins. "Off we go, Josie Storm," he said joyously. "Egad, but I can scarce wait to see Yolande!"

The chaise picked up speed.

Tyndale gazed after it for a moment, then followed.

Steep Drummond was constructed of red sandstone and, perched on the top of its hill, turned a defiant eye to the rest of the world as though it were a fortress, maintaining stern guard over its domain. It was a large house, uncompromisingly square, and with gardens so neat and trees so uniformly spaced they gave the appearance of being prepared at all times for a tour of inspection.

On this grey spring morning, smoke curled from several chimneys, one of which led from the morning room where the fire blazed merrily. Standing before the hearth, hands clasped behind his back, General Sir Andrew Drummond's craggy face did not, however, look in the least merry. As was the way of his house, he was a tall man, and his well-built frame was as lean and erect as ever, although the thick, once-red hair was now iron-grey. He had the Drummond chin, which had lost not one whit of its belligerence and was, at the moment, decidedly aggressive. "Yon wee hoond," he proclaimed, "has seen fit tae sink his fangs intae ma mon, and nip twa o' the hoosemaids! I've held ma peace the noo, Arrrabella, but enough 's as guid as a feast! 'Tis a chancy business tae lure a decent chef up here, forbye. I'll nae hae him run off by an scrrruffy mongrel! Do I make m'sel' clearrr, ma'am?"

The question was debatable. Blinking at him, his daughter-in-law asked uncertainly, "Yolande, what did your grandfather say?"

Exasperated, the General's fierce green eyes rolled at the ceiling, his moustache bristled, and he uttered a sound midway between snort and groan—a sort of "och-unnh!"—while reflecting that from among all the women in the world, his eldest boy had seen fit to choose *this* silly widgeon!

Regarding him with fond amusement, Yolande said, "I see you still become pure Scots when irked, sir."

"All Scots are puir!" he asserted.

"Their whisky, at least," his irreverent granddaughter chuckled, winning an immediate answering grin. "It would seem, Aunt Bella, that Socrates had been partaking of the servants, and Grandpapa's chef has threatened to leave. You really will have to muzzle him, if—"

"Muzzle him!" exploded the General. "I'd a sight sooner shoot the wretched pest oot o' hand!"

430

This, it developed, Mrs. Drummond did understand, for she uttered a shriek and clapped handkerchief to tearless eyes. "Oh! How could you be so—so unkind?" she sobbed. "My d-dear little Socrates! All—*all* I have left in the . . . whole, wide world!"

The wiles that worked so well with Lady Louisa did not so much as check the General. "Then," he said dourly, suddenly becoming punctiliously English, "do you wish your worldly goods to remain intact, madam, I would suggest you confine your pestilent pet to a leash!"

"Cruel!" wept Mrs. Drummond. "Cruel!" And wailing, departed.

"Whisht!" the General erupted as the door closed behind her. "How do you abide that caper wit, Yolande? I'd have thought you could have delayed your visit until one of your brothers could escort you. Or at least, that young scapegrace, Devenish—though I canna abide the boy!"

A frown shadowing Yolande's eyes, she said, "Papa would have come, save that poor Rosemary is miserably ill with measles and Mama draws so much support from him at such times, you know. As to Aunt Arabella, why, I suppose the poor soul needs to be needed. And I needed a chaperon."

"At your age?" he snorted, tactlessly. "Gammon! Besides, you'd that fella Garvey to escort you, in addition to the outriders and your abigail. I'd have thought 'twas an ample sufficiency."

"We met Mr. Garvey quite by accident, sir, and it was indeed good of him to stay with us for the rest of the journey. Although he denied it, I suspect we took him out of his way."

"Very likely. Young Hamish MacInnes told me he saw the man bowling along north of Kilmarnock, so he canna have stayed long with his retired servant, if indeed there is such a creature. He probably told you he was to visit there purely to set your mind at ease. He seemed a well-bred sort of man, for all he cries friends with that Germanic clod who'll next usurp the throne."

Yolande threw up her hands in mock horror. "Heavens! Treason!"

"Fiddlesticks! Well, miss? Well?" He glared ferociously at her, even while thinking how pretty she was, gracefully disposed on the green damask sofa, wearing a morning dress of palest lime muslin, and with her hair arranged into glossy curls, soft about her face. "I suppose I'll next be forced to play host to your would-be spouse, eh? Chances are he's hot after you, as usual!"

"Perhaps not, sir," Yolande answered quietly. "We had a small—er, difference of opinion and Dev seems to have gone off in a huff."

"Good! You're well rid of him. He's no more ready to settle down than Brummel would be to wear Petersham trousers!"

She smiled. "You make it all sound very simple, Grandpapa."

"Aye. Well, so it is. If ye dinna care for the laddie, ye shouldna wed him. And—if ye *do* care for him, ye shouldna wed him. Hoot-toot, whar's the hair-tearing in that?"

Laughing, Yolande reached out her hand to him and, as he came to take it and sit beside her, scolded, "Alain is truly a fine young man, dearest. Why do you so dislike him?"

A frown tugged at his bushy brows. "Partly," he said softly, "because he is all frivolity and foolishness, and has never stuck to, nor accomplished aught in his ne'er-do-well life."

"I shall be so bold as to pull caps with you on that score," she argued in her gentle fashion. "Alain is, and I know this for a fact, a brave and fearless fighter, who stood by Tristram Leith when they were hopelessly outnumbered in Brittany last year. When he was hurt, he endured a great deal of misery with no complaint, so Leith told me. He is full of spirit, and if he has not yet settled down to managing his estates and—and setting up his nursery, why, it is for no worse reason than that I have made him wait so long."

Watching her narrowly, he said, "Which brings me to my other reason. I collect you must care for him very deeply, lass. And I'll own I've heard a few things of late to his credit. Yet, I've a wee suspicion that you have been pushed into this promise because my son and Louisa wish it. And that is an utter folly that I'll no—" He checked, glancing with irritation at the door as it opened and his stocky little butler entered to announce, "Mr. Devenish, Mr. Tyndale, and Mistress Storm, General."

Yolande started, and her heart began to pound in a most ridiculous way. *"Mistress Storm . . . ?"* She turned, gave a gasp, and came instinctively to her feet as she saw the signs of battle on the faces of the two young men.

Standing also, General Drummond welcomed Devenish with cool dignity. Upon being introduced to Tyndale, he stared, frowned, and said, "Tyndale? Strange, I'd not even known of your existence until my granddaughter told me of you. Yet I feel we've met before. Gad, but I know we have! Wasn't it—"

"At the Horse Guards, I believe, sir. Though I was presented to you as—"

"Winters! Major Craig Winters! Right you are!" The General extended his hand. "Heard great things of you, young fella, but never dreamt you was a Tyndale! Don't use the family name, eh?"

Tyndale smiled, his eyes very empty, and moved to shake hands with Yolande.

Quite bewildered by these disclosures, she said, "Why cousin! I'd not the faintest notion you were in the army."

"And at Waterloo, m'dear," said Devenish, coming up jealously to claim her hand and press it to his lips. "I was fairly bowled over when Montclair told me of it. Never heard such wicked deceit!"

Sir Andrew's sharp glance at the Major surprised a wistfulness in the lean face. "Oho!" he thought. "So that's the way the land lies!"

Yolande was still striving to recover from the all too familiar lightning bolt that had again struck her the instant Tyndale touched her hand. She said in pretty confusion, "Well, well— never mind that now. How glad I am to see you both! But how naughty of you, firstly to have vanished, and now to come here!"

"You never thought to keep me away?" Devenish grinned, squeezing the hand he still held. "The fact is, Tyndale and I were set upon. Robbed, carried off, and dumped miles from anywhere!"

"By Jove!" fumed the General, his whiskers bristling alarmingly. "Do not just stand there, laddie! Set ye doon. You too, Major. Yolande, never loiter about with your mouth at half-cock! Pour these fellows some cognac! Now, Alain, tell us of it!"

Devenish obliged in his usual exuberant fashion, Tyndale inserting an occasional quiet remark of his own. Listening with indignant incredulity, Sir Andrew variously smothered oaths, snorted his outrage, or applauded the cousins' resourcefulness. Just as intent, Yolande was soon very pale, her horrified gaze darting from one young gentleman to the other. Devenish was only halfway through his tale, however, when the General suddenly flung up a hand. "Lord! Where is my mind? Devenish—do we not neglect someone?"

Devenish blinked. "Eh? Who?"

"The child!" Tyndale exclaimed in dismay. "By gad! What's become of her?"

"I be here," came a scared little voice, and Josie, her eyes huge and fearful, peeped from around the back of a tall wing chair.

"Jupiter, but I forgot her," cried Devenish. "Come here, elf, and make your curtsy to Miss Yolande Drummond and General Sir Andrew Drummond."

Trembling with nervousness, Josie crept out and essayed two clumsy curtsies.

"Really, Dev!" Yolande scolded. "You could at least tell us the poor child's name."

"Enderby announced her," he said defensively.

Josie flushed. "I be Josie Storm now," she piped. "I was Tabby, but Mr. Dev found me and when I grow up I going to be his—"

"Housekeeper!" Devenish inserted, in the nick of time.

Tyndale chuckled, and a corner of the General's stern mouth twitched appreciatively.

"*Found* you?" echoed Yolande, much intrigued. "Dev, whatever have you been about? You've never kidnapped the child?"

"'Course he hasn't!" said Josie scornfully. "I followed Mr. Dev because I don't want to be sold to no Flash House. He didn't want me, but he's going to train me for a abigail if *he* don't want me when I be growed."

Devenish sank his head into his hands. The General gasped. Tyndale turned away, smothering a grin. Yolande, her warm heart touched, stroked the child's dusky curls and, not deigning to pretend unawareness of such horrors as Flash Houses, said gently, "Poor little girl, what a dreadful time you have had. Are you parents living?"

Kindness was a blessing Josie had known but seldom, and at this, tears blinded her. Dashing them away, she blinked up at this fairy princess of a lady and divulged huskily that she had been stole and didn't, if you please, know who her parents had been.

"The devil!" muttered Drummond. "You did perfectly right, Devenish. What d'you mean to do with her?"

"I was hoping Yolande or Lady Louisa could advise me, sir."

Yolande, whose grave regard had not left the child, said, "Did you and Cousin Craig buy her this dress, Dev?"

"Yes," he answered proudly. "Jolly good—what?"

Yolande shook her head at him in the time-honoured sympathy of a woman for a helpless male, and asked, "Josie, would you really like to be an abigail?"

"I'd like to be a lady, like you." The child sighed wistfully. "But I'd a sight liefer be an abigail than be sold to some bloody Flash House!"

Tyndale and the General dissolved into mutual mirth. Devenish groaned and clutched his locks. Yolande, her face scarlet, was momentarily struck dumb. Horrified, Josie threw both hands to paling cheeks, and her gaze darted to her god. "Oh," she wailed, "I said something drefful again! Don't ye be cross with Josie, now! Don't ye!"

"Of—of course he will not," stammered Yolande. "It is only, er—you will soon learn. Dev, excuse me, please. I will hear the rest of your tale later. Come, Josie, we will see what we can do about that—dress."

She extended one dainty and exquisitely manicured hand. Staring from it to Devenish, Josie demurred, "If you please, ma'am, I'd like to stay with Mr. Dev."

"Castle Tyndale," cautioned the General softly, "is no place for a child, Devenish."

"No, sir," Devenish agreed. "And what's more, my elf, you'll be a sight better off with Miss Drummond than jauntering about the countryside with two rogues like Tyndale and me." He threw up one hand, silencing the forlorn attempt at a plea. "Do as you're told! Lord, but I am surer than ever that I should have left you in Cricklade! Which reminds me— Yolande, where is that reptile, Garvey? Still trying to fix his interest with you?"

She frowned. "Oh, never start that again! Mr. Garvey was the essence of courtesy, which is more than could be said for you, Dev! Only see how you have made the child weep! Truly, you should be spanked!"

"Don't you never cut up stiff with him!" sobbed Josie, turning on her in a flame. "He can make me cry if he wants. He don't mean it. It's just—he don't want me. And why should he? I ain't got a pretty face, and I'm just—just a nuisance to . . . to him. . . ." Her voice broke, and she stood there in choked silence, the tears coursing down her gaunt little face.

With a muffled cry, Yolande pulled the child into her arms. "Of course he wants you! We all want you!" Over Josie's shoulder, she flashed a fuming glare at the hapless Devenish, then murmured, "Come, dear. We'll visit the kitchen first, for I'm sure you would like a glass of milk and there may be some cheese tarts left. Then I'll take you down to see our new filly—should you like that?"

Her woes forgotten, Josie dragged one skinny arm across her eyes, and said eagerly that she would like that very much, adding an anxious, "Providing Mr. Dev do not go off without me."

Devenish, his own eyes rather inexplicably moist, promised gruffly that he would not desert her.

"All right," said Josie sunnily, accepting Yolande's hand. "I'll go with you, miss. I loves animals. Though I ain't got the way with 'em like what Mr. Dev has. Did you know," she went on chattily, "that he's got the Rat Paws?"

As an amused Tyndale closed the door behind them, Devenish turned to find the General's fascinated gaze upon his hands.

"Be dashed if I ever noticed it," said Sir Andrew. "Let us have a look—poor fellow."

❧ *Chapter 9* ❧

The clouds had lightened, but a brisk wind blew Yolande's pelisse and tumbled her hair as she leaned against the paddock fence, watching Josie romp happily with the two-week old filly. She could scarcely wait to see Devenish and hear the rest of his adventures. From what she had heard, Tyndale had been quite brutally beaten. Her heart turned over as a picture of his pale bruised face came into her mind's eye. Whatever must he think of England, being so newly arrived and so savagely dealt with? But, he was not newly arrived, of course. He was a major, and had survived the terrible Battle of Waterloo. She thought with a sudden surge of irritation, "Oh, how I wish they had not come here! I wish Dev had not brought Craig!" But in the next breath she was wishing that Devenish would hurry to her.

The child did not look so scared any more, poor mite. And they would soon find some decent clothes for her. That awful dress! How could those two great moonlings have thought it became her? It was at least three sizes too large, and that hideous red-and-white check was downright ghastly! Already Peattie and Sullivan were quarreling happily over an ell of cambric and several pattern cards, and if she knew those two redoubtable women, their nimble fingers would have fashioned a far more attractive frock for the little girl by morning.

"Here you are, my delight!"

She jumped and, relieved to see that Devenish was alone, reached out both hands in welcome.

Devenish took them strongly and kissed each. "Lord, but I've missed you!" he said with unusual fervour. "Are you ready to go home yet?"

"I just arrived, silly boy," she laughed. "And you have no business to have come!"

Deliberately misinterpreting, he said a blithe, "Oh, I slipped away as soon as I could in good conscience do so. Luckily, Tyndale's taken your grandfather's fancy, and they're jawing like a couple of old campaigners." His merry eyes slipped past her. "Josie found a friend, I see. Gad! What a fine filly! Who's the dam? Is she—"

"Never mind the filly, sir," said Yolande, trying to look stern, while thinking how hopeless a case he was to take it for granted so breezily that they had nothing more important to discuss than that Molly-My-Lass had dropped her foal. The marks of combat were very evident upon his classic countenance and, touching his perfectly straight, slim nose, she murmured, "It never ceases to amaze me that through your many battles you've managed to keep this article from being broken."

"Tactics," he asserted, seizing her finger and kissing it. "I was born to be a general, but the Horse Guards lacked the sense to snap me up."

Despite his light manner, she thought he looked tired and said gently, "Poor Dev. What a dreadful time you have had." And then, teasing him, "Are you quite sure it is not all a hum designed to cover up the fact that you and Craig fought all the way up here?"

"You're not so far out, at that," he chuckled, reluctantly relinquishing her hand. "Though not one another. We've both—more or less ... er, taken vows not to—to come to blows. Ever." As always when he was in earnest, he stumbled and flushed, and darted a self-conscious glance at her. "Curst n-nuisance, ain't it?"

"Indeed not! I think it splendid! And splendid that you rescued the child. Did you ride Miss Farthing all the way up here?"

"Oh, no. She and Lazzy grow fat in St. Albans. I fancy we will have a very large reckoning at the posting house."

Dismayed, she cried, "But—Dev! Your horses were taken from there. Did not you and Craig call for them?"

"Devil we did! What d'you mean—taken?"

"Well—oh, heavens! We all thought— Oh, you never think they were stolen? Craig thinks the world of that queer animal of his, and Miss—"

"That slippery rogue!" raged Devenish. "I'll call him out, by God! Where is he? Not too far from you, I'll warrant!"

"What? Who? If you mean Craig—"

"Not Craig, m'dear! Not this time!"

"Then— Dev, do you *know* who is responsible for these dreadful things?"

"Assuredly! Your gallant, conciliating escort! And as for—"

She stiffened and stepped back a pace. *"James ... Garvey?"* she whispered, staring at him incredulously. "Oh, but ... you cannot be serious?"

"Oh, can I not!"

"Then you must be all about in your head! No, really—you allow jealousy to go too far. My aunt and I—"

"Were properly gammoned," he rasped, flaming with wrath over the loss of his beloved mare.

"I was not 'gammoned,' as you so crudely put it," she declared angrily. "I am truly sorry you were set upon, but since you were last seen in the tap you were probably very well to live, and—"

"Well, if that don't beat the Dutch! Here I've been lured into an ambush, drugged, robbed, tossed into a ditch and left to wander over half England with not so much as a groat in my pockets. And every moment half out of my wits with worry for you! And you meanwhile, allow that treacherous scoundrel to—"

Her chin lifting haughtily, Yolande countered, "Since you

are so sure Mr. Garvey is a treacherous scoundrel, one must presume he introduced himself before clapping the drugged rag over your face."

"No, he did not," he fumed. "Nor did he hand Tyndale his calling card before breaking his head! But that don't mean he wasn't behind everything! And if you was half as shrewd a judge of character as—"

"Then dare I ask, O infallible judge, upon what—save your despicable suspicions—you base this wicked slander?"

Devenish marched closer, grabbed her shoulders, and held her firm despite her struggles. "My opinion, ma'am, is based not upon suspicions, but upon something that happened whilst I was in Dinan last autumn."

Shock came into her eyes, and her struggles ceased abruptly. Any lover with an ounce of wisdom in the ways of women would have allowed those ominous words to sink in. Devenish, however, was as inexperienced in courtship as he was swift in temper, and swept on disastrously. "And furthermore, I have every right to be both concerned and jealous as bedamned over you! As soon as you stop playing off your coquettish airs and set a date, we will—"

"*Coquettish . . . !*" she gasped, wrenching free. "Why, of all the—"

"Well, dash it all, Yolande, when *are* you going to permit me to announce it?"

Her heart fluttering, she said. "Perhaps never, if I must face a future in which you are ready to call out every gentleman I chance to speak to!"

"*Never?* My God! You do not— Dearest girl . . . you never mean to cry off?"

She felt miserable now and close to tears, and darting a glance at him saw that he was very white, a stark desolation in his face. She loved him dearly and, struck to the heart, reached out her hand. "Forgive me. That was very bad. But, you know, Dev, I have almost as—as nasty a temper as do you."

He clasped her hand between both his own, scanning her beloved features anxiously. She had spoken in the heat of anger, merely. She had not truly meant that she might not wed him. For a moment, the prospect of a future in which Yolande played no part had stretched out, bleak and terrible before him, but that was silliness. They were meant for each other; they always had been meant for each other. He must learn to handle her more gently was all. It was difficult sometimes, when one had grown up with a chit, to see her as anything but a pigtailed schoolgirl . . . But Yolande was far from that now, and other men—too many, blast them!—saw her with far different eyes. "I'm a crazy clunch," he said repentantly, "and you are perfectly right, I'm jealous as a link boy's torch. I love you, you know. Very much. But—I wonder you tolerate me, much less accept me as a husband."

The declaration was as clumsy as it was rare. Overwhelmed, Yolande tightened her grip on his hand and smiled mistily.

Devenish knew a great surge of relief. Her affection was plain to see. He was reprieved! Offering his arm, he said with his engaging grin, "A stroll around the riding club, m'dear?"

She took his arm, and as they strolled along together he told her most of what had transpired. He spoke lightly, but at the finish she halted and stood regarding him in no little perplexity.

"However can you laugh at it? You might very well have been killed! I can certainly understand your aversion to Mr. Garvey, and I will be honest, Dev, and admit I cannot quite like him, although I have no complaints as to his treatment of us. I assure you he made no attempt to engage my affections. He was kind and considerate, and apparently with no other object in view than to be of help to us. He said his adieux very politely when he delivered us safely here, and I've not seen him since. Why would he have gone to the trouble and risk of having you abducted, as you suspect, if he did not mean to try and fix his interest with me?"

"Perhaps he had another motive." He thought, "Perhaps he was hoping to please Sanguinet," but he knew that would sound farfetched, so said nothing more.

Yolande eyed him uncertainly. "Are you thinking that Craig might pose a threat to him? But—how could he? Craig knows so few people over here."

"I wouldn't refine overmuch on that, m'dear. That varmint knows a sight more people than he'll admit to."

"Now that—" she smiled—"sounds much more like dear Dev."

"How so?"

"Why, when last I saw you it seemed only a matter of time before you two were at it with sword and dagger! Yet just now, when you were telling me of your adventures, one might have thought Craig your dearest friend."

"Good God! How could I give you so revolting an impression! Only because he saved my life, I'm not like to change my opinion of the rascal."

"Saved your life? Heavens! When?"

"During our scuffle with Messrs. Akim and Benjo. I told you of it."

"You did not say your *life* was endangered!"

"Oh. Well, I was downed and just for a minute or two knocked clean out of time. Old Craig stood over me when one of the louts made to kick my ribs in, and fought like a lion till I could hop up again."

Her eyes glowed. "How splendid!"

"Yes. I'll admit it was, rather. I was surprised to see how well he handled himself, for he's such a quiet type. I was never more shocked than to hear he'd served at Waterloo."

"It does seem incredible. And at first he was at pains to make us think he had only just arrived in England."

"Well, I suppose he had. He likely joined up in Belgium. Never look so doubtful. He was at Waterloo all right, and got himself properly stove in."

"He was wounded! Are you sure there can be no mistake?" And she knew that there was no mistake, but that she asked purely to learn more of Craig.

"Quite sure. For one thing, I saw the scar on his chest—beast of a thing! For another . . ." He frowned a little. "When we was at Longhills, Montclair's place, you know, Craig and I were given a room to share—if you can credit it."

"My goodness! They must have been very full of guests."

"Lord, no! There was only Montclair and the Trents—and Selby was from home, thank God! But, never mind about that. The point is that Craig started to talk to me in the night—or so I thought, only it turned out he was dreaming. Had the deuce of a time with him. He kept saying that he was 'all right' and that they must hold their position at all costs. There wasn't much doubt what he was re-living and I'd judge the real thing to have been—" he kicked at a clump of dandelions—"rather grim."

For a moment Yolande stood silent and very still, staring also at the dandelions. Then, drawing a deep breath she said, "I see. No wonder you name him a shifty scoundrel! He deceived us all."

Devenish glanced up, met her smile, and grinned responsively. "Didn't he just! Which—"

"Mr. Dev! Oh—Mr. Dev!"

Mounted on the back of the filly's mother, Josie ambled towards them.

"My Lady Fair," Devenish laughed. "How did you manage to get up on that mighty charger?"

"By Jove!" exclaimed Tyndale, wandering up to them with the General. "What a magnificent animal! A Belgian, sir?"

"Clydesdale," said Drummond, proudly. "The breed was founded in my father's youth. That's Molly-My-Lass you're looking at."

They all walked closer to the fence, and Tyndale reached up to stroke the neck of the great horse, who suffered his caress for only a moment before moving to nuzzle at Devenish.

Nodding at Josie, the General observed, "That must have been a large climb for you, little lady."

"Oh, I love horses, sir," said she brightly. "And they like me. Mostly. I just climbed up the fence and then hopped on. But I think I'll come down now please, 'cause her back's so wide it's making me legs stretch awful!"

Devenish put one hand on the fence, but hesitated. Craig swung with lithe ease over the bars and into the paddock, and lifted the child down.

A part of Yolande's mind registered the fact that poor Dev's leg must be troubling him again, which was natural enough after so long and violent a journey. Most of her awareness was centred on Craig, however. How kind that he had moved so quickly to spare Dev any possible embarrassment. He was smiling at something Josie had said, the wind ruffling his light hair, the sunshine bright on his face, accenting the laugh lines about his eyes.

The filly came flirting over, and Josie made a dart for the pretty creature, but with a flaunt of her tail and a roll of saucy eyes, the filly bounced off again. Craig swept Josie up and settled her on the fence, and Devenish reached up to collect her. Climbing the rails, Craig swung one leg over the top, glanced at Yolande, and paused, struck into immobility as his eyes met hers. The clear grey gaze seemed to pierce her heart and she could not look away. Time had halted. Yolande seemed scarcely to breathe and was so entranced that it was all she could do not to move towards him, and Craig sat astride the topmost rail as one hypnotized.

Devenish whirled Josie around, and the child's shrill joyous squeal shattered the spell. Tyndale gasped and jumped quickly to the ground.

Her breathing very fast and her cheeks very pink, Yolande called, "Josie, I think we should go inside now and change for luncheon." Not daring to look at Tyndale, she asked, "Are you gentlemen coming?"

Devenish was beside her at once. Tyndale declined, however, saying with a somewhat fixed smile that he would like to know more of the Clydesdales, if the general would be so kind as to tell him of the breed.

Sir Andrew was more than willing. "A Dutch stallion was the founder," he began. "They brought him up here from England, and we've bred many fine animals since. Molly's one of the larger specimens—weighs in the neighbourhood of two thousand pounds. Did you mark her fetlocks, and . . . ?"

As she walked back towards the house, listening with only half an ear to Josie's merry chatter, Yolande's eyes were troubled.

Tyndale now found himself in the unenviable position of longing to be near Yolande, yet dreading each moment he spent in her company. In an effort to end his misery, he remarked in a casual way that he would start for the castle after luncheon. Sir Andrew, however, had taken a liking to the tall young Canadian, and was determined he should stay on, at least for a few days. In this he was abetted by his widowed daughter, Mrs. Caroline Fraser. This angular, kind-hearted, but rather sharp-tongued lady ran the Drummond household with inflexible efficiency. She mistrusted Devenish and had privately advised Yolande that no gentleman possessed of such extraordinary good looks could be expected to be a faithful husband. Mrs. Fraser had no use for "foreigners" in the general way, but Craig's rather shy smile and gentle manner had made an impression on her. Sensing that Yolande was not indifferent to him and aware that Arabella Drummond (whom she detested) loathed him, she joyously added her own voice to that of her father in urging that both men make Steep Drummond their temporary headquarters.

Desperate to escape, but dreading to offend, Craig suggested that he should go on alone, while Devenish remained. Mrs. Fraser brushed his hesitancy aside, and the General's eye began to take on a frosty glare, so that Craig had no recourse but to accept the hospitality so generously offered. He did so with sufficient grace that the old gentleman's suspicions were lulled. Delighted, he clapped him on the shoulder, admonishing,

"Dinna fash ye'sel, laddie, we'll nae demand ye don sporran and kilts!" this drawing a laugh from almost all those present. The exception was Yolande. She sensed the real reason behind Craig's attempt to leave, and directed a sober glance at him that caused his beleaguered heart to cramp painfully.

Contrary to what others might think, sporran and kilts were not unknown to Tyndale, but to Josie they were both new and vastly intriguing. It was the custom at Steep Drummond for the colours to be taken down with full ceremony each dusk, and when the child's eyes first rested on one of the General's retainers in all the glory of kilts, tartan, and bagpipes, she was speechless with awe and astonishment. They all followed to the roof and the small platform around the flagpole. The pipes rang out their unique song, the Scot marched proudly, the cold wind blew, and the kilts swung. A glint of curiosity grew in Josie's eyes. She edged closer and, her watchfulness unrewarded, appeared to experience some continuing difficulty with her shoe. When the flags were down, folded, and being reverently borne away, the child contrived to head the small procession and was obliged to pause on the stairs and again attend to her recalcitrant shoe buckle. Craig, his mind burdened with other matters, did not notice this behavior. Devenish was both aware of and amused by it. Coming up with Josie, he gripped her elbow and propelled her along beside him.

Scarlet, she gulped, "I was—only wondering—"

"I know just what you were wondering," he said *sotto voce*. "And they *do*, so have done, wretched little elf!"

She saw the laugh in his eyes and knew he was not angered, so accompanied him cheerfully enough, but at the foot of the stairs was evidently still fast gripped by curiosity, for she murmured, "Then they must be awful tiny not to show under that—"

"I beg your pardon, dear?" asked Yolande.

"I said, if that great big man wears—"

"She—ah, said she didn't—er, know about tartans," Devenish blurted.

His beloved turned an impish smile upon him. "Oh," she said meekly.

There were many tartans at Steep Drummond that evening. Word that the General's lovely granddaughter was visiting him had spread lightning fast through the Scottish hills. Several dinner guests had found their sons extraordinarily willing to accompany them, and by nine o'clock a steady stream of chaises and sporting vehicles was bowling up the drive, well escorted by riders. Yolande, clad in a gown of creamy crepe, wore also the plaid of her house, held at the shoulder by a great sapphire pin. The soft blue, green, and rust of the tartan became her, lending her a dignity that enhanced her beauty. She was hemmed in by ardent young gentlemen and a few just as ardent but less youthful. Devenish was as admired by the ladies as his love was worshipped by the gentlemen. He was impatient with what he described as "doing the pretty" and parties bored him, but he was much too well mannered to show it. His pleasant laugh rang out often; he managed to convince all about him that he was thoroughly enjoying himself, and when Mrs. Fraser sat down at the pianoforte in the music room and an impromptu hop came into being, he danced politely with Yolande's very good friend, Miss Hannah Abercrombie, who had red hair and a high-pitched giggle; and next with Miss Mary Gordon, a dark pretty girl who, harbouring a secret *tendre* for him, trembled so much that she succeeded in conveying her nervousness to him, so that at the first decent opportunity he contrived to wend his way to Yolande's side.

With equal determination, Craig stayed as far from his lovely cousin as manners would allow. Having carefully rehearsed a means of escape when he should ask her to dance, Yolande was denied the opportunity to put it to use. She knew perfectly well why he did not approach her, and told herself she should be grateful for his common sense. But she was woman enough to be disappointed. She was not alone in this. Craig fell short of being a handsome man, but no one could have denied that he was attractive, and many a feminine eye turned to the corner of the room where his tumbled fair hair could be glimpsed above the heads of the other gentlemen. He, however, was quite unaware of this attention, and had anyone told him of it, would have laughed and decried it as rank flattery. Embroiled in a discussion of the quarter horses that were gaining much popularity in Canada, he was asked by a well set-up gentleman with a fine military moustache if he had as yet seen Scotland's Clydesdales.

"I have," he replied, his eyes kindling. "And they are magnificent, if I do right to judge by Molly-My-Lass."

"Och, ye do, laddie," said his new acquaintance with enthusiasm. "Did ye hear that the noo, Drummond? 'Tis a bonnie braw laddie ye've claimed for a guest. We'll make a good Scot oot o' him yet, eh?"

The General smiled and rested one hand on Craig's broad shoulder. "I don't know about that, Donald, but he's a fine soldier, that I do know. He was at Waterloo. Served with—was it the Forty-Third, Tyndale?"

An admiring crowd had gathered at these magical words. Flushing, Tyndale stammered, "Thank you, but—er, that's not quite it, sir. I was—"

"With a line regiment, perhaps?" asked young Hamish MacInnes, who had his own aspirations for the fair Yolande's hand and would have given his ears to have been at Waterloo.

Tyndale said quietly, "I was with the Union Brigade."

MacInnes opened his eyes. The General muttered, "Were you, by God!"

"And—your regiment, sir?" persisted Mr. Walter Donald, eagerly.

"The Scots Greys."

Shouts and cheers arose. Grinding his teeth, MacInnes retreated. There was no fighting that! Tyndale was the hero of the hour. When the uproar eased a trifle, General Drummond drew the uncomfortable cause of it towards the door. "Tyndale," he murmured. "There's a wee favour ye can grant me—if ye'll not find it unco' ghastly!"

Thus it was that, half an hour later, leaving the floor on Devenish's arm after a country dance, Yolande was surprised by a sudden quieting in the noisy room, followed by a crashing chord from the indefatigable Mrs. Fraser.

All eyes turned to the General, who was ushering a newcomer from the hall—a tall young Scot, with unruly fair hair, but who was elegant in his kilts and plaid and black velvet jacket, with lace foaming at throat and wrists. He halted and looked up, and Yolande stared in disbelief. It was Craig, his grey eyes flashing across that silenced room to meet her own, a tentative smile trembling at the corner of his wide mouth. She thought numbly. "Oh, how superb he is!" and, choked with pride, went to him. Never knowing how her eyes glistened, nor how fine a sight they were, the two of them, she said huskily, "My goodness, how grand you are!"

"Aye, he is that!" The General laughed, vastly pleased with himself. "What d'ye think of our 'good Scot' now, Donald?"

"Why, I think ye're a muckle old fool, Drummond," scoffed his friend. "Ye've wrapped the boy in the wrong plaid!"

"Lord, what a sight!" Much amused, Devenish came over to them, his manner earning an irate scowl from the General. Taking Tyndale aside, he added murmurously, "You've won the Fairs with your boney knees, coz. But—I give you fair warning—look out for Mistress Josie Storm!"

Tyndale's answering smile was strained. Looking sharply at him, Devenish detected a hunted look in the clear eyes. He uttered a crack of mirth. "Don't care to be the centre of attention, eh? Well—" He checked to glance around curiously for the cause of a new commotion that arose in the hall. Two footmen and the butler were remonstrating with someone. Devenish glimpsed a sleek, blue-black head towering over the throng, and grinned hugely. "Beastly luck, coz," he commiserated, "but your glory is about to be considerably eclipsed."

He was right. The footmen were sent reeling back. The butler chose discretion as the better part of valour and effaced himself. Through a sudden awed hush, Montelongo strode across the floor, tall, bronzed, pantherishly graceful, totally out of place, yet ineffably proud as he made towards his employer.

One swift glance told him that the Major had suffered a few hard knocks since last they met. He stopped before him. In an oddly measured way, his dark head bowed very slightly. He said in that deep rumble of a voice, "You very fine?"

Recovering his own voice, General Drummond stalked over to demand, "What the deuce is all this? Who is that—fella to come bursting in here, flinging my servants about?"

Behind him, the ladies were whispering excitedly behind their fans. The gentlemen, only slightly less intrigued, had missed no part of the Iroquois's leathern garments, the long knife that hung, sheathed, at his lean waist, or the beaded moccasins.

Tyndale smiled into his man's keen eyes. "Perfectly fine, thank you," he answered, before turning to his irate host. "My apologies, sir. Montelongo is of the Iroquois Nation. He is a chief's son, but has been so good as to look after me for some years. I ask your pardon for this intrusion, but I've no doubt he was concerned when we did not rendezvous as I'd instructed. May I present him to you?"

Sir Andrew's brows bristled alarmingly, and his outraged eyes shot sparks. Tyndale met those eyes and said in cool challenge, "Monty, this gentleman is General Sir Andrew Drummond. Sir—Montelongo."

Some small titters arose behind him. The General's jaw set.

447

He gave a frigid nod. Untroubled by protocol, Montelongo put out a broad, bronzed hand. To one side, Devenish grinned his delight, while beside him Yolande wondered if Craig had lost his mind. Slanting a molten glare at Tyndale, Sir Andrew encountered steady eyes of steel. A reluctant grin took possession of his strong features. He took the Indian's hand and wrung it, but could barely refrain from gasping at the answering pressure that was, he suspected, carefully restrained.

Montelongo's lips parted in the brief, white flash that served for a smile. "Proud to meet great warrior," he rumbled. And again, his head nodded in that quaint suggestion of a bow.

"Jove!" chuckled the General. The look in Tyndale's eyes had softened to a mute "thank you." "Rogue!" said Sir Andrew. "Off with you. I'm sure the butler will know where to put him." And turning to his entranced guests, he remarked, "What a night this has been, eh?"

Making his way through the curious and admiring throng, Montelongo stalking behind him, Tyndale led the way out. Once they were in the hall, he said urgently, "Monty, I'll tell you what happened, later. I cannot guess how you found us, but—have you brought the horses?"

The Iroquois emitted a grunt, the timbre of which indicated an affirmative reply. "When you no come, me go back to St. Albans. Desk man say you leave. Me trail. Find horses with thieves. So take Lazzy."

"Good God!" Tyndale checked his stride. "They must have been Montclair's people! But—no. That couldn't be, they've not had sufficient time to get down there as yet." He frowned thoughtfully. "I wonder who the devil they were."

"Bad men."

Tyndale scrutinized the impassive features. "For Lord's sake! You never killed them?"

"Bad men," Montelongo repeated. A twinkle lit his dark eyes. "But very good runners. Me and Lazzy find this place. Have mare of beautiful man, too."

Tyndale laughed, but threw a quick glance around. "Don't ever let Mr. Devenish hear you say that! No matter how he looks, he's a splendid fighting man, Monty. He saved my life."

The Indian was briefly silent. "Him Monty's brother. Why you wear petticoats?"

It was a term that had been used in Belgium to describe the Scots. It was also a term of high respect, for none had so endeared themselves to the Bruxellois as the Scottish regiments.

Nonetheless, leading his man down the hall to the kitchens, and happily unaware of how many awed household eyes were watching, Tyndale carefully explained it was an expression that might better not be used. At least, in front of the uninitiated.

Montelongo grunted.

The night was crisp and clear, a half-moon illuminated the walkways, and Yolande followed them aimlessly, lost in thought, her plaid wrapped about her shoulders. The attraction she had felt when first she met Craig Winters Tyndale had not diminished. To the contrary, the sight of him tonight in all the glory of formal Scots attire had stirred her heart in most disquieting fashion. Even now, to visualize him, the way his grey eyes had sought her out, that charmingly uncertain smile, made her pulses leap and brought a warmth to her cheeks. Were these emotions merely the result of gratitude because he had come to her rescue? Was this rapid heartbeat brought about by admiration of his military record, or interest because he was different from any other man she had ever known? She closed her ears to the wretched voice that sought to whisper "nonsense!" and, not a little frightened, decided resolutely that she was not falling in love with Major Tyndale. She *must not* be falling in love with Major Tyndale! The difference in their stations could not be ignored, and there were other loves—Devenish and her parents, for instance. And as for Grandpapa—she shuddered. No, it was quite impossible. Besides, the Major had paid no more attention to her than would be required by the dictates of good manners. How foolish to be constantly mooning over a Colonial gentleman who had made not the slightest push to court her—and should not of course, do so, when she was promised to dear Dev. The chastisement did not seem to make her either more sure, or less miserable, and yet it was the only possible verdict.

Thoroughly irritated with herself, she swung around very suddenly and gave a little cry as she came face to face with the very object of her thoughts. "Oh, my!" she gasped. "How you frightened me!"

"My most humble apologies, ma'am," said Tyndale, remorsefully. "You passed me by just now and I—er—had been hoping for a word with you, so I followed. Will you permit that I walk with you?"

"Of course, though I must return to the house. Had you come out for a breath of air, cousin?"

"And a smoke," he nodded, holding up the cheroot that glowed in his hand. "A wretched habit I picked up in Spain."

"I was indeed surprised to learn that you had served with our army over there. I'd no idea you were a military gentleman."

"How should you?" He said awkwardly, "We—er, scarcely know one another."

"True. And have had scarce two words together since you arrived. I had, in fact, begun to think you might be avoiding me." And she thought in dismay, "Oh! Now, why did I say *that*?"

"Perhaps I have," he admitted, his grip on the cheroot tightening. "Devenish is—well, he's a good man and—and, you and he are— That is, I mean—you are to be wed. No?"

Even in the moonlight she could see that the cheroot was now quite badly bent. Her own heart was thundering, which was too ridiculous. She said with desperate calm, "It has been understood for many years that we will—will marry."

"I see."

He did not, to judge by the hesitant words, and, wondering vaguely at the need, she felt obliged to add, "Our estates march together."

Their progress had become very slow. Tyndale halted to drop the wreckage of his cheroot and grind it into the dirt. "Not a compelling reason for wedlock," he remarked, gravely.

Flustered, she answered, "No. Of course. I did not mean to imply— Suffice it to say he is my choice. And—and that choice is much applauded by my family."

"Very wisely," he said. But he thought, "And how horrified your family would be did you wed a Colonial about whom all they know is that his father was a murderer!"

Watching him from beneath her lashes, she saw the bitter twist to his mouth and her heart was wrung. Fighting an inclination to burst into tears, she said with forced lightness, "You seem to like my grandpapa, sir."

"I do. He is such a fine old fellow."

"Yes, he is. I wish he lived closer to us, but he loves this old house."

"I can see why he would. It has great character. I am—very glad he invited me to stay. Though—I'm surprised he did so. Under the circumstances."

She caught her breath and, dreading what he would say

next, yet longing to hear him say it, faltered, "Cir-cir-cumstances, cousin?"

The moonlight on her lovely upturned face was driving him to distraction. Clenching his fists, he mumbled, "My—er, fa-ther. And—and Devenish's father."

"Oh." Of course that was what he had meant. What a ninny she was! "But, you see, Grandpapa does not know about that."

"No?" Tyndale's heavy brows drew together. "I thought everyone knew."

"Only those who were there at the time knew. It has been kept very quiet down through the years. I did not know of it myself until very recently."

"But—there must have been dozens of people—servants, workers on the estate . . . ?"

"They were loyal, and were paid well to hold their tongues." She smiled. "Besides, Scots tend to be a secretive people. They have had to be."

Somehow, they had stopped walking. Not speaking, they stood gazing at one another.

The wind sighed softly through the trees. In the stables, a horse stamped and snorted restlessly. High on the hill, the windows of the house shone bright amber, and from them came the distant sounds of laughter.

Tormented by Yolande's nearness; by the faint scent of her perfume; by the terrible temptation to sweep her into his arms and kiss those sweetly curved lips, Tyndale wrenched his eyes from her face and stared down at the path. He thought, "My Lord! I *must* get away from here!" And he said, "If your grandfather *did* know that my father is believed to have murdered Stuart Devenish, would I still be welcome?"

She did not answer. He raised his down-bent head and looked at her gravely. Her eyes fell away, and she turned from him.

"Yolande," he persisted, softly. "Would I? Would he give me the benefit of the doubt? Or—would he be outraged?"

With slow reluctance she answered, "He, would be out-raged. He has introduced you to so many of his friends. And they would—would feel . . ."

He stiffened. "Insulted. I see. Then I had best be upon my way as soon as may be."

Spinning around, not wanting him to go, she protested involuntarily, "Why? After all these years, the secret is not likely to suddenly become public knowledge."

"It could." Ah, but how sweet, how unbearable to see the concern in her dear face. "Our presence here might awaken old memories; set people to talking."

It was true. She could only ask miserably, "Then—what shall you do?"

"Tell the old gentleman I simply *must* leave tomorrow. But there is no reason why Devenish should accompany me."

"If he promised to go, he will," she said, adding stoutly, "he is the soul of honour and will not break his word."

He said with a wry twinkle, "His honour may be severely tested. If the castle has not been lived in for twenty years and more, it must be in a sorry state, and probably beastly damp into the bargain."

"Oh, no. I doubt it is that bad. Colonel Tyndale comes up at least once a year, and there has been a caretaker of sorts, until recently. I know most of the furnishings are under Holland covers, and I suppose you will find the carpets rolled up, and the linens stored away. I will ask our housekeeper to pack some bedding for you, but I believe you will find cedar chests very amply supplied with linens needing only to be aired."

"You are too kind, Cousin Yolande," he said gratefully.

She thought, "No. I am only afraid," and avoiding his gaze, she began to walk on once more. "Well," she responded, "you are, after all, one of the family. And—you have, I believe, become a good friend of Alain's, no?"

He hesitated, then said slowly, "Not exactly. There is—ah, too much between us, you see."

Yolande glanced at him and found in his eyes a smile touched with sadness. Her face flamed. She knew suddenly that she herself was one of the reasons why the cousins could not be friends. And she knew also that Craig Tyndale loved her. She thought numbly, "What a fine bumble broth it would create did I love him also. Dev would kill him!" Fear closed an iron fist around her heart. She said something, heaven knows what, and hurried back to the house, Tyndale silent beside her.

❧ *Chapter* 10 ❧

The morning dawned clear but cool, and by the time they were ready to depart the sun was growing warmer, giving rise to hopes for a nice day. The General had been at first amused, then irked by Tyndale's quiet insistence that he must leave, but had capitulated at last. Since Devenish would not draw back from his promise to accompany his cousin, the end result was that they all would go. "If only," grunted Sir Andrew, "to detairmine if yon pile o' rubble is fit fer human habitation, regarrrding which, I hae me doots!"

It had been decided that Josie would stay at Steep Drummond until Devenish returned, and he would then take her back to England with him, hoping to obtain the benefit of Lady Louisa's wisdom in the matter of her eventual disposition. Meanwhile, however, she formed part of the small cavalcade, her peaked face bright with happiness as she nestled beside Yolande in the open curricle Devenish drove.

Yolande was outwardly as bright as she was inwardly disturbed. The ravages of a sleepless night had been concealed by Peattie's deft hands, and she was radiant in a primrose muslin dress buttoned high to the throat, a beautifully embroidered yellow shawl about her shoulders, and the poke of her bonnet a foam of primrose lace.

Despondent because he was leaving her, Devenish rallied when she smiled at his glumness and assured him she would anxiously await his return. She was so affectionate in fact that he was soon in high gig, all his dismals flown.

Sir Andrew led the parade, riding a fine bay gelding, with on one side of him, Mr. Walter Donald, his friend of many years who had over-nighted at Steep Drummond, and on the other, Tyndale, astride his big grey. Next came the chaise containing Arabella Drummond and Caroline Fraser, who quarrelled politely all the way, each convincing herself she was scoring the most hits. Following, Devenish drove the curricle, and, bringing up the rear was a landaulette bearing two footmen and various hampers and bottles that promised an excellent luncheon.

Yolande exerted herself to maintain a cheerful façade, responding with every appearance of gaiety to Devenish's easy banter. Josie, impressed by his proficiency with the reins, eventually interjected the observation that he was "a regular top-draw-yer!"

He laughed. "That's 'Top Sawyer,' my elf. Where did you learn that term?"

"Benjo," she replied, gazing up at him, ever hopeful of bringing the approving smile to his eyes. "He said I could manage the pony and trap so good because my old man was a Top Draw—I mean, Top Sawyer."

Yolande murmured, "Dev, we really *must* try to discover something of her background." She lifted the child's hand that was confidently tucked into her own and, marking the fine bones and long, slim fingers, said, "There's good breeding in her, I'm sure of it."

"*We* must?" he said eagerly. "Yolande, does that mean you're ready to allow me to announce our betrothal, at last?"

Yolande shifted her glance from the child's hand to Devenish's handsome, hopeful face. Dear Dev. She *did* love him. And surely countless women had married gentlemen with whom they were not deeply *in* love? She knew she could make him happy, unless . . . "Dev," she said, watching him steadily, "are you quite *sure* you are in love with me? No—do not answer so quickly! Think on it for a moment. You love me, of course, just as I love you. But—is there no one else? Are you really *in* love with me?" And, realizing what she had said, she could have bitten her tongue.

Devenish had suspected that his passion was not as fully returned, but the confirmation was like a knife being turned in his breast. He managed to keep his face from revealing his hurt, and said staunchly, "I really am, m'dear. But if you ain't in love with me, it's only to be expected, and I don't mind. That you love me at all is far more than I deserve."

It was the most romantic speech she had ever heard him utter, and she reached across the child to him, her heart touched.

Taking that small, gloved hand, Devenish searched her face, waiting.

"Yes, you may announce it," she murmured, smiling at him. "We will settle the details when you return from the castle."

He gave a whoop of joy that brought the heads of the riders twisting around, and so alarmed his horses that he had to relinquish Yolande's hand and give his full attention to his driving.

"Jove!" he said with a guilty grin, succeeding in quieting the teams at length. "Almost had us in the chaise with your aunts! A fine set-to that would have been!"

Josie's head was bowed. Yolande stroked the dark curls and asked gently, "What is it, dear? Are you sad?"

The child nodded. "Josie *is* sad. If Mr. Dev marriages you, you won't never let him have me fer his—"

"Abigail?" Yolande inserted swiftly.

Devenish chuckled. "Perhaps Miss Drummond will let you be *her* abigail," he suggested, buoyant at the promise of a glowing future.

"She's got a abigail." Josie sighed. "I'll be all growed in a year or two."

"Or ten," he qualified.

"Even when I be *that* old, Peattie might not be dead."

"Good heavens!" gasped Yolande. "What things you do say! Oh—see, Dev! There is Castle Tyndale!"

They had passed through a hilly area of lush pastures dotted with black-faced sheep and threaded by the hurrying sparkle of the river. Ahead, the hills fell back to reveal, far off, the wider sparkle of the sea and a distant misty looming of islands. The skies were threatening over the Firth of Clyde, creating a fitting background for the castle that soared at the top of the cliffs. A tall structure, its three conical topped towers upthrusting stark and grim against the clouds, its Gothic windows dark holes against the massive grey walls, it presented, from this distance, a desolate picture of brooding power.

"Jupiter!" Devenish exclaimed. "Old Craig cannot mean to dwell alone in *that* great pile?"

"It could be spectacular, were it brought up to style," mused Yolande.

"Yes, but that would take a mountain of blunt, and—What's wrong now, elf?"

Clinging to his jacket, Josie whimpered, "I don't like it! It's a bad place! I don't want to go there!"

Devenish experienced a deepening of his own inner apprehensions. Those were the battlements from which his youthful father had plunged to his untimely death. Within those walls his heart-broken mother had lost her babe and grieved herself into an early grave. He shivered suddenly.

He was not alone in his apprehensions. Surveying his birthright with troubled eyes, Craig was deeply shocked, not because it looked so forbidding, but because it was so exactly as he had pictured it. He had no sense of strangeness or unfamiliarity, but rather a feeling of inevitability; of a homecoming that had been planned and long awaited—not by himself, but by that great grey pile of stone and mortar and memories. He turned to find Walter Donald's keen brown gaze fixed upon him with so gravely speculative a look that he flushed and was seized by the feeling that the gentleman knew more of the tragedy at Castle Tyndale than he had said.

They still had several miles to drive before they came to the heavy lodge gates and the winding drive that led up to the castle, and with every mile Devenish's unease increased. When Tyndale dropped back to ride beside the curricle, he said, "Well, there's your ancestral pile, coz. What d'ye think of it?"

His face expressionless, Tyndale countered, "What do *you* think of it?"

"I don't like it!" whimpered Josie, holding tightly to Yolande's hand. "I got a bad tummy about it!"

"It's—rather grim," said Devenish.

Tyndale nodded. "Certainly not Prince Charming's castle."

"Lord, no!" Devenish elaborated tactlessly, "More like Bluebeard's demesne. I pity the poor princess who was carried in through those doors!"

Yolande kept her eyes on the child. "Pity the poor princess, indeed!" she thought.

They soon came to the gates, hanging rusted and broken upon massive pillars. The lodge house was abandoned, the windows boarded up, and a padlock upon the door.

"Small need of a lock!" the General snorted.

"None at all," Mr. Donald agreed, watching Tyndale.

Tyndale met that grave regard squarely. "Why?" he asked curtly, his chin well up, and irritation gnawing at him. If this man fancied he was ashamed, or held his father guilty, he was vastly mistaken!

Donald smiled and said rather apologetically, "Your pardon, but—it *is* said to be haunted, you know."

They passed through the gates and began to clatter up the winding, neglected drivepath.

The General declaimed his friend's fears as "gilliemaufrey nonsense!" To which Mr. Donald responded by asking Sir Andrew if he had ever been inside. "I have," he went on, "and I'll no deny it had me shaking in me shoes, and I'm no a supairsteetious mon! Not," he went on in purest Oxford accents, "that I mean to deter you, Tyndale."

"You would be wasting your time, sir," said the Canadian determinedly.

The General grinned his approval. "And that gave you back your own, Donald! Gad, it's no wee cottage, is it?"

It was not. And the closer they came, the larger loomed the castle until they were in the dark shadow of it, as it towered above them.

With a stirring of pride, Tyndale thought, "How grand it is! The home of my ancestors! And it is mine now."

His thoughts taking a different direction, Devenish noted that there were no small boys intrepidly exploring the great pile. And how odd that a hush seemed to have fallen upon their own small party, even the shrill titters from the chaise having been silenced.

The General pulled his mount to a halt beside the spread of some great old trees, and swung from the saddle. "Shall we picnic here?" he called with rather determined gaiety. "What d'ye say, ladies?"

Tyndale dismounted to hand Mrs. Fraser from the chaise. "It's well enough," she allowed, her shrewd eyes flickering over the bulk of the castle.

Following, Mrs. Drummond clutched nervously at Tyndale's arm. "Oh, my!" she twittered. "I think I shall not awaken Socrates. The dear little fellow would be petrified."

Mrs. Fraser threw a disdainful glance at the terrier, who snored on the seat " 'Twould take a mighty fearsome bogle tae scare that wee grouch!"

Innocently watching Arabella, the General asked if the ladies would prefer that they picnicked inside.

Mrs. Drummond uttered a small squeak. Mrs. Fraser cast disgusted eyes to heaven, and the General chuckled.

Yolande shook her head at him. "Wicked rascal!" She slipped her arm around her aunt's trembling shoulders. "We will do nicely out here. There is still plenty of blue sky, but if it begins to rain you and the gentlemen may go inside and light a fire for us."

"May we?" the General said with an amused chuckle, "Well—let us have the baskets down! I'm famished." The two footmen busying themselves at once, Sir Andrew said that the ladies could supervise the disposition of the picnic whilst the gentlemen took "our new property owner to view his home, the noo." He and Devenish led the way. Walking beside Mr. Donald, Tyndale asked softly, "Am I mistaken, sir, or do you know something of my . . . background that causes you to hold me in aversion?"

"Let us say rather that I have recently learned that which causes me to believe Drummond will be vastly incensed when *he* hears it."

Tyndale drew a deep breath. "I see. I trust you will believe me, sir, when I tell you that when I first arrived here, I thought everyone knew the—the details."

"And when did you find your assumption to be incorrect?"

"Last night. Which decided me upon leaving this morning."

"You do not mean to return to Steep Drummond?"

"No, sir. My man was packing and is likely already following."

Donald nodded and said a judicial, "As well, perhaps."

Angered, Tyndale lifted his chin, and, noting that prideful gesture, the older man said, "When the word gets out, you'll be cut—I warn you."

"And I warn *you*, sir. Whatever you have been told is not truth!"

A twinkle coming into his eyes, Donald said mildly, "If ye dinna ken what I've heard, laddie, how can ye know it for a lie?"

Tyndale flushed, his mouth tightening.

Taking pity on him, Donald gripped his shoulder briefly. "I'll tell ye what I *do* know, which is precious little. I was acquainted with your sire. Oh, never look so hopeful, lad! Not well acquainted. But enough to know that if Jonas brought about Stuart's death, it was because of a blow dealt in anger. Not a deliberate attempt at murder. Of that I am perfectly sure."

Mollified, Tyndale said, "Thank you, sir. But—may I ask who told you of it? And when? Yolande thinks it a deep buried secret."

"Aye. It was, that. For four and twenty years. Who let the

458

cat oot o' the bag, I dinna ken. But oot it is! And——whisht! I'd as soon not be nigh when Andy learns of 't!"

Before Craig could respond, the General called a testy summons, and they hastened to join him atop the debris-strewn steps before the main door. The castle rose from a veritable jungle of overgrown shrubs and trees. Several window panes were broken, but it did not now appear to be in as sorry a state as it had seemed at a distance. It was perched at the very edge of the cliffs, and from below came a steady booming as waves broke against the great rocks offshore that rose as if to shield the bay from further inroads of the hungry tide. Devenish gazed up at the soaring battlements. Donald glanced meaningfully at Tyndale, who flushed darkly, drew from his pocket the heavy key his solicitor had given him, and fitted it in the lock. He had expected the door to prove recalcitrant, but it swung open smoothly enough, and like guilty schoolboys, they did not at once enter, but all stood at the top of the steps, peering inside.

They looked into a great, flagged, baronial hall. About forty feet distant, there was a gigantic fireplace, with beside it a steep flight of stone stairs, leading to a railed balcony. To the left of the fireplace an enormous door, half-open, offered a glimpse of a long corridor, and in the right-hand wall was a similar door that they later discovered led to the kitchens, servants quarters, and stableyard. Several well-preserved bishop's chairs were grouped about the hearth, and the walls were hung with occasional large and faded tapestries. At the foot of the stairs, a suit of armour had toppled, and lay rather pathetically strewn on the dusty flagstones.

Tyndale gathered his courage and walked inside. The General and Mr. Donald followed, but Devenish stood as one frozen, making no attempt to accompany them. He had never fancied himself to harbour a belief in the occult, but now he was gripped by an all but overpowering terror, so that it was literally impossible for him to put one foot before the next. It was as much as he could do, in fact, not to dash madly back down the steps.

"Jove," Tyndale murmured, considerably awed, "but it's big!"

"It was a bonnie sight when I was a lad," said the General. He turned to Donald. "D'ye recollect when——" He stopped and, following his friend's gaze, called, "Well, Devenish, d'ye not mean to come inside?"

Devenish wet his lips. Glancing at him, Tyndale said, "I fancy the ladies are ready. We can leave this until later."

"Hoot-toot!" exclaimed Sir Andrew irascibly. "What ails the boy? He's no afraid o' ghosties, I—"

Donald frowned and leaned to murmur something in his ear, and Sir Andrew looked mortified. He said contritely, "My apologies, Devenish. I must be getting daft in my dotage! I'd clean forgot that both your parents died here."

"It was—just an odd sort of—feeling." Devenish gave a ghastly grin. "I shall do very well now, thank you." Nonetheless, to make himself walk forward was one of the most difficult things he'd ever had to do, and it seemed an age before he stood beside Tyndale, who was inspecting one of the tapestries.

"I would really as soon look over the castle by myself," the Canadian muttered. "And I am sure you would rather be with Yolande, so—"

"Stuff! I mean to stay and lend you a hand. Besides, I want to see—" The words ended in a yelp of shock as Socrates shot between his legs and disappeared into the dimness beyond the half-open door.

"That imp o' Satan!" growled the General. And then, brightening, "Happen a bogle'll get him!"

"I would never be forgiven," Craig said, going over to swing the door wide. There was no sign of Socrates, but he went into a broad corridor that gave onto several large rooms, some provided with heavy doors, and others having only broad archways to afford entrance. The first of these latter led into a formal dining hall that boasted two modern chandeliers above a fine oak table lined with about thirty ponderously carven chairs. There were fireplaces at both ends of this large chamber, and daylight shone dimly through three sets of closed curtains.

Devenish wandered in, remarked that the atmosphere in the room was less frigid, but dashed gloomy, and went over to fling back the draperies. He was at once enveloped in a dense cloud of dust, his resultant explosion of sneezing amusing the General and Mr. Donald, who mocked him gleefully.

Tyndale, however, paid no heed to his cousin's plight, but stood staring down at the oaken table top, his brows drawn into a thoughtful frown.

Clouds began to drift in from the sea while they were still sitting around the luncheon cloth, but the sunshine, although not constant, was sufficiently warm to take the chill off the air. The chef had provided a varied and tempting repast, to which they all did justice. Yolande was surprised to find herself hungry, despite the fact that she was heavy-hearted. Josie was prey to no such affliction, and soon forgot her initial fear of the castle. Not for as long as she could remember had she eaten as well as during her travels with Devenish, and she applied herself to the food with joyous appreciation, yet with a mannerliness that brought curiosity to Sir Andrew's eyes.

"I'd give a few guineas to know where you hail from, Mistress Storm," he said, waving a bannock at her.

"So would I, sir," she replied, serenely unafraid of this old gentleman before whom grooms trembled and maids were tongue-tied.

"D'ye hear that?" he demanded of Donald. " 'So would I, sir.' Proper as you please! D'ye recall nothing, child? Nothing of your lady mother, or a fine papa, belike?"

"I only remember Akim telling me I'd fetch a good price at the Flash House," she said. And watching Mr. Donald choke on the tart he'd just sunk his teeth into, went on, "Only Benjo said I might not, 'cause I ain't pretty."

"Whatever is a—a Flash House?" enquired Mrs. Drummond naïvely. "A place where they manufacture gunpowder, I suppose. Though," she tilted her head dubiously, "why one should be pretty for that occupation, I cannot understand."

Devenish gave a muffled chortle of amusement.

"Your supposition is incorrect," said the General, irritated. "And never mind what it *does* mean!"

"Ladies," conveyed Mrs. Fraser grandly, "are not supposed to know such things, my dear Arabella. Or so the gentlemen hold."

"Then that would certainly explain why it is I know nothing of such a term." Mrs. Drummond replied with a smug smile. "For indeed, I have been sheltered by gentlemen all my days. My late husband, God rest his soul, would have flung up his hands in horror had any unsavoury remark soiled my ears." She raised her brows, all arch innocence, and enquired, "You, certainly, do not comprehend what the poor waif said, do you, dear Caroline?"

Mrs. Fraser fixed her with a look of searing a contempt. "Ay, I do. *My* late husband was not one to value a widgeon."

The General, his thoughtful regard on the child, now daintily wiping greasy fingers upon her petticoat, asked, "How would ye like to stay at Steep Drummond, girl? My housekeeper could instruct you in the ways of a parlourmaid, I don't doubt. 'Twould be a good life. A clean life, y'ken. And ye'd not go hungry or abused—I'd see to that!"

Josie stared at him and wondered what Peattie would wish her to say. Mr. Dev was gazing at an apple he held and gave no sign of having heard the offer. She thought it a grand one, but sighed, scrambled to her feet, and dropped the old gentleman a curtsy. "Thank ye, sir General," said she. "But I'd liefer stay with Mr. Dev, if you please."

"I do not please! And nor will Colonel Tyndale, let me tell you. Ain't fitting! 'Tis a bachelor's dwelling, and they'll no be needing a young female growing up there."

The child paled, and her lips trembled. "No, b-but—I will *soon* be growed! I won't be no trouble!"

"Mama may be able to help, sir," Yolande put in kindly.

His own heart touched, Mr. Donald suggested, "Or perhaps Devenish will make her his ward."

The General slanted a glance at Devenish, who still tenderly contemplated the apple in his hand, wholly unaware of this conversation, torn between joy that he had secured his lady's promise and unease because of his reaction to that blasted great castle wherein he'd given his word to remain for a few days.

"Well?" fumed the General, eyebrows bristling. "Well, sir?"

Tyndale nudged his cousin and Devenish jumped, saw every eye upon him, and gulped nervously. "Eh? What's to do?"

"God! What a block!" snorted Sir Andrew.

Laughing, Tyndale said, "General Drummond is interested in Josie, Dev, and wants to know what you plan for her."

"Me? I have not the vaguest notion. Lady Louisa will have some splendid scheme, I expect."

Close to tears, Josie pleaded, "But, I want to stay with *you!*" And turning to the General, explained, "He don't mind if I'm not pretty, do you, Mr. Dev?"

"Lord, no. I don't mind if you're plain as a mud fence," he said, carelessly.

"Really, Dev!" scolded Yolande.

The General glared at him. "Insensitory puppy!"

These words exercised an extraordinary effect upon Mrs. Drummond. Her eyes widened alarmingly, and she became rigid. She squawked, "My sweet love has gone!"

"Been gone for twenty years at least, Arabella," the General pointed out, viewing her askance. "Don't go into a funny turn, now!"

Ignoring this, the distraught dowager, her eyes searching about frantically, wailed, "He was but now nibbling my fingers!"

"Nibbling . . . your fingers?" gasped Sir Andrew. He drew back a little and glancing to Donald, muttered, "She's off the road! Suspected it this twelvemonth and—"

Mrs. Drummond, lost in anxiety, shrieked, "My angel! Where are you?"

"Good God!" whispered Drummond, goggling at her.

His daughter-in-law's cry rose shrilly "Soc-ra-*tees*—? Oh! Surely he has not fallen over the cliff?"

The General cast her a look of both relief and disgust, and muttered something about "unlikely blessings."

Tyndale stood. "I think he is in the castle, ma'am. I'll go and find him."

Reaching out to be helped up, Yolande said, "Dev and I will come with you."

He lifted her to her feet but when she attempted to pull away, his grip tightened. He said a quiet, "Thank you. But Dev or Mr. Donald will help."

"What's this?" asked Devenish, belatedly becoming aware that something was brewing. "Who needs help?"

"Socrates!" wailed Mrs. Drummond. "My poor baby is lost, and Mr. Winters just stands and talks. And you sit! Will *no one* help the poor darling?"

"Lord save us aw'!" The General snarled.

Devenish promptly joined the search party, and Yolande again voiced her willingness to assist. "Famous!" Devenish nodded brightly, ignoring his own unease. Noting Tyndale's dark frown, he added hastily, "But it is dusty in there, m'dear. Might spoil your pretty frills and furbelows."

"Pooh!" said Yolande.

Side by side, they walked up the steps and into the Great Hall. As before, Devenish was seized by the same unreasoning terror. He felt the blood drain from his face and, dreading lest he betray his craven fears in front of the girl he loved, forced his rubbery knees to obey him, and walked briskly to the rear door. The corridor stretched out in a dim, chill menace. Clenching his teeth, he walked on and began to call the missing dog.

In the Great Hall, Tyndale looked after his cousin, his lips a thin line of vexation. Yolande, uneasily alone with this disturbing gentleman, said brightly, "Why, it is not near so bad as I had feared." She started forward. "Whilst we are here, we can find where the linens—"

A firm hand seized her elbow, drawing her to a halt. She swung around, her heart thundering, her brows raised enquiringly.

Craig had a soft but determined, "No. I thank you."

He was very near, and yet the grey eyes were devoid of expression, telling her nothing. Puzzled, she demanded, "But, why ever not, sir? Do you fancy me thrown into a pucker by a little dust?"

"No, ma'am. But—I could not endure to see that very pretty frock sullied. Castle Tyndale is—is not yet ready to receive you." Brave words, spoken with the most honourable intention, but his heart cried out to her, and he did not remove his hand from her arm.

Yolande knew that she should leave. Hastily. Instead, she murmured a vague "Most . . . inhospitable . . . Major."

For Craig, all other matters and individuals had ceased to exist. "Why must you be so unforgivably lovely?" he thought yearningly. "I shall never see you again, my dearest, my darling girl . . ."

Yolande did not know that her lips were slightly parted, her eyes dreamy, but she saw the emptiness in Craig's eyes change to an expression of tender worship that took her breath away. It seemed to her that he was bending to her, but she neither moved, nor experienced the least desire to break this spell. The seconds slipped away and not one word was spoken. But two hearts met and the message they exchanged was as clear as though it had been shouted from the battlements.

And then, somewhere close by, Devenish whistled for Socrates.

Craig started. Dismayed by his shameful weakness, he said brusquely, "You had best wait outside—cousin."

His words restored Yolande to reality. Equally shocked, she turned from him and, without a word, walked across the Great Hall and onto the steps.

Craig watched her go. He whispered, "Goodbye, my lovely one . . ." and, sighing, went to assist in the search for Socrates.

The sky had become white. Yolande lifted a shielding hand against the sudden glare and walked as slowly as she dared down the steps and along the path. Her head was a whirl of confusion, impressions chasing one another at such a rate she could scarce comprehend them. She knew only that she was very unhappy, and that her once neatly mapped-out life had become a chaotic muddle. But she also knew that if she betrayed the slightest sign of discomposure, one of her aunts was sure to notice. She must bring her rioting emotions under control or there would be anxious enquiries with which she was in no state to cope.

Luckily, however, Mrs. Drummond had other matters on her mind and, before her niece had quite come up with them, was calling anxious questions as to the whereabouts of her pet.

"I can be of no help, alas," Yolande answered. She summoned a smile for Mr. Donald, who stood courteously to assist her to sit beside her aunt. "I have been banished."

"Would not let you stay, eh?" The General chuckled. "Speaks his mind, does Tyndale. Fine young fella, but he bears little resemblance to his sire. You'll recollect Jonas Tyndale, Donald?"

"Aye," said Mr. Donald, laconically.

"Wild as any unbroke colt." Sir Andrew nodded. " 'Tis Devenish takes after him, had ye noted that, Donald?"

"Aye," said Mr. Donald.

"He has nae a mean bone in his body," observed the General, glancing covertly at Yolande. "But he's a feckless, reckless laddie, just like his uncle was, and no good end will come to him does he not bend his energies to something better than—er—"

"Than—murder?" interposed Mrs. Drummond, her anxious gaze on the castle.

Yolande gave a gasp and dropped the lemon tart she'd just taken up. Mr. Donald directed a fuming glance at the bereft dog lover, and the General frowned, "Losh sakes, woman! What cockaleery nonsense are ye blathering at?"

Alarmed, Mrs. Drummond prattled a defensive. "Why—why, what's in the blood will out! And you yourself said that Alain takes after his Uncle Jonas!"

"And what has that to say to anything? Jonas Tyndale may have been wild, and fought him a duel or two. But he didnae murder!"

"I seed a duel once," Josie began, reminiscently. "It was—"

"Of course not," Yolande put in, fixing her aunt with a look of desperate warning. "You must be thinking of someone else, Aunt Arabella."

"No such thing!" retorted that lady huffily. "No one was *supposed* to know, of course, but I chanced to hear Mrs. MacInnes speaking of it to Sir John Gordon at the party last night. Jonas slaughtered poor young Stuart Devenish in cold—"

"Aunt!" Yolande blurted, her heart hammering with dread. "You really must not say such things!"

"Losh! What a prattle box!" Mrs. Fraser muttered scornfully.

Mrs. Drummond's gaze darted from Yolande's white face and imploring eyes, to her sister-in-law, to the General's intent glare. "Oh, dear! Have I . . . spoke out of turn?" she wailed.

"Now—by God!" breathed the General. "Have I been kept i' the dark all these years? Damme, but I'll have the straight of it the noo! *Be still*, Yolande!" He turned glittering eyes on his friend. "Donald? D'ye ken aught o' this? Caroline . . . ?"

Mr. Donald scowled at his plate. Mrs. Fraser put up her chin, pursed her lips, and finally announced that she was not, nor ever had been a gabble-monger!

Walter Donald met Yolande's distraught gaze and shrugged helplessly. " 'Tis nae use, lassie. The word's oot, I fear. Hamish MacInnes told me 'twas all over the county, yesterday, so—"

"You mean *it is truth*?" Drummond's voice cut like a knife through those reluctant words. "Jonas Tyndale *murdered* his fine young brother-in-law? And 'twas put out as an accident?" His face purpling, he sprang to his feet, Mr. Donald and the ladies following suit. "Now—blast it all! Why was I not told? Am I held too senile—too decrepit and irresponsible a gabble-monger to be trrrusted wi' family secrets?"

"You were in India," Yolande said faintly. "*Nobody* knew— save a few servants. And—my mama, because she went to nurse poor Aunt Esme, but—"

"Do ye tell me, girrrl, that my blitherhing idiot of a son fancied I must nae be trusted wi' the truth?" raged the General, beginning to pace up and down like a hungry tiger. "That puir wee lassie! Her ain brother had murrdered her husband! 'Tis nae wonder she lost her babe! My Lord! What infamy! Stuart was in every way a fine gentleman, wherefore that wild creature Jonas hated him with a passion and judged him unworthy! How did he do it? Shot? Steel? Poison? I'd nae put it past the

466

scoundrrrel! Well? *Answer* me, someone! The cat's frae the bag—no use trying to wrap things in clean linen at this stage!"

Josie had slunk away and was cowering behind the landaulette with the two footmen who had speedily made themselves least in sight—and were listening eagerly. Mrs. Drummond, cringing before her father-in-law's wrath, mumbled, "Jonas p—pushed him from—from the battlements! And old Mr. Tyndale banished him to the Colonies and forbade him ever to use the family name, or return to England. Which is the shameful reason his son used the name Winters!" Encountering Yolande's seething glare, she wailed, "Now—never be cross, love! By what Mr. Donald says, your grandfather must soon have heard it, at all events. Better it should come from one of the family, than—"

"Aye," snarled the General. "And better yet had either of those two alleged gentlemen had the decency to have owned to it!"

Mrs. Drummond gave a joyous cry as Socrates reappeared and raced to fling himself, shivering, into her eager arms.

Tyndale and Devenish were also returning. Yolande's attempt to speak was cut off by a savage, "You will be *silent*, girl!" And her grandfather, tall, austere, and rigid with anger, ground out, "So ye found the pesky creature!"

"He found us, more like, sir." Devenish grinned blithely. "Shot down the stairs like the devil himself was after—" The tension of the group conveyed itself to him, and he stopped speaking, looking uncertainly from one to the other. "Something wrong? Cousin Craig and I wasn't gone too long, was we?"

"Nae, laddie," purred Sir Andrew with an awful smile. " 'Tis only that I'm a mite fashed that ye'd address yon deceitful upstart as 'cousin'!" His chin thrust forward. "The *son* of the man who *murdered your sire*!" he roared.

Devenish stiffened. Tyndale, the colour receding from his face, snapped, "There is no proof of that, sir!"

"Is there not? I am told that your father deliberately pushed young Stuart Devenish from the battlements of yon accursed castle!" The General threw up an authoritative hand to silence Devenish's attempted intervention. "Donald"—his contemptuous gaze seared past Tyndale and Devenish—"I know *you* to be an honourable gentleman. If you will be so good as to tell me what you have heard I shall not question the truth of it."

Tyndale clenched his hands and flushed darkly, but said

nothing. Devenish, his own colour rising, flung up his head and frowned, waiting.

With a commendable paucity of words, Donald sketched the tragedy that had occurred here twenty-four years earlier. And all the time, Sir Andrew's cold gaze drifted from one to the other of the young men standing so silently before him.

"And that," Donald concluded regretfully, "is all I know, Andy. I might add that I only learned of it yesterday afternoon."

"Would I had done so!" said Sir Andrew, shooting a brief, angry glance at him. "I'd have known better than to introduce these two—individuals—to my friends, or allow either of 'em to make sheep's eyes at my granddaughter!"

"Sir," said Tyndale, with his share of hauteur, "I can understand your anger, but—"

"Then ye're in the wrong of it tae starrrt with! I've no anger towards you, Tyndale. Ye've my sympathy, rather. Aye, my deepest sympathy for the black shame that has been handed doon tae ye! No, sir! Ye'll no speak till I give ye leave. Which is not yet!"

Tyndale subsiding, though he was white and trembling with rage, the General turned his attention to Devenish, who fronted him pale but proud, a slightly condescending droop to his eyelids that served merely to further infuriate the old gentleman. "As for you," snorted Drummond, "what manner of man is it cries comrade with the son of the rogue who killed his sire? I knew you for a wild young scalliwag. I dinna ken ye were withoot honour! Ye're just like Jonas! Ah, ye've heard *that* before, I see! Well, ye've heard the truth on't! And had I known ye for the man ye are, ye'd no hae set foot in my hoose! Either o' ye!" Scarlet with wrath, he spun around to shout, "Verra well, you two skulking behind the coach there! Come and clear this away as fast as may be!"

"Grandpapa!" Yolande began tearfully.

"By your leave, ma'am," Tyndale intervened in a voice she had never heard. "Sir, you have judged on hearsay. I shall not. Somehow I mean to prove my father innocent of intent to do murder. And Devenish—"

"Will speak for himself, if you please," said that individual, his tone as cold as his cousin's. "General, my initial reaction to the truth of my father's death was very similar to your own. I have since discovered my cousin to be a gentleman. One to whom I probably owe my life. I mean to help him come at the real truth of the tragedy, but whatever comes of it has little to do with the fact that I have offered for your granddaughter, and been given reason to believe she—"

"Well, she don't!" Drummond overrode harshly. And loftily disremembering that two of his sons had married English-women and that Yolande was half-English, said, "I would suggest that since ye've very little Scot in you, sir, you hie yourself back to your homeland and wed a girl closer to your own unfortunate background! Ladies—into the carriages, if you please!" With sublime arrogance and a spate of snapped-out orders, he marched towards his bay, but turned back, coming full circle to announce, "The bairn is innocent and can stay at Steep Drummond until you, Devenish, are ready to return to England. Then, you may come and collect her." Not so much as glancing at Tyndale, he finished a brittle, "Alone!" and stamped to where the grooms were saddling his horse.

For an aching moment, Tyndale looked squarely at Yolande, then he strode off to find Lazarus.

Wrenching her gaze from his tall, erect figure, Yolande faced Devenish, who came to her side, one cautious eye on the General. "Whew!" he breathed. "What a devil he can be. Bad as my own tyrant, and worse! Understandable, I suppose, but—not entirely justified. Craig's a good enough man, Yolande."

She smiled wanly. "He said the same of you. Dev, whatever shall we do?"

He took her hand and gripping it with a confidence he could not feel, said firmly, "You will do nothing. Don't let the old fellow scare you. He's all huff and puff, you know. Chances are he'll go off the boil and begin to think he was a shade hasty. At all events, I must stay with Tyndale—for a while at least. When I come to get Josie, you'll—you'll not back off from what you promised?"

Suddenly, he looked very anxious. Yolande returned the pressure of his hand and said staunchly, "I'll not back off, dear Dev."

The skies darkened while Devenish and Tyndale were exploring the castle, and soon rain was pattering down, the gloomy weather and clammy chill adding to the forbidding aspect of the great, silent, high-ceilinged rooms.

Scanning a vast bedchamber, the bed hangings and furniture swathed in Holland covers, Devenish remarked, "You know, coz, Yolande spoke truly—it could be jolly fine if you was to bring the place up to style. It would cost a mountain of blunt, though." And he wondered which of the rooms his parents had occupied, and how it had all looked when his gentle mother was alive.

"Might be worth it," Tyndale mused. "I wonder what scared Socrates so badly."

Following him from the room, Devenish did not voice his thought that the scruffy hound was not alone in finding Castle Tyndale daunting. "A cat, probably," he said lightly. "A black one, of course!"

The next corridor they came upon was dim and very chill. Tyndale opened the first door, "Perhaps," he agreed. "I must—" He stopped. A pleasant bedchamber was before them; a room of painted ceilings, soaring leaded windows, a graceful canopied bed, its blue silken hangings free of dust covers, and a fine carpet of great size laid down in readiness for the new occupant. A stone fireplace was between the windows, and hanging over the mantel the portrait of a lovely fair girl, looking down with proudly tender eyes at the infant she held: a tiny infant, richly gowned, and having tufts of golden hair and deeply blue eyes. There were portraits of Esme Devenish at Aspenhill, and an impressive family group at Devencourt, but this portrait had a rare charm and warmth and, captivated,

Devenish gazed up at it. Beside him, Tyndale was again struck by the stark pathos of the tragedy. He glanced from the radiant joy in the face of his long-dead aunt, to the awed features of her grown son, and guilt fastened steel claws in him. Only a short while ago he had been standing beside this man's love, wanting nothing so much as to sweep her into his arms and claim her for his own. The slightest encouragement from Yolande would have been all the impetus he would have needed to speak his love and try to win her from Devenish. Disgraceful behaviour in any man, but especially dishonourable in his own case, to attempt to steal the betrothed of a man who had already been so cruelly wronged, whether deliberately or accidentally, by the Tyndales!

"Was she not lovely, coz?" breathed Devenish.

"Indeed she was. I collect the caretaker must have been told you would wish to have this room. I suspect it was occupied by your papa when he—" It seemed to him that he heard something odd, and he stopped abruptly.

Devenish seized his arm and hissed, "Listen . . . !"

At first, the silence was absolute save for the faint drumming of the rain on the high Gothic windows. And then, faint and stealthy, came a soft shuffling, followed by a muted thump. Aghast, the two men looked at one another through a moment so intensely still that the air seemed to throb in their ears. All too soon another sound disturbed the quiet: an echoing wail, muffled with distance, but unutterably forlorn. The hair lifted on the back of Devenish's neck. His eyes grew dim, and his breath was snatched away. Of a less imaginative nature, Tyndale's calm was considerably shaken. Then, "Oh, good gad!" he exclaimed bracingly. "It must be that fool, Montelongo! Likely having the deuce of a time with our trunks and never dreaming his howlings would petrify us!"

Very aware that he had betrayed terror, Devenish coloured up and disclaimed, "I trust you apply that term to yourself, Tyndale!"

"Oh, but of course." Tyndale held open the door and bowed with a flourish. "You were perfectly controlled." But as Devenish sauntered past, he added mischievously, "A little green, perhaps."

His cousin's head tossed upward. "Your own colour was a trifle off. Though I doubt you would be honest enough to admit you were afraid."

There was a glint of anger in the blue eyes, and Tyndale

made a disarming gesture. "No, seriously, Dev. I *was* uneasy, I'll own, but I must confess I am out of charity with such flights of fancy as shades and goblins, witches and warlocks, and their brethren. Childish nonsense; or the promptings of an uneasy, er—" And he checked, dismayed by the bog into which he had blundered.

"Conscience?" flashed Devenish, partly infuriated by those tactless words, and partly sickened by a terror that, instead of fading, became ever more compelling. "Faith, but you surprise me! Here I had thought *your* conscience would rest less easy than mine—in *this* place!"

Tyndale's lips tightened and for an instant he experienced a pressing need to apply his fist to that high-held jaw. Then he shrugged and stalked out of the room and towards the main staircase.

Montelongo was halfway up the first flight, struggling with Tyndale's heavy trunk.

"Idiot!" his master scolded affectionately. "Small wonder you howled. Mr. Devenish and I thought for—"

Propping the trunk, Montelongo leaned on it, panting. "I not howl!" he denied vehemently. "I think *you* do that!"

His blood running cold, Devenish grinned and said a forced, "Well, that's hell's own jest!"

"Tell you what," said Tyndale. "Let us leave the trunk on the landing for the present, and bring the rest of the paraphernalia inside. It seems to have stopped raining—for a minute."

He helped Montelongo deposit the heavy trunk on the landing, and they all started down the stairs. Glancing uneasily about him, the Iroquois muttered, "Me no like big wigwam. Me sleep out. Under stars. You too, sir."

Sighing as they crossed the great hall, Tyndale remonstrated, "Why must you persist in using that pidgin English?"

Montelongo responded woodenly, "I shall take my rest *à la belle étoile.*"

Devenish halted, staring his astonishment.

"I engaged a tutor," Tyndale explained, "to help Monty learn English. It turned out he has a very quick mind. Speaks fluent English, French, and German."

With a shout of laughter, Devenish asked, "Then, why in the deuce do you do it, Monty?"

The Iroquois shrugged. "It is expected of me. You sleep outside, sir?"

Still chuckling, Devenish said that he might just do so.

"In that case," grunted the Iroquois, "me stay in the—er . . ."

"Heap big wigwam?" Tyndale offered, helpfully.

His minion's dark features broke into a broad and rare grin.

"Faker!" Tyndale scoffed and, coming to the chaise and the groom who waited on the drivepath, he walked to the rear of the vehicle and began to work at the straps that held the second trunk. "Devenish," he said softly, "there is no reason for you to remain here. Do you prefer to return to—"

"What you are saying, I think," said Devenish, bristling, "is that you take me for a poltroon!"

Tyndale glanced at him and ventured with caution, "I have heard it said that certain types of men have—er, perhaps more awareness of things that are not quite so—ah—readily apparent to—to others."

"And you do not believe one word of it!" His anger flown as swiftly as it had come, Devenish laughed. "Jove! What a windy wallets! My thanks for the offer of a gracious escape, but I shall stay. If you hear a drumming sound in the night, however, it will likely not be your Indian friend here, but my knees."

Montelongo, who had carried a large box of bedding from the interior of the chaise and stood watching, grunted his approval, and put down his burden.

Tyndale said, "Good man, Dev! I'd hoped you would stay. But—tell me, do you *really* believe the old pile haunted, or were you hoaxing me?"

Devenish hesitated. With his eyes lowered and stubbing one boot at the uneven drive, he said slowly, "My uncle and Drummond both say I'm the living image of your father. I—begin to fancy I do indeed take after him—in more than looks."

"He held the castle to be an evil house." Craig nodded thoughtfully. "Is that what you mean?"

"You will think me daft, but . . ."

"But—so do you."

Devenish looked up in a shy, shamefaced fashion. "I expect it sounds purely crazy but—but there *is* something here. Something not of—this world."

Montelongo folded his arms and, having privately made up his mind to stay as close to Tyndale as was possible, rumbled, "You speak of Evil Spirits! Me *very* sure me sleep out!"

"Well, before you do, you Friday-faced fraud, pick up your

box!" said Tyndale. "I can manage this trunk. Dev, can you bring the greatcoats and dressing cases?"

Laden, they started back to the castle, Tyndale calling to the groom to take the chaise around to the stableyard which he supposed to be further along the drive, beyond a stand of elm trees. It began to rain again as they were climbing the steps, and the wind blew up gustier and colder.

"First thing—" Montelongo shivered—"me build one fine campfire."

"Hey!" shouted Devenish, stumbling forward with his load. He was much too late. The door slammed shut before he reached the top step.

"Oh—damn!" he groaned. "Hurry and fish out the key, Tyndale!"

Craig set down his trunk and began to grope in his waistcoat pocket.

Montelongo offered a disgruntled, "Me lay twenty pounds you no find it! This place bad magic!"

"Nonsense! I'm sure . . . I put it— No! By Jove! I left it in the lock!"

Montelongo uttered a triumphant exclamation. Tyndale said indignantly, "I didn't take your bet! Put down that box and help find the thing, you pagan mushroom!"

Amused by this appellation, Montelongo put the box down and began to prowl about, keen eyes searching. Fearing the worst, Devenish dumped the greatcoats atop the bedding and made his way to a window. Shielding his eyes with both hands, he peered inside. "Never mind the key," he called. "It's lying on the floor just inside the door. Craig, you dolt, you must have dropped it!" He tried the window. "Locked, blast it! Well, we'll have to try the others."

Up to a point, the idea was a good one. A few windows could be reached from the wide front steps; the rest, however, proved to be set too high to be investigated. At some time in the recent past the castle had been fitted with comparatively modern windows, but the three that were accessible were also securely locked. Montelongo was dispatched to the stables in search of a ladder, while Devenish and Tyndale roamed the building, looking for a likely means of entrance. By the time Montelongo reappeared, carrying a serviceable ladder, they were all soaked, but no closer to entering Tyndale's new home. It was, in fact, another half-hour before they were able to do so, having been obliged to break one of the panes so as to reach the lock.

"An inauspicious beginning," grumbled Devenish, peering around the dimness of a cold, shrouded saloon.

"It will be more inauspicious did someone see us creeping in and fancy us to be burglars," Tyndale pointed out, crossing to the door.

Montelongo hurried to unlock the main door and carry the boxes inside. He and Tyndale then took up the large trunk and prepared to haul it upstairs. Devenish, his arms full, kicked the door closed and followed them to the stairs. "I hope there's some food about," he remarked. "Ain't too hungry now, but by—"

"Look out!" shouted Tyndale. He and Montelongo dropped their burden and leaped aside. The trunk they had earlier deposited on the first landing had apparently not been securely settled. It had gradually yielded to the pull of gravity and now came hurtling down the stairs to fetch up with a crash against its fellow, missing Devenish by a hair. It was a sturdy trunk, metal-bound and heavy, and he whistled his relief that it had missed him.

"Are you all right?" Tyndale asked. "Why in the deuce didn't you jump for it?"

"I was behind you, if you recall. Did not see the blasted thing coming. What the devil made it shoot down like that?"

Tyndale glanced up to the landing. "I suppose we must have failed to anchor it securely. We were in such haste to bring the things in out of the rain."

"Almost," grunted Montelongo, "Mr. Devenish got brain box broken."

"Yes." Tyndale scanned his cousin frowningly. "And I wonder what people would have said of that!"

"Oh, pshaw! You would scarce murder me with a trunk, coz! Besides, Monty was here—he could swear it was purely accidental."

"You think folks believe word of ignorant savage?" Montelongo uttered a scornful, "Hah!"

"And if my pagan was Caucasian as you or I," said Tyndale grimly, "this little island is largely populated by people who consider those dwelling in the next *county* to be 'foreigners' and as such, quite untrustworthy. Can you not imagine how much confidence they would repose in the word of a *Canadian*? A man in *my* service, known to be very loyal to *me*?"

475

The cousins looked at one another.

Devenish said rather uncertainly, "Well—nothing happened."

"No. But do you know, I begin to think your presence is a decided hazard. To me! Are you quite convinced you'd not prefer to return to your gentle Sussex?"

"Perfectly sure. All you have to do, coz, is make very sure nothing happens to me."

"That may well prove to be a two-edged sword," Tyndale warned, his eyes sombre.

"Fustian!" Never one to remain glum above a minute, Devenish scoffed, "We shall likely go on comfortably enough."

The evening that followed was, however, somewhat less than comfortable. As a result of their perfunctory tour of inspection, the book room was selected as the initial headquarters. The dining room was warmer, but the long table was rather daunting, and Devenish had taken an aversion to the tapestry that hung above the long oak credenza against one wall. This monumental work depicted a boar hunt undertaken by a number of individuals caught in unlikely poses, their flat, pale faces and gory pursuits causing him to express the conviction that never had he seen such a set of rum touches, and that to spend an entire evening with them staring at him was more than he could endure. The book room, despite a pervasive odour of mildew, was a large chamber made considerably less forbidding by the addition of a modern pegged-oak floor and, when some fine Sheraton chairs were unearthed from dusty Holland covers, was pronounced more the thing.

While Devenish and Tyndale embarked on a search for candles, Montelongo descended into the lower regions in the hope of finding firewood. He returned in a great hurry, clutching a scuttle full of logs and shavings, and with his bronzed features markedly pale. He insisted that he had been "watched" throughout his foragings, and advised Tyndale that much as he appreciated his situation, if the Major decided to dwell permanently at Castle Tyndale, he would be obliged to find himself a new valet! Tyndale laughed at him, and said his megrims were the result of the roast pork they had enjoyed at dinner last evening, but he noted that the Iroquois was even less loquacious than usual, and that often during the balance of the evening, his dark gaze would flash uneasily to the dimmer corners of the large room.

As soon as the fire was established, the box of bedding provided by the housekeeper at Steep Drummond was brought in to be set by the hearth. By that time, the pangs of hunger were at work and a small table was also borne over to the fireside to serve their dining needs. Thanks to the friendship Montelongo had struck up with General Drummond's irascible French chef, they were enabled to eat quite well. The chef had provided a basket containing slices of a fine ham, some excellent cheeses, two fresh loaves with an ample wedge of butter, a cold roast chicken, some grapes from St. Andrew's succession houses, and two bottles of a fair Burgundy. The inroads made on this fare by three healthy young men served to impress upon them the need for Montelongo to journey into the village next morning. A discussion as to the supplies needed resulted in the compilation of a list, at the head of which were a cook, housekeeper, footman, and two maids, these prospective employees to repair to the castle immediately.

The food, wine, and warmth produced a pleasant feeling that all was not as black as had at first appeared. Evening deepened into night, and they chatted drowsily, but always at the edges of two minds nibbled the sly demons of unease. Devenish, his easy grin and cheerful commonplaces giving no least sign of his inner apprehension, could not dismiss the grievous cry they had heard that afternoon, and Montelongo alternately pondered the rapid and unexplained descent of the heavy trunk and his persistent sense of being under constant but invisible surveillance.

The candles were burning low before Tyndale stood, stretched, and said he was going up to bed.

"Up where?" asked Devenish, staring at him.

"I think I'll take the large bedchamber on the west front. It has apparently been prepared for me, and I fancy it must have been the master suite."

"But—it will be freezing up there! Why not bed down here tonight, and—"

"I will be damned," said Tyndale, "if I'll allow myself to be scared into bivouacking in my own house!"

"Who said anything about being scared?" Devenish demanded, jumping up and snatching up blankets and sheets. "It just seems stupid to leave such a fine fire."

With a broad grin, Tyndale shrugged. "Then by all means, stay down here."

Devenish glared at him and stalked from the room.

The bedchamber he had selected was next to Tyndale's. The large canopied bed was free of Holland covers but not made up. Grumbling to himself, Devenish began to spread his blankets atop the mattress. Montelongo stalked in, stared from the blankets to Devenish, and with one sweep of his long arm cleared the offending articles away. Devenish meekly assisted him in the business of sheets and blankets and eiderdown, each in its correct order of business, until a very tidy arrangement had been completed. The Iroquois departed while Devenish was disrobing, and came back a few minutes later, carrying a warming pan which he tucked between the sheets while eyeing the young man appraisingly. "You," he imparted, "peel good. For small white man."

Devenish stiffened and prepared to devastate him with some well-chosen words. There was a twinkle in the unfathomable dark eyes, however, and it was dashed difficult to devastate anyone while one's teeth chattered so. Clambering hastily between the sheets, his feet encountered the comfort of the warming pan and he forgot indignation. "You," he shivered, "are—are a j-jewel! If ever you l-leave my cousin, come to me. My own man stayed with the m-military when I—er—left it, and now that I'm to be sh-sh-shackled, I'll have to find myself a valet."

Montelongo thanked him gravely and went off to the adjoining room, where he advised Tyndale he meant to stay by him all night, just in case an uninvited guest should put in an appearance. Tyndale chuckled and enquired as to who was protecting whom, but he was disturbed, nonetheless. He had never before seen the proud Indian show fear.

Devenish had set his candle on the table beside his bed and had instructed Montelongo to leave it burning. The room was so large, however, as to make the circle of light pathetically small. He found himself straining his eyes into the surrounding darkness, whereupon he closed them and tried to go to sleep. It had been a long, tiring day, and downstairs he had almost dropped off several times, but now that he wooed slumber his brain became fiendishly wide awake, his thoughts whirling helter-skelter fashion from one worry to the next. The shadows of past events weighed heavily on his mind until he felt crushed by sympathy for the mother he had never known, and for his father's sad death.

Outside, the night seemed full of movement and noise; the rain pattered, the wind sighed in the chimney and set the windows to rattling. Normal noises, of course. Certainly nothing to cause alarm. He concentrated on his beloved Yolande ... her sweet face, and those heavenly eyes that could be so tender, or ... sometimes, so vexed with him. ...

He could not have said what woke him, but he started up suddenly, his heart thundering. The candle was out, the room oppressively dark with only the lighter squares of the windows relieving the gloom. The storm was still blustering. Perhaps a branch had come down, or a gate had slammed somewhere. He pulled the eiderdown closer around his ears and settled down again.

"Alain ... Alain ... !"

His breath congealed in his throat. His eyes shot open and he lay tensely unmoving. Tyndale never called him by his Christian name. Monty certainly would not. And besides—it had been the voice of—*a woman!* How stupid! He must have dreamed—

"Alain ... oh—Alain ... my son ..."

His mind reeled. He thought dazedly, "My God! My *God!*" And leaping out of bed, grabbed for his tinderbox, only to pause, frozen with new terror.

A faint glow shone from the mantel. By that unearthly light, he could see his mother's portrait distinctly. His own infant likeness and the rose arbour wherein they had posed was gone, and there was only her face, transformed into a nightmare countenance like some hideous caricature of the beauty that once had been. The eyes stared from great, hollow sockets. The cheeks were sunken, the mouth gapingly down-trending as if in a despairing scream. Only the hair was as lovely as before, of itself seeming to render the other features even more ghastly.

Devenish wet dry lips and battled a sick weakness. "M-m-mama ... ?" he croaked.

"Avenge me ..." came the poignant moan. "Alain ... avenge us ... !"

The outer door crashed open. Tyndale, holding up a branch of candles, and with Montelongo's dark face peering apprehensively over his shoulder, said, "Dev? Are you all right?"

The familiar faces seemed to ripple before Devenish's eyes, like reflections on the disturbed surface of a pool. "The—the portrait ..." he managed, gesturing towards it.

Tyndale walked closer, holding his candelabra higher.

Devenish saw the puzzled expression on the strong face and, dreading to look again, turned his own gaze to the mantel.

The portrait was just as he had first seen it, his mother smiling lovingly down at the babe she held.

Dimly, he thought, "I am going mad . . ."

Tyndale gave a cry of alarm, and Montelongo ran to steady Devenish as he swayed uncertainly. Considerably unnerved, the Iroquois demanded, "When we go home, Major? We got no haunted teepees in Montreal!"

For many years General Sir Andrew Drummond had served his country with distinction. He had left the military when the death of his elder brother brought him both the title and estates and, although he sometimes remembered the camaraderie of army life with a nostalgic sigh, his most bitter battles had been fought and lost behind a desk in Whitehall, so that he had never really regretted his decision to resign. He had proven a conscientious and just landlord, a fair-minded employer, a good neighbour, a bruising rider to hounds, and an excellent judge of horseflesh, the which sterling qualities had won him both liking and admiration. He was also, however, a man who drove a hard bargain, his manner was brusque, he was impatient with foolishness (of which he had been heard to remark the local society had more than its share), and his temper was notorious. Further, he had an unfortunate habit of refusing to bow to the dictates of protocol: he attended the social functions which pleased him, rather than those to which it was expedient to respond, and invited to his home people he enjoyed, not necessarily those who might some day prove of use to him. Needless to say, these praiseworthy practices had aroused a good deal of ire, albeit subdued, in certain quarters.

Nonetheless, General Drummond was the last man one might have suspected of improper conduct, and the entire County was astounded to learn that he had committed a horrifying social solecism. Unsuspecting guests, lured to his home so as to renew their acquaintanceship with his granddaughter, had been introduced to two young gentlemen distantly related to their host. Never dreaming that these same two men figured prominently in a shocking scandal, trusting parents had allowed their daughters to be presented to the newcomers and had watched indulgently as those carefully nurtured flowers flirted, chatted, and danced with them. Prominent citizens had greeted them cordially and had deigned to introduce them to their own friends. And then, after four and twenty years of lies and deceit, the sordid truth concerning the tragedy at Castle Tyndale had exploded through the County.

When the first wave of shocked incredulity abated, it was reasoned that the General must certainly have been aware of the long-kept secret, and had deliberately sponsored the son of a murderer into society. Young Tyndale had a fine military record, even if he was a Colonial, but that was no justification for allowing him to mix with the cream of the local gentry. His blood was tainted with the dread stain of murder, his house was disgraced, and he must forever be a pariah. As for Alain Devenish—surely *his* behaviour was utterly beyond the pale! By all the laws of Polite Society, he should have faced Tyndale across twenty yards of turf, aimed down the barrel of a duelling pistol, and done what he might to obliterate the scion of the man who had orphaned him. Instead, he appeared to regard his dastardly cousin with an affability that was, opined several indignant gentlemen, sufficient to turn the stomach of any honourable, God-fearing man!

Thus, having arrived at their variously damning conclusions, the County, deliciously scandalized, proceeded to beat a path to the door of the miscreant. Such honeyed sympathy was extended by reason of his having been "hoodwinked" by the pair of young scoundrels; such heartfelt condolences offered upon the "unfortunate proceedings" at the castle; and such bland amazement expressed that the tragedy had been "so artfully concealed all these years," that General Drummond became almost purple in the face with rage, even as he parried thrust with block, and attack with evasion. "Curse and confound the pack of 'em!" he raged to his stoical daughter. "I canna fight back, y' ken? That's what galls, Carrroline! I canna say a worrrd in me ain defense! And if one more sanctimonious hypocrite comes fawing here wi' his treacly grin and sairpents' teeth, I'll chop him tae bits and stuff him intae his own sporran! And be damned tae him, if I dinna!"

Life at Steep Drummond was thus become a tense business of late. Mrs. Drummond, never at ease with her father-in-law, avoided him as much as possible and took care to say nothing at the dinner table that might provide fodder for his simmering rage. Yolande, having endured a thundering scold all the way back from Castle Tyndale on the fateful day of the picnic, had since refused to discuss the matter, regarding her grandparent with cool but respectful silence whenever he attempted to take

her to task for not having informed him of the true state of affairs. He had, he snarled at her, written to his bacon-brained
son, and in such a way that he had no doubt but that her father
would "soon come posting up here to see what he might do to
make amends." Yolande replied calmly, "How lovely," which
drove her grandpapa into strangled choking sounds and gri-
maces that might have alarmed her, did she not know the old
humbug so well.

She had her own share of callers and did what she might to
point out that for whatever had occurred four and twenty years
ago, Craig was in no way responsible, and that Devenish
would be a clod indeed, if he refused to give at least a hearing
to the man who had saved his life. Not surprisingly, her most
sympathetic listener was her friend Mary Gordon, whose dark
eyes would glisten with tears at the very thought of "dear Mr.
Devenish" being so unjustly accused. "How very said it is,
Yolande," she mourned. "And you just aboot to announce your
betrothal. Do you suppose your papa will be able to bring the
General about his thumb?"

Yolande said that if Sir Martin was unable to do so, her
mama would probably succeed, for Lady Louisa had so much
charm her fierce father-in-law was usually putty in her hands.
"It is not that which worries me, Mary," she confided one day,
as they took tea together in the drawing room. "There are
things I simply cannot understand. The real facts of what happened between Stuart Devenish and Jonas Tyndale have been
buried for all these years. Yet within days of the arrival of my
cousins, the entire County was fairly buzzing with it! Do you
have any notion of who set it about?"

Miss Gordon shook her sleek head. "Hamish MacInnes told
my brother, and Jock gave him a rare setdown for spreading
such vicious gossip, I can tell you!"

"And spread it a little farther," said Yolande, dryly. "Oh, never fret, dear. I cannot blame Jock. It's just—" She hesitated.

Miss Gordon slipped a consoling arm about her. "Of course.
I understand. You must be fair daft with worry, to have the
love of your heart dwelling in that dreadful old pile and never
knowing if yon Colonial wild man has taken it into his head
to exact vengeance by pushing poor Devenish off—"

"Do not *dare* to say such wicked things, Mary Gordon! Or
I shall positively shake you!" raged Yolande, springing to her
feet and rounding on her startled friend like a fury. "Craig is

as honourable as he is brave, and would no more attack Dev than raise his hand against—against little Josie!"

"Oh—I'm s-sure you are perfectly right," quavered her friend, variously frightened and elated. "Is a fine man, Major Tyndale. I never meant aught but to console you, and pray you will forgive me for being such a great gaby."

Yolande saw the gleam in the big eyes and knew what her friend was thinking. Scarcely caring, she resumed her seat, apologized, was forgiven, and sat staring miserably at the great bowl of sweet peas on the occasional table. What were Dev and Craig doing at this moment? Were they cold and uncomfortable, and not eating properly? Or had that strange man of Craig's managed to find them some servants? And what possible hope had they of ever proving Jonas Tyndale's innocence?

A warm little hand was placed over her own. Mary said softly, "I've known you a good many years, dearest, and never seen you sae doonhearted. Can I no help ye?"

Such warm understanding brought a lump to Yolande's throat. She pressed her friend's hand responsively. "Cousin Craig holds his father died swearing his innocence," she sighed. "I believe him, but—how he can hope to prove it, after all this time . . ." And she sighed again.

"Well, it certainly wouldnae hurt to try. And twenty-four years is not sae very long, Yolande. At least, so my papa holds. The older you get, says he, the faster pass the years." She added with rather doubtful logic, "To people of *his* age it likely seems no more than a year would seem to you and me."

"Yes," said Yolande dubiously. "But even so, a lot has changed since then. The only people who have even a glimmering of knowledge about what really happened that day are the servants who worked in the castle. And many of them may have moved away, or gone to their reward."

"Fiddle! Who would wish tae move from Ayrshire? Or leave their families? They are likely most of them within a few miles of here at this very minute. At least, Major Tyndale must be of that opinion, for he seems to have been pester—I mean—questioning everybody he can reach, and those he misses, Devenish finds."

"Oh!" cried Yolande, encouraged. "How wonderful if they learn something to help! Do you know if they've done so, Mary?"

"I—I hae me doots, Yolande. Sorry I am tae say it, but," she smiled wryly, "they're a close-mouthed lot at best, and from all I can detairmine, are not being—well, they seem to hae put up a—a wall of silence."

Yolande's hopes died. It was no more than she had expected, really. The Scots country folk with their fierce pride, their unyielding sense of family, their stern adherence to proper behaviour, had judged both Tyndale and Devenish and found them wanting. "What a frightful mess!" she thought. "No one will help them."

Moved by her friend's despairing attitude, Miss Gordon said a tentative, "If there is anything I can do, I'll nae hesitate. There may be old folks knowing something of it all who would never be found by Tyndale, but who my papa might be able to approach."

Brightening, Yolande clasped her hand tighter. "Oh, bless you, Mary! I shall ask my Aunt Caroline, also. She is well acquainted."

"Nae—d'ye think ye should?" Mary demurred. "Will she no tell your grandpapa?"

"Why, she's a dear, despite her gruff ways, and I feel sure . . . Oh, my! It would put her into a difficult position, wouldn't it? And my poor dear old gentleman is so upset just now. There must be *someone* I could ask. . . ." She knit her brows, then exclaimed a triumphant, "Yes! There's Mrs. Mac-Farlane, the gardener's wife. She has the dearest little girl who sometimes plays with Josie, and I believe the family has been here for centuries. I'll go and see her at once!" She stood, the bloom back in her cheeks again. "Mary—how good you are! Thank you, thank you!"

On the front steps they embraced and parted, Yolande to hurry into the garden and walk across the park towards the copse of trees beyond which was the gardener's cottage, and Mary to be driven home, her pretty head full of wonderment that Yolande Drummond, whom she had always thought a sensible girl, could have such a *tendre* for that lanky Canadian boy who was well enough in his quiet way, but had not one jot of Alain Devenish's looks or personality.

Yolande, meanwhile, was diverted from her route when she heard childish voices coming from the new summer house that was the General's pride. Sure enough, Josie and her friend were inside, solemnly conducting a tea party with two elderly dolls and a large black cat that seemed not to mind the dress it wore.

"Miss Yolande," called Josie gaily, waving the hand of the

doll seated next to her. "Come and have a cuppa tea. These are Maisie's dolls. That's Mrs. Crump, and mine is Lady Witherspoon. Ain't they lovely?"

Yolande was suitably impressed with the company and, having been presented to the cat (first) and to Maisie, said with her kind smile, "Never look so frightened, dear. I'll not hurt your dolls."

The child, rather frail and all eyes and elbows, backed away, remarking in a breathless fashion that she didn't mean no harm and that "Mum said I wasna tae play wi' Miss Josie."

"No, did she? We must see if she will not relent. Meanwhile, I'm sure she would not object if I joined you."

Fears were forgotten, and the two junior matrons welcomed their guest and plied her with lemonade "tea" and broken biscuits. The black cat, who went by the odd name of Mrs. Saw, considered the newcomer at some length before deciding that she had an acceptable lap and occupying it.

"Oh, dear!" said Maisie, alarmed. "He's kneading your pretty dress, ma'am."

"It doesn't matter," Yolande reassured her. "I like cats, and she's such a lovely one, aren't you, Mrs. Saw?"

"It's a 'he.' And he doesn't like nicknames," Josie corrected primly.

A dimple peeping, Yolande said, "My apologies. But why do you call him 'Mrs.'?"

Both girls dissolved into shrieks of laughter, and when Yolande was at length able to enquire the reason, she learned that they had "said it so funny."

"We *don't* call him 'Mrs.,'" giggled Maisie.

"His name's *Methy-slaw!*" Josie elaborated with a shake of the head for the density of some adults.

For a moment Yolande was unenlightened. Then, she exclaimed, "Oh—Methuselah! A biblical name."

Josie nodded. "Like Mr. Craig's horse."

Intrigued, Yolande said, "Lazzy is short for Lazarus, then? Do you know why?"

"It's because when he was a wee colt, he was caught in a flood or something," said Maisie, all importance. "He almost drowned, but Mr. Craig jumped in and got him out, and that's why that funny Red Indian follows him all over the world, even to Waterloo."

Yolande blinked. Josie, incredulous, demanded, "How do *you* know all that?"

"Me mum told me. She knows all about Mr. Tyndale. I heard her tell me dad that we ought to make it our business to find out—"

"Maisie! Whatever be ye doing, child?" A thin, nervous, dark-haired little woman hurried up the path, wiping her hands on her apron.

"Good afternoon, Mrs. MacFarlane," called Yolande. "Will you not join us?"

Mrs. MacFarlane not only would not join them, but was apparently most distressed. "I *told* ye, never to come up here, you bad girl!" she chided. "Do ye ken what happens to bairns that do nae heed their mums?"

Beginning to cry, Maisie picked up her doll.

Yolande stood and walked forward, pleading, "Pray do not scold her, ma'am. I am the culprit, for Josie is so short of playmates I asked your daughter to stay. It would be lovely if Maisie could keep her company now and then."

The lady fairly clutched her child and, standing very stiff and straight, replied a frigid, "We thank ye, Miss Drummond. Is best they dinna meet." She bit her lip and added with a sort of desperation, "And besides, we'm moving away verra soon noo. Good day tae ye."

She bobbed a curtsy and backed away, her attitude all but fearful.

Josie snatched up the other doll and ran forward. "Don't forget Lady Witherspoon," she said sadly.

Maisie ran to retrieve her doll. A ball that had snared the chair with "Lady Witherspoon" fell to the floor. Yolande took it up. "Catch," she called, and threw it to Josie.

Mrs. MacFarlane, standing just beyond the little girl, uttered a piercing shriek and sprang back, throwing up a protecting arm.

Astonished, Yolande cried, "Oh, I do beg your pardon. Did I startle you, ma'am?"

The distraught woman returned no answer, but burst into tears, took her frightened daughter by the hand, and all but ran back across the park.

It was very apparent, thought Yolande, that she could expect little help from that quarter. Maybe Mrs. MacFarlane thought they were *all* murderers!

"Now," said Josie forlornly, "I got no one to play tea party with."

"Not only that, you have no tea party left." Yolande nodded

at Methuselah who was on the table, busily crunching the remaining biscuits, with the empty cream pitcher overturned beside him.

"Silly creature," Josie giggled. "There wasn't no cream in it. And cats do not like biscuits!"

Yolande smiled, "I suppose no one has ever told him," she said, thus awakening a little peal of laughter.

As they started back towards the house together, Yolande thought, "I wonder how Mrs. MacFarlane knew so much about Craig. . . ."

❧ *Chapter 12* ❧

The village of Drumdownie had seen many changes during the march of the centuries. It was thought to have been extant during the Roman military occupation, it had endured through the wars of the tribes, the Norman invasion, and a mighty battle with Norwegian hosts. It had known Robert the Bruce with pride, and Oliver Cromwell with hatred. But it had never as yet seen an Iroquois Indian clad in leathern tunic, trousers, and moccasins, and riding bareback with the demeanour of a conquering monarch. As a result, Montelongo's process along the cobbled old street became more a procession, with children, dogs, and a growing number of adults following in his train, many of the latter, greatly diverted, calling out eagerly to learn where was the rest of the circus.

Ignoring the uproar, Montelongo drew his bay mare to a halt outside the blacksmith's shop where were seated several of the village elders. He swung one leg across the mare's back, preparatory to slipping down, but stopped as an ancient man tottered to his feet, his rheumy eyes as wide as his toothless mouth, to pipe in broad Scots, "The puir savage will be needin' a body tae translate. Now dinna everyone press in—he's nae tae be trusted too close, like as not!"

Montelongo decided this old gentleman was as unintelligible as most of the other Scots he had met, and eyed him imperturbably.

"Dinna fash ye'sel' laddie," urged the aged one. "Me name be Roberts an' I ask ye tae light ye doon and open y'r budget wi' us. How much will they be chargin' fer tickets? And d'ye ken whar the tent will be pitched?"

Very little of this was clear to Montelongo, but one word stood out. "Tent," he said in his deep, resonant voice. "Where big wigwam? Where Chief?"

Mr. Roberts cackled. "Not sae fast!" he admonished. "Show us some tricks, first."

An eager chorus echoed this request, shouts of "Aye, gie us a show!" ... "Whar's a skelpie?" ... "Will ye nae dance fer us?"

The minister, a mild gentleman with a soft heart and patient eyes that blinked behind thick spectacles, managed to work his way through the throng. "Och! A Red Indian, is it?" said he admiringly. "Will ye no stand back and give the puir chappie air. They're accustomed to great spaces, d'ye ken. Are ye lost, me guid mon?" And then, misinterpreting Montelongo's incredulous stare, he said with careful articulation, "You ... come here ... for ... why?"

The fathomless gaze of the Iroquois drifted up and down the good minister and his black robes; around the circle of faces, variously grinning, mocking, curious, or awed; and returned to the reverend gentleman. "I have come here," he said in flawless English, "to hire servants for Major Win—Tyndale."

A new chorus of astonishment arose, a markedly less friendly outcry.

"What manner o' jiggery-pokery be that?" quoth Mr. Roberts, indignant.

"A iggeramous aping his betters!" the baker sneered.

"Servants, is it?" laughed the butcher. "Tae worrk at Castle Tyndale, eh?"

A sharp-faced matron asked snidely, "Why hae ye come all this way? Could ye no hire at Drumwater, or Kirkaird?"

Ignoring this unfortunate question, Montelongo proclaimed, "Major pay well. We need housekeeper, cook, parlourmaids, a footman. A gardener, perhaps. People come early tomorrow morning."

"Ye'd best hae the gates wide, big Chief," chortled the blacksmith, "else they'll like to be beat down by the rush!"

This witticism sent the crowd into whoops, the following derisive comments causing many to become so hilarious that there was much side holding and moaning that no more mirth could be endured.

And the end of it all was that Montelongo returned to Castle Tyndale, a thunderous scowl upon his face, to inform his employer that everyone in the village of Drumdownie was crazy as a loon, and there was no servants to be had there, either. "Them say," he imparted with a disgusted glance around the great hall, "castle is bogle-ridden and they'll not set foot in it!" And taking himself gloomily to the pile of dirty dishes in the kitchens, reflected that he was much in agreement with the locals, loony though they may be.

"It passes all understanding!" Mrs. Arabella Drummond tilted her parasol against the afternoon sun as she wandered with her niece along the village street. Following, Josie was obliged to adjust her pace to the meanderings of Socrates since that pampered darling paid little heed to tuggings at the red ribbon that served for a leash. "Simply," Arabella went on in high dudgeon, "because my sweet baby chanced to forget himself in the greengrocer's shop, one might have thought the world would come to an end! I shall speak to your grandfather about that wretched man, I do assure you! Never have I been so insulted!"

In Yolande's opinion the shopkeeper had been quite restrained, especially in view of the fact that they had entered his neat establishment in an attempt to gather information, and not as customers. The greengrocer had been able to supply little more than had been garnered from her previous informants. Of the inside servants who might be able to shed new light on the happenings of 1792, few were still in the neighbourhood. There was the Hewitts, he said thoughtfully. "But Mrs. Hewitt was a sickly woman who passed to her reward three years ago, and Mr. Hewitt went for head groom to a gentleman in India. Their daughter stayed, but she was only a wee bairn at the time of the tragedy."

Reflecting that it all seemed hopeless, Yolande murmured something placating to her aunt. That lady, her feathers still ruffled, remarked that she could not for the life of her see why Yolande must make all these enquiries. "It is downright embarrassing," she declared. "Had I known you meant to do so, I should not have accompanied you, for to be connected even remotely with such persons as Major Winters, er, Tyndale, is stigma enough, let alone to remind others of it! Were you wise, my love, you would allow him to do his own investigating. Much good will it do him, for the locals are not likely to tell him anything, even was there anything to tell!"

"Which is exactly why I am trying to help," said Yolande. "They think of—"

"Oh—only look at that darling doggie!" Mrs. Drummond interrupted, rapturously eyeing a china spaniel in the window of the draper's shop. "How that would brighten my poor little room at Park Parapine! Not that I mean to appear critical of the quarters allotted to me, for I am after all only a poor relation, and your dear mama is more than kind to allow me to serve as her constant stay and support, so I can scarcely expect to be given a chamber suitable for family or guests, can I? Of one thing, Yolande, I am very sure; none can brand me ungrateful. Not a night passes but that I remember your dear mama in my prayers! As indeed I should, for it must be so tiresome for her there, all alone with the children. Save for your father. Sir Martin is not a garrulous man. Often have I remarked how little he contributes to the conversation when I am with your mama, which must make her life just now so very dreary. Though that was not what I had intended to remark, and . . ." She paused, at a loss to know what she *had* intended to remark.

Yolande seized the opportunity to remind her aunt of the china dog (which she herself thought quite revolting, for surely no dog had such enormous and soulful eyes, or hair the colour of raw liver). "Should you like to go inside, dear? I can wait out here with Socrates, if you wish."

Mrs. Drummond did wish. Yolande and Josie remained outside, but it developed that the lady proprietor was both an ardent faunophile and overjoyed by the patronage of one of the ladies from "up tae the hill." As a result, in a very little while Socrates had to be taken inside to be exclaimed over and, Josie also soon succumbing to the fascinations of the cluttered little shop, Yolande was left to her own devices.

It was a beautiful afternoon, the warm sunlight causing the old sandstone cottages to stand in sharp relief against the blue of the skies, and a light breeze flirting with the trees and swinging the weathervane atop the minister's cottage next to the quaint old church. The door of the church stood wide and, as Yolande passed a woman came out, head bowed and handkerchief pressed to tearful eyes. Wondering if she could be of some assistance, Yolande hesitated. The woman looked up, and Yolande thought she had never beheld so desolate a countenance. Her kind heart touched, she moved forward, stretching forth one hand and saying, "Mrs. MacFarlane! Oh, my dear ma'am, whatever is wrong? Is there anything I can do for you?"

But the gardener's wife only shrank away, uttered a gasping, unintelligible remark, and hurried past.

"Puir wee lassie," said the minister sadly, walking to join Yolande. "She carries a heavy load, Miss Drummond. A crushing load, indeed!"

Yolande nodded. "So I have thought," she agreed, still looking after that frantic retreat. "I know you cannot betray a confidence, but—is there any way in which I could help her?"

He sighed heavily. "In company wi' the most of us, ma'am, puir Mrs. MacFarlane's best help can come frae but one source. Her own self!"

He was probably in the right of it, thought Yolande, and she said no more. Just the same, when she returned to Steep Drummond, she sent a note down to the MacFarlane cottage, in which she reiterated her offer to be of any assistance, and urged that if Mrs. MacFarlane ever felt the need, she not hesitate to come to her.

"Six days!" Devenish observed wrathfully, following his cousin down the main staircase. "Almost a week in this miserable damned pile, and what have we accomplished? Nothing! Not a word! Not a hint! Not a clue!"

Tyndale frowned. "It is not a 'miserable damned pile'! In fact, I think the architecture superb for the period. Most edifices of this type are stately and impressive from the outside, and like a rabbit warren inside. Castle Tyndale has large, bright rooms; corridors that are straight and functional; and ample storage facilities."

"As you should certainly be aware," grumbled Devenish, "since you've paced off and sketched every blasted room we found."

"I really fail to see why that should so annoy you."

But it did annoy Devenish, because he judged it to be a bourgeois pride of ownership. His disgust had been so obvious that one day his cousin had met his irked glance, paused in his pacing, and murmured, "You certainly understand why I do this, Dev?" He had replied disdainfully, "Oh, it is quite obvious that you cherish every brick and stone in the place!" To which Tyndale had retaliated, "And, like my father, you do not." The reminder of his close resemblance to Jonas Tyndale had further infuriated Devenish. His head flinging upward he had snapped, "Very true. I am also becoming more aware of the murderous side of my nature of late. You had best never venture onto the battlements in my company, cousin!" and stamped away, fumingly aware that their relationship was fast deteriorating.

Now, however, knowing he was very tired and overwrought, he turned from an argument, saying merely, "I would think you had better things to do, is all, when we accomplish so little of what we'd hoped for."

"No, but I think we have accomplished a good deal."

"The devil! All we've managed to do is alienate the whole damned county! The yokels mistrust you, and now they've turned on me because I'm trying to help you."

"Yes, I know. And I wish you will go back to London. You do not look at all the thing."

Devenish was silent. That he did not look well was very true. There were dark shadows beneath his eyes and a drawn look to his pale face. His nerves were taut, his temper flaring more frequently these days, his frustration over their lack of success finding expression in an irritability that he was at times unable to contain.

Watching him, Tyndale said, "You have spent too much time in the saddle."

"And learnt nothing! But they know—damn them! Some of 'em, at least! They know *something*, but will tell me nought!" He added moodily, "Besides, you have ridden as much as I."

"I do not have a game leg." Tyndale saw the immediate drawing together of the slim, dark brows, and went on hastily, "And *I* sleep. Why you must sit up half the night when you come in worn out, I cannot fathom."

Again, Devenish returned no answer. The truth of the matter was that these six days had been a nightmare such as he had never before experienced. Despite his carefree demeanour, his life had not been completely free from care. He had endured a good deal of merciless mockery because of his good looks, and although his friends were numerous, he had also made bitter enemies, many of these because some admired lady's eyes had wandered wistfully in his direction. He had known deep disgrace, and a prolonged siege of physical suffering that had not entirely left him. None of these experiences, however, had served to extinguish his ebullient optimism, or to daunt him for very long. But he was close to being daunted now. Just as, with every day that passed his cousin admired his heritage the more, with each hour that passed his own dread and loathing of it was increased. So long as he was inside Castle Tyndale, whether by day or night, he was tormented by the instinct that he was watched by other-worldly eyes. Often, he'd had the sensation that something stood so close beside him that his skin would creep with the fear of being touched by some cold, invisible hand. Prompted by the conviction that he was followed, his glance flashed constantly over his shoulder. His hesitant attempts to explain his experiences to his cousin had been met with a faintly incredulous simulation of understanding, but the sensitive Devenish had thought to detect amusement beneath Tyndale's gravity, and pride forbade him any further reference to the matter. If Tyndale thought him either over-imaginative or a poltroon, he would be driven into his grave sooner than add to either suspicion.

His terror of betraying cowardice forced him to retain the same bedchamber despite his first ghastly night in the castle. Each evening he lingered by the book-room fire for as long as he could maneuver either his cousin or Montelongo to remain with him. When he did seek his bed, it was as much as he could do to open the door, and he avoided looking in the direction of his mother's portrait until shame forced him to glance at it. Only once, on the third night, had the gruesome transformation been repeated. He had sat up in bed, determined to keep his eyes upon the portrait to see if the change would take place while he watched. But he had dropped off to sleep and awoken, as before, to find his candle extinguished but the room illuminated by that soul-freezing glow emanating from the ghastly portrait. His teeth chattering, his limbs weak as water, he'd somehow driven himself to spring from the bed and rush to the painting, but he had tripped over some unseen object and by the time he'd picked himself up, all was normal again. The second and fourth nights had been entirely free from any manifestations, but he had been unable to sleep, his ears straining for the first sound of his unwelcome visitors. On the fifth night he had slept at last, only to awaken to a man's voice calling his name repeatedly, this swiftly followed by the sound of a woman's heart-rending weeping. Sick with fear, he had pulled the covers over his head and slept again from pure exhaustion, to awaken half suffocated when dawn lit the tall windows.

Even the memories were sufficient to make him shiver, and he was horrified to find Tyndale eyeing him curiously. Flushing, he said, "Instead of worrying about my sleep, cousin, you would do better to reflect on our failure to prove what we came here to prove. Dash it all, here we stay, achieving nothing, freezing with cold, victims of Monty's 'cooking,' ghost-ridden, and—"

"Nonsense! I have seen no ghosts, and if Monty has good luck in Kilmarnock today, we may soon have some servants to provide you with the comforts without which you evidently cannot exist."

They had reached the main floor and were starting across the echoing vastness of the Great Hall. Devenish wrenched Tyndale to a halt and expostulated angrily, "I have existed without comforts before this, blast your eyes! But it was in the good clean open air, not cooped up in a clammy, brooding—"

"Well, God knows you have often enough been invited to leave!"

"D'ye take me for a flat? I'm well aware of how eagerly you would gloat and sneer and spread about that 'poor old Devenish's nerve has gone!' Well, it has not! I can last as long as can you—and longer!"

His own nerves somewhat the worse for wear, Tyndale grated, "Devil take you! I would do no such thing!"

They stood in the middle of the big room, glaring at one another, and were both shocked when a discreet cough warned that they were not alone.

Mr. Hennessey, an Irishman who owned a small farm nearby, stood just inside the front doors, hat in hand, and an embarrassed expression on his ruddy face. "Sure and 'tis sorry Oi am did Oi disturb yez, gentlemen," he said in his soft brogue. "Oi've fetched the eggs your haythen—Oi mean, your man ordered. And some bacon and pork and chickens, besides. Oi'll bring 'em inside if 'tis convenient and will not disturb yez at your brawling."

The tension eased. Devenish laughed, and explained, "This was one of our quieter discussions, Hennessey. By all means, bring in the provender."

"Well, Oi tried, y'r honour, so Oi did. But 'tis beyond me poor powers to get the kitchen door open. If you could be so kind as to unlock it, Oi'll be fetching the stuff."

The cousins at once preceeding to the kitchen found the outer door not only unlocked, but standing open, a fact that caused Mr. Hennessey's dark eyes to become very round and his mouth very solemn. He carried in the supplies with marked rapidity, so eager to be away that he all but drove off without the flimsies Tyndale offered.

"So much for your 'large, bright rooms'!" grunted Devenish as they loaded the food into the stone pantry. "Do you decide to live here, you are not like to be pestered to death by company!"

"Gammon! Hennessey said he'd been trying to get the door open. Likely he had got it almost free by the time he came for aid, and the wind did the rest. As for living here, I may very well do so. There must be *some* rational folks hereabouts who do not shiver and shake and fancy every sound the work of shades and goblins!"

Devenish flared, "You refer, perhaps, to me, sir?"

"Good God!" groaned Tyndale, swinging shut the door of the pantry. "He's off again!" He turned, half laughing, but was given pause by the stark fury in Devenish's blue eyes. His own eyes narrowed. After a silent moment, he said thoughtfully, "We have been here almost a week. Time we looked at the battlements—if that would not cause you to be overset."

Why he would choose this of all moments, Devenish could not comprehend, but he as damned if he would show alarm, and so followed his cousin into the hall.

In stern, unsmiling silence, they went side by side to the stairs and up until they came to the winding side steps that led to the northwest tower. It was too narrow here to walk abreast, and Tyndale took the lead, Devenish following until they reached a certain narrow window, where he paused. He had fought against looking out, but now his Uncle Alastair's sombre voice echoed again in this ears. . . . "I saw a darkness flash past the window. I heard this . . . this terrible scream. . . ." He stood immobile, gazing at the narrow aperture. How terrible a thing to have seen what Alastair Tyndale had seen. How frightful to see someone of whom you are fond, plunge—

"Well? Are you coming, or not?"

A look of irritation on his face, Tyndale waited at the next landing. "Insensitive clod!" thought Devenish. "*He* should be plagued by guilt and remorse!" Yet it was very obvious that if Tyndale felt anything at all, it was merely impatience. Cursing under his breath, Devenish resumed his climb. They must, he was sure, have negotiated literally thousands of steps when the stair at last ended before a diminutive landing and a Gothic arched door. Tyndale hesitated briefly, then raised the heavy iron latch and the door creaked open.

They stepped out on to the battlements and into a brisk, clear afternoon with the wind coming straight off the sea and full of the damp, clean smell of it. On their first day here they had found two flags in the basement, one the Union Jack, and the other a banner bearing the arms of the House of Tyndale. Montelongo had decided that these must be flown, and they were now whipping merrily at the flagpole. A line of clouds was building in the northeast; westward, the wind raised little whitecaps on the waves and sent surf crashing against the guarding rocks, and, far off, the islands in the Firth of Clyde were clearly visible.

Postponing the inevitable, Devenish sauntered to the east battlements to scan a fair prospect of rolling hills, lush meadows, and forest land. He breathed deeply of the bracing air and could not wonder that his mother had been so fond of this home of her childhood. Craig stood at the western side between two merlons of the battlements, at the very edge of the embrasure, looking straight down. Devenish thought, "My God! How simple it would be! There's nothing to stay his fall. . . ." He went over and murmured a dry, "You're a trusting soul, I'll give you that!" His cousin neither replied nor moved and, reluctantly, Devenish looked down, also. It seemed terribly far to the jagged rocks. What had been in his father's mind as he fell? Only the ghastly certainty that death awaited him? Or had he thought of the wife and little son he loved? Shrinking, Devenish wondered what he himself would think of at such a moment. And he knew: Yolande.

Tyndale said huskily, "I had so hoped the roof would be faulty. That your father might, perhaps, have stumbled over an uneven or sloping surface. But—see, it is clear, and level." He drove one fist against the parapet and cried, "I still cannot credit it! I *cannot*! He may have been wild and reckless; resentful, perhaps. Obsessed with his conviction that the castle is haunted. But—he adored your mother. He would never have sent the man she loved to so cruel a death, knowing it might very well kill his twin also!"

"You surprise me," said Devenish, with a curl of the lip. "I had come to think you cared not a button for the whole ugly business."

His despairing gaze still fixed on the beach, Craig muttered, "Dolt." He drew a hand across his eyes, then, regaining his control, said, "Now—tell me what has you up in the boughs. I've seen no trace of 'em. Have you?"

Devenish stared his astonishment. "Trace of who?"

"Whoever else is dwelling in the castle. Good God, Dev, you surely have realized we're not alone here?"

"Not . . . *alone*? You—you mean you also have felt—"

"That we are watched? Oh, yes."

"But—but you s-said you had seen nothing!"

"I said I had seen no ghosts. Which I have not." Peering at his cousin's astounded face, he asked keenly, "Lord, is that it? Have you been subjected to more—er—jousts with the Unseen?"

Devenish fixed him with a defiant glare. "Several!"

"The deuce! Tell me!"

So Devenish told him and, because he was extremely angry, spared no details but did not embellish with dramatics, biting out his words in such terse fashion that the fearsomeness of the episodes he described became very vivid to his listener. "Well," he finished, "do not deny yourself, Major Tyndale, sir! Tell me what I already know; that you do not believe a word of it!"

Instead, watching him with wide, shocked eyes, Tyndale breathed, "By Jupiter! And you faced that all alone . . . ! What a total clunch! Why in the *devil* did you not tell me?"

"Because," snarled Devenish, "I knew what a fine laugh you would have at my expense, and how you would delight in telling me I ate too much rich food for dinner, or some such fustian. As you did to Monty on that first night!"

"Gudgeon! Had you only swallowed that ridiculous pride and told me all this sooner! I had my suspicions, but—"

"You had your suspicions, did you? And kept them to *yourself*!" His eyes fairly speaking, Devenish raged on, "While I endured hell's own misery. One word from you—one hint that it was all contrived would have spared me! But—no! Because you have no sensibilities yourself, you just sat back and watched. Gloating! Dammitall! I should . . ."

He had paced nearer, thrusting his flushed face under his cousin's nose, and stepping back instinctively, Craig teetered on the brink, and made a grab for the edge of the parapet. "*Will* you control that insufferable temper of yours? We must take no chances up here!"

Devenish paled at the reminder and all but leapt back. "Then let us go inside at once so I can punch your smug head!"

Tyndale moved away from the sheer drop behind him and caught his cousin's arm. "Don't be such a fool! Can you seriously judge me so base as to serve you so vile a turn? I thought *someone* had been racking up in the castle, but I fancied them vagrants merely, or homeless soldiery. Nothing more. This sheds a new light on it."

"Vagrants, indeed! And where did you think these poor starving soldiers hid themselves so that we never saw them—or their belongings? You have inspected every inch of your ancestral home!"

"Why, in the secret rooms and passages, of course. I thought you had guessed that when you quizzed me about pacing off and measuring all the rooms."

"Secret . . . rooms . . . ?" breathed Devenish, his eyes kindling. "By thunder, but you're right! I recall Uncle Alastair once telling me that the old place is fairly riddled with them. But—what did your sketches and measurements prove?"

"That there is a wide discrepancy between interior and exterior dimensions. When we were locked out in the rain and prowling about trying to find a way in, I paced off the exterior measurements, and—"

The elation that had begun to dawn in Devenish's face vanished. "Then—you knew *very* early in the game! When *exactly*, Major Tyndale, sir?"

Tyndale stifled exasperation. "The first time we went inside I noticed that although there was dust everywhere, one end of the dining table was free of it. I surmised that the table had been in use. No, Dev! Hear me out! I really thought they were demobilized soldiers, and I suspect you have little use for the military. Some of the poor devils have had such a bitter time since the war ended. It seems every man's hand is against them, so I thought—"

"You thought I would have them hanged for trespassing!" snarled Devenish.

Tyndale reddened and his eyes fell. "I—don't know . . . but they seemed to be causing no trouble. I thought they would either leave, or show themselves and we—I—could offer them work. I even said as much once, when I was alone in the book room." He shrugged, embarrassed. "Perhaps no one was listening."

"Likely not! They were all too busy 'haunting' me!"

"Well, dammit, I did not know of any of it! I knew you were a trifle shaken that first night, but it seemed perfectly understandable—in the circumstances. When you said no more of it, I thought you had adjusted, and—"

"Adjusted! My God! To what? Bedlam?"

"No, really, Dev. You seemed calm most of the time, so I—"

"Thunderation, man! I came near to losing my mind!"

Tyndale hung his head, looking and feeling like a chastened schoolboy. "What an unobservant fool I am." He looked up with his crooked, apologetic grin. "I never even suspected what was going on right under my nose. Poor Dev. A harrowing week you have had!"

Touched, Devenish cleared his throat and grunted, "Gad, there's no call to be so damned patronizing. I'm near as old as you, you know!"

Scanning him, Tyndale thought, "Not really. You are just a boy; a likeable, warm-hearted, but rather too impulsive boy." And aloud he said, "Oh, but I was born a greybeard."

"I'll agree with you on that point." Devenish chuckled and went on, "So tell me, O Ancient Sage, what is it all about, think you?"

Tyndale knit his brows for a moment. "I had thought," he answered carefully, "it was a relatively minor problem. It is not, very obviously. That portrait business took not only scheming, but either the talent to create such an atrocity, or the funds to commission it done. It could, I suppose, prove an excellent means of frightening away curious children or occasional vagrants, but . . ."

"I wonder," Devenish mused. "By daylight, only those who have seen the original painting, or who remember my mother would be really scared by it. Strangers might merely fancy it an excessive ugly painting—of which there are many, God knows. And I rather doubt many people wold wander to so lonely a spot after dark, so as to get the full effect." He frowned. "How the deuce did they manage it, d'you suppose? How could they have switched 'em so fast?"

"A hidden panel, perhaps."

"What—in a rock wall?"

Tyndale argued, "Well, perhaps it isn't rock. Perhaps there is a wooden section, carven and painted to resemble rock, that can be slid aside—lots of priest's holes have steps leading from a chimney, you know. Someone could have opened the panel while you slept, substituted the changed portrait, and then contrived to wake you. The night you said you tripped over something in the dark, obstacles could easily have been moved into unexpected spots just in case you did have the gumption to charge before they had a chance to switch portraits."

Gratified by this small compliment, Devenish nodded. "It fits, all right."

They began to pace slowly towards the door to the stairs, each deep in thought. "It was planned from the start," muttered Tyndale, "with one end in view. I was to be scared off. So terrified that I decided to live anywhere but here."

"If they wanted to scare *you*," Devenish protested indignantly, "why am *I* the one to have been victimized? The picture was in the room intended for *me*!"

"Not necessarily. Perhaps I was meant to choose that room."

"Hmmn. Perhaps . . . No! The voices, coz! They called *'Alain!'* and begged I 'avenge' them." And recalling the anguish he had suffered because of that trickery, he fumed, "Those miserable blasted vermin!"

"True," Tyndale acknowledged. "Unless they planned to thoroughly panic you, so that you would leave. And then—go to work on me. They certainly have succeeded in frightening the local people away."

"And Montelongo. . . . But—why? Regardless of *how* they went about it, why go to so much trouble? All this skulduggery, when there ain't nothing hereabouts save for hills and cows and sheep and such."

"And . . . the sea," murmured Tyndale.

Devenish caught his breath. "Jove!" he breathed, awed. "You have it! The sea! Free Traders! Of course, but—no, surely this is the wrong coast?"

"Sometimes the longest way is the quickest. And the safest. I believe there is at least one large cellar here I have been unable to find. If it has been stocked by smugglers, only think how perfect this is for them. They could sail from France, around Land's End, up through the Irish Sea, slip through the channel, and land here any night there's moon enough, secure in the knowledge that no one would be the wiser."

Devenish eyed him askance. "It may not seem far to someone who's done as much travelling as you, old boy, but it seems a devilish roundaboutation to me!"

"It is a bit of a haul, I grant you. But—only think, they could offload into wagons with perfect safety, for no locals would dare venture near the castle by night, and be well on their way before dawn. Why, they could likely even hire Pickford's in Kilmarnock, or Glasgow perhaps, and have their smuggled goods shipped to London, free as air. 'Twould be worth the long journey, I'd say. And unless I'm fair and far off, there is an entrance to the castle somewhere down among the cliffs. A cave, perhaps!" His eyes bright with triumph, he exclaimed, "That *has* to be the answer! No wonder they're so desperate to drive us away, Dev! They've the ideal hideaway and do not mean to give it up!"

Devenish swung the door open and, lowering his voice, murmured, "If you *are* right, we're likely to find ourselves nose to nose with some very irate gents! At any moment!"

"Yes," Craig acknowledged with his slow smile. "In which case, I should not have been so irked with Monty today. He was convinced we were going to wake some morning with our throats cut. Advised me, just as he was riding out, that he meant to report our uninvited guests to the Constable at Kilmarnock. He means to bring reinforcements this evening!"

"Good old Monty!" said Devenish blithely. "By George! And to think I fancied this would be a dull journey! With a little bit of luck, my bonnie Colonial, we shall land ourselves a jolly good scrap before your reinforcements arrive!"

Even as one part of his mind marvelled at his cousin's transformation from a brooding man of mercurial temper to a cheerful, high-couraged youth, Tyndale still pondered the one detail that plagued him. He had the uneasy feeling that the substitute portrait did not fit into his solution of their puzzle.

The wind was brisk this morning, hurrying the clouds across the pale blue sky, and setting the heather to whipping about beneath the hooves of the horses. Their habits fluttering, the two ladies urged their mounts up the hill beside the pass road, from the top of which eminence Castle Tyndale could be seen, a distant, darkly powerful thrust against the encompassing slate of the sea. The eyes of both riders were fixed upon the fortress, and in green eyes and brown was longing and a measure of hopelessness.

Heaving a deep sigh, the smaller of the pair murmured, "Whatever will I do if he don't never come back?"

Yolande pushed her own dreary reflections aside and, forcing a smile, said reassuringly, "Of course he will come back. And very soon."

By mutual accord they stopped the horses. "I'd like him to see me new have-it," said Josie.

"I know you would, dear." The child looked quite ladylike in her pink velvet, a demure little bonnet tied over her dark curls. Watching her, Yolande pointed out gently, "But the word is 'habit,' Josie."

"It is? I thought a habit was something you did when you shouldn't ought to have."

"Yes. But it is also a riding dress. And you look very pretty in yours. Mr. Devenish will be pleased."

"I hope so." Josie sighed again.

Yolande suggested bracingly, "Only think of the future. We shall all drive back to England together. Will you not like that?"

"Not Mr. Craig. He cannot go. Not if you marriages Mr. Dev." Josie turned to look up at this beautiful vision beside her and ask hopefully, "I don't 'spect as you would sooner marriage with Mr. Craig, would you?"

Yolande's heart gave a terrifying jolt, and she stared at the child speechlessly.

Alarm came into the small, pointed face. "You ain't never going to have a bad turn, is you, Miss Yolande?" cried Josie. "Old Ruby used to have 'em, and stagger about carrying on something dreful 'bout her poor old eyes and limbs. But Benjo said it was the gin, and I ain't never seed you swig blue ruin. Your face is awful red, though, so p'raps—"

With a shaken laugh, Yolande denied an addiction to blue ruin. "What—whatever," she asked, "would cause you to think I might wish to marry Mr. Tyndale?"

A third sigh was torn from the child. "I didn't really think it. I knowed there wasn't much hope. What lady would want Mr. Craig when Mr. Dev is there? Only I knows how bad Mr. Craig wants *you*, and—"

Her breathing becoming highly erratic, Yolande intervened, "Good—gracious, what an imagination! I—I thank you, dear Josie, but—there are lots of ladies much prettier than I for—for Mr. Craig to—er, choose."

"Are there? I never see one." A gleam coming into her dark

eyes, Josie asked thoughtfully, "Is there one up here? Like—in Drumdownie, p'raps? I like Mr. Craig. He's kind, and he has scrumptious eyes." She thought for a moment, then said sadly, "It'd be *so* much easier if you would just marriage Mr. Craig, ma'am." And with a rather pathetic desperation, she enquired, "Are you *quite* sure as you wants Mr. Dev?"

"Are you *quite* sure as you wants Mr. Dev . . . ?" For an aching moment, Yolande saw a strong, lean, rather pale face, with steadfast grey eyes and a wide, humorous mouth. Her own eyes dimmed. Wracked by anguish, she thought, "Dear God! Is there never to be an end to it?" And afraid her misery might be seen and understood by the discerning small woman beside her, she spurred her horse forward. "Come dear, I'll race you back to the house!"

Josie gazed remorsefully after the graceful retreating figure. She'd really gone and done it now. She'd made Miss Yolande cross, and Miss Yolande was good and gentle, and had promised to help, just in case Mr. Dev didn't take her to live with him. Starting her pony and following the chestnut mare, Josie could not wonder that Miss Yolande had not bothered to answer such a silly question. No lady could resist Mr. Dev, with his beautiful face and happy nature. Just to think of the smile that could so suddenly warm his blue eyes was enough to give her goose bumps, and she was only a little girl. As from a very great distance came the echo of a soft voice, *"Aide-toi, le ciel t'aidera."* Her small chin set. It was possible. If she helped herself, heaven might indeed help her! She touched one heel to her pony's sleek side and began to weave plans. Lost in her own introspection, Yolande did not notice how quiet the little girl had become, and two subdued ladies made their way back to Steep Drummond.

When they arrived they found the grooms all agog because young Mr. MacInnes had come to show off the paces of his fine new hunter. Yolande went at once to join the small crowd gathered in the meadow, but Josie stayed to watch as the mare and the pony were unsaddled, rubbed down, and turned out to graze. She declined the offer of Mr. Laing, the head groom, for a piggyback ride to the meadow, saying that she wanted to play with Molly-My-Lass's foal for a little while, and watched as the genial man hurried off to join his colleagues in the meadow. They would be busied there for a good half hour, she knew. Ample time, surely, for her to get to Castle Tyndale and dear Mr. Dev. How she was to plead her case did not concern

503

her. Time enough for that when she faced her god. She went over to Molly-My-Lass, and the Clydesdale nuzzled her affectionately. Molly wouldn't mind helping, though it was unfortunate, Josie admitted, that she did not herself possess the Rat Paws, and did dear Mr. Dev. Nonetheless, it was the work of a few seconds only, to climb up the first few rungs of the fence and hop onto that broad back. A kick of heels, a tug at the thick mane, and they were off, Molly-My-Lass perfectly willing to get some moderate exercise.

Josie wasn't too sure just how to get to Castle Tyndale (having only been there once), but she could smell the sea, and once they were safely out of sight of the house, turned confidently in what she imagined to be a lane leading westward.

Half an hour later, she was a rather frightened little girl harbouring the uneasy suspicion that she was a wee bit lost. The sun was starting to be blotted out by clouds, and she wished she had brought the new cloak Miss Yolande had given her. She looked about worriedly. Scotland was nice, and the hills was bigger than in England. The trouble was, there wasn't never many folks about, and not many houses nor signposts, neither. How a body was to know which way to go was hard to tell. If the sun would start to go down she would know where was the west, but the sun, uncooperative, was high in the sky. Her heart gave a jump when she heard a cantering horse, and she guided Molly-My-Lass into some tall shrubs by the lane, fearing the grooms from Steep Drummond were after her. She was vastly relieved to see Major Craig's Indian man riding up. She almost called out to him, but then realized he would be just as liable to return her to Steep Drummond as would the General's grooms, and so sat quietly while he went on past. She watched him, admiring the easy grace with which he rode, almost as if he was one with the sleek bay mare. He was headed for the castle, that was sure.

Josie coaxed Molly-My-Lass into a trot and followed, careful to stay out of sight and earshot.

In all his life Montelongo had never seen such a climate as that which bedevilled the occupants of the British Isles. Nor had he imagined that so small an island could manage to be so perplexing. He had been quite sure of his route when he left the castle this morning. Now, not only was he lost, but he would wager a paint pony that the last knock-in-the-cradle who had assured him it was only three miles at the outside from the

504

Kilmarnock road, "give or take a half-mile" was more lost than he! That had been at least five miles back, and he still had not come to the promised large signpost and the turn he was to take. To add to his indignation, the bright weather that had blessed his departure had given way to heavy clouds, so that he could not now judge the position of the sun.

Thus he was pleased to observe two mounted gentlemen a short distance ahead. They were riding at a walk and turned to him amiably as he approached, evincing neither surprise nor curiosity by reason of his unorthodox appearance.

"Hello there," called the taller of the pair, a well set up individual wearing a frieze coat. "You'll be Major Tyndale's man, eh?"

Montelongo nodded.

"Heard of you. I'm in the service of Mr. Walter Donald," vouchsafed the stranger. "Name of Wood. This here gent is Mr. Barnham."

Montelongo acknowledged the introduction and asked, in his tense fashion, if they could direct him to Kilmarnock.

They could. They were, in fact, going that way themselves and would be glad to set him on the right road if he wouldn't mind waiting a minute while they stopped at Mr. Wood's house. This detail having been agreed to, they rode along all three, the two Englishmen chatting slanderously about their employers, and Montelongo listening with no small amusement.

Mr. Wood's cottage was located across a field, some way from the lane and so isolated that there was not another house in sight. Messrs. Barnham and Montelongo waited before the battered picket fence while Mr. Wood went later. He reappeared after a few minutes to say that his wife was off somewhere, and if the gentlemen would care to dismount and step inside, he could offer them a spot of ale to wash the dust away before they resumed their journey.

It was the first time the Iroquois had met with such instant hospitality in a strange land, and he willingly accompanied his new friends into the cottage.

Ten minutes later, the shabby parlour swimming dizzily before his eyes, he lowered his head to the table and with a heavy sigh sank into sleep.

Mr. Wood bent over him, seized his shoulder and shook him, at first gently, then roughly. He lifted his eyes to smile with gratification at Mr. Barnham. "Well, that's done!" he observed. "Now we'll truss him up all neat and tidy. Just in case."

"But I thought," demurred Mr. Barnham, "that we wasn't to leave no signs of force."

"No more we won't. We'll loose him come dawn. But mark them shoulders, me lad. This here savage has probably got muscles what you and me never dreamt of! There ain't no telling how long he'll sleep, for one thing I didn't dare do was to give him too much. I ain't taking no chances he'll wake up whilst you and me is having a nice convivial chat as you might say!" Mr. Barnham applauding this decision, they proceeded to bind their unwitting victim. "Very tidy," said Mr. Barnham. "If he does start to wake up early, what you going to do?"

"Leave his knife close to hand. It'll take him some time to get it and get loose, 'cause he won't be thinking clear—spite of all them muscles. Either way, we'll be least in sight and he can go strolling off, free as air, back to the castle, tripping through the daisies in the dawn. Just like Mr. Shotten wants." He laughed. "By which time," he added, "he'll be what you might call a Johnny-come-lately!"

"You mean a Monty-come-morning!" leered Mr. Barnham.

"Aye. Morning. Spelt *m-o-u-r-n-i-n-g*," said Mr. Wood.

This clever play on words so titillated them that they repaired to the kitchen and found a bottle of much stronger content than ale, with which they decided to celebrate their success.

They went back to the parlour, settled down, and enjoyed the bottle together, while Montelongo slept.

❧ *Chapter 13* ❧

Unwilling to provide the smugglers with any cause for suspicion, the cousins agreed that they would proceed in their usual

manner while awaiting Montelongo's return with the "reinforcements." They spent most of the afternoon, therefore, in
thoroughly inspecting the stables and barn, returning to the
castle in a chilly dusk with a long list of necessary repairs.

The fact that Montelongo had not as yet come back was
worrying Tyndale. Devenish, however, reasoned that the Constable at Kilmarnock might have felt it advisable to refer the
matter to a higher authority, or might at this very moment be
positioning his men about the castle. "Suppose they do come,"
Devenish whispered as they walked across the stableyard.
"What in the deuce are we to show them? We don't know how
to find either Free Traders or contraband! The Constable will
laugh at us!"

"I don't think he will take action yet, but if he does, we will
at least be enabled to make a proper search of the basements.
That's where the hidden rooms are, I'm sure of it. And even
if we are laughed at, someone in authority will have been
warned of what's going on here. Just—in case."

Those last three last words caused Devenish considerable
disquiet as he walked along the hall towards his bedchamber.
It had not occurred to him that the smugglers might really be
willing to commit murder. If they did decide to cut up stiff and
were able to put a period to him and Tyndale, it would be a
proper bumble broth, for everyone would merely think the
feud had been fought over again. He was dismayed and, as he
opened the door, called down a blessing on the head of the absent Montelongo. It was a jolly good thing that—

He checked, his hand still on the doornob, his eyes glued to
the opposite wall. The portrait was macabre once more and,
even knowing that the cruel distortion of his mother's loveliness was a ruse, goose bumps rose on his flesh. He drew a
hissing breath, then sprinted along the corridor to his cousin's
room. "Craig!" he gasped, plunging in without ceremony. "The
portrait!"

Tyndale was in his shirt sleeves, in the act of pouring water
into his washbowl. He looked up, startled, as Devenish flung
the door open, and at once set down the water pitcher and ran
with him to the adjoining room. The sight of the portrait
checked his hurried progress. He paused in the open doorway,
gazing at it. "Lord!" he breathed. "Small wonder it so distressed you!" And he wandered closer, drawn by that monstrous image.

"At least you've seen it!" said Devenish. "This time we were quick enough."

"And there wasn't no need," sneered a crude London voice. " 'Cause it's all done, coves. All over with!"

The cousins spun about as the door slammed shut. Four men leaned against the wall, watching them with various degrees of amusement. The one who had spoken was a large, powerful individual, dressed without elegance in a brown riding coat, breeches, and topboots. He was whistling in a soft, hissing monotone, as ostlers whistle when currying a horse, and his small, hard eyes were fixed on Devenish in leering mockery.

"Shotten . . . !" breathed Devenish. "So—*Sanguinet* is behind this?"

Shotten laughed. "Monsewer's a vindictive man, 'e is."

Glancing at his cousin, Tyndale said, "Your French—er, acquaintance in Dinan? Aha! So this is a vendetta. Whatever did you do to so upset the gentleman?"

"Yer kinsman was so foolish, sir," volunteered Shotten, "so downright stupid as ter kick Claude Sanguinet in the jaw and then throw him in a nasty wet pond! Monsewer, 'e hadn't never bin treated like that afore. And 'e didn't take to it!"

Devenish made a swift appraisal of the others. One was lean and leathery, his narrow face holding an expression of sneering malevolence. The other two were as burly as Shotten, and both held horse pistols. This, he thought, his pulses beginning to race with excitement, would be a close-run thing. . . .

With unruffled calm, Tyndale drawled, "If you expect us to believe that Monsieur Sanguinet has expended all this time and effort on a simpler matter of revenge—"

"You mistake that, sir," said Shotten, with that infuriatingly oily deference. "Fact is, we don't give beans fer what you believe. And just look at me, fergetting' me manners! That there thin little cove as ye see aholding up the wall—that's Fritch. The chap with all the pretty curls"—he gestured to a man who was quite bald—"his monicker is Jethro—he's a very gentle, friendly type o'cove."

The "friendly type" uttered a roar of mirth at this witticism, displaying a few crooked teeth. The younger, sandy-haired man next to him stood away from the wall and interrupted harshly, "You talk too much, Shotten. They can live without knowing of my name!"

"Ar," giggled Fritch. "But not fer long, Walter, me bucko!"

The cousins exchanged swift glances. "A fine set of rum

touches you cry friends with!" protested Tyndale. He turned from Devenish's irrepressible grin to Shotten's beady-eyed antagonism. "When shall we meet your master?"

"You know what, Major War Hero?" said Shotten, strolling forward. "I don't like yer face, nor yer way o' talkin', nor nothing else about yer. Ain't no man is *my* master! No man! Clear?"

"The words." Tyndale shrugged. "But they are of doubtful veracity."

Shotten's little eyes narrowed, and the pistol in his hand swung upwards a trifle. "And wot might that jawbreaker mean?"

The sandy-haired man laughed. "He means as you be lying, Shotten. Which you is. Sanguinet's *your* master just as much as what he's *ours*."

"Keep yer dirty fat mouth in yer pocket!" Shotten snarled murderously.

"Never mind about Walter," Fritch advised in his nasal, whining voice. "He's a bit upset like."

"*You'll* be upset if we make a hog wallow of this," snapped Walter, his pale eyes glinting. "It could mean the nubbing cheat for the lot on us!"

"You would do well to heed him," Devenish corroborated. "Else you will most certainly end up swinging on Tyburn."

"Well, don't worry about it, my dear old friend," said Shotten with a broad grin. " 'Cause you won't be invited ter watch us kick!"

Devenish clicked his tongue. "Pity. I would so enjoy it."

"I think it all a Canterbury tale from start to finish," Tyndale interposed hurriedly, misliking the way Shotten advanced on his indomitable cousin. "You were using my castle long before we chanced up here, and for something more profitable than pure vengeance, I'll wager."

Shotten halted abruptly. Fritch looked shaken. Jethro and Walter exchanged scared glances, and the bald man wiped off the top of his head with a grimy sleeve. "If the soldier come at that much," he muttered uneasily, "maybe he told that old devil up at Steep Drummond."

"And maybe that 'old devil' is bringing up his men this very minute," taunted Devenish. "My military cousin is full of tricks, I warn you. You had best scamper whilst yet you may."

"Shut him up, Shotten!" whined Fritch, his cunning eyes darting about. "As well snuff him now as later."

"Wot?" exclaimed Shotten, much shocked. "Rush me dear old friend off quick and easy? Oh, no, my cove. I want Mr. Devenish ter be give plenty o'time ter think of it . . . afore he follers his poor dad orf the roof."

Something very cold clamped around Devenish's heart.

Tyndale, his fists clenching, said, "I see. You mean to keep the legend alive by a repeat performance. So it was Sanguinet who spread the news of the original tragedy. Had he planned this from the start?"

" 'Course not," jeered Shotten. "We didn't know nothing about *you,* Major, sir. Monsieur didn't even know as the owner o' this ruin was related ter our old friend Mr. Devenish. But— well, strike a light, guv, you can't 'ardly blame him. I mean— arter all, it was fair made to order, eh?" He sighed and shook his head dolefully. "Wot a shame as you went and bubbled it. We was so hoping ter surprise yer."

"I doubt you will surprise anyone," Tyndale said contemptuously. "If I am believed to have pushed my cousin off the battlements, how shall you explain my own demise?"

"Simple, sir. Mr. Devenish will be found with a pistol still clutched in his cold meat hand. He shot you, Canada, just afore he went over!" He laughed his triumph and added, "Tidy, ain't it?"

Devenish swore under his breath and took a step forward. The pistols were raised at once, and Tyndale put a restraining hand on his arm. "You must all be deeply devoted to Monsieur Sanguinet," he said dryly, "to be willing to commit two murders for him."

Walter scowled. Fritch said with exaggerated innocence, "But *we* ain't goin' ter murder no one, Major, sir. You two loving cousins been a'fighting and a'quarrelling halfway 'cross England. And only fancy—just s'arternoon you was almost coming ter blows, right in front o' Mr. Respectability Hennessey. Most shocked, he was. *Most* shocked!" He folded his hands piously, his eyes mocking, while his friends hooted their mirth.

Tyndale threw his cousin a wry look. "We properly set the scene for them."

"You are, like the flash coves say, all consideration," Fritch agreed.

Leering, Shotten added with relish, "And ternight when it's nice and dark so no gawking yokels can't see what's goin' on, we'll 'ave the final act. And arter that, me fine coves, there ain't none o' these country blubberheads what'll set foot within a mile o' yer cozy castle Not a one, gents. Not a blessed one."

Devenish looked grimly from one face to the next. They were savagely inflexible. Even Walter, who seemed to have sufficient sensitivity to know nervousness, if not conscience, looked merciless.

Tyndale glanced to the windows. Already it was dusk. Within an hour, it would be full dark. "Monty," he thought, "please do bring your reinforcements. And soon!"

At about the same time that Mr. Hennessey was delivering the supplies to Castle Tyndale, Josie, concealed by an overgrown hedge, was waiting for Montelongo and his friends to come out of the cottage. She had been quite dismayed by their meeting, but had followed them, believing it to have been a chance encounter, and that the Indian would soon resume his journey back to the castle. After a while, when he still did not come out, she dismounted, tied Molly-My-Lass's halter to a branch and began to wander up and down. She really should not stay away from Steep Drummond much longer. Molly's foal would be needing to be fed, and the family had probably noticed by now that both the mare and herself were missing. Dismay seized her as the thought came that because she was a gypsy they might fancy she'd stolen the valuable animal. She glanced apprehensively at the cottage. It must be at lest an hour since the men went inside. Goodness knows how long it would take to get to the castle, and then Mr. Dev would probably make her go back to Steep Drummond and everyone would be in a proper pucker. She'd likely be walloped and sent to bed without supper. Well, she would simply have to go and ask Mr. Monty the way. Sighing and reluctant, she crossed the weedy lawn and knocked on the front door.

A roar of laughter was the only response, but it was sufficient to send her scuttling around the corner of the house, for she had seen men when they were shot in the neck, and she knew from bitter experience that they were best given a wide berth. If they went on drinking much longer, she could not hope for any help from Mr. Monty. She waited undecidedly, and, full of nervous fears, wandered around to the back of the house. The laughter was louder here, and the voices more clear, but the conversation, such as it was, puzzled her.

"Lor'!" howled a man's voice. "How I'd love to've seen

them throw the Frog in the pool! Wonder he didn't drown of hisself!"

"Frogs don't—don't drown, friend," advised another voice. "They just gives a sorta hop . . . and out they come!"

This sent them into guffaws again, though why a frog being tossed into a pool should be amusing was more than the child could fathom.

"I'll tell you one thing," said the first man. "I'm g-glad as bedamned *I* didn't do it! The Frenchy will hold that grudge as long as Devenish lives!"

"Then he ain't got long to hold it, has he, my cove?"

Another roar of laughter, but Josie didn't think it funny at all. Whatever did they mean? Mr. Dev was a young man. He wasn't going to die for years and years! Especially now there wasn't any wars what killed all the nice soldiers. She worried at it while the rough talk went on and on, growing ever more raucous, until it dawned on her that through it all, not once had she heard Mr. Monty say anything. She was quite frightened by this time, her fears having nothing to do with whether or not she had been missed at Steep Drummond. A window of the room stood open, the curtains flirting in the rising wind. She thought, "I must not be a coward. I must have a look, for Mr. Dev's sake."

The very thought of serving her god strengthened her. She crept nearer, but the window was too high. Her glance around discovered some bricks piled against one wall and, the fear of detection spurring her on, she trotted back and forth carrying one heavy brick at a time, until three were piled below the casement. They were a bit wobbly, but it was the best she could do. She stepped up, crouching, then slowly straightened.

An involuntary gasp of horror escaped her. Mr. Monty was slumped in a chair. He looked dead, but he was tied hand and foot and one does not tie a dead man, so she supposed he must have been struck on the head. At a table to one side, the two men she had thought to be his friends sat with a half-full wine bottle between them, their flushed faces and another empty bottle on the floor testifying to their state. Even as she gazed, petrified, the taller of the pair glanced to the window, lurched to his feet, and with an oath stumbled towards her. Sick with terror, she tried to run, but her legs had turned to water and would not stir. The slurred voice, just above her, snarled a profanity. She sank against the wall, eyes half closed, waiting in a helpless panic to be seized and dragged into that horrid room. Dimly, she saw a large hand thrusting at her. She felt sick, and the bright afternoon grew dim. A coarse voice snarled, "Blasted damned wind!" The window was slammed shut, the lower edge of the frame brushing her curls.

He had not seen her! By some miracle she was still free! She clapped her hands over her mouth to muffle her terrified sobs, and collapsed to the ground, a small, crumpled heap, weeping softly, and whispering fervent players of gratitude for her narrow escape.

It was several moments before she was sufficiently recovered to think coherently, but gradually her numbed mind began to function again. What it was all about, she did not know, but those two men were bad. They had tied up poor Mr. Monty, and it looked as if they had hurt him, besides. He might be, as Mrs. Arabella was fond of remarking, a "heathen savage," but he had never done anything savage that she'd seen. His voice on the few occasions he'd spoken to her had been gruff, but kind, and Major Craig thought the world of him. He had very nice eyes, that Major Craig . . . not that he was a patch on Mr. Dev for looks, but eyes were important. And that was another thing: those men had said something about Mr. Dev dying. Soon, they'd said. Perhaps that was why the Indian was tied up. So he couldn't go and help Mr. Dev. Her blood ran cold with the fear that a plot existed to murder the only person who had ever really befriended her. If that was so, she must get away quick, and warn him!

The window was tight closed, the curtains drawn, but if there was anyone else in the cottage she would be in full view if she ran across the lawn to the mare. Shivering with fear, she tried to be as brave as Mr. Dev would want her to be. Perhaps, even if they saw her, she could climb onto Molly-My-Lass and be away in time. How fast the Clydesdale could run, she had no idea, but an animal so big simply had to be powerful and would likely be a fine goer.

And so, a very young lady gathered up her sadly tested courage and made a wild dart across the open space of the lawn. She reached the hedge and trees that shielded the cottage from the meadow in a flash, and with no enraged shouts following. With a hand over her madly pounding heart, she paused to catch her breath, only to utter a moan of despair. Molly-My-Lass was gone!

* * *

"I cannot understand it!" Yolande exclaimed distractedly. She turned to Mrs. Drummond, who was brushing a disgusted Socrates. It crossed her mind that the General might not care to see the dog standing upon the piano bench while being groomed, but it was a thought that did not linger, her main concentration being upon the missing child.

"*I* understand it *perfectly* well," said Mrs. Drummond, with the condescension of superior wisdom. "The child went to see her friend, is all. She is lonely here, Yolande, and it is but natural for her to want to be with her own kind, and to grieve when forcibly removed from her natural environment. Far be it from me to criticize, but it was wrong of Devenish to abduct the child so thoughtlessly. His besetting sin, alas! I could have told him no good would come of it, but he would not have attended me—or anyone else, for that matter!"

Sorting the wheat from the chaff, Yolande decided that her aunt was very likely in the right of it, at least in so far as Josie's destination was concerned. It was foolish to indulge this frightening sense of something being very wrong. After all, what could happen to a little girl at Steep Drummond? "I'll go down there," she murmured.

Astonished, Mrs. Drummond glanced up. "To the MacFarlane cottage?" she asked, in the tone she might have employed if told the minister had run naked through the village. "Good gracious, why? There is no call for you to so demean yourself. Besides, I heard the MacFarlane girl has contracted measles. Send one of the footmen."

"Send a footman where?" enquired General Drummond, wandering at that moment into the music room.

"Down to the gardener's house," supplied Arabella, casting a wide smile at her father-in-law. "If you can credit it, dear sir, *Yolande* was about to go!"

"Josie has wandered off, Grandpapa," Yolande explained. "I thought I would go and see if she is there. In fact, since Aunt Arabella tells me little Maisie is ill, I've no doubt that is where I shall find her."

"Very likely," he said, rather pleased to discover his granddaughter was speaking to him in a friendly way and that she had not held a grudge because he'd forbidden those two rapscallion cousins to call on her. "I'll go with you."

"Oh, in that case," purred Arabella, "nothing could be more proper."

The General escorted his granddaughter to the door, and

turned back to fix his son's widow with a minatory eye. "How glad I am that we hae your approval, ma'am," he said cuttingly. "Tis an emotion I canna returrn however; not while yon beastie distributes his fleas over my pianoforte! Be sae good as tae remove the wee currr tae the barrn whar he belongs!"

He ignored Mrs. Drummond's flustered protestations that Socrates would not be caught dead with a nasty flea on him and, ushering Yolande from the room, growled his thanks for providing an excuse to escape that "absurd female! You must, however," he admonished as they started into the gardens, "impress upon little Miss Storm that she should not wander off like this. If the child's to become an abigail, m'dear, she must learn proper behaviour."

But when they reached the gardener's cottage, it was to discover that Josie had not visited that establishment since the day Maisie had been caught at the summer house "tea party."

Her eyes dark shadows against her tired, pale face, Mrs. MacFarlane said, "The wee lassie is nae lost, I hope?"

Losing some of her own colour, Yolande turned a frightened glance to her grandfather. He patted her hand and said bracingly, "Wandered off, merely. I fancy she's lonely here, poor mite."

"I'm sorry for that," Mrs. MacFarlane said. "Wherever can she hae got to? I—" And, as if suddenly becoming aware that she kept her illustrious guests standing on the step, she flushed darkly and stepped back, gesturing for them to enter. "Ye're more than—than welcome tae come inside," she stammered. "Unless ye've nae had the measles."

The General nodded. "We both have, I thank you." He stepped over the threshold immediately dwarfing the small, immaculate parlour, and, when Yolande had seated herself on the ornate red sofa, followed suit, and enquired as to Maisie's condition.

Mrs. MacFarlane, who had perched on the very edge of a straight-backed cane chair, sighed. "Och, but she's awful bad, puir bairn." Her eyes distressed, she added brokenly, "I never saw her in such a waeful state."

"I am so sorry, ma'am," Yolande sympathized with her customary warm-heartedness. "She's a truly delightful little girl. Can we help? You've had the doctor out, I—"

Mrs. MacFarlane sprang up again and backed away, an expression almost of frenzy on her face. "I dinna wish . . . your aid. . . ." she gasped out. "We none of us—want nothing frae ye!"

From the corner of her eye, Yolande saw the General's whiskers bristle alarmingly. Not glancing at him, she placed a gently restraining hand on his arm. "I quite understand, ma'am," she said. "You likely wish us at Jericho, so we will take ourselves off and ask only that, if you should see Miss Storm, you will send word up to the house."

"Aye." Mrs. MacFarlane's lip trembled. "I will, that. I—I'm sorry, Miss Yolande. It's not—I dinna mean—I'm a mite fashed, y'ken."

"Of course you are. Any mother would be." Yolande stood, her grandfather at once, almost protectively, standing beside her. "Measles is a wretched illness, and we—"

"Aye! If it *be* measles!" And with a sudden resumption of her former hostility, this strange little woman said fiercely, "I pray to the good Lord it is nae something worse. Heaven only knows what may be brought in tae the district when we're infested with foreigners and heathens! Ye'll mind that MacFarlane can read, sir? He told me he'd read somewhere that red men are awful subject tae—" Her eyes all but starting from her head, she gripped and wrung her hands and whispered, awfully, "tae—the smallpox!"

"Good God!" the General exploded. "What utter balderdash!"

"Dear ma'am!" cried Yolande, "I beg you will not so distress yourself! If Major Tyndale thought his man to be ill, he would have called in a doctor at once, I do assure you! And certainly you would have been warned if—"

"Oh, aye!" the woman interposed shrilly. "Warned we *should* hae been! Mark my words, miss, that savage and his foreign master will bring death and destruction doon upon us all! If little Miss Storm is missing, *he's* likely responsible! And if my bairn should dee—" She passed a distracted hand across her brow, darted to the door and, swinging it open, regarded her astonished callers more wildly than ever.

Yolande thought, "She is mad, or near it, poor creature!" and as she passed the woman, murmured a compassionate, "God bless you, poor soul!"

Her only answer was the door, slamming behind them.

" 'Pon my soul!" gasped the General, unnerved. "You've more charity than I, m'dear! Perkins told me distinctly this morning he had examined the bairn and she's only a verra mild case of measles! The woman must be fair daft!"

"Listen," said Yolande, pausing as they started down the path.

From behind that closed door came the sound of weeping so intense and so laced with despair that she hesitated, directing an anxious gaze up at her grandfather.

He drew her hand firmly through his arm. "Let her be!" he commanded. "No telling what she might do next! I'll have to speak with MacFarlane, poor devil. His wife is plainly ready for Bedlam! A sad thing for so young a woman."

"Young?" Yolande said uncertainly. "Why, I'd thought . . . that is, she looks to be forty at least, no?"

"She looks it, poor lass. But, no. She's a decade younger, to say the least of it."

"Good heavens! I can scarcely believe—Grandpapa, has she been ill?"

"Not that I'm aware. Fey, perhaps. She was a strange little girl, I mind, full of odd fancies. But she was pretty enough. I recall her at the castle when old Tyndale was alive. A bonnie wee lass she was, but—"

"At the *castle*?" Yolande intervened, breathlessly. "She *lived* there, sir?"

"Aye. With her parents. Her mama was abigail to poor Esme Devenish, and her father a groom or a gardener, or some such." He caught Yolande's arm as she turned back. "Hey! Hey, my lass. You'll nae disturb the woman the noo?"

"But I must! I *must*! She might know something that could be of help to Cr— I mean, to Devenish!"

Watching her, frowning a little, the old gentleman growled, "She doesnae. She was a wee lassie—maybe six or seven at most—when it happened."

"Old enough to have some recollection, then," she persisted stubbornly. "I can remember things that happened when I was six—can not you?"

"I've my work cut oot to recall what happened yesterday," he said with a grin and, becoming very English again, added, "You'll do well to let the lady alone now, Yolande. She has her hands full and her poor mind is obviously hovering on the brink. Besides, I'll own I'm becoming a touch concerned for our own missing young lady."

"Oh, my goodness! How could I have forgotten Josie!"

"Hmmmn," said the General. "I wonder, indeed! Come, m'dear. We'll send the grooms out seeking her, can we find any. The place was empty as a drum when I looked in a wee bit ago. The rascals were up to no good, I'll be bound. They'd best be about their business now, or there'll be much explaining to be done!"

When they reached the stables, however, it was to find them far from deserted, grooms and stablehands milling about, and an air of exultation very apparent.

"Here comes the guv'nor!" the head groom proclaimed, as the General and Yolande crossed the yard. "All's bowman, sir! We found her."

"Oh, thank heaven!" gasped Yolande, not until that moment realizing just how worried she had been.

"That saucy rascal!" the General exclaimed. "Good work! Who found her?"

"It was Graham, sir. He was fair beside himself! Thought he should've kept a closer eye on her."

The General nodded. "Commendable. Where was she?"

"Halfway to Tarbolton, by what I gather."

"Tarbolton! The devil you say! What did she want up there?"

The groom shrugged. "Who knows what goes on in their minds, sir? Such as they have!"

"Oh, come now, Laing!" Yolande protested. "Females are not completely blockheaded, you know!"

"I'll not deny that, miss," he allowed with a chuckle. "Though she was blockheaded enough to be frisking about in the stream that runs alongside Mr. Willoughby's east field."

"Good heavens! Whatever possessed her? The wind is quite chill today, and this is no weather for a swim. Oh, I do hope she has not taken a chill."

"Tush, child," the General said reassuringly. "Do I know anything of the matter, she's being thoroughly pampered and cossetted. And after all, we must not forget her background. I doubt she was even slightly remorseful, eh Laing?"

The groom laughed. "Not the slightest, sir."

"A sound night's sleep, snug under her blankets, and she'll be good as new. She should be spanked, but I'll own she's lots of spirit. Strong as a horse, too, don't you agree, Laing?"

Yolande, who had always thought Laing to be a sensible man, began to wonder if she had rated him too high, for at this he gave another shout of laughter, so hearty that the General stared at him in surprise

"That's a good one, sir! And glad I am that you're not angered. It's a bit of luck it was Graham who came up with her.

Eyes like a hawk has Graham, else he'd never have noticed her nose sticking through the branches."

The General's jaw dropped in a most undignified fashion. "Her . . . nose?" he echoed faintly.

"Sticking . . . through the branches . . . ?" gasped Yolande.

"Aye, miss. Chewing them leaves like she'd not ate for a week, Graham said, or—"

Having recovered itself, General Drummond's jaw began to chomp alarmingly. "Are ye gone puir daft, mon?" he exploded. "What a'God's name are ye babbling?"

Yolande asked urgently, "Of whom are you speaking, Laing?"

Paling, the groom faltered, "Why—why, Molly-My-Lass, of course, miss. Wasn't that—"

"Molly . . . My . . . Lass!" The General's lung power made Yolande jump. "Why, you bacon-brained gapeseed! You let my prize mare wander off and stand about in a cold stream all day? Dammitall! That's what I get for allowing a Londoner at my cattle! Of all the—" He glanced, fuming, at Yolande, and closed his lips, his whiskers continuing to vibrate like reeds in a high wind.

Her hopes dashed. Yolande seized her chance and explained, "We were speaking of Miss Josie. She seems to have wandered off, also. Is Molly all right?"

"Quite all right, miss." And with a cautious look at the fiery old gentleman, Laing ventured, "As the General said, we've pampered her and she's warm and—"

"I was not speaking of a *horse*, blast your impudence!" howled Drummond. "If you but had the brains you were born with—"

"Sir!" Yolande cried, tugging at his sleeve urgently. "Sir! We must do as you suggested and send the grooms out to search! It is starting to rain, and if Josie is trying to reach Devenish at the castle, the poor child will still be walking after dark."

"That curst boy!" the General raged, quite willing to turn his anger from Laing, who really was an excellent head groom. "He should never have brought the lassie here in the first place. A fine bog we'll be in, does she come to grief! Well, talking pays no toll. Turn oot the men, Laing, and set 'em tae the west road. But—do *you* stay with the mare!"

Laing knuckled his brow respectfully. "I'll set the men out, right enough, sir. But I don't think Miss Josie took the west road. Two of the stablehands rode that way while we were looking for Molly. They went clear to the Pass, and would certainly have seen the little girl."

"Unless she did not want to be seen," argued Yolande. "If she was running away again. She adores Dev, you know, Grandpapa."

"Lord knows why," he grunted. "You're right, though. Saddle up Crusher for me, Laing. Yolande, I'll change my clothes and be off. Never worry, lass. We'll find her."

"I'm going with you. Please, Grandpapa! I feel responsible. I could not bear to just sit here and wait."

He frowned, but in the end, of course, was won over, and they hurried to the house together. Ten minutes later, having changed into her habit in record time, Yolande hurried downstairs, train over one arm, a dashing hat set upon her curls, and riding whip and gloves in her hand.

Her aunts walked into the Great Hall as she descended, and Mrs. Fraser said with one of her rare smiles, "What a bonnie green that is! You look very fetching, Yolande. May one ask whither ye're bound at this hour?"

"I wish I knew, ma'am. Grandpapa has asked Laing to send all the men out to look for Josie. She's wandered off somewhere, the tiresome child."

Snatching up Socrates and thus foiling his attempt to nip her sister-in-law's ankle, Mrs. Drummond murmured that he was a very naughty doggie today, then expostulated, "You never mean to ride *with* them? Yolande, your wits are gone begging! You must let the gentlemen handle such things!"

"I would, did I not feel so wretchedly responsible. I might have known she would try to find Devenish."

"Aye." Mrs. Fraser nodded. "The poor wee mite idolizes the lad." She looked at her niece enigmatically. "Children and dogs. He canna be all bad."

"Bad!" flared Yolande, her cheeks flushing. "Dev is a very fine young man! He is not at all bad!"

"Well, you love him, of course. Your pardon, dear, I keep forgetting. I had in fact meant to ask you for the date you've selected."

The voice was mild, but Yolande's eyes fell before her aunt's steady gaze and, concentrating on adjusting her gloves, she answered, "We have not quite decided on the exact date, but mean to set it and make the formal announcement as soon as Dev returns." She looked up and said gratefully, "Oh, there you are, Grandpapa. Have the men started yet?"

"They wait for us to join them. Never fret so, girl! We'll likely find her long before she reaches the castle." His whiskers twitched. "I hope we do, for I've nae wish tae encounter that Canadian mushroom!"

Aware that her Aunt Caroline's covertly amused gaze was upon her, Yolande did not utter the indignant retort that trembled on her tongue, saying instead that she did not see how Josie could possibly have reached the castle by this time, even had she left at ten o'clock.

Mrs. Drummond caressed Socrates fondly, and murmured, "Well, she did not. It was well after noon, as I recall."

With his hand on the doorknob, the General stiffened, glared at the panelled door, assumed a smile that might well have caused the paint to blister, and turned to his daughter-in-law. "You *saw* the child leave, Arabella?"

"I suppose that is what she was doing. At the time, I merely thought she was going for a little ride."

"How grand in ye tae inform us of it the noo," said Mrs. Fraser ironically.

"Ride—ye said?" Sir Andrew snapped. "Upon what, ma'am?"

"That great big animal. Jolly Nelly—or whatever it is called."

"Molly-My-Lass?" said Yolande. "Oh, Aunt! If only you had told us!"

"But, I *am* telling you, my love! And I cannot think why you should go to the castle, for she never meant to go there, unless perhaps she experienced some difficulty in guiding that monster, which I own she did not seem to, as the horse moved off in quite a docile fashion."

His brows beetling, the General snarled, "Which *way* did the wee girl go?"

"I am striving to tell you that, sir. It was *not* in the direction of Castle Tyndale, for to reach there one would have to take the estate road to the west, I do believe, and—Sir Andrew! Are you feeling quite the thing? Your face is alarmingly red, and—"

"Fer losh sakes, woman!" cried Mrs. Fraser. "Put it in tae simple English if ye please! If Josie Storm dinna take the western road, which way *did* she go?"

"She took the north road, my dear Caroline. As if she meant

to go north, do you see? Though *why*, or whom she meant to visit, is more than I could say!"

"Och-unnnh!" snorted Drummond. "At last the gem is extrrrracted! Come lassie, we must come up with the wee girl before dusk!"

With Yolande hurrying beside him, he stalked to the hall and the stableyard, from whence he could soon be heard roaring orders to Mr. Laing.

"Good gracious," murmured Mrs. Drummond, nervously. "How you ever stand it here, Caroline, is quite beyond me! My father-in-law's temperament would drive me distracted!"

" 'Tis a mutual emotion," Mrs. Fraser informed her dourly.

Arabella smiled. It was nice, thought she, that for once they were in accord.

❧ *Chapter 14* ❧

The small store room in the second basement was musty, icy cold, and pitch-black. From the moment they had been thrust down the short flight of steps and the great door slammed and barred upon them, the cousins had explored in frantic search of a way out, or something with which to defend themselves when the door was opened. Neither effort met with success. Now, shivering and defeated, they sat against the wooden door, shoulder to shoulder, in an attempt to keep warm.

"They could at least," Devenish grumbled, "have left us a lantern."

"Probably thought we'd burn the door down," said Tyndale, and the faint note of strain in his cousin's voice having been noted, asked, "That leg bothering you?"

"Just a trifle."

"If you had managed to refrain from advising that nasty little weasel he was a nasty little weasel, he might not have pushed you down the steps."

"But he might. And I am not in the habit of grovelling to such as he."

"Very true, Master High and Mighty. Are you instead in the habit of escaping predicaments such as this? I gather you've had more experience in these matters than I have."

"You refer to my little jaunt with Tristram Leith?" Devenish grinned into the darkness. "What a jolly good adventure that was! I'll say one thing for that rascally Frenchman, it was all conducted on a far more gentlemanly plane than this! We'd interfered with his plans, so he meant to kill us. But there was none of this shutting people up in haunted dungeons and then shoving 'em off the top of a . . . a damned great tower!"

There was a rather heavy silence, the imminence of that horror daunting them both, if only for a moment.

Tyndale said coolly, "I wonder if it's dark yet."

"I suppose it must be. We've been in here at least an hour, wouldn't you say?"

"At least. In which case they're liable to come for us at any minute. Dev, we must *think* of something!"

"Simple. The instant they open the door, we'll toddle out and lay about right and left. Likely they'll not expect it, and we'll grass the lot!"

His optimism proved ill-founded, however. Another long hour crawled by before the door swung open, revealing the pallid features and sandy hair of the man Walter, standing well back, with a large musket aimed unerringly at Tyndale, so that Devenish's well-planned charge was brought up short.

"That's a good lad," sneered Walter.

"You do not dare shoot," said Devenish, his eyes flashing to the grim faces of the three who watched.

"Oh, we wouldn't shoot *you*, sir," Fritch admitted, a sly leer illuminating his narrow features. He nodded to Tyndale. "But if you try anything, *he* gets snuffed. You're going to shoot him anyway, so it could just as well be now."

This information, intended to terrify the helpless victims, was ill-judged. With a shout of triumph, Devenish sprang directly in front of the musket. "Go on, Craig!" he howled.

Tyndale needed no urging. He experienced a brief sense of awe that his cousin should have the pluck to throw himself against that yawning muzzle, then he sailed into action. Simultaneously, Devenish sent a right hurtling at Walter's jaw. His was a slender fist, even when clenched, but his slim grace had deceived men before this. When in Town, he had seen a good deal of the interior of Gentleman Jackson's Boxing Saloon and, while he was not muscular, he was tough and wiry and had proven an apt pupil. Besides that, he was both angered and in the grip of the exhilaration that always seized him when action or danger beckoned. Thus, Mr. Fritch was amazed to see his cohort reel backward to bring up with a crash against the far wall of the corridor. His surprise was brief. Craig had height, reach, and solid power to complement his cousin's steel. An uppercut to the point of Mr. Fritch's very pointed chin sent him first to the tips of his toes, and then diving to join the crumpled Walter. Recovering from their momentary stupefaction, Messrs. Jethro and Shotten now plunged into the fray, and the narrow hall, lighted only by the flickering flames of torches set in iron brackets, was suddenly very busy indeed. Craig was jolted to his knees when Shotten rammed a large fist under his ribs. spinning triumphantly from his encounter with Walter, Devenish was too late to block the left that Jethro smashed at him. Dazed and half blind, he struck out instinctively and, howling, his nose streaming crimson, Jethro staggered, colliding with Shotten, who had also turned his attention to Devenish. Reprieved for an instant, Devenish fought away dizziness and scooped up the fallen musket. The quarters were too close to fire it without hitting Tyndale, so he swung it instead, and Jethro went down. Tyndale, who had struggled to his feet, tapped Shotten on the shoulder and, as the bully whirled to attack, drove home a jab that dropped him like a sack of oats.

"Hah!" panted Devenish, bruised but exuberant.

"Come on!" cried the more practical Tyndale.

They ran for a door at the far end of that long, descending corridor. The door burst open. A bearded man appeared; a voice shouted, *"Ils se sont échappés! Alors! Alors!"*

"Whoops!" Swinging sharply about, Devenish panted, "Retreat, coz! No—*ahead* of me! Hurry! They don't want a bullet in *me!*"

Thus protected, they safely reached the stairs leading to the kitchen quarters. Many feet pounded behind them. Never had Tyndale mounted stairs with such desperate haste. But there must, he knew, be a reargurd action, and as they reached the landing and sprinted for the Great Hall, he gasped, "Dev. You run like hell when you—get outside. I'll . . . hold the doors!"

"Noble," Devenish acknowledged breathlessly. "But pointless. If either one of us . . . stays . . . he will be killed and— and the survivor accused of his murder! It's—all or nothing, coz!"

It appeared perilously likely to be nothing, for as they rounded the corner and headed across the Great Hall, voices could be heard on the drivepath, and one, ominously close, howled, "Something's wrong inside. Hurry!"

Tyndale swore.

"The back!" gasped Devenish, and once more they wheeled about.

They were too late. Already, their pursuers were between them and the rear corridor. A pistol in Shotten's eager hand was pointing at Tyndale. The explosion was shattering, but he missed his shot and the ball thudded into the wall.

"Upstairs!" Tyndale shouted, leading the way in a mad dash for the main stairs.

Fritch howled, "We've got 'em! There's no way out, and they're goin' where we want 'em, lads!"

"Blat him! He's . . . right!" Tyndale panted as they toiled upward.

"We'll set fire . . . to . . . the blasted pile!" Devenish clutched his leg painfully. "That'll attract half the . . . countryside."

They reached the first floor balcony ahead of their pursuers. It was, thought Devenish, too close, besides which, his blasted leg was becoming too much of a nuisance for him to climb any further. Belatedly, he realized he still clutched the musket. "You—go on, coz! I'll hold 'em while—you build . . . a bonfire." Not waiting for consent, he swung around, musket levelled. "Platoon . . . halt!" he shouted. "Guided tour . . . stops here!"

Behind him, Tyndale hesitated, but the fierce gallop had halted before the wide mouth of the musket that waved gently to and fro. "Go *on*, dash it all!" urged Devenish.

Tyndale plunged into the nearest bedchamber, which chanced to be the one his cousin had occupied, and began dragging chairs, tables, draperies, into a pile before the windows. Inspired, he wrenched down the ghoulish portrait, propped it against the pile, and smashed the still burning oil lamp at it.

A gout of fire exploded. Tyndale leapt back. The flames licked upward, reaching hungrily for the draperies. They caught, and in a trice the windows were edged with fire.

Smoke began to billow out, and Tyndale, coughing, ran back to his cousin, still at bay on the balcony.

"He done it, damn him!" howled an enraged voice. "He's fired the blasted place. If it reaches the stores . . . !"

Strong faces blanched. Murderous glares faded into unease. The rear rank began to edge downwards. "Shoot! You perishin' fools—*shoot!*" raved Shotten, brandishing his empty pistol.

The front door burst open. A new arrival ran in, shouting, "There's a damn great bunch of riders coming!"

"Hurrah!" Devenish exulted.

The smugglers hesitated, exchanging scared glances. A thunder of hooves could be heard outside. Simultaneously, a great billow of smoke gushed onto the landing. It was the *coup de grâce*. As one man, the group on the stairs broke and ran. From the corner of his eye Tyndale saw Shotten wrest a pistol from the newcomer and turn—aiming. With a cry of warning, he leapt to push his cousin out of th line of fire. The pistol shot cracked deafeningly, even above the tumult. Tyndale staggered and clutched his shoulder. Devenish steadied himself and fired, his shot sounding as an echo to the first, the twin retorts almost simultaneous, and Shotten gave a howl, grabbed his arm and reeled away, assisted by a comrade.

Tyndale swayed, missed his footing, and fell, tumbling limply down the precipitous stairs even as the front door was flung wide.

General Drummond, Yolande behind him, rushed in. They halted, and stood as though rooted to the spot. Yolande gave a small, shrill scream. With an appalled groan, Devenish started to hurry to his cousin, but Yolande was before him. She flew to sink down beside Tyndale's sprawled form, another despairing cry escaping her as she saw the blood that stained his shirt. Tearing his cravat aside, her distraught gaze flashed up to Devenish and the still-smoking pistol in his hand. "Murderous savage!" she sobbed, in fierce accusation. "*Had* you to try to kill him, then? Would *nothing* satisfy your vengeance, your insane jealousy, but his death?" And bending to investigate the wound high on Tyndale's shoulder, she pleaded brokenly, "My darling, my darling! Oh, my dearest beloved—do not die! Please, *please*, do not die!"

Two steps above her, Devenish halted and groped blindly for the banister rail. For years to come that scene would haunt him: Craig, sprawled and silent, Yolande weeping over him;

the General standing as one dazed, while the grooms and stablehands from Steep Drummond crowded noisily in behind him to gaze in awed condemnation at the dramatic tableaux before them.

"It is not true," he thought numbly. "It *cannot* be true! She is *mine*. We are betrothed. She does not love Craig. She *must not* love Craig!" But Yolande's tears, her tender efforts to help the wounded man, and above all else the bitter, accusing words that rang in his brain, left no room for doubt. She *did* love Craig. That terrible knowledge seared like a sword through him. Her love was forever lost. The Colonial bastard had stolen her away, and in so doing had taken every hope for the future, and all meaning in life. . . .

Craig struggled feebly and came to one elbow. His eyes were full of pain, and he must have struck his head in falling, for blood was streaking down his face, but he held back Yolande's ministering hand, his gaze fixed on his cousin. "Dev," he gasped faintly, "Dev—I tried . . . not to love her, but . . . but I—I did not—I would . . . not . . ." And he slumped down again, Yolande supporting his fall so that his head sank into her lap. Her tears fell like bright diamonds onto his unresponsive face. She lifted her head to glare up at Devenish and demand through clenched teeth, "Are you satisfied now? Oh—may God forgive you! I never shall!"

The General moved forward, breaking the spell that had held them all still for what seemed like a long time, yet had actually been only seconds. "Good God, man!" he breathed. "Have you entirely lost your wits? I'd not thought to find something like this when the child said there was trouble here!"

A door, distantly slammed, brought his head swinging around, and jolted Devenish from his personal misery. "The smugglers!" he cried.

Montelongo staggered into the hall, saw Tyndale, and ran to him weavingly.

The General brightened. If there were smugglers about, this tragedy might not be so black as he had at first surmised. Smoke was boiling out of one of the upper rooms. "Some of you men," he roared, "get upstairs and put that fire out! Todd and Blake—stay with Miss Yolande. The rest of you, come with me!"

"This way!" shouted Devenish. He sprinted to the kitchen hall and the basement stairs and with whoops of excitement,

527

the General and his men followed. At top speed, they clattered down the stairs and raced along the hall. The door to the store room in which the cousins had been imprisoned was still open. The rear door stood wide, but as Devenish ran through it, he slowed. A large cupboard just beyond the door jutted crazily into the corridor, revealing a small aperture in the wall behind it, and a glimpse of deep-cut steps leading downwards.

Holding up a flaming torch that he'd snatched from its bracket, the General muttered, "Have a care, lad. They may be waiting!"

Devenish smiled without mirth. Much he cared! He stepped over the low wainscot and onto the first step. The darkness was intense, the light of the torch penetrating a very few feet ahead, but the steps wound steadily down. They were slippery and treacherous, but he went on with reckless haste, and as he went the smell of the sea came ever more clearly to his nostrils. Had not Tyndale once made some remark about the possibility of an entrance to the castle through a cave? His heart began to hammer with anticipation.

The steps curved around a wall, and suddenly they were in an enormous chamber, one side of which was formed by the living rock of the cliff-face. Torches still burned in wall brackets, but of Sanguinet's minions the only sign was the open door at the far side of the room, a door of solid stone, so formed as to be invisible from without once it was securely closed.

Coming up with Devenish at the foot of the steps, Drummond exclaimed, "By God, but this is a fine haul! There's a deal more here than brandy and perfumes and the like!"

And indeed, there were innumerable boxes, bales, and barrels of every shape, row upon row of them, stored very neatly by their various sizes.

"No wonder there were so many of them," muttered Devenish.

"D'ye see any of the rogues? Be damned if I do!"

They quickened their steps, but when they had run across that great storage room and passed through the open door, they encountered a misty, deserted cove, with only the fast-diminishing sails of a yawl to vouch for the hurried flight of the Free Traders.

Devenish cursed bitterly. "They're safely away! And I've not one witness to attest to the fact that I did not shoot my wretched cousin!"

"Tyndale will attest to it," said the General. "The wound did not look to be serious. Not much more than a deep score across the base of his throat. D'you know which one shot him?"

"Yes." Devenish said reluctantly, "The leader of that unsavoury crew was a lout named Shotten. He fired at me. Tyndale ran to push me clear, and so took the ball himself."

"By Jove!" exclaimed the General, eyes kindling. "That was well—"

"Sir!" called one of the grooms, his voice ringing with excitement. "Come and have a look here!"

They went back inside. Several of the crates had been broken open, and the grooms were busily unloading bottles of rum and cognac from one large barrel. "Let that stuff alone, men!" Drummond ordered crisply. "The Excise people will want to find it undisturbed." His eyes fell on a bottle of '71 port. He amended hurriedly, "Or relatively so," and grinning into Devenish's stern face, murmured, "Finders keepers—eh?"

Devenish shrugged and wandered to a clear area of the room. It had very obviously been occupied recently. There were scratches and grooves in the rocky floor indicating that heavy objects had been dragged across it, and from the disposition of dust and straw it appeared that many large crates must have been removed. "I'd give a good deal," he muttered, "to know what was stored here. . . ."

The General nodded briskly, "Likely a cargo bound for London markets. And more likely, there's many a gentleman will be the better of a case or two of duty-free brandy before another week's out. Oh, well—this haul alone must be worth a fortune. There may be a reward, m'boy. You're liable to become famous. But you cannot stay here alone. You must come and rack up at Steep Drummond for a while."

With bleak control, Devenish thanked him. "I will impose on you sir, only until I can be assured of my cousin's condition. Then, I must get home."

The General slanted a compassionate glance at him. "Of course," he agreed understandingly. "Only natural you'd want to go."

Yolande closed the bedchamber door softly and trod her weary way down the hall. Reaching up to push back an errant strand of hair, she stopped, her heart contracting. Devenish had been sitting beside an ornately carven old chest, but came to his feet when he saw her, and waited, his face pale and expressionless. She reached out to him tentatively.

He did not take her proffered hands, saying in a voice she did not know at all, "How is he?"

She blinked, allowing her hands to lower again. "Not very good, I'm afraid. The gunshot wound is slight, but—but it seems he struck his head when he fell. He keeps going off into unconsciousness, and the doctor . . . just—" Her voice scratched a little. "He does not really know . . ."

He had not expected this and, shocked, stepped a pace closer, peering at her in the dim light of the one lamp that was lit and asking, "He must have come around, surely?"

"He spoke twice. You are quite exonerated, Dev." Tears blinding her, she said pleadingly, "Oh, Dev . . . dear Dev. I am—so sorry. I wish—*how* I wish I had not said it!"

He did not answer, and she dashed her tears away, impatient because she was so very tired and distraught and could not seem to see him clearly. He had moved over to the window and stood looking into the night, his back very straight, his hands loosely clasped behind him. Humbly, she begged, "Can you please tell me what has been happening? I heard people coming and going all night long, I think."

"Oh, yes. There has been a very great fuss. Your grandfather sent riders to Kilmarnock, and the Constable came and Sir Hugh somebody-or-other called out the militia, who are guarding the castle until the powers-that-be arrive. And—" The clasped hands was gripped tighter. His head tilted upwards as though he was bracing himself. He asked hoarsely, "Do you—Yolande, do you mean to wed him?"

She bit her lip, her heart aching for him. But said firmly, "Yes. If he lives, I will marry him."

"If he lives!" He spun around. "There's no question of *that*—is there?"

"I . . . I don't know. He has been unconscious for hours now." Her lip trembled and she said with unknowing pathos, "I am—very frightened."

How strange that the sight of her grief still had such power to move him. How strange that, even now, he loved her, worshipped her, wanted so desperately to make her his wife. And yet somehow, he heard himself saying, "He saved my life again, you know. The bullet that struck him down would likely have caught me in the head, had he not pushed me aside. I . . . I suppose you must resent that fact."

With a muffled whimper, she shrank, turning from him, her face buried in her hands. "Do not . . . oh, please, Dev. Do not hate me!"

"Hate you!" He stepped closer to seize her shoulders, pull her against him, and press desperate kisses on the cool silk of her hair. "I *adore* you! I always have—you know it. Yolande— for the love of God—*think!* What are you doing? We have been promised all our lives! Do you really—"

"I know!" She wrenched free and faced him. "I feel sick and ashamed. But I cannot change my heart. I have broken my promise to you. But—but at least our betrothal was never made public. You will not have to suffer that humiliation."

"It is no less binding because it wasn't published! You gave me your word!" And knowing he could choose no worse time to plead his cause, driven by desperation he plunged on. "You said you would name the day when I came back from the castle."

Her eyes fell. She wrung her hands and admitted miserably, "I did. Oh, I know how I have hurt you. I—I cannot tell you . . . how I wish I might not."

"*I* can tell *you!*" Again, he took her by the arms, gazing into her strained upturned face, and demanding, "Admit to yourself that he is not for you. Could you adapt to his way of life? Could you give up everything you have ever known? Home, family, friends, even your country. Admit you will break the hearts of all who love you! Can you do it? Yolande—*can* you? And not care?" She was weeping openly now, but he shook her a little and rasped, "*Think*, love! Stop and think what you are doing!"

"Dev . . . oh, heaven, how . . . how frightful it is . . . ! How can I make you understand? I love my family . . . my friends—my country. But . . . I love Craig more. I—I would follow him . . . to the ends of the earth."

He flinched as if she had struck him. A groan was torn from him, and he again turned from her. Sobbing, she took his arm and leaned her cheek against it. And despite himself, his hand went out to caress her bowed head. Despite the aching anguish within him, he soothed, "Never weep, my—my dear one. What a—a dolt I am. Just as . . . clumsy as ever, you see."

"No . . . you are not at all . . ."

"I should not have spoken. You are too upset to think clearly. I do apologize. But, Yolande—" he looked down at her, forcing a smile. "It will pass. You'll see. It is just an infatuation."

She stiffened and drew away. Her sobs eased as she stood there, gazing at him in silence. Then she said with a quiet resolve that terrified him, "No, Dev. It is not infatuation. I know now that from the first moment I met him, I have loved Craig. And that I always will love him. The only thing ever to come between us will be—death."

His face convulsed. With typical abruptness, his mood changed and he looked so maddened that for the first time in her life, Yolande was afraid of him. Fists clenching, eyes narrowed and blazing with passion, he snarled, "Then, I pray to God he *dies*!" And strode rapidly away, leaving her to gaze after him, her eyes wide with shock and an emotion that would have further enraged him—pity.

The days that followed were busy ones for all concerned, which was perhaps as well. The authorities from Glasgow arrived and were soon superseded by the authorities from Edinburgh. Writers from several newspapers and periodicals descended upon Steep Drummond and infuriated the General by conducting understanding and sympathetic interviews, then writing articles that grossly misrepresented the facts. Devenish said nothing of Sanguinet's part in the matter, nor would he until he had reported to the Horse Guards. But the newspapermen promoted the smugglers to "Bonapartists"; Drummond and his men had galloped to the rescue of his "headstrong young nephews," arriving in the nick of time, and driving off the ruffians by means of a pitched battle during which half of the castle had been burned to the ground. The ultimate offence was a piece by one writer describing Drummond as "a peaceable little old gentleman," which so infuriated the General he all but foamed at the mouth. Devenish was questioned interminably, praised lavishly, and then depicted in the newspapers as having sadly mismanaged the affair. It was, it appeared, very obvious that had the authorities been "properly notified," the criminals could have been seized and brought to justice. Instead of which, thanks to Devenish's ineptitude, not only had they escaped but war hero Major Craig Tyndale now lay at death's door.

Devenish read this with fuming resentment and joined the General in calling down maledictions upon all newspaper writers. Even Mrs. Drummond was offended. "It is not," she sniffed, as they sat in the drawing room after dinner one evening, "as if Devenish did not do all that he was capable of doing. They surely must realize he is *not* a big strong fellow. And he certainly did not *mean* Major Tyndale Winters to be hurt." She turned curious eyes upon the seething Devenish and murmured, "Now, did you, Alain?"

"I must own, ma'am," he answered with a brittle smile, "that I'd not had the wit to consider it."

Arabella blinked at him, uncertainly. Mrs. Fraser uttered a faint snort and took up her embroidery. General Drummond fixing Devenish with a stern eye, said, "I understand you'd a letter from Alastair Tyndale today. Does he mean to come up here, may I ask?"

"He did not say so, sir. I had written to tell him of what transpired, of course, and of Craig's condition. He asks that I remain until— Well, one way or the other. If this goes on much longer, I shall take myself to the Gold Florin in the village. Lord knows you have been more than kind to allow me to stay here, under the circumstances."

"The circumstances," the General said with deliberate emphasis and a darkling look, "have changed. You have redeemed yourself. In my eyes, at least." He noted Devenish's faint, cynical smile, and frowned. "The lass is properly in the boughs now, and little wonder. She is grateful to Tyndale, and is besides a good girl who would bend every effort to help *anyone* in so wretched a condition."

Mrs. Fraser did not look up from her embroidery, but her scornful, "Hoot toot!" was quite audible.

Devenish said politely, "Thank you, sir. But I think that is not all there is to it."

"It had best be! Your cousin has shown himself a right gallant gentleman. What's gone before cannot be changed, nonetheless, and I'll not give my approval to my granddaughter's marrying into such a house. No more, I doubt, will her parents."

"She is of age, sir."

"Aye, she is that. But if you think she would wed over the objections of her family, *I* do not. And besides—whatever else, Tyndale is a gentleman. He'd neither propose marriage to a lady he well knows is already promised, nor allow her to go against the wishes of her family. Give her time, lad. She'll come to her senses!"

For the next five days and nights, however, Yolande rarely

emerged from the sickroom. Her grandfather had installed competent nurses to care for the injured man, and the devoted Montelongo seldom left him, so that her help was not needed, but she dreaded lest Craig regain consciousness and did not find her at his bedside. Often, during those weary days, she would think his awakening imminent, for he would begin to toss about and mumble, and sometimes he tried to get up, shouting incoherently. Always, hers was the only hand that could quiet him. But always, he sank back into the depths without having recognized her.

The nurses who shared her vigil were kind and capable, but uncommunicative. The doctor talked to her gravely of Tyndale's splendid constitution, but of the often bewildering effects of concussion, and the fact that only last year Craig had almost died of wounds received at the Battle of Waterloo. " 'Twould be a shock tae any man's system, ma'am," he observed, nodding his white head ponderously. "We must gie the body time tae recover!"

But it seemed to Yolande that her love was not recovering. Each day, he appeared to her anxious eyes to become more gaunt and thin. The periods of activity were fewer, and on several terrible occasions she feared he had ceased to breathe. When she begged the doctor to do *something* to help him, he patted her shoulder and said kindly, "Ye gie me more credit than I deserve, lassie. Better you should broch the subject tae the good Lord. And be wiling tae abide by His decision."

Those ominous words sent a shiver down Yolande's spine. She sank to her knees beside the bed and prayed as she had never prayed before. The nurse, coming silently into the room following a quiet consultation with the doctor, saw that sad little scene, and her heart was wrung. She went quickly into the adjoining dressing room where they had set up her trundle bed and offered up a few prayers of her own.

There was a hill on the General's estate from which one could obtain a very fine view of the surrounding countryside and, on a clear day, see all the way to the Isle of Arran. It was a pleasant spot, the thick turf providing a soft blanket underfoot, and several large old trees offering sprawling patches of shade if the sun should prove too warm. Josie and her friend Maisie had sometimes brought their dolls up here, and the hill had served variously as the afterdeck of a great galleon deliciously pursued by bloodthirsty pirates, or as the topmost parapet of some mighty castle from which the two "ladies" had watched their knightly lords set forth to battle oppression and tyranny, with an occasional dragon thrown in for good measure.

To this peaceful retreat on a warm afternoon some eight days after the confrontation at Castle Tyndale came Alain Devenish, head down bent and heart as heavy as his dragging steps. He strolled to the tree that was closest to the western side of the hill and settled himself down with his back propped against the trunk. The valley between this hill and the one whereon stood Steep Drummond stretched out lush and green below him, smoke wound lazily into the air from two chimneys of the great house, and, far off, the sea, incredibly blue under the azure bowl of the heavens, stretched into a misty distance.

The young man's brooding gaze saw none of this beauty, but saw instead a slim girl on her knees in the vast hall of Castle Tyndale, her great eyes, hate-filled, flashing up at him.... Down in the meadow, a small disgruntled creature named Socrates came upon a placid milk cow and hurled himself into battle, barking shrilly. The sound travelled all the way to the hilltop on the warm air, but Devenish heard only a beloved voice railing at him as it never had railed before. "Murderous savage ... May God forgive you! I never shall!" And he thought with longing that was a pain, "Yolande ... Yolande ..." Her face, fondly smiling now, was before his eyes, wherefore he closed them and leaned his head back.

Perversely, it was Tyndale he saw then. Tyndale, standing astride him during the fight with Akim and Benjo; laughing when he was staggered by a blow, and fighting on dauntlessly; Tyndale, looking so confoundedly magnificent in his Scots regalia, with that uncertain grin on his face. Tyndale, shouting a warning and leaping forward to push him clear, thus taking the ball that had been meant for him ... Somewhere at the back of his bedevilled brain a soft voice whispered, "Greater love hath no man ..." He swore and bowed his head into his hands, and though he would fiercely have denied it, his grief was not entirely for his lost love, but some was for the man he had come to like and admire; and who had betrayed him.

For a long time he remained thus, trying to form some plan for the future; trying to envision a future in which there was no sparkle of laughing green eyes, no soft, teasing, musical little voice, no warmth of hearth and home—and children.... But gradually he sensed that he was not alone and, looking up, found a small figure kneeling beside him. When the wistful dark eyes encountered his own, the child said nothing, but thrust a small, rather wilted bouquet of tiny daisies at him. Touched, and faintly smiling, he took it, and she sighed, murmuring regretfully, "I got nothing else to give you."

"This is just right," he said. "Thank you." And, with an attempt at lightness, "But it is not my birthday, you know."

"I picked 'em for you 'cause you was hurting so bad. I'd have bringed hundreds of roses and great big dailies, if I could. Or I'd have made him better for you. I asked God to make him better, so p'raps He will." A small grubby hand was placed comfortingly on Devenish's immaculate sleeve. "Don't you never grieve so. If God needs him in Heaven, you shouldn't ought to angrify about it."

He looked away from her earnest face, flushing slightly. "I expect you are right." Her eyes seemed so piercingly intent. There was no telling what might be going on in her funny little head. Hurriedly, he asked, "What have you been up to these past few days? I fear I've neglected you. Have you been playing with your friend?"

"No. Her mum wouldn't let us. Don't you remember?"

"Oh, of course. Maisie, wasn't it? And she has the measles."

"She's better. But Mrs. MacFarlane's poorly. I thought she was cocking up her toes, 'cause they asked the vicar to come and see her—only they call him a minster. Next day when I went to take her a rose, she was up, and she was lots better. I was s'prised. That minster must be God's bosom bow to make her well so quick. P'raps we should get him to come and make Major Craig better."

"Perhaps," he gritted. "Was Mrs. MacFarlane cross because you went to her house?"

"No. I thinked she would be, but she wasn't. She was nice, even when she talked so funny."

"Funny?"

"Mmmm. She asked me how Miss Yolande was, and I said I hadn't hardly seen her, because she's been so busy nursing of Major Craig. And she started to look all weepy and said something about how good Miss Yolande is, and now her heart is breaking 'cause her love is dying under her very eyes. I told her she'd got it all wrong, 'cause *you* are—" She faltered to a stop, Devenish's suddenly bleak expression causing her own eyes to become very big indeed. "Oh . . . my!" she gasped. And without warning she threw her frail arms around his neck, hugging him so hard he all but choked. "Never look so, dear soul! Oh, my poor, dear soul!" she said with a sob. "I'll take care of ye. Ah—never look so!"

Succeeding in freeing himself from her stranglehold, Devenish regarded her wonderingly. "What are these?" he smiled, removing a glittering drop from her cheek. "Tears? For me? No need, m'dear. I'm fine as fivepence, I do assure you!"

His grin was as bright and cheerful as ever, but she was undeceived. She buried her cheek against his cravat and hugged as much of him as she could reach. "How *could* she?" she gulped. "Oh, how *could* she like him best—when she could have *you*?"

Devenish's grin took on a set look. But, after all, there was no need to dissemble with the child. "Tell you the truth," he said wryly, "I've wondered as much myself. But—no accounting for tastes." Once more, he gently disentangled himself and, looking down at her woebegone face, said, "And there really is no cause for all these high flights and tragic airs, milady elf. I wasn't thoroughly set on getting leg-shackled. This is probably—probably better for everyone."

Having been deprived of throat and cravat, Josie hugged his arm and, looking worshipfully up into his face, said with a sigh, "You say that, but I know how your poor insides really feel. Anyone else, they'd be waiting for Major Craig to get up, so they could shoot a hole right through his breadbasket. But not you! He's lucky you love him, else—"

"*Love* him?" exclaimed Devenish, revolted. "I cannot *abide* the fellow!"

She gave a rather watery giggle. "I know. And you'll say you don't give a button if he saved your life, or 'cause his dad and your dad was such fine friends. You both pretend you don't like each other. But you fights together, and you keeps together. You didn't run off and leave him alone at that horrid castle, however creepy it is. And I think he's very lucky that you ... cannot 'bide him. Poor Mr. Dev! You want her for your lady wife, but you're so good you'll probably wish her happy—even if she's hacked your poor heart to little pieces!"

Shattered, Devenish scrambled hurriedly to his feet. He strode to the brink of the hill and stood staring across the valley to that other hill and the great house wherein was a quiet bedchamber and a lovely lady—waiting. And he thought in stark misery, "Perhaps when my dear cousin wakes up—if he wakes up—I *shall* shoot a hole through his breadbasket."

✄ *Chapter 15* ✄

Yolande came swiftly down the stairs and hurried to the small parlour into which her unexpected guest had been shown. "Mrs. MacFarlane!" she said, walking forward, hand outstretched. "I heard you had been unwell. I am so glad you came to me. Is there some way in which I may help you?"

The emaciated little woman sprang up to take her hand shyly and drop a curtsy. Her own fingers trembled as she said in short nervous gasps, 'Ye-ye have always been sae . . . sae verra good tae me. I tae come find oot—how the poor gentleman goes on."

"How kind. Will you not sit here beside me? There, now we can be comfortable. Major Craig remains the same. There is—no change, I'm afraid." For an instant a look of desolation crossed that beauteous face. Then Yolande bit her lip, raised her chin a little and, putting aside her own sorrow, asked, "How is your little girl?"

"Och, sae much better, miss. She'd like fine for Miss Josie tae come and see her, if it's nae forward tae ask it."

"But of course it is not." Yolande searched her face; it seemed calmer. "Maisie is—quite better?" she asked, wondering at this new demeanour.

"Aye. Thank you. But if ye fear Miss Josie might catch it, we could wait a wee while."

"No, no. I expect Josie was exposed when they played together at all events. She might already have had measles. I only wondered . . . you seem less, er—"

"Troubled, Miss? Well, I am. I've come tae—" She drew a deep breath. Almost, thought Yolande, as though she were nerving herself for some tremendous task. "I'd not thought tae ever do this," Mrs. MacFarlane said, gripping her bony hands.

538

"Likely I'd nae be doing it the noo, but—ye've been sae good. And even with your man lying there, ye came doon, thinking I had need of ye. I felt fair horrid, and I could nae—" She broke off with a gasp, her frightened gaze darting to the open doorway.

Yolande glanced around. Devenish stood there. His fair curls were disarrayed, and he looked out of breath as though he had come in haste, but in his eyes was an expression she had never thought to see there again, and that brought hope to brighten her heavy heart a little. So it was that for one of the very few times in her life, Yolande Drummond was so discourteous as to completely forget a visitor. She stood, saying eagerly, "Dev . . . ? Oh, Dev—have you forgiven me, then?"

"No," he replied tenderly, reaching out to her. "For the only one who needs forgiveness is this hot-tempered idiot."

With a glad little sob, she flew to take his hands and then allow herself to be enveloped in a hug.

Devenish closed his eyes for an instant, savouring to the full that bitter-sweet embrace. "Lord," he said, his voice low and husky with emotion, "what an ill-grained clod I am! The most important challenge of my life, and I was so unsportsmanlike as to lose without grace—without honesty; having the un-speakable arrogance to suppose that merely because I so love you, it must follow that—"

She put up one soft hand to silence his words, then said very gently, "I do love you, Dev. I always have. That is what made it so very hard. But—it wasn't in . . . in just that very special way, do you see?"

The same cruel lance was piercing him, but he managed a smile. "I do—now. And if I cannot have you for—my wife, I . . . I hope I may still have you for my friend."

She blinked tears away. "Always, Dev. Dear Dev. Always."

"It's as well you agreed," he said shakily. "Else I might not have told you." Her lovely brows arched enquiringly. How he longed to kiss them. . . . Instead, he took his handkerchief and carefully dried her tears. "There is a curst great clod of a Co-lonial upstairs," he imparted, "of whom I have, unhappily, be-come quite fond. That starched Amazon of a nurse tells me that—he is calling for you."

Yolande uttered a gasp and, paling, put a trembling hand to her throat. She searched his face and as he nodded, she sped to the door. Watching her, Devenish's fond smile faded into a wistful sadness. He had to replace the smile very quickly when

Yolande paused and spun about, but she had seen that changed expression and suffered her own pang. "Dev," she said timidly. "Will you—come? I'm . . . afraid. . . ."

He went at once to her side. "Silly chit," he said.

They entered the room together. Montelongo stood beside the bed, beaming. Craig's eyes turned to them eagerly, but saw only Yolande. With a glad little cry she went to take the hand he raised and clasp it between both her own. For a few moments, neither spoke a word, but looking from one rapturous face to the other, besides grief and yearning, Devenish experienced a sense of awe.

"Oh, my dear," breathed Yolande at length. "You have come back to me at last. How are you?"

"I feel . . . splendid," he said, faint but radiant. "Only—a touch pulled. What a clunch to have gone off like that, yesterday."

Devenish chuckled, and his cousin's eyes flashed to him. "It wasn't yesterday, gudgeon. It was eight days since. And if you doubt me, feel your chin!"

Tyndale's hand wavered upward. He touched the thick beard and gasped a disbelieving, *"Eight . . . days . . . ?"*

"Slugabed," said Devenish, and thought, "Lord, but he looks a rail!"

Briefly, bewilderment held sway, then remorse rushed in on Tyndale. He started up. "Dev! Yolande—what she said in the castle—I mean— There was nothing ever— She didn't mean . . ." The words trailed off, and he gave a helpless gesture.

Devenish said with a wry smile, "Do you tell me I have so nobly stepped aside for no cause? If you do not want the lady . . ."

"Want her. . . ?" Tyndale gazed at Yolande with total adoration. "There are no words. But—" Again, his hollow eyes turned to Devenish. He said with sober intensity, "I swear to you—I have done nothing—said nothing, to betray you, Devenish. Nor to bring dishonour upon her."

" 'I could not love thee dear so much, loved I not honour more . . .'?" Devenish quoted softly. He walked to the bed and looked squarely at Tyndale. "You are in that bed, cousin, because you took something meant for me. It was bravely done, and I thank you."

Tyndale's thin cheek flushed. "It was not done with any thought to claim as reward your every happiness!"

Devenish kept his eyes from Yolande and said lightly, "You rate the lady high."

"I do indeed. And so do you."

"Dear," Yolande inserted in her most gentle voice, "I think you are talking too much. We must not allow you to tire yourself so soon."

The term of endearment caused his hand to tighten on hers. "No, really, I feel perfectly fit. And have so many questions, but—"

"Aha!" cried the General, marching briskly into the room. "So our sleeper has come out from hibernation at last! Jove, but it's good to see you with your eyes open, m'boy!" He shook Tyndale's hand cautiously. "You did very well oot at your castle, but I surmise Devenish has told you what happened."

Devenish said, "I've not had time to—"

"Is he awake, then?" Mrs. Drummond bustled in, followed by her sister-in-law. "Oh, my!" She fumbled for her handkerchief. "What a blessing that you did not die after all, Tyndale. We all thought you would, you know. But—"

"But we're powerful glad tae see ye didnae!" said Mrs. Fraser, adding with an irked glance at Arabella, "Of all the bird-witted things tae remark!"

"Never mind, dear," purred Mrs. Drummond. "We do not expect you to be brilliant, after all. Oh!" She blinked rapidly. "Is it not affecting? See how they gaze into each other's eyes ..."

The General, having already noted this blissful gaze, scowled, "Pairhaps I should warn ye, Tyndale—"

"Not now, Sir Andrew!" Mrs. Fraser inserted with a warning frown.

Devenish said hurriedly, "The smugglers got clean away, Craig, but—"

"But we found a damn—a dashed great stockpile o' contraband hidden in a cellar," the General put in, his eyes sparkling with excitement at that memory.

"And you should have seen all the newspaper reporters ..." said Mrs. Drummond.

They all began to talk at once, so that poor Tyndale was quite bewildered and struggled to comprehend Montelongo's kidnapping, the dramatic arrival of the rescue party, and the fact that not once was Sanguinet's name mentioned. Watching him narrowly, the Iroquois abruptly strode forward and pronounced, "You tired. Me show door to these people."

The General uttered a snort of indignation, and Devenish laughed, but Yolande was relieved. "Perfectly right," she agreed. "You must rest, Craig. We will have plenty of time to explain everything."

"Just one more thing, I beg of you," he pleaded, smiling at her in a way that warmed the hearts of most of those gathered in the bedchamber. "Monty, how did you escape your two new friends?"

"Little squaw, sir. She peep in through window." Montelongo forgot his customary pose in the recollection of that moment, and said with enthusiasm, "It was very brave. She was shaking with fear, but she managed to find a way into the cottage and used the kitchen knife to cut me free while those two rogues snored!"

"Goodness me!" gasped Mrs. Drummond, staring at him in astonishment. "Whenever did you learn to speak English so well?"

The Iroquois folded his arms across his chest and assumed a characteristic stance. "Monty talk good," he declared woodenly.

"We were searching for the child," said the General, impatient with this digression, "and came upon the wee lass trying to help your man, who was in a sorry plight, I do assure you. He could scarce speak at all, and the child told us there was trouble at Castle Tyndale, so we turned aboot and galloped hell-for-leather to investigate!"

"And arrived in time to see me murder you," said Devenish. Yolande flinched a little.

Tyndale gasped, "Good God! They never thought—"

Mrs. Drummond emitted a trill of laughter. "Well, we know better now. Though one could scarcely blame poor Alain had he indeed done so dreadful a thing. . . ." And she glanced coyly from the flushed Yolande to Tyndale's enigmatic face.

"Dinna talk such fustian!" the General barked. "Say rather, all's well that ends well. Yon smugglers are routed; Tyndale here can live in his castle in peace and be assured of the good will of his neighbours. Or most of 'em, at least. And Yolande and Devenish can—"

"Grandpapa!" Yolande interpolated desperately. "This is not the time or place to speak of these things."

"Aye, the lass is right. Tyndale, we'll leave ye tae your

slumbers. Come everyone. Oot! Oot! Devenish, ye're welcome tae stay here wi' us for as long as suits, but I fancy ye'll be wishful tae escort your lady back tae London Toon, eh?"

Devenish smiled rather bleakly; Yolande blushed and looked distressed, and Tyndale lay in helpless silence, watching them all leave. Having ushered everyone from the room, the General turned back at the last minute. He said nothing, but the warning contained in his grim stare was very obvious. Alain Devenish might be so unselfish as to step aside, but the barriers between Tyndale and his love were as insurmountable as ever.

Outside, the westering sun laid soft shadows upon the scythed lawns. The air was warm and the summer house loomed cool, quiet, and inviting. Approaching that charming structure, Mrs. MacFarlane glanced around. There was no sign of anyone. She went timidly up the steps, remembering the last time she had been in this little house, and how kind Miss Drummond had been to her Maisie. "Puir wee lassie," she thought, "she'll nae have the man o' her heart, I doot." But she had tried. It had taken days and days to gather sufficient courage to go up to the great house as she'd done today. She *had* tried! She directed a small, silent prayer at the cloudless heavens, apologizing for her inability to have completed her task. Leaving the summer house she began to walk across the lawns. The smell of the freshly cut grass wafted about her. The golden afternoon was like a benediction. It could only be viewed as an omen; she had been spared. With a small sigh of relief, she hurried back to her cottage.

At the edge of the Atlantic Ocean, off the northwest coast of Scotland, lie the islands called the Hebrides, and among them, remote and often uncharted, one small cluster is known as the Darrochs. The first three, bleak, inhospitable, and uninhabited, form a rough circle about the fourth. This, the largest, enjoys a milder climate than its fellows, being protected to an extent by a high range of hills on the eastern side, which cut off the freezing winds. Despite this redeeming feature, it falls far short of being a beauty spot, and no one was more surprised than the impoverished owner when, in 1812, all four islands were purchased by a Greek company, the president of which allegedly intended to make the big island—Tordarroch—his home.

For a while, all was as before; the gulls continued to shout and circle undisturbed among the rocks and along the shore; the breakers pounded an incessant assault upon the impregnable cliffs to the east, north, and south, and on its high hill, the ancient structure called Tor Keep squatted mouldering under the chill skies, as it had done for centuries.

Early in 1813, however, a ship put in and anchored in the western cove of Tordarroch; many men landed, and much cargo was unloaded. When the ship sailed away, most of the men remained. A week later, another ship put in; and the next day was followed by yet another. Suddenly, Tordarroch became a beehive of activity: the debris-strewn beach was cleared; the little bay was deepened and new docks were constructed; several buildings appeared; Tor Keep swarmed with workmen; new roads were built, and the face of the island changed in other ways as tall shrubs and trees that were able to withstand the harsh climate replaced the rough broom and bracken and stunted pines. The trees grew rapidly. Within two years they had formed a screen that completed the work of the eastern hills in shielding Tordarroch from any chance sailing vessel with a prying spyglass. The workmen completed their tasks, but did not depart. Instead, they moved onto first one, then another of the three outer islands, and started to labour all over again.

It was to Tordarroch, however, that most shipping travelled, and it was to the much improved harbour that a fishing boat sailed one afternoon in early summer of 1816, and despatched a dinghy to the dock. A gentleman disembarked from the dinghy, entered a dog cart, was duly conveyed into the courtyard of Tor Keep, and thence to a magnificent chamber, part-library, part-study, where the powdered lackey bowed low and requested that Monsieur Garvey should be *"à l'aise, s'il vous plâit."*

Mr. James Garvey did not obey this behest, but instead scrolled about, gazing in awe from the massive hearth whereon a great fire licked up the chimney, to richly panelled walls, to elaborate plastered ceilings. Thick carpets deadened his footsteps, *objets d'art* delighted his eyes, the warm air was faintly scented, and he'd have been not in the least surprised had a trio of minstrels put in an appearance and serenaded him. When the door opened, however, it disclosed a comparatively plebeian figure clad without ostentation in a maroon jacket of peerless cut, pearl-grey unmentionables, and an off-white waistcoat embellished with embroidered maroon clocks.

"Claude!" Mr. Garvey smiled, advancing to take the hand that was languidly extended. "What miracles you have wrought here! I might have known! In five years or less you will boast another such showplace as your chateau in Dinan."

"I never boast," Monsieur Sanguinet murmured in French. "And you are inaccurate. The gardens of Dinan required the better part of my father's lifetime to bring to perfection. In five years I will have no need of this place. Besides which, my so dear James . . ." He wandered to seat himself in a fine Chippendale chair beside the glowing hearth. "Flattery does not prevail with me. You waste your efforts."

He interlaced the fingers of his hands and looked up benignly. To any casual observer he would appear as mild as any rural clergyman. But deep in his light brown eyes burned an echo of the fire's glow that was yet not of the fire.

Garvey's nerves tightened. "You are displeased." He shrugged, turning away and taking up a position against the edge of a superb walnut desk. "I did my best. The crates you wanted removed were gone long before your men bungled matters with Devenish."

"How clever of you to remind me that they were 'my men.'" Sanguinet demurred with a silken smile. "They really are not, you know. They are my brawn, rather. And it is because I know their brains are small and ineffectual that I required Shotten to take his orders from—you."

Garvey folded his arms and said sulkily, "It should have gone off perfectly. We had the portrait ready and used it to good effect, I assure you. Shotten said Devenish turned fairly green when first he saw it, and the pivoting panel in the wall worked perfectly. His cousin all but laughed when he was told of the matter. Devenish said no more, but Shotten reported his nerves were ready to snap, and the dislike between the cousins deepening hourly."

"So that you were sure our plans would come to full fruition, and they would kill one another."

Garvey grinned. "How choice that would have been!"

"Poetic justice," said Sanguinet broodingly. "My dear brother Parnell died for this cause. By rights—I should be in deep mourning at this very moment. . . ." He stared into the fire and was silent.

From all that Garvey had heard, Parnell Sanguinet had died while attempting a brutal murder that had little to do with Claude's ambitious plans. If Claude was capable of affection, thought Garvey, that affection had been given to his brother Parnell—as depraved a sadist as ever lived. Yet even his sudden death had neither swerved Claude from his self-appointed task nor caused him to go into blacks. "He is without mercy," thought Garvey. "Without warmth, or kindness, or feelings!" but when the sombre gaze turned to him, he said apologetically, "It was very close, you know. They were so often at each other's throats the world would have believed Tyndale took vengeance. A lovely plan . . ." He sighed. "Who could guess that lunatic would do so crazy a thing as to toss himself at the wrong end of a musket?"

"I could," purred Sanguinet. "And you should. He is of a type, Garvey. The British public schools mould the type and inculcate into it a worship of valour and chivalry, and a fear of one thing—fear itself." He waved a finger at his companion, and went on, "Your own Wellington knew it. He said, 'The Battle of Waterloo was won on the playing fields of Eton.' Honour, my James. Integrity. Sportsmanship. Had your country one single brain in its collective head it would take that remark and spread those values through *all* its young men. Expensive? Pah! How expensive is a war? I tell you this—you call it lunacy—but could I inspire my men with such lunacy, I should rule the world!" Garvey stared at him, his incredulity so obvious that Sanguinet was irked, and remarked in his gentle fashion, "I cannot think, my dear, how *you* came to avoid such—ah, contamination. . . ."

Garvey flushed and in an effort to turn aside the attack, said, "You will likely rule the world soon or late, at all events."

"Not, James, if one of these—*only one!*—is discovered in the store room at Castle Tyndale." He held up a round lead ball of about three-quarters of an inch diameter. "Tristram Leith, or Redmond, or my very dear friend General Smollet—any of them would only have to see such as this, and know Shotten was there, and—they would know *everything*, James!" He leaned forward, half whispering, "They would *know!*"

Garvey said irritably, "Nothing was left, I tell you! Only the brandy was sacrificed as a red herring. Besides, if they found something they'd likely think we were gun runners, is all."

"No! Damn you! I tell you, *Leith* would know! Harry Redmond would be quick to suspect. And through either of those thorns in my flesh, the Horse Guards would know! Our friend Devenish is the catalyst. He must be silenced. See to it!"

The glare in those strange eyes had flared, and Garvey quailed inwardly. He loathed Alain Devenish and would have been delighted to see him die as slowly and painfully as possible, provided that someone else was responsible. Not that he shrank from murder, but he had plans of his own to bring to fruition, and any public scandal would ruin these. He dare not mention this, however, and avoided Sanguinet's keen scrutiny, muttering, "Nothing would please me more. But I doubt it is necessary, and the least fuss would be our best protection, no?"

Sanguinet continued to regard him for a long moment. Then he settled back in his chair, the flame faded from his eyes, and in a faintly contemptuous tone he enquired, "Why is it not necessary, *mon ami*?"

"Devenish is mad for Yolande Drummond. I have learned she's chosen Tyndale and that Devenish is a broken man. If Tyndale dies, all his energies will go to winning back his light o' love. If the Colonial lives, I fancy he will slink back to England like a whipped cur, with his tail 'twixt his legs. Either way, he will present no further threat to us."

Sanguinet uttered a soft laugh. "You are a philosopher, James. This comes from your own vast experience with *affaires de cœur*, eh?" The sly gleam in his eyes brought a deeper flush to Garvey's countenance, and Sanguinet laughed again. "Perhaps you are right. We will see. Devenish must be watched closely, and destroyed does he make one false move! I have been twice thwarted and now must find another distribution point. Annoying. And it will delay me. I had thought to strike this year. Now—it must be next. Who ever would have dreamed the Canadian would survive Waterloo, much less come to claim our castle! Fate can be so wayward!" he sighed. "I doubt we will ever again find an end for Devenish that would have been so well accepted as our lovely ploy in Castle Tyndale. And how well it would have served us. . . . Such a great pity. . . ."

For a while there was silence, each man busied with his own thoughts.

Sanguinet glanced up at length. "It could have been worse. And—what is it you English say? Better luck the next time? Let us drink to that, my dear James."

They did.

The following Saturday afternoon was sultry, with clouds piling up over the sea and a warm fitful breeze occasionally stirring the banner atop Steep Drummond. The great house was quiet: Mrs. Drummond was laid down upon her bed, softly snoring, with Socrates at her feet, loudly snoring; Mrs. Fraser had gone into the village to supervise the flower arrangements for tomorrow's church service; and in the kitchen, Montelongo was comparing bread recipes with the General's chef. In a certain small study, three people were involved in an intense discussion, the outcome of which would most logically spell defeat and despair for two, and a hollow victory for the third. And because of that same discussion, Alain Devenish was as far away as possible, riding through the hills with a very small person at his side.

These two also had plans to discuss, and Devenish, having just been dealt what he was later to describe "a leveller," turned in the saddle to demand, "What the deuce d'you mean—'thank you, no'? Lord, child, do you not know the future you would have as the General's ward? The old gentleman has taken a great liking to you. He's vastly well breeched and can offer you the best in life. You'll have a splendid education, and when the time comes, be presented, I shouldn't wonder! You'll have a Season in London, and—and everything any chit could wish for! And you say—'thank you, no'? You're wits to let is what it is!"

She peered at him anxiously. "You bean't angry with Josie?"

"No, but—" He straightened and muttered, "I should have more sense. You are too young to understand what's best, so—dash it all—I must make your decisions."

Staring straight ahead between her mount's ears, Josie rode on. She was not a sullen child, but Devenish had come to know that mulish set to her small mouth and, covertly watching her, he waited in amused anticipation for the next move.

"I don't know why he wants me," she said, judicially. "I bean't pretty, Mr. Dev. I don't think I ever will be. Not a Beauty, anyway."

"No," he agreed. "But there are more important things."

She stifled the hurt and said stoutly, "Yes. And I don't give a button for being one. Nor would you, if you stopped to think of it."

"Me?" he exclaimed, startled. "But I've no wish to be a Beauty, elf!"

She giggled, "*Me*, I mean, silly! I might not grow up to be pretty like—" She checked, seeing a muscle ripple in his jaw, and went on quickly, "I mean, I c'n *do* things, Mr. Dev. And in a year or a bit, I'll be all growed and you can—"

"Jo . . . *sie* . . . !" he uttered trenchantly.

"You can turn off your housekeeper," she went on, twinkling at him. " 'Cause I'll be able to keep house for you and sew on your buttons and cook, and—"

"And scrub the floors and wash the windows and do the laundry, I suppose? Devil take it! Can I not make you understand that the General offers you the life of a Lady of Quality? I remember you once said that you wanted to be just like—like Miss Yolande. This is your chance."

She said rather wistfully, "If I *was* like her, would you like me then?"

Devenish's heart twisted. If she were like Yolande . . . Poor little plain, ignorant, lowly born child, how could she ever begin to be like the exquisite lady he had lost . . . ? But the poignant note to her voice had not escaped him, and therefore he shifted in the saddle and, drawing his mount to a halt, appraised her critically. It was not an unpleasant face. It simply had no one feature that was noteworthy. The eyes were bright and alert but neither large nor of exceptional hue; the dark curls showed a regrettable tendency to frizz, the chin was too pointed, and the nose, although straight, lacked distinction. And yet, despite the many hardships she had endured in her short life, her mouth seemed always to tremble on the brink of a smile, and whenever he spoke, her eyes would fly to him with a look of eager expectancy. He thought, "She is like a cheerful little bird, waiting confidently for the crumbs of happiness she knows will come," and realized he had become fond of her.

He said with a smile, "I like you just as you are, but I've nothing to offer you, little one. You cannot live in a house with two bachelors, it wouldn't be right."

"But—but couldn't you ward me, like the General was going to?" she asked desperately. "I want to stay with *you*, Mr. Dev."

"You think you do now, but the time will come when you'll thank me for making you stay here. I've scarce a feather to fly with, but General Drummond's an extreme wealthy gentleman."

"I don't give a button!" she declared fiercely. " 'Sides, you're getting older all the time. I heered you tell the Major that you'll come into your 'heritance soon. So then we could go to your other house to live, and I wouldn't have to live with two bach'lors."

"No. With one. Infinitely worse!"

"No, oh no!" She reached out, tears glistening on her lashes. "If you don't take Josie, who will take care of you? You don't like that other house of yours. You'll go there and be lonely and sad inside, 'cause of—her."

Astounded, Devenish gasped. "How do you know I don't like Devencourt?"

She dashed tears away with an impatient hand. " 'Cause I know your looks," she said, sniffing. "And you get such a funny one when you talk about it."

He was silent. It was true, he still had the same feeling of being trapped whenever he thought of living in the old place. When he had planned to take Yolande there as his bride it had been so different; the house had been often in his thoughts, then, and he'd known a sense of contentment, envisioning their life together, and the improvements they would make. With Yolande at his side, he could have been perfectly happy. Now . . . "I will not be going to Devencourt," he said slowly. "I shall stay with my Uncle Alastair, until—" Cold drops struck his face. "Heigh-ho! Rain again! Come along, Milady Elf! I'll race you back to the house!"

"Sir," Tyndale said earnestly, leaning forward in his chair, I will most gladly lay my financial expectations before you. I think you will find them not contemptible."

General Drummond was miserable, but this remark diverted him. "You've the castle, I'll admit, and some very fine land about it. But I had supposed that to be the sum of your fortune."

"I doubt you were the only one to do so," Tyndale said, adding with a wry smile, "It does not seem to have occurred to anyone that my mother may have been an heiress."

The General blinked. "It didnae occur tae me! Is that the case? Have ye a respectable competence, perhaps?"

"No, sir. I rather think I'd have to name it a—a considerable fortune."

Yolande gave a gasp and stared at her love in astonishment.

Tyndale turned to take up the slender hand resting on the arm of her chair. "I'd not intended to deceive you, my dearest girl. You did not seem to care, one way or the other. And I thought my chances to be nil, so said nothing."

"And did not press your suit, because you are so honourable a gentleman," she murmured.

He was silent, mesmerized by the look of adoration in her

550

beautiful eyes, and they gazed at one another through a breath-less moment.

The General gave an irritated snort. "Oh, do stop your fon-dling! How can I discuss business matters with you looking at each other like a couple of moonlings? This is a perfect exam-ple of why the ladies are usually excluded frae such confer-ences." He cast a darkling glance at his granddaughter's radiance. "As they should hae been this time, too!"

"Yes, and I know just what would have happened had I not insisted upon coming," she asserted with rare defiance. "You would have convinced Craig of his unworthiness—"

"I need no convincing of that," murmured Tyndale, pressing the hand he still held.

"—for my sake," Yolande went on, a dimple appearing briefly beside her pretty mouth. "And he would have agreed that it would be inhuman to tear me from family, friends, and country—"

"Very true. But I've no intention of so doing," he inter-jected, again.

"Also for my sake," she continued resolutely. "And the up-shot of it all would have been that—for my sake—he would have walked out of my life. Only, *for my sake*, I cannot let that happen."

"I apprehend," the old gentleman said gravely, "that the Ma-jor is a splendid young fellow. I've had word from a friend at Whitheall concerning his military record, and I'd be a clod not to be impressed. Now, it would seem he is eminently qualified from a more practical aspect to seek your hand. Besides which—" a faint smile warmed his troubled eyes—"any fool can see you care for each other."

Yolande's fingers gripped very tightly about Craig's lean hand. Two young hearts thundered as they waited tensely for the decision.

"Accidents do happen," said the General with slow deliber-ation. "I had one myself was almost fatal. I was just a lad, and shot an arrow into a rustling bush. Nigh killed my favourite cousin. . . . Never have been able to touch a bow and arrow since. But—had I the slightest proof that Stuart Devenish died as the result of such an accident, however foolish, I'd with-draw my objections in a trice, and do all I might to convince my son and his lady to accept you, Tyndale. But . . . dammitall! I'll be honest, even though my words will be un-welcome to you both. It is my belief that Jonas, with his wild temper and intolerance, did just as he stood accused of doing. That he deliberately pushed his unwanted brother-in-law to his death. And to have my beloved granddaughter sneered at and derided because she had wed the son of a murderer . . . ! No! Tyndale, I've no wish to distress you. But—*that* is what I cannot countenance. I wish—I really wish that I could offer you hope, but . . ." One powerful hand was raised in a helpless gesture, then fell back onto the mahogany desk again.

Tyndale's head had lowered. It was no more than he had expected. And one could not blame the old fellow: He was doing his utmost to protect his beloved granddaughter. Lord knows, the decision was one he himself would likely have made, under the circumstances. But . . . how could he bear to part with her, knowing that she loved him, and loving her so much that life had taken on so new and glorious a glow of happiness?

"No!" cried Yolande, jumping up. "This is so wrong! Grandpapa, you must see that Craig has done *nothing*! Oh, do not, I beg of you—do not drive me to run away with him!"

Craig, who had stood also, said gently, "That you will never do, my beautiful lady. I'll wed you with honour, or not at all."

General Drummond grunted his approval of these sentiments. Yolande, however, watched Craig with frantic eyes, and said a shaken, "Not even if you know I will never marry anyone else?"

He took her hand and kissed it and, holding it in both of his, said softly, "I came to Ayrshire with two aims in view. One was to find my inheritance. The other was to clear my father's name. I've found my inheritance, but I've scarcely begun an enquiry into what really happened out at the castle four and twenty years since. Have faith in me, dear heart. I'll prove it was an accident—I know it!"

Her heart sank. She said miserably, "and what if it is not possible to prove it?"

"Then I shall be so crude as to go to your papa over your grandfather's protest, lay my claim before him, and beg his understanding."

He smiled at her confidently, but her answering smile was wan, for she sensed that his hopes for a happy resolution to their problems were as forlorn as her own.

The General said kindly, "Never despair, Yolande. We'll all throw our efforts into discovering the truth of matters. Between us—" He paused as a knock sounded.

The door swung open, and Devenish entered to say cheerfully, "Only look at who we found coming up the drive!"

Colonel Alastair Tyndale strode briskly into the room, shook hands with Drummond, bestowed a kiss upon Yolande's cheek, looked with obvious shock at Craig, and exclaimed, "Good God! Dev wrote you was better, but you look in very queer stirrups still, poor fellow. The effect of this beastly climate, I suppose."

"There speaks a fugitive from London's clammy fogs!" Drummond retaliated, laughing. "Devenish, be so good as to pour your uncle a glass of Madeira. You'll stay with us, of course, Alastair, and very welcome. But what brings you up here? We'd understood you didnae plan a trip."

"No more did I." The Colonel raised his glass to the assembled company and sipped the wine appreciatively. "Three things brought me. The first, naturally, was to see for myself how Craig goes on. Secondly, I received a rather strange letter from a lady who lives on your estate, Andy. And, thirdly"—he reddened and said with boyish shyness—"and to me most importantly, to announce my forthcoming marriage."

Sir Andrew, in the act of sampling his wine, spluttered and choked. Devenish, who had put down the decanter, fumbled with the stopper, caught it, juggled it frantically, but dropped it, fortunately onto the carpet. Yolande clapped her hands and cried a joyous, "Oh, how lovely! To Lady Grenfell, sir?"

"Thank *you*, at least, my dear," he said, his eyes glinting with amusement at these reactions.

"At *your* age . . . ?" wheezed the General.

Devenish, utterly incredulous, gasped, "The Silver Widow? B-but—she's the most sought after lady in Town!"

"And the best catch, I heard!" Craig grinned broadly. "Congratulations, sir!"

"Thank you, Craig. Have I quite bowled you out, Dev?"

"What? Oh—er, no, of course not, sir. I only thought— That is to say, I *didn't* think— Well, what I mean to say is—at your time of life, who would guess you'd do such a thing?"

"Devenish!" said Yolande indignantly. "Uncle Alastair is in the prime of his life! And is, besides, a very handsome gentleman. Lady Grenfell has been setting out lures for him this age!"

Colonel Tyndale laughed. "Oh, no! You put me to the blush. I count myself a very lucky man."

"Well, so you should, by Jove!" said the General heartily,

coming around the desk to shake his hand again and pound him on the back. "A beautiful lady, The Grenfell. I'll own my eyes have strayed in that direction a time or two since poor Stephen got himself killed, although I know she is too young for me, despite that pretty silver hair of hers."

Recovering himself, Devenish hastened to also offer congratulations but, shaking the hand of this man who had been his family for so long, chided, "What a sly dog you are, sir! I do think you might have let me know you was contemplating becoming a Benedick. I was never so taken in."

"To tell you the truth, Dev, I should probably have delayed my announcement until after you and Yolande are wed. But now that is . . . imminent . . ." He was struck to silence by the sudden bleakness in his nephew's eyes and, glancing quickly at Yolande, saw her face flushed and distressed.

"The lady won't have me, sir," Devenish imparted with a forced grin. "Prefers a dashed Colonial bumpkin, if you can credit it."

It was the Colonel's turn to be bowled out. His gaze flying to Craig's grave features, he gasped, "Does she—by God!" And then, ruefully, "Gad, but I properly wedged both feet into my mouth!"

"Not at all," said Devenish, filling a sudden awkward silence. "But, it's as well I'd intended to remove to Devencourt before the summer's out."

The Colonel frowned. "No need for that, Dev. There's more than enough room at Aspenhill for all of us."

"Do you seriously expect me to live bodkin between two newlyweds?" Appalled by such a prospect, Devenish made a swift decision. "I've a lady of my own now. You've not met my—my ward, sir."

Colonel Tyndale's jaw dropped. Then he uttered a hearty laugh. "Young varmint! you really had me for a moment. Lord, if there was ever a here-and-thereian less qualified to take on an adopted daughter!"

"How I am maligned!" mourned Devenish. "I assure you, sir, Josie don't share your opinion of me. Does she, Craig?"

"Viewing you with the trusting eyes of childhood," said Craig with his slow grin, "I'd say she has endowed you with halo and wings."

"Oh, Dev!" cried Yolande with delight. "Do you really mean to make her your ward? She will be in heaven!"

"The devil!" exploded Sir Andrew. "She's mine, you rogue! I've already spoke for her!"

"Yes, but I've stolen her away, sir."

"You mean ... it really *is* true?" the Colonel stammered. "But—"

From the door no one had heard open, Enderby announced, "Mrs. MacFarlane!" and absented himself before his indignant employer could request that the gardener's wife be denied at this particular moment.

Yolande went at once to welcome the little woman, exclaiming, "Good heavens! I completely abandoned you when you came last week! I do pray you will forgive me such disgraceful conduct."

The hand she took was like ice and violently trembling. Mrs. MacFarlane's sharp eyes darted about the room, finding curiosity in some faces, amusement in others, and annoyance in the eyes of the General. She mumbled a response to Yolande and nodded to Alastair Tyndale. "I seed you come, sir, and I reckoned I'd best do it the noo, before I—I lose my ... courage. It's—" she drew herself up, gripped her hands tightly, and finished—"it's right ye should all be here."

Yolande's heart began to race. She said, "Do sit down, ma'am, and tell us whatever troubles you."

Mrs. MacFarlane allowed herself to be settled into a comfortable chair, but when Yolande made to draw back, she tightened her hold on the girl's hand and said huskily, "It's yourself has brought me to this pass, Miss Yolande. Your gentle ways and kind words, even in your own sorrows, were an endless barb in my immortal soul! The Good Book says 'there is no peace unto the wicked' and so it is. So I've come here." Tears began to glitter in her eyes. She bit her lip and finished threadily, "I didnae think I'd find the courage tae come again. ... I only hope I can—can go through wi' it!"

Intent now, the General returned to the chair behind his desk. Alastair Tyndale sat on the leather sofa, Craig stood behind Yolande's chair, and Devenish settled his shoulders against the bookcase.

"I expect," Mrs. MacFarlane began nervously, "I expect ye all ken I lived at Castle Tyndale when I was a wee bairn."

Devenish tensed, pushed himself away from the bookcase, and the smile vanished from his eyes, to be replaced by a keen stare. Yolande reached up, and Craig at once took her hand in a strong, brief clasp.

Pleating and unpleating a fold of her dress with trembling fingers, Mrs. MacFarlane quavered, "I should've told . . . years syne . . . what happened that day, b-but—"

"By thunder!" the General ground out, leaning both hands on the desk top as he bent forward. "You *saw* it? Now, why in the name of— Why did ye not come *forward*? Why did your *parrrents* nae speak?"

His tone of voice and fierce mien caused the little woman to become even more nervous. She shrank and pressed both hands to her lips, a stifled moan escaping her.

Colonel Tyndale said, *sotto voce*, "Easy, Andrew. Easy."

Craig and Devenish exchanged glances of flashing excitement.

Yolande stood, and clinging to Craig's arm, whispered, "Oh, my dear—I have prayed for this, but . . . I am so afraid!"

He patted her hand and drew her closer.

"We are more than grateful to you, Mrs. MacFarlane," said Colonel Tyndale kindly. "But—can you tell us why nothing has been said in all this while?"

She blinked at him. "Me mum and dad didnae dare speak, sir. They was terrified they'd be turned off. And besides, we're only simple folk. It—it don't always do tae—tae tell truth to the Quality." Her drawn face twisting with emotion, she wailed wretchedly, "Oh, if ye but knew how I longed tae speak oot! All these years I've knowed the truth! I've knowed the murderer!"

Craig was jolted as though he had been struck. *"Murderer?"* he echoed, his hopes crashing.

"Whatever ye've tae tell us," said Sir Andrew, his own heart sinking, "ye'll be fairly dealt with here, ma'am. As well ye know."

She closed her eyes for an instant, then began almost inaudibly. "I was only six, then. I minded my ma verra well, usually. But—I'd a toy. Me brother Ian had carved it out fer me, and—and it was me most favourite, but Ma didnae like tae see me always playing with it, and bade me tae put it by and tend tae me chores and schooling. She was teaching me tae read and write." She sat with head bowed, her eyes fixed on the hands that wrung and wrung in her lap. "I hid it, though," she said chokingly. "I daren't leave it aboot or it would've been taken and burnt, so—so I hid it, and every afternoon when Ma was busy with her sewing of Miss Esme's pretty things, I'd go and—and take oot me toy. And play with it. Oh!" She gave a wail and clutched her head in near frenzy.

" 'Twas wicked! I ken that well!"

"Poor soul," said Yolande, touched by such anguish. "As if anyone could condemn so natural a thing. You were scarcely more than a babe, and likely had very few toys. Was it a doll your brother made for you?"

For a moment the unhappy woman seemed too lost in remorse to hear the gentle words. Then she looked up at the girl's sympathetic face and answered, "No, miss. But it was my only real toy. Och, but I thought it the finest Diabolino ever . . ."

Baffled, Craig murmured, "Finest—what?"

"Diabolino," rasped the General, more than a little impatient with all this talk of toys. "A wooden ball on a string that is swung up so as to fall into a cup."

"I was playing that day," Mrs. MacFarlane muttered, her wide gaze very obviously looking back into the past that so terrified her. "I heered someone coming. I was awful scared, for me ma had always told me I was *never* tae go up to the battlements. So I ran so fast as ever I could, and hid on t'other side of the tower. Only . . . I dropped me toy."

Again, she paused, and now the room was so still that the soughing of the wind outside sounded like the voice of a hurricane. They waited, breathlessly, for no one dared to ask that Mrs. MacFarlane resume her tale lest her obviously teetering intellect should be pushed too far and completely give way.

"Stuart Devenish, it was," she said in a half whisper. "And he walked over tae stand where he always did, looking oot tae sea. I remember praying he'd soon go inside, but he didnae. And then—then Mr. Tyndale come. He was running almost, and I could tell he was cross again. Mr. Devenish turned round and said, 'Hello, Jonas' in his nice, friendly way, but Mr. Tyndale started ranting and cursing. And all this time I was sae afeared they'd see my toy, for it was close by them."

Under his breath the General snorted, "The devil fly away with the toy!" He asked, "Can you recall ma'am, what the two men were discussing? I suppose 'tis a lot to expect of a lady who was only six at the time."

"I can remember," she said, her stare still fixed and vacant, "as if it was yesterday."

"Can you, by God!" breathed Devenish, moving to stand beside his uncle.

"Miss Esme—Mrs. Devenish, I should say," muttered Mrs. MacFarlane, "was increasing, ye'll mind. Her brother wanted her back in London Town. 'She dinna look right, Stuart,' he said. 'I be afeared fer her! If ye'll nae go, let me take her back with me.' Mr. Devenish said he couldnae allow it, for 'twould be a weary way fer her tae travel. He was verra quiet and calm, and the quieter he was, the angrier Mr. Tyndale got. I was sure as they were going tae start fighting, and so was Mr. Devenish, fer he said, 'Jonas—mon, ye dinna understand! I canna take her back! I *canna*!' Mr. Tyndale shouted, '*Will* not, ye mean!' and he took hold of Mr. Devenish's arm and said, 'Ye *want* her tae die, sae ye can get your hands on her fortune!' Mr. Devenish told him he was a fool, and then he said in a funny sort of voice, 'If she must die, it will be here, where she's been so happy.' I remember it was all quiet then, and they stood there, staring at each other. And Mr. Tyndale asked what was meant by that, and Mr. Devenish says, near weepinglike, 'I'm going tae lose her, Jonas. The doctor says she canna survive this birthing.' "

She stopped speaking, and there was a long, hushed pause. Then, she went on slowly, "Mr. Tyndale wouldnae heed him at first. He kept ranting it was all none but lies, and Mr. Devenish kept saying it was truth, and he looked so sad and sounded so—sort of lost, that I reckon poor Mr. Tyndale had tae face it at the last. He put his head in his hands and began tae weep. Mr. Devenish tried to comfort him, but he was fair crazy with grief. He shouted, 'If ye knowed she would die, why did you get her with child?' And he marched smack up tae Mr. Devenish, like he meant tae throttle the life frae him. Mr. Devenish said he *hadn't* knowed until a few days syne, fer the doctor hadnae told him of it. But Jones Tyndale wouldnae listen. He screamed oot that Mr. Devenish was nae better than a murderer. That he'd murdered Miss Esme. Lor', but I was scared! He was throwing his arms aboot and raving sae wild. Mr. Devenish grabbed him and said sharp-like, 'Have a care, mon! Ye're tae close tae the edge!' Mr. Tyndale pulled free and then—he hit Mr. Devenish. Not hard-like. More as if he didnae want tae be held. But . . . but Mr. Devenish jumped back and then . . . and then . . ." She cowered, bending over and rocking to and fro in a paroxysm of grief.

Through that hushed silence, Tyndale said, "And then my uncle stepped on your toy. Is that it, ma'am?"

Devenish gave a gasp of horrified comprehension. The General whispered, "My God! Oh, my God!"

Mrs. MacFarlane looked up and gulped, "Aye, sir. Oh, how terrible it were tae see him fly back like that! And . . . and tae think I done it! *I* murdered your poor papa, Mr. Devenish! A eye fer an eye, says the Good Book. And . . . and here I be, sir, I owned up . . . at last. . . ."

❧ *Chapter 16* ❧

Sprawling comfortably on the bed in his nephew's spacious bedchamber, Colonel Alastair Tyndale watched Devenish bestow gratuities on the abigail who had cared for Josie during their stay at Steep Drummond, pinch her blushing cheek, and escort her to the door as though she were a duchess. "The boy has changed," he thought. "A month since, he'd have demanded a kiss!" And, as Devenish closed the door and turned to take up his hat and gloves, he said, "I apprehend that you're eager to be on your way, Dev. But—will you please spare me a minute before you go?"

"Of course I will, sir," said Devenish, regarding him fondly. "Are you quite sure you won't ride with us? Lord knows there's room in the coach, and nothing would please me more. Or Josie."

"Thank you, my boy. But I'm promised to help Craig plan the refurbishing of the castle. Still—since you mentioned the child, it is of her that I wish to speak."

He hesitated, and Devenish, limping to pull up a chair, straddle it and watch him over the back, was fairly sure of what was going to be said. He was correct.

Cautiously feeling his way, the Colonel said, "I've no wish to discourage you, for it's a fine thing you plan. But—you really have no notion of what may lie behind her, you know. Blood will out. In a few years you may regret your kindness."

"Forgive me, but I cannot agree, sir. You'd not believe how Josie has blossomed since I found her. And I've a notion there's good blood in her. She may, I think, be of French parentage, for she sometimes will speak the language, and with a flawless accent."

The Colonel's brows went up. "Will she, indeed? I take it you have questioned her in the matter."

"Oh, yes. But to no avail. She remembers only that she was stolen, and—" He frowned. "And—brutality."

"Poor mite! Small wonder she worships you."

Devenish grinned. "All the ladies worship me," he quipped. And thought, "Save only the one *I* worship. . . ."

The Colonel knew him well and thus knew how deep was the wound he had suffered. He kept silent for a moment, dreading to add to that hurt, and at last, tracing the design of the eiderdown with one well-manicured finger, asked softly, "Have you told her you mean to make her your ward?"

"Er—no. Not yet, sir. I—er, I thought I would break the news on our way back to Devencourt." He stared rather blankly at his uncle's muscular hand. The truth was that he still had not really decided to adopt Josie. At the back of his mind was the thought that he'd see if he could land a position on the staff of an ambassador. His blasted leg would keep him out of the military, but he'd as soon leave England for a while. He might even go out to India, as Justin Strand had done; which reminded him that he must drop in on Justin and see if a date had been set for his wedding. Everyone seemed to be getting leg-shackled these days . . . lucky dogs. . . .

"If you do tell her," murmured Colonel Tyndale shrewdly, "and later change your mind, I think it would break her heart."

Devenish started and, glancing up, found those keen blue eyes fixed on him as piercingly as they had done when as a small boy he'd quailed before the Colonel's desk. He wondered resentfully if the guv'nor really could read his mind, and, aware he was flushing, said, "Whatever I do, sir, you may believe she will be well taken care of."

"I was not speaking of material things. I do not mean to prose at you, but—this is a very serious undertaking, and a potentially lengthy one. You mean to take upon yourself the responsibility for another living being. Another soul, Dev, to be shaped and moulded and—provided for, through many years to come. If you are to do it well, it will entail selflessness, compassion, and—love. A large order. Are you—quite sure . . . ?"

Rage, swift and white-hot, tightened Devenish's lips. He had been judged yet again, and found irresponsible! He stood and, taking up his many-caped drab coat, shrugged into it and said with a taut smile, "Well, I collect I'd best say the rest of my goodbyes."

Shocked by this unfamiliar hauteur, the Colonel came to his feet also. He had been very distinctly warned off; a door closed in his face as it never had before. "I'll not detain you longer," he said politely. But his love was deep, so that with his hand on the doorknob, he swallowed his pride and turned about. "Dev, lad, I am so sorry. I only meant— Don't be too hasty in your plans! This—infatuation of Yolande's . . ."

Devenish flinched. "It is no infatuation, sir. Have you not seen them together? It is . . . as though they were—one being."

His heart aching, the Colonel gripped the younger man's shoulder. "If only there was *something* I could do! I know how—how deeply you have loved her all your life. It must be . . ." And he stopped, the words eluding him.

Devenish lifted a hand almost absently to cover the one that rested on his shoulder. "If I thought," he muttered, "that I would have the least chance of winning her, I would call Craig out and . . ." He was silent for a moment, then raised his brooding gaze, saw the helpless sympathy in his uncle's eyes, and smiled wryly. "But, do you know, sir? Of late I've begun to wonder . . ."

"What, Dev?"

"Only that . . . I have loved her, as you said, all my life. But—when I see her with Craig, I think . . . perhaps, there are degrees of loving, and—and theirs is something . . . almost holy. That I will not ever be granted."

The Colonel had the same thought about the relationship he shared with his own lady, and so it was that his affection for this valiant young man, and his comprehension of the grief that he knew must be intense, overmastered him. He spun around and strode rapidly to the window, to stand staring blindly into the sunny morning.

A quick uneven step. A strong arm, tight about his shoulders. And his nephew's voice, husky with emotion, said, "Now, God love you for that sympathy. You always were true blue. The best and kindest uncle who ever took in a lonely scamp, and was curst seldom thanked for it! But—" Devenish turned the Colonel to face him, and smiling rather uncertainly into those blurred eyes, said, "You know—sir, I have always felt . . . I have always, er . . ."

Tyndale gripped his elbow. "Yes," he said huskily. "I know."

"You were not going to leave without saying goodbye, I hope?"

Craig! Devenish thought, "Damn!" but turned, and said lightly, "Lord, no. I just came down to see if Monty has assembled the luggage. My elf seems to have acquired a prodigious amount of paraphernalia since we came."

"Yes. Dev, I—"

"Don't, Craig!" Despite himself, Devenish's voice was harsh. "You saved my life, and you're a damned good fellow. If I had to—to lose her, I could not wish . . . . it to be to a better man."

Craig swore furiously at him. "What a perfectly wretched thing to say! You might at least have knocked me down."

Devenish laughed. But the worst, he knew, was yet to come.

Yolande's eyes were red, but she put out her hand like the thoroughbred she was, and said composedly, "Ride safely, my dear. And take care of your little lady."

He took her hand, stared down at it, so sweetly resting in his own, and released it hurriedly. Looking up, he saw that she was blinking rather fast and, reaching back into the many happy years he had so stupidly taken for granted, feigned indignation. "Now, dash it all, Yolande. If you're going to turn into a watering pot . . ."

She laughed shakily. "Odious creature! You always did treat me as if I were a tiresome little sister."

"Is that what drove me to the ropes?" The words were out before he could stop them. He saw her mouth twist and said a swift, "I shall have to be more careful. And I shall expect a very special invitation to the—ceremony."

"You shall have it—of course. And . . . Josie shall be a flower girl, if she would—like . . ." Her voice broke. "Oh . . . Dev . . ."

She was in his arms, weeping. He held her very tight, hoarding these priceless seconds. "Yolande . . ." he whispered. And, fighting for control, said, "No tears, if you please. I seem to—bring you very often to tears, of late."

"I love you, Dev," she sniffed. "I wish I did not love you—quite so much." And she pulled away, looked up at him for an instant, the tears bright on her cheeks, then leaned to kiss him.

"You will ... find your happiness ... my very dear," she managed, and fled.

Josie had been granted her wish to ride Molly-My-Lass to the edge of the Drummond estates; beside her, Devenish rode his beloved Miss Farthing, and the carriage followed with a groom behind, to lead the Clydesdale back to Steep Drummond. Montelongo had ridden ahead to arrange rooms for them in New Galloway, so that they were now quite alone, and Josie thought she had never been so happy.

"Oh," she sighed, looking with glad eyes at clear heaven, lush meadows, and contentedly grazing cows. "Oh, ain't it a 'licious morning?"

"What?" muttered Devenish. "Oh—er, yes. Delicious."

"I doesn't see," she persisted, "how everything in the whole world couldn't be anything but filled with happy on a day like today."

"You cannot be filled with *happy*, my elf," he protested. "Frightful grammar."

"Yes, Mr. Dev." She slanted a mischievous glance up at him. "Just the same—I is."

He smiled, his heart like lead.

" 'Course," said Josie thoughtfully. "You ain't. Not just at this minute, p'raps. But afore you knows it—*voilà*! you will be."

As always, her use of French intrigued him so that for a moment he forgot his misery. "How so? What I mean to say is, I *am* happy. As a cursed lark, in fact."

"No." She shook her small head so that the curls bounced beneath the bonnet of primrose straw that Yolande had bought her.

"Nonsense. After all, we're going to Devencourt, my, er, home, and—"

"And you hates Devencourt."

He stared at her. "Josie—are you *quite* sure you're only eleven?"

"I be very old sometimes," she said, matter-of-factly. "All ladies is. And I be a lady—or, I will be, when you—" She broke off, looking guilty.

"When I—what?"

"I'm not s'posed to know."

He thought, "Oh, God!" "But," he said rather stiffly, "you, ah—*do* know?"

"Yes. Oh, yes!" She all but jumped up and down in the saddle, her small face radiating joy. "And you won't be sorry, Mr. Dev. Not never! I'll be the bestest daughter what ever you had! I'll take care of you and be perlite and learn to talk pretty like—her. I know I won't ever *be* pretty like—her, but you won't have to go to that great crawly place and be sad all alone."

Torn between dismay and laughter, he asked, "Who told you?"

"Oh, the servants knew." She said airily, "You cannot keep nothin' from the servants, you know. Aunty Caroline says."

He blinked. "*Aunty* . . . Caroline?"

"She told me to call her that. I was frighted of her at first, but she's a dear. Monty says she talks too much." She giggled.

They rode in silence for a while, then he said carefully, "I hope poor General Drummond may not be utterly cast down because I took you away from him."

She thought about that. "I 'spect he was. But some folks gets to dance on a bubble, and some gets to be casted down. Like me and you."

There should be an answer to that, he thought dully. But he could not seem to find one. They were at the brow of the hill. In another minute Steep Drummond would be out of sight. It was as well. He did not want to see it. Never again. But somehow he was drawing his horse to a halt, motioning the carriage and groom to move ahead, and turning aside to guide his mare to the brow of the hill and the shade of a great tree where he had sat once before. His mount began to crop at the rich grass, and Devenish, quite forgetting the child beside him, leant forward in the saddle and gazed across the lush green valley to Steep Drummond. Was she at one of the windows that twinkled in the morning sunlight, looking out, trying to see him? Was she—out of the affection she bore him—grieving to see him go? Yolande . . . my own, my love . . . Yolande. . . .

A small sound roused him from this hopeless yearning. He glanced around and straightened in dismay. Josie's head was bowed. Even as he watched, something bright and glittering splashed down upon Molly-My-Lass's broad shoulder. He reined closer. "Child . . . ? Josie? Do not! Whatever is it? Please—do not cry!"

"I can't . . . help it," she sobbed, raising a woebegone countenance. "I cannot bear it when your eyes gets . . . so awful sad. Like you was all full of tears inside. I—I *wants* to make you happy. I *wants* so for you to not—not give a button for her. But—I cannot help! I cannot *help* you. And, oh, Mr. Dev—Josie *loves* ye so!"

Who could not be touched? A heart of stone must have melted before that youthful anguish. And however cracked it might be at present, the heart of Alain Devenish had never resembled stone. He reached out, Josie leaned to him, and in a trice she was sitting across his saddle bow, sobbing gustily into his cravat and clinging to him with her skinny little arms.

"Milady Elf," he said, stroking her soft curls, for her bonnet had fallen back during the change of mounts. "Hush, now. If you keep weeping, you will make me even more full of tears."

She at once wiped fiercely at her flowing eyes. Devenish groped for and offered his handkerchief. Josie dragged it across her face, blew her nose stridently, and tucked the handkerchief into the front of his jacket. It was quite soggy, but he gave no sign of his inner dubiety. "That's better." He smiled. "Now"—he slapped the reins against the neck of the mare and started her towards the waiting carriage, Molly-My-Lass following amiably—"am I to understand then, that you are willing to be a dutiful and obedient daughter, brightening my declining years, and caring for me in my dotage?"

Josie gave a watery giggle.

"I see." He fought against looking back as they started down the hill. "In that case, we shall have to arrive at an understanding, my elf."

She peeped at him, uncertainly.

"I will have no more popping off at the least little whim to consort with drunken rogues," he adjured.

Josie chortled.

"To say nothing," he went on, "of going about putting bears into the toolsheds of respectable farmers."

She snuggled against him. "Oh, Mr. Dev," she sighed, blissfully aware that Steep Drummond was now safely out of sight. "What a complete hand you are."

"That is *precisely* the sort of remark you must not repeat!" he groaned. "Now—pay heed to your papa, child, if you please. . . ."

On they went, Devenish speaking with grave earnestness, and the child's piping laugh threading through his remarks like quicksilver. Now, whether it was because of the infectious happiness in that youthful laughter, or because, in seeking to lead Josie from sorrow, Devenish briefly forgot his own woes, who shall say? Certain it is that the sharpness of his anguish eased a trifle, and despair's dark shadow began to lift from his heart. After a while, he restored the child to her own saddle. They resumed their journey then, travelling side by side through the brilliant morning, towards England, and home, and whatever the future had in store for them in that bright promise that is called—tomorrow.

❧ *Epilogue* ❧

Major Craig Tyndale ushered his lady up the deep steps of the castle. "We've done very little as yet," he said with a trace of anxiety. "I hope you'll not be disappointed, Yolande."

"No, but how could I be? This is to be my home. I've been so anxious to see it ever since you and Uncle Alastair began the work."

"And I have longed to bring you these whole ten days. It was very kind of your papa to let you come."

"And even kinder of him to travel up here. But, now that we are officially betrothed, it is not very shocking for me to be here alone with you—is it?"

He smiled down into her face, so enchantingly framed by the pink ruffles of the dainty bonnet she wore. "A little, perhaps, but Laing is with us, after all."

He threw open the heavy door, revealing the majestic sweep of the Great Hall, gleaming with fresh paint, brightened by rich carpets, and mellowed by the careful placement of fine furniture. Watching his love with no little anxiety, he said, "It is rather isolated, I daresay, but we'll only spend the summer here, you know. I thought we would purchase a house in Town for the Season, if you should care to. And you will wish to spend time with your parents of course."

"And you will want to take me to see your home in Canada—no?"

"You would not object?" he asked eagerly. "It would be a long, tiresome journey, but I thought perhaps, if we should be—er, that is—when we have set up our—our nursery, perhaps you might be willing to go."

"Foolish, foolish man." Yolande looked up at him, her eyes soft with love. "I can see that you have done beautifully with Castle Tyndale, and I shall enjoy being here with you. Or in Town—with you. Or on the high seas—with you. Oh, Craig—my very dearest love . . . do you not yet know? My happiness lies not in *where* we are—only that we are . . . together."

Mr. Laing, checking the chestnut mare's harness, shook his head bodingly. "Did you see that, Heather?" he enquired. "Picked her up in his arms and carried her across the threshold like they was already wed! Shocking! These young people today have no least notion of how to go on!"

He was quite mistaken. Standing in the Great Hall, a slender girl clasped against him, her arms about his neck, and his lips pressed crushingly to hers, Major Craig Winters Tyndale knew exactly how to go on.